CROWN PROPERTY

CROWN PROPERTY

by Wes Fulton

For Beverly Lanza Fulton

"Body and Spirit I surrendered whole
To harsh Instructors — and received a soul ..."
— Rudyard Kipling, "Epitaphs of the War"

PART ONE

THE WARRENS

1

ootman Sesh came by again today and asked me if I was ready.

I looked over my bandaged wounds. "Actually, I think I'm going to pull through, Holy Father, so I won't need your final blessings. If you could maybe say a prayer for my ass, though, because it won't stop itching and I can't scratch it..."

He told me to quit joking around and said he'd brought the paper and ink with him.

Footman Sesh has been after me for at least a month about writing down my story — ever since I healed up well enough to hold a pen and paper. I keep telling him I don't think anybody wants to hear the story I have to tell, but he keeps saying all stories need to be told.

I'm not sure I agree. But I suppose someone, somewhere should tell the truth. They tell me there are long-bearded scholars out there in academies and monasteries who only want to hear the truth, and not the prettied-up tales told in taverns, schoolrooms and pulpits. If there are such people, I guess I'm writing this for them.

You will want to know my name, I suppose, even though I don't think it's all that important. But you can't really tell a story without a name, and I had to come from somewhere, right?

My name is Lashan Pearl. I was born in Solta, the capital city of the Kingdom of Selva, and for my first seventeen summers, my feet never took me beyond its walls. My mom told me "Pearl" was not her family name — it was some long word I can't pronounce. When I was little, she told me that when she first came to the capital, she wanted to leave her old life behind, and when she got the job at the factory the foreman told her she could pick any name she wanted, so she chose "Pearl," because she always thought pearls were pretty.

My mother was always an odd one. I never knew another like her. Even today, she's still a wispy little thing — it's hard to believe such a small and skinny woman could be so fearless. But she said she came by her long red hair honestly — centuries ago, she said, her people were the last wild tribe to submit to Selvan rule, and she still treasured the wild spirit of their ancestors. It was said, she told me, that her people were the last human descendants of the fairies — she would point to her small nose (which I shared) and the way her smile seemed to be too big for her cheeks, and the freckles that still covered her face when I was a child.

"My grandmother told me, 'those are the marks of fairy blood,' and the marks upon my face were strong indeed," she said.

I asked if it was true. "ARE you descended from fairies, Mommy? Are you really?"

And she would shush me and remind me that those were just old stories, because the light of Auld Father had rescued all of us from such superstitions. "We are, all of us, children of the Great Father on the Mountain."

Speaking of fathers, I suppose now you'll want to know why I don't have my father's family name. Well, it's because I don't know it. My mom knows it, but won't tell me. All she'll say is that he was a soldier from the Molan Isles, a Molan Strongblood who came to Solta with a battalion from his homeland. They were to be put on a ship to go fight somewhere. My mom said he promised to write her and come back to her, but he never did. She said he probably got killed fighting.

But that's why, growing up, I looked a little different from most of the other kids in Solta — it's my blood. Don't ask me about the Molans, though — aside from a few that I'd sometimes see passing through, I never knew any other Molans growing up. I don't know anything about their language, and all I know about their customs is what I've read in books.

One last thing you should know is that I was born blind. For my first two summers, I lived in total darkness. I think that's why my mother has always been so protective of me. Looking back today, I find it hard to recall much about that time. I don't remember being very bothered about it; you can't miss something you've never had.

I was cured when the great, elderly holy man, Footman Bet Sorish, came to preach in the capital. My mother couldn't miss that, of course; I'm pretty sure my mother would have become a Footman herself if they allowed women, and she told me once she would have become a Consecrated Daughter if it weren't for the little problem of, well...my existence.

I asked her if that made her upset.

"No, because if Auld Father had wanted me to honor him in that way, he would not have given me the precious gift of you," she said, and laughed as if that were the most obvious thing in the world.

Anyway, when Footman Sorish came, my mother of course went to hear him deliver the word every chance she got. I've heard it said that Auld Father's power rolled through the streets like a flood at that time, and the black demons of Gruun suffered a terrible thrashing. One of Solta's richest merchants was even inspired to give away all his wealth to the poor and take up the life of a poor Footman.

Thousands who came to see Footman Sorish "received the Father's Touch," speaking in tongues and having visions of the future. They say that receivers spoke in detail about the imminent coming of the Reckoner, although I've never been able to find any good description of the things they said. Considering all I've been through, I think it would make for interesting reading.

Footman Sorish, of course, rebuked anyone trying to claim he was the Reckoner. "I am just a poor herald of Auld Father," he would say. Even so, his powers were legendary; it's said that hundreds were healed from terrible ailments when Sorish laid hands on them and, with nothing but his mighty voice, cast out the demons that afflicted them. As my mother tells the story, after waiting in line for nearly half a day to come before the great man, she finally presented me. She said before she could even speak, he knelt down and looked at me, and took my small head in between both of his hands, looking me over.

"It is a powerful demon indeed that possesses this boy," he said, becoming very serious. "Gruun must want very dearly to keep his eyes sewn shut to send such powerful forces against him."

My mother claims she never told him I was blind — he just seemed to sense it. She asked him if he could heal me, and a very grim look came upon his face, as if he were about to say no. She started to cry, and when he looked at her, his face changed and softened.

"It is not Auld Father's will that any of us should be left in Gruun's darkness," he said. "And not even the greatest of demons can stand against the Father." And with that, he clutched my head hard between his hands and bellowed a loud prayer, and commanded the demon to leave.

I don't have any memory of this moment, but my mother says I began crying and screaming in terror when, for the first time, I perceived light and didn't know what it was. She said it was not until she got in front of me and pressed my tiny hands against her face, and let me run my hands through her long red hair — something which had always soothed me whenever I was upset — that I gradually began to calm down and understand what was happening.

My mother said she thanked the old holy man profusely, begging him to accept some sort payment, but he waved her off. "Just see that he is raised up in the faith," he told her. "And stop calling me 'Father,' young lady. You can call me 'Bet.'" Then she said he glanced once more at me, laughed and added, "Both of you can."

My mother said that for months afterward, I seemed to regard even the most humble sights in the world with awe — because, I guess, I was experiencing it all for the first time. As it happens, the first event of which I have any fully formed memory was the King's Coronation Week, about a year later. It's just images, really, but I remember being dazzled by all the colors that suddenly sprung up all over the city — clothes, costumes, paints, banners, displays, even food and drink in every imaginable hue. My mother says I spent nearly the entire week pestering her to find out the name of every new color I encountered.

GROWING UP, IT WAS just me and my mom and all my aunts. They weren't really my aunts; they were just the other ladies who lived in the rooming house, but my mom said they were like our family, so I had to call them my aunts. My mom worked nights and had to sleep all during the day, so my aunts spent a lot of time taking care of me.

When we did have time to spend together, one of my mother's favorite things was for us to go up to the roof of our tall, creaky rooming house — it was seven stories full of unmarried women, along with whatever children any of them had who hadn't yet come of age. Mom said Aunt Rossie, who owned the house, had given her a key to the roof; it was one of the few places outside of our little room where we could be alone. We would go up there and she would tell me stories about her life, or point out different sights and explain their significance.

I remember once when I guess she was off work for the evening, she took me up there at night. All three moons happened to be in the sky that night, and she explained how the names of the moons were actually taken from the Auld Tongue, which she said had been the original language of her people, before they submitted to Selvan rule.

"The largest one, the one you see in the sky most often, is called 'Arban,' which means 'King.'"

"Like our King, the one who lives in the Palace?"

"No, the last Arban lived many hundreds of years ago."

"What about the others?"

"The second-largest one, the one that moves through the sky the most quickly, that's 'Siran,' which means 'queen.' Only it's not like our queen; in the old days, the Siran was actually almost as important as the Arban; she was the one who handled many of the day-to-day duties of running the realm. That's why they say she moves so fast; they say she's always moving from place to place, keeping tabs on the realm."

"And the little one?"

"Ah, that's 'Tarissa!' It means 'little princess.' If you watch the moons for long enough, you'll see Tarissa sometimes disappears behind Siran. They say that's because she's shy, and trying to hide behind her mother's skirts!"

She laughed as she told me that, I guess thinking I would find it funny, but it just reminded me of how much I missed my mom when she had to leave for her job. I asked her why she had to leave me alone every night.

"It's for my job, love. Your mother needs the money. I suppose if I'd married your father I might have earned a widow's pension, but..." She didn't finish, but just gazed up at the moons.

"But what do you do for your job? Where do you go?"

I must have looked pitiful then, because I remember her wrapping her arms around me and squeezing me tightly, then keeping one arm around me as she pointed to the harbor. "See all the ships?" she asked.

I nodded.

"Well, every one of those ships needs rope — hundreds, even thousands of yards of it. Mommy works in a place that makes the ropes for all of those sailing ships."

She said that was why her hands were always so rough — they got rough from working all night with all that scratchy rope.

I remember being amazed — there were so many ships! I asked my mom if she'd ever been aboard one. She told me no, but that when she was younger she'd sometimes dreamed of sailing away on one with a pirate captain.

"You wanted to be a pirate?"

"Not exactly," she said with a grin.

She also told me when she was pregnant with me, she used to come up to the roof of the rooming house alone sometimes — that's why Aunt Rossie gave her the key — and look out at the ships and dream of boarding one, and traveling off to a distant land.

"Where did you want to go?"

"As a little girl, I always loved hearing stories about the Kingdom of Garlund — it's to the west, on the other side of those mountains…" She pointed to the rocky peaks rising up in the distance west of the city. She'd said she'd also heard fascinating stories from sailors about a new land far to the north across the Sea of Songs.

I asked her what had stopped her from going, and she explained that she couldn't very well go aboard a ship with me in her tummy. I didn't understand why, and told her I would have liked to have been born and raised aboard a ship — maybe even a pirate ship, like she'd dreamed of as a little girl.

"Oh, Lash," she said, rubbing my head and kissing my forehead. "Lash, my dearest one. It's just not that easy."

"It's not that easy." That's what my mom would always say when I asked something and she didn't want to give me the answer. I suppose she thought I probably couldn't understand back then, and she was probably right. My mom was really smart — a lot smarter than I'll ever be. But now that I'm older I think sometimes she wouldn't tell me because she didn't know the answer herself.

It's not that easy. It's probably doubly true when you grow up in the Warrens. That's where I'm from, I should say, because I know a lot of you reading this will think that's important.

When I tell people that's where I'm from, there's a certain sort that always gets a look in their eye, because they've heard all the stories. If it's a guy, he'll stiffen up a bit, like he half expects you to pull a knife out and cut his throat. If it's a woman, she might pat your head and curl her mouth down like she feels all sorry for you.

To be honest, it wasn't that bad, but I guess I only think that because it was all I knew at the time. Just as when I was blind, I couldn't miss something I'd never known.

And anyway: Being from the Warrens has its advantages. There's no tavern, no alley anywhere on either side of the Striped Mountains that I'm afraid to walk into. When you're a Warrens kid, there's nothing the civilized world can throw at you that will shake your nerves.

It took going to war for me to find out what real fear felt like.

2

Soon as I was old enough to wander off out of sight of my mom, I was out roaming the streets of the Warrens. At first I'd just hang around the rooming house because I was too scared to go very far, what with all the loud and angry grownups about. But it didn't take me too long to figure out that if I hung around the rooming house, one of my aunts would put me to work on some chore, and who wants to be stuck doing chores?

I must have been around four or five summers when I fell in with this gang of boys over on Frog Street — they called themselves the Craller Square Wolves, even though, back then, I don't think any one of us even knew what a wolf actually was. The stories my mother read to me sometimes talked about the ferocious five-eyed wolves of Garlund, but my mother said those weren't real. But all the boys insisted that regular wolves — the kind with just two eyes — were real, and we figured "wolves" sounded intimidating.

At first, some of the boys made comments about my appearance, me being half-Molan and all. I tried to ignore it, but one day one boy made the mistake of calling me a "scaleback."

After what I did to him, no other boys around our part of the Warrens dared to call me that. They say us Molans are born fighters, and my father was bona fide Molan Strongblood — the best of the best. So I've been fighting since the first time I had something to fight.

The "Craller Square Wolves" didn't actually hang around Craller Square — I think we just picked that name because that was the main hub of our little corner of the Warrens. I'm sure you long-beards probably know who Lord Craller was and why they'd name a square after him, but all I know of him was his name written on a big granite block in the middle of the square. People said there used to be a statue of Lord Craller sitting on that block, and that the trash heaps around that block used to be a fountain, like they have in the squares over in the Palace District. But it was gone now. Some folks said it had been torn up in a riot, and other folks said it was because the King and the nobles decided one day that Lord Craller wasn't so lordly after all, so they hauled off his statue for scrap metal.

They say Gruun's demons often come to us in the form of men, and I reckon the first one to pull me off the Path was this older boy, Lemon — he must have been about ten — who was in charge, more or less, of the Wolves. He knew all kinds of jokes and seemed to have a funny story about nearly everybody or every place around the Warrens. I don't know how true any of it was. For example, Lemon claimed the Lord Craller statue fell down because nobody ever cleaned the bird-shit off it and then the birdshit finally ate right through the metal and it collapsed. I don't know if I believed that even back then, but the way Lemon told the story always made us laugh.

Lemon was always smoking a pipe, and I remember he would light it and hold it just like the grownups did. And he always wore this brown jacket. Somewhere in that jacket, I remember, he had a stash of sweets, though nobody could figure out where, because it didn't have any pockets — at least none that anybody could find. He'd even take it off and let us younger kids mess around with it to see if we could find a secret compartment, but we never could.

Anyway, Lemon would give you a sweet from his mystery stash if you'd lift him a copper off somebody coming along Frog Street — if you've never been to the Warrens, it's one of the main streets that cuts through the southern quarter. It wouldn't do to just lift one off one of your parents, or whoever you lived with — if you lived with anybody. He wanted you to actually steal it off a stranger, and if possible he wanted to see you do it.

Lemon would goad us on by insulting us. "Here, Lash, pick a card," he told me once, holding out the deck he'd been fooling with. I pulled one and looked at it. "Which one do you have?"

"The five-eyed wolf."

"It fits you."

"Why?"

"Because it's just like your pickpocketing skills — nonexistent," he said with a snort.

And because we all wanted Lemon's approval more than just about anything, even the sweets he gave us, we worked for it.

You might ask how in Gruun's name a bunch of kids knew how to lift a copper off a grownup. Lemon taught us a few tricks at first, but we quickly started coming up with our own. We'd practice on each other until we felt like we had a hang of it, and then we'd go out and try it.

You do it first on drunks, of which we always had plenty around the War-rens. Now I don't mean the regular bums, because they didn't have money — the Crown sees to it that the wine and ale is free at all the public halls, after all. I know what you silk-wearing fops think of the public halls and the drink they serve there, but remember, this was the Warrens, so most people weren't too particular about that sort of thing. No, if you're looking to lift a copper, you're looking for a drunk who looks like they might have a spot of coin.

And if you're a Warrens kid, you learn quick how to spot who's carrying coin and who isn't. Sometimes it's just as simple as watching how they walk. Some folks — the ones who aren't regulars in the Warrens — are always feeling around at their pockets while they walk, which is a dead giveaway that they're carrying something worth stealing. But most folks we saw in our corner of the Warrens were a little sharper than that. If you saw clean fingernails or a flash of jewelry, that was usually a clue. Shitfaced sailors on leave were always an easy mark.

Drunks are the easiest to lift from, both because they're usually not paying attention and because if you do get caught, it's easy to give them the slip. A guy or gal who's shitfaced isn't gonna have the best coordination anyway, and being little kids gave us an advantage — we could slip through crowds and dive under carts, or squeeze into tight alleys and passages where they couldn't fit.

But you only get so much going after drunks. People aren't stupid, after all — even the drunks were usually smart enough to figure out what we were up to and they'd mostly try to avoid us. Apart from the rare occasions when some dandy from the finer parts of the city somehow got lost in our neighborhood, most of the folks passing through our area had their wits about them.

One thing I put together on my own, without Lemon or anybody else clueing me in, was to look for scary old men who had big scars or missing limbs. Those, I learned, were often former soldiers.

My Aunt Shen at the rooming house had a man who came around to see her every Seveneve — she said he was her dad. He looked like one of those men. I remember he wore something strapped across his face covering his nose, and my mom said it was there because half his nose had been cut off in battle. Anyway, I noticed he always had a little bag of coppers, and I found out from asking around that a lot of those old soldiers often had a nice spot of coin, especially at the beginning of the week. Everybody said it was from something called a "pension."

Now being a kid, that word didn't mean a thing to me. You proper types reading this can sit here and judge me all you want, but I didn't know any better. All I knew was that it made them easy pickings for prying little hands in search of a copper.

Using this knowledge, I quickly became one of Lemon's favorites. My Aunt Rossie used to tell my mom that she'd better watch me close, because the demons were always drawn to the brightest brains. I don't know that I'm particularly bright, but even back then I could see I had a little bit more brains to work with than the average street urchin.

But just like Gruun is always whispering in their ear, Auld Father is always ready to chastise His wayward children. Late one day, when I was about to call it quits and head back to the rooming house, I spied a short fellow limping down the lane on an old wooden leg. I knew from his height he was a klanger — well, a dwarf. I mean I'm only calling him a "klanger" because I didn't know enough back then to know you're not supposed to call them that — it's like calling a Molan a "scale-back." But at that age, I'd never even heard the word "dwarf"; everybody around the Warrens just called them klangers, even to their face.

He wore his hair and beard short, in the proper style of a pious follower of Auld Father. I'd never seen a klanger — I mean a dwarf — wearing his hair that way; I thought the dwarves had their own so-called "gods" that they followed. Strange. But with his scarred hands and wooden leg, and the way he carried himself, I knew immediately that he was an old soldier.

I also knew that the klang...I mean dwarves, were all supposed to be rich. Well, that was what everybody said, anyway. And so here comes this dwarf, and he's a former soldier, and I figured if he's a rich dwarf, well, maybe that pension thing the old soldiers have is bigger for him. I know, I know, but it made sense in my head as a kid.

And I thought, hey, this might be an opportunity. If he's rich, maybe he's carrying more than a few coppers. Maybe he's carrying some sixcoins. Maybe he's even carrying a silver.

A silver. I'd only seen those a few times; my mom sometimes had a few that she paid Aunt Rossie with. When us boys brought Lemon a sixcoin he'd give us a handful of sweets, or even give us a sip of ale — he always had a flask handy that he'd take swigs from. I wondered what Lemon might give me if I came up to him and held up a shiny silver.

By this point I was probably the second-best pickpocket in the gang; a boy named Gammon was better, but only cause he had long, bony fingers that looked weird. So I figured I'd go for it. I signaled to a couple of other boys to watch my back and be ready to run interference. Then I sized up my target: He was dressed rather lightly for such cool weather. There was a fat coin purse dangling from his belt, but it was bound to his belt quite snugly and didn't look like it would be easy to remove, even if I could distract him for a moment. It was made of thick leather that didn't look like it could be easily sliced open, either.

So that was out, but even so, I knew most people usually carried a few loose coins somewhere else, so they wouldn't always have to fuss with their coin purse. There was usually a small pocket or opening...

There. I saw it — a small slit cleverly concealed in the folds of his tunic. It was near the front of his tunic, which meant I wouldn't be able to sneak up behind him unnoticed — I'd have to come in from the front.

I could try the bump and frisk approach, but I thought this fellow looked a little too wise for that. I noticed there was a cart and a draft horse off to the side of the street, and the drover was unloading kegs of ale to haul to the public hall across the street. That would work.

As soon as the old dwarf got close enough, I slipped up next to the horse and stuck it with a needle, which startled it. It lurched just as the drover was trying to pull a keg off the cart, and the sudden movement knocked him off balance and he tumbled to the ground.

I'd actually been hoping he'd be knocked against the old dwarf, but the little bastard was sure-footed enough to step out of the way, even with a wooden leg.

Luckily, though, the dwarf stopped to check on the drover to see if he needed any help. That was all I needed. I came over and crowded up next to the dwarf, acting like I was trying to get a better view of the commotion. I easily slipped two fingers into the hidden slit in his tunic, felt the cold metal of something, and slipped it right out. As the dwarf was helping the drover to his feet, I quietly faded back into the street crowds. I ducked into an alley — one which was jammed with a broken-down old ox-cart I could easily slide under, but any grownup pursuing me would have to noisily climb over in order to chase me. Confident that I was safe, I examined my ill-won gain.

I'd known immediately from the size and weight that it wasn't a copper, so my hopes were running high. But when I opened my hand I was greeted with a puzzle.

It appeared to be nothing but a block of steel, though of a strange color I'd never seen before. It had a strange, angular design of sharp edges that reminded me a little bit of a gemstone, and a curious set of indentations. There were some numbers and letters crudely stamped into the bottom, but since I couldn't read yet, they meant nothing to me.

"Not what you were hoping for, son?" a gravelly voice behind me suddenly said.

I whirled around in astonishment. It was the old dwarf. He'd seemingly appeared out of nowhere — somehow he'd managed to make it past the broken ox-cart without making a sound. Not even with his wooden leg.

He held out his hand.

"I believe you have my ingot."

I hesitated, then handed him the object. He held it up between two fingers, inspecting it.

"Tell me, boy, do you know what this is?"

I tried to remember what he'd called it.

"Of course," I lied. "Everybody does. It's an 'inket.'"

That drew a smile.

"Ingot," he corrected. "Do you know what it does?"

No use in lying. I shook my head.

He smiled wider, and gently tucked the strange object — the ingot — back into the slit in his tunic.

And then — well, I know now what happened, but at the time it was hard to understand. At that point in my life, I'd never seen anyone but Footmen use magic before.

It was like one second I was there, standing in an alley, and then quicker than you can blink an eye, I was on the roof of Mallee's — that was the big sporting house that took up one whole side of Craller Square.

Except I wasn't on the roof, actually. That klang... I mean, that dwarf was on the roof. As for me — he had me by one of my ankles. And he was dangling me over the side. It was nine stories straight down.

It took me a second to understand what was happening, but once I figured it out, I wanted to start crying. Except I couldn't — you know that feeling where you're trying to say something, or trying to yell, and it just feels like all the air is trapped in your throat and you can't get any of it to come out? It's like you're so scared even your voice wants to go and hide?

Well, that was what it was like. After a few moments, I thought I could hear some squeaking sounds escape my lips, but I couldn't manage anything else.

"I'll tell you, lad, I've half a mind to drop you right here. You know how many good dwarves I saw fall to keep these bloody lands free? And most of them dead by my own hand!"

I looked at him. The skin on his angry face had changed color, just barely enough to be noticeable. His expression then changed — although since I was looking at it upside down, I couldn't tell if that was good or bad. Was his new expression angrier? Or softer?

Softer, I guess. At least that's how he sounded when he spoke.

"You're not like the others from around here," he said — I guess in the light of Craller Square, he finally saw I was half-Molan. "Do you know your parents?"

Well, he knew a thing or two about the Warrens, that was for sure. I managed to stammer out: "I...I...l-l-live with m-my m-mom..."

I waited for him to say something, but he just kept looking at me. So I stammered out a little more. "At the...the r-rooming house, across from the b-black-smith..."

Again, it was like someone snapped their fingers, and we were standing in front of the rooming house.

I looked up at him.

"Mister? How did you...?"

He ignored me and rapped on the door. After a moment, Aunt Rossie opened it.

"The boy tells me he lives here with his mother," he said. "Is she about?"

I hoped she might have left early for work, but felt my gut drop when Aunt Rossie said she was in and she'd go get her. I had to wait in the front parlor with the old dwarf; grown-up men weren't allowed on the upper floors, no matter how bent over with age they might be.

My mom came down into the parlor, still fastening the cuffs on her work dress. The dwarf introduced himself as — I forget. One of those dwarf names — Fartknocker, son of Shitstain, you know how they go.

"The boy has been up to no good, ma'am," he said. "He tried to lift one of my valuables. I saw him running with a bunch of other boys; I suspect it's a pickpocket ring. That's usually how they start them off."

The color drained from my mom's face. I had sort of hoped that, well, maybe she knew — I mean I knew there were other boys in the gang, even some who lived in the rooming house, whose moms knew what they were up to, and they didn't seem to mind.

I should have known better. As devout as she was, I'm sure it never occurred to her that I could be anything but a perfect little saint. Every night before she left for work, she'd read to me from The Walk and lead us in prayer. We were in chapel every Seveneve, and if there was a feast at the house I never got to eat goose, because it was forbidden by the Scriptures.

No, not me — not her darling little Lash.

Still and all, we lived in the Warrens. What did she think I did with my time? The demons call to you from every door and alleyway down there. Now that I think of it, though, my mom must have been no more than a young girl back then. Maybe it's understandable that she was so naive.

"I noticed the boy was part Molan," the dwarf said. "So I figured there must be something...well, I can see that..."

He nodded at her. She reached up and touched the Father's Arrow she always wore around her neck. It wasn't until I was a bit older that I noticed her wearing that made some folks — not all, but some — treat her a little different.

"Call it intuition," he continued. "I fought alongside a Molan lad, a Strongblood, back in the service. Finest Raider I ever saw."

The word "Raider" caused my mom to — I don't know. It was a small movement, almost like she was about to bow, but then stopped herself.

"Anyway, I think he's probably really a good boy — just fell in with the wrong sort, is all. I figured bringing him back to his mother instead of...well, bringing him to you is a step on the Path, right?"

She thanked the man profusely, and led me back upstairs. I knew when she got her hairbrush I was about to get the worst thrashing I'd ever got. Well, the worst up until that point, anyway.

3

"I'd been hoping to put this off until you were a little older," my mom grumbled as she straightened my clothes, "but I guess we'll have to start now."

Even if I didn't know enough to know there was a better life outside the Warrens, my mom knew it. So the morning after that dwarf had brought me home, my mother was putting me in the finest clothes she could scrape together, to get me ready to go enroll in the Temple School.

Now I don't know how much you know about Solta, though I assume if you're one of those long-bearded scholars you've probably at least visited there. But for those of you who may not be familiar with it, Solta's built on three hills surrounding a harbor. The part of the city in and around the smallest hill, which is right next to the harbor, is the Palace District, where the king and all the nobles and wish-they-were-nobles live.

Most of the city's built around the two taller hills. Right at the very tippy-top of the tallest hill is where they put the Patriarch Temple.

Now, the Warrens are next to the docks. Which is to say, as close to the bottom of that hill as you can get. And even though she was dog tired from working all night, my mom got me spiffed up and we marched all the way to the top of that blasted hill.

At that point, I'd only been to the Temple complex a few times. The first two times I couldn't remember — right after my birth to have my name recorded, and once right after I first started walking, to take my first step in the Sacred Soil. I'd also been there during the last Winter Festival, where I'd watched the Temple's Master of the Arcane wave his staff around and use nothing but magic to levitate a giant statue of St. Baur onto a pedestal overlooking the Temple Plaza.

But on this day, we walked right past the rows of statues and past the front of the Temple to this ugly stone building off to the side that looked more like some sort of gaol. It was just a big stone box four stories high, with rows and rows of bored-looking windows half-heartedly jabbed into it. There was an ornate bridge that led from the second story over to the Temple itself.

At the front of the ugly stone building was a big door with an elaborate carved sign above it. It said simply, "Temple School," but as I couldn't read just yet, it might as well have read "YOU ARE FUCKED, FUCKED, FUCKED."

My mom pulled me through the door into a large room ringed with hundreds of cubbyholes, which made it look like the inside of a giant beehive. All the cubbies were stuffed with various papers.

Off to one side was a small wooden desk, covered with stacks of paper, a bowl of ink, and a container stuffed with quills. A tall, bony man with long white hair surrounding a shiny, almost pointed bald spot was hunched over it, scratching something on a piece of paper laid out on the only open space on the entire desk.

The man continued scratching on the paper for several seconds. I expected my mom to say something, but she just stood there pleasantly.

Finally the man raised his quill and looked down at the paper as if to inspect it. He must have been satisfied, because he nodded and smiled, then slowly reached over to put the quill in the container with all the others.

He then looked up at us, his expression brightening as if we were a pleasant surprise that had suddenly appeared, even though he had to have known we were standing there the whole time. He had bulging eyes framed with spectacles that looked much too small, and was dressed like one of Auld Father's Footmen.

"May I help you?" he said in a musical baritone.

My mother explained who she was and said she would like to enroll me in the Temple School. She said she knew the school year had already started and she had been wanting to wait a few years, but had recently come to the conclusion that for the sake of my immortal soul, the hour had come. She was gracious — my mom did everything gracefully — but the worry in her voice was obvious.

The Footman stared at her, smiling, his face frozen. When she finished, he looked down at me.

"Is the child — Pearl, did you say? — is he registered at the Temple?"

She nodded. "Registered, as am I. And he has taken his first step on the Path," she said, and gave them the date, though don't ask me what it was.

"And you are the mother? Your name is...?"

She gave him her name and explained why it was different.

"'Pearl' is his father's name," she lied, and gave him some sob story about how they had been engaged to be married, and then him and his whole family had died of plague or something, and this after her parents had died only the year before, leaving her all alone to raise the child...it went on, and she looked like she was genuinely beginning to get teary-eyed, and her freckled face was beginning to flush, although when I asked her about all that later she told me to hush and not be silly.

It must have worked, because the Footman's eyes drooped in something I suppose must have been pity. He rang a bell and got another worker to go fetch some paperwork.

In an hour I was waving bye to my mother as I was led down a hallway that ran down the length of the big stone building.

"You must obey the Footmen," she told me before I left, "as if they were me — as if they were your father. Because in a way, they are." I was whisked away before I could ask her what she meant by that.

The boy leading me was a few years older, maybe about Lemon's age, but he didn't look anything like Lemon. He stood straight and looked very serious, and didn't speak a word to me.

Finally, he came to a halt in front of a door, just one among the rows of wooden doors that lined both sides of the hall. I could hear a raspy voice droning on somewhere on the other side of the door. The older boy rapped the door three times. I heard the raspy voice shout "enter!"

We came into a room with a big lectern at one end. The lectern was atop a raised platform a couple of steps up from the floor. Behind it was another man dressed in Footman's attire. He had a big tuft of snow white hair hastily brushed back, and a weatherbeaten face with a jaw like bouncer at Mallee's. From the wrinkles around his mouth he looked like he'd been frowning for a hundred years without stopping.

To this day I can remember his eyes. They were small, black with a glint like fire. The older boy exchanged words with the old man, and he was introduced to me as Footman Graus.

The rest of the room was taken up by rows of long tables arranged like the pews in our local parish chapel. Seated at the tables were a bunch of young boys who all looked about my age. They all looked at me wide-eyed, like I had just let out a huge fart.

The old Footman introduced me to the others as "Mr. Pearl," and told me to find a seat. I found a place in the back, and he continued droning on.

I DON'T REALLY REMEMBER the first few days. I think I was still in shock — there was nothing like this where I was from. Everybody seemed so stuffy, and the kids were all so quiet. None of the kids were from the Warrens, or anything close to it. A lot of them were from the Bells, which is farther up the hill from the Warrens, and several steps above it in quality, and a few of them were from the Bronze Terraces, which is where I used to think all the rich people lived, before I saw how REAL rich people lived.

But once I got my bearings, I decided real quick I didn't much like this school bullshit. I mean, you had to sit still and couldn't talk or anything, except to repeat the stuff from the instructors — and in the beginning, it seemed like that's all we did, was just repeat stuff, over and over and over. And there didn't seem to be any point to it at all.

And nobody really liked me, either. The other kids didn't like me, but they didn't give me much trouble — they'd heard all about the Warrens, so I think they were probably scared. But the instructors REALLY didn't like me. It seemed like most of my time was spent getting yelled at or beaten for doing something wrong.

And I was always doing something wrong. It seemed like every time I took a breath I was breaking some rule. I had no idea there was so much you could get in trouble for. I remember feeling a little pinch of relief every time I managed to figure out something that WASN'T against the rules.

Anyway, that's what put me on the road to the first real lesson I think I ever learned in life, and that lesson was to never try and grow a brain around my mom.

4

For the first few weeks, my mom would walk to school with me, even though she was tired from working all night. But once she figured I knew the way, she started letting me go on my own. And that's the first time in life I decided I was really clever.

See, I was the only boy from the Warrens who went to the Temple School. And nobody I knew from the Warrens ever came around up there. So I figured it wouldn't be any harm if I just stopped going. I mean I pretended to go, of course, to make my mom happy, but as soon as I was around the corner I'd go hang out with my gang. Lemon was glad to see me back. He liked the fancy clothes my mom had me wear, because it made me look less suspicious — which meant I had an easier time lifting coins off people.

I didn't figure it would be any trouble. I mean, how was my mom going to find out? Most of my aunts from the rooming house didn't care, and the ones that did never came around the parts where our gang hung out.

You're probably laughing right now, reading that, and I wouldn't blame you. But I was just a small boy, remember, and nobody ever explains these things to children. Nobody explains much to me now that I'm a grown up, come to think of it.

Anyway, I didn't know better, and the school was all the way at the top of the hill, and it was farther away than anywhere else I'd ever been in my entire life. And there were so many other boys at the Temple School, I didn't think anybody would notice if I wasn't around. By Auld Father, as much as the instructors seemed to hate me, I figured even if they noticed I was gone, they'd be glad to be rid of me.

And even if they did have a problem with it, the Temple School was so far away I didn't think the people there would have any way of telling my mom. What, would they walk all the way back down the hill, all the way down to the Warrens, just to tell my mom I hadn't shown up that day?

It never occurred to me that they might ride down on a horse, or catch an ox-trolley. And I didn't know anything about the Crown Post. I was just a little kid. The world still seemed small, and I thought I had it figured out.

Well, they noticed real quick that I wasn't at school, and they wasted no time in telling my mom. I think it was about a week after I started ditching, after a day of pickpocketing with the gang, I came into our room and my mom wasn't asleep, like she usually was. She was sitting there at our tiny table looking all serious, and she asked me where I'd been. And of course I told her I'd been to the Temple School, and I was so happy to be home, and she let me go on and on for about five good minutes before she got up from the table and came over to me and gave me a good thrashing with her hairbrush, calling me a liar the whole time.

Of course, I had plenty of experience with my mom's thrashings by this point because, as my Aunt Rossie said, Gruun's demons had obviously taken a liking to me. But I remember this time in particular because my mom started crying while she was beating me, and she was crying so hard she actually stopped whipping me long before she usually did, and sat down on the bed with her hair all mussed up and falling half across her face.

I started to think something was wrong with her, like she might be sick or something, because I'd never seen anything like that before. I'd seen her cry before, of course, but she was always quiet about it, and she always tried to do it when I was asleep. I asked her what was wrong and I remember she stopped crying long enough to yell something at me, asking if I wanted to grow up to be like the men who spent all day at the public halls drinking on the King's coin.

I got scared at her yelling and started crying myself — well, worse than I already was from the whipping — and then Aunt Gresa came barging in and wrapped her arms around my mom and rocked her back and forth, telling her it would be okay. I asked her if my mom was okay and she gave me a look that would melt steel, and told me to go downstairs to the kitchen and help Aunt Rossie with the dishes.

Well, needless to say, the next day, one of my aunts came along to escort me up the hill to the Temple School. For the rest of that fall and winter, one of my aunts would always go with me to the school, and would always make a point of checking that the clerk — the tall Footman I'd met that first day, who I came to know as Footman Olney — knew I had arrived.

There wasn't a need for that, though. After seeing how bad I'd hurt my mom that first time, I resolved never to hurt her like that again. It wouldn't be the last promise I'd end up breaking.

I don't think Lemon would have been all that thrilled to see me, anyway — a few days after I started going back to school, I saw him limping along the streets sporting a bunch of bruises and a nasty black eye. When he saw me, he ran as fast as his limping legs would carry him in the other direction.

I figured that was Aunt Rossie's doing.

5

One thing stuck with me, though. Even though mom made me go to the Temple School, I knew there were other schools. We even had one in the Warrens — just a few blocks over, facing Leeds Square, they had the King's School. Most kids in the Warrens didn't go to school, but the ones who did all went there. I asked my mom why she didn't make me go there, and she just shook her head and said nothing good ever came out of the King's School.

Now, at the time I didn't really understand that. I knew Mr. Thed, the man who came to fix things around the rooming house when they broke down, had gone to the King's School, and he seemed nice enough. But looking back Mr. Thed wasn't, well — he wasn't what you would have called "presentable." I didn't know that word back then, and I don't think my mom knew it, either, but I think that was what she wanted for me — she wanted me to be "presentable."

She figured if I went to the King's School, I'd never get out of the Warrens. She knew there was something better out there and she wanted that for me, but at the time I didn't understand; it just seemed like another one of those crazy things adults do that don't make any sense.

There was also another school, one that you could pass right by on your way up the hill to the Temple School, if you took the eastern thoroughfare. It was a big fancy place, with a big fence around it, and the fenceposts were all topped with gold stars. There were words above the gate, but even after I learned to read, I could never read them — the shopkeeper across the way said they were in the Auld Tongue, like the names of the three moons. He claimed the words said something about educating the body, brain and spirit. Now that I think of it, I guess that sounds like a fancier version of what they always used to tell us back in the Blue Wood: "Sharpen your limbs; polish your mind; and master your will" — but I'm getting ahead of myself now; I'll come back to that later.

Anyway, the full name of this fancy school was "St. Kendophal's Academy of the Noble Arts," but everybody I knew, even the teachers at the Temple School, just called it St. Kendo's. At first I didn't even know it was a school; I thought it might be one of those houses where the King or his nobles lived, except it was strange to have such a grand home sitting around so many ordinary homes. One day when Aunt Twos was escorting me to school I asked her if the King lived there and she laughed and told me it wasn't a house, it was a school.

I asked why I couldn't go to school there, since it was closer. It looked a lot nicer than the Temple School, too.

I remember Aunt Twos laughed, which started her coughing — she smoked a lot, those awful smelling cigarettes from Lyndan — and when she finished coughing she laughed some more.

"By Auld Father's Foot, I bet your momma wishes you could go there!" she said. She told me that it cost money to go there, and when I said my mom had money, she laughed and coughed again and said it was a lot more money than my mom had, a lot more money than I'd ever seen. I asked her how much and she said she didn't know, but she reckoned it would be so much money it would weigh as much as the big table in the rooming house where we would have the meals on Seveneve.

I was pretty sure Aunt Twos was lying, because back then I didn't think there was that much money in the entire world. But from what I know now, she might not have been that far off.

Later on, I learned that St. Kendo's is actually a bit middling, as far as schools like that go. I learned that there's schools a lot fancier and richer, even in Solta. Skunk — I haven't gotten to him yet, but I will — said he went to a school in Komat that made St. Kendo's look like a four-hole shithouse with no dividers.

But even if the Temple School wasn't as fancy as St. Kendo's, it was a damn sight nicer than any of the buildings in the Warrens. I reckon that's what set me on my path to ending up with the Raiders, now that I think of it — going to the Temple School. I didn't know much about the Raiders then, but people always talked about them as if they were tough — for a while I thought they might be some big-time gang, like the Tritons were back home in the Warrens. It was a fellow student who finally set me straight.

I remember it was a hot day, and Footman Tan was lecturing at the front about how to use a counting board to figure fractions, and I was bored almost to tears. To try and keep awake, I focused on the big scar on Footman Tan's face.

Footman Tan was on the short side, and a bit rounded, though not exactly fat. He was beefy, like a stevedore down by the docks. His head was completely bald, and the only hair anywhere on his head poked out from his ears. You might think that's disgusting, but that's not what caught most people's attention. What people noticed when they looked at Footman Tan was his face — it was marked by a long scar that went all up one side and over all the way to the back of his skull; it made one of his eyes a little bit higher than the other. I looked at it, and the more I looked at it, the more I wondered how he got it. I'd seen tavern brawlers with scars like that, but Footman Tan didn't seem like he spent much time around taverns. He was more the type who could turn a mug of ale into vinegar just by looking at it.

Where did he get that scar? I couldn't get the question out of my mind, so I leaned over and whispered to the boy beside me, asking him if he knew the story. He didn't answer me at first — he didn't want to catch a beating — so I had to keep pestering him. By that point, beatings didn't bother me — well, not much, anyway. The instructors would only beat you with those little leather straps they carried on their belts, and a beating with one of those was nothing like a beating from my mom's hairbrush.

Finally the boy — his eyes locked straight ahead — whispered out of the corner of his mouth, "what is it, scaleback?"

Oh, he'd pay for that. But that could wait. At the moment, I just wanted to know about Footman Tan's scar, so I asked him.

His eyes swiveled slightly towards me.

"You don't know?"

I didn't say, "no, you dumb fucker, that's why I'm asking" while slapping the back of his head, like I would have done back in the Warrens; I just played dumb.

"Footman Tan was in the Raiders," the boy hissed.

Later, after school got out and I pulled him aside and gave him a few lumps for calling me a scaleback, I told him I'd hold off on taking the rest of my payment out of his Bronze Terrace ass if he'd tell me more about the Raiders. (One thing I figured out really quick was that flashing Warrens cred was a good way to get the snootier kids at the Temple School to take me seriously.)

I think the boy thought I was putting him on at first, but when he finally got it through his head I was serious, he told me the Raiders were like soldiers, except different.

"You mean like the King's Guard?" I asked.

"No, no, the King's bodyguard, that's different. The Raiders are — well, they're like really, really tough soldiers. The ones they send out to handle the toughest fights. You know," he said, looking directly at me with a burning contempt, "like if there was a pack of five-eyed wolves..."

"Fuck you, I know they're not real."

He rolled his eyes. "Okay, like a rampaging troll. Or a goblin eruption. They used to fight dragons, back when there were enough of them still around to still be a threat."

I tried to squeeze a little more info out of him, but he said he didn't know much else, and if I wanted to find out more I should go read a book.

6

By that time — I must have reached nine summers — they'd actually managed to teach me to read.

For a while there I was pretty sure they'd never manage it. I just didn't see the point in memorizing all those stupid letters, which just looked like squiggles to me, or what sounds they made. I couldn't see any good use for it — almost nobody else in the Warrens could read, and they all seemed to get along fine.

But if there's one thing they believe in at the Temple School, it's reading. Footman Tan in particular was pretty hard on that point — he said every one of us had to learn to read, because that was the only way we'd be able to study the Holy Scriptures in The Walk, which was the only thing that could keep Gruun from snatching our useless souls and turning them to his wicked plans.

Footman Tan was really big on The Walk. I mean, I guess all Footmen are, or are supposed to be, but Footman Tan was something else. He had a huge, thick, leather-bound copy of The Walk that he carried everywhere and which sat open on his lectern when he was teaching. I don't know why he actually needed a copy of it, because it seemed to me that he had the entire thing memorized.

And Footman Tan seemed bent on making us all as crazy about the Scriptures as he was. Even when it came to big words, the ones that real people never use, like "sanctification," Footman Tan still made us learn them, because if it was in The Walk, it meant Auld Father wanted everyone to know them.

And once I'd spent about a hundred thousand hours repeating the same stupid exercises, I found out that in spite of myself, I was actually starting to make sense of this reading stuff. One day when I was walking to school I found myself looking over at the posters and murals alongside one of the buildings and I realized I could understand what they all said, and I didn't even have to sound out the different letters to myself.

All those endless lessons and endless thrashings had somehow set my brain so that all the steps I used to have to go through were just done in a flash, without thinking, the same way I'd learned pickpocketing. Point is, I'd picked up something just by doing it over and over again, and it didn't seem to matter whether you hated or loved it — it worked the same either way. Much later on, I'd run into that again.

So when that smart-ass kid from the Bronze Terraces told me to read a book, it was something I actually knew how to do. Up until then I'd never thought books were worth anything, but my interest had been sparked. I remembered how that klang…I mean, that dwarf who'd hauled me to my mom that one night had said something about being a Raider, which seemed to impress her.

That was something; there wasn't much in the world outside of the faith that impressed my mom.

I decided I needed to find out more about these Raider fellows. So the next day I went to the Temple School library, and for the first time in my life I got myself a book to read on purpose.

That first book didn't do much for me, I'm afraid. I can still remember the look the library keeper, Footman Crain, gave me when I asked for a book about the Raiders.

"We don't have any books like that for someone…for a student your age," he said, and tried to interest me in some little kids' book that had stupid pictures of a knight wearing purple armor. I kept pestering him, and finally he sighed and pulled a big volume off a high shelf and shoved it across his desk at me, telling me it had to be back in two days. It was a big, thick book, bigger than all my schoolbooks stacked on top of each other.

I brought it home that night and tried to read it, but I couldn't make much of it — all the words were big and it was all too stuffy. I thought it was gonna have stories about guys hacking each other up with battle axes, but there was nothing like that. Most of the pictures were boring, too — a bunch of charts and maps. But there was this one page that had a painting of a battle on it — it was the famous painting of the Battle of Crooked Canyon, the one that's in probably every book anybody's ever written about the Raiders.

I was dazzled by that painting. You know the look that Captain Elex has on his face, and the way he's standing there with his sword as the dwarves are just starting to pour out of the fog? And I mean, you just know the second he saw that, he must have known he was going to die, but he just stands there with that look on his face like, yeah, you filthy klang…I mean, dwarves, do your worst.

It was just about the greatest thing I think I ever saw. I remember sitting on my bed looking at that by the light of the lamp, and thinking to myself, man, if that's what a Raider is, then I want to be a Raider.

I remember that changed the way I looked at Footman Tan, too. I mean don't get me wrong, I didn't like him any better. Just thinking about him now makes me flinch, like he's gonna suddenly pop up out of nowhere and yank me up by the neck and drag me off to pound my ass with his strap in front of the whole class.

But once I got a line on how badass the Raiders were, those beatings didn't seem so bad. My hatred sort of dried up and got replaced with something more like respect. Heck, I even started trying to straighten up and behave a little better. Oh, I was still a nasty little shit, don't get me wrong. But for the first time I sort of picked up on why behaving yourself could be a good thing — it was good because it could get you the respect of a man like Footman Tan, and that might actually be worth something.

Respect — you know, that reminds me of something. Now that I think of it (and I didn't think of it much at the time, what with my ass always being sore), I remember the way Footman Tan called me MISTER Pearl. I mean all the teachers did that, called you Mister, or I guess Miss or whatever if you were in the girls' classes — we never saw the girls except at daily prayers in the Temple. But there was something about the way Footman Tan said it — he said MISTER in a way that sounded very mean, except...not mean, really. More like serious. Like he saw you as...well, not like you were an equal, but maybe like you weren't a piece of horseshit to be scraped off the bottom of a boot. And I remember he said that MISTER-whatever exactly the same to all the other boys. Like he didn't think any of us were better than any other.

That meant something to me, because I reckon I stuck out like a pink goat at the Temple School. The kids there would rag on me a bit for being from the Warrens — but not too much, because like I said, flashing some Warrens cred could usually shut them down. But even if they didn't give me shit to my face, they still treated me different, and I knew they said stuff about me behind my back.

But Footman Tan wasn't like that at all. He just always called me MISTER Pearl, like I was no different from any of his other students. The other teachers, they had a way of saying "Mister" to me that was just a bit different, you know? They said it girly-like, or sad-like, or something, like they thought I was just a bit lower than the other "Misters." But Footman Tan just sounded the same, even when he was pounding my ass for the millionth time for farting in class.

7

Now I know, from reading the books they had at the Temple School, that I'm supposed to tell you here that even though I was a wretched poor boy, I worked hard and was smart and that I showed up all the other boys at the school. I guess that's probably what my mom was hoping for by sending me up that hill every day in the first place. They had whole stacks of books with stories like that at the Temple School, some which they made us read and others I guess they expected us to read for fun.

But I said at the start that this wasn't gonna be one of those stories, because I think somebody has to tell the stories where real stuff happens. Oh, I got to the point where I'd at least give my schoolwork a good try, just because I didn't want to let down my mom. For example, I learned that the whole repeating something over and over again until it became second nature was something that also worked with numbers and arithmetic — though for some reason, that never worked as smoothly for me.

But even if I was learning, it was pretty obvious I wasn't cut out to be any kind of scholar. I think most of my teachers probably just gave up on me, although not all of them did. I mean, I don't think they were ever proud of me or anything — I don't think I ever got so much as a "good job, Mister Pearl" or anything like that. I mean, the ones who didn't give up just wouldn't lay off me, even when I was obviously a hopeless case.

And Footman Tan was the worst. By Auld Father, how sore my ass was coming out of his classroom. But I guess some of it must have stuck, because I suppose he's the main reason I can read and write. I know I'm not good at either, but I'm writing this and you're reading it, so I can't be that bad can I? At any rate Footman Sesh said I do a pretty good job, which is why he kept hounding me to write all this down.

Still, I got something out of all that schooling — something more than thrashings, I mean. There weren't that many folks in the Warrens who could read, after all. My mom could read, and I knew of a few others, but it was pretty rare. I found out quick it was something I could do to impress the grownups. When I got good enough, Aunt Rossie would sometimes ask me to read a bit from The Walk before Seveneve meals. I always thought it was kind of weird that there were folks like my Aunt Rossie who had copies of The Walk but couldn't read them — and now that I think of it, I reckon Footman Tan probably thought that, too.

But it didn't take me too long to find an even better reason for reading. If I couldn't read, I'd have never found the stories about Vast the Brutal.

I can just about see you long-beards turning white when I mention that, at least those of you who know who Vast the Brutal is. After I got to where I could read a bit, I started taking an interest in those books they call two-coppers, because they only cost two copper coins. Before I learned to read, I used to notice them because they were always the ones they put in the windows of the bookshops. They had paper covers, like some of the books we had at school, but they didn't have any of those boring pictures on them, the ones of little boys and girls dressed in finery sitting in a garden and drinking tea. Instead, these books always had drawings of monsters and big fighting men with swords, guys with giant arms like the bouncers at the sporting houses. They also had lots of pictures of big-bosomed girls that didn't have hardly any clothes on, which I didn't really notice when I was a kid, but I noticed when I was a little older.

Anyway, once I got to reading well enough, I got tired of reading boring stuff and got curious about those two-coppers, so I filched a few of them from a book-cart. We used to call that the Warrens discount, because even though they were only two-coppers, I didn't even have that much. I mean I guess I could have lifted some coins off people I passed in the street and bought them honest, but that somehow seemed even worse. I figured stealing those books direct was the most honest thing to do.

Now before you get on my case, I'll tell you I tried first like they tell you in the stories, where the good boy goes to the lending library to get the books he needs to make himself better. The trouble was, I didn't really know where I could find a library, which is how I know none of those books about wretched poor kids I read at the Temple School were ever written by somebody who used to be a poor kid. I'd heard of something called the King's Library, but I had no idea where it was, and anyway I doubted they'd have any of the books I was looking for.

Oh, yes, I know: They had a library at the Temple School, and I swear to Auld Father I went there first. When I went and asked Footman Crain about one of those books with monsters on the cover, I remember I got a right good thrashing. Footman Crain thought I was making another of my pranks by asking about such things in Auld Father's house. But I wasn't really clear back then on the idea that some books were good and some were bad; as far as I'd seen by then they were all just awful and boring.

So I lifted a few of those two-coppers, and one of the first ones I snagged was about Vast the Brutal. He was from some wild land called Thongamara. It sounded a lot like the stories my mom used to tell me about the place where she grew up, except she said there weren't many men who were hunters or fighters anymore, or even farmers. She said that was one reason she left — all the men spent their time drinking on the King's coin down at the public hall, or whoring about when they managed to scrape a few coins together for themselves. I guess she was disappointed when she found pretty much the same thing in the big city.

Maybe that's why I took such a quick liking to Vast the Brutal. Even though Vast wasn't a city boy from the Warrens, and never seemed to like cities all that much, he seemed like he'd be able to make his way just fine in the Warrens — in fact, we could have used a lot more of his kind. He was always going about killing monsters and bad men and sometimes both, and he never did it for selfish reasons, or at least not totally selfish — it's not like he was a criminal or something. He might be on the lookout for some gold or women, but he seemed like he was usually out to help folks while helping himself.

It might sound silly, but when I first started reading those two-coppers, I didn't realize they were all made up. I figured if somebody bothered to write it down, it must be true, because why go through all the trouble to write a book full of stuff that never happened? I got excited thinking that maybe one day, Vast would come by the Warrens during one of his adventures, and he'd meet me and find out I came from fighting stock, and would want to take me with him, so he could show me the ropes on becoming a great adventurer. So I was kind of let down when my mom explained to me how Vast was just made up, and pointed out that all the stories about him had the same name at the beginning, somebody called "Igon Laerax." That, she said, was the guy who was making up all the stories. She said some people made a full-time living just making up stories like that, which I didn't really believe, because that sounded like the dumbest job in the world.

Even after that, though, I kept reading those two-coppers, because even if the stories weren't true, they were still a lot of fun. I mostly read the ones about Vast, but I also read some others — there were other guys who tried to write stories that were like Vast the Brutal stories, but they'd change the names to something else, like "Humongous the Bloodthirsty," or "Last the Brute." They were pretty good, but they were never as good as the ones written by that Igon Laerax guy. I liked other stories, too, like the ones about Captain Juska and his band of pirates, or Rustan the Wizard, who traveled with a pet rooster that could talk and was always cracking jokes at his expense. There was even a bunch of stories about a long-bearded scholar named Doctor Artyn, except instead of sitting in a library all day reading dusty old books like most of you fellows, he was always traveling to exotic lands to find lost books and scrolls for other long-bearded scholars to read, and getting into adventures along the way. One time, he even used a big slingshot to travel up into the sky and land on Arban, the largest moon, which was pretty strange even for a made-up story.

I learned real quick, though, that even though those two-coppers had words just like any other book, they weren't the right words, or they weren't the kind you were supposed to read, no matter if you liked them or not. One day when I was at about ten summers, I was sitting in Footman Tan's class reading a two-copper story about Vast and how he was fighting to save this princess from a giant spider with wings. And I guess I was really into it, because I didn't notice when the whole classroom got real quiet, but then I suddenly heard this booming voice:

"MISTER Pearl," Footman Tan said, and he clapped that big paw of his on my neck and yanked me up out of my chair. "WOULD you CARE to tell the rest of us WHAT you are reading that is more IMPORTANT than Footman Rom's speech before the Council of Murak?"

And I probably should have known better, but one thing I liked about Vast the Brutal is that he always told the people he talked to exactly the truth, none of that sidestepping talk that clever folks like to use when you ask them a simple question. So I told him what I was reading, and how I liked it better than the stuff we usually read, and I probably should have stopped there, because that one eye of his was starting to twitch like it always did when he was getting angry. But I kept on shooting off my mouth and asked him why we couldn't read fun books like that instead of boring stuff? It's all words and reading, right?

By Auld Father, what a beating I got then.

8

The rest of my learning at the Temple School can be summed up as: I learned how to keep my mouth shut and sit still and pay attention, how to take a beating when I didn't, and how to get up early in the morning and walk a long ways. Those turned out to help me later, though I can't say they were welcome lessons.

When I got to around 13 summers, Gruun's demons managed to bend my ear once again and lead me away from the Path. I can still remember the day I made my decision, and how it happened.

The Temple School would give older students a bit of free time after daily prayers. A lot of students used it for studying, of course. But you didn't have to study; you could do other things. Some kids would grab a bite to eat at one of the stalls in the nearby market; some would just find a quiet spot and catch up on sleep. Some of the more religious kids would just remain in the Temple pews, silently praying.

Of course, it wasn't like me to gravitate to kids like that. Instead, I used to join a group of other boys who would sneak up to the top of the Temple's great bell tower. Somehow, one of them had learned about a hidden door in an out-of-the-way little space right off the Temple's side entrance hall, which was where the walkway over from the school connected to the sanctuary — I remember I spent a lot of time in Footman Pol's correction class for all the times I got caught tossing stuff out the windows of that walkway, trying to hit people going by on the street.

If you wandered over to this little corner that was kind of hidden from the main part of the entrance hall, there was an elaborate wooden wall carving, and if you grasped a carved wooden flower and turned it, the carving opened up, revealing the staircase that led up to the Temple's belfry. Up there, shielded from the eyes of the Footmen, we'd use our free time to drink, smoke, play cards, trade dirty jokes, and whatever other schoolboy mischief we could dream up. It would break my mom's heart if she'd known, but hey, I was still going to school, wasn't I? We obviously weren't the first Temple School boys to stumble upon the place, because there was a bunch of trash and markings left behind by earlier generations of students. A lot of people had scratched their names into the wooden beams, along with dates — some went back nearly 100 years, which Footman Sesh tells me was around the time the current temple was built to replace the old one.

Anyway, it was right after we'd gotten our scores back from this big exam, which was supposed to determine which classes we'd take in the next term. Nobody in our little group had done very well, so after prayers we snuck up there to grumble about it. Somebody had brought along a bottle of Ytter's, so we took turns sipping from it and sharing gripes.

It was a gray, overcast day, and very cold; we were bundled up in our winter cloaks. Everyone was real quiet at first; I remember taking a sip from the bottle and looking south towards St. Rom's Arch; it's the largest and most elaborate gate along Solta's city walls, and the one every first-time visitor always wants to enter through, because it's supposedly the one Footman Rom came though when he first came to Solta to preach about Auld Father.

I was reflecting on the fact that I'd never been beyond those walls when this kid named Zam finally broke the ice. When he spoke, the knot in his skinny throat would always bob up and down in a way I found funny. So the second I heard his nasally voice I turned to look.

"It's been nice hanging out with you guys," he said, "but after tonight you'll need to carry me up here, 'cause my dad is gonna break my legs." I chuckled at that — Zam was a thin, bony kid; the image of his twig little legs being snapped was almost as funny as the bobbing knot in his throat.

He turned to me. "What's so fuckin' funny?" he snarled, which made me laugh harder. Zam could never pull off the tough guy act; he had a weak chin and a gap in his front teeth, which seemed too big for his mouth. His hair was always cut very short, yet somehow it still seemed messy.

"Oh come off it, Zam. You barely even use your legs as it is." It was another kid, I can't even remember his name, but I still remember what he looked like: Short and pale, with golden blond hair cut like a bowl, bright red lips and a face that was already starting to be covered with acne. "You come to school every day in a private carriage."

"I told you it's not ours," Zam said, the fire draining from his voice. "It's one of my dad's clients. It's a favor for my dad."

"Man, you don't see any of us coming here in a carriage. And anyway I've been to your house. Your dad's got his own stable."

Zam seemed to shrink at that. "Yeah, it's probably where he'll have me working the rest of my life after I graduate," he mumbled. He took the bottle from me and took a swig. Then something caught his attention. "Hey, what's going on over at the stadium?"

We went over to the eastern side of the belfry to get a better look. The Royal Stadium is the largest arena in Solta; they mostly use it for equestrian crap, but every so often they'll use it for something worth watching, like the skram match finals. They also use it for big public celebrations, since the stadium floor is one of the largest open spaces in the city. They say it's large enough to run a full-length horse race while still leaving enough room in the track infield for two skram matches on regulation-size pitches.

From where we stood in the belfry, we could see the whole structure lit up with colored lanterns. Rows of flagpoles with the Royal Standard had been erected all around the top ring of the arena. Listening carefully, I noticed the faint sounds of an orchestra playing a fanfare.

"It's the prince's investiture, when he formally receives his titles. It's been on the front page of the Ledger for weeks." It was another kid, name of Sesol; thick-bodied, but I wouldn't call him fat. He had a flat face and a flat head, but I think he was probably the smartest of our little group; the "Ledger" was the Capital Ledger, the closest thing to the Crown's official newspaper. Sesol was the only one among us who read it, since his dad was a butcher who worked in the Palace. Even though Sesol was built like a brick, his full dark hair and the thick fingernails on his stubby fingers were always perfectly trimmed.

"The prince? Which one?" — Zam again.

Then another voice: "If you don't know, Zam, your dad really is gonna have you working in his stables."

I turned to look. It was the last of our little crew, Gotto. He'd arrived late; his fleshy face had a permanent smile pressed into it, filled with crooked teeth. His sculpted nose was flanked by two happy black eyes under a mop of curly brown hair. While nobody in our group would have ever been judged handsome, Gotto was the only one I occasionally overheard girls describe as "cute." If you squinted, he did look a bit like a puppy dog. Maybe that was it.

"Eat my ass, Gotto. Just eat my whole ass," Zam said, flipping him a finger.

Gotto just laughed and grabbed Zam by the shoulders, then physically turned him back around to watch the spectacle in the distance, and leaned in beside him: "How do you ever expect to be registered at Stag's Hall if you don't know which prince is which?"

Zam shoved Gotto aside, and took a sip of Ytter's. "Stag's Hall. Shit. You sound like my dad." Another sip. "I'm telling you: After that fucking exam, I'll be lucky if he'll even let me be his apprentice."

Zam's father was some kind of clerk. I was never clear on exactly what he did, but I knew it was stuff to do with numbers and that he did work for people in the Palace District, like the "client" whose carriage brought Zam to the school each day. But Zam's old man apparently dreamed of his son becoming a barrister, and Stag's Hall was the snootiest barrister's registry in the capital. That was about as high as a commoner in Selva could expect to rise, powered by his own farts. Any higher and you'd need to be lifted by someone whose dick was swinging up in the clouds.

Gotto just grabbed the bottle of Ytter's and took a long swig. His eyes immediately popped out, and the face he made caused us to burst into laughter. He swallowed hard, let out a painful-sounding groan, then doubled over, his hands tightly clutching his knees. For a second it looked like he might throw up, which caused Zam to laugh even harder. Gotto staggered a bit, then managed to stand again, his ragdoll grin still gleaming.

"FUUUUUUCK. You should have…" — he made as if to heave, but caught himself — "…warned me. I thought it was just ale."

"Don't even start, you fucking pussy," I said, and took an equally big gulp. It burned my throat and nostrils, but I ignored it; I clenched my teeth, then let out a roar, the way I'd seen drunks do in taverns when they did shots. The other guys applauded.

Gotto stepped over to the edge of the belfry, moving very carefully on his boozy legs. He looked out at the bustling stadium. "Well, at least we're all in good company."

"What do you mean?" Sesol asked.

Gotto took the bottle from me as I stepped up beside him, and lifted it in a toast towards the distant celebration. "I mean someday, that prince is gonna let down his dad as badly as we all are."

"Not cool, man," the pale-faced kid said.

"Yeah, kid's five," Sesol said. "And that's our future King you're talking about."

Just then I caught a rare sight: Gotto's smile sagged just a bit, which was the closest he ever came to being serious. "I love our King," he said. "I love the Queen, I love the prince, I…" There was a long pause, then he continued. "I mean, it's just: Fuck, imagine the weight that kid carries around."

"I'd give my right nut for some of that weight," Zam said, still downcast.

I looked at Zam. I opened my mouth to say something, but closed it again. Fuck if I was going to help anybody at the Temple School feel better about themselves by reminding them that at least they didn't have my life.

Pale-face kid grabbed the bottle and raised it to his lips. I noticed he didn't actually take a sip; the other guys had their heads turned, so they didn't catch it. "I get it, actually," he said. "I mean sure, look at his life. But can you imagine what it's like, all those eyes on you every waking moment? Everybody just waiting to see you fail…"

Pale-face kid sounded like he spoke from experience. I knew, or thought I'd heard, that he was the only son in his family, with two older and two younger sisters. His dad was a heavyweight in one of the city's guilds — was it the dyers? Or maybe it was the cordwainers; I knew it had something to do with garment work

— and I guessed he was the one on whom his family's hopes were riding.

"Yeah. But he's the prince. They won't let him fail," Sesol said. "Even if he does fail, they'll find a place for him. They've got his brother, after all. And you didn't hear this from me…but the queen's already expecting another." Sesol took the bottle, sniffed it, and took a swig. "Least that's what my dad says…"

At just that moment, a loud, majestic shriek pierced the air, and a flight of five giant birds came soaring across the gray sky in a tight formation. They banked into a turn that brought them within a bowshot of the top of the belfry, close enough that I could see their riders. One of them saw us there gawking and waved to us.

"Hawk cavalry!" Sesol exclaimed, and raised the bottle of Ytter's in salute. "Hey, Zam, maybe there's something you could do, instead of cleaning out your dad's stables."

"Only nobles can be cavalry, dumbass," Zam said, seizing the bottle and taking another swig.

"Not if you join the Raiders. They've got a hawk cavalry division. And they damn sure don't have any nobles."

"Raiders! Fuck, I might as well jump to my death right here. My whole *family* would disown me."

Sesol just shrugged. The flight formation dropped lower as they approached the stadium. I noticed each rider had something strapped to his back. As they neared the stadium, the lead rider gave a hand signal and all five riders pulled something attached to their weird backpacks. The backpacks all began billowing out streamers of colored smoke as the formation passed over the stadium, and the lead hawk let out another stirring call.

Gotto continued to stare out at the stadium with the same odd smile. I noticed he'd gotten unusually quiet. I nudged him. "Hey, man, you OK?"

He turned to look at me, and for a second he didn't seem to recognize me. Then his usual grin spread wide across his face. He turned back to look at the stadium.

"Let's ditch," he said. "Fuck this place, fuck the exam, let's go join the party over there. If we go now we can avoid Footman Olney…"

Zam looked confused. "How the fuck are we supposed to get in?"

Gotto grabbed the bottle from him and took another swig. "You guys don't trust me?"

"It's a Palace event," Sesol said. "Even my dad couldn't get…"

Gotto held up a finger to shush him, and reached into his cloak.

"Well, *my* dad is the secretary of the Printer's Guild, which comes with certain… benefits." And with that, he produced a handful of palm-sized cards on thick, velvety paper, each with intricately-engraved printed designs: Tickets to the investiture celebration.

He handed one to each of us. I took mine and studied it. There was a problem. "Uh, Gotto, buddy…this isn't my name."

He craned his neck over and looked at it. "Oh, shit. You're right. I must have grabbed the wrong one. Well, it doesn't matter. Nobody cares who you are or where you're from if you've got the right credentials."

"You think they're going to fall for fake tickets?" pale faced kid asked.

"Oh, but that's just the thing — they're not fake. These are real. Well, more real than any other fakes out there, at least. My dad was in charge of the print run, and I helped out. Normally he won't let me because he wants me to focus on school-work, but this was an important job. And, well, I might have managed to slip in a few extras when he wasn't paying attention."

"He'll kill you if he finds out," Zam said. "Shit, and I thought I was in trouble…"

"Oh, I assure you, I'll be in much bigger trouble from that exam. This…this is nothing." He twirled the ticket playfully in his fingers, studying the designs. "And hey, I needed the experience — you're not the only one who's gonna be begging his dad for an apprenticeship, when it's all said and done."

And so, for the first time since I'd been caught all those years ago, I ditched class, and we made our way over to the stadium. The guard merely glanced at the tickets held by Zam, Sesol and pale-face kid, and waved them on through, but when Gotto produced his, the guard took it from him and examined it very closely. For a second I worried we'd been found out, but Gotto just smiled and said, with confidence as sturdy as granite, "Is there a problem, sir?"

The guard handed the ticket back to him.

"Just checking, my lord," he said. That cheeky bastard Gotto had made sure all of the tickets gave us titles of nobility. "We've had a few people try to come in with counterfeits."

Gotto retrieved his ticket and shook his head. "Counterfeit tickets? To the prince's investiture?" He clucked disapprovingly. "What is the kingdom coming to?"

"My thoughts exactly, my lord," the guard said. "You should see how bad things have gotten in The Warrens. With all the trash they have down there, the Reckoner can't come soon enough." With that, he turned to me, looked at my ticket, and waved me on through.

Even though the stadium wasn't quite full, it was still an awesome sight, seeing that huge mass of people cheering and waving banners. When we came in, I saw that they had set up lists for jousting, and two knights decked out in old-fashioned looking armor were riding their steeds to each end, preparing to charge. Each knight bore the crest of one of the noble families.

"What the fuck?" I said. "Isn't jousting…I mean didn't they…I thought the nobles…"

"Just watch," Zam said.

At each end of the lists, the knights lowered their helmets and pointed their lances, and at the sound of a trumpet, they charged. I stood there for a moment in nervous suspense, wondering why the rest of the crowd didn't share in my wide-eyed breathless silence, when the first lance struck...

...and simply crumpled up.

"Paper," Zam whispered in my ear as the crowd roared in approval. "It's just for show. For tradition."

I nodded, and we made our way to our seats.

Since we'd come in so late, the only open seats were high up, but we didn't mind. Even though we couldn't hear much of what was said, we could follow along well enough, and we could continue to finish our bottle of Ytter's in peace.

There were more jousting matches; Sesol gave a running commentary on all the noble houses, and where each one stood politically. None of it meant anything to me.

The jousting was followed by chariot races, again with contestants from each noble house. There was a troupe of dancers, a choir sang a bunch of songs, and then a solo singer, an incredibly fat guy, performed a song accompanied by the Royal Orchestra.

Sesol said it had been written especially for the occasion. I have to admit, the fat guy's voice was spectacular, and the lyrics were very stirring — something about how even though Selva was the greatest kingdom, and our King was a wise and mighty King, and our prince would no doubt be a great King too, we were all princes of the blood under Auld Father, who was the greatest King of all. I noticed the singer had a lot of people, including Sesol, tearing up; truth be told, I felt a little misty-eyed myself. When he finished, the entire stadium erupted in the night's biggest round of applause.

Finally, the King, Queen, and the prince, along with a bunch of other fancily-dressed people I didn't recognize, made their way to a small stage that had been erected there in the stadium. A klang...I mean, a dwarf dressed in the garb of a Footman Magnus stepped forward and gave a long speech that I couldn't make out, even though everyone in the stadium stayed silent for it, and many bowed their heads in prayer. At the end of it, the King, Queen and prince stepped forward, and the klang...the dwarf Magnus placed his hands on the prince's head and reeled off a bunch more things I couldn't make out.

And with that, I guess the celebration was over; the orchestra struck up another tune, and people began cheering and filing out of the stadium. Even though I was very drunk by that point, I can still clearly remember the King holding the young prince in his arms, beaming with pride as the boy waved at the departing crowd.

Making my way back to the Warrens that evening, I remember thinking about how the prince seemed to have an entire golden future already set to welcome him. Even in their disappointment, all of my school friends still had a vision of a future in front of them — maybe it wouldn't be as cozy as they'd been raised to expect, but they had a future all the same. But try as I might, I couldn't see anything like that for myself.

I mean, what was I going to do, once I graduated? I suppose I could have tried for an apprenticeship in one of the trade guilds, but even there I'd be up against guys like the ones I hung out with, who already had connections. If I managed to be accepted for anything, it would probably be for the worst trades, under the cruelest masters. I just thought I wasn't cut out for that.

Gruun's demons were whispering to me that the Warrens was where my future was, and after that day, their whispers were sweet indeed. So about a week later, I just quit going to school. I had four summers left at the Temple School, but I decided I was done.

By this time I was wise enough to add a few coins to the school clerk's pocket to make sure his mouth stayed shut and my mom didn't find out. But I know she quickly put it all together in her head. Like I said, the first lesson I ever learned about my mom was to never try to grow a brain around her, because she knew more than she said, and what she didn't know, she eventually found out. She never actually said anything to me about it — I guess she decided that I was old enough at that point to make my own choices. But I could see she was disappointed in me.

9

If I was going to make my way in the Warrens, I needed some kind of hustle, the kind you couldn't learn at the Temple School. And I needed to learn fast — at the end of my seventeenth summer, my mom would kick me out of her place at the rooming house. It wasn't entirely her call; those were the rules — can't have a bunch of horny young guys roaming about a respectable place for single women. My mom always warned me about that date when I was a little boy, I guess to scare me, but as I started to get a little older and sprout up a bit, she seemed to stop talking about it. I think it might have made her a little sad.

Now I know a lot of you folks who've never been to the Warrens, or whatever passes for it in other cities, think we're all just a bunch of criminals there, but you've got it completely wrong. It's actually probably only half that are criminals — I mean, those are the ones who actually make their living committing crimes and whatnot, and never have anything legitimate going on. I guess if you were going strictly by the King's Law, there'd be a lot more criminals, but those don't really count.

And by Auld Father, I had no intention of being one of those criminals, or at least not one of the ones you'd be scared of. I just wanted to be one of the ones who made money.

At first I thought maybe since I knew how to use a counting board I could be a bookie, because they always seemed to have lots of coin and they weren't mean and never beat anybody up, at least not personally. The small-time bookies worked at the animal-fighting pits, so I figured that was the place to break into the business. But when I went to the pits to talk up some of them and get a clue about the business, I learned real quick that there was more to it than just knowing some numbers on a counting board. You had to have a real head for numbers, and I already knew that I didn't.

When that didn't work out, I started hanging out around the part of the Warrens they called the Improvement District. Don't ask me why it was called that, because I never saw any improvement there. It was the part of the Warrens closest to the docks — all just muddy flats and streets that flooded every time it rained. If it rained hard enough, all the privies overflowed and the streets flooded with shit and piss, but since it was right next to the ocean it would just wash out into the harbor, so it was no big problem.

The Improvement District was, I guess, the only part of the Warrens most outsiders were likely to see; it was the part where all the high and mighty came when they wanted to go slumming. It was full of the better sporting houses and taverns, at least by Warrens standards — the kinds that actually charged for drinks and food instead of handing out the slop funded by the King's coin.

One of the first things folks ask you when they find out you're from the Warrens is if you know anybody from the Tritons. I used to scare the kids at Temple School all the time by making like I was in tight with the Tritons, but to tell the truth, back then I never actually knew anybody who was a member. I knew lots of guys who claimed they were members, but you could pretty much throw them out right away, because everybody knew if you were in the Tritons you weren't supposed to brag about it.

But even if I never really saw any Tritons, I heard all about them — if you believe all the stories you heard on the vine in the Warrens, the Tritons were the secret power behind everything. They got blamed for anything mysterious, and even stuff that wasn't that mysterious.

A rooming house burns down? It was the Tritons. Some guy dies in a bar brawl? The Tritons did it. Some people even blamed them for stuff they couldn't have any control over, like storms or girls dying in childbirth. If a fly cut a fart somewhere in the Warrens, people would tell you the Tritons fed him the beans.

So I wasn't a Triton, that didn't mean I was keeping my face clean. Every Warrens boy worth his salt was in a gang, because that's the only way you stay safe. The Craller Square Wolves were no more, but a few of the boys I'd known from back in the day ran with a gang called the Stonegate Clubs, named after a street a bunch of them lived on, and they put in a word and got me my buttons.

Footman Sesh was just in here reading over my shoulder again, and he was yammering about how I need to explain to you long-beards about the buttons. Okay, well, that was how you told what gang someone was in — the buttons. Everybody wore slouchers — well, I think you outsiders call them roach coats. Those are the brown leather jackets like the one Lemon wore back in the day. I didn't realize it at the time, but Lemon was in a gang — a real gang, that is — and the Craller Square Wolves were just one of his hustles, a bunch of street urchins he was running to make coin.

Anyway, the slouchers were what all the young guys wore, because anybody who looked our age and wasn't wearing one was considered fair game. Even a boy who didn't want anything to do with crime and just wanted to earn an honest living — I told you we actually had a few — had to get a sloucher just to go about his business without anyone bothering him; once I was old enough, I had to wear one just to go back and forth to the Temple School. And the way you told different gangs apart was the buttons. The Stonegate Clubs had buttons that looked like a balled fist, and they were painted red — it was supposed to symbolize our bloody knuckles, showing how tough we were.

I still remember the day I got my buttons, and how proud I felt over something that, looking back, is pretty stupid. It's not like you had to undergo a trial or anything — if you were a boy who lived near Stonegate Street and you were the right age and breathing, you were pretty much in. But I was still proud, because after years of being kind of a weirdo for going to school up at the top of the hill, it felt nice to actually be a bit normal.

And being in a gang had other benefits. Having other guys to back you up in a fight was the big one, but there were others. People treated you with a little more… well I wouldn't say respect, but they gave you a lot less friction. The buttons on my sloucher even got me my first girl. It's not like that was a huge achievement, either — girls outnumbered boys in the Warrens by a lot, so if you could talk and didn't look like trash you were pretty much set. But my buttons were what sealed the deal for me.

When I first got my buttons I had to sew them on myself — I couldn't ask my mom or any of my aunts for help, because they all knew what those buttons meant and they weren't about to help me with them. So I borrowed a needle and thread from one of my aunts — I didn't tell her I borrowed it, of course — and found myself a place to hide for a few hours while I figured out how to display my new pride and joy.

When I got finished, I knew the result didn't look very good, but I was proud of it anyway. I put on my sloucher and headed off to meet the gang, with my chest puffed out like I was the finest cock in the quarter. Then, while passing through Craller Square, I heard this giggling sound, and looked over and noticed this girl laughing at me.

Now, on the inside, I felt just about as silly as I could be. I knew she was laughing at how bad I'd done my buttons; I wanted to shrink up to the size of a gnome and run away.

But growing up in those parts, you learn to never clue people in on when you've got feelings like that. So even though I felt about as solid as a bowl of welkberry jam, I stalked over to her with my chest puffed out while trying to find the right words for the situation.

I tried to growl, "Girl, what's so funny? I know you aren't laughing at me; why don't you point out what's so funny so maybe I won't be so angry." I once heard a pimp say that to one of his girls, and she shut up real quick, but that was probably because he was built like a boulder and his voice boomed like the door of the Temple being slammed shut.

When it came out of my mouth, though, it just sounded scratchy, and I heard my still-breaking voice go real high at the end. She'd been trying to keep a tight smile, but that caused her to burst out in laughter. She dropped the bag full of cotton she'd been carrying over her shoulder. I wanted to shrink from the size of a gnome to the size of a gnat.

She must have seen the look on my face, because she zipped her lip and tried to keep from giggling more as she kneeled down to pick up her bag.

"You're a new one, aren't you?" she said. She was three summers older than I was, and had a hoarse voice that probably came from too many cigarettes. Tightly-curled rings of blonde hair spilled out from around the scarf which wrapped around her head, and when she smiled, your eye was drawn to her broken front tooth.

I opened my mouth to say something, but all that came out was an "uhhhhh." I was distracted by her cleavage, which was impossible to ignore when she was bent over picking up the bag.

She noticed I was looking, then gave me a fake frown with smiling eyes as she ran a finger down my cheek.

"Awwww," she said. "So CUTE!"

It was her big green eyes that did it, along with that broken tooth. She looked like a beautiful, clumsy doll.

She asked me to walk her to the place where she worked, so I did; it was a spinning mill over in the industrial section of the docks, near where my mom worked.

Her name was Salah, and she admitted she'd been with a lot of other guys before me. She said she thought her days as a gang moll were over, but that when she saw me I looked too adorable to pass up. Later that night after she got off work, I lost my cherry to her, and afterwards she fixed up the buttons on my sloucher and went with me to meet up with the other Clubs.

I suppose if any of you long-bearded scholars are women, you'll want to know if I loved her. Girls always want to know that — do you love her, do you love me, does that guy love that girl, does she love him. And I guess I could say I loved her — I loved her the way a wide-eyed boy of 13 summers loves the first girl who hikes up her dress and opens up her bodice for him. I loved her a lot when she was right in front of me, but I don't think you can really love anything or anyone until you start to worry about them when they're not right in front of you, or worry about where they will be in the future. And the future just wasn't real to me back then. Salah was great and all, and we had a lot of fun, even though we were only together a few months. I had a few other girls after her, but it was never quite the same.

So there: Salah will always have a special place for me. Even today I can feel chills when I remember the first time she ran her finger down my face and said I was "so CUTE." I guess that's a kind of love.

But it wasn't the sort of thing girls giggle and coo and sigh about — I wouldn't really understand that business until later. It was more like what I had with some of the friendly dogs I used to play with on the way back and forth to the Temple School — except, you know, different, because I wasn't fucking dogs. I know you long-beards think I'm disgusting, but even I'm not that depraved.

10

People think gangs are all about the crime. That's what the newspapers always made it out to be — yeah, we followed all the stories in the papers. Since I could read, I was always the one who read the stories to the rest of the crew when we got together in the tavern. That was always good for a laugh. One thing I learned from that is that you can never trust anything you read in newspapers. Even when they did manage to tell the truth — instead of just making things up, which is what they usually did — they always got everything scrambled.

That was the thing people never got — besides protection, the main reason for being in a gang was just to have a crew to hang with. It was like a kind of second family — and for some guys, it was the only real family they knew. Where we came from, it was like everybody in the world was against you — it felt good to have one group of people who would stand shoulder to shoulder with you for a change, and would always give a whistle to warn you when trouble was around the corner.

For a lot of us, the crime was never a big part of it. I mean sure, there were guys in our gang who were straight hustlers, who'd sometimes tap the rest of us for muscle. But the main thing was partying. Well, that and fighting. Those two things always seemed to go hand in hand. There was a joke people used to tell: "I went to a brawl last night, and a party broke out." We didn't have a whole lot else to do in the Warrens.

The highlight of the week was always Sixeve. We'd be up early in the morning to hit the public halls to get good and plastered on the King's coin, then we'd head out to the local arena for the games — skram was the big one, of course, although sometimes they'd stage equestrian stuff in the summer. While the horse games could be impressive, it was hard for us to get too wrapped up in them, since none of the competitors were the sorts we would ever have the chance to rub shoulders with — they were all either rich and highborn, or they were yokels from the far countryside who'd been in the saddle since before they could walk.

Playing skram, on the other hand, only required a ball and a gang of guys who didn't mind getting roughed up, and we had plenty of those in the Warrens — there were countless players for the big-time skram teams who'd come up from the Warrens, and from other equally scuzzy places in other cities that we'd only heard about. There were always scouts crawling around our haunts looking for some undiscovered skram star.

I know there's this notion that a lot of you outsiders have that all of us Warrens rats are skram experts. And maybe it's true, for the most part — but not in my case. At least not by Warrens standards, anyway. All of those years the boys back in the Warrens were spending their days playing skram in empty lots or back alley courtyards, I was spending my day up at the Temple School. I don't mean to say my skram game was terrible — I was an ace blocker in the short game — but since I spent most of my early years in school, I never got to be anywhere near as good as I could have been. I've always wondered how far I could have gone if I'd had a chance to pour myself into it, but you know what The Walk says: "Weep not for the turns you have missed; be thankful only that you are on the Path today."

But yeah, the idea that us Warrens rats love skram — *that* part is true. Even the skram guys who grew up in much nicer places tended to fit in well with us Warrens degenerates. By Gruun's cock, I remember the star forward for St. Pola's — one of the two main teams followed by folk from the Warrens, and the one we were loyal to in the Stonegate Clubs — came from an actual noble family, like the fourth family in line for the throne or something like that. Quick little bastard named Jais — small guy, but moved like a weasel that got loose at the dog pits. Even though he was the highest of highborn, he was a regular at taverns in the Improvement District — always with a couple of choice pieces of ass on each arm, always ready to spread coin about and drink and gamble with the locals.

The closest arena to us was Rainbow's Court, where St. Pola's played most of their matches. I don't know if you long-beards would even see fit to call it an arena — the stands on three sides were made of wood that looked like it might fall apart from rot at any moment, and they'd creak and groan like an old lady when the crowd filled them up and began stomping and cheering. The stands on the fourth side of the field were built into a hillside and were much sturdier, but the Crankers — the St. Pola's supporters — took pride in braving the rickety wooden stands. We left the hillside seats for whoever was stupid enough to come out and root for the visiting team. It was usually empty, except when the visiting team was Shaver's End — they were the big rivals of St. Pola's, from the west side of the Warrens. When that happened, it was a matter of honor for the west side crews to show up, as it was for us to show up at their arena when St. Pola's played them on their home turf. They always had an extra regiment of the city guard out for those games, because rumbles before, after and during the games were a certainty.

After the games, we'd gather up the crew and either head for the taverns back in the Improvement District, or — if we were feeling spicy — head out to find a bit of trouble. Although we preferred to brawl with westside crews, we could usually work up some reason to rumble with fellow eastsiders — though if they were eastsiders, the end of the night would usually find us drinking with them.

Now that I look back on it, a lot of it seems pretty silly — someone would flash the wrong gang sign while we happened to be strolling by, or they'd hit on one of our girls while wearing the wrong buttons. It was like we were looking for excuses to get in brawls.

And the girls! That's another thing you outsiders don't get — the girls were the worst ones. If there was a fight, you could be damn sure a girl had something to do with it. If somebody from another crew was stepping out of line, it was usually the girls who saw it first. Same when one of our crew stepped out of line — which, truth be told, we often did. They have a saying in the Warrens — the measure of a man is how far he can swing his dick before someone cuts it off. So everybody was always testing the limits, and everybody else was always pushing back.

Anyway, when somebody "broke the rules" — don't laugh, that's how we actually described it — the girls would notice immediately, and they'd start raising a fuss about it. And if we tried to brush it off, they'd raise an even bigger fuss. And that usually did it — you can't look like a coward in front of your gang molls.

I know you might not believe it, but the gangs tried as best we could to avoid bothering regular folks in our brawls. For big brawls, we'd usually schedule them ahead of time, some place like an abandoned warehouse or a vacant lot. That way we could be sure to keep it just between us. For REALLY big beefs, we'd usually try to have a "clean" fight: No weapons, two men only — our toughest guy against their toughest guy. Clean fights were always a big deal, and sometimes we'd go as far as charging admission, like it was a regular pit fight. They didn't happen very often, though.

But when it came to ordinary scuffles, we usually just had it out right there in the street, where regular folks sometimes got hurt through no fault of their own. I never felt great about that, but then again, there were a lot of things in the Warrens I didn't feel great about.

For weapons, we'd mostly use coshes or weighted belts — coshes were easy to make, so you could throw them away if the city guard arrived, and belts? Well, belts were clothing! There's nothing in the law that says you can't wear clothes, right? But like I said, it was the Warrens, so people like to push the line — in big fights, you'd sometimes find guys with slings, clubs, spikes and small knives. You'd even see rusty old swords, despite the fact that commoners caught with swords, if they weren't in the military, were subject to flogging.

I'm not gonna lie, people got real banged up in our brawls — sometimes killed, though I never knew of anyone getting punished for killing someone during a brawl; you could never prove who'd actually struck the killing blow. And it wasn't like the city guard cared much what happened in the Warrens, anyway. The guard would occasionally show up during a brawl and round up everybody for fighting, but at most that meant a few hours in the tank at the district gaol, which wasn't punishment at all — the tank at the Warrens gaol was practically another tavern, since we all knew each other there, and the guards didn't care what you did as long as you weren't fighting. They'd even give you dice or a deck of cards if you asked. I was a card man myself; I may not be too smart, but I knew enough about numbers to know that dice are pretty much all about luck, while card games like Cooper's Crown need a bit of skill. For somebody who'd already been dealt a bad hand in life, I liked that aspect — while you couldn't control which cards were handed to you, how you played them was entirely up to you.

This was one thing where my time at the Temple School gave me an edge back down in the Warrens. I'd cut my teeth playing cards against boys who could always afford to lose a little bit of money, while I could never afford to lose any. So learning how best to keep my money while taking everyone else's was a skill I'd honed through hard practice. I can't claim I was the best card player in the Warrens; if I was, I wouldn't be here writing this. But whatever cards you put in my hand, I'll figure out a way to play them the best I know how.

But most brawls never got to the level where people died or the city guard got involved. It seems weird to outsiders, but a lot of our brawls ended quite friendly. We'd all shake hands and even hug, and if anybody was hurt real bad, we'd band together to haul them off to the King's Hospital. It's a shithole, but it's the only one in the city that's free.

After nightfall on Sixeve, we'd usually go catch a fight — like the official kind, with guys who did it professionally. There was pit fighting, of course, both with weapons and without. (No blades, though — that was one rule where the city guard held firm. If you wanted to see men fight with blades, it had to be an illegal match that was invitation only — and we never got invitations; that was strictly high-roller stuff run by the Tritons.) But my favorite fights were when the different fighting schools would put on "exhibition matches" in our part of town, both to boost their own rep and to scout for talent. They'd have a few of their best guys fight a few matches to show off what they could do, then their toughest guy would stand up and accept challenges from all comers. And the exhibition guys almost never lost.

Now, I'm sure a lot of the "challengers" were probably ringers, but a lot were genuine, because I knew more than a few guys who gave it a shot, only to come back banged up and sore (and as heroes to the rest of us for defending the honor of the Warrens). What I found interesting was how *different* the exhibition guys looked from pit fighters — like there was an order and purpose to what they were doing. You saw all sorts of wild and acrobatic fighting styles, with guys who jumped and flipped around and all the rest, but the ones that caught my attention were the wrestlers. They weren't flashy, they didn't bounce around, but they weren't fazed by anything that came their way. A lot of times you'd see a small, wiry little wrestler take on a half-dozen guys twice his size and leave them groaning in pain. The calm determination they had, and the way they could just slowly and methodically take apart any attack, left a big impression on me. Bigger than I might have guessed at the time, as it turned out.

There were other evenings, particularly if we wanted to treat the gang molls, when we'd skip the fights and head to a music hall to watch the shows. I should probably explain that the music halls in the Warrens aren't like the proper music halls you long-beards are used to — they're what I guess you folks would call "unrefined." The plays and puppet shows and concerts are — what's the word? — I think Footman Sesh would call them "lewd." He uses that word a lot when I tell him about my life, so I think it's the right one.

One thing that always got me is that the singers and actors in the music halls seemed to know about us in the Warrens, because they'd always have little lines and jokes that only we could understand. Footman Sesh tells me that's how all entertainers are — he called it "playing to the audience." Whatever it was, it was terrific — sometimes it was enough to start a brawl right there in the theater, though we'd try to hold off until everybody was outside. I don't think the city guard had to show up more than three or four times that I remember. Maybe it was more, but anyway, it wasn't very often.

Anyway, the night would always end in a tavern — the paying kind, because the last thing a bunch of young folks want on a Sixeve night is to be in one of those gloomy public halls surrounded by gray old folks drinking their cares away on the King's coin. Even the food in the public halls is depressing — it seems like every dish is made from potatoes.

Whenever we could, we'd hire a band of musicians. That's another way out of the Warrens, by the way — through music. Some of the biggest singers and musicians that all you long-beards love to go on about got their start in places like the Warrens, where they probably spent many a night performing "lewd" songs for us degenerates. You'd be surprised how many of us are walking among you right now. I'm a perfect example, now that I think of it.

A lot of the gang would keep partying into well into the next morning, but I always had to come up with a way to duck out early — because, no matter what, no matter how hungover I was or what mischief I'd been up to the previous night, I always had to go with my mom to the noon service at the local chapel on Seveneve. That was the one thing which she absolutely demanded, no matter what. And considering all the other stuff she seemed to overlook, I figured it wasn't a bad bargain.

"When the day of the Reckoner comes," she used to say, looking at the sorry state of the Warrens while on our way to the chapel, "this will all be swept away."

11

Partying costs money. Everybody in a gang is supposed to chip in to the party fund, though they're not too particular about where you get the money. I mean, sure, a lot of guys get it through hustling on the streets, and I wasn't above that myself, but you don't actually have to do that. And all the lessons from the Temple School and Seveneve services must have had some effect on me, because doing anything too illegal always felt wrong. I mean, I don't think there's anybody in the Warrens with clean hands, except maybe my mom, but that doesn't mean you feel the same about every law you break. I guess it's her doing that Gruun's demons could never work their claws that deep into me.

Even with magic doing a lot of heavy work these days, there's still a lot of shit work where it's cheaper to pay a few coins to Warrens scum than to pay for enchanted ingots and the mages to use them. For a youngster around my age, you could go down to one of the factories around the docks — a lot of them are powered by stepwheels, and they'd pay you two coppers an hour to join with a couple of dozen other fellows holding a bar and treading a wheel. It's more boring than listening to the crier read out the King's Law every Seveneve morning, but for a young, healthy guy it's not too difficult. Sore legs for a few hours, and then you're fine. A lot of guys even claimed it helped their skram game.

I grabbed more than a few of those jobs. But since I could read, I also had a better option — I could pick up rush jobs from the Crown Post.

The Post has a big office down by the docks for all the mail coming in off the ships. It looks like a small warehouse from the outside, save for the big windows, and the aviary on top for the courier gulls. Inside, though, it's filled with rows and rows of shelves where they sort packages and letters. They had their own men for normal deliveries, but they also have a lot of urgent messages or parcels that come in at odd times.

My mother was friendly with the man who ran the office. He was a regular at chapel and he would always try to flirt with her, though it was a funny kind of flirting — my mother had taken a vow of chastity after I was born, and he was a bit too old for my mom, anyway. Plus, I knew for a fact that he still carried a torch for his deceased wife. But they seemed to enjoy their verbal banter all the same. I chalked it up as one of those mysterious things grownups do.

Having an in with the Post Master meant that he trusted me enough to let me make rush deliveries if I happened to be hanging around the office when they came in. I didn't start out hitting him up for honest work — the first time I came by his office, I was pretending to be interested in the Crown Post's courier gulls. See, I knew that's how the skram scores came in from distant parts of the kingdom, and I figured if I could find out the scores before they made it to the Solta newspapers, maybe I could work out some kind of betting scam to make a little extra coin.

The Post Master was no fool, though; he let me carry on for a bit while I fed him a line of bullshit about how I admired the the gulls' blue plumage and had been fascinated by them ever since reading a book about them back at Temple School before finally cutting me off and explaining why the grift I wanted to run wouldn't work. Bookies, he said, knew the schedule for the courier gulls and stopped taking bets well before they arrived, so there was no window where I could use an insider bet to hustle them. If I tried to run the con on random strangers, they'd just assume I had some kind of connection at one of the papers — or at the Crown Post. Instead, he offered me a more respectable gig.

The pay wasn't great, but the jobs were fun. He'd give me a cap and badge to wear while making deliveries; that getup worked better than any sloucher buttons I've ever seen — better than a Tritons pin, even. By Gruun's ass, I might as well have had a warding spell cast on me by a high sorcerer.

See, the minimum punishment for stealing from the Crown Post was 30 lashes. I'd seen a few lashings over at the public gallery at the main City Gaol — the lashes were always given by the Chief Lictors, who also did the public executions. They were big guys who wore hoods and had huge muscles like Vast the Brutal. Just hearing how people screamed after only a few lashes was enough to make most folks barf, so nobody would mess with you if you were running an errand for the Crown Post. I'm pretty sure even the Tritons would have kept their distance from me when I was wearing the hat and badge.

Running those Crown Post errands was what first got me a real good glimpse of all the parts of the city outside the Warrens. In most parts of Solta, the city guard would send you packing if you came around looking like you were from the Warrens, but come through with the Crown Post and they'd just tip their hat and wish you a good day. I could even roam through the Palace District without being bothered! If it wasn't a 40 lash penalty for wearing counterfeit Crown Post gear, I reckon a lot more people would have tried it; I think it was the closest I ever came to feeling like royalty.

I WISH I COULD remember the first time I met Kanin. All I know for certain is that it must have happened during one of my rush jobs for the Crown Post.

If this were a proper story, like the kind you read in a two-copper, I'd be able to tell you the exact moment I first saw her, the things I felt, the way her hair looked, and all kinds of little details to mark it out as something special. But *that* kind of moment didn't come until much later.

For reasons I didn't much care about at the time, a lot of my rush deliveries brought me to her father's house. By that point I'd learned enough to only use the servant's entrance for deliveries at homes like the one she lived in — even Crown Post gear only gets you so far! But I remember that whenever a job brought me to her place, she was often the one who appeared to sign for the package, instead of leaving it to the house staff.

Hand on The Walk, I don't even remember the first time we exchanged names. I just remember the little pinch of anticipation I started to feel every time I approached her house, the tiny little hope that today would be one of the days when the pretty girl with the freckles would throw open the door and greet me with a "hi, Lash!" Even if I happened to have a gang moll waiting for me that same evening back in the Warrens, it somehow didn't feel like cheating, because when I was out of the Warrens and roaming about the city with my Crown Post cap and badge, with important people nodding at me and treating me with respect, I felt like a completely different person, living a different life. That boy back in the Warrens suddenly seemed like a stranger. What would a respectable young man like this Lashan Pearl have to do with some kind of filthy Warrens rat?

That was where my head was at everytime I ran into Kanin. She wasn't the only pretty young girl I met on my rounds; she wasn't even the only one I ran into regularly. But with the others, it always felt like there was a kind of barrier between us, just like I'd felt with the boys I hung with back at the Temple School. I don't know if they could smell the stink of the Warrens on me, or if they were judging me because of my accent — or maybe I was the one who was unthinkingly judging *them*, I don't know. Whatever it was, there was always a moment with those girls where it felt like a lock clicked shut and we became nothing more than a customer and a clerk.

Not with Kanin, though. She always greeted me warmly, and even someone as dumb as me could figure out it wasn't an accident that she was almost always there to meet me when I arrived with a delivery. What amused me was how she didn't seem to know quite what to do with that.

See, where I came from, if a girl wanted you, she would tell you. Not directly, necessarily (although that happened a lot); some wanted you to put on a bit of a show of wooing them before things moved on to the unlacing and unbuttoning.

But if they were interested, they'd find some way to make it clear that the invitation was there. The Warrens wasn't a place where people kept their feelings under wraps.

Kanin was clearly a stranger to all that, which wasn't surprising. What was odd was that her awkwardness seemed infectious, robbing me of whatever fake cockiness I could usually summon up almost by instinct. When I rolled into a tavern with 20 of my gang brothers, all our slouchers hanging just right, like we were a band of nobles on a hunting trip in the King's Forest, I knew just how to handle any Warrens girl. I knew how to cock my head, what tone of voice to use, what words to throw at her to either call her bluff or get her into a dark corner ready to hike up her skirts. But when I was with Kanin, it was like all of that knowledge just vanished — all of her nervous small talk, her forced laughter, her blushing (I felt a pleasant shiver every time I saw her blush bloom beneath her freckles) — all that somehow managed to echo in me.

And I...liked it? I didn't know why, but thinking back on it, I realize I enjoyed it because it was one of the rare times when I didn't feel like I was wearing some kind of costume. Whether it was wearing a sloucher around the Warrens, or wearing a cap and badge for the Crown Post, or wearing the face of a dutiful son for my mother, I was always playing a role. But for a few brief moments with Kanin, I didn't have to be somebody else. I could just be plain old Lash, because she seemed to like that guy just fine.

Not that there was ever a chance that there could be anything between us. I mean, I lived in a cramped room in an old rooming house; she lived in a *house*. And even if it wasn't quite up to the standards of the houses in the Palace District, it was finer than any house I'd ever be able to live in. I wasn't a rich skram player or musician, and I'd pissed away my one ticket to an honest, if unspectacular, trade when I'd left the Temple School. I was stuck in the mud and dirt forever. Wasn't I?

But if any of that bothered Kanin, she never let it show. I mean, she had to have known I was poor. She didn't know just *how* poor I was, but there was no hiding my station. While I always made sure to wear my nicest clothes when I went on Crown Post runs, there was no way to disguise the faded colors or the worn-down spots; seeing me among all the other people strolling through her neighborhood, I looked as out of place as a mule among stallions. But despite all that, she still greeted me with the same bright smile, the same giddy "hi, Lash!" everytime we met.

ONE TIME I HAD a particularly weird package — it was a long, heavy, but very narrow box, and it was awkward to carry it. When I finally reached her house, I couldn't just hand it over to her the way I usually did.

"Here, try to carry it," I said, holding the box out to place into her arms. I let her feel the weight of it, but kept it securely in my grasp.

"Oof, that's heavy," she said, dropping her arms to shift the weight back to me. "How far did you have to carry that?"

"I just brought it here straight from the office," I told her. I was always careful not to mention which "office" I was coming from, lest she figure out where I lived. "It was no trouble," I added, ignoring my aching shoulder.

"Can you bring it inside for me? I've got somewhere to store it until father gets home," she said.

"Sure," I said, and she led me inside, down a short hallway and through a large kitchen. To one side of the kitchen were a large set of folding doors, and she scurried over to unlock and open them, revealing rows and rows of shelves stocked with food and ingredients. My Aunt Rossie would have fallen to her knees to sing a hymn to Auld Father if she'd seen such a bounty.

"The pantry!" Kanin said brightly. "The chief steward is off right now, but he'll be able to fetch it from here later. If you'll just put it down here…"

I placed the oddly-shaped box where she indicated. "By His Foot, what is in that thing?" I asked. "Oh, I mean — you don't have to tell me," I quickly added, remembering the Post Master's warnings about confidentiality.

"Oh, it's just for father's business. He has a network of buyers all over Selva. He says you don't always have the luxury of waiting, in his line of work. That's why we get so many rush deliveries. Can I get you some tea?"

Tea? The only people I knew who drank tea were some of the older ladies back in our rooming house, and after hauling that weird, heavy box, what I was more in the mood for was a good mug of ale. Surely, I thought as I watched her close the pantry back up, there would be some fine ale in a place as well-stocked as this. I thought about asking, but then decided not to press my luck. Because what I really wanted was just a few more minutes with her.

"If it's not too much trouble…"

"Oh, it's nothing. Anything to avoid getting back to rehearsal."

"Rehearsal?"

"Harpsichord," she muttered. "Father insists that I master it. He says that all proper young ladies must…oh, never mind."

The subject seemed to irritate her, so I let it drop as she busied herself making the tea, which she served us at a small table in one corner of the kitchen. I tried to hold the tiny, fragile little cup the way I had seen my aunts do — I didn't know if there were any rules to drinking tea. Was there a way of drinking it that would mark me as a Warrens rat?

So I thought, what would Vast the Brutal do? And I remembered that Vast never worried too much about things like etiquette or manners, because he said a true hero is a lord in every kingdom and a prince in every palace. Well, I didn't know if I was "true hero" — I hadn't saved a village from a two-headed giant or anything — but I had just performed an honest service; maybe that would get me enough credit to cover any screwups.

If I was doing anything wrong, though, Kanin either didn't notice or was too polite to point it out. She kept focusing on the dark amber liquid in her own cup as she stirred it nervously. Every few seconds she looked up at me and smiled and blushed again, then went back to looking at her tea.

The silence was getting awkward, and I was about to speak up when she finally looked at me, took a deep breath, and said, "So how does one get a job with the Crown Post?"

"Oh, it's only a part-time job. But in my case, I was lucky enough to know the Post Master."

"Father always says success is all about who you know! Does it pay well?"

"Well enough, I suppose. It gets me some spending money. So me and the…so I can hang out with my friends. Skram matches aren't free, you know."

"I've never been to a proper skram match. I mean, the boys at my school play it in the courtyard sometimes, but I've never been to one of the real matches. Father says it's a vulgar game." She looked at me, and quickly added, "not that I think…"

I rolled my eyes and chuckled. "You wouldn't be the first girl who hates skram." Most of the gang molls loathed it, I thought to myself.

But Kanin answered with a mock frown. "Are girls not allowed to like skram?"

That caught me a bit off guard. "No! I mean sure! Wait, I mean…"

Kanin started to giggle. I felt my cheeks getting warm, but I started laughing too. I hung my head for a second, then straightened back up and looked at her. "It's just…a lot of girls are turned off by it, for whatever reason. But not all of them. Some really get into it. I think they just like seeing men tussle with each other."

Another frown. "So they can't just enjoy the game on its own terms?"

I didn't know how to respond. I was trying to think of what to say when Kanin gave me a light punch. "Don't do your eyes like that, I'm only teasing you!" she said.

I didn't know what I was doing with my eyes, but I felt myself relaxing; I hadn't even realized I'd tensed up. I smiled and sipped my tea.

And there it was. If I'd been with a Warrens girl, I'd have known how to press forward at that moment. I would have known how to steer the conversation, how to move in closer and start touching her…just lightly at first, just a few taps on her thigh or a brush of a hand on her cheek. And then some more talk, and some more touching, until we had to take things somewhere more private.

I would have liked to have done that with Kanin. Maybe I would have had to take things a little more slowly with her (although you never know; girls can surprise you), but it was clear from her giddy nervousness that she wanted it too. But something held me back. I could lie to you and say I was worried because she had a house full of servants, and they could have stumbled upon us at any moment;

I think that's what I told myself. Imagine the outrage if a filthy Warrens rat had been discovered violating a respectable young lady under her father's roof!

That's not the truth, though. The truth, which was always shuffling around in the back of my mind, was that I knew I had no future with a girl like her. There was no scenario I could conjure up in my head where she could be with someone like me. Even if I dropped the gang life and tried for the Warrens version of respectability — what, would she come and live there with me in a two-room flat next to the docks? Maybe get a job to help support us? She could join my mother at the rope factory, and work for hours until her soft and tender hands got as rough and calloused as my mom's. I just couldn't see that happening.

Or maybe her father would take pity on me, and find me a job with...whatever he did. But everybody would understand then that I was just a charity case. Behind my back, they'd still call me a Warrens rat.

No, Kanin was just a beautiful dream; there was no future there, and thus no reason to try and take things further. There were guys I knew who wouldn't have let that stop them, because they could put any consequences completely out of their mind. But as a boy who'd watched his mother struggle every day for his entire life, there was no way I could — at least not with her.

I said before that Kanin seemed to like me — the regular me, the me who wasn't fronting any fake bullshit — just fine. But I don't know if she knew what "liking me" really meant. Warrens girls knew what they were getting into when they gave me the side-eye and pouty lips. Kanin, with her bashful giggles, her huge house, her delicately trimmed, carefully-stitched dresses and her blushes beneath her freckles, had no idea. And despite the funny, warm feelings she gave me, I was in no mood to put her straight. A few moments of the real Lash Pearl was all I could give her — or myself.

Not that I was in any hurry to give any of that up! I was still selfish enough to want those few moments of that illusion, no matter how fleeting.

"Do you...want to know about skram?" I asked.

She smiled and glanced down nervously into her cup, then picked it up and leaned back, looking directly at me.

"Tell me," she said.

So I used the cups and saucers from the tea set to show her the basics of the game — there wasn't enough room on the little table where we were sitting, so I had to use a large countertop. I used saucers to represent the goal circles, and cups for the players.

"So you've got your ten players on each team, right? And when your opponent has the ball, on his third round..."

"Can you have more than ten players? Or fewer?"

"Well, in an official match, it has to be exactly ten. But if it's just guys playing out on an empty...um...plaza, or what did you say the guys at your school use?"

"The courtyard?"

"Yeah. If it's just a bunch of guys playing for fun, they might use more or less than ten. If you've only got a small area, you can use 'half-pitch' rules, which only uses five men per team, but that's a whole other..." I stopped for a second, distracted at the sight of all those teacups placed out on the counter. "Do you ever actually use all of these?"

"Oh, back when mother was...still with us, we would. She used to host quite large receptions several times a week." Kanin gestured at the empty kitchen. "We used to have at least a half-dozen cook staff then; the kitchen was always a hive of activity. You never saw it empty like it is now. Which reminds me, the cook, Mrs. Lodi will be here any minute, and I'm sure you've got other deliveries to make. And I need to get back to the harpsichord..."

When I showed up at her house a few days later, Kanin had a copy of a newspaper turned to the skram section, ready to pepper me with more questions.

TEA WITH KANIN BECAME a regular thing. I don't know if she ever fully understood skram; some of the questions she'd ask me were pretty funny. I mean, she couldn't seem to understand a simple hangman's knot play no matter how carefully I tried to explain it: "Look, you've got five of their men locked up on the flank; the other five have to cover the rest of the field. So if you set up a sock-and-nail attack..."

"Wait...explain the sock-and-nail thing again?"

"Like the saltbox formation? But you know, in reverse?"

"I forgot...how does the saltbox formation work?"

See what I mean? Still, she tried. It would have been a lot easier if I could have taken her to an actual match. Seeing the game played on a proper pitch, with official rules and referees, would have made things much clearer. She did say that she was beginning to understand why the boys at her school were so obsessed with skram.

"Where do you go to school, anyway?" I asked.

"St. Kendo's." She must have read something in my face when she said that, because she quickly added, "please don't think I'm a snob because of that."

I held up my palms. "No! No, it's not that. It's just...I've never met anyone from there."

"Honestly...it's probably a little more than father can afford. Some of my classmates are actually from the Palace District! But father says it pleases him to be able to give me things he never had."

Oddly, Kanin never asked me about my own schooling. Not that the Temple School was anything to be ashamed of, but...well, I wasn't going there now, was I? But Kanin never brought it up. I think she sensed a lot more about me than I ever actually shared with her; I've never understood how girls manage to do that. But she seemed to instinctively avoid anything that would have made me feel awkward.

Skram wasn't all we talked about, though. I was curious about her own life. Had she ever been out of the city? (Many times; she'd been all over Selva and beyond. She'd even been far enough south to see the frozen peaks of the dwarven realms, if only from a distance.) What was up with the harpsichord? (Her father had given her a choice of which instrument to learn; she'd picked the harpsichord because their nasty neighbors, the Phelgans, apparently hated harpsichord music.) How many servants did they have? ("Fewer than we used to; my mother had her hands in everything, so there was a lot to keep up with when she was still alive, but father prefers a quieter life.")

I never did meet her father, and only rarely encountered the servants — usually the chief steward, who was there to accept packages when Kanin wasn't available. While it was always a letdown to see him emerge from the door, he was never anything but kind to me — a relief, considering some of the snooty servants I had to deal with.

I tried to avoid talking about her mother. Not so much to spare her feelings — I got the sense that while she had happy memories of her mother, they hadn't been close; she seemed much more attached to her dad — but because that might raise the question of her own future. And...well, I didn't want to spoil the time I had with her by bringing that up.

Presumably, she would be a wife and mother herself one day. Women in Kanin's world didn't go out and get jobs, the way my mom had. And because of that, they couldn't just marry any man who caught their fancy. I found it funny, in a sad way, that for everything she had, Kanin was in some ways even more trapped by her situation than I was. (I asked Footman Sesh if there's a word for that; he told me the word I was looking for was "ironic," though I don't know what iron has to do with any of that.)

I think the closest we ever came to the subject was once when she appeared at her door to greet me not in one of her neatly-tailored dresses, but in a dull, shapeless robe of some sort.

"Don't look at me that way," she said quickly. "I'm being fitted right now, I have to wear this while they make adjustments. I need something I can pull off in a hurry when they're ready for me again."

"I...didn't know I was looking at you."

"Oh, yes you were. You still are! I look like a Footman shuffling around in this."

I clasped my hands together. "Forgive me, Father," I teased. She gave me a shove, and I laughed. "I'm sorry, it's just...what do you mean, 'fitted'?" I asked.

"For a dress. For my cousin's wedding," she said, taking the package I was holding and heading into the kitchen. I wasn't sure if I should follow until she stopped and looked over her shoulder at me.

"Oh, come on, it's all happening upstairs, you're not going to see anything." I shrugged and joined her in the kitchen where she was already setting things up for our usual tea.

I was still a bit confused. "Why do you need to be…fitted? Don't you have a dress you can wear?"

She smiled when she rolled her eyes at me. "It's for a *wedding*," she said. "I'm a *bridesmaid*. You need a special dress. And it has to fit *perfectly*. You want everything to be just right for the bride, don't you?" There was an edge of sarcasm in her voice with that last bit. I got the idea she wasn't especially fond of this cousin of hers.

But I still didn't quite understand. While we sipped our tea — she really did look kind of silly trying to sit down gracefully while wearing that robe — I tried to learn more. Why did the bride get to tell her what to wear? Did she get to keep this dress afterward? Could she just wear it whenever she wanted?

She shook her head at me and smiled. "Don't they have weddings where you're from? Haven't you ever been to one?"

I didn't answer, but I must have reacted in some way because her forehead instantly knotted up in worry. "I'm sorry. I didn't mean…"

I smiled and touched her hand, to let her know it was fine.

That touch. I wished I could have held it longer.

She blushed. That blush. Oh, man.

Then she quickly picked her cup and sipped from it nervously. She looked back at the door that led in towards the rest of the house. "They aren't always like this, you know," she said. "Weddings, I mean. Not everyone does it this way. You're supposed to, but…"

She continued looking at the door, her eyes locked there, not once looking back at me.

"I don't want that, myself. When I get…when it's my time, I don't want any of that. I want something simple. I don't need bridesmaids. I don't need fitted dresses."

She kept looking back at the door for a long moment, then turned back to me. She made a sweeping gesture across the piled-up folds of her robe.

"What's wrong with getting married in this?" she asked, with a beautiful fake grin.

I just smiled back and raised my teacup in a toast.

IT WAS WHILE WORKING a Post job that I first heard about the Arcanter. I'd noticed that a lot more rush deliveries had been coming in, so I had become a regular at the office. It wasn't just rush deliveries, I noticed — everything in the office had been busier. The Post Master even offered to give me an actual job, but I wasn't quite ready to join my mom in taking up the ball and chain of an actual schedule.

Still, I couldn't resist asking what all the buzz was about.

"The war," the Post Master growled, pipe firmly clenched in his teeth. He didn't turn to look at me; he was focused on scratching entries into a large ledger on his desk. "Over in six weeks, they said. They always say that. Been more than a year now. And the worst isn't even here yet. Something big planned for this summer, I think."

"War? What war?" I asked. Back then, they weren't yet calling it a "war," so I'd missed anything about it when reading the papers. Because who cared about some nonsense on the other side of the world?

The Post Master stopped writing, and turned to regard me, with his big untrimmed eyebrows raised in curiosity. He was a fat man, but not in the way of some of the nobles you see being ferried about the Palace District. It was the honest gut of a fellow who worked hard and felt he deserved an extra cake and mug of ale at the end of a long day. I remember now that his faded green uniform was clean but heavily wrinkled, not that you could see much of it behind his thick gray beard when he was sitting in a chair.

He leaned back, eyeing me while taking a long drag on his pipe.

"I thought a clever boy like you would know more about the world," he finally said, a lazy ribbon of smoke spilling out the side of his mouth.

I didn't know what to say, so I just shrugged.

He pointed to a large map hanging on the wall, showing the great continent in full, with the Striped Mountains running like a slash down the middle. "You know, I assume, where Selva is?"

I rolled my eyes. "Yes. We're on the eastern side of the mountains. Garlund is on the west. They worship cats there."

"Well technically just the one cat, Ghant. And he's a lion, not a cat. But…you know about our dealings with them? The treaties?"

"From the Great War, I remember from school." I might not have remembered much else about history, but the war stuff, I could get into. "Wait — are we fighting the klangers again?"

"Dwarves," he said slowly, leaning forward as he said it. He gave me a quick grin, then leaned back again. "And no, they're still saying quiet in their frozen kingdom down south, at least as far as anyone knows. No, it seems the Suzer and his court have a little problem on their hands, one serious enough that they've chosen to call on their beloved brothers to the east to come give them a helping hand. Just a small thing, really, they said. Maybe a thousand troops. And they wouldn't really need our troops for fighting, they said — just that good old Selvan logistical knowhow, so their men could stay focused on the actual killing."

He smiled, and took another drag on his pipe. "Six weeks, they said," he chuckled.

Now that he mentioned it, there HAD been a bunch of troops that had come through the docks and been shipped off about a year before. And then there were a lot more a couple months later. And then I remembered another, much bigger group had come through several weeks before, though they'd been loaded onto ships and sent off so quickly it almost seemed like the whole thing had been a mirage.

"So the part about not fighting…"

"Oh, yes, it turned out very quickly that our troops would be needed for more than just pack mule duty. It turned out their problem was…not so small as their emissaries had represented to us."

Well, fighting WAS what soldiers were paid to do, I thought. But even so…

"Why are we still helping them? It sounds like it's their problem, not ours. What is this problem? Some kind of goblin swarm? A lycanthropy outbreak? A witch wielding a horde of undead thralls? There's no dwarves involved, you said."

"No, nothing like that. Even the sorry troops of the Suzer would be more than a match for any of those foes. You might call it…a civil war."

"A civil war? Why should we care if someone opposes the Suzer? He did ban our Footmen."

That was one thing they never let you forget in the Temple School: The Suzer and his idolatrous priests had banned Auld Father's Word in their lands — the very home of the great apostle Footman Rom himself! St. Rom had tried to bring the good news of the true faith to his own people and been cast out, and had to bring his teachings east.

And for that, Footman Tan would always remind us, the west had been cursed, sinking deeper and deeper into evil and corruption, while the we in the east had been blessed by Auld Father's favor.

I know you long-beards know all that, but considering where I had grown up, I confess that I found it hard to believe things could be so much worse over there. Then again, the bloody stories you heard about the cruelty of the Suzers and their priests did send shivers up your spine. Say what you will about Selva, but our King had always been a fair man. Perhaps there were worse places to grow up than the Warrens…

"Yes, well, as much as we may despise them," the Post Master said, "we do have treaties with them. And how does it reflect upon Selva if our King does not keep his word?"

I was about to say that I didn't see how I should care one way or the other when the Post Master continued: "But, that is not quite the whole story. There is the issue of who our western brothers are fighting."

"A civil war, you said. Somebody trying to overthrow the Suzer."

"Yes, but this 'somebody' seems to be more than just another disgruntled subject. Some sort of rogue priest, apparently. But he wields some terrible dark form of sorcery, and inspires a fanaticism in his armies that is unlike anything we have record of."

I shrugged. "A sorcerer with a pack of hypnotized warriors? That's nothing new."

"No, not hypnotized. That's the thing. It seems their devotion is quite genuine. His captured followers show no signs of ensorcellment."

"Well, if the Suzer is the bastard they say he is, can you blame them?"

"Perhaps not. But the King's advisers seem to think he may pose a unique threat." He leaned in close. "There are whispers that he is one of Gruun's demons, raised up in the flesh. There are whispers that...this might herald the coming of the Reckoner!"

He winked, I rolled my eyes, and he let out a laugh.

"They were telling those same kinds of tales back when I was your age," he said, shaking his head. He took another drag on his pipe. "Even so, this foe really seems to be a new thing. And they say — well, they say the Reckoner will be the one to finally liberate the world for Auld Father."

"Well, that's one interpretation," I said — a chance, for once, to use something I'd actually learned from reading The Walk. "In Temple School, the Footmen told us that there are many..."

He waved me away with his pipe. ·

"I know, I know. I'm just saying — it does seem the case that this is an enemy of an entirely different order."

"What do they call him, this dark sorcerer?"

The Post Master took the pipe from his mouth, and said, speaking each syllable clearly: "The *Arcanter*."

It would be nearly a year before I had reason to think of that conversation again.

12

Though I usually didn't stop by the Crown Post office until later in the afternoon, one day I stopped in early on a lark to ask the Post Master if there were any rush jobs.

I was in luck. A message had just come in on a ship, and it had to be delivered to the Palace immediately.

"I was just about to make the delivery myself," the Post Master muttered, "but I have much work to do, and since you have proven yourself reliable, I will entrust it to you."

Whatever it was, it was a small folio sealed with an elaborate wax seal I'd never seen before. The wax was blue, mixed with streaks of what looked like gold — I'd never seen anything like it.

The Post Master signed the front, indicating it was being discharged from his office and placed in my possession, and told me to deliver it to the address on the front.

The address was at the Palace.

"Will they let me in there?"

"Just display the package, along with your badge," he said, handing me the badge and cap. "Now run along. This is an important delivery."

So off I went. I'd never heard of the Post Master making a delivery himself, so I figured whatever it was had to be important. I took a route through the docks and up through the fisherman's quarter, which I usually avoided because of the awful smell. I took it this time because it was the quickest way. Sometimes people will tip you a sixcoin for a prompt delivery; maybe the Palace would give a handsome tip, too.

I had never actually gone past the front gate of the Palace, because of all the guards. I was worried they were going to hassle me, and as I got closer to the huge archway, I could feel my teeth clacking together in fear. But it turned out my cap and badge worked their magic even here. The guards gave me stern looks as I walked past, but then swiveled their heads back as soon as I was through.

Once past the gate, I looked around to figure out where to go. I was in a big courtyard, and there were doors and gates leading off of it on all sides. Lots of soldiers and guards and finely-dressed sorts I assumed were nobles or councilors or whatever were going in and out of all of them and walking quickly back and forth through the courtyard, looking like they all knew exactly where they were going. I was the only one who looked out of place, but nobody even seemed to notice me.

At the opposite end of the courtyard was a huge staircase leading up to the actual Palace. The bottom of the staircase looked almost twice as wide as a skram pitch, narrowing as it rose up to end at a row of columns, each as high as a ship's mast. The staircase was flanked by two huge statues of stags, each sporting an impressive pair of horns.

A lot of the fanciest-looking people went walking up that staircase. Figuring somebody would set me straight if I was wrong, I followed along with them.

At the top of the stairs you went through a giant door into this huge room that was nearly the size of the Temple sanctuary. There were more doors leading off from it, and more staircases headed up to Auld Father knows where. There wasn't anything to give me a clue where to go.

I looked up at the ceiling of the huge room. It was this giant dome with paintings of butt-naked folks all over it. At first I thought it might be a picture of an orgy, but all the naked folks looked incredibly serious, like they were at a Seveneve service at the Temple, though I couldn't imagine looking that composed if I was walking around with my dick hanging out.

I was trying to figure out what they were all doing when I noticed somebody standing beside me. It was this short fellow with a thin little mustache, and he was wearing a red outfit that looked the same as what a lot of other people around were wearing, which I guess was some kind of uniform.

With a voice that seemed way too deep to come from such a pipsqueak, he said "may I HEEEEELP you, SIRRRRR?" He stretched the words out just like that. I think I was supposed to be scared, but I had my Crown Post hat to make me feel invincible, so I didn't flinch.

I pointed to my cap.

"I've got a delivery for the Palace," I said.

The man gave me a smile like he had just spit in my drink.

"Deliveries are made outside at the CLEEEERRK'SSS office. Here let me SHOOOOW you..."

As he was beginning to turn, his eyes suddenly popped open and he froze.

"May I see that package?" He didn't sound all high and mighty now; all the big shot went right out of his voice.

I held it out as if to let him take it, but he took a step back.

"No, no, you can't give it to me. Actually I'm not even supposed to touch it."

He bent down and examined the wax seal.

"Has the package been in your control since the Post Master gave it to you? Has anybody else touched it or opened it?"

I shook my head.

"Follow me," he said, turning abruptly and heading up the largest of the big staircases.

We went through a bunch of other rooms — some of them were empty, some were full of people hunched over tables; all of the rooms looked so nice I was pretty sure the stonework in each one cost more than Aunt Rossie's entire rooming house. Twice we had to make our way past mean-looking armed sentries, but both times they immediately waved us through when the little man in red had me show them the seal on my parcel.

Finally we came to this one empty room. There was a big window at one end looking out over the harbor; at the other end was a giant painting of some old man with angry eyes and a hand propped on a shield, like he was using it to stand himself up. He was super old, like the sort of old man you'd expect to be hunched over, but he was standing up so straight it actually hurt to look at him. He was dressed in armor, so I guessed he must have been a soldier or something — but it was that old kind of knight's armor you only see in history books, with all the etchings and inlays and delicate metalwork.

The shield that he had his hand on was painted with what I recognized as the King's coat of arms, which featured a drawing of a great red stag. A light came on in my skull as I connected that to the big statues of stags next to the staircase outside.

"Wait here," the little man told me, and went through a big set of wooden doors across the room from the small door we'd come in.

When he went in, he didn't latch the door right, and it slowly swung open a bit so I could see inside the room. I looked, but couldn't see anything other than some bookcases on the other side of the room. But the door was open enough for me to hear men speaking.

I heard what sounded like an older man talking, and he had his voice raised — he wasn't yelling or anything, but it sounded like he was trying to make a point.

Now it's hard for me to remember it exactly, because you have to understand, I didn't know anything about anything back then. But trying to piece it together, I think this was about what I heard:

"...and the forces he's stationed there are quite formidable. In addition to doubling supply shipments, we should also send a fresh brigade of troops, and..."

"Again, I am not sure how much more we owe the cat worshipers," a tired voice cut in. "We've honored the terms of our treaty, but at some point they need to stand on their own. We cannot carry them. We cannot fight all their battles for them."

That voice sounded familiar. Was that...?

It was. The older voice confirmed it: "Normally I'd agree with you, Your Majesty, but the Arcanter isn't some spoiled, sulking noble leading a bickering little pack of conspirators. He is brilliant, capable and charismatic, and seems driven by forces we do not understand. If the considerable resources of Garlund were to fall under the control of such a man..."

"All of Garlund?" the King exclaimed, a sarcastic, skeptical edge in his voice.

And then another voice — this one with a dwarven accent: "We think it's likely that he will have effective control of much of Garlund's southern regions within a year."

"Is the Suzer's army really so incompetent?" the King asked.

"They are...well, they are not up to our eastern standards, Your Majesty," the dwarven voice said.

"And from what we have gathered from the Arcanter's captured followers," the older voice said, "it seems clear that he views the defeat of the Suzer as a mere stepping stone to an eventual confrontation with us. And if he has rediscovered the power of necromancy..."

"Again with the talk of necromancy. Have any of our sorcerers confirmed that? How would they know?"

"Not confirmed, no — but our master sorcerers are certain he wields a magic unlike any they have seen before, and it seems consistent with the descriptions of the power in the ancient scrolls."

There was an exhausted sigh. "Perhaps the time of the Reckoner finally approaches," the King said, though without the hope people usually have when they say that.

There was a long silence.

"Yes, well...we expect the Suzer's forces will put up more resistance in the north," the dwarven voice finally said.

Yet another voice spoke up, this one high-pitched and sounding all fancy, like one of you long-beards: "We believe the northern highlands to be more strategically...um excuse me...um...yes...?"

I heard a whisper — it sounded like the small man who'd brought me there.

"Very well. Show him in," the King announced.

13

The little man sheepishly pushed the door open. All the attitude had definitely gone out of him by now, though he was still trying to put up a front that he had it all under control. He jerked his head, motioning me to come.

I walked through the door into what looked to me like a kind of library. In contrast to the brightly lit room I'd just been in, this one was as dark and serious as the painting of the old man in the armor.

The walls were all covered with bookcases — big, serious-looking books with rich leather bindings, all lined up perfectly. There were some windows looking out towards the ocean, but the light coming in through them formed thick cones of swirling dust. All the dark wood and elaborate carvings made it seem like the whole space had been whittled out in one piece from the trunk of an enormous tree — the biggest tree in the world, carved by a giant.

The huge table in the middle of the room was the only part that didn't look trimmed and perfect — it was covered with documents and some kind of big map, which I recognized as a map of Garlund.

I looked at the map. There were big marks and writing all over it. Then I looked around at the men in the room.

There must have been at least a dozen. In a flash, I recognized the King, and automatically dropped to my knees and bowed my head.

"S…S…Sire…Your H…Highness…" I stammered out, trying to remember the correct form of address.

"Rise, my son," he said. I struggled to my feet and looked around, fighting against the urge to keep my eyes looking down.

The King was dressed in very fine clothes, even if they weren't as flashy as what he wore when he appeared in public. It was kind of weird to see him without his crown on. He was standing at one end of the table, all casual like, as if he were just waiting for an ox-trolley. But even there, looking fatherly and relaxed, he had the face of a man who could command armies.

The crazy thing was that even though the King was probably middle age, he was easily the youngest man in the room. I didn't recognize any of the other men, though I knew many of them must be from the Army or the Navy, on account of their dress. Others were dressed in the fashion I associated with Palace District nobles. It seemed like everybody except the King had bushy white beards and mustaches.

I held the folio in my hand, and looked around for some sign of who I was supposed to give it to. It must have taken everybody a second to figure out what was wrong, because it seemed like an eternity before the King finally spoke: "Son, I believe that letter is for me."

I walked over to him, my legs feeling soft as fresh dog shit, and held out the folio. He smiled as he took it, turning it over in his hands as he examined it.

"The seal with the blue and gold wax means the bearer must deliver the package directly to my hands," he explained as he opened it up. "I know it must seem silly to someone from — where are you from?"

"The Warrens, sir," I said, hoping my voice didn't crack.

He pulled a document out of the folio, but didn't look at it, keeping it clasped in his hands. Instead he looked at me with a smile. I know that it sounds silly, but I can only describe his smile as "loving." The way he spoke to me, it was like we were the only two people in the room — in the entire palace, even.

"The Warrens? You look like a Molan, though."

"Yes sir. My dad was a Molan." I stood a little straighter. "He was a Strongblood," I said with pride.

He nodded, then continued. "Yes, I know this all must probably seem silly to a youngster from the Warrens, but there are good reasons for it. You must be an extraordinary young man if the Post Master was willing to entrust you with this."

It was the first time I could remember anyone saying something like that to me.

"Who's the Post Master over there?" the King asked, looking up as if he was trying to remember something. "I believe I know this one. Grast, isn't it?"

"Grelle, Your Majesty," came the reply. It was the pipsqueak who'd brought me here.

I'd never known the Post Master's name — to me he'd always been just the Post Master.

"Oh, yes, I know him. Fine fellow. My, my, if you've won his trust, you must be quite the promising young man indeed. Now, let me see here..."

The King began fishing in his pocket with one hand while he held the folio and the document in the other, looking over them. He suddenly frowned, and everything got really still and quiet. He looked around the room at the other men — and that was when the illusion ended. We were back in that stuffy library with all those people.

The King handed the document to the man beside him, a dwarf with cold blue eyes who looked at me suspiciously. I judged him to be the one whose voice I had heard before.

The dwarf took the document from the King, only taking his eyes off me when he had the paper fully in his hands, ready to read it. He looked down at it, his jewel-like pupils swiveling back and forth as he read it. The way his eyes moved seemed so exact, it reminded me of the ticking motion of a watch hand.

The King pulled something out of his pocket, clenched in his fist. He looked off into the distance, as if waiting for something.

The dwarf's thick brow folded up in what was obviously deep disappointment. He looked up and opened his mouth as if to speak, then stopped.

He looked over at me, and then right past me. A hand clapped down on my shoulder — it was the little man in red.

"Time to go," he whispered.

"One thing," the King said, before I could turn to leave. He took my hand and pressed something into it and closed my fingers around it. Then he pushed my fist down into my pocket.

"People see something in you, boy," he said, scruffing my hair. "You owe it to Auld Father to find out what that is, and don't let us down."

Us. He didn't say "don't let *them* down." He said "don't let US down."

And with that, the man in red whisked me out of the room, back through the palace and out the gate past the guards.

"Have a good day, SIRRRRRR," he said, his old iron voice now back to full strength.

It wasn't until I'd made it halfway back to the Warrens that I thought to look in my pocket to see what the King had given me. I pulled it out.

It was a brand new, bright, shiny gold piece.

14

The Post Master didn't look up when I came back to the office and turned in my cap and badge. He was sorting through a big stack of letters.

"I met the King," I said, quivering. After the initial joy of and surprise, I was now shivering with fear for some reason.

I looked at the Post Master. "You knew I would meet him when you gave me that package to deliver."

He grunted, and kept sorting.

"If you're expecting me to give you a life-changing speech now, you can go fuck an orc," he said. "You're a good kid. Well, as good as any kid can be in these parts. You don't have a demon-gripped soul in you like some of them do. And you've got a head on your shoulders. And you've got a mother who's done her best to steer you right."

He smiled when he mentioned my mom. You saucy shit, I thought.

"Bottom line, son, is you could be one of the few to pull yourself out of this shithole. What did you think of the Palace?"

He stopped sorting and suddenly looked at me, his face serious.

"It was…" I tried to think of the words, but nothing came.

"You know you could work there someday. Well, probably not in the part of the Palace you saw. But at the Palace complex."

I wanted to tell him he was full of shit, but I let him keep talking. I wanted to find out his angle.

"It's not just spoiled nobles and rich shits who work there. We're not like those corrupt degenerates in Garlund. Our King needs good men — men who know something of the real world. And he can't find them in those flouncy finishing schools where our nobles send their spawn."

"Who do you know from the Warrens that has ever got a job in a place like that?" I asked.

He smiled.

"I did," he said. "I grew up in the Warrens. Got a job with the Crown Post, worked my way up. I worked in the Palace complex for 20 years — they even gave me one of those stupid red suits you probably saw over there."

His smile grew wider when I rolled my eyes thinking back about that.

"When the Post Master slot here in the Warrens finally opened up, I was the obvious choice. And here I am today."

I was about to make a smart-ass remark about how that didn't seem like much of a come-up to me, but I stopped myself, because was I really sure I believed that?

I thought about the other men his age in the Warrens. The ones who were still alive were mostly drunks who spent their last few years staggering back and forth to the public halls. There were a few older fellows who weren't total wrecks, but they were nearly all criminals and gangsters, and they all ended up coming to a bad end. Most of the folks who ran legitimate businesses around our quarter didn't come from the Warrens and didn't live there, either.

Instead of answering the Post Master, I just handed him my cap and badge and headed back to the rooming house.

WHEN I GOT HOME, I woke my mom up and confessed to her that I'd quit school years before. She knew, of course, but I'd never actually spoken the words to her. I told her I didn't know what I was going to do with my life, but I didn't want to lie to her anymore.

Then I pulled out the gold piece, and told her where I'd gotten it from — how it had come from the King's own hand, and now I was giving it to her.

I thought for certain she'd thrash me with her hairbrush, but she just looked at me and started crying. She looked like she was disappointed in me, but there was something else mixed up in there, too. She hugged me and held me real tight.

That night after she left for work, I didn't go out to hang with the gang. Instead, I sat in my bed, thinking about things, and where my life was headed.

When Footman Sorish had cured my blindness all those years before, he had told me that Gruun wanted very badly to keep my eyes closed, but Auld Father's power had opened them. Whatever it was Auld Father wanted me to see, I was pretty sure I wouldn't find it in the Warrens.

I thought about maybe becoming a sailor. That would get me out of the Warrens for sure, and would probably be an exciting life, even if it didn't pay shit.

Then there was the Crown Post. The Post Master had already offered me that route. It wasn't exciting, but — well, if I worked my way up, maybe I'd eventually make enough that I could move my mom and myself out of the Warrens. My mom wouldn't have to work at the factory anymore. Maybe in a few years I could even save up enough to get us a place in the Bells. Maybe I'd even find a decent girl who might marry me — nobody like Kanin, of course, but at least I'd have someone to cook my meals and look after me as an old man, and that was a lot better than what any man in the Warrens could boast of.

I kept coming back to what the King said. He said people saw something in me. The KING told me that! The King himself!

"Don't let US down," he said. The more I thought about that, the more it sounded like he was saying, "don't let ME down."

I went to sleep that night with the King's words ringing in my head.

15

I spent the next several months without much direction, trying to sort out what I was going to do. But in the end, the choice was sort of made for me — you might say Auld Father kind of grabbed me by my shoulders and gave me a kick in the ass in a certain direction.

Now all of you know that one of the big things for any Selvan youth is the day you reach your seventeenth summer, because that's the day you're reckoned to be a man, and enjoy all the privileges of a man. In the Warrens, it's not quite the step up it is in other places — there, it mainly just means you can go to the sporting houses without running afoul of the law. I know for you outsiders it's more of a milestone, because it's also the age when you can sign contracts and get licenses and permits and all that shit. But being able to have your pick of a woman to lay with, and not having to bother with any of that wooing or gifts or crap besides, is something I reckon any young man with blood in his veins is excited about.

For me, the start of that summer was also the beginning of the countdown until I was tossed out of the rooming house for good, but that was still a good twelve weeks away — which might as well have been twelve years in my mind, because I was thinking of something else. See, on the first day of summer, gangs always throw a big bash for all their members who'd reached that magic milestone. The Stonegate Clubs were no different — that year there were three of us, and we were told to go at midday and stand under the big tree in front of the Sailor's Chapel.

The other lucky fellows were Lyco and Rupens. Lyco was a short, dark-haired fellow with darting eyes. He was one of those guys that tries to make up in other areas what he lacks in stature — for one, his stringy dark hair was always done up perfect. He was always checking it in mirrors, and I never did figure out how he got it to stay so slick and straight. Gangsters in the Warrens aren't supposed to use any of that fancy perfume crap that the swishy types over in the Palace District use, and Lyco insisted he didn't wear anything like that, either — but if you got close to him you could catch a whiff of something that smelled a bit like fresh cut timber. If you asked him about it he'd crack some line about how it was his natural scent, and how ladies couldn't get enough of it. Then he'd follow it up with a crack about how maybe you liked it too, because you were one of those boy-humpers. That usually set people off, but Lyco would always manage to talk his way out of it before things came to blows.

That was the other thing about Lyco — he had a fast mouth. If he wasn't using it to talk trash, he was either using it on the ladies, or using it to talk up all the stuff he'd done with the ladies. We'd all been around him enough to know it was mostly lies (mostly — he did have a way with women, even if he did slap a thick coat of bullshit on it), but no one ever outright called him on it, because his stories were too funny. Instead, we'd just slide in some question marks here and there, as a way to spur him onto even more epic lies to keep us all laughing.

Rupens was one of the Clubs' best all-out brawlers. He stood a head taller than anyone else in the gang, with a chest wide enough that two of Lyco could have fit behind it without so much as a stray fingernail casting a shadow.

To look at him, though, you wouldn't think he was that tough. He had a big red face covered with baby fat, with a big grin pressed into it like dough. His teeth were huge and white but crooked, and he was topped with a mess of sandy hair that always looked like he'd just stepped in from a cyclone.

Rupens wasn't dumb, but he definitely wasn't the brightest torch you've ever seen. Luckily he didn't need that much of a brain, because there weren't many problems he ran into that he couldn't solve by punching them over and over. If it had been possible to learn reading by punching books, Rupens would have been the greatest scholar in all of Selva.

Naturally, he was the guy everyone wanted to be next to in a brawl. I reckon most of our brawls looked like people-colored whirlpools swirling all around Rupens — a big, grinning muffin face shooting fists in every direction.

We showed up at the appointed place at the appointed hour. Nobody told us what we were supposed to do there, so we just sort of stood there dressed sharp in our slouchers, cracking knuckles and trying to look intimidating. Most folks didn't pay us any mind, though; everyone knew that the streets around the Sailor's Chapel were neutral territory — not just among the gangs, but among all the thugs and trash and lowlifes that infested the Warrens. It was sacred, I guess you'd say — the walls of the Chapel were lined with inscriptions and memorials to men who'd been lost at sea, and nearly everybody in the Warrens had a friend or family member with a name on those walls.

We waited, and waited, and waited. We were all starting to feel a bit silly standing there when a man walked up to us wearing a weird hat — it seemed to be adorned with bird feathers in almost every color you could think of. The other thing about him was his boots — knee-high, with sharply pointed toes, they were studded with fake gemstones arranged in crazy patterns.

"You gentlemen look lost," he said, flashing a row of perfect white teeth. It was a conman's smile if I've ever seen one.

Me and my fellow louts looked at each other and shrugged. There was nothing else to do; no sign of the rest of the gang. Might as well amuse ourselves.

I cocked my head at the stranger.

"We're not lost. We're waiting for someone. What's your story?"

That smile again.

"I am a salesman, of sorts."

He gave a deep, exaggerated bow. I was sure that silly hat of his would fall off, but it stayed on his head like someone had nailed it down.

"Not of hats, I hope," Lyco said.

The stranger winked.

"You're the clever one, I suppose. No, not of hats. More like — experiences."

He drew what looked like a deck of cards from his pocket, and fanned them out. They weren't playing cards — they were covered in fancy writing.

"Tickets," he explained.

"To where?" Rupens asked, scratching his head. "You got a show or something?"

"A show, you could say. Or something..."

He waved them tantalizingly before us. I think it was supposed to look clever, but it just looked silly.

"We've got somewhere to be," I said. "And besides, we don't have any money."

"Oh, this will not take long, I assure you. And as for money — well, consider this a free demonstration."

I shrugged. If this were a trick, then between the three of us, I figured we could handle it. There's not much you can slip past a bunch of Warrens toughs.

I reached out and took a card. Rupens quickly followed, and Lyco — after hesitating a second — did the same.

With a dramatic flourish, the stranger folded up the rest of the cards back into a deck and deposited them in a pocket.

"Well?" Lyco asked.

"Examine your tickets," he said.

We looked down. I was the only one who could read, so I began reading aloud for the benefit of my companions. I noticed the ink had a metallic sheen to it.

"'The bearer of this ticket is entitled to a private audience at the Kabinet Kuriosum. Prof. Omi Van Omi, prop.' — hey, what the...?"

Aside from the writing, the card was decorated with numerous shapes and swirling designs. These suddenly began to move and rotate. I flipped the card over to see a printed picture of a pair of eyes, surrounded by more intricate designs. The left eye suddenly winked at me.

Okay, I yelped like a girl when that happened. I know some of you reading this have probably seen stuff much more sophisticated, but this was the first time since that damn klanger (NOTE FROM FOOTMAN SESH: I *give up*) I met as a kid that I'd experienced real magic up close. And as strange as it sounds, it was much scarier now than it was back when I was a youngster. When you're a kid, you don't know the rules — stuff just happens, and you just kind of accept it, no matter how strange it is. But by the time you reach seventeen summers, you've got it set in your head that the world follows certain rules, and when it suddenly doesn't, well, different parts of your body suddenly get the idea that they're gonna do their own thing — I reckon it's like when you're in a brawl and suddenly everyone panics and starts running in every different direction. Suddenly, your ass goes one way and your mouth another and none of it is what your head, which is usually the boss, would have advised. So that's why I yelped like a girl.

Actually, if I'm being honest, it was more than a yelp — it was more like a scream. If I'm being completely honest, it was a long, downright sissy kind of scream, the kind my fellows might have mocked me for, if...wait, where had they gone?

I felt my hands let go of the card — my head didn't ask them to, they just went and did it on their own. Instead of falling to the ground, the card just floated there for a second, then vanished in a puff of smoke, and that was when I saw for the first time that I wasn't standing in front of the Sailor's Chapel anymore.

Right about the moment I noticed the jagged rocks was when the first spray of seawater splashed into my face. I looked around. Lyco and Rupens were gone — along with all of the Warrens.

Also gone was the mild, warm air of summer. Instead, everything was suddenly brutally cold. That was the part that was hardest to take in, at first. You know how when you suddenly plunge into really, really cold water and for a few seconds the cold is pretty much all you can think of? It feels like your eyes see nothing but ice and your ears hear nothing but howling winds? That's what this was like.

When my eyes finally adjusted, I saw I was standing on a small, rocky island in the middle of the ocean. The sky was nothing but silvery clouds, and the water itself was a dark blue tinged with flecks of gray, with waves whipping back and forth like a horde of angry trolls. Every few seconds a wave would smash against the rocks I was standing on, and the bite of the spray on my skin was like one of those trolls' clubs had just grazed me, its splinters singing against my flesh.

Seeing another wave throwing itself into the rocks, I instinctively raised my hand to protect my face from the angry spray, and noticed I was no longer wearing my sloucher. Instead, my forearm was sheathed in some kind of heavy, dark leather studded with black feathers. I looked down at myself, finding the rest of my body clad in what looked like the traditional garb of a Molan Strongblood. In my left hand I held a Molan Breaker, a type of small shield, and in my right I held a Molan seaspear. I'd never seen any of these things in real life; up until then, my only knowledge of them had been through drawings or paintings.

You might think if all this suddenly happened to you, you'd have some questions. You might, you know, yell out and ask what the heck just happened. But for some reason, all this funny stuff felt completely natural when it was happening to me.

Some instinct caused me to crouch and scan the horizon. I immediately noticed another small, rocky island not far away — it was about the same size as the one I was standing on, but unlike mine, this one rose sharply up out of the sea to a peak maybe the height of a sailing ship's mast. Standing on the peak, well beyond the spray of all but the tallest crashing waves, was a dark figure who looked a lot like Vast the Brutal. Even though he was standing motionless, I somehow got the feeling that the figure wanted me to come to him.

The island I was on was long and thin, and pointed like an arrow towards the island with the tall peak. I was on the part that was farthest away from that island, so I began jogging across my strip of sand and rock, still keeping in a crouch. For some reason I had suddenly gained the surefooted grace of a cat as I leaped from one jagged rock to the other, my feet effortlessly avoiding sharp spots. I seemed to be moving noiselessly, too — not that anyone would have noticed over the crash of the waves.

It took me maybe a half hour to reach the other extremity of my island. When I got there, I saw a long but extremely narrow boat of some kind hidden between two large rocks. The construction was odd. On one hand, it appeared very primitive. I couldn't see any metal parts, for one thing — it was made entirely of wood and the same kind of dark leather that formed my clothes.

But despite the primitive construction, it was covered in intricate, finely-wrought designs and what looked to be inscriptions in a language I didn't recognize. Some were painted; others were carved into the wood or pressed into the leather. The leather strips which functioned as rigging were woven into complex patterns studded with exotic sea shells.

My hands somehow knew how to handle the craft. I located a pair of oars that had been lashed to the side and pushed the strange boat out into the crashing surf, and quickly scampered aboard. There were mounts for the oars, and a set of brackets which I quickly realized were for my seaspear; I slipped my weapon into the brackets with what felt like practiced ease, lashed my small shield to the deck in front of me, and began pulling at the oars.

Even though I'd never spent more than a few hours aboard a boat in my life, and certainly never had to pilot one, some deep instinct showed me how to direct the thin boat through the choppy seas without flipping it over. I made my way as quickly as I could towards the craggy peak I'd spied before. Looking over my shoulder every so often, I could see the dark figure was still there. He had turned his body to watch me. I still couldn't make out his face, but his powerful build left little doubt that he was, if not Vast the Brutal, at least one of his close relatives.

Turning back to the task at hand, I suddenly saw a watery bulge surging up in the trail of foam that formed my boat's wake. It disappeared, and I was trying to sort out what I'd just seen when I felt the front of my boat rising, and turned to see a huge hill of water looming up in front of me — the biggest wave I'd seen yet.

The instincts I was allowing to guide me told me to orient the craft so I was pointed straight up the face of the wave, and pump the oars furiously to pull myself over the top before it crested. The muscles of my arms were burning by the time I felt the boat start to level off, signaling I'd reached the top, but I barely had time to catch my breath before the boat started to tip down, and I had to look over my shoulder to steer a course plunging down the back side of the wave into what looked like a small canyon with sides made of ocean instead of rock. I tried to steer so that I'd be in a position to tackle the next wave when I reached the bottom.

As my boat skidded down the steep incline of foam and seawater, I noticed movement. Looking into the slope of the water, I could make out — something. It looked like a mass of scaly skin rushing through the water just inches below the bottom of my boat. I shook my head — was this an illusion? If it was a creature, it must be huge — the flowing skin streamed by for what seemed like forever.

Then it was gone. I reached the bottom of the huge wave, and the front of my boat briefly dipped into the water, then rose back up as the wave receded.

I reached and felt for my seaspear; it was still there.

After tackling a few more big waves, the water calmed down and I saw that I was over halfway to the other island, and began scanning it for a promising place to land my boat. I thought I spied one little inlet between two tall rocks — similar to the place I'd launched from — when I turned around to try to adjust my bearing. What I saw caused me to shiver worse than any gust of wind or splash of icy seawater.

It was a set of — I don't know if there's an official word for them, but I'll just call them horns. There were four of them, long and sharp, sticking straight up out of the water, and speeding toward me. The two in front were shorter; the two in back were taller than a man.

Once again, my body seemed to know what to do before I could form anything in my mind. I grabbed the seaspear, and jumped to my feet, standing on the narrow boat in a crouch. My muscles made small twitching movements, slight adjustments that kept my body perfectly balanced against the undulating movements of the ocean. As the horns drew closer, I could see a pair of crystal blue eyes glowing in the water just beneath the surface. When the horns got within maybe a dozen feet of my boat, the creature rose out of the water.

The beast I saw — I've never actually seen one before, even in drawings in books, but when it revealed itself, there was something about it that felt familiar. Whatever it was, it was very long. I don't know if I was looking at the creature's body or just a long neck connected to some massive bulk hidden beneath the waves, but the part I did see was thickly-muscled and covered in silvery, streamlined scales.

I couldn't tell if it was a fish or a reptile — there were flaps near its head with long fringes that whipped back and forth in the wind, almost like a mane of hair. I guess those flaps could have been like the flaps you see on fish that hide their gills, but the dancing fringes made them look more decorative than useful.

On second thought, "decorative" might not be the right word to use. The flaps and fringes seemed to work in concert with the creature's head to make it more intimidating. And that it was! I mentioned the four horns, but then there was the rest: The head was long and flat and lined with thin, long teeth, including two very long fangs at the front that extended well below its chin.

I felt my hands roaming over the seaspear, searching for something — and finding it: A little loop of leather cord that attached to a band around my wrist. The loop attached to the band with an amazing little clasp made from interlocking seashells. The loop in turn was attached to a springy leather cord that was formed into a thick coil wrapped around the haft of the seaspear.

The beast opened its mouth, unsheathing its rows of needle-like teeth, and let out a scream which somehow combined with the crashing sound of the waves to set my body shivering like I'd been thrown naked into a snowbank. I felt the misty sting of the creature's breath, and noted the smell — like I'd shoved my face into a pile of rotting fish. I heaved a bit, but managed to hold back from barfing.

You'll pay for that, I thought, as I hefted the seaspear into position, thrust out my free arm to aim, then hurled the weapon at the monster's head in one quick motion, feeling like I'd done it a thousand times before.

I was a little surprised when the spear flew sharp and straight, the coil of leather cord spiraling out behind as it unfurled. For a moment it seemed like the spear was going to strike the beast dead between its eyes — but I guess the blasted thing wasn't in any mood to be a notch on someone's belt. It looked at the weapon arcing up toward it with something that I swear was contempt, let out a snort, and quickly leaned out of the way at the last second. The seaspear whistled through empty air and tilted downward. I began pulling on the leather cord to reel it back in.

Out of the corner of my eye I saw the creature's head swing down, and then it was skimming across the surface of the water toward me. It opened its mouth as it closed in on me, those sharp blue eyes showing something between hatred and lip-smacking anticipation, like I was a fresh-baked pastry sitting in a shop window.

I remembered the Molan Breaker still lashed to my boat. I grabbed it and tore it free, snapping the leather lashings, shoving my hand through the straps. What with my having to balance myself against the rolling waves, it would take me a few seconds to turn and get into a proper forward stance to face the beast. But something told me I didn't have that long.

I stood up, my back now towards the animal, and looked over my shoulder to see it lifting its head up and opening its jaws, ready to plunge them into my exposed back.

I leaped into the air and swung my shield arm towards the creature's face, backhanding it hard across its snout with the Breaker. I heard a shriek and then a gurgle, and as I was still spinning wildly through the air I saw the head of the creature disappear into the water, the rest of its neck or body or whatever it was sliding after it. I felt a momentary twinge of satisfaction, until I hit the icy water. Slipping beneath the waves, my head bumped into something — my seaspear, still attached to my wrist. That nifty spin through the air had served to reel it back in all the way.

I pulled my head up above the water to see how far away my boat was — just in time to see the beast's jaws emerge from the water and snap shut on the very part of the craft I'd just been standing on. The force of its bite snapped the vessel in two as if it had been made of twigs.

Moved by instinct, I plunged beneath the water, swimming as fast as I could toward the creature, my seaspear clutched tight in both my fists and held straight out before me — my weapon and I moving together as one deadly creature, a kind of living spike. While the creature still had its head above the surface, I plunged the seaspear into its neck just behind its head with all the violent force I could muster.

Still gripping the haft of the spear, I suddenly felt myself being lifted up out of the water, up, up, up above the waves. The creature let out another chilling shriek, and I could see a purplish liquid gushing out of its skin where my weapon was still lodged in its body.

Snapping its needle-like jaws, it tried to swing its head around to attack me, but I was too close to the head — it could not bend itself enough to reach me. I could see one of its cold, lidless blue eyes fixated on me — it could see me clearly, but couldn't reach me. There was an eerie burn in the way it tracked my movements.

I felt at my waist and my hand found something — a handle. I pulled a long, thin knife from a sheath — until that moment, I hadn't even realized I had it with me.

I reached out and plunged the knife right into the monster's staring eye. As I released the handle and wrapped both of my hands around the haft of the seaspear, I heard something like a deep gasp escape the creature's throat. I gripped the seaspear and hung on while the creature writhed in agony.

The head crashed down into the water and the beast thrashed about, trying to shake me loose. I held.

I held even though my shoulders were now wrenched with agony, even though it felt like at any second they could be pulled straight apart from my body.

I held, focused so hard on simply tightening my grip that I didn't notice being pulled underwater, didn't notice that I could no longer pull air into my lungs.

I held, even as I felt my vision fading, the sights before me slowly fading into a red fog.

I held, but at last I could hold no longer. The fight had been beaten out of me.

I released my grip on the seaspear's haft, to allow my muscles one last moment to relax before the creature whipped around and skewered me in its jaws…

…But nothing happened. The creature's body was no longer thrashing about. Every few moments it would twitch, but other than that, it hung lifeless there in the water. I looked up — I was now maybe 20 feet below the surface, and my lungs suddenly began to sting. My mouth fought to open and drink in the air that was still out of reach. With what little strength I still had, I swam back up and gulped in the salty air.

Looking around, I spied some heavy shards of wood bobbing on the surface — the wrecked remains of my boat. I swam over to them, and after pausing to regain my strength, used them as a float to help swim the rest of the way to the tall, rocky island.

Dodging the sharp rocks, I made my way up onto something like level ground, or at least a place where I could lie back and rest for a moment. I didn't realize until I was lying on my back staring up at the sky how exhausted I was. The feeling hit suddenly, as if someone had thrown a heavy sack onto my chest and knocked the wind out of me.

Then I remembered the man I'd seen standing at the top of the rocky spur. I began to pull myself up to look for him, but at first my body wouldn't move — the exhaustion was now gushing through my body. Finally, feeling like my legs and arms were made of stone, I painfully hauled myself to my feet and looked up to the high point of the island. The man was no longer there.

My gaze dropped down, and I saw he had come down from the peak and was now walking towards me. He was still some distance off, but I could now begin to make out his features more distinctly.

The man I saw was definitely Vast the Brutal, exactly the way I'd always pictured him. And yet…and yet there was something about him that was off. His face — where had I seen that face before? He was now close enough that I could see him smiling. It was a broad, warm smile…

And that's when I heard a voice cut through the crashing waves like a clap of thunder: "Okay, Lash, that's enough there. Up and at 'em!"

And the image froze, like a painting. Then it slowly dissolved into smoke.

16

It was the sound I noticed first. A slithering tune played on some kind of flute, with a low drum beating out a lazy rhythm somewhere in the background. And the air was suddenly different. No longer cold. Warm. Cozy.

Then there was a loud sound of fingers snapping that seemed to have come from just in front of my nose.

"Lash! Lash! Come on now, you'll miss the show!"

My eyes opened, and there was Taygor, one of the older members of the gang, looking me direct in the eye and grinning.

"Not bad, eh?" He leaned down and pressed his ear against my chest, then began laughing. He came up and fixed me again with that grin. It was a grin that always left me feeling a bit uneasy, like a butcher who enjoys the blood and gore of his job a little too much. Taygor always sported a bit of stubble, even though that wasn't the fashion for gang members, and his dark brown hair was longer, too, though normally he kept it neatly slicked back, as it was this evening. I could smell the oil as he pressed his ear against my chest to listen.

"By Auld Father, your heart's popping like a woodpecker," he said, bringing his head up and giving me a sharp punch in the bicep. "Old Omi's always got just the thing, hasn't he? Once you're done with one of his trips, any party you go to afterward is going to feel like the best thing that's ever happened to you."

I looked around. I was in some kind of great festival hall — but not one I'd ever visited before. This one looked expensive.

I was on the bottom floor. I was sprawled out on some soft, luxurious sofa. On either side of me were Lyco and Rupens. I wondered if my own eyes looked as bleary and stunned as theirs did.

"Wheressshhhhhhh...wheresh the guy...the hat..." Rupens snorted. "I'm-a killsshhhhh...Tear hissshhh...I'm-a...Where issshhhh...."

"Professor Omi?" Taygor said brightly. "Oh, he's actually around here...somewhere. I don't think he wanted to actually be present when you boys…"

"Men," Lyco said, running his hand through his hair — I guess to check that it all looked perfect. "We're men now, remember?"

"Men," he said slowly, nodding. "He figured his face probably wouldn't be the first thing you saw when you came to."

"Yoursssssh ain't much better, Taygorrrr," Rupens rumbled, "making usssh fight a fu…fucking fi…fi…five-eyed wolf…" With that, he made a wide, bleary swing with his fist at Taygor's face. But our host laughingly ducked under the slow-moving hammerblow, causing Rupens to lose his balance and tumble forward.

Taygor seemed like the kind of guy who had a lot of experience dodging fists, actually. That unsettling grin was all of a piece with the rest of him. Everything about him was average, but you got the idea that it was on purpose, to keep people from looking too closely at him. He always reminded me of a cat which would lazily lick its paw while the mouse was watching, but slink up to strike the second it had its back turned.

I rubbed my eyes again and tried to get a better feel for the surroundings.

"Is this Mallee's?" I asked.

Taygor smiled. "Mallee's? Oh, no. We're the Stonegate Clubs, pal. We're not trash like the March Alley Mutts or the Rye Court Roosters. We wouldn't bring our newest men to some place so common."

"I can't say I've ever thought of Mallee's as common."

"It is compared to this place," came a raspy voice from off to the side. I looked over to see the chief of the Clubs, Lusseau. He was just walking up with three large tankards of ale, which he handed to me, Rupens and Lyco.

Lusseau was the oldest member of our gang, right on the edge of that age when it starts to seem creepy for a guy to be hanging around a bunch of young punks, the point where he either hangs up his sloucher and tries to be something like a respectable citizen, or when — and this was what usually happened — he gets nabbed by the city guard on some beef and finds out they no longer see him as a poor wayward youth caught up in the wrong crowd. Then it's off to a few years in prison and the next time you see him, he's a hardened criminal who wants nothing to do with kids.

We all three gratefully snatched the offered ales and took deep draughts. Rupens drained his and tossed it aside — and suddenly found another placed in his hand.

"Another, master?" the serving wench cooed, gliding in with barely a sound. She was so beautiful I blinked a few times to make sure my eyes weren't still deceiving me — I'd never seen a serving wench like THAT before.

"Where are we? We can't be in the Warrens."

The wench winked at me and sauntered off, with my eyes fastened to her swaying hips.

"Oh, but we are," Taygor said. "If you stuck your head out of this building, you'd be within shouting distance of the Sailor's Chapel."

I tried to think of which sporting houses would be in that area, but Lusseau must have read the question on my face.

"Oh, no, this isn't a place you've seen. There's nothing about the building we're in that gives a hint of what's inside. This is the Dead Scorpion, the most exclusive… ah, 'pleasure hall' in all of the Warrens."

"Veeeery exclusive," Taygor added, "and frankly, you boys aren't quite exclusive enough to know the location. So we had to sneak you in here in a way that would keep you from knowing how to get to it. Not that any of you could get in anyway, without knowing the passphrase."

"By Gruun's hairy balls," Lyco swore. He was straightening out a last few strands of his barely mussed hair and looking around for a mirror. "Why didn't you just throw hoods over our heads, spin us around a few times and throw us in the back of a cart?"

"Oh come now, and have you miss one of Professor Omi's shows? You boys — excuse me, men — are Stonegate Clubs. We knew you could handle it."

I sighed, stood up, took another draught of ale — it was incredibly good ale — and looked around.

The crowd was a respectable size, though on the smaller end for a place with this much room. Other than Lusseau, Taygor, Rupens, Lyco and a few other random Clubs who were milling about, I didn't see anybody I recognized. They weren't kidding about it being exclusive, though — I don't know if gold has a smell, but if it does, it would have been thick in the air.

The hall itself was fully three stories high, with no windows I could see. The second and third floors were galleries that ran around three sides of the hall, over-looking the main gathering area. Two large golden chandeliers adorned with light crystals hung from the ceiling.

The fourth wall was dominated by a stage raised a few steps above the main floor. The stage was mostly dark, save for one corner where a reddish-yellow light crystal illuminated a small group of musicians. There were a couple of rag-ged-looking elves playing flutes and a dwarf pounding gently on a set of large drums. Behind them, I could also make out the dim outline of a human who was playing rhythmically on some kind of stringed instrument.

Our sofa was one of several set right in front of the stage — I guess this was for the bigshots. The sofa just to the side of us was occupied by older, serious-looking men smoking cigars — from the aroma, I could tell they were the richest kind, imported from Kassor. They wore the sort of clothes you only saw in the Palace District, but their faces and hands were pure Warrens — scarred, rough and men-acing. I saw the telltale glint of Tritons pins on their lapels — theoretically, those were illegal, and wearing one in any public place was grounds for immediate arrest. I took it, though, that this wasn't a place where they figured they'd have to worry much about that. I saw one of them exchange a look with Taygor. Did they…know each other?

Another couch further away was occupied by a group of very loud, boisterous young men about my age who were most certainly not from the Warrens — if the clothing and grooming hadn't given it away, their accents did. Young highborns on a gutter crawl, though they were several cuts above the type that usually come down to our part of the city to play.

I told the others I wanted to walk around a bit in order to clear my head.

"Don't take too long," Taygor said brightly. "You don't want to miss the show — this is the best seat in the house."

I mumbled a reply and headed over to the far side of the hall, which was dominated by a large bar. I noticed the walls of the hall were covered with paintings that, even now, kind of make me blush when I think of what they showed. They were a bit like those pictures on the covers of two-coppers, the ones with the big-bosomed girls, except these girls didn't have a stitch of clothes on, and they were with big muscle men who didn't have any clothes on, either.

I'd say they were fucking, but that word can't really capture what was shown — they were doing all sorts of things I'd only heard people whisper about, and up until then wasn't sure I actually believed. I didn't have a main girl at that moment, but I made a note to myself to ask Salah about some of those things next time I saw her — back when we'd been together, she always seemed to know a lot more about that stuff than I did.

The bar was long and well-stocked, but there weren't many people sitting at it. Most people seemed to be getting their drinks from the serving wenches — and no wonder. I saw many a pinch and slap on their shapely, barely-clad bodies — none answered with a knee in the groin or a fist in the mouth, as would have happened in any other place in the Warrens. The girls were acting (it had to be an act, but still) as if they positively enjoyed it.

On the wall behind the bar they'd mounted the head of a goblin — first time I'd seen one outside of a museum. The bartender, who was slim and well dressed, with a thin waxed mustache, had some sort of small creature perched on his shoulder. It was shaped like a human, but incredibly scrawny, with two tiny wings jutting out of its back. It seemed to be eyeing me with hatred.

The bartender must have noticed my reaction.

"Don't worry, he always looks like that. He's actually friendly."

"What is it — I mean, he?"

"A kobold. His name's Woon. Say hello, Woon."

The creature chirped out some gibberish.

The bartender nodded at the tankard of ale in my hand. "Top you off?"

"No, not now. Hey, I've never seen a kobold in the flesh before. I didn't know you could tame them."

"Only race of the Little Folk that can be tamed — though with great difficulty."

"Why do you have him?"

The bartender smiled. "He's my assistant. Watch. Woon, Stalk Valley Slider, double."

As the bartender casually grabbed a glass and reached for a bottle on a high shelf, Woon leaped into the air and somersaulted several feet down the bar, grabbing a small shot glass as he sailed by. Landing on a railing, he grabbed a small bottle of something off a bottom shelf in one hand while his long spiked tail rummaged around on the top shelf.

In one motion, the creature popped the cork from the bottle and poured some into the shot glass, while his tail knocked a small vial off the top shelf. As it fell, one of his wings kicked out and smacked the vial, sending it arcing through the air, where his other wing smacked it back. The two wings juggled the vial back and forth in the air while he replaced the cork on the bottle and placed it back on the bottom shelf.

The vial then fell out of the air and into one of Woon's hands, and he carefully placed a few drops from it into the shot glass. He then threw the vial into the air where it was caught by the tip of his tail, which placed it back on the top shelf. While he was doing that, he pressed a coaster over the mouth of the shot glass and shook it vigorously.

In another smooth motion, he placed the shot glass on the bar and slid it down to where I was, simultaneously launching into another aerial somersault. In mid-air, his tail flicked out and flung yet another small vessel off a shelf, where it flew through the air and banged into a beam above my head.

Just as the bartender had finished filling the glass in front of me, Woon landed beside it, and the shot glass finished its slide, right into Woon's waiting hand. The vessel he'd knocked off the shelf that had crashed into the beam was caught by his tail.

He used his tail to bring it down over the glass, where he removed the stopper and shook a little bit of powder into the drink. He reclosed it and tossed it into the air, where it was once again caught and juggled back and forth between his small wings.

Woon carefully poured the mixture from the shot glass into the drink. He produced a long stick which he used to slowly stir the mixture, all the while juggling the vessel containing the powder.

Seemingly satisfied, he allowed the vessel he was juggling to fall into one of his hands, and he tossed it in arc towards the shelf he'd knocked it off of. He did a backflip, using his clawed feet to catch a ceiling beam, which he hung from. His tail flicked out and caught the vessel he'd thrown, and placed it back on the shelf. He did another flip and landed back on the bartender's shoulder, and resumed his motionless posture, once again staring at me.

I couldn't help but clap.

"Don't clap yet," the bartender said. "Try it first."

I picked up the glass. The drink was a swirling mix of gold shades. I took a sip. There was a short burning sensation that was quickly replaced with a lovely honey-like taste. My head felt light.

"Wow," I said. I paused for a moment, trying to think of something to say. Then I said it again: "Wow."

I looked at Woon. Damn if the little bastard didn't take a bow.

I fished into my pocket and pulled out a stack of coins, which I slid over to the bartender.

"Oh, no sir, no charge for your drinks. Your friends paid in advance."

"It's a tip," I said, "for the drink, and for that dazzling little display." It occurred to me just then that getting a fat tip was the entire point of the kobold's little routine. Pretty slick.

I nodded at Woon. "Where in Gruun's name did you ever get a creature like that?"

The bartender's gaze flicked back and forth.

"I actually — ah! Let me introduce you to him."

He pointed with his chin to the end of the bar. I looked and saw Professor Omi settling onto a stool. The crazy hat and boots made him unmistakable, but the insouciant cheer was gone from his face.

"Usual, professor?" the bartender trilled.

"Yes. And leave the bottle, Arn." He removed his feathery hat and sat it down on the bar. He stared ahead glumly. Taking the hint, I suppose, the bartender gave Woon a break while he mechanically fetched a black bottle labeled "Ytter's" from the shelf and brought it down to the Professor with a small glass. I took my own drink and walked down to join him.

"So you're the one to see if I want my own kobold," I said.

He looked at me. Without his hat, I noted that he had a mane of long, unkempt-looking black hair. And without his phony, pasted-on grin, I realized his eyes looked sad and tired.

"You again. How did you like the show." He didn't ask it so much as state it, as he poured a glass of dark liquid and took a swig.

I took a sip of my own drink, savored the burn-then-sweet taste, and thought of how to respond. I realized I didn't have any words in my stunted brain to easily describe it, though I suppose most of you long-beards would be able to sum up those feelings perfectly.

"How'd you do it?" I finally asked.

A tiny grin flashed, then disappeared, and he took another drink.

"Simple tricks. Smoke and mirrors. See?"

He rolled up his sleeve and spread out his hand, showing me both back and front. Then he snapped his fingers and produced a coin.

He placed the coin on the bar, and put his glass over it.

"And with a wink and a wave and a whistle..." — here he whistled out a few notes from a children's nursery song — "...we have...magic!"

He lifted the glass and the coin was gone.

"Now be a good fellow and pay for my drink," he said.

"I'm not paying for your drink."

"I never said YOU were. It's my money. Just take it and toss it to Arn down there."

"I don't see any money."

He reached and picked up my glass. The coin was sitting there underneath it. He picked it up and tossed it to Arn, who caught it, smiled, and put it in his pocket.

"Smoke and mirrors," he grumbled, and took another drink.

I wasn't having it. The Warrens is full of con men claiming to be mages, but I knew the real thing when I saw it.

"Don't bullshit me, Professor. I used to be a pickpocket. That out there in front of the Sailor's Chapel wasn't just a case of quick hands and slippery fingers."

He frowned and stared straight ahead.

"No. No, it wasn't."

"Then how'd you do it?"

He seemed to think about it for a moment before answering.

"You know how magic works?"

"Sort of. Uses metal, doesn't it?"

"Mostly. You can use crystals too, but only elves can really get them to work effectively. Or..." — he took another swig — "...if one believes the stories, you can use necromancy. But that...well..."

I waited for him to continue, but he just sat there. I figured that meant it was my turn again, so I pressed further: "Can anybody do it? Work magic, I mean?"

"Not really. Only about one in ten humans, on average, possess enough native ability to do anything useful with it, and even among those, the power varies considerably. It seems to run in certain bloodlines. It's also different in non-human races — among dwarves, it's much rarer; among elves, it's much more common."

"I thought dwarves were the ones who first discovered magic."

"That's what the dwarves say; the elves say they were the first. But it was dwarves who taught it to humans."

"Yeah, the dwarven outcasts — the ones who allied with the humans, against the ice dwarves — taught us the secret to help us win the Great War. I remember from school."

That got a chuckle from him. "A Warrens rat? School?"

He quieted down real quick when he saw my face.

"I just think it's interesting that dwarves have so much trouble with it. First mage I ever saw was a dwarf."

I almost added, "He's the one responsible for getting me hauled off to school in the first place," but I didn't want to give him a chance to make another smart-ass remark that would force me to smack him.

"Yes, an irony indeed." He looked at me for a second — I could tell he wanted to ask if I knew what "irony" meant — but then added, "especially since they are the only source of the telluric component — what my old instructor used to call the 'hocus pocus sauce.'"

"The metal, you mean."

"Yes. It's essential. I mean unless you use crystals..." — he gestured at the light crystals hanging from the ceiling above us — "...but like I said, only elves can seem to get that to work. Or if..." He trailed off, and his eyes seemed to lose focus for a second.

"If what?"

"Nothing. Like I said. Metal, or crystals if you're an elf."

I suddenly realized why elves all wore crystal jewelry, but kept that revelation to myself. "What did you mean, that dwarves are the only source?"

"Only master dwarven smiths can forge magemetal, and there aren't many of those."

"So where did you get yours? And anyway, I don't remember you using any metal when you did...whatever it was you did to me back at the Sailor's Chapel."

He pulled the pack of tickets from his jacket, once again fanning them out with a flourish.

"The ink. Notice anything about it?"

Not daring to touch the damn things again, I leaned in closer. Once again, I noticed the metallic sheen.

"It's some type of metal?"

"Close. It's regular ink that's been mixed with shavings from a magic ingot," he said.

"An ingot — of the type made by dwarves?"

"The hocus pocus sauce, yes. It fuels spells like oil in a lamp."

"So...the ink is magic?"

"Not by itself. I have to activate it by saying, or thinking, a spell. The magic does the rest."

"A spell. Like saying, 'hocus pocus.'"

He rolled his eyes.

I eyed the shimmering ink some more.

"So I took your card, and then — what? I was whisked away to some rocky island in the middle of a freezing ocean?"

He grinned. "Is THAT what you saw?"

"Well...that's what I saw. I think my friend saw a five-eyed wolf, which I know is just a myth. I only hope the thing I saw was just as mythical…"

He chuckled and took another sip. "You, my friend, merely fell asleep. Whatever trip you took was largely a creation of your mind."

"How long was I asleep?"

"Five minutes, maybe? Probably less. However long it took for your friends to pick you up, bring you here and plop you on yonder couch."

"It felt much longer."

"The passage of time can be elusive during a dream state," he mused.

I thought back to all the time I spent rowing that boat across that ocean. And the fight I'd had with that horrible beast. Now that I thought about it, there was something about it that felt like a dream — the way I suddenly had mastery of so many new skills; skills that felt like second nature. Still, there was something about it that felt more real than any dream.

"So — it was all just my imagination? Everything I experienced?"

"Not entirely. The spell is…well, in simple terms, it's a sort of wish fulfillment spell. The spell sets the parameters, if you will, but your imagination fills in the details."

"That didn't fulfill any wish I ever had."

"I did say 'a sort' of wish fulfillment spell. It's more about fulfilling a nameless yearning. But just looking at you and knowing where you're from, I think I probably have an idea of what you went through."

"Really."

"Let me guess. You saw a man in the distance beckoning to you, and to get to this man, you had to endure a kind of trial? And the experience ended with him showing you some sign of approval? And let me guess — the man looked vaguely familiar? Almost like he might be related to you, somehow?"

I just looked at him. He rolled his eyes.

"So predictable," he said.

I wanted to say something rude, but instead I steered things back to how he'd done it.

"You never told me where you got your magemetal."

"From my former employer." He held up one of the tickets, examining the ink closely. "I don't have that much, so I have to resort to things like this to… economize, I guess you'd say. Dwarven smiths don't exactly fill special orders for washed-up old priests of Ghant."

"Ghant? You're a cat-worshiper?"

He put down his glass hard. He didn't slam it, but he was firm. He stared straight ahead as he answered: "There was a time I could have had you publicly scourged for uttering such an insult in my presence."

"Not here in Selva, you couldn't. You're from Garlund, then? What brings you east of the Striped Mountains?"

He turned to face me.

"I take it you don't follow international affairs much."

"You think anybody around here does?"

I hoped that might get a smile from him, but he just took another drink.

I thought about my encounter a few months back with the King. I wondered how much I should say; I decided to play dumb and see what the old cat-priest would tell me.

"I know there's something going on in Garlund right now that seems to have the nobles excited, but I don't know why that should be any concern of a Warrens rat."

The Professor's eyebrows twitched slightly. I decided to press it a bit further.

"Something about an enchanter fighting the Suzer, or something, and for some reason you cat-worshipers..."

"Not an enchanter," Professor Omi cut in. "'The Arcanter.' That's what people call him."

"The 'Arcanter?' Like, an 'arch enchanter?'"

"Possibly. Nobody is quite sure. The meaning is obscure."

"And you came east..."

"Well, west, actually. I came here on a boat that sailed west across the Glass Ocean."

"You came here — east of the Striped Mountains — to escape from this Arcanter?"

"In a manner of speaking, yes. I was a victim of the initial purges."

I had no idea what "the initial purges" were, but they didn't sound pleasant. Even so...

"You seem to have fallen pretty low for a former priest," I ventured.

"Yes," he grumbled, taking another drink. "There is, as you might imagine, no demand for my priestly vocation in the happy lands under the gaze of your Old Man on the Mountain." He spit out the words as if they burned his tongue.

I was about to ask him more, but at that point the music that I'd heard in the background suddenly ended, and a small fat man dressed in clothes similar to the bartender walked up on stage.

"Ladies and gentlemen — oh, I'm sorry, how silly of me, this is the Warrens! Brutes and brawlers, welcome to the most SEDUCTIVE, most SALACIOUS, most SINFUL den of deviancy in all of SELVA — the Dead SSSSSCORPION!"

I heard hooting and lewd boasting coming from the general direction of the couch I'd seen earlier, where the young nobles had gathered.

Professor Omi gestured in the direction of the couch with my fellow Clubs.

"I think THIS is the show you were probably hoping for," he said, with an air of dismissal. I eyed him for a second, wanting to say something. But I just picked up my glass and walked away to join the others.

Taygor slapped me on the shoulder as I sat down, and leaned over to whisper in my ear: "I'll tell you what I told the other two — now this is something they don't offer to just anybody, but any girl you see working here tonight, you just say the word and you can have her."

He paused for a second, seeming to think about something. "Or — I'll look past it only for tonight — any boy. Just don't let Lusseau know."

I gave him a look.

"I didn't think so, but you never know. It is YOUR night to celebrate, after all. Oh, and there is one girl who's off limits."

"Which one?"

"You'll know."

I sat up and looked around, curious to get a glimpse of what I figured must have been an incredibly choice piece of ass, but Taygor placed a hand on my shoulder.

"I said, 'you'll know.' Now relax and enjoy the show."

The music started up again, sounding naughtier and nastier than before, and the fat little man on stage announced the first number and bowed out. The lights around the stage got brighter while some unseen hand dimmed the chandeliers. For the first time, I noticed the lifeless husk of a golden scorpion mounted on the wall behind the stage — hence the name of the place, I guessed. I'd never actually seen one before, and the sheer size was enough to give you chills — its stinging tail was as thick as a man's thigh.

But it didn't hold my attention long — a quartet of four ladies leaped onto the stage and began dancing. And it was quite a sight — all four of them looked like those big-bosomed girls on the covers of a two-copper, and they were dressed to match. I blinked my eyes in astonishment and leaned in closer.

I turned to look at Taygor. I mouthed the words "any of them?" He grinned wide enough to reach the walls and nodded. I began mentally weighing my options, trying to decide between the light-skinned brunette or the tall, dusky-hued one who kept to the back to keep from blocking the shorter ones.

More whoops and hoots from the slumming young lords off to the side, along with some shouted propositions. Normally me and the other Clubs would have strolled over to their spot to teach them some Warrens manners, but tonight we let it slide — we all knew that tonight, WE would be the ones enjoying a royal feast after hours.

I sat back to enjoy the sights and lovingly ponder my options, when a voice rose up from the stage, coming from somewhere in back. It was a husky female voice, crooning along with the music.

A softly glowing orb descended from the ceiling, and began dancing lazily in the air above the stage. I looked over at the bar and saw Professor Omi moving his hand around with a look of concentration — the orb was another one of his spells, I realized.

Each of the girls took turns dancing a little number with the glowing orb, acting as if it were a male partner they were trying to seduce. As they twisted and wiggled their charms, the orb shimmied and whirled and cast light and shadow just so, now hiding, now revealing their curves in an intricate little play of tease and temptation. All the while, the husky voice continued its song of slow-burning lust.

As the song drew to a climax, the girls suddenly whirled out of the way, and the glowing orb brightened, revealing a new figure walking forward, no longer hidden in the shadows. It was…a young girl?

Wait…it WASN'T a young girl. She was dressed in a similar fashion as the other ladies, accented with an elaborate metal headdress and metal wristbands. Her skimpy attire, though, left no doubt that she possessed the body of a fully grown female — but shrunk down to about two-thirds the size.

It was an elf maiden, I realized, noticing the pointed ears and large, oddly shaped eyes.

I looked over at Taygor once more, and gestured towards the singer. He drew his finger across his throat.

Okay, so SHE was the one who was off limits.

Not that I really would have been interested. I mean, I suppose every man has heard whispers about what she-elves are like in the bedroom — but you also know how every man on both sides of the Striped Mountains claims he's packing a cock the size of the hitch-pin on an ox-trolley once he's got a few ales in him. Myself, I couldn't quite get past those odd elven proportions. Yes, the big eyes are titillating, I'll grant, but the rest just seems…not quite right.

As she stepped forward, belting out the tune and shaking her body with the other girls, I suddenly noticed her skin — bare at first, it suddenly sprouted dozens of elaborate whirling designs — like tattoos. Or was my head playing tricks on me? I looked at my drink — what had the bartender put in it?

I sat up and leaned forward. No, I was pretty certain I wasn't seeing things. And then the designs began to…move. First slowly, then more quickly, in whirling, dizzying patterns. I might have decided right then I was seeing another of the Professor's illusions, except that everyone else in the place began cheering at this display. It couldn't be a shared illusion, could it?

The elf reached out her arm, her open palm facing us as she emphasized one particular verse — the image of a multicolored butterfly shimmered into view on her palm, as if it were painted there. And then it began flapping its wings, still looking like a flat tattoo on her skin, but moving like it were a living creature.

She drew her hand in and touched it to her chest, just above her breasts, and the flat image of the butterfly seemed to slide off her hand and onto her torso. Stepping up to the edge of the stage, right in front of our couch, she cooed out a few seductive lines as she jutted out her chest, giving our gang an up-close view as the butterfly flitted back and forth between her breasts. She looked me directly in the eye and winked.

I shuddered. Even though I wasn't exactly attracted, I wasn't pushed away, either. And again, the stories about she-elves...

She turned, looking back at us over her shoulder with a look of pouty innocence. The butterfly swirled its way around her body, seeming to come to rest on one of her half-exposed butt cheeks. She gave her hip a pop, and the butterfly acted startled, flitting its way up her bare back.

Turning back to face us, she finished the song with a powerful crescendo, as she struck a statue-like pose with her arm held high. The animated tattoo flapped its way in a spiral up her limb, settling back into the flat palm of her hand.

With the last notes of the song, she balled her palm into a fist, bowed her head, and then all the lights in the hall — the glowing orb, the candles in the chandeliers and along the walls — winked out. Cheers erupted, and when the lights suddenly flickered back on, the elf maiden's skin was once again bare of any marks. She bowed as she took in the applause.

17

I settled on the tall, dusky girl — what swayed me was, when the girls were being introduced to us after the show, she seemed excited to see that I was half-Molan. I suppose it was just an act, but it did the trick for me. All three of us — me, Rupens and Lyco — got deluxe suites for the night. While me and Lyco went with one girl apiece, Rupens took two — that big appetite of his wasn't limited to food.

The next few hours were better than anything I could have even fantasized about. No other girl I'd been with until then had ever seemed as into it as I was, but Trin — that was her name — seemed even more on fire with raw passion than I could ever be. She even introduced me to some of the things I'd seen painted on the walls downstairs — man, I had a LOT to learn…

I was finally spent sometime around midnight, and though she gave me a lustful pout that almost got me going again, I was done. I fell asleep with her long, smooth body wrapped in my arms.

Sometime in the early hours of the morning, I felt rude hands shaking my awake. I rubbed my eyes and found myself staring into Taygor's ugly mug once again. Considering what had happened last time, this couldn't be good.

"Up and at 'em, slick," he whispered.

I pulled myself into a sitting position. Trin was still sleeping soundly at my side. She stirred a bit and murmured softly, but didn't wake up.

"Rom's curses on you, you bastard. What is this?"

"The night's not over yet. We're going on a little adventure."

I looked back at Trin, her achingly perfect body outlined underneath the covers.

"I think I'm good."

"It's not optional. Get your pants on and get out in the hall."

I threw the covers off and stood up. I saw Taygor look down at my cock. Now, I'm not gonna claim I've got the biggest bed-serpent you've ever seen, but I think it's fair to say that I live up to the stories you've heard about Molans. Taygor groaned and rolled his eyes, but I could see the jealousy.

"Whatever. Just put your pants on and get out there." He turned to leave.

"You sure don't need a better look?" I said. "Your hand might thank you later."

"Let me ask it. Oh, here's its answer now," he said, flipping me a middle finger on his way out the door.

When I emerged into the hallway a few minutes later, pulling on my sloucher, I wasn't surprised to see Lyco once again looking at a mirror, checking his hair. His clothes were still perfectly creased, and he still smelled fresh. He made a fine contrast to Rupens, who didn't notice his shirt was on backwards until I pointed it out to him.

"Rupens, by Auld Father's Foot, what is that smell?" I asked.

"He was still going when I came in to fetch him," Taygor said. "You should see the sheets in there. The girls are still catching their breath."

"You saying they didn't like it?" the big guy growled as he pulled his shirt over his head — the right way, this time.

"Oh, I didn't say that. I think it was the best night of their lives. I just think they need an hour or so before their eyeballs once again face forward."

Rupens smiled.

"Are we doing this or what?" Lyco snapped, turning to face us.

Taygor pushed off and wheeled around.

"Follow me."

He led us to a door at the far end of the hall which led to a cramped stairway, which obviously wasn't designed with full-sized men in mind. With some squeezing and scrambling, we made our way down it to a little room, where Lusseau was perched on a crate, holding something in his hands.

"Sorry guys," he said, coming towards us. "Like I said, you're not quite ready to know the location of this place."

"If you come at me with another spell..." Rupens growled.

"No, no. This time we're doing it the simple way."

What Lusseau was holding proved to be three hoods, which we somewhat reluctantly donned. They further made us put on thick cloaks, and then they led us along a twisting path through the building — we went through a kitchen at one point; I could tell from the sounds and smells — and then out into the street, where we were herded into the back of a cart. There we had to wait until Lusseau — who was driving the cart — believed we were far enough away to let us take off the hoods.

Pulling mine off, I looked around. The cart had a lantern that illuminated the filthy streets and buildings around us. In the light of the lantern, I finally noticed how grown-up Lusseau looked now — though he'd always been a lanky guy, even the small patches of baby fat were now entirely absent from his bony face, and he looked tired and bored. Taygor, meanwhile, had the sleepy but contented look of a cat with a belly full of its prey.

I looked around for something that I might recognize — then I saw it. While passing through a square, I saw a huge stone pedestal with four rusty horse's legs pointing up from the top. It was what was left of the monument to Count Gravener — most of the statue was gone, but the legs of the horse Count Gravener had been perched on were still there. The story I heard was that since the legs were made from iron (painted to match the rest of the statue), they were the only parts not worth stealing, which was why they were still stuck there.

That meant we were in Gravener Heights, which was on the far west side of the Improvement District. It was a part of the Warrens I'd seldom been to; it was dangerous territory for eastsiders like us.

I looked at Taygor.

"So you mind explaining this to us? Where are we headed?" I figured it might be some stupid initiation ritual — the old cemetery was nearby, and it was the site of a lot of that sort of nonsense.

"You'll see," he said, with the hint of a smile.

So it was going to be like that, I thought. I settled in and reviewed the night's events. Something occurred to me.

"Hey, Taygor. Was that another one of the Professor's tricks back there?"

"What, you being able to satisfy a woman? The only magic there was the magic of money, you dumb ape."

"Yeah, I'm sure that's the only thing that works for you, needledick. I mean the elf. With all the shit she did with her skin."

"Come on, you klanger-banger, I'd think someone who went to Temple School would know elves can change their skin color."

I was about to explain that I did in fact know that and follow it up with a "yes, but," but I decided to let the matter drop for the moment, because I noticed we were passing across Sack Lane.

I was suddenly aware of why we were all wearing cloaks — Sack Lane marked the boundary of Black Stars territory. We couldn't very well be showing our buttons around these parts.

Of all the westside gangs we brawled with, the Black Stars were the ones we hated the most. Nobody ever pulled punches in those fights, and everybody usually came away with a lot of scars. To this day I have a scar running from the wrist to almost the shoulder of my left arm where a Black Star gashed it open with a whip in a brawl outside the Crooked Horsehoe Tavern.

Rupens and Lyco noticed where we were, too.

"What in Gruun's name are we doing here?" Lyco hissed.

Taygor looked like he might burst out laughing, but he merely gave an amused snort.

"What, did you think tonight's pleasures were free? We've given you something, but now you have to return the favor."

"By what, getting our heads bashed in?" Lyco said.

Rupens just cracked his knuckles. "Tell me who I have to fight," he rumbled.

Taygor patted him on the shoulder. "Easy, big guy. If this all goes well, you won't have to fight anybody. It's not that kind of hustle."

I sighed. I thought I knew where this was going, and Taygor quickly confirmed it.

"You boys aren't here to fight. You're here to steal. Specifically, you're going to steal Pissing Pip."

"PISSING PIP" WAS A statue of a smiling little boy standing and holding his tiny cock, just pissing himself silly. I've heard it was originally part of a fountain, though who'd want to make a fountain of some little boy pissing is something beyond the imaginings of this Warrens rat.

Anyway, he wasn't part of a fountain anymore, though there was a hole hidden in his back where you could pour stuff, and it would come out the hole in his little cock like he was taking a whizz. Pip was sort of the mascot of the Black Stars — for what reason, I don't know. I've heard probably a hundred explanations, but the one you hear most often is that he shows how the Black Stars piss on all their enemies. I've also heard it said that you're not a full member of their gang until you've swallowed a pint of ale from Pip's cock.

Of course, gangs stole stuff from each other all the time. A couple of years before, some Black Stars had stolen the sign from our main tavern hangout, the Anders Arms. And the year before that we'd stolen the sign marking the corner of Star Road and Black Creek Lane, which was where the Black Stars got their name.

But Pip was something else altogether. He wasn't just sitting out in the open where you could wait for the right moment to come up and snatch him. He was actually in their hangout, the Burning Wheel tavern.

"That's a suicide mission," Lyco said, right as I was opening my mouth to say pretty much the same thing. Rupens just cracked his knuckles again.

"No, it's not. We've already cased the place. The only people there at this hour who are even awake will be the barkeep and a handful of drunks. You three shouldn't have any trouble handling them."

"Yeah, but this isn't like stealing a sign," I said. "Stealing Pip will be a big deal. It'll start a damn war. They won't rest until they have him back."

"They'll get him back. In a few days they'll get a note telling them where they can go fish him out of a privy. And if you guys do this right, they won't ever know it was us. We're not the only enemies they have, you know."

The Burning Wheel got its name from the giant painting of a sun that took up one whole side of the building. At least people said it was supposed to be a sun —

it had a crazy, whirling design with ribbons of flame shooting out from it. Lusseau backed the cart into an alley a few blocks down the street from the tavern and killed the lantern; we were instantly in pitch darkness. We got out and made our way to the street.

Lights were still on inside the Burning Wheel, but the whole neighborhood was eerily quiet.

"It's real easy, fellas — you've done strong-arm jobs before, right?"

Rupens and Lyco both growled their assent. Taygor looked at me.

"Oh. That's right, I guess when Rupens and Lyco here were getting their hands dirty you were up at the Temple School getting your nails painted."

I just stared back. I didn't want to give him the satisfaction.

"Well, stick close with these two, they know what to do. Now like I said, the only folks you should have to deal with are a few drunks and the barkeep. The drunks will be no problem, but the barkeep might be. Info we have is he's a former pit fighter. Now, now, don't get that look — he's been retired for years, and he's getting pretty long in the tooth. He'll probably put up a fight, but I have no doubt the three of you can handle him. Be careful, though — story is he was pretty tough in his day. He might still have a few tricks up his sleeve."

Lusseau chimed in. "Get it done quick and you boys will be back with your ladies in no time."

I could practically hear the wink in his voice.

The street was not quite deserted — figures shuffled along in the dark even at this hour. I assumed most were laborers or delivery people working odd shifts, but some of them might be Black Stars. Even though the tavern was only a few blocks away, the last thing we needed was to be challenged.

I looked at Lyco and Rupens. They looked like gang toughs even with cloaks on — and I assumed I did too.

I reached down and grabbed some dirt and rubbed it over my face, and told them to do the same.

"Why?" Rupens asked warily.

"We're trying to look like a band of old drunks. And try to slouch and stumble a bit when you walk. There's only three of us, and this isn't our territory. I'd just as soon not raise any suspicion."

There was a bit of hesitation.

"Do it," Taygor finally hissed.

I heard a couple of sighs, and both my companions reached down and grabbed some filth and dirtied up their faces, though Lyco moaned about getting dirt in his hair. He sniffed his handful of muck and glared at me.

"There damn well better not be any horseshit in this," he said, before smearing it on his face.

Suitably filthy, we ambled off down the street. When we were about a block away, two big guys wearing slouchers with Black Stars buttons came out of the front door of the Burning Wheel. Both were almost as tall as Rupens.

"See you tomorrow, Razor," one called back through the door, and then they both came walking down the street right towards us.

Shit, I thought.

"Shit," Lyco hissed.

Neither of the two showed any signs of being drunk, so we didn't have that working in our favor. I thought quickly.

"You two just keep your mouths shut. Let me try something."

Pretending to limp, I hobbled straight up to the two Black Stars with my dirt-covered hand out.

"Spare a coin?" I wheezed. "We've almost enough for a bottle of Ruddy," I said, nodding at my companions.

Not even bothering to glance in my direction, one of the two Black Stars flipped me a silver.

"Don't kill yourself with that poison, old man. Get yourself a bottle of Ytter's," he said, and they both kept walking past us. A few moments later, the other looked back over his shoulder and shouted "it's on the Black Stars, don't forget!"

Now let me just take a moment here to salute those two fellows for being fine and upstanding examples of Warrens hospitality, something so rare I can probably count on my hands the number of times I've seen it, and I'd still have fingers left over. If I'd thought about it, I might have taken that little incident as an ill omen, because you only get so many lucky moments in a day and that one just about used up all of ours.

But I wasn't thinking about much except getting back to the Dead Scorpion. I pocketed the coin.

"You're going to split that with us," Lyco muttered as he came up alongside me.

"Fuck off. Let's get this over with."

We stumbled our way to the door of the tavern, and I opened it and motioned to the other two to go in first — they'd done this before, after all.

My two companions charged in, and I heard commotion from inside. I carefully looked up and down the street, making sure we weren't noticed. It all seemed as sleepy as ever. The only sound was the laughing of the two Black Stars we'd seen, now several blocks away.

I ducked in and locked the door behind me.

18

I was confused at first. The inside of the Burning Wheel didn't look like any tavern or public hall I'd ever been in.

Maybe it's different at the fancy places you long-beards go to, but in your usual trash watering hole, there's pretty much a standard design: There's a long bar up against one wall. There's a bunch of tables and chairs, including a couple of big tables for groups. Depending on the place, there might be a dance floor or a stage or both. Some of the nicer places — nicer for the Warrens, at any rate — have second- or even third-level galleries looking down on everything, generally reserved for bigshots.

The Burning Wheel wasn't anything like that. Instead, the bar itself was — well, it was a big circle, right in the center of the hall. The shelves holding all the liquor bottles were arranged in a smaller circle behind the bar, and the barkeep ran around in a space between the two that sort of reminded me of a castle moat.

Behind the shelves with the liquor was a raised platform visible from everywhere in the hall. It took me a few moments to realize this was supposed to be a stage for performers.

I heard some kind of scuffle — I realized it was coming from the opposite side of the circular bar, which I couldn't see from the door. From where I was standing, there was only one person visible — a fat fellow whose head was slumped over on the bar next to a bottle of Ruddy. He was snoring loudly.

I circled around to find — I'm not sure what you'd call it.

Laid out on the floor was a limp body, bleeding from the head. It was a shirtless man, small and thin but with taut, wiry muscles covered in tattoos. Lyco was behind the bar holding a large — well, it was a large spoon. I think he had just grabbed the first thing he'd laid his hand on. Rupens was on my side of the bar, holding a large chair. Cowering behind the bar was a frail-looking old man waving a rapier. The old man's shaky grip didn't exactly inspire fear, and the thing looked rusty and dull.

There was also a pudgy but hardy-looking man with a big mustache sitting at the bar, gripping a mug of ale and watching the whole scene as if it were completely normal. His eyes were glassy and his face was very red.

He didn't notice me at first. He gestured toward the barkeep with his mug: "Better just give them what they want, Razor. Somebody who rubs horseshit all over their face is not likely to be quite right in the head, and that blade was just there for show. I don't think it's seen action since...oh, look, we have a third guest," he said, finally spying me from the corner of his eye.

"Geni and Barc just left a minute ago with the night's take. I'm afraid all that's left for you boys is some petty cash and whatever Razor there has collected in tips. Oh, and I guess whatever's in Halmer's pockets over there..."

He nodded at the limp, shirtless man on the floor. A moan rose up from the motionless form, but he didn't move.

"I don't know if Cresh is still here," the man continued. "He usually sits over on the opposite side of the wheel — we don't get along. He might have a few coins, but I doubt it. As for me, this I'm drinking on the King's Coin" — he raised his mug in a mock toast and smiled broadly — "and I don't have a copper on me. It tastes like ox piss, but it gets you drunk just the same."

The barkeep looked at me with pleading eyes. If he was a former pit fighter, you could have fooled me. But looks, I knew, could be deceiving.

"Look, mister," I began. "We're not here for money, and we don't want to cause you any trouble. We're just here for Pip."

The red-faced man drinking ox piss snorted. "Pip? What, is this an initiation thing? Which crew are you boys with, the Winfield Vampires? Cheapside Vandals? Bond Street Butchers? If you think he's going to help you with that, you're dreaming. The Black Stars scare him much more than you do."

I was about to say something to the man when the barkeep suddenly swung the rapier hard against Lyco's hand. Lyco shouted "Owwwww!" and dropped the spoon; the man ducked under the bar just as the chair Rupens was wielding came crashing down right where he'd been standing.

I shoved Rupens out of the way and leaned over the bar to see the barkeep scurrying around to the other side of the circular bar, hunched down. As he disappeared around the curve I leaped over the bar and began chasing him, but once I'd reached the other side of the circle — where the drunk was passed out beside a bottle of Ruddy — I came to a hatch in the floor that was just closing. I reached for the ring attached to the top to yank it open, but as my fingers wrapped around it, I heard a tiny "click" from beneath. I pulled at the ring to confirm: Yep, he'd locked it.

Damn it.

I heard Lyco and Rupens coming up clumsily behind me. Turning, I could see Lyco gripping his hand.

"Are you okay?" I asked.

"Yeah, he didn't cut me. Just slapped my hand hard with the flat part of the blade. Clever."

I tapped the floor hatch with my foot.

"It's locked," I said.

I looked down at the hatch and had a sudden realization.

"You two stay right here," I said, jumping back over the bar. I ran toward the back of the hall. I'd noticed a door there earlier, and I reached for it — it opened.

I ran through some kind of kitchen and then out the back of the kitchen into a storage room. The storage room had a set of large, warehouse-style doors — and one of them had a smaller, human size door built into it. I unlocked it and opened it, finding myself in an alley.

Just to my left, there was a large set of service doors that led down to the basement, and they were wide open. I saw a set of fresh footprints leading away from the doors, down the alley and around a corner.

I broke into a sprint and quickly caught up with the barkeep, who could only manage a slow jog. I grabbed him by the shoulders and threw him against the wall of the alley. His eyes stared back at me in fear.

I sighed.

"Look, mister," I said, trying to sound reassuring. It was difficult, since my excitement was still up from the pursuit. "We just want Pip! I don't want to give you any trouble. I don't want to hurt you. Honestly, I think this is all just stupid. I just want the damn statue."

He looked at me. I could feel him shaking.

"I can't...they'll...they'll..." Then his eyes hardened. "If I was 30 years younger, boy...I'll have you know, I was at Silver Ridge!"

Now I know all you long-beards will recognize that name right off — and I do, too, nowadays. But back then, at that moment, it was just a dim memory of something I'd heard about back in Temple School.

When he mentioned Silver Ridge, his eyes seemed to drift off and lose focus, as if he were thinking back about some mighty deeds he'd done as a young man. I slapped him to remind him of where he was at that moment.

"Pip, old man."

His eyes narrowed.

"Would you tell, boy, if you were in my shoes?"

That sent a chill up my spine, and I was struck all of a sudden with the thought of where I was and what I was doing.

I thought back to the smile I'd seen on the face of that man back in...back in the illusion I'd been given by Professor Omi. He'd smiled at me because I'd fought and defeated some demon sea creature — a creature much stronger and more powerful than I could ever be. And now here I was, threatening a helpless old man in a dark alley. I could feel his tired skin wrapped around weak, weak old bones; there was nothing threatening about him.

Except — hadn't Taygor mentioned he was some kind of ex-pit fighter? And that he might try something sneaky? The frail old man thing could be just a front. I thought, maybe, I felt some hints of muscle underneath that sagging skin.

I pressed my arm into his throat.

"Pip," I growled.

He gasped for air, but his eyes spit defiance at me. For some reason, that made me angry.

I'd been trying to be nice. But he wasn't playing along.

I released my arm and slugged him hard, and he collapsed with a wail of pain.

"The statue, damn it. The statue! Right. Now."

He was blubbering, and blood was coming out of his mouth and nose. But when I grabbed him by the neck and looked into his face, he tightened his jaw. I kicked him in the ribs, and he doubled over, coughing up blood. Then I slammed him down into the mud, just because it felt good.

His whole body wrenched with sobs. I was about to hit him again when I heard a voice.

"Lash! Lay off him and come back to the tavern. We got Pip."

It was Rupens. He had just come around the corner. I followed his gaze down to where the old barkeep was on the ground, just pulling himself to his hands and knees.

I grabbed the old man and lifted him up, and stared into his muddy, haunted-looking face.

"Get out of here. Go back to whichever shithouse you call home. Don't even think of dropping a clue to any of the Black Stars, or we'll know who to look for — 'Razor.'"

I tossed him down the alley and turned to go back to the Burning Wheel.

Back at the tavern, the first thing I saw was how all the paintings and tapestries had been torn off the wall and were thrown about the room. Where one of them had been — a painting of a man looking up at a night sky, I noted — there was a tough-looking door set into the wall: A strongbox. Lyco was trying to pry it open with the rapier the old barkeep had been wielding, but he only succeeded in bending the blade.

He threw the useless weapon away in disgust.

"Not very creative, are they?" he said, wiping the sweat from his face.

He noticed my confused expression. "You work enough of these jobs, you learn where people like to hide things," he explained. "Still, I thought the Black Stars would come up with something a little sneakier. Now if we could only get the blasted thing open..."

"Obviously you haven't worked enough of these jobs," Rupens said, running his beefy hand over the sturdy-looking door. It was very thick, made of what looked to be solid iron.

"Oh, I suppose an oaf like you is an expert locksmith?" Lyco said.

"Not at all," Rupens said over his shoulder. He had his back to us, and was walking over to the tavern's large fireplace. "Don't have to be. You said yourself they're not very creative."

Rupens grabbed the ax for the firewood, held it up, swung it around a few times, as if getting the feel for it. I noticed the guy at the bar drinking ox piss watching the scene with some interest.

Our big blond companion walked over, ran his hand over the wall surrounding the iron door, then stood back and began attacking it with the ax. Me and Lyco just stood and watched.

Rupens used the ax to methodically cut through the wooden wall around the iron door, leaving just a little part at the bottom where the strongbox and wall were still attached. Then he grabbed the top and pulled. There was a loud crack, and the strongbox came crashing down out of the wall and onto the floor.

He walked over to the strongbox, now sitting face-down on the floor, and rapped on the back with his knuckles.

"Yep," he said. "Figures. Cheapskates."

He then grabbed up the ax again and swung it hard down on the back of the strongbox, where to my shock it made a deep dent. He kept swinging it until he managed to gouge a large hole in the back. He then grabbed a nearby chair, snapped off a leg, and used it to pry back the metal to open the hole wider.

"I used to run with a cat burglar when I was a kid — back when I was small," Rupens explained, as he laboriously peeled back the metal. "He used me to get into tight spaces where he couldn't fit. One of the things I learned from him was about strongboxes set in walls like this. Lots of time, the door is the only part that's worth a shit. The front's built like a fortress, but the rest of the box is flimsy. Heck, sometimes the rest is even made of wood! Nobody ever expects you to just pull the whole thing out of the wall."

He struggled a bit more to bend back the flimsy metal. Finally, he dropped the wooden chair leg and wiped his brow.

"There you go, gentlemen," he said, nodding at the thin metal that had been peeled back like a fish-tin. Me and Lyco leaned over and looked inside, finding ourselves facing the stone-carved ass of a childlike figure, just slightly smaller in size than a real toddler. There was a hole in its back, right where the figure's neck connected to the torso.

I reached in and tried to lift it. It was surprisingly heavy. Lyco pitched in and we lifted out the figure and flipped it over.

There was a fresh crack in the figure's nose, I guess from where it had tumbled around when Rupens had pulled the box out of the wall, but otherwise it was just like I'd always heard it described: It was a carving of a little boy pissing. The tiny cock was worn smooth, unlike the relatively rough texture of the rest of the figure.

I nodded at it. "Looks like the stories are true," I said.

We all laughed at that.

"Let's get out of here," I said. Rupens reached to pick up Pip, but I stopped him.

"No, man. You opened that strongbox. I fought an ex-pit fighter. It's Lyco's turn to bust his ass tonight."

I heard a loud scoff from the bar. I turned. It was the ox piss drinker, who had helped himself to a free bottle of something else, which I assumed tasted better than ox piss. He was using it to refill his huge mug.

"Pit fighter? Did you say ex-pit fighter, boy? You mean Razor?"

"Yeah. What's it to you?"

"He's no ex-pit fighter, boy. You're thinking of Mernon. HE'S the ex-pit fighter — and he was a great one, in his day! He has the night off — and lucky for you three, because he would have given you a fight. By Auld Father's Foot, that would have been something to see! Razor's just a harmless old man. He just got that name because he makes extra coin as a barber-for-hire. Hands like an artist, he's got — will give you the closest, smoothest shave this side of the Palace District."

I felt queasy. The drunk must have noticed, because he let out a great guttural laugh.

"You REALLY thought that old man was an ex-pit fighter?" he said, nearly choking on his ale. "What do pit fighters look like in your part of the Warrens, boy?"

He was still laughing when we left the bar. I carried Pip, with no help from the others, ignoring the burning feeling in my muscles the whole time.

19

There were still several hours of darkness left, and Lyco and Rupens were in a hurry to get back to the Dead Scorpion. But I told Lusseau to just drop me off at Craller Square. I was done for the night. I whipped off my cloak and threw it into the back of the cart.

I headed back to the rooming house, but then I remembered my face was still covered in filth. I wondered about what Lyco had said earlier when he was smearing it on his own face — was there horseshit in it? I scraped some off my cheek and sniffed it. Maybe it was — maybe it wasn't. I couldn't tell. Everything in the Warrens smelled like horseshit. Or ox shit. Or dogshit. Or people shit. I realized I'd been living in shit so long I barely even noticed the smell anymore — ever since I'd quit going to the Temple School, I'd forgotten what a shitless world smelled like.

They say Gruun, down there in his dark kingdom, lives in a whole lake of shit. That was where his seductions would bring you, in the end. They say he seduces us with lies, but here I was, someone who'd willingly rubbed shit all over his own face. What lies had the dark one ever told me? It looked more like he was keeping his promises — what did it say about me that this was something I wanted?

I bent over a watering trough and did my best to wash the muck off my face. When I got back to our place at the rooming house, my mom was there — I wasn't sure of the time, so I had no idea if she was early or late or right on schedule. Nevertheless, she was sitting in her chair, reading a copy of The Walk. When she looked up at me, she had tears in her eyes.

"So you're a man now," she said.

I wasn't sure what she was getting at, so I played dumb. Played being the key word there, because once again I was trying to grow a brain, and I've said before that's something that's never smart to do with a mom.

"It's only first day of summer, mom," I said. Then I remembered the time. "Well, second day now, I suppose. Anyway, you always said I was born in midwinter, right?"

She closed The Walk and looked at me. She looked at me for a long time, but didn't say anything. Even when I sat down on my bed, and began to get ready for sleep, she just looked at me.

"How was the Dead Scorpion?" she finally asked. "Oh, don't give me that look, I've been here in the Warrens longer than you have. I know everything that goes on."

The look I now saw in my mom's eyes — it was something I'd never seen before. And the tone in her voice — it was like she was shuffling off a heavy costume she'd worn for years. I didn't get it at the time, but I realize now she'd been wearing it for me.

But sitting there on my bed, I was just confused. I saw the tears in my mom's eyes starting up again.

"Mom. I..."

She cut me off.

"I did the best I could by you, Lash. I'm poor, and my life has been hard, but by Auld Father, I've done the best I could! What else could He ask of me?"

She leaned her head forward and began to sob silently. I came over and just put my arms around her, trying to calm her. Finally she straightened up, and took both of my hands in her own. She looked at me.

"Three days. Aunt Rossie says I shouldn't even give you that much, but Auld Father help me, you are my son and I love you, and I can't just toss you out."

"Mom. Mom...what do you mean...?"

I knew what she meant, of course, but I'd been hoping I still had time, that I still had until the end of the summer. My thought — it had only been a hazy thought — was that I'd somehow get my life sorted out, and then I'd be able to stand before my mom like a man and say I'd found my own place and could make my own way. But that happy thought which I'd been holding in the back of my mind was now being snatched away.

"Three days. You'll need to be completely out of here, along with anything you intend to keep." She wiped a tear from her eye. "Aunt Rossie already has your bed rented to another girl."

I felt cold. I looked over at my bed, at all my books, at my clothes...it had been the only home I'd ever known. I'd taken my first step on the floor between our beds. My mom said I'd spoken my first word while she had me on her lap in the very chair she was now sitting in. I don't think there's any shame in saying I started to cry myself.

And when I did, for a brief moment, my mom was mom again. She put her arms around me and helped me to my bed, and tucked me in. She kissed my forehead and looked down at me while she stroked my hair.

"It's not goodbye, my son," she said. "Just goodbye from here. You're a man now. You need to live as one."

Despite my tears, I could feel my eyelids getting heavy.

I was glad, at that moment, that my mom worked nights. I was glad to have her there with me that morning as I drifted off to sleep. If she had left me just then, I'm not sure I could have handled it.

20

When I woke up later that day, I sat in bed reading some stories about Vast the Brutal. I wasted the whole day doing that. I was trying to avoid thinking about what would come next. It wouldn't be that hard — I knew Lyco had a place of his own somewhere. He could take me in for long enough to get things settled. If nothing else, I could rent a bed at a bunkhouse — even if Lyco wouldn't let me stay with him, he would at least let me store some of my stuff with him.

But I didn't want to deal with any of that right now. I just wanted to enjoy what little time I had left in this little room where I felt so safe.

As darkness crept in — one day down, two more left — I glanced over at my sloucher, hanging on the wall. I could go join the rest of the gang down at the Anders Arms. I wondered if the Black Stars might have managed to put things together about our caper — if they might come around looking for a brawl.

Just then, my mom started to climb out of bed to get ready for her shift. I pushed away the thought of going out that night — no, I wanted to stay the night right there, warm and safe. I could find solutions tomorrow.

As I began to get sleepy, I thought again of the vision, or the hallucination, or whatever it was that Professor Omi had shown me. He'd said it was some kind of yearning. I thought of the man there on the island, looking at me and smiling with approval.

Maybe that's it, I thought. Maybe I'm meant to be a sailor. Or something. Something on the ocean, as I'd seen in that vision. The Molans were sea people; maybe that's where I belonged.

I made up my mind to go down to the docks the next day and sign up to work aboard a ship. Sure, I could be gone for years. But at least I'd be doing something that...well, that my mom might view as honorable. Maybe I could come back in a few years, and look up the old Post Master, and get a job with the Crown Post.

One thing was sure: I needed to get out of the Warrens. There was no future here. I remembered the man sitting on that barstool back at the Golden Wheel, boasting about ale that tasted like ox piss. I remembered how clever I felt smearing shit on my face to look like a worthless beggar.

I'd find my way out. First thing tomorrow, I'd be down at the docks.

I went to sleep feeling good. For the first time — well, for the first time in my life, really — I felt like I might be going somewhere.

IT DIDN'T LAST. NOT even eight hours. I was woken up early the next morning by my mom shaking me.

"Get up. There's a man downstairs. Says he's here to see you."

"What man?" I said, trying to wipe the gunk out of my eyes.

"He says he's with the City Constabulary."

That got my attention. I pulled myself up and looked at my mom. Her face was hard. I could see her eyes were moist, but she wasn't crying.

I splashed water on my face and got dressed. My mom picked out something for me to wear — I didn't ask her to, but somehow she just seemed to know. It was a plain white shirt and gray jacket, with brown trousers. I might have been a regular workman off to his morning job.

It was something about us stealing Pissing Pip. It had to be. I knew none of my fellow gang members would rat me out on that, so maybe it was that drunk at the Golden Wheel. Or maybe somebody at the Dead Scorpion had overheard something? The important thing was not to panic, keep your mouth shut — if everybody kept their mouths shut, there would be no problem. They couldn't pin anything on us.

As I was about to head down the stairs, my mom pulled me aside.

"Son. Son, before you go...I just want to remind you..."

She pulled out something that had been hanging from a string around her neck, hidden in the folds of her dress.

I recognized it. It was an impression of my first footprint in the sacred soil of the Temple, after I'd first learned to walk. It was cast in copper. My mom took my fingers and ran them over the tiny impression.

"You've taken your first step on the Path. That was my doing. I've done everything I knew how to do. Your feet are your own now. Just remember, Footman Rom has written, 'no matter how far a seeker strays from the Path, only one step is needed to find it again.'"

She kissed me on the cheek. I made up my mind at that moment that I would confess everything.

My resolution lasted for as long as it took me to walk down the stairs. For at the bottom was not the tall, stern, forbidding officer that I expected, but a plump little man with long hair that spilled down from the sides of his shiny, red bald head. Just beneath that red dome was a smiling red face with a pair of tiny spectacles set on top of a bulbous nose and fat, bulging cheeks.

The man was almost short enough to pass for a dwarf, and his round body was wrapped in a dark green suit trimmed with lace. On another man it might have looked girlish, but on him it just made him look like an overgrown doll. Aunt Rossie herself was bubbling with joy as she poured the man a cup of tea. When he asked for three lumps of sugar, she pinched his cheek and wagged her finger.

"Mr. Bogg, really! I hardly think your daughter would approve!"

"Ever since my dear wife passed on, I have resolved to savor the few delights left to me, Perna!"

He smiled broadly, and Aunt Rossie blushed. It was the first time I'd ever heard anybody but Aunt Rossie's brother call her by her first name.

"My daughter needs to worry about other things at her age, anyway. I was telling her the other night, Perna, that…oh, I take it that this is Mr. Pearl!"

With more ease than I would have thought possible, the little man shot up out of his chair and extended a hand. I'd had my dealings with the law before, but none of the encounters had been pleasant. The members of the city guard who showed up in the Warrens looked like they might have been first cousin to ogres — you half-expected them to walk about on their knuckles.

This guy was not at all like that. If it hadn't been for the shiny — VERY shiny — constable's emblem pinned to his chest, I never would have took him for the law.

What, in Auld Father's name, was this about? I'd never seen a law man like this before. I'd been ready to confess, but now I had no idea what was going on.

Perhaps this was something else entirely. Perhaps it had nothing to do with me after all. Maybe the hand of Auld Father had only meant to give me a start. I silently swore to myself that I would take the hint.

I shook the man's hand and managed a confused-sounding greeting: "Pleased to…meet you? Sir?"

"Pleased to meet you as well, sir!" he said as he shook my hand firmly. "I am Bogg. My men call me 'Captain' Bogg, but that's just because they're required to. I prefer 'Bogg' — or 'Mr. Bogg,' if you insist on formalities! I'm just here to clear up a few matters, son. Please, sit down!"

He settled down into his chair and studied his cup of tea with delight. I sat down opposite him. My mom and Aunt Rossie stood off to the side; we were in the entrance hall to the rooming house. The little table holding the tea set had been put in a few years before. I stared for a moment at it; I remember that was the exact spot where that dwarf veteran had stood all those years before when he'd brought me home to my mom.

Mr. Bogg took a sip of his tea and then flashed a phony-surprised smile at Aunt Rossie. She let out a small giggle in response. Then he looked at me, still smiling.

"Now. Mr. Pearl. Can you tell me where you were the night before last?"

I looked at my mom. "At the Dead Scorpion," I said. "Celebrating with friends," I quickly added.

Mr. Bogg looked down at his tea, still smiling. He stirred it with a dainty motion.

"I see. Were you there the entire night?"

"Pretty much. I mean I was there until morning. My friends could tell you that. Their names are..."

"No need, son. You are quite sure you didn't go anywhere else?"

"No, sir." I'd meant to confess, but here I was, already lying — it had become a reflex with me, to lie like that. Still, I wasn't quite sure what was going on — why would a Constable who looked like this care about Pissing Pip? What, exactly, was I supposed to confess to?

I decided to keep on lying, on the off chance that this wasn't something that involved me at all. But I tried to at least hew close to the truth: "I mean on the way out, they made us put masks over our heads and ride around in a wagon for awhile, because they didn't want..."

"They?"

"Two of my...my friends. They were the ones that organized the celebration. First day of summer, you know? They're...older. They're the ones who knew where the Dead Scorpion was. We — me and my other friends — weren't ready to know, they told us. So we had to wear masks and ride around in a wagon."

Mr. Bogg took another sip of tea and scratched his head.

"These friends of yours — I assume they are fellow members of your little organization? The Stonegate Clubs?"

I felt my heart sink.

"Gang," I said. "We're a gang. You can call us that."

Bogg gave a little nod.

"Not against the law for a group of young men to have their own little — 'gang,' as you call it. If it were, I reckon I'd have half the young men in the Palace District locked up in the gaol," he said kindly. Then, as if noticing my expression for the first time: "Why so sullen? Do you not like this — 'gang' you belong to?"

"No, sir. I mean, not anymore. I've been thinking it's probably not the best thing for me, sir."

He gave an approving nod.

"You seem like a sensible fellow, Mr. Pearl, so I'll talk to you man to man. With your permission — your mother has already given it, but I'd like yours — I would like to look through your room."

What could it hurt? I didn't have Pip with me. I told him that was OK by me if it was OK by my mom, and we went upstairs.

Once we got to our room, Mr. Bogg walked up and down the length of the small space, with his hands clasped behind his back. He never did stop smiling. Everything he saw seemed to bring delight and a twinkle in his eyes.

He gave an appreciative nod to my mom's copy of The Walk, lying open on the table beside her bed, and shared a look with her after doing so.

Finally, he took off his glasses and began cleaning them.

"Have you ever met, Mr. Pearl, a gentleman by the name of Ton Fernnis?"

"No," I said truthfully.

"Mr. Fernnis is a veteran of the Goblin War. The FIRST Goblin War, mind you," he said, returning the glasses to his nose. By his tone, I gathered that I was supposed to be impressed by that detail. "He is a somewhat FAMOUS man from the first Goblin War, as a matter of fact. There's actually much that's been written about him — you went to the Temple School, did you not? You may have heard about him in one of your classes."

I shook my head. "Name doesn't ring a bell."

Mr. Bogg took a step towards me.

"Mr. Fernnis was the only man in that war ever awarded the Order of St. Mersa twice."

Bogg must have seen the confusion on my face. "The Crimson Star," he explained. That, I had heard of — it was Selva's highest military award.

"I still haven't heard of him."

"Yes, well, Mr. Fernnis is a modest man, and he prefers a quiet life. He doesn't like to give interviews, so historians — my brother is a historian, that is how I originally met Mr. Fernnis — often have trouble locating him. So I was a bit surprised yesterday when he showed up in my office and presented me with this..."

Mr. Bogg held out his hand. There was something in his palm. I leaned over to get a better look at it.

It was a red button, in the shape of a fist.

Reflexively, I jerked my head over to look at my sloucher hanging on the wall. Bogg grinned and followed my gaze, then stepped over to the sloucher and lifted it off its hook to study it. He then showed it to me.

One of the buttons had been torn off.

IT WASN'T ABOUT PIP — well, not specifically. It was about the barkeep, the old man I'd beaten up in the alley. I'd assumed he was a nobody, but it turned out he was a somebody. He was a somebody people listened to. And when he told the City Constabulary how some young punk had beaten him nearly to a pulp — and provided a button he'd ripped off my sloucher — the law didn't have to look very far.

They knew the button was from our gang, obviously, because when you're on the wrong side of the law, the most helpful thing you can do for the authorities is to go around wearing a sign advertising your affiliation. And since Mr. Fernnis

— "Razor" — was a great war hero, the Constabulary was pretty keen to catch whoever was responsible for giving him a beating. Palms wouldn't be greased — instead, skulls would be cracked. As he was leading me back to his wagon with my hands chained together — my mom bawling the whole time — Mr. Bogg calmly explained that, with a little bit of this kind of "persuasion," my pals — my gang, the guys who were supposed to stick with you through the worst the Warrens could throw at you — had been only too happy to give me up. So much for brotherhood.

On the way to the gaol, I asked Mr. Bogg what would happen next. I sort of knew, from stories I'd heard from other gang members who'd been arrested, but I needed — well, I needed to talk to somebody just then. I needed a friend, and Mr. Bogg, who still wore a smile and doffed his hat to people he recognized on the street, seemed as good a person as any. There was another man in the wagon with us, a Constable with a thick mustache and stabbing eyes pointed straight ahead, but he didn't look nearly as promising.

Mr. Bogg looked at me with that same broad grin that never seemed to leave his face — but this time, his eyes grew soft. I figure it was as close as he could get to looking somber. He patted me on the shoulder and told me what was coming.

21

The City Gaol itself wasn't in the Palace District, but it was built right beside it. On one side, the windows of the cells looked right out at the Palace District — the top-floor cells would have given you a clear view of the Palace itself.

I didn't get one of those cells. The cell I was in looked out over the fishermen's docks. Beyond that I could see the harbor, and the sails of the ships going to and fro.

I could have been on one of those ships, I kept reminding myself. I could have left all the stink and filth of this wretched city and this wretched land far behind.

But now I was stuck staring through iron bars at what could have been.

There were four bunks to a cell, so I shared my space with three other men. One was a very old man who seemed terribly confused. He didn't speak a word. The whole time I was in that cell, it never did seem like that old man had any clue where he was.

The second man wouldn't shut up. Not that he'd talk to you, that is: He just talked endlessly about the gremlins. And he didn't speak to anybody in particular — he just jabbered on about the intricacies of gremlin society, and how, as I gathered, gremlins lived inside the walls of all the buildings everywhere and came out at night on their "disruption missions." To hear him tell it, this mostly involved stuff like randomly moving socks and cups and lamps and other things around in order to confuse people. It was a conspiracy, he explained to nobody in particular, and it was all part of the gremlin master plan.

The last fellow was the only one I could talk to. He was a lanky middle-aged man with ugly, patchy stubble and most of his teeth missing, and he called himself Jop.

My first day in the cell, he saw me staring at our constantly jabbering cellmate.

"You know what he's in for, don't you?" Jop suddenly asked.

I said I had no idea.

"Killed three people. Butchered them with a fishknife. Said they were being mind-controlled by gremlins."

I gave him a look. I sensed bullshit.

He picked up on my skepticism immediately.

"No, I'm serious. Carved out their livers. Brought them to the local chapel and presented them to the presiding Footman. Said you could tell from the color that they were from gremlins. That's how he said the gremlins controlled people — by replacing their livers."

I looked at our cellmate and felt a chill.

"How long has he been here?"

"He's been here since I got here, and that was two weeks ago."

I gulped. Two weeks? Or more? Was that how long I'd have to wait?

He chuckled. "First time, I take it? What are you in for?"

"What are you in for?"

"Me? I'm a con artist. This is, oh, probably my 29th, 30th visit. This time was a beaut, I must say. Sold shares in a nonexistent gold mine outside of Yant. It would have worked if one of my investors hadn't turned out to have a second cousin serving in the army there. What are the odds?"

I looked him over. I'd never seen such an ass-ugly con artist before, but maybe that was part of his act. Still, he had the look of a man who'd been through this before.

"How long does it usually take to get a hearing?" I asked.

"A hearing? Oh, by His Foot, it can take months. Usually only a week or two, though. It depends on the case — and it depends on who you know. You don't know anybody, do you?"

I just hung my head. I'd been holding it back, but I no longer had the strength: I started crying. Jop left me alone, and I curled up in my bunk and cried myself to sleep.

To my surprise — and the surprise of Jop — it only took me two days. I was lying back on my bunk, chewing on a piece of salt bread they'd shoved into the cell for breakfast, when someone started banging on the bars of the door and a disgusted voice spat out my name.

"Pearl. Pearl, you in there? Get up here. Your public counselor is here."

Jop stared at me with wide eyes as I shuffled off of my bunk and headed over to the door. I think he might have been thinking I was a potential bigshot that he'd let slip through his fingers.

They led me down several flights of stairs and threw me in this little room all by myself, and I had to wait there for what felt like hours, but probably wasn't more than 15 or 20 minutes.

I heard the door lock snap and this fellow in fine clothes who smelled of some flowery soap came in carrying a big folio.

Without even thinking about it, the words just tumbled out of my mouth: "Can I see my mom? I want to see my mom."

The man stopped, but he seemed — unsurprised, I guess you would say. For the life of me, I felt myself starting to tear up again. It was embarrassing.

The man leaned out the door and whispered something to a fellow outside, and a few minutes later my mom was there, and I couldn't remember the last time I've been so happy to see her. We hugged tight, both crying — but even with her tears, she seemed so peaceful now. She patted my back and shushed me, holding me like I was a little boy who'd stubbed his toe.

The counselor just stood there watching us, until he finally did that coughing thing that uppity sorts do when they want you to cut out whatever you're doing and pay attention to them.

He opened up his big folio and laid out some papers, and he began telling me about all the trouble I was in, but he used all those fancy words that the long-beards like to use to pretty up their language and make it sound like it's something other than what it actually is. I was too dumb and blubbery to make perfect sense of what he was saying, but I picked out some stuff about "violations of the King's Laws in Section 3" and something about "prescribed sentences" including six lashes and six years in prison.

At this point I was sniffling and trying to dry my eyes and look serious. Truth be told, it was about what I had expected, but it set off my mom to crying again, so I just put my arms around her and told her five years wasn't that long and it might do me some good to be away from the Warrens. I lied and told her I'd heard that lashings weren't all that bad. She kept on crying, so now it was my turn to hug her and pat her on the back and shush her.

The counselor did that coughing thing again, and I gave him a stone-cold Warrens look like I was going to punch him in the throat. To my surprise, he didn't flinch.

"That," he said, "is the worst-case scenario here. Luckily..." — and with this he turned one of the papers around and slid it toward me — "...this is a first offense, and that gives us some options."

He nodded down at the sheet, which was smaller than the others; when I reached out to pull it closer, I noticed it was actually made of thick cardstock. It had "A CONFESSION" written at the top in big, elaborate script, then I guess what was supposed to be a description of what I'd done filled in underneath.

I bent over and read it carefully. It was full of big words I didn't understand, but the basics seemed to be more or less right. Heck, the way it was described, in those flowery poet words, it made my beating a poor defenseless old man sound nearly like a polite disagreement.

Nearly.

I pointed to one phrase: "What does 'with malice aforethought' mean? Is that saying I planned to beat him up?"

I saw the counselor's eyes flicker a little bit.

"You can read?" he asked.

"Yeah. I can write and do some figuring, too, if I have a counting board."

At that, his eyebrows rose up a little.

"If you sign this document," he finally said, "the Crown Prosecutor has graciously agreed to three years' imprisonment — subject to good behavior."

"Where would they send me?" I asked. "Would I go to a prison ship?"

In the two days I'd been in my cell, between bouts of crying, I'd already done some thinking. I knew I'd probably get prison, and I knew that Selva had a fleet of prison ships. I wasn't sure exactly what "prison ships" were, other than that they got sent to do ugly jobs that even the lowest-paid sailors wouldn't take, like harvesting birdshit off the Crooked Bow Islands. (Footman Sesh tells me that's actually an important job, and that birdshit can be used for all sorts of important things. All I know, though, is that collecting it is an awful enough job that prisoners are the only ones who'll do it.)

I reckoned if I got sent to a prison ship for a few years, I could learn myself the basics of sailing, and get a job on a trading ship once I was let go. Then I could either spend the rest of my life working the seas, or just get a few years of honest work under my belt and come back to find a decent job here in Solta. By the Warts on His Toes, maybe that Post Master job was still something I could aim for.

The counselor crinkled his brow.

"Typically a first-time offender would serve a sentence at the penal compound on Mule Island," he said. Mule Island was just off the coast from Solta. On clear days you could just see the edge of it on the horizon when standing on the roof of the rooming house.

I reckon he could see the disappointment on my face.

"However…" he said, letting that hang there in the air like he was some stage actor. "It's not unheard of for a first-time offender to join the prison fleet. It's an unusual request, but I can put it before the judge."

He nodded at me, and added "…IF you sign the confession."

"Fine," I said. "Give me a pen already and I'll sign."

The counselor said he'd see me in court at 10 o'clock the next morning, and collected all of his things in his big folio and left, and it was just me and my mom. I talked with her and told her what I was thinking with learning the sea trade on a prison ship. That made her a little better, I guess, but she was still bawling when a guard came in a few minutes later and told her she had to leave.

At this point, I was actually feeling a little bit relieved. I knew from my talk with Mr. Bogg that I wouldn't be going back to my old cell, with my twisted gaggle of cellmates. Instead, they marched me down a hallway and up a set of stairs, and down another hallway. They put me in a long cell with a dozen or so other prisoners to spend the night. Though many of those men looked quite frightening, I swallowed my fear and tried to act casual. I knew — or at least Mr. Bogg had claimed — that these men would be on their best behavior. This was the holding tank for the next day's court session, and there were three guards who patrolled the hallway outside the cell around the clock, constantly on the alert for trouble. I found a spot against the wall to sit down and consider my looming fate.

The next morning after another salt-bread breakfast, we were all supplied with wash-basins, soap, and clean clothes. Some of the prisoners ignored the offered niceties, but I eagerly scrubbed myself down and tried to make myself as present- able as possible. Then I stood there, waiting until my name was called. I was the fourth person called up.

My counselor was there, along with a guard. They led me down another hallway and into a courtroom.

I'd never actually been in a courtroom before — just seen them in pictures. This one wasn't as nice as I'd always imagined they would be. It was small, not much bigger than the dining hall at Aunt Rossie's rooming house. There were sev- eral rows of chairs taking up about half the room, and I could see my mom sitting in one, wiping her eyes. Me and my counselor sat down next to her to wait for my turn.

At the other end of the room was a big desk sitting high up, with a squat little fellow sitting behind it who had a face like a toad. It looked for all the world like he might shoot his fat tongue out of his mouth and snatch a fly out of the air. I could tell by his scarlet robes and hat that he was the judge.

Behind the judge was a huge portrait of the King. He looked remarkably like he had that day I'd met him in the Palace, except this portrait wore a very differ- ent expression. Instead of the kind face I remembered, he now looked very stern and — I looked long and hard at the picture, so I'm sure of this — just a bit sad.

In front of the judge's big desk there was a lectern, and there was a dandy-look- ing fellow with a ruffled shirt standing at it, yelling about something. Off to the side of the judge's desk there was a box, and there were two folks standing in the box. One of them was a guy I recognized from the holding cell, as he had scars all over his face and his clothes didn't fit quite right. The fellow standing next to him — his public counselor — had obviously gotten his own getup from a tailor in the Palace District.

The fellow in the ruffled shirt, I realized, was the Crown Prosecutor. He was going through a long list of awful things and pointing across the room at the ugly fellow in the box, saying he'd done all of them. The judge who looked like a toad didn't look at the supposed criminal. He just sat there looking sleepy-eyed, watching the Crown Prosecutor. When the Crown Prosecutor finally wound up, the judge swiveled his head and sleepy eyes over at the box. He didn't look at the public counselor — he just looked straight at the man with all the scars, who glared back at him like he wanted to kick him.

"And the accused, Mr. Hellick, has signed a confession attesting to the truth of all these charges?"

The scarred fellow rolled his eyes, and I knew enough about criminals down in the Warrens to know a fellow like him probably wasn't used to being called by his proper name.

His public counselor spoke up: "He has, your honor."

That toad-like face turned to the Crown Prosecutor.

"What sentence does the Crown put forward as a recommendation for Mr. Hellick?" the judge croaked.

"Twenty years, your honor, to be served at Mule Island."

The judge stared at the prosecutor for a second, then back at Mr. Hellick.

"Twenty years, then," he said.

The criminal's public counselor began to gather his things together, and one of the big guards stepped up to put his hand on Mr. Hellick's neck as if to lead him away, when another croak came from the judge's mouth.

"Not Mule Island, though."

The public counselor stopped and looked back at the judge.

"Your honor?" he said, looking a little surprised, like a statue had suddenly spoken to him.

"Not Mule Island. Among his other crimes, Mr. Hellick confessed to a rape, did he not?"

The public counselor began to fumble with his papers, but the Crown Prosecutor quickly spoke up.

"One count of rape — of a widow of not less than 70 summers, your honor."

The judge eyed Mr. Hellick. "Seventy summers..."

"Seventy-nine summers, to be exact," the Crown Prosecutor said.

The judge's eyes flicked over to the prosecutor, then back to Mr. Hellick.

"And a widow..." he added.

There was a longer-than-normal silence before the judge spoke again.

"The court believes Mule Island to be insufficiently capable of focusing the mind of Mr. Hellick regarding the severity of his offense."

The judge gave Mr. Hellick a long, silent look, then croaked out: "The court believes it would be more appropriate for Mr. Hellick to serve his sentence at Gilford Rock."

I'd never heard of Gilford Rock, but I reckon it must be a rough place, because I heard my own public counselor gulp at those words.

There was another moment of silence, and then without turning his head to look back at the Crown Prosecutor, the judge croaked out: "Assuming that is acceptable to the Crown?"

"Um..." the prosecutor coughed and pretended as if he was looking over some papers, then looked up. "Um, yes your honor. Quite acceptable."

Mr. Hellick's public counselor didn't show much reaction, but Mr. Hellick's eyes got wide, and I reckon he turned white as a sack of my Aunt Rossie's flour.

"Very well then," the judge said, turning away. "Twenty years, to be served at Gilford Rock, sentence to begin immediately."

He rang a bell on his desk. "Next case," he croaked.

They led away Mr. Hellick, who — even though he probably could have torn the heads off three of the guards before someone could stop him — looked like someone had just socked him in the stomach with a ballast stone.

It was my turn. I shuffled into the little box with my counselor, then looked over at my mom, who was trying to keep a good face on while the prosecutor in his silly ruffled shirt read out the charges against me.

The judge turned and looked at me with his sleepy eyes.

"And the accused, Mr. Lashan Pearl, has signed a confession attesting to the truth of all these charges?"

My counselor straightened up.

"He has, your honor."

And they went through the whole mess with asking what the Crown recommended for my sentence, and them giving their recommendation. And that's when my counselor spoke up.

"Before the court pronounces its sentence, Mr. Pearl has a request," he said.

The brows above the judge's sleepy eyelids went up, which I guess was the signal for the counselor to continue.

"Mr. Pearl has no objection to the Crown's proposed sentence, but requests that his term of punishment be served aboard the prison fleet."

The judge's eyebrows rose even higher at that, and his sleepy lids looked like they might have even opened a little wider.

"Would Mr. Pearl care to provide the court with an explanation for his request?" the judge asked.

The counselor leaned over and whispered in my ear that it was my choice, but that he thought I should go ahead and take it, so I nodded and looked straight in the judge's eyes.

"Sir...your honor? My mom's over there, and looking at her right now, all I can think of is how much of a disappointment I've been to her. Your honor, my mom...well, she's not like any mom I know. She wanted me to be better, expected me to be better, pushed me to be better. She hauled me off to chapel every Seven-day and sent me off to the Temple School, and all I did was...sir, all I did was let her down. And now I'm standing here and I've confessed to something that, well, sir..."

Again, I remembered the face of the man I'd seen in Professor Omi's illusion. I looked up at that portrait of the King, and suddenly felt very, very ashamed.

"Sir...I want...I want...sir, I feel so awful about what I've done. It's not something that..."

I felt my eyes getting moist, damn it. Not now. I paused for a second to get those tears properly plugged up again.

"Your honor," I began again, "When my mom heard what I'd done, the way she looked...your honor, that's a look nobody wants to see in their mom's eyes. I don't ever want to see that look in my mom's eyes again. I know when I walk out of here I probably won't see my mom again for a long time, but the next time I see her, I want her to be proud of me. I want her to know she did right by me, that everything she's had to go through was worth it. Your honor, all I want is to find a way out of the Warrens. If you just throw me in a cell for a few years and then send me back there, I'm afraid all I'll do is keep on making my mother cry.

"I just thought, your honor, that if I could serve on a prison ship — maybe I could learn an honest trade and get out of the Warrens. Your honor, if I never see my mother again, if I die at sea doing honest work, I'd rather that than coming back to the Warrens to keep bringing her shame and disgrace."

I could hear my mom quietly sobbing through everything, but with that last bit the sobs got sharply louder.

Through it all, the judge just looked at me with no feeling, like he was looking at a lump of coal. When I finished, he looked back at the crowd — I guess at my mother. Then he looked back at me.

"You said your mother had you attend the Temple School?"

"Yes, your honor."

He looked down at a paper on his desk.

"And I gather from your confession that you can read and write? This is your signature, is it not?" He held up the paper for me to see, and there was my name at the bottom, just as I'd written it.

"Yes sir. And I can do some figuring with numbers, but I need a counting board."

The judge looked over at the Crown Prosecutor, and I could tell from the way the prosecutor looked back that he knew what was coming next.

"Public counselor," the judge finally said, turning to look at my counselor, but not me, "would Mr. Pearl be willing to approach the bench?"

The counselor leaned over and whispered again that it was my choice. I looked at him and nodded.

"He's willing, your honor."

A guard opened the door to the little box and directed me up to the front of the judge's desk, where he looked down at me, with eyes looking sleepier than they'd been before.

"So you're from the Warrens. Lived there all your life, have you?"

"Yes, sir. With my mom, in my Aunt Rossie's rooming house. She's not really my aunt, but..."

He smiled and held up a palm, signaling to me to stop.

"I don't have many Warrens boys your age come through my courtroom who can read and write," he said. "How long were you at the Temple School?"

"I reckon I quit going around the time I'd reached 16 summers," I said, though that was a lie, and I reckon the judge probably knew it, too.

He looked at me like he was thinking.

"Did you have Footman Tan as an instructor while you were there?"

"Yes, sir."

"And did you enjoy having him as your instructor?"

It took me a second to figure out how to answer that, because I knew it wouldn't sound good to the judge if I told him what I really thought. But at the same time, I knew if Vast the Brutal were in my shoes, he would have told the judge Auld Father's hard truth.

But I wasn't sure I was quite ready to do that. So I tried to say the truth, but I prettied up as best I could.

"Well I'm not sure if I enjoyed it," I said. "But I respected him, you know? He didn't treat me any worse than anybody else, and I reckon I always had good feelings about him for that."

The judge nodded.

"And you are sincere in this desire you express to — better yourself?"

I nodded vigorously — automatically. Because that WAS Auld Father's honest truth, at least.

He nodded again, and then tapped his fingers lightly on the desk.

He called the Crown Prosecutor over to the side of his great desk, and they had a quick, whispered conversation. I couldn't make out much, but I heard "Garlund."

And I heard the Crown Prosecutor say that name again: "The Arcanter." Even in a whisper, it seemed to ring out clear as a bell.

Finally, the judge dismissed the prosecutor and turned back to me.

"You know who the Raiders are, boy?"

I nodded sharply. "Yes sir. They're like soldiers, but tougher!"

The judge smiled at that.

"I suppose that's one way of putting it. They are very tough, but a young man who came up in the Warrens might very well be the kind of tough they're looking for. And they — well, they have something of a reputation of taking boys like you and giving you...well, MAKING you into something their mothers could be proud of."

"That's all I want, sir."

He frowned. "Well this isn't about you, young man. You ARE here to be punished."

I reckon I must have looked sad when he said that, because his frown disappeared, and he went back to looking just like a frog.

"Nevertheless, you are a *young* man. And punishment for someone your age — well, if it can be turned to a beneficial purpose, we owe you that. We, this Kingdom of Selva, have failed you as much as you have failed us."

That "us" felt like a thump on the head. "Us" — that was the word the King had used, when he'd pressed that gold piece into my hand. Don't let US down, he'd said.

The judge continued: "But perhaps we can yet do right by you, and you can do right by us. You do not yet seem completely lost."

He turned to the prosecutor.

"Does the Crown object if the court sentences Mr. Pearl to a term of service with the Raiders?"

Before the prosecutor could answer, the judge turned back to me. "With a suspended sentence of three years — to be served at Mule Island, of course — should Mr. Pearl fail to complete the terms of his enlistment."

His face a mask of impenetrable stone, the prosecutor nodded, and said: "The Crown would not object."

"Very well. Mr. Pearl, does that sound acceptable to you?"

I looked back at the counselor, but he gave no hint of what he might be thinking.

"Or we could go with the terms of the original agreement," the judge said, "and you could serve your term as part of the prison fleet..."

"No, I'd like to serve as a Raider, sir."

"Very well. Mr. Pearl is to be remanded to the custody of the Raiders, who, if finding him a suitable candidate, shall press him into service immediately."

He rang a bell, and the guard came up and took me back to the holding cell.

22

Not more than an hour later, they pulled me out once again, took me down another flight of stairs and into a room with a big desk that was nearly entirely taken up with a huge ledger. A man was sitting at the desk with a fountain pen, comically large compared to his small, almost childlike hand. He barely glanced at me as I was marched into the room.

Standing on the other side of the desk was a man who looked like he'd stepped right out of a painting. He was very tall, fully as tall as Rupens, but without the dumb face or beefiness. This man's chiseled head was perched on massive shoulders that were made even bigger by a pair of gold-colored epaulets.

He was dressed all in blue, except for shiny black boots. His tightly-tailored tunic, adorned in the front with a row of highly-polished buttons, plunged inward from his wide shoulders to a trim waist and flat stomach.

From his waist emerged a long pair of legs. Though wrapped in hard muscle, his legs weren't the powerful, thick limbs you would have seen on a guy like Vast the Brutal; instead, they were lithe and springy, like a racehorse.

His clean-shaven face was topped with a cylindrical hat with folded-up ear flaps on either side. It was cocked to one side at an angle that was confident, but not sinister or arrogant. Short but well-groomed red hair peeked out from beneath his headgear.

I knew, of course, that he was a Raider, but this was my first time seeing one of them up close. He looked impossibly perfect. I could not believe there was any way I could ever look so immaculate.

The man extended a hand, which poked out of a perfectly creased wrist collar with three bright buttons.

"My name is Sergeant Casco. You are Mr. Lashan Pearl, I believe?"

I shook his hand and confirmed it.

"I am here to take charge of you until you leave for training. I am told you hail from the Warrens."

"Yes, sir."

He brightened at the "sir."

"We don't get many young men from the Warrens, but the ones I know of have been impressive. My senior DC was from the Warrens, and I don't think Auld Father ever built a man more impressive than Sergeant Gul."

That was hard to believe, since I couldn't imagine someone more impressive than this red-headed god standing in front of me.

Sgt. Casco nodded to the man at the desk, who made some florid inscription in his ledger, calling out "inmate zero three zero five five two, Pearl, L. Remanded to the custody of Sgt. C. Casco, Raiders."

The guard who'd led me to the room undid the chains around my legs, and I followed Sgt. Casco out a door and into a waiting wagon.

On the ride back to the Raiders' HQ, Sgt. Casco told me a little about himself. He'd been a printer's son in Toka, which was how he learned to read and write. He was the youngest of four children, two brothers and a sister, so he had no hope of taking over the family business. His father, a deeply religious man, had wanted him to become a Footman, but that had held little appeal for him. Failing that, the options he'd had were becoming a scribe or clerk, following his father into the printing trade while either starting his own business or working for his brother, or learning some other trade. None of those held much interest for him.

"I'd always been athletic," he explained. "I won the footrace at the Summer Festival two years in a row, and one of my father's clients had told me about the Raiders. It sounded far better than anything else I could have done, so I signed up the day I reached 17 summers. It was the best decision of my life."

I asked him if there was any chance I could join the hawk cavalry. "I've heard the Raiders have them," I said.

He chuckled. "I have no control over something like that, I'm afraid. You've still got a ways to go before that decision gets made; all I can tell you is to do the best you can in the coming months, and if that's something you're still interested in, you'll be considered for it."

Sgt. Casco hadn't explained what would happen when we got to the Raiders' HQ, but I took it I would be required to stay there. When we arrived and went inside, I was surprised to find that they had a cell there, built right within Sgt. Casco's private second-story office. There were bunks for four men inside, but I was the only occupant.

"I apologize for this, but until you are sworn in, you are technically still a criminal serving a prison sentence, so we have no choice but to treat you as one."

I looked over the cell — in sharp contrast to my lodgings back at the City Gaol, they were tidy and clean. The privy built into the wall even had a curtain that could be drawn around it for privacy.

I was still a bit dumbfounded at the arrangement, but he must have grasped my confusion.

"There's actually another cell in the office of my colleague, Sgt. Holk. Right now, you're our only...inmate. We don't get many during the summer. Peak time for our...our guests...is during the winter."

"How long will I be in here?"

"You are actually in luck there. The next group ships out in four days; you'll be going with them."

I walked into the cell. All four of the bunks were neatly made up, and on each one were two books: A copy of The Walk, and one labeled "Raider Hand Book."

"Just a hint: You'll want to read up on both of those," Sgt. Casco said, as he closed the door and locked it.

THE NEXT MORNING BEGAN with Sgt. Casco pulling me out of my cell and having me run through some physical exercises. None of them were hard; afterward, he gave me a written test; that, too, was fairly simple. I asked, and Sgt. Casco confirmed, that they were just making sure I possessed the basic ability to do what was required. The rest of the morning passed with Sgt. Casco doing work at his desk; after lunch, he spent the rest of the day downstairs — I could tell from the sound that he was talking to people, but I couldn't make out anything. He stopped in to check on me and deliver supper right before he left for the day. There was another fellow in Raider dress who patrolled the building at night, but I never spoke to him or even learned his name.

That was how it was for the rest of the time I was there: Sgt. Casco would come in and deliver breakfast, then work at his desk until lunch; after lunch, he'd disappear downstairs, where I'd hear him talking to people. He was never anything but perfectly friendly, which made me wonder just how tough this Raider outfit really was.

I flipped through the Raider Hand Book, but found it pretty dull. Had I the ability to go back in time and talk to my old self, I probably would have told me to buckle down and learn as much of it as possible, but as they say, the glance over the shoulder is always the sharpest.

Instead, I read The Walk. It was still as dull as I remembered from Temple School, but I amused myself reading over the few parts I liked — mostly Footman Rom's time in the Stalk Valley. I also read over Footman Rom's debate with Ellu — before Ellu converted and became Footman Ellu. I seemed to recall it had something to do with duty, which I figured I ought to read up on.

The day before I was to ship out, my mom came to visit me.

Sgt. Casco let me out of my cell, and let us have a room all to ourselves. I could tell it was some room that must have been used for important stuff, because once again I was face to face with a portrait of the King, staring back at me with cold authority. My mom was on the verge of tears; her eyes looked moist all through our meeting. But she also seemed happy.

"That nice man says we'll be able to write to each other," she said. "You have to promise me that you will write to me."

"I will, mom," I said.

"I have given prayers for you every morning and evening. I went to the Temple yesterday when I got off work and lit a torch for you, to light your way along the Path. I promise I will return every week to light it once again."

"Mom. Mom, you don't have to do that."

"I do, Lash. I know you are a young man yet, and the Path probably seems like foolishness to you — but I know there are hard days ahead, just like the hard days I faced when I was raising you. It was by following Auld Father's Path that I was able to find the strength to go on, and I want you to have that same strength now. If you feel yourself growing weak, if you feel like you can no longer go on, do not be afraid to call on Auld Father. He will make straight the Path. He has done it for me, and he will do it for you."

"I'll try, mom. But if I...if I can't do it..."

She put her hand over my mouth.

"You WILL do it. I know you will. Do you know why?"

"Why?"

"First, because I will be tugging at Auld Father's cloak the whole time, begging him to keep you on the Path. Second, because I know you will be doing the same, though it might take some time. And third, because I look at you..."

She placed her hands on my arms and looked me up and down.

"I look at you, and I see your father, and my father. I even see some of my grandfathers — you walk the way my father's father walked.

"I know the blood that flows through your veins. And your own father — I only knew him for a short time, but he was a good man. He gave me something to give to you — he said to give it to you when you were ready. I asked him how I would know you were ready, and he said you would be ready when you became a man.

"I have long feared that day would never come. It never does for most boys in the Warrens, no matter how old they grow. But I believe now that it will come for you. I can already see it. You stand straighter than you were last time I saw you. Your voice, the way you talk to me — I can see that you are different. You are beginning to change."

She squeezed me. I hugged her back, awkwardly. She looked up at me, her eyes still moist, but still with no tears.

"Come back to me as a man, Lash."

SGT. CASCO WOKE ME up early on the morning I was set to leave. He hustled me downstairs and into a big room with about 20 other fellows. They all looked as confused and bleary as I felt.

Sgt. Casco had us hold our hands over our hearts and recite a short oath: "I swear upon my blood to sharpen myself and to defend the honor of my King and my country, guided by the wisdom of Auld Father. Under my watch, Auld Father's children will be ever protected."

He congratulated us, and hustled us out to a waiting ox-trolley. It was still dark outside; the light of dawn was just starting to reach out over the eastern horizon, but the sun was still tucked away.

A few of the other guys smoked cigarettes. Not a single one looked like they might hail from the Warrens, though they didn't look highborn — a lot of them had the plain look of tradesmen's sons, like I'd known back at Temple School.

The ox-trolley hauled us slowly through the soundless streets of the city, up over the ridge and down through the outskirts that spread towards the plains. I'd only been to this part of the city a few times — it was mostly made up of the stockyards and storehouses where the rest of Selva brought its goods to trade with the imperial capital. As the sun finally started to crawl its way over the horizon, we passed under St. Rom's Arch and beyond the embrace of Solta's big stone walls.

It was the first time in my life I'd ever been out of the city.

23

I was a little nervous as I watched the city walls recede into the distance. As we made our way further inland into the surrounding hill country I noticed the air was beginning to lose its salty tinge. The sun climbed higher, and I saw the land around us dominated by fields of crops and pastures for livestock; here and there in the distance you could see lone buildings poking up; I guessed those were barns or farmhouses. The spooky thing was how it was so QUIET. I know how this sounds, but the quiet was almost as loud as the loudest thing I'd ever heard back home.

We passed through a few small towns — "town" is being generous, actually. They were really just little villages. We kept going all day, only stopping a couple of times to let people piss and shit and have a bite to eat. The ox-trolley continued on as the sun drooped below the Striped Mountains to the west and it got dark. Right after the sunset, we came to a village where our ox team was replaced with a waiting group, and our drovers switched places with a couple of other men. The switch made, the trolley headed out along the main road once again. It was clear that we wouldn't be stopping to sleep; they expected us to get what shut-eye we could while the ox-trolley rambled on through the night.

Some of the fellows started to cry then, and I can't say I really blame them. If they were like me, it was the first time they'd been in the dark — the REAL dark, with no lights other than the moons and the stars and the swaying lanterns of our ox-trolleys. And of course being from the city, you hear the stories about the bandits out at night on the country highways, though I tried to reassure myself that no bandit would be stupid enough to attack an ox-trolley full of Raider recruits… even if we were just a bunch of scared boys.

I didn't cry, but I didn't feel too good, either. I tried to sleep, but that was tough, too. The seats in the ox-trolley had no padding, they were just solid wood, and it didn't feel like the springs on the axles were doing much good. On top of that, there were funny noises coming from everywhere, the kind us city folks aren't used to. A lot of them sounded like insects, though some might have been birds. The ones that bothered me were the ones I kept on hearing that sounded like animals moving around in the brush beside the road. It was too dark to see them, but you could hear them moving — or even breathing.

Cows, they had to be, I thought. Or sheep, or horses. Some kind of livestock. Right? But...what if it was something else? Wolves...or bears...or worse. How would I have known? They say hunters can identify an animal just from the sound of its breathing, but I'd never hunted anything but wharf rats.

After a few more days of this, we came out of the foothills and onto gentler, rolling terrain. Now the fields of crops and pastures began to spread out and cover much of the land in every direction. After about a day of this we finally came to a city perched along the banks of a large river. Somebody said it was Toka; the guards confirmed us as we passed through the city gate. I noticed the walls were much less formidable than the ones that ringed the capital.

They brought us to a place where a lot of ox-trolleys were gathered, and had us get off and head into a big warehouse-like building with a bunch of other young guys, including a bunch who were dwarves. I'd never seen so many dwarves in one place before.

There were more guys there dressed like Sgt. Casco. They gave us some food and pointed out a little stand set up where we could buy sweets, cigarettes or newspapers. A bunch of guys headed over there, but I just sat on a bench and waited. A lot of the other guys were chatting and laughing, mostly about either girls or skram matches. There was one group over on one side playing dice, but I just kept to myself among a group of other guys who were all blank-eyed and silent. I guess we all dealt with our looming fate in our own way.

While I was sitting there meditating on how I'd ended up here, a guy sitting next to me suddenly got up and tossed away the newspaper he was reading; he walked quickly over to the guys playing dice, announcing loudly that they were all amateurs and he was about to show them how it was done. I listened for a minute, wondering if he might try to slip in a trick pair to try to cheat the other guys out of their money, but it quickly became clear he was just as full of hot air as any of the others.

I looked at the paper he'd crumpled up and tossed aside. The thought suddenly struck me that it might have skram scores from the capital. They'd have to be a few days old, of course, but I had been out of the loop for several days anyway, so they'd be news to me. I picked up the crumpled ball and unfolded it, but before I could flip to the sports section, the main story on the front page caught my eye.

"KING ARRIVES IN GARLUND TO REVIEW TROOPS, HOLD TALKS WITH SUZER," the headline read. I suddenly felt my limbs grow numb.

The story made it sound like the trip was just some kind of routine diplomatic tour, like the kind the King occasionally made to the small border kingdoms to the south. But I knew better — I knew from the histories we'd read in the Temple School that a King never traveled any place where there was actual fighting unless he planned to take part in it himself somehow. And that meant...well, I wasn't really sure WHAT it meant, except that kings who went off to battle tended to show up a lot in history books, and the battles they were in always got big, thick chapters.

Sitting there, I realized we'd entered into one of those parts of history again, even if nobody seemed to want to say it out loud. In fact, everybody seemed to be stumbling all over themselves to say that everything was just fine, and nothing had changed, and that us commoners shouldn't worry our heads about it. And maybe some commoners — maybe most of them — had no idea anything was amiss.

But I knew better. And I also knew I had just signed up for three years, minimum, with the band of fighters that some people called "the King's right fist."

Suddenly, I really, really wanted a tall tankard of ale. Which, as new recruits, we were forbidden to have. I spent much of the day trying to figure out what this business with the King might mean for me, but it was hard to think straight. The numb feeling seemed to extend to my brain. It was hard to concentrate on anything except the mysterious fate looming directly before us.

Late in the afternoon, a few men in Raiders gear herded us out to a train of ox-trolleys. None of them looked like the one we'd come in on; I took it that these were all fresh teams. We headed out in a convoy, six ox-trolleys, one after the other.

I was in the one at the front. The guy beside me was a dwarf with an arrow hanging from a string around his neck, just like the one my mother wore. He closed his eyes and held his palms up and mumbled a prayer to Auld Father.

As the sun went down, we could see we were headed towards the Striped Mountains. As the sun began to disappear, I noticed the terrain growing steeper and the farmland giving way to forest. I drifted off to sleep — sleep came easy now, either because I had gotten used to the wooden bench, or because I reached that point of tiredness where even a stiff plank of wood feels like a feather bed.

The guy sitting next to me shook me awake the next morning. Rubbing my eyes, I looked around — we were now entering steeper woodland terrain, leaving the huge open fields and pastures behind. I looked and saw the Striped Mountains growing closer, looming up above the western horizon. As we drew closer, they seemed to grow impossibly tall — it seemed incredible to me that anything could rise up that high in the sky.

Around nightfall, we entered an especially thick forest. The next day I awoke to see that we were very deep in the woods — looking around, I could see nothing but trees on either side. Only the looming mountains above us broke the endless armies of trees.

About noon, we came to a town, where the oxen and drovers were switched out again, and they fed us once more. They loaded us back up and took us deeper into the forest, and even closer to the looming mountains. The trees had slowly started to get much bigger — they were now taller than the masts of ships, or even the tops of temples, with trunks bigger around than the stone pillars in front of the Palace back in Solta. That, and the high peaks to the west, blocked out the sun and caused darkness to fall much sooner than usual. Even though it was pitch dark, we could still see a glow in the sky for a few more hours, but eventually we were once again shrouded in total darkness.

This was even worse than the darkness from before, because now we were completely enclosed in this strange, forbidding wood. None of the moons were out that night, and the stars were mostly blocked out by the branches above us; the only lights were the lanterns on each trolley, and they looked pretty lonely, just swaying back and forth in a whole world of darkness with nothing but a little patch of road that you could see in the light. Even though I was surrounded by others, I still felt incredibly lonely. I looked around at the other guys — they were all just strangers. I'd exchanged a few words with some of them, but all of them seemed a thousand miles away. If a dragon attacked our convoy right that second, I felt like I would die alone, with no help from anybody. All of us would. We would all just burn to death, looking up at the sky. Even in the midst of a crowd of other souls, I would be totally alone.

It was a loneliness that would not last much longer.

After hours of just making our way through what seemed like nothing but an ocean of tar, we finally came to this one little stone building with a large lantern on a post out front, sitting next to a big gate that spanned the roadway. The train of ox-trolleys came to a stop there, and this short fellow in a Raider uniform came out of the building.

He said something to the lead drover, who said something back. I tried to listen, but couldn't make out anything.

I guess the man at the gate was satisfied with whatever the drover told him, because he walked quickly over and opened the gate, and we passed on by. I tried to get a look at the guard's face, but he wouldn't look at us; he just stood there staring off back down the road, like he was expecting somebody to come roaring up behind us out of that bleak, endless darkness.

I watched the little guardhouse get smaller as we moved further along the road. That image — that guardhouse getting smaller in the distance — is the last thing I remember of my old life.

PART TWO

THE BLUE WOOD

24

I looked and up ahead I could see lights. As we got closer, I saw there was a group of stone buildings laid out next to a big stone wall crowned with battlements. In the darkness, the stone wall — which was spotless, with no graffiti or anything — seemed to go on forever; wherever it might end, or turn a corner, was lost far out in the darkness on either side.

We pulled up next to a long stone building, which was next to a long pit filled with mud and rotting garbage and — judging by the smell — probably worse. Now those of you who know all about the Raiders know what comes next, but I didn't, so I'll just tell you about it the way it happened to me.

All six of the ox-trolleys lined up right alongside this pit. It was very long but kind of narrow, and somewhat shallow — I reckon it came up to about my eye level, or a little more. It looked like a rubbish tip, except I'd never seen one so long and so, well — neat. The grass along the sides was trimmed and immaculate, as if somebody was treating this area like part of the Royal Gardens. The pit itself was like an ugly scar in the middle of perfection.

Several dozen men came out of the long building and gathered around, watching us. Most of them were carrying buckets, which they set down beside them. I pegged the ones with buckets as recruits — they were young men about our age. But other than age, they were a world apart from those of us in the trolleys. These fellows were lean and straight and corded with muscle, with short cropped hair. Even the dwarves among them seemed to be walking a bit taller. Every one of them, even the small ones, looked like he'd be a terror in a tavern brawl.

They looked sweaty and tired, but that didn't seem to dull their energy — they were laughing and talking loudly with each other. A few guys in the trolleys called out to them.

"How long have you guys been here?" one asked.

A recruit shouted back, "since you got your first period, sugar tits!" which brought a roar of laughter from their side.

A guy from our side shouted something about how they looked like pussies and he could take any of them in a fight. Instead of attacking us — which is what would have happened back in the Warrens if you'd thrown that insult — they just laughed, and a few of them made mocking gestures of recoiling in fear.

Along with the young guys were several men who were a few years older, and were obviously in charge. These men looked even more terrifying than the younger ones; one of them looked like he'd ripped the arms off an ogre and sewn them on his shoulders to replace the ones he'd been born with. These guys, which the younger men invariably addressed as "Sarge" or "Sgt. So-and-so," all wore hats which were different from the hats I'd seen on other Raiders so far. The "Sarges" had hats with wide brims and tall peaks. Each hat was adorned with a long, frilly yellow feather jutting out cockily from the side.

Like the man back at the gate, these guys paid no attention to us. They just stood there silently, apparently waiting for something. I heard a guy in the ox-trolley behind us trying to talk to one of them, but they didn't even acknowledge his existence.

Then, for no reason I could see, the "Sarges" took up places alongside our ox-trolleys. I reckon some of the guys I was with knew what was coming, because they began to straighten up and look nervous.

"UHreeeeehDEE!," one of the Sarges said, and they all grabbed iron rings that were hanging off the side of the trolleys. I'd seen the rings before, but had paid no attention to them. I figured they might have been used to tie down cargo or something.

"ON MY MARK!" said the apparent leader. "ONE, TWO, THREE...NOW!!!!"

At that, they all pulled on the rings, which proved to be attached to big metal pins that slipped out of the sides of the trolleys. I had the briefest moment to wonder about that when I suddenly felt myself tilting. It was gradual at first, then suddenly it felt like the entire trolley was tipping over. I saw the garbage pit swinging its way toward me. I got the idea to grab hold of something, but it was too late — I was already falling. For what it was worth, the putrid garbage guaranteed a soft landing, but my face slammed directly into a rotting melon.

As I pulled myself to my feet and wiped off my face, I looked up at the ox-trolleys, which were now pulling away. I could see now that the passenger compartments had been rigged to tilt sideways when the pins were pulled. Shit.

As the trolleys moved out of the way, the "old" recruits came forward and began pelting us with garbage they had stashed in their buckets. They seemed to find this hilarious, and hurled taunts at us. A few guys from our side tried to crawl out of the pit to go after them, but the "Sarges" stomped on their hands and screamed at them to get back.

A few of our tormentors came up to the side of the pit and tossed the entire contents of their buckets all at once. One recruit, a dwarf, aimed the contents of his bucket right at the dwarf I'd been sitting beside on the trolley and scored a direct hit. Even my Warrens-dulled nose immediately recognized the smell as a big mess of wet oxshit, some of which splattered onto me. A few recruits whipped out their cocks and began pissing into the pit. I don't know why they bothered; we could easily step out of the way, since not one of them had any distance. I guess it was more just the principle of the thing.

This went on for a bit before one of the fellows wearing a hat blew a whistle, and at that they all tossed their buckets into the pit with us and booed loudly.

Then there was another loud whistle, and I heard a voice bellow, "FORM UP! FORM UP!"

It was the craziest thing I ever saw. In no more than a few eye blinks, the unruly mob that had been tormenting us instantly sorted itself into neat little rows. It was like watching the smashed pieces of a plate jump up from the ground and reassemble themselves.

"SOUND OFF!" came the cry, and in perfect unison, the recruits boomed out a chant that made my teeth rattle: "I AM THE SHINING SWORD! I AM THE SHARPENED BLADE! I CLEANSE THE PATH WITH THE BLOOD OF THE WICKED! KILL! KILL! KILL!"

...followed by dead silence.

Us new guys just sort of stood there, looking dazed. I looked around for hints of what I should be doing, but *everybody* just looked dazed. Here and there, I heard quiet sobs.

A new guy appeared, a bit older than the "Sarges." He didn't have the funny hat the Sarges wore; he wore a regular Raider hat, like the one Sgt. Casco had back in Solta.

He looked us over with a smile, and then said, in a thick East Selvan accent, "Boy, it looks like someone really fucked up." He paused, as if waiting for a response, but nobody dared utter a word. Then he continued.

"See, we were expecting a new shipment of recruits this evening, but it seems the ox-trolley caravans must have got mixed up along the way, because it looks like we got a bunch of girls headed for the Royal Finishing School.

"Ladies, I'd like to extend my sincerest apologies for that mixup. This is Fort Harrel — or as we like to call it, the Blue Wood — where with the grace of Auld Father, we take the most worthless bums and layabouts in the Kingdom and turn them into the finest, meanest, bloodiest, toughest fighting men on either side of the Striped Mountains. Why, we can take garbage right out of this pit you're standing in and turn it into hard, polished steel. For those who are willing to do the hard work we demand — the ones who are willing to scratch and claw and pull themselves up out of the garbage — they will find themselves walking through the Turquoise Gate and standing on the Glorious Field."

I had no idea just then what the "Glorious Field" was, but it sounded a hell of a lot better than where I was now.

"Whether any of them make it that far, well — that's up to them. Those that do make it, like the men standing here before you — who will be standing on the Glorious Field less than 48 hours from now — have earned something priceless. I've had men tell me the day they climbed out of this pit was the day they were born.

"But obviously I couldn't expect anything like that from any of you ladies; this has obviously been a terrible mistake.

"You're in luck, though! It just so happens that we have a team of the finest chefs in all of Selva, and as I speak to you now, they are preparing a seven-course meal fit for the King himself! We have a selection of the finest wines and ales to accompany it, along with a bath, a warm bed for the night, and a new set of clothes. Tomorrow morning we'll have a luxury coach ready to take you back to Toka, and from there, we'll pay for your passage back to wherever you came from."

A gust of wind blew the scent of cowshit up into my nostrils. I wondered if I should take him up on his offer.

"If that's what you want, all you have to do is remain in this pit for exactly one hour. You can sit, you can stand, you can jerk off — we don't care. Just stay for one hour, and we'll pull you out and this whole awful nightmare will be over.

"But if there's the slightest chance — I know, I know, it's crazy — if there's the *slightest chance* that any of you girls think you might have what it takes to stand on the Glorious Field, then when the whistle blows, grab one of those buckets and climb out of the pit, and we'll see if we can do something with you."

He executed a crisp turn and marched away. As soon as he was gone, one of the guys in hats shouted a few commands, and the recruits standing there in neat rows pivoted in unison and began marching away, with one of the guys in hats calling out a cadence.

As soon as they'd disappeared into the darkness, someone standing behind us blew a loud whistle. I hesitated for a second — I thought about that warm bed — but then I picked up the nearest bucket and climbed up out of the pit.

25

Up until then, every Raider I'd met — save those damn recruits — had been either friendly, or at least not hostile. Now it all changed. The second we got out of the pit, we had big, red-faced guys in Sarge hats screaming at us.

I'm no stranger to fights, obviously, and I'd had more than a few grownups chew me out for stuff I'd done wrong, but in the name of Footman Rom, I'd never seen anybody as angry as this group of men. They acted like I'd just told them I heard their mom was running a special and charging half-price down at the sporting house and had no takers.

"HOLY FUCK RECRUIT. WHY THE HELL DIDN'T THE MIDWIFE STRANGLE YOU WITH THE UMBILICAL CORD?" said one giant red face when I was trying to figure out the correct way to stand. I tried to stand a little straighter, but he didn't stick around long enough to let me know if I was doing it right — the giant red face had whooshed away to torment some other poor recruit, leaving me with a blob of his spittle running down my chin. I didn't dare reach up to wipe it away.

They had us line up in a long queue, packed uncomfortably tight together. I kept my gaze fixed firmly on the back of the head of the fellow in front of me — apparently, one of the biggest sins was allowing your eyeballs to point in any direction other than straight ahead.

"IF I WANT YOU TO LOOK SOMEWHERE ELSE RECRUIT I'LL PICK YOUR ASS UP AND POINT YOU THERE," someone screamed.

"I don't think I've seen one of them stop to breathe," a voice behind me whispered. I felt a smile coming on, but was smart enough to murder it before it reached my face.

I don't have really good memories about the next several hours. At some point they herded us into one of the stone buildings. Under the brightest, most blinding lanterns I'd ever seen, they first had us strip naked, and then ran us through some kind of gauntlet where men with mops and buckets of water cleaned us off. They shaved our heads, and then herded us into another room where we got poked and prodded by various long-beard doctors. The doctors pulled two guys out of our group and took them away; I never saw either of them again.

Still naked, they made us clean our buckets. That was memorable, because the whole time we were cleaning them we had a guy screaming at us about how we now owned absolutely nothing; from this point forward, every piece of equipment, including our bucket, was the property of the Crown, and we should treat everything, including the bucket, as if we were going to present it to the King himself at the end of our training.

The Crown's ownership, he explained at the top of his lungs, extended to our bodies: "YOUR HEAD IS NOW CROWN PROPERTY. YOU WILL NOT USE IT FOR ANYTHING NOT APPROVED BY YOUR SERGEANT. YOUR HANDS ARE NOW CROWN PROPERTY. YOU WILL NOT USE THEM FOR ANYTHING NOT APPROVED BY YOUR SERGEANT. YOUR DICK IS NOW CROWN PROPERTY. YOU WILL NOT USE IT FOR ANYTHING NOT APPROVED BY YOUR SER-GEANT. IF YOU JACK OFF WITHOUT PERMISSION FROM YOUR SERGEANT, YOU ARE ABUSING THREE SEPARATE ARTICLES OF CROWN PROPERTY!"

One guy laughed at that; a guy in a Sarge hat leaped across the room and un-furled a string of curses, upbraiding the poor fellow for "abuse of the mouth" — which, he was reminded, now belonged to the Crown. The Sarge then forced him to run laps around the room shouting "I love the King! My mouth exists to pleasure him!" Two more guys laughed at that; they were forced to get up and join the first guy.

We were herded into a big room with a series of little service windows along one wall. Holding our newly-clean buckets out in front of us, we went from one window to the next; at each one, some surly faced fellow in white would toss something into our buckets. We were issued soap, razors, towels, brushes, a padlock and key, and sewing supplies.

The last two items that were piled into our buckets were two books: A copy of The Walk, and the Raider Hand Book. These were the only two items that weren't tossed haphazardly; the man passing them out placed each one gently and rever-ently on top of the jumble of other stuff.

At various points, they had ledgers which you had to sign — I don't know why. Finally, after what seemed like hours of standing around naked, we were all given two sets of uniforms, each consisting of undergarments, socks, a pair of sturdy sandals, a pair of light boots, a pair of long trousers, a pair of short trousers, a belt, a short-sleeved shirt made of light cotton which tucked into the trousers, and a long-sleeved overshirt made of heavier cloth, worn untucked, which buttoned up in the front. These were just to start us off, the supply clerks explained; we'd get our actual fighting gear later.

Along with the plain peasant-like garb, we also got a single, dressier ensemble — a fine-looking doublet, collar and hose with a fancy dress belt and fancy-looking shoes — which we were told was "for Sevenday services." None of it came close to fitting right.

In the next room, one man barked at us, we would be issued one of the most important pieces of equipment we would receive during our time in the Raiders. That got everybody excited, because naturally we all expected that these would be our swords. Imagine our disappointment when it turned out to be...wristwatches.

Now don't get me wrong, a wristwatch was incredibly cool to a boy from the Warrens — I'd never known any but nobles to have them. A few people in the Warrens owned big, beaten-up looking pocket watches. But here they were giving each of us a brand-new wristwatch, as good as any you'd see around the Palace District. Still, it was a bit of a letdown after the excitement of a few moments before.

They gave everybody a short lesson in how to operate a wristwatch — they had to be rewound every night — along with a stern warning that any damage due to carelessness would be deducted from our salaries.

"These have been purchased at great expense from the leading watchmaker in Kassor," the quartermaster sternly explained. "Believe me, you don't want to find out how much they cost."

After everybody set their watch in unison — "don't even think of setting them wrong and using that as an excuse; recruits have been trying that trick for over a hundred years now, and we haven't been fooled yet," the quartermaster said — they informed us that we were now on Blue Time, and we'd better start acting like it.

"If you need to check that the time is correct on your watch, ask your sergeant. He will ALWAYS have the correct time — at least as far as you are concerned."

Newly outfitted with clothing and timepieces, we filed into a large room with rows of benches, where we were treated to another lecture by another guy in a Sarge hat.

Unlike all the Sarge types we'd seen so far, this guy did not scream. He wasn't exactly friendly — he had a tired face and voice, and he seemed to look at us with a mixture of contempt and pity — but other than that, he was polite.

He spoke slowly. He began: "Listen carefully to what I'm about to tell you. It won't be repeated again."

He gave us a brief rundown on what to expect, and an introduction to Raider terminology. He explained, for those who hadn't put it together yet, that the guys in Sarge hats were indeed sergeants — specifically, they were Drill Chiefs, or DCs, for short. You could always tell a DC by his hat — they were the only ones who wore the "Sarge" hats, which we learned were called, naturally, DC hats.

"Under no circumstances," he told us, "are you EVER to refer to a DC hat as a 'fowling hat.'"

Ah. THAT'S where I'd seen those before — nobles were always wearing those hats, or hats like them, in bird hunting paintings.

DCs were to be addressed only as "Sergeant," followed by their last name. He told us his name: Sergeant Something I Don't Remember.

He also informed us — in the gravest and most serious tones — that beginning right at that moment, we could only refer to ourselves as "recruit," followed by our last name.

"The word 'I,' and all of its associated forms, is henceforth a stranger to your vocabulary," he said. "Raiders are part of a team, not individuals. The faster you absorb that principle, the easier this whole process will be."

BATHED, SHAVED, DRESSED AND loaded with our gear, we were feeling pretty frisky by this point. We thought we were starting to get the hang of this place — there was less slack in our movements; we were getting used to responding quickly to commands. Well, we thought it was quick, anyways. We were still moving as slow as tree sap for Raiders, but at least we had the principle down.

They then herded us through another building — there seemed to be an endless hive of buildings — slightly different from the others. When we stepped into this one, the light was different — it was soft and warm, lit by torches and candles. The sterile, soapy smell of the other buildings we'd been through was replaced by delicious aromas of all kinds.

They filed us past a table of young guys who seemed to be in the middle of enjoying a mouth-watering meal of roast pheasant with all the trimmings.

I recognized one of them as a guy I'd seen back on the ox-trolley. It clicked: These were the guys who'd stayed behind in the pit.

A DC was standing off to the side, giving us new recruits a sales pitch: "No need to put yourself through this, gentlemen. You could be sitting at this table, too. Last chance: Say the word now, and we'll pull you aside and let you join them. A warm bed, fine wine, and a luxury trip to Toka tomorrow morning. Just say the word."

The guy standing directly in front of me immediately stepped out of line and marched over to the DC.

"I'm out, sir!" he said. The DC nodded and directed him to a waiting servant.

26

I felt a hard smack from an open hand against the back of my head. The spoon flew out of my mouth, out of my hand, and rattled as it hit the table.

"Recruit, who told you to start eating?" a voice roared. I heard several other spoons slamming down onto the table all around me.

After what felt like hours of being shouted at while the perpetually outraged DCs ran us through drills and exercises, we had finally ended up in what I recognized as the chow hall. After lining up to receive a bowlful of slop — I was too tired at this point to really care how it looked or tasted — I thought I was finally, finally going to at least be able to enjoy the simple pleasure of eating. I'd heard about "the Raider way" of doing things about 500 times already, but certainly there couldn't be a Raider way of eating, could there?

It turned out there was, at least if you were a recruit. Nobody was permitted to so much as touch a utensil until the DC at our table did so. I still hadn't affixed a name to any of them yet; they were just screaming voices and faces that all blurred together, and I was too frightened to look at any of them long enough to size them up.

As the very blade of Auld Father, we could not rightly begin our meal without giving thanks to Him. Thus I was introduced to the official "Raider Prayer." With our eyes tightly shut, chins raised, and palms up, we listened as the DC belted out the words:

"Auld Father, we are the guardians of the Path!

"With the power that you lend our unworthy bodies, we vow to make the way straight and clear! We beseech you to cede but a thimbleful of your strength, that we may thwart the enemies of the righteous!

"May the bruises of their flesh be a psalm to your majesty!

"May the breaking of their bones be a song to your wisdom!

"May our steel be rinsed in the blood of barbarians, whose taste is clean and sweet on your tongue!

"May the scent of their burning corpses be to you as the delicate perfume from a field of summer lilies!

"May we compel from the mouths of the wicked screams of bitter agony, which to your ears are like unto a gentle lullaby!

"Auld Father! We beg through tears to be the instrument of your chastisement! We weep to hear that a single hair on the head of the righteous has come to harm! We plead to be the emissaries of your kind and merciful wrath!

"Our hands are open, Auld Father — they yearn to caress the hilt of your peace-giving blade!

"Amen!"

When we were finally permitted to eat, I saw from the corner of my eye that the DC was wiping tears away from his eyes.

"**WHAT THE HELL, RECRUIT?** WERE YOU JUST CHECKING OUT MY DICK?" the DC screamed at me.

It all started because I was apparently "slouching." After chow, we'd spent hours being introduced to the basics of drill. As with everything else, it seemed like nothing we did was right, no matter how closely we tried to follow the instructions. Every so often, the DC would single somebody out to correct something. And at one point, I got singled out for "slouching" — which I didn't think was unreasonable, considering how long I'd been awake by that point. I kept stealing glances at the sun, silently praying that Auld Father would yank it down a bit faster so that, at some point, they might finally let us sleep. While I was thinking this, the gruff DC muttered, "shoulders go on top of your back, recruit, not hanging there in front like your granny's tits. Neck stiff; eyes straight ahead."

"Like this, Sgt. So-and-so?" I said, using the name I saw written on the tag attached to his chest.

He took an exaggerated step back, as if I'd taken a swing at him.

"Sgt. So-and-so? SGT. SO-AND-SO?! What in Auld Father's name makes you think I'm Sgt. So-and-so?!?!"

Not quite sure what I'd done wrong — which, at this point, was everything, including breathing — I innocently flicked my gaze down at the name tag on the DC's chest.

"Damn it recruit, WHAT THE HELL DID I SAY ABOUT YOUR FUCKIN' EYES?!?!"

I instantly snapped my gaze back at the guy standing in front of me. The DC leaned in close, and I could feel his hot breath on my cheek.

That's when he began screaming about whether I'd been looking at his dick. He had paused, apparently expecting an answer.

"No sir?" I offered.

"No sir? You either were or you weren't recruit! Which is it?"

"No sir."

"I'm sorry, recruit, I COULDN'T HEAR YOU."

"NO SIR!"

He sucked in a deep breath, and then said, "well why the hell NOT, recruit?"

"Sir?"

"Why weren't you checking out my dick? Is there something *wrong* with it? Not as big and juicy as the ones you've usually got stuffed in your cum-catcher? Does one of my balls hang too low? Are the veins not thick and purple enough? Auld Father's Mercy, IS THERE SOMETHING TERRIBLY WRONG WITH MY DICK, RECRUIT? SHOULD I BE WORRIED?"

"NO SIR!"

"No sir? Are you saying you want to SUCK MY DICK, recruit?"

I wasn't sure at this point what the right answer was — I suspected anything I said would be wrong — so I just told the truth: "NO SIR!"

"Well WHY NOT?"

"Sir..."

"Why not, recruit? Why does my dick not live up to the lofty standards of your mouth?"

There was some muffled laughter, which suddenly vanished — I guessed because of an evil glare from the DC, even though I couldn't see him with my eyes locked straight ahead.

"I'm waiting, recruit! My entire self-image is hanging by a thread!"

I sucked my stomach in, tried to stand a little taller, and shouted: "SIR, I..."

"'I'?!?!?!?!" he wailed, his voice somehow getting even louder. "'I'? WHO THE FUCK IS 'I'? THE ONLY EYES AROUND HERE ARE THE ONES I'M GOING TO RIP OUT OF YOUR HEAD BEFORE I SKULLFUCK YOUR BRAIN RIGHT OUT OF YOUR FUCKING EARS!!!!!!"

He pulled me out of the group and told me to stand beside him, then ordered everyone to drop to the ground for push-ups. They got it good and hard, too. Except I — "I" — wasn't part of it. While they were sweating it out, the DC had me stand there and sing a song with him called "My Beautiful Boy Wears Raider Blue."

That was how, on Day One, Recruit Pearl got his official Raider nickname: "Lips."

FOR THE REST OF the day, I put up with evil looks and a few "accidental" kicks and jabs from my fellow recruits. Although it took every ounce of strength I had to muffle my natural instincts to strike back at every "accidental" blow, I just gritted my teeth and ignored the hostility. I didn't blame them — I knew I would have felt the same way. Instead, I directed all my hate at the damnable DC, while pledging to myself to earn my place back among the other recruits — which, I suppose, had been the DC's intent all along. This "I" was suddenly eaten up with a burning need to be part of the "we."

27

I've heard from a lot of guys that they don't remember dreaming for the first few weeks of their time in the Blue Wood. But I've probably got more imagining in my head than most; back at Temple School, Footman Tan used to beat me at least once a week for daydreaming in class.

So once I fell asleep, I found myself immediately in a dream. I remember that I was on an island — it was like the island I'd seen in Professor Omi's illusion that night at the Dead Scorpion.

Except now the sea was calm and the skies were clear. Everything was warmed by the light of a lazy sun. The only chill was the tingle from a breeze coming off the water. I plodded across the warm sand and dipped a hand in the ocean — it was cool, but not stinging cold, as it had been in Professor Omi's illusion. I splashed some on my face, then stretched out on the warm sand, and I noticed I was wearing nothing but a loincloth decorated with Molan designs.

I closed my eyes and soaked up the clean ocean air, letting the sun bake my skin. It felt like I was only there for a few minutes when a shadow fell across my body. Shading my eyes with my palm, I gazed up into the face of the powerfully-built warrior I'd seen before, the one with the face that seemed familiar.

"Get up," he said gently, with a knowing smile.

I propped myself up on my elbows.

"What did you say?"

"GET UP! GET UP! GET UP!"

The dream blinked out, and my head was suddenly ringing with the sound of a shouting voice and an enormous crashing sound.

"GET UP, LADIES! UP AND AT ATTENTION! GET UP! RIGHT NOW! You have FIVE seconds, starting NOW, two, three…"

The voice didn't sound anything like the DC from our first day, the one who'd been so worried about what I thought of his dick. That DC had merely sounded pissed off. THIS voice, a clear tenor that would have been soothing in some other context, sounded like it was on the verge of murdering us in our bunks with a battle ax. It wasn't until somewhere around "three" that my brain finally realized where I was.

AFTER RUNNING US INTO the ground the previous day, they had finally marched us to the place that would be our new home for the next six months. Though there was a village-sized collection of comfortable-looking stone buildings clustered around the chow hall, it turned out we wouldn't be resting our weary skulls there. Instead, they led us off into the woods. About two miles north of the chow hall, we came to a wide clearing where four single-story stone buildings were laid out on either side of a large rectangular open area paved with huge flagstones. There was another group of recruits out on the flagstones as we approached, hauling our buckets full of gear. Unlike us, these recruits had weapons and were decked out in full combat gear, practicing drilling maneuvers; even in their heavy gear, they looked about a hundred times sharper and more coordinated than we did.

On the third side of the rectangle was a tall pole; the Royal Standard fluttered from its top. The fourth side was dominated by a big round wooden structure with a roof shaped like a shallow cone. Off to the side of that building, I could see two long pits, one filled with sand and the second filled with wet muck. Beside them was a long wooden beam of some sort — it looked to be a fallen tree that had been carefully stripped of its branches. Next to that were a series of stone spheres lined up in a row, each a little larger than the next. The largest ones looked too heavy for a man to carry.

Rising out of the forest nearby, I spied a featureless stone tower. A bell tower? Some kind of guard tower? It took me a second to place it — it was a water tower. They had them back in Solta, where they supplied the public taps in places like the Warrens; in nicer parts of the city, they supplied the public baths and fountains and even, it was said, private homes in the Palace District. So we'd have running water, at least.

The four single-story stone buildings, I'd later learn, were each home to a separate platoon, each one in a different stage of training — and one of those buildings was about to become ours. But they didn't explain that to us at first, just like they never explained anything. They just herded us into one of the buildings, where we were greeted with a long room whose stone walls were painted bright white, containing two long rows of wooden bunks. Ahhh, my weary brain sighed — sleep! Finally!

No such luck.

The DC instructed us we had until the count of ten to each find our beds, put our buckets down and then stand at attention alongside them.

Since there was nothing else to indicate who belonged to which bed, and nobody was going to have enough spine to ask the DC, each of us just ran to the first empty bed we could find. Nobody could fail to notice that near the foot of each bed, facing the aisle that ran down the center of the room, there was a pair of footprints painted on the well-worn stone floor. Even a group as lunkheaded as ours could manage to figure out that this was supposed to tell you exactly where to plant your feet. Finally, everybody found a place and assumed a position of attention — conveniently just as the DC reached "ten." I was beginning to suspect that "ten seconds" didn't always exactly equal ten seconds, and that the DCs might be slowing down the count or speeding it up in order to fuck with us, but I wasn't about to sneak a look at my watch in order to find out.

The DC ran us through some other nonsense with our gear, which I guess was supposed to familiarize us with everything, but by that point we were all so, so tired that we were just going through the motions. Then we went through another set of drills learning to pack everything correctly in our footlockers, which sat at the foot of each bed right beside the spot where the footprints were painted.

"Auld Father help your soul if your footlocker is ever found unlocked," the DC growled.

It was just one thing after another, the same as it had been all day long. I thought for sure the DC would be running us through drills all night long. At some point, though, we were finally commanded to undress and climb into bed. After another bloody-sounding prayer asking Auld Father to help us destroy our enemies, the DC went around extinguishing the lanterns. Before the last one was out, I was already asleep.

NOW IT WAS THE next morning, and before the mist in my brain had even lifted, my body had somehow pulled me up and into a position of attention beside my bunk. That feeling — where your body has gotten so used to doing something that it doesn't take the time to check in with your head, so your brain somehow ends up being the last one to know what's going on — was something I grew increasingly used to over the next six months.

One thing I did notice, once my head and limbs had gotten everything sorted out, was a large clock hanging on the wall at the end of the bunkroom. At first I thought I might have just missed it the night before, but no, that couldn't be right. The face of the clock was huge, the size of a large wagon wheel — to make it easily visible even to someone on the very far end of the bunkroom, I guessed.

The crashing sound stopped. My eyes instinctively locked themselves straight forward. I was staring straight at a big, hairy greasy guy directly on the other side of the bunkroom. Since he stood a full head taller than me, I was staring right at his neck, which already sported a healthy stubble.

I heard boots clacking smartly on the stone floor, coming down the aisle between the rows of bunks. The top of a yellow plume passed in front of my field of view, but I didn't dare look down to see what was connected to it. Then the voice boomed forth again: "The door to the right of the clock will take you to the washroom. The door in the back of the washroom leads outside, behind the building, where you'll find the latrines. All of you on the western side of the room — that's those of you on the side with all the windows — you have 30 minutes to shave, shit, shower, and be back here standing at attention, starting NOW. Go, go, go!"

The recruits on the other side of the room — I was on the eastern side — scampered off to the washroom, although most had to come back to grab their soap and razors, which they'd managed to forget in all their drowsiness.

"Those of you on the other side, come over here, it's time for a lesson."

We hustled over in the direction of the voice, where I first laid eyes on its owner: A dwarf — a motherfucking klanger.

He was standing beside one of the empty bunks on the western side of the room, which I noticed was neatly made up and empty. In a fog, I tried to think back to the previous day — I was absolutely sure that when we'd gone to sleep the night before, all the bunks had been occupied, but this one looked like it had never been slept in — at least before the DC began ripping the sheets off and piling them on top of the bunk in a messy pile.

This DC looked immaculate. Like all DCs, he was clothed in splendid attire that put our drab and functional training outfits to shame. Well-formed muscles bulged and strained against the fabric of his uniform. His tall DC hat, with its ever-present yellow feather, was set at an angle that looked pissed off.

Placed carefully off to his side, I noticed a huge drum — the source of the crashing sound that had startled us awake. The man's face, which had been beet red from shouting, was slowly returning to its natural pale color. He had a heroically-sculpted jaw, powerful blue eyes, and his close-cropped hair was a brilliant golden blond. If he hadn't been a runty little dwarf who barely came up to my chest, he could have passed for one of those shiny knights on the cover of those stupid romance tales my Aunt Twos used to read.

"I am going to instruct you ladies on how to make a bed, after which you WILL return to your bunks and follow my example to the letter. Is that understood?

Still sleepy, we muttered "yes, sir."

"Am I going DEAF?" he bellowed.

"Yes, sir!"

"Louder!"

"Yes, sir!"

"Did I fucking *stutter*? I said LOUDER!"

"YES, SIR!"

I watched the puffed-up little klanger through bleary eyes, trying to memorize exactly what he was doing. His hands moved quick — it was obvious this routine had been burned deep in his muscles. Even so, he carefully explained each step — "a six-inch fold here, a 45-degree fold here" — and it seemed like no time before he was up and standing once again, admiring his work.

"Okay, now you ladies do your own bunks, and snap to attention when you're done. You have five minutes starting NOW." I saw him ripping up his own work as I turned on my heels to race over to my own bunk.

I made my bunk as fast as I could, but it didn't look anywhere near as nice as the one the DC had done. I was still making adjustments when I heard: "and five, four, three..."

I resigned myself to getting chewed out and jumped up to attention, just as the DC shouted "...DONE."

Eyes straight ahead, I listened to the DC's boots coming down the row. They stopped in front of me for just a second, and I steeled myself for the coming storm.

"Recruit, your girlfriend lied to you about what six inches is," he grumbled, and then the top of his cap moved on. I heard his boots finally come to a stop at the bunk several down from mine.

"Recruit, what did your mom call you after the midwife stopped screaming?"

"Berrit Camlin, sir!"

"Recruit Camlin, where did you learn to make a bed?"

"Sir, this recruit learned from the servants when he was growing up."

"SERVANTS, recruit? Did you say you learned from the SERVANTS?"

"Yes, sir."

"Oh, now this is something we don't see every day! You grew up in a home with SERVANTS. And they taught you how to make a bed?"

"The ones at...sir, yes they did, sir."

"The ones at what, Recruit Camlin?"

There was a tiny pause, then: "The ones at the summer house did, sir."

Just out of the corner of my eye, I saw the DC reel back in pretend surprise as if he was some ham actor on stage.

"The SERVANTS at your SUMMER house taught you to make a bed, recruit? How many houses did your family own?"

Recruit Camlin took a deep breath. "Fi...two, sir."

"Recruit did you just LIE TO ME? You were going to say five, weren't you?"

"Yes, sir."

"Why did you say two?"

"Sir, those are just the ones that belonged to my mother, where this recruit spent most of his time. His father also had three more."

The DC let out a low whistle.

"By Auld Father, it's not often we get a highborn here at the Blue Wood. I suppose that explains the way you've made your bunk, recruit. Look at these folds. This bunk is truly fit for a noble!"

"Thank you, sir."

"You're welcome, recruit, except there's one thing."

"Yes sir?"

"This isn't your summer house, and that is the WORST EXCUSE for a properly-made Raider bunk out of all the disgraceful bunks in this barracks!"

As he screamed this, he picked up Recruit Camlin's entire bunk, frame and all, and hurled it to the other side of the bunkroom.

Then he charged up and down the row, ripping the sheets off all the bunks and flinging them aside.

His face turned red and the veins in his neck popped as he screamed, "you goat-fuckers have FIVE MINUTES to get those bunks made up right, starting NOW!"

So we went through the whole routine again, although Recruit Camlin had the added trouble of having to go fetch his entire bunk and drag it back to its normal spot. From the amount of effort it took him, it was pretty clear that those bulging muscles under our DC's uniform weren't just for show.

I thought my second attempt was looking pretty good, when I heard the count off again and shot back up to attention. But it still wasn't good enough, so the DC had us do it again.

And again.

By the time we'd been through it a fourth time, the recruits on the other side of the bay were all back and standing at attention. The DC suddenly lost all interest in us and marched up and down their side for an inspection. Then he snapped back around to face our side and told us we had 30 minutes to shave, shit, shower and be back at attention. We grabbed our gear and headed to the washroom, where the whole time we could hear the DC's voice in the next room, a constant reminder of what was in store for us.

ONCE EVERYONE WAS BACK in the bunkroom, the DC gave us another count-off to get dressed, and when we were back at attention, he suddenly snapped to attention himself, his boots giving a sharp "crack" as they hit the wooden floor.

I heard a heavy door open and shut, this one far back in one corner of the bunkroom. I had noticed it before but thought little of it, thinking it might lead to a storage closet or something.

That door — which I later learned led to a private bedroom and office for the DCs, which everybody called the Cage — would come to loom as large in my thoughts as the smoking-hot mouth of a dragon's den.

From the door, I heard a new set of boots stepping firmly down the length of the bay. The voice I heard next sounded like it came from the man with the biggest dick in the world.

He couldn't have sounded any cockier if he'd just finished wearing out every girl in a sporting house. You could actually hear his wide-ass self-satisfied grin in his voice.

"This is recruit training platoon One! One! Five! When I say sound off, you say One! One! Five! Sound off!"

"One! One! Five!"

"Which platoon is this?"

"One! One! Five!"

"Which platoon are we?"

"One! One! Five!"

"What's the best platoon at the Wood?"

"One! One! Five!"

"What's the only number that matters?"

"One! One! Five!"

"What's the only name that matters?"

"One! One! Five!"

"Auld Father can't hear you!"

"One! One! Five!"

"Come on, shake the roof!"

"ONE! ONE! FIVE!"

"Come on, break those beams! Again!"

"ONE! ONE! FIVE!"

He let it hang there in the air for a moment as he paced up and down the room, giving each recruit he passed the once over. When he passed by me, I got my first good look at him.

I was right about the smile — it sprawled across his face like a lazy noble riding a litter. His upper lip sported a thin, astonishingly well-trimmed mustache.

And I gotta be honest — while I couldn't tell you anything about the size of his dick, the son of a bitch had a breathtakingly handsome mug. With a face like that, I'd imagine he could make women faint just by tipping his hat.

I'm not saying I'm one of those kind of guys, because I'm not, but by Auld Father, it would have been a nice face to look at if it wasn't the cause of untold piles of misery for me in the coming weeks. It looked tough enough for a tavern fight, yet fine and dainty enough for a formal ball at the palace. If that dwarf DC had a face like a knight in some stupid romance, this DC had a face like the sculptures of ancient kings I used to see in the Palace District.

Unlike the dwarf, this new man wasn't wrapped in thick muscle — not that he was scrawny or anything. He had a strong but smoother build, like an athlete, and was almost exactly my own height.

His DC hat, topping a head of thick, dark, but closely-trimmed hair, was cocked at such an exact, prickish angle that I wondered if he'd used a surveyor's tool to set it. I noticed he had small red stripes on the shoulders of his uniform, which the dwarf DC didn't have. His uniform also sported a red ascot, where both the klanger and the nameless DC who'd run us through our first day had green ones.

Again, unlike the dwarf, whose attire seemed to have been cut just a hair too small to emphasize his muscles, this man's DC uniform was, like everything else about him, irritatingly perfect. The fit was so flawless I doubt the Royal Tailor could have done a better job.

"I am Sgt. Sculler, and I will be your senior drill commander for the next six months," he began. "You've already met Sgt. Taba over there. Don't let his size fool you. He can take down any one of you girls without even breaking a sweat. Sgt. Taba will be assisting me over the next six months. Any order that comes out of my mouth is the same as a command from Auld Father himself, and any order that comes from Sgt. Taba is the same as one that comes from me.

"How about that? You motherfuckers got a direct line to the Almighty. Can I get an AMEN?"

"A-men!"

"What was that?"

"A-MEN!"

"Was that an 'amen' or an 'a-fucking-men?'"

"A-FUCKING-MEN!"

"Okay."

Another several seconds of silence as he continued to pace around the room. Then he continued.

"Now the first thing you cretins should know about me is that I LOVE my fucking job. In fact, I like to think of this whole building as Sgt. Sculler's personal House of Love, because everything I do here comes straight from my own over-flowing heart. And you maggots are lucky enough to be here so you can be showered with it. How wonderful is that? Can I get an A-men?"

"A-MEN!"

"Auld Father, praise be upon his glorious and merciful name, has given me the greatest job in the world. The SECOND greatest job in the world is to spend all day, every day killing the living shit out of any man, beast, or spirit who blocks the Path. Gruun and his hell-demons spend every night crying and pissing their beds at the thought of the Raiders, because they know that somewhere there's a Raider blowing a load in his sleep with fantasies of drinking their blood. But the GREATEST job in the world is building more Raiders, because the only thing our Patriarch likes more than dead enemies is live sons.

"Auld Father's sons are the one who fill his shoes while he's waiting for us up on His Holy Mountain. Now Auld Father has two feet, so he has two shoes. He uses one foot to mark the Path. And since this isn't seminary, and you disgusting half-trolls could never hope to be Footmen, that means we're here to be the foot that fills the other shoe — the one Auld Father puts in the ass of any motherfucker who gets in his way.

"Now, if I were a lady — maybe you disgusting swine have heard of those, not that you could ever get within a bowshot of one — I could make Auld Father happy by squeezing out more sons from my blessed lady parts. Sayeth The Walk, 'blessed above kings is she who bears many sons.' Can I get an A-MEN?"

"A-MEN!"

"But since I was born with a dick, I can only build sons the hard way. And even though you are a bunch of pussies, you were still born with dicks, so unlike your mommy, you can't bring glory to Auld Father by laying back and getting railed all day by one of His blessed Raiders. Your mommy made a baby, but I'm your DAD-DY, and I'm about to make your ass a man. Can I get an A-MEN?"

28

I was looking forward to morning chow, but that wasn't what they had in store for us. Before that, we got our introduction to that big log I'd seen the day before. Forming us up outside, Sgt. Sculler explained that this was the Toothpick. "You girls are gonna have fun with this," he promised.

It was still dark outside; I heard somebody yawn, and Sgt. Taba snapped, "don't get excited recruit, it's not a dick. You're not gonna suck it."

What we did have to do was lift it — half the men in the platoon on one side, half on the other — and carry it around on our shoulders. All the humans were bunched at one end; the dwarves were all bunched at the other, with the middle unsupported. Sgt. Taba somehow scrambled his klanger ass atop the damn thing and was strutting back and forth along the length, issuing orders. For the briefest moment, I wondered how he was able to keep his balance so easily.

It sounds easy, but my shoulder quickly got sore, and the rough bark bit into my skin. And it's not like we were just lazily strolling — Sgt. Taba kept barking at us to pick up the pace. It seemed like no time at all until our crisp new clothes were soaked with sweat.

"The more you sweat, the less you can cry," Sgt. Sculler sang as he marched alongside. "You girls don't want to cry around me. I bottle that shit and spike my whiskey with it."

When we finished that, they lined us up on the ground in a row with the Toothpick on our chests. As one, the whole group had to do sit-ups while lifting that thing. Most of us couldn't do more than five without collapsing, though a few idiots kept going, trying to do more.

"Pathetic," Taba said. "Recruit, where are you from?" he asked one guy.

"Millsark, sir!"

"Good, now I know where to go so I can kick your recruiter in the nuts."

THEY DROVE US INTO the ground that day, never stopping for morning or mid-day chow. The gnawing hunger made everything foggy, so I don't remember much other than more endless drilling and exercising.

One other part I do remember was when we learned the purpose of the stone spheres I'd seen earlier: We had to pick one up and carry it through each of the long pits — first the one filled with wet muck, then the one filled with sand. You started with the smallest one, then did it again with the next largest one and kept going until you got to one you couldn't lift. I noticed even the scrawniest dwarves could manage to lift all but the very heaviest of the spheres, even if they couldn't carry them very far. At the time I thought that was a bit odd, but was otherwise too wrapped up in my own troubles to spend much time pondering it.

Once we got done with that, they paired us up and we got to do it all over again, with each pair of men carrying one of the massive spheres that were too heavy for just one man to carry.

Of course, our brand-new uniforms got absolutely filthy from all this. When we'd finished, Sgt. Sculler casually mentioned that our uniforms would need to be clean and presentable each and every morning, noting that there were a set of stone washbasins built into the back of the barracks, near the latrines.

By the end of the day, when the sun began to dip beneath the mountains, it felt like every single one of my muscles ached. I feared they would keep at us all through the night, and it was all I could do to just avoid collapsing into a crying heap. I probably would have, actually, if it hadn't been for Recruit Camlin, the guy with all the houses — he'd suffered a breakdown earlier in the day; he'd just stopped right in the middle of a drill exercise and sat down on the ground cross-legged and began blubbering. Sgt. Taba called us to a halt and stalked over to where Camlin was sitting, looking like he was going to tear the poor guy's head off, but then he stopped short and simply stared at him, breathing heavily.

"What's wrong, Summerhome?" he growled softly. "Still need a few more gulps from your mommy's tit? Not ready to play with the big boys?"

Then, to my shock, Recruit Camlin stood back up, wiped his eyes, sniffled a little bit, and marched right back over to join us. Sgt. Taba resumed the drill as if nothing had happened.

Well, after that, there was no way this street kid was going to let himself collapse like a soft-handed noble. I swallowed my agony, but it wasn't easy. I wasn't sure how much longer I could go when Sgt. Sculler finally told us to head back to bar-racks and assemble in the washroom.

I was filthy by this point, so I was looking forward to the luxury of those show-ers. Now, I know what you're thinking — by His Foot, they've got running water; what other useless luxuries does the Crown lavish upon these brutes? Silk for their bedsheets, perhaps? Maybe servants on standby to fan them when they perspire?

I can assure you that this washroom was not something you'd ever encounter in one of those fancy public baths. The walls and floor were bare stone, with no decoration, unless you counted the bright white paint.

Along one wall was a row of showerheads which would dispense water of whatever temperature the air outside happened to be. The wall directly opposite was hung with mirrors to be used for shaving. The mirrors were quite a bit larger than what I was used to, but they were plain — no ornate frames or anything like that. Attached to the wall beneath each mirror was a copper basin that could be plugged up to hold water; you had to fill it by hand using your trusty bucket.

There was a row of thin windows above the showers that let in some light during daytime, but at night the only illumination came from a row of lanterns along the same wall as the mirrors. These lanterns were kept burning constantly during the night — which, I later learned, was one of the duties of whoever was on firewatch.

"In short," as the Footmen back at the Temple School liked to say — in short, I'd been in stables that offered finer amenities.

Once we'd assembled in the washroom, I saw Sculler's skirt-raising grin was looking particularly wide. "I hope you gents are happy with our facilities here," he purred. "Because I want to share something with you."

He leaned in with a conspiratorial smile. Since we were all crowded together in the room, we instinctively mimicked the gesture.

"We Raiders," he whispered, "are a bit misunderstood, you see. The world only sees our armor, our swords. But inside our studded shells, behind our fearsome masks, we have a secret — before we are warriors, we are something else: We are *lovers.*"

He uttered that last word softly, with a hint of lewdness. We responded with nervous laughter, which he answered with a wicked grin. That brought more laughter, now less nervous.

"As a lover, a Raider's heart has two deep and abiding objects. The first, of course, is the everlasting glory of Auld Father and the Path he has set out for us."

The DC closed his eyes and inhaled. When he opened his eyes again, the lewd grin returned.

"But the Raider has another passion, another object he lusts after. It fills his dreams at night and focuses his mind during the day.

"Though it's unyielding at first, it flowers with careful caresses. Eventually, with enough attention, it changes from cold and dry to warm and yielding. Then, in its full bloom, when it is *slick* and wet, it unlocks its sweet treasures, and offers up its gifts for the hard and manly flesh that presses against it. It delivers ecstasies undreamed of by mere mortals.

"This rose of our hearts, this star of our strivings has a name, gentlemen. Do you know what it is?"

Sculler's grin grew even more obscene.

The room was silent. From somewhere in our group, a whisper came: "Pussy?"

"No," Sculler said, leaning in closer — causing us to do likewise.

In a tiny whisper, he said: "SOAP."

Then he snapped back to attention, and his deep, loud voice barked out: "You filthy sacks of shit have until the COUNT OF TEN to go back to your bunks, strip butt naked and report back here with your CROWN-ISSUED blocks of soap held in one hand above your head, starting NOW. Two, three..."

By "three" I was back at my bed, my shirt and one sandal already off. By "seven" I was completely naked, digging through my footlocker for the block of soap. The DC bellowed out "ten" just as the last man came through the door of the washroom.

So there we were, a bunch of naked, shaved-head boys huddled together in a washroom, shivering with shrunk-up dicks as we stood there holding those stupid blocks of soap in the air. I'm sure you long-beard scholars reading this are probably laughing your wrinkled old asses off. But to tell the truth, none of us even cared at that point. They'd managed to burn every last bit of dignity or self-respect out of us, which was a good thing considering what came next.

Sculler proceeded to give us a class in what he called "hygiene," a word I'd never heard before that night, but one which, as promised, quickly became more dear to us than any piece of plump and smooth ass we would ever see or even dream of.

We got a crash course in the proper Raider manner of accomplishing the three "S's" — shave, shit, shower. The true and correct Raider way, we discovered, extended even to pissing and taking a dump, activities which I had managed to forget might ever be a subject of general interest. Sculler reminded us, though, that it had not always been so:

"Plug up those eyeballs, recruit," he bellowed at one fellow who started to tear up. "Your mommy once taught you how to do this, even if you managed to forget it. For her sake, you'd better learn it again. You don't want us to send you home and tell your mommy you got KICKED OUT of the Raiders because you FORGOT how she taught you to clean up after taking a SHIT, right?"

By the time we'd finished, most of us had managed to finish off at least half our blocks of soap. No matter: As Sculler helpfully pointed out, there was a bin right at the entrance to the washroom which would always be stocked with fresh blocks.

"We restock it twice a day," he sang, as if he were telling us it would be refilled with pastry. "Can I get an A-MEN?"

ONCE WE WERE SUITABLY scrubbed and attired in clean clothes — thank Auld Father they'd given us an extra set — they marched us off to the chapel.

When we arrived, it was the first time since we'd arrived at training that nobody was screaming or angry or disappointed in us. I felt like a condemned man who had suddenly been freed — which I'm sure was the whole idea.

Sgt. Taba, speaking in a hushed voice all of a sudden — it was the first time any of us had heard him use something like a normal tone — directed us to our seats at the front of the cavernous hall, which was filled with the haunting sound of a group of chanting Footmen standing up at the front. The chapel was easily the largest building in the Blue Wood; it was maybe half the size of the Temple back in Solta. Although there were enough benches to seat a thousand or more, most of the building was empty except for three platoons of recruits and their DCs. I recognized the two other platoons as recruits who'd come in with us on the ox trolleys; at some point early on, they'd been split off from our group and taken elsewhere. Through whispers, I learned that they each had been sent to barracks in other parts of the Blue Wood, and were now platoons Two One Five and Three One Five. They confirmed that their time so far had been just as awful as ours.

Behind the chanters at the front of the chapel, sprouting up from the plants of the Sacred Soil, there was a huge sculpture of an arm. In the hand of the arm was a massive sword, which looked to be made out of real steel, with its blade fully polished and sharpened. I'm telling you, it looked real enough that you could imagine a man wielding it — although it would have to be a true giant of a man, since the blade reached up as high as the mast of a schooner.

Once we'd all been seated and the chanters finished, another Footman, this one bearing the garb of a Magnus, appeared and led us through a prayer service, where he gave us a little sermon about the importance of our mission in helping bring Auld Father's children back to his bosom at the summit of His Holy Mountain.

"A blade, in order to fulfill its task, must be ground hard and true on the whetstone," the Magnus said, "and it is to that purpose that you have been gathered here in the Blue Wood."

He reminded us that we'd all been given a copy of The Walk, and to turn to it in the weeks ahead for comfort and solace and blah blah blah.

Footman Sesh scolded me for that last sentence, but I'm just trying to follow his instructions and put into words what I was really feeling. I'll just say that the weeks and months that followed gave me more than enough opportunities to reflect on the flippancy I felt just then. At the time, it was all I could do just to rest my worn-out muscles and drink in the blessed peace of the moment. There would be many days ahead when that serenity, that cool oasis in an endless desert of sweat and strain and anger — which arrived every Sevenday thereafter, without fail, and on all major holy days — was the only thing that kept me going.

I'll allow that it was a head game they were playing. They wanted to give us nothing but good feelings about Auld Father, about His Scriptures, about his holy places and our holy mission. But I like to think of it as another form of training. One of the main things training is supposed to do is to make it so doing the right thing is automatic. In the middle of a battle, you don't have time to think through things, so having the right reaction at the right time can be the difference between life and death.

Chapel was just doing the same thing for our spirits — training them where to go automatically when Gruun's whispered lies threatened to disarm and defeat us. Plant your feet on the Path, and keep your eyes on the summit, where Auld Father awaits.

Lest we forget where we were, though, we ended chapel with the same bloody prayer we had every morning at chow — indeed, it was a prayer which accompanied every significant event in the Wood, and which I rapidly came to know by heart. It would be some time before I'd learn a more respectable, civilized prayer.

29

They play a lot of head games with you in training. One that I figured out pretty quick, because I'd seen so much of it back home, was the little back and forth between Sgt. Sculler and Sgt. Taba.

Taba, the junior guy, was obviously the attack dog, the enforcer. When two gangs had a sit-down in the Warrens, he would have been the guy standing off to the side, quiet, frowning, just cracking his knuckles or cleaning his fingernails with a scary knife. Not that Taba was ever quiet — that klanger fuck had a set of lungs that would put the announcer at a skram finals match to shame — but the principle was the same. He was there to ruffle your feathers, make your hair stand up.

Sgt. Sculler was the guy who came in to smooth everything back down. Not that he was there to hug you and dry your tears, understand. And not that he couldn't be every bit the terror that his sidekick was. He just — he did more with less, you might say. Instead of a screaming fit that would leave your ears ringing, he'd hit you with little more than a sharp glance or a sigh of disgust, and somehow it cut worse than anything Taba could do. All you wanted from that damned dwarf was the chance to punch his smug face straight in the nose, but when it came to Sculler, you wanted something else — you wanted his respect. Because if a guy like THAT respected you, it made you feel like you could do anything. Just a word of praise from the big guy would have you feeling like you were a lord being hauled about on a litter for the rest of the day.

There was never any schedule that I could work out for when Sgt. Sculler or Sgt. Taba, or both of them together, would be leading us, or when one of them would appear or disappear to take over from the other. Sometimes it felt like days went by without us seeing one of them; other times, we'd get bounced back and forth between them like a skram ball. I understood — the idea was that they never wanted you to get comfortable and fall into a routine with one or the other of them.

Taba was, of course, permanently unimpressed with anything we did — that was his role, of course, but there was nothing about him to indicate it was just an act. If you got any praise, it came from Sculler. But don't get the wrong idea — it took a LOT to get any praise from Sculler. If Taba spent most of his time yelling at us, Sculler spent most of his time pointing out things we were doing wrong.

"Recruit, that button on your shirt is loose. Knee bends, right now — count 'em off until I say when. You there, Shorty," Sculler said to the tallest guy in our platoon, "those sleeves are too loose. Have that sorted out by tomorrow morning. You're on fire watch tonight."

We were formed up after morning chow, our third day. None of us knew what in Gruun's asshole a "fire watch" was at that point, but nobody was about to ask.

Sculler stopped to face one of the dwarves in our platoon.

"Now here's a fellow who knows his way around a needle and thread!" he said. "Excellent work on those cuffs. Your fellow recruits could learn a thing or two from this. What's your name?

The dwarf straightened up and announced, with obvious pride, "Malok, son of Maudok, of the House of Teryn, sir."

Sculler let out a sigh. "Do you love Platoon One One Five, Malok, son of Maudok?"

"Yes sir!"

"Then you should know, Malok, son of Maudok, of the House of Teryn, that there's only one first name in Recruit Platoon One One Five, and that name is 'Recruit.' Do you want to be a part of One One Five, Recruit Teryn?"

"Yes sir!"

"Do you think you're better than the rest of One One Five, Recruit Teryn?"

"No sir!"

"Do you think you're special, Recruit Teryn?"

"No sir!"

"Do you WANT to be special, Recruit Teryn? I saw the way you smiled when I complimented your tailoring skills. Do you like that, Recruit Teryn? Do you want to be different from your fellow recruits?

A little quieter now: "No sir."

"Do you think Sgt. Taba is going to be nice to you because he's a klanger like you, Recruit Teryn?"

"No sir."

"Are you sure, Recruit Teryn?"

"Yes sir."

There was a long, long pause as Sculler walked around Recruit Teryn, sizing him up carefully. I thought he was gonna let loose with a bunch of criticisms — your arms aren't straight enough, your feet are at the wrong angle, you missed a spot while shaving, anything — but instead he said, very slowly:

"I don't believe you, Recruit Teryn. I don't think you want to be Recruit Teryn,

Raider Recruit Platoon One One Five. I think you want to be Malok, son of Maudok, of the House of Teryn. I think you hate it here, Recruit Teryn. And since you're just a little klanger…"

With this, Sgt. Sculler flashed his skirt-raising grin and stepped right up to Teryn, so that the recruit had to crane his head back to look up at him.

"…Maybe I'll go easy on you. Really easy. Since you're so special."

Then he stepped back, and surveyed the rest of us, still smiling.

"Maybe I'll go easy on the rest of your fellow recruits, too. Perhaps a few of them would like to be just as special as you." He let that sit there for a few seconds, still grinning. Then he sighed and shook his head.

"But I just don't know how I'd ever explain it to Sgt. Taba…"

OH, HOW WE HATED Sgt. Taba. I was pretty sure he had a set of bloody fangs where his heart should have been. We learned real quick to avoid tripping his temper if at all possible.

Most of the time, though, it seemed like getting on his good side wasn't possible. He was just a tiny golem carved out of anger and perfection. There were times I had to force myself not to take a swing at him. I think the only thing that stopped me was the knowledge that if I did, I imagined he'd easily be able to snap my arm off and stab me to death with the broken edge of the bone.

But you probably know that wherever you find a nasty bastard with power, you'll always find another guy willing to fall on his knees and suck the guy off just to get on his good side. (Though you'd have to get down pretty low indeed to reach that klanger bastard's cock…)

And we had a guy like that with us. His name was Avor, and he wasted no time trying to work his way into Sgt. Taba's good graces.

For one, he was a bit of a show-off. It was just little things at first, like yelling just a little bit louder than the rest of us, or being just a little faster or doing things with a little bit more polish. But Sgt. Taba picked up on it.

"Recruit, do you think you're better than the rest of One One Five?" he said.

"No, sir," Avor said. "This recruit is just eager to get to killing Auld Father's enemies."

"You think the other recruits don't want that too?"

"No sir! This recruit believes all of his fellow recruits share his enthusiasm!"

Taba smiled.

He quickly started calling Avor "A-1," and made a point of singling him out: "Come on, girls, do it like A-1 over there," or "come on, A-1, shine for me."

But unlike Recruit Teryn, who quickly faded into the background once Sculler had singled him out, Avor just couldn't hide his cockiness. He wasn't foolish enough to crack a smile, but you could see just by the way he carried himself that he was beginning to get a big head.

And Avor quickly took on the role of an unofficial assistant DC. He slid into the role with such ease that I could tell it was a costume he was used to wearing. I heard him whispering friendly corrections to different people as we went about training. That was great and all, but it was his tone that rubbed me the wrong way — like he was some kind of old hand at this, showing the rest of us the ropes.

Sgt. Taba noticed it too, and he seemed fine with it. At one point, while he was making Avor duck walk across the drill field in front of the barracks, he casually asked his stud recruit where he was from.

"The Stennen foothills, sir. East of Toka," he grunted, with a bit of pride.

"Oh? You wouldn't happen to know a Jaal Bardam, would you?" I recognized that name. He headed up one of the boxing schools that would sometimes swing through the Warrens to put on exhibition matches.

"Yes sir! This recruit trained for four years under Master Bardam, and achieved the rank of Lion, Second Class. The recruit won his division at the provincial tournament three summers in a row."

"A trained fighter, huh? That's why you joined the Raiders, I take it. Wanted to see some real action for a change."

"Yes, sir. This recruit believes he has a gift, and wanted to put it to use for the glory of the King and Auld Father."

Sgt. Taba didn't reply; he just grinned some more.

That evening, when we came back to the barracks, Sgt. Taba brought us to the big round wooden building that stood flanking one side of the drill deck. At that point, our platoon hadn't yet been inside it, though we'd seen the platoons from the other buildings filing in and out of it regularly.

Sgt. Taba slowly opened the door, and beckoned us inside, where we found a large, well-lighted space. The floor was covered with a thick layer of sawdust. Taba strode purposefully into the center and told us to form up in a circle around him — "not that close, guys, make it a little wider. I don't want you grabbing each other's dicks when I'm not looking. I know you want to."

He folded his arms and looked around us.

"Even though bringing you here makes me want to vomit, I feel obligated to give you girls a look at the furnace where real Raiders are forged. Not that any of you will ever get that far, but maybe sniffing the sweat of real men will cause you to realize your true calling as painted two-copper girlboys in a sporting house, and then I'll be rid of you for good.

"The training arena is the place where Raiders perfect the beautiful and sacred practice of cold-blooded murder of their fellow man. Yes, I said 'murder.' I didn't say 'kill.' To 'kill' is simply to end a life as a matter of routine business. It's to take a scythe to crops or a butchering blade to livestock. It's to crush an insect under your boot.

"'Murder' is altogether different. It is to take a life and also revel in the pulse-quickening pleasure of it! Someone has probably told you somewhere along the way that murder is wrong. You may even remember it from The Walk: 'Do not take the life of your fellow man, for that is murder, detestable in the eyes of Auld Father.'

"That's what we like to call a 'white lie,' which is something parents tell their children. You there, Gorgeous," he said, stopping to look up at Recruit Pesh — the greasy, flat-nosed guy who had the bunk right across from mine. He was easily the ugliest bastard in our platoon. "When you were a kid and caught your mom and daddy fucking, and they told you they were just playing horsie, was that a lie?"

"No, sir!"

"You're damn right it wasn't, because your mommy would never lie, would she, Recruit?"

"No, sir!"

"You sure about that, Gorgeous? I don't know about you. You got the stink of the sporting house about you."

"Sorry, sir! It's probably coming from my trousers, sir, this recruit..." He hesitated for just a moment, like he was gathering up his courage, then smiled and said: "This recruit just can't control himself around all these *men*, sir!"

Everyone roared with laughter, and even Sgt. Taba cracked a smile at that one.

"Okay," Taba finally said, instantly shutting everyone up. "So you know what I mean about a 'white lie.' Fact is, Auld Father doesn't detest murder — he loves it! But ONLY when it's directed against his enemies — Gruun, or any of his evil lackeys who dare to turn his beloved children from the Path.

"And that was why He made Raiders: We're the only ones permitted to give him that finest of pleasures. Every time you cut an enemy's throat, every time you stab an enemy's heart, every time you dash out an enemy's brains, it's like Auld Father is popping off a load all over your face! Recruit Lips," he said, wheeling to face me, "do YOU want Auld Father's spunk on your face?"

"Sir, this recruit dreams of it day and night!"

"That's what I'm talking about! And this..." — Taba swept his arms around theatrically — "...is where we'll teach you how to make that happen!"

Trying not to be obvious, I looked around a bit. I noticed the other guys were doing the same. Sgt. Taba wasn't yelling at us, so we loosened up a bit, even going so far as to turn our heads.

The western wall of the room was dominated by a large mosaic portraying a stylized picture of an arrow, pointing up: The symbol of Auld Father, just like the one my mother wore around her neck. The other walls were adorned with various types of what I took to be training equipment. Much of it was strange to me, but I recognized the implements hanging from a rack on the eastern wall: Wooden versions of various types of hand weapons — swords, axes, spears, maces, halberds, morningstars and shields. There were also a number of large boxes and cabinets which were securely locked.

"Tell you what," Taba finally continued, "since I'm in such a good mood today, I'll give you ladies a taste of what it's like to be a real Raider. Strip off your overshirts, fold them up and put them over next to that wall."

When we finished, Sgt. Taba — who had stripped off his own overshirt and stowed it somewhere — led us over to one of the larger cabinets, which he opened up to reveal a large assortment of clubs.

These weren't war clubs. They weren't even "training" war clubs. Instead, they were oddly misshapen — from the thin handles, the long end suddenly ballooned outward. They reminded me a little bit of wine bottles.

Taba directed us to the clubs on the bottom rung of the cabinet, which were painted soft pink. Some had flowers drawn on them. He had each of us grab a pair and told us to assemble back around the ring. But as we started to head back to our places, he suddenly called out:

"Hold up there, A-1. Come back here; I've got a special pair for you."

Taba locked the first cabinet and went over and opened another one in the far corner. He pulled out a pair of clubs that were far larger than the ones the rest of us had. Unlike the ones we had, these were painted Raider blue.

The DC handed them to Avor with a look I couldn't quite read. He gave him a firm pat on the back, and nodded for him to join the rest of us.

Taba also grabbed his own set of clubs — bigger than the ones we had, but smaller than Avor's. His, too, were painted Raider blue. Returning to the circle, he gave us a rundown.

"What you girls are holding in each hand are called meels. Raiders have been using them to train since our outfit was first founded. They come in different weights — obviously, you've been given the children's size, since I doubt you can handle anything else."

Well, that explained the pink.

"Except you, A-1," he added, and he gave Avor a wink.

"We use meels to build arm strength. You need arm strength to properly wield a hand weapon. And that's important because every Raider — every single one — is a swordsman. Even mages and medics and siege engineers — even balloon scouts and hawk cavalry. And you can't be a swordsman if you can't swing a sword. A trained Raider swordsman can chop a man's head off with a single swing of his blade.

"We'll start with some basic exercises. Just copy what I do, and don't stop until I give the order."

We launched into an arm swinging exercise, waving our meels up and down like fans in simple patterns. Taba stood in the center, doing the exercise right along with us, calling cadence in a haunting tone that sounded, well, dwarf-like. It was how you'd imagine the dwarves would sound when hammering out metal at their mountain forges in the far south.

Although my arms quickly got tired, Taba remained spry as ever. Seeing him there with the tight short-sleeve shirt molded around his torso with a light sheen of sweat, I finally got a good look at his mighty muscles. They strained against his skin, with thick veins forming little webs all around them.

As we exercised, he slowly pivoted his body, so he could get a good look at each one of us. He would occasionally offer a note of correction or admonishment.

"Recruit Gorgeous, move your wrists more, like you see me doing. God knows your right wrist has probably had enough practice. The way your arm fat slaps your side is disgusting. If I lose my lunch, you'll be cleaning it up."

Finally he swiveled around to face Recruit Camlin — the highborn one whose family had the five separate houses, and who'd had a momentary breakdown the day before.

"You there, Camlin, are you having trouble? Do you want us to fetch your servants to come down here and carry you home on a litter?"

"No, sir!"

"Come on, Camlin. You know this isn't the place for you. Why are you putting yourself through this? Shouldn't you be going to parties and riding in gilded carriages and paying for abortions for all the well-bred girls you knock up?"

"No, sir!"

"I don't believe you, Camlin. I believe the only reason you want to be here is so you can use the Raider uniform to get more pussy than you already get as a highborn. Recruit, I'm going to make it my personal mission to break you and send you crying home to your servants and your five houses and your featherbeds and full wine cellars and fine food! Do you know how many great men had to lay down their lives so you could enjoy that life? You're not even fit to polish their boots! Come on, FASTER!"

Taba picked up the pace. Camlin gulped in air and matched him. Taba began doing more complex swings. Camlin matched that, too. His face became a mask of utter hate, and I could see his eyes getting moist. The rest of us tried half-heartedly to follow along with Taba's movements, but it was clear that this was now just a personal match between the DC and the recruit.

Taba increased the pace once more. Camlin matched him again, his chest heaving and his face in utter anguish. He closed his eyes, let out a piercing cry, and the clubs flew out of his hands. He fell to the floor and vomited.

At that, Taba halted. The rest of us did, too. He looked around at us angrily.

"I didn't say stop!"

We went back to the routine, but without Taba calling time, we fell into a much slower rhythm. The DC didn't notice, though, because he was kneeling down checking Camlin, who was looking a little better, but still full of hate. The thoroughly drained recruit quickly pulled himself to his feet and made as if to go fetch his clubs, but Taba stopped him. Instead, the DC grabbed "Recruit Gorgeous" and told him to accompany Camlin to the medical building.

"Once you've signed him in, get back here on the double," he barked. Then he grabbed his clubs and started up again as if nothing had happened.

He kept pivoting around until he was facing me.

"Lips, right? You're the one who's everybody's best friend, right?" Even though I was completely worn out by this point, there was no fatigue in Taba's voice; he spoke just as casually as if we were having a pint of ale at a tavern.

Between gulps of air, I forced out my answer: "Yes, sir!"

"Yeah, I bet you wanna be everyone's friend. Where are you from, Lips?"

"Solta, sir!"

"Solta! The capital city! Well it's obvious you're not a silk-shirted fop like Camlin. What are you, some bureaucrat's brat looking for more excitement than a life spent slinging ink?"

"No, sir! This recruit grew up in the Warrens, sir!" I kind of puffed out my chest, hoping that the name would carry a little weight.

"The Warrens! Why, I hear that's where the limp-wristed nobles go to find back-alley boys! By His Foot, I can tell just from the way you grip those clubs that's something you're used to. I bet you were disappointed we didn't issue you lipstick and..."

My eyes had only drifted for the briefest second to look at something, but Sgt. Taba caught it. Cutting off our conversation in mid-sentence, he whirled around to see what I'd been looking at, and came face to face with Avor, who had stopped exercising and was hunched over, using one of his big meels to support himself.

"A-1! Did you hear me give the order to stop?"

"No, sir," he wheezed.

"Well then why are you not participating in the exercise, A-1? Do you think you're too good to join the rest of us?"

Avor lifted his head and shook it.

"The meels you gave me — they're too heavy," he said, forgetting to use the correct form of address. "I can't do it."

Sgt. Taba stopped, and told the rest of us to stop, too. My arms were burning. The DC walked up to Avor and looked up at him.

"Recruit A-1, I believe you specifically told me you had trained under Master Bardam. You specifically said you had achieved the rank of Lion, Second Class. Didn't you say that, Recruit A-1?"

"Yes, sir."

"I've never been to Master Bardam's school, A-1, but it's my understanding they use meels to train there, don't they?"

"Yes, sir."

"But not as large as these," Taba said, gently taking them away from the worn-out looking recruit and setting them down.

Avor shook his head. "No, sir."

Taba picked up one of the large meels and inspected it. He made a motion like he was going to put it back down — then he suddenly swung it at Avor's midsection with terrific speed.

I expected to hear ribs crack, but Avor, who had looked like he was about to collapse, suddenly dove out of the way, rolled to Taba's flank and jumped up into a fighting stance.

"Well, you seem to have the reflexes of one of Master Bardam's pupils, if nothing else," Taba said, throwing the meel aside. "The rest of you sit down."

The DC strode quickly over to one of the wall racks and grabbed a wooden fighting staff. He whipped it around a few times, making it clear that he was no stranger to the weapon. Even with his small frame, he looked plenty fearsome.

Avor hadn't moved from his fighting stance. Taba gripped his staff firmly, smiled at his opponent and took a few running steps and lunged.

Avor smoothly dodged his attacker's thrusts and swings. Each time, he seemed to jump or whirl out of the way just in the nick of time. A couple of times he dodged the staff with dramatic flips that got whoops and applause from the rest of us. The second time that happened he smiled. He was starting to enjoy this.

Sgt. Taba's expression was unreadable.

Then Avor managed to grab the staff; with a hard shove he threw Taba off balance and wrested control away from the dwarf. Now he began attacking with the staff, with many of the same moves Taba had used, and a few that were new. His own technique used considerably more flourish than Taba had shown, as if to emphasize that he'd had lots of practice.

For his part, the DC was plenty quick at evading the blows — but not as quick as Avor had been. A few times he was too slow and got grazed, but he never took a full blow. I still couldn't read the expression on his face.

Suddenly, Avor unleashed a quick and furious volley of moves. It was sudden but calculated, as if he had seized an opening. Taba took a step back and dodged a swing and then took another step, but he came down wrong and stumbled and fell onto his back, and Avor was instantly on top of him, the butt of the staff thrust into his face.

"Yield?" he said.

Taba looked at him. "Yield."

The recruits roared with approval. Everybody clapped. Avor spread his hands wide in an expression of victory, strutting around the room like a champion.

And before anybody could say anything, Taba jumped up off the ground and slammed his fists into Avor's back.

I wish I could describe the look on Avor's face when that happened; "stunned" doesn't really do it justice. For a second it seemed like time slowed down as Avor stumbled forward, then awkwardly tried to move back into a fighting stance, trying to thrust his staff out to block another blow. He barely missed having another fist smash into his jaw.

Now the two opponents began circling each other warily. It looked different now — Avor's movements were more hesitant, and Taba was tighter and more controlled. They reminded me of nothing so much as a pair of fighting dogs in the pits back in Solta.

Avor feinted, then swung hard — he let out a yell as he swung, as if he really meant to hurt his opponent.

And...the blow connected. The staff slammed into the dwarf's body with a sickening smack. The little klanger grunted loudly in pain. But he never seemed to lose his balance, and quickly lunged forward.

Avor quickly jabbed him in the ribs and hit him in the head, enough to open a gash in the DC's forehead. Taba let out a sound like a bark, but he pressed himself forward and grabbed the staff near where Avor held it — first with one hand, then both.

The two foes wrestled with the staff for a moment until Taba — with a sharp and powerful flex of his huge muscles — executed some kind of move that caused the staff to snap in half, then managed to wrench one half out of Avor's hands. Avor shifted his weight and tried to jump back into a defensive crouch, but Taba rammed the blunt end of his half into Avor's ribs in midair.

The recruit flopped to the floor, just in time for Taba's foot to smash the hand that was holding the other half of the staff.

The stunned recruit looked up at Taba and said, in a bewildered voice, "yield..."

Taba then used his half of the staff as a club, beating it against Avor's prostrate form several times. The "thunk" of wood hitting meat was like a sickening drum. Avor wriggled and tried to roll himself into a ball. The rest of us were silent.

In the midst of his beating, Avor tried to shout out "yield!", but his voice was cracked and raw with pain. When he did so, Taba rammed the broken edge of the staff into the floor right beside Avor's head. When he let go, the broken half was lodged several inches into the floor, sticking up like a crooked ship's mast.

Taba, who was barely out of breath, stood up and looked around at us, and then looked down at the stunned Avor.

"War," he announced, "is not a game. It is not a sport."

He then looked away from Avor, and around at the rest of us.

"Most of you — maybe all of you — are here because you think you're some kind of badass. Because you think, in some way, you've got something other men don't.

"Maybe you are, though I haven't seen any proof of it yet. But just because you're a badass somewhere, doesn't mean you're a badass everywhere.

"And let me tell you this. There's no system here. There's no 'rules' to figure out. There's no tricks to it. We're building warriors here, and war's got nothing to do with how smooth you are, how cool you look, or how many points you can score. You'd better get used to it being unfair, because EVERYTHING about war is unfair.

"You win when your enemy is sitting there holding his own guts in his hands, trying to stuff them back in his ripped-open torso while crying for his mommy. You win when the enemy is dead, and your ass is still up and breathing and walking around.

"Whether you do it as a gentleman or whether you do it as a snake doesn't really matter. It doesn't matter to me. It won't matter to your commanders. And it sure as hell doesn't matter to Auld Father."

He looked down at Avor, then looked around at the rest of us.

"Head to the barracks. Inspection in 15, starting NOW."

I TOSSED AND TURNED for several minutes after lights out, but even though I was exhausted, sleep wouldn't come. I could still hear Avor several bunks over, silently sobbing.

There was some commotion as Recruit Camlin came back from the infirmary. Camlin sounded angry and gruffly dismissed another recruit who tried to ask him if he was okay.

I was thinking about trying to say something to him when I heard my own name in a low whisper:

"Pearl."

I thought I had to be imagining things at first, but it came again.

"Pearl. Pearl. Hey, Pearl."

It was coming from the bunk on the other side of me. I cocked my head and whispered over my shoulder: "'Lips' is fine. That's what everyone else says."

The voice whispered back, kind of nervously, "'Lips?'"

I turned over. In the dim light, I could make out a face. It was a dwarf — the one who'd been single out earlier that day.

"I'm Malok, son of...I'm Recruit Teryn."

His whisper was punctuated by a pitiful moan from Avor's bunk.

"I know. I'm Pearl," I said.

There was a moment, and then he said, "you said to call you Lips."

I sighed.

Another moment passed.

"Lips?" came the whisper again.

"Yeah?"

"Do you think we're gonna make it?"

I thought about that, then said, "'We?'"

"Never mind."

"No, no. Sorry, just being a jerk. It's been a hard day for...well, shit. I guess I wasn't the only one."

"I know what you mean," Teryn said. "I'm not sure I'm cut out for this."

"I don't think any of us are cut out for this, pal."

When they woke us up the next morning, three different bunks — including Avor's — were empty, and neatly made up.

30

"Fuck yeah," I heard Gorgeous mutter after we were lined up inside the building.

There was a long table along one wall, with several starched-looking men standing behind it. But behind them we could see the reason we were here in this building: swords, knives, armor. Finally, I thought to myself, we're going to get to at least LOOK like real Raiders.

I'd have many opportunities over the coming months to curse that enthusiasm.

Sgt. Sculler was in charge, and he was his usual self, strutting about, supervising the show. He was peppering us with insults and occasionally questions, followed by a good smoking for anybody who couldn't produce the right answer, which was everybody.

"Lips, what's the Sixth Raider Command?"

"Sir, the Sixth Raider Command is…is, um, 'the blade…'"

"'Um' isn't a word, Recruit, it's what your girlfriend is moaning right now while she's back home and your best friend is balls deep inside of her. Get over here and do squats until I tell you to stop. You're first on fire watch tonight."

I guess here is where I should explain about the Raider Hand Book. It was, to quote Sculler, "the second-most important book ever written." The Walk, of course, was the most important, because as our DC told us, the Scriptures would clean our souls, and soap would clean our skin, "but the Hand Book will clean the filthiest part of your disgusting bodies — your minds."

Sculler assured us that between The Walk, the Raider Hand Book, and the wise and enlightened guidance of our DCs, we had access to a complete library of every possible thing a budding Raider might need to know — "if you can't get the answer from one of those places, you don't need to know it."

The book was full of things like the Eight Raider Commands, the Raider Prayer, an overview of the complete chain of command — we were at the bottom, while

Auld Father was at the top — dress and presentation, the basics of weapons handling (with such handy information as diagrams showing the seven deadliest locations on the body for a blade strike — there were separate diagrams for humans, dwarves and elves) and a very long section on "customs and courtesies," which explained all the nitpicky etiquette we had to follow when dealing with superiors.

Since we were a fighting outfit, you might think weapons handling would be the biggest and longest section of the book, but no — that was actually the shortest. The LONGEST section was the last, and was titled simply, "The History of the Raiders."

That, at least, was something I could work with. Year after year, history was my best class back at Temple School — not that that's saying much. I won't ever be one of you long-beards sitting in libraries poring over those big lists of royal bloodlines or the records of the Holy Councils. Mostly I just liked learning about wars and battles and big-shot generals, and Raider history was nothing but that.

At any given moment, a DC might decide to pull you aside and quiz you on some bit of knowledge from the Hand Book, and if you failed, punishment was certain — just for you, if you were lucky, though if you botched a big one, like the name of the battle where Maj. Braborn — whose massive statue dominated the center of Fort Harrel — had earned his first Crimson Star, the whole platoon might have to sweat it out. Needless to say, our copies of the Hand Book quickly became worn and dog-eared from constant use.

Once Sculler figured I'd paid my penance for forgetting the Sixth Command, I joined the others in collecting the tools of my trade. I went down the long table, facing each starched clerk in turn. Each had a big book laid out, and would hand you a piece of equipment, being careful to mark down in the book a number stamped on each item.

They saved the swords for last. The clerk in charge of giving out swords was a dwarf, a bit heavyset for a Raider, with a wispy ring of red hairs crowning a shiny bald head and a thick but carefully trimmed mustache. I marveled at how even that mustache was — even the hairs on the little klanger's upper lip stood in stiff military ranks. He had small, angry eyes, which flicked up and down, watching each of us suspiciously as he jotted down the number of each weapon before handing it over.

Much of the equipment they gave us was in pretty bad shape — the leather was worn and smelled of sweat, and the metal parts were scratched and dented. Only the blades of the swords looked shiny, though the handles and scabbards showed evidence of heavy use. Sgt. Sculler produced his own set of gear from somewhere, which I noticed looked far more presentable than ours, and then walked us through our kit.

We each had a pair of extremely sturdy thigh-high boots and long trousers of heavier fabric than our normal gear. For our torsos, there was a light, long-sleeved cotton shirt, over which we wore a long, thickly padded sleeved gambeson. Over that went a stiff brigandine, fastened at the front, which covered only the torso, and pauldrons on the shoulders. A tough leather belt cinched everything up around the waist. We had steel vambraces for our forearms, and tough but surprisingly flexible leather gloves. For the head, we donned a mail coif underneath a metal helmet. The helmet was the famous Raider helmet you've seen in all the pictures — it has an open face and sharp crest along the top, with a wide flange covering the neck.

As we stripped off our light training outfits, I suddenly became aware of just how warm the day was. I was certain Sculler had somehow managed to conspire with the sun as I worked to bind myself up in a sweltering leather and metal cocoon. Sculler carefully supervised us through the whole ordeal, finding fault with every detail. But when we were finally done, I could have kissed the man full on the mouth when he instructed us to fill up our newly-issued water flasks and drink as much as we wanted.

"We've got taps and water pumps all over the camp," he said. "You'll want to keep those flasks full as much as possible."

Then came our introduction to our weapons. The first was a large knife worn at the waist, which we were supposed to use anytime we needed a blade — our sword, Sculler sternly told us, was to remain in its scabbard and NOT be used for anything except combat. Along with that was a smaller, thin-bladed fighting knife to be used for close-in fighting to slip in through gaps in an enemy's armor.

The sword was a basic cross-guard arming sword — the blade was a little larger than on most swords I'd seen, yet it was surprisingly light and easy to swing, which I was told later was due to the quality of steel demanded by the Raiders. We also had curved wooden shields which were slung over the backs when not being used.

And in addition to all that was the spear — 8 feet long, made from light but incredibly strong Firegum Tree wood, topped with a pointed steel head with stubby "wings" at the base of the head. I'd had chances to see other recruits drilling with them since arriving — it always looked like a moving, steel-tipped forest. We'd shortly become another one.

If all this sounds like it would be incredibly tiring to carry — it is. Over the rest of training, I would grow to loathe the phrase "turn out in full kit," which was often shortened to just "full kit"; as in, "be in formation outside in 10 minutes — FULL KIT." And that doesn't even get into all the extra packs and sacks we'd have to use to haul supplies during long marches. But all that would come later.

For now, Sculler ran us through the basic drilling maneuvers. We already knew some of the basic commands and could sort of manage to do them in unison, but doing them in full gear was like having to learn it all over again, but worse, because our sense of balance hadn't yet adjusted to all the extra weight. We spent most of the rest of the day trying not to look like "a bunch of fuck monkeys in greased slippers dancing on ice while trying to hold in a wet fart," as Sgt. Taba said of us when he suddenly arrived shortly after midday chow.

By the end of the day, we were more or less able to get the basic maneuvers — or at least, we'd managed to advance from looking like "a giant explosion of shit in a fuck-up factory" to just "shit." We'd gotten there the hard way — several guys had bumps and bruises on their heads from the mishandled spears of their fellow recruits. It was a good thing they'd also given us those helmets to soak up the blows.

One of the guys whose helmet got several good whacks, courtesy of me, was the guy directly in front of me — Recruit Parsa, a sour-looking guy from East Selva with a stocky build.

"Watch it, faggot," he hissed after the second time I bopped him. After the fourth time, he simply looked over his shoulder and gave me an evil glare which I recognized immediately as an "I'll get your ass later" look.

Sgt. Taba noticed the exchange.

"Holy shit, Lips," he said, "your dumb ass couldn't fuck your way out of a box filled with pussy."

A FEW DAYS LATER, though, another guy washed out, and for me, it was a bit of a stunner: It was a guy I only knew as Miro, from the Kassor Hills. He was a big guy, the only recruit with muscles like the DCs; I had him pegged as the guy most likely to win the purple sash at the end of training — the reward for the top recruit in each platoon.

But Miro's muscles apparently extended to his brain, because he wasn't the smartest guy I've ever seen. By this time most of us had more or less memorized the Eight Raider Commands, even if we couldn't get the wording exactly right or weren't exactly sure of the correct order. But I never saw Miro get even one of them right. It might have had something to do with the fact that he never seemed to study his Raider Hand Book, though most of us had realized by that point that it was a good idea to crack it open and study it any time you had a spare moment.

Anyway, Miro was gone after chow that morning — when he dropped out, or was pulled out, I couldn't say, but I noticed that evening that we were one short on our side of the barracks — his bunk was empty, and was later removed.

Seeing that called up some kind of feeling inside me, which I'm sure you long-beards have a name for, but I don't. See, up until then, I wasn't entirely sure I'd made the right decision in coming to the Wood. I mean, I was beginning to think time on a prison ship wouldn't be so bad, seeing as when you're a prisoner, no-body cares about you when you're not on duty. At the Blue Wood, though, there was never a moment when you felt like the DCs weren't watching you. Later on, after a few more weeks, they even began showing up in your dreams — you'd be holed up in the Seraglio of the Suzer of Garlund, with all his concubines pawing at you and wanting to pleasure you, and all of a sudden one of the girls would whip off her veil, and there would be Sgt. Taba screaming at you about why there was a smudge on your gloves, and why the fuck aren't you wearing your damn helmet?

That's what the pressure was like, and already at this early stage I wasn't sure how much longer I could take it. But when Miro left — for some reason, that was a watershed moment for me.

I'd already figured out it wasn't about the muscles. I mean it is, but not really; I felt sore at the end of every day when I climbed into my bunk, but it was nothing compared to what I sometimes felt at the end of a gang brawl back when I was running with the Clubs back in the Warrens. It was nothing like what I felt like after a beating from Footman Tan back at the Temple School. It was nothing like a good licking from my mom's hairbrush.

So I knew, being a Warrens boy, I just KNEW I could take the physical part. It was the mind part I was worried about. And seeing a big strapping guy like Miro, a guy who could have been an absolute beast in a Warrens gang rumble — seeing a guy like that fold, it was like a revelation. Somehow, I knew then that the fucking DCs didn't have what it took to make me quit. I don't know HOW I knew, because I also knew they had a lot more they could dish out to me — but I KNEW. I knew they didn't have what it took to break me.

31

Sgt. Taba was in the middle of a lecture on proper maintenance of our knives and swords — particularly our swords, which had to remain sharp and polished at all times. For once, he wasn't yelling at us. His voice was calm and even, as if to underscore the solemnity of the lesson.

They weren't kidding, by the way, about maintaining your gear — sword blades, like everything else we carried, were subject to spot inspections at any time. The inspecting DC would test the blade by removing the feather from his hat and running the blade over the tips of the feathervane; a properly sharpened blade was supposed to make a clean cut.

It was our first time actually getting to handle our swords, and of course I couldn't resist clowning around with mine. When I thought everybody else was caught up in Sgt. Taba's presentation, I tapped Teryn on the back.

"Hey, check it out," I whispered, holding the sword up to my crotch like a boner. He smiled and stifled a laugh. I looked around at the rest of the platoon. Parsa had still been giving me shit, so while motioning to Teryn to keep quiet, I sneaked up behind him and held my sword to my crotch while miming humping motions. When I saw Teryn's face turning red, I turned it up a notch, making faces and acting like I was popping a load.

Teryn tried to cover his mouth, but a sharp giggle escaped. I immediately tried to look innocent as Sgt. Taba growled, "something funny, Recruit Teryn?"

"No, sir."

The DC's eyes flicked over to me. "Lips, wouldn't your boyfriend back home be jealous if he found out you'd been flirting with a klanger?"

Everybody laughed except me and Teryn.

"Sir?"

"Oh, don't play dumb, Lips, I saw you with your sword there, pretending to buttfuck Recruit Parsa. That's why Recruit Teryn was laughing."

Parsa turned and looked at me, his face full of hate. Everybody else turned to look at me, too.

"Sorry, sir. It was a joke."

"I know that, Lips. You are only the ten millionth recruit to think of it. Now pay attention, this is serious..."

To my surprise, the platoon didn't get smoked for my offense. Sgt. Taba just carried on with the lesson. I realized, though, that he'd just painted a target on my back for Parsa.

THAT NIGHT RIGHT BEFORE lights out, Sgt. Sculler made another of his miraculous appearances. Right after Taba gave us our final inspection, the head DC emerged from the Cage, the mysterious room at the end of the bunkroom. He was uncharacteristically calm.

"Before we go any further, does anybody have any questions?" he asked.

At first, nobody said anything, expecting another mind game. But he continued, in a reassuring tone: "No need to fear, we're just trying to get a sense of where you boys are. We're taking your temperature, so to speak."

It'll be hard for you long-beards to understand this, but when he called us "boys," it felt like fireworks had just gone off and we'd just received a promotion. The whole time we'd been there we'd been "girls," or sometimes "ladies" — that is, when we weren't fartnozzles, shitbirds, shits, shitsacks, pukes, cum bubbles, abortions, fuckwads, fuckers, maggots, faggots, ladyboys, or noodledicks.

Somebody asked about mail. Sculler said all our families had received notice that we had entered training and had received instructions on how to contact us; it usually took a couple of weeks for letters to start to arrive, but once they began arriving we would have a regular mail call.

Another guy — a lanky fellow I recognized as being a few bunks over from me — raised his hand, and Sgt. Sculler nodded.

"Sir, Recruit Birchen has a problem with the food here, sir."

"What's wrong with it, recruit?"

"Sir — with all due respect, sir, this recruit has puked up stuff that was more appetizing."

There was nervous laughter at that.

Sculler smiled. "I suppose you'd prefer roasted pheasant, recruit?"

"Sir, this recruit was actually thinking of Lyndan Suncake, if possible."

Murmurs of approval, and more nervous laughter — a little louder now. Even Sculler chuckled.

"Well I see you gents still have your sense of humor. You're gonna need it. Anyone else?"

Parsa raised his hand. The DC nodded at him to go ahead.

"Sir…are we going to be sent to Garlund? To fight with the King?"

Sculler looked down at the floor for several moments, as if he was thinking about his answer. Finally he said, "recruit, do you WANT to go join the war?" He pointed at the western wall. "I mean, you could go join the fight right now, if you can make it over the Striped Mountains." I heard some soft, nervous laughter from Teryn, on the bunk beside mine.

"Just because nobody's made the crossing in 200 years doesn't mean you can't do it, recruit," Sculler continued. "If you want to abscond and give it a shot, we're certainly not going to make an effort to chase you down." He paused, then flashed his grin. "The ice cats will thank us; they'll have a feast."

There was some more laughter at that, but Parsa didn't join in. He looked somber.

"Yes, I…this recruit wants to go," he finally said. I noticed Sculler didn't jump on him about the "I," but just looked at him thoughtfully. "To be there when the Reckoner…"

"What makes you think the Reckoner will be there, recruit?" Sculler said, cutting him off. He didn't say it in an angry way; he was still calm. But there was some steel in his words all the same.

"Everybody says…"

"'Everybody,' recruit? Who is 'everybody'? Did I say it? Did Sgt. Taba? Does it say it in the Raider Hand Book?"

"The recruit has heard rumors…"

"The Raiders don't run on rumors, recruit."

Parsa's brow wrinkled as he seemed to consider this.

"The point is, recruit," Sculler finally said, walking slowly over to where Parsa stood, "the King and our soldiers are not in Garlund as conquerors. They are there merely to assist our allies in putting down a small but particularly stubborn insurrection. We are not on the cusp of a grand crusade, and we have certainly not reached the time when we should look to the coming of the Reckoner." He stopped right in front of Parsa, and looked him directly in the eyes. Something unspoken seemed to pass between them, but damn if I could tell you what it was.

Then he turned away and began pacing back down the center of the bunkroom.

"As far as what any of you might face when you finish training — IF you finish training, and if I feel like any of you are even fit to wear Raider Blue — this little squabble in the west will probably all be over by then, and you can look forward to the next three years at an isolated garrison post where you will barely have to get mud on your boots."

I HAD FIRE WATCH that night — two hours of sitting in a chair at the end of the barracks, watching the other guys sleep. Every 15 minutes you had to make a circuit of the building — both the sleeping area and the washroom. Everywhere except The Cage — the door to that remained closed, what lay beyond it, still a mystery. If there had been a fire in there, I wouldn't have known until it was too late, but something told me Sgt. Sculler, who was asleep in there that night, wouldn't be in any danger.

I thought about what the DC had told Parsa. Sculler had lied — at least in part. Every single man in that room understood that the King would not be traveling to the West to merely "assist our allies" with putting down a "minor insurrection." But if he'd lied about that — what else might he have lied about? Were we indeed going to be sent off to a crusade? Was that what awaited us at the conclusion of training — being shipped off to be dumped straight into the dragon's maw? And were Parsa's suspicions right — were we, at long last, living in the time of the Reckoner? And how would we even know him when he arrived? I remembered nothing in The Walk about him arriving with signs and wonders and miracles. Maybe he was just a man. If so — would we even know him when he finally showed his face?

If Parsa had been troubled by any of Sculler's evasions, he showed no sign of it. Before lights out, he had gone through his nightly ritual of prayer — I had seen enough of him to understand that he was obviously one of the more religious among our ranks — and he drifted off to sleep easily, showing none of the distress of a recruit with something on his mind. Perhaps that's one of the benefits of putting such enormous stock in Auld Father. My mom had always been the same way.

For me, though, the questions lingered, gnawing at me and helping me keep awake for my shift. From time to time, I looked at the door to The Cage, and wondered what other things our dear daddy Sergeant was keeping from us.

32

My next fuck-up came a few days later when we were in the training arena and Sgt. Taba was giving us an introduction to fighting with a shield and spear. The practice spears had a padded bumper at the end instead of a sharpened spear point, and Taba, with the help of Recruits Parsa and Gorgeous, was showing how one man armed with a spear and shield could easily fend off two men armed with swords.

"Now let's make it a little interesting and add a third," he said. "Let's see…Lips? Lips are you even fucking paying attention?"

I hadn't been, because I was too busy staring at a bird that had somehow made its way into the building and was flitting about in the rafters. I sat up and tried to look engaged. "Sir! Yes sir!"

"Lips, what is the Sixth Raider Command?"

"Uh…the Sixth…uh…is 'the blade…'"

"Shut up. If you ladies aren't engaged enough, maybe some exercise will get those hearts pumping and bring your focus back. Everyone grab a pair of meels and let's run through some exercises. NOW!"

Amid mutterings from the others of "thanks again, asshole," I got up to join the rest and take my punishment.

When Taba finally judged that we'd had enough, he herded us back over to finish the lesson. Throwing me a wooden practice sword, he had me join Parsa and Gorgeous, saying "think you can pay attention now, recruit?"

Gorgeous clapped a big paw on my back. "Don't worry about Lips here, sir," he said, smiling at Taba. "He'll know just what to do when something long and hard starts poking at him." And with that he mimed a blowjob.

That brought a laugh, and I was happy to join in. One of the few things that made training tolerable was the way Gorgeous was always ready to step in and lighten the mood. Even Taba cracked a smile.

The only one not smiling was Parsa, who continued to eye me with hate.

"With all due respect, sir," he began, "I don't understand how it would do me any good to have this sewer rat by my side on a battlefield."

"Did I hear you correctly, Recruit Parsa?" a voice suddenly boomed from the door to the training arena. It was Sgt. Sculler, making another of his miraculous sudden appearances. "Did you just refer to yourself as 'I?'"

The arena felt eerily silent as the DC made his way over to where Parsa stood, now looking dejected. You could see he was mentally preparing himself for whatever punishment came next.

But when Sculler reached him, he didn't start bellowing. Instead, he looked at me, giving me a good once over, then back at Parsa.

"Recruit, if you're looking for the cause of any problems you might have on a battlefield — assuming I ever let you make it to one — you're not going to find it with Lips over there. Instead, you can start with that word, 'I.' What are you, recruit?"

"Recruit Parsa, Training Platoon One! One! Five! Of the..."

"Spare me that bullshit, recruit, I know you can give me the official answer. I'm asking who YOU are. Where are you from? Who were you before you came here? Who's the scared little boy still stowed away inside this piece of Crown Property?"

Parsa blinked. He opened his mouth as if to speak. Held his mouth open. Blinked again.

"We're waiting, recruit."

"Sir...this recruit..."

"You can say 'I,' recruit."

Parsa looked at the DC in confusion.

"It's not a trick," Sculler told him.

Parsa began again. "Sir, this...I was a farmer. Well, I wasn't, really, at least not...I mean, my father was one. I came from a town — well, I mean, my name was enrolled at the Temple in a town called Caford. Our farm — my father's farm — was out farther in the country."

"Caford. They grow rye there."

"Sir, yes, and oats! A lot of people don't know it, but our oats are the most prized feed for top racehorses. It's said that 21 of the last 25 winners of the King's Derby were raised on oats grown within our county, and that the other four got oats from the county right next to ours." He gave a small smile of pride.

"Did you grow the oats, Parsa?"

"Sir?"

"Did you grow all those oats yourself? Pack them up, prepare them, ship them to the horse breeders?"

"I mean — not me, sir. My father...what I mean is...I used to help with the harvest. Back before..."

"So that's a no, then."

Parsa thought for a second. "Correct, sir."

"So back there in Caford…they're getting along just fine without this 'I' standing before me right now, aren't they?"

Parsa flinched. "Uh, yes sir."

"Sure about that, recruit? Sure the whole town hasn't dried up and blown away without you there to see to things? I know your mom bawls her eyes out every night now that you're gone, but what about everybody else? Don't say your girlfriend — I can guarantee you that the second you left she was getting railed behind the barn by the first young buck who came by swinging his scythe."

Sculler let that one sink in for a second, then continued. "So this 'I' that you keep referring to — he didn't really do shit, did he?"

"I…I…" Parsa gulped, stood a little straighter, like he was trying to get something out of his mind by focusing. "Sir, this recruit would agree with that."

Sculler turned away from Parsa, and looked at the rest of us.

"Recruit Parsa has just illuminated a great truth for us, and explained why none of you are an 'I.' You are not you. You are where you came from, you are a product of a community — of a people. They don't need you, but you need them, because a man without a people is a man from nowhere; he's nothing, just a fleeting spark in the darkness. But sparks together build a flame, and flames can build a great fire. That fire is the family, the team, the village, the town, the city — the nation.

"A people — not an individual, but a community — can be great at many things. Recruit Parsa's people grow oats for horses. Recruit Birchen's people breed horses…" — at this everyone looked at the named recruit, who shrugged and nodded — "…and Recruit Camlin's people ride those horses to victory."

I looked over at Camlin, but his face betrayed nothing.

Sculler gave me a glance. "And I guess Recruit Lips's people shovel out the stalls," he added, to a chorus of "OOOOOOHs." But I played along, giving a series of bows that got some chuckles.

"The point is, none of you are individuals, however much you might treasure the thought that you are. All of you are children of one people or another. But none of those people, none of those communities were built to fight and win wars. And that's what we're building you into now. Once we've succeeded — if we do succeed — only then do you earn the right to call yourself an 'I.' Then you'll be speaking as a member of THIS people — the Raiders."

He turned back to Parsa. "Does that answer your question, recruit?"

"Sir…Sir, this recruit still doesn't see how a Raider of Recruit Lips's…caliber… is going to help with that."

"Oh, we'll eventually teach Recruit Lips how to recite the commands and swing a sword well enough. We've got 433 years of practice at it. By His Foot, my five-year-old son can recite the Eight Commands perfectly, so I think there's still some hope for Lips."

Five-year-old son? Did I hear that right?

Did Sgt. Sculler just imply he had a life apart from torturing recruits? I looked at his hand and, sure enough, there was a wedding band there. Son of a bitch.

"But you're still seeing it wrong, recruit," Sculler continued. "No war was ever won by a single man wielding a sword or a spell. They are won by groups of men working in concert, each doing his duty. And not every one of those men is necessarily hefting a sword, but every single one of them is necessary.

"Think of a great building — the great Temple of Lyndan, for instance. Its greatness comes from the fact that every stone, every beam, every nail, every pane of glass is ordered and put together and in its proper position. No piece by itself is great — indeed, many of the individual pieces have been replaced over the years. The greatness comes from all the pieces together. Everyone talks about the great statue of Footman Rom atop the high dome, but if the statue were to switch places with one of the foundation stones, which is buried under the ground where it can never be seen — the greatness would be diminished. Indeed, the whole structure would likely collapse — the dome could not bear the weight of a foundation stone placed atop it, and the statue could never bear the weight of the structure above it if placed as a foundation stone. The problem, Recruit Parsa, isn't with Lips; the problem is that we haven't yet found out where he belongs."

Sculler stood there for a second eyeing us, then something caught his attention. "Yes? Recruit Teryn? Did you have a question?"

All eyes turned to the direction Sculler was looking at. Recruit Teryn was lowering his hand and straightening up, trying to bring his compact dwarven frame to its full height.

"Sir, all this talk of communities and cathedrals is well and good, but what about a great athlete? Or a great artist? Don't they, by definition, achieve what they do entirely from their own efforts? You talked about the Temple of Solta — what about the architect who designed it? Did not all that greatness ultimately spring from him alone?"

Someone let out a sigh. Sculler heard it and pounced. "Recruit Camlin, you have something to add?"

Camlin, he of the five houses, was sitting on the ground, head down while he idly dug at the dirt floor of the arena. Since the beginning of training, Camlin had rarely said anything or interacted with the rest of us. At first I'd just chalked it up to blue-blood snobbery, but since I'd seen more of him it became clear that it wasn't that. Camlin always seemed on the verge of giving up, admitting defeat and asking to leave the Wood, but he somehow managed to power through, no matter how much ragging he got about his background. He just silently dropped his eyes and did whatever was asked. I was actually starting to admire him a bit for it.

Aware now that all eyes were on him, Camlin shrugged. "The so-called 'Great Man' is an illusion," he said.

"I'm surprised to hear such sentiments from one of noble blood, recruit," Sculler said.

The recruit shook his head, not looking at Sculler. "A seed is only as good as the gardener."

"Fenson, I believe. From 'The Arguments.'"

At that Camlin looked up, a bit surprised.

"You've read Fenson?"

"All six of his surviving works, yes. Believe it or not, recruit, 'DC' doesn't stand for 'dumb cunt,' despite the whisperings among the bunks in the barracks at night — oh yes, me and Sgt. Taba are well aware of what you ladies gossip about when you think we're not listening. Where did you encounter Fenson, recruit?"

"We studied him at…at…St. Layre's…"

I'd never heard of "St. Layre's," but from some of the murmuring around me I could tell it must be a big deal. Sculler himself raised an eyebrow.

"I must say, it has been a long time indeed since one of your station has graced these quarters, recruit. A long time indeed. Care to expand on that quote from Fenson? For the benefit of us commoners, understand."

Camlin suddenly looked uncomfortable at all the eyes on him. He looked down and sighed.

"A great man is as much a product of others — of a people, if you will — as of his own native talents or genius. The greatest artist still requires teachers. The greatest athlete still requires coaches. The architect who designed the Temple at Lyndan, Footman Garmo, began as the apprentice of Footman Chion, who designed the great Sailor's Chapel at Agellos.

"Throw a born genius into the street and demand that he develop himself entirely on his own, and his growth will remain forever stunted. He may achieve a measure of success, but he will never reach anything close to what he could have been capable of. This recruit is sure there are plenty of talented graffiti artists wasting their talents in the back alleys of Solta; there are only a few painters whose works hang in the Palace Museum."

I wondered if he was talking about me there. He went on: "The difference isn't the degree of talent; the difference is the degree of cultivation, and cultivation only happens when talent submits to authority. Fenson used the example of a Kassflower plant that was said to have the most beautiful blooms in all the realm. He said you could take two seeds from that plant, and throw one off somewhere into the wild to grow on its own and have the second cultivated by a master gardener. Though both seeds contain the possibility of greatness, only the one raised by the master gardener will actually achieve it."

Camlin was still looking down when he finished, still digging aimlessly in the dirt. Sculler looked around at the rest of us.

"You ladies have a long way to go before you bloom," he said, and turned and left. Taba quickly went back to the lesson, but I noticed that he left Camlin alone with his thoughts.

LATER THAT DAY THEY split us up into our squads. Raider squads are supposed to have eight men each, but since the platoon only had 35 now — we'd started with 40 — there were three guys left over who got assigned as extras.

I was in Squad Three with Recruit Teryn, and Sculler tapped Recruit Gorgeous as our squad leader. Which made me Recruit Pearl, Second Sword, Squad Three, Recruit Training Platoon One One Five of the Recruit Training Battalion, Fort Harrel. I know that by heart because one time when I forgot it, I had to stand in front of a mirror, slap myself and repeat the entire thing, slap myself, repeat the entire thing, and so on for over an hour, with Sgt. Taba coming by to scream at me for not doing it with enough enthusiasm.

There didn't seem to be any reason Sculler picked Gorgeous as our squad leader — maybe because he was the tallest? As far as I could tell, there weren't any perks to being a squad leader. The only difference was that if one of your squad members fucked up, you often got smoked right alongside them — which made squad leaders awful keen on getting everybody under their "command" squared away. That, as far as I could tell, was the only real responsibility a squad leader had, although I suppose being a leader is one of those things where you can make it as big as you want.

Take, for example, my nemesis, Recruit Parsa. He got tapped as leader of Squad Two, and took to his new job right away, bossing around the guys "under" him like he'd been doing it all his life.

Recruit Camlin-with-the-five-houses was in Squad Two, and Parsa seemed to take particular delight in ordering around a highborn. When Sgt. Taba took us on "short run" a couple of days later, I overheard Parsa talking to his new subordinate:

"Those berrycakes at chow looked delicious, Camlin. Have one ready for me tonight after lights out."

"You gotta be kidding. There's no way." The dessert table, as Parsa well knew, was not only off limits to recruits — it was on the other end of the chow hall from where we ate.

"I gave you an order, Camlin. Figure it out," Parsa growled. "If all else fails, you can use your dad's name to pull rank."

Camlin didn't respond, but that night when Parsa came back from the showers, there was a berrycake sitting in the middle of his bunk, for everyone to see. He quickly hid it and whispered something to Camlin, I imagine about being a little more sly next time — what if one of the DCs had seen? But Camlin had made his point, and before the lights went out, Parsa was slapping him on the back and sharing a joke with him.

33

Once the shock of our introduction was over, training began to take on a familiar rhythm. A typical day began with a workout — sometimes a run, sometimes stationary exercises, and sometimes training with meels in the arena. When training with meels, they'd move us to a heavier pair at the start of each week.

After our workout it was off to the showers, then morning chow. From morning to midday chow was nonstop drilling. We'd started off drilling on the grass, but as soon as we were issued our full kit, they had us drilling on the central square of flagstones — mopping marble, they called it. Afternoons were a mixture of mopping marble, learning how to use our weapons and gear, and lectures on Raider history, doctrine, and life in the military in general.

The day wasn't over after evening chow. Usually the DCs would follow up that meal with more drilling, but sometimes they'd change it up and take us for weapons practice in the arena.

Of course, the platoons in the other barracks around the drill pad, who were all in various stages of training, also needed time to use the arena, so occasionally we'd be taken off on "conditioning" marches, which were two-day affairs. Not only did we have to load up with all our regular battle kit; we had to haul extra supplies for an overnight camp in the wilderness. We'd have to march for hours at a regular pace no matter what the terrain or the weather — the marches were always timed — and when we finally reached our destination, we couldn't relax because we had to spend even more time setting up camp in a fashion that satisfied the DCs. If they didn't like how we'd set it up, we'd have to tear the whole thing down and do it again. Then it was up early the next day for the long march back to barracks.

On nights when we actually were in the barracks, we had a half-hour of "personal time," before lights out, though it never felt like a half hour, and precious

little of it was spent on "personal" matters. Most of it was spent on studying, practicing, or otherwise getting squared away. Recruit Teryn, whose bunk was right
next to mine, was always busy helping other recruits mend or adjust their clothes.
Sculler had been right about his skill with a needle and thread; the House of Teryn,
it turned out, was a family of tailors.

"The 'house of' stuff is just tradition," he explained. "It used to be your warrior
clan name — for our ice dwarf cousins down in the far south it still is. But our
kind long ago settled into more civilized ways."

Oh, and the cleaning. Cleanliness was starting to become an obsession. If there
was dirt on my boots or a smudge on my armor, I could feel it gnawing away at
me all through the day, and I couldn't wait to get back to the barracks to work on
cleaning it up again. They weren't kidding about developing a love affair with
soap. I started to carry a small chunk of soap around in my pocket in case I got the
opportunity to touch up during the day. I used to love playing in the mud and
getting dirty when I was a little kid; now the thought of getting dirty almost made
me ill. All I could think of was Sgt. Sculler telling me how the great Maj. Braborn
would cry if he could see one of his beloved Raiders so filthy, and how heartless did
I have to be to make the great Maj. Braborn cry?

Sgt. Taba was more direct. "If you like being so damn disgusting, get down
there in the dirt and start pounding out pushups!" he'd scream. He'd insist you
press your face deep into the dirt, to soak up the maximum amount of filth.

Weather provided no relief in our daily routine. If it was raining outside, the
DCs would sometimes sweatbox us — have us seal up the windows and doors of
the bunkroom and work out until the air in the room grew damp.

The first time that happened, I remember the sweat gathered up so thick on the
ceiling that it started falling down on us in drops, like the rain falling outdoors.
Sgt. Taba noted this and said for every drop that fell on Death Row — the strip of
floor in the middle of the room between our bunks, so-called because you would
die if you were caught there without permission when a DC was present — we'd
get one minute of extra free time before lights out. I remember working my body
so hard that I became light-headed and started seeing spots — but it was worth
it, because when we were done, Taba counted out 14 drops of sweat along Death
Row, giving us 14 precious extra minutes at the end of the day.

THERE WERE ONLY TWO sources of relief. The first came every Sevenday — we'd
get an extra hour of sleep and no workout, followed by morning chow, chapel,
then back to the barracks for an hour of mandatory silent reading of The Walk. We
still trained on Sevenday, but they seemed to go easier on us, and later on in the
cycle also got a lot more personal time on that day, too.

They weren't kidding about the mandatory reading part, by the way — the

DCs would patrol the room all during the hour and would give you a good thwack on the back of the head if they caught you sleeping. But they only had to do that a few times — I don't know about other recruits, but speaking just for myself, that hour was one of the highlights of my week.

Funny thing is, they weren't allowed to tell us WHAT to read, just so long as it was from The Walk. Sgt. Sculler warned us they could ask us afterward to name the chapter we'd been reading and then quiz us on it, to make sure we weren't lying — but I never saw that happen. For my part, I needed no threats. I always used the time to read up on stuff that I'd always wondered about. Thanks to my mom, I'd been attending services and mouthing the words of prayers and verses since I was a child. Of course I knew the main stories about how Auld Father had chosen Footman Rom as his first apostle, and how Footman Rom had spent the rest of his life bringing Auld Father's children back to the Path. But much of the rest was lost in the mist of my memory, if it had been there at all. The weekly reading hour was the beginning of my travel back to the Path — or maybe, come to think of it, my first real step onto its sacred soil.

The other source of relief was mail call. After a few days of training, it began to seem like the world outside the Blue Wood had ceased to exist, and that everybody back home had forgotten you even existed. I noticed more quiet sobs at night after lights out — some of which might have come from me.

So the first mail call was like a bolt of lightning — it came without warning; we were back in the barracks after evening chow when Sgt. Sculler emerged from the Cage and announced it with no fanfare, like it was just a normal part of the day.

I don't know how to explain the effect that mail call has on soldiers, but it was the same way from that first time back in training and continuing all through my service. For a lot of guys, getting mail is like the fuel they need to keep their fire going — when they're without it for too long, they start to lose their drive, and then when a letter for them comes in, it's like BOOM — they're back, they're high, they're ready to kick the shit out of every damn thing you put in front of them.

I honestly think that's the only thing that got a lot of us through training. When your thighs are burning from spending an entire morning trying to perfect the movements of the "close-order spears" command, and Sgt. Taba is screaming in your face again because you brought your spear down just a half-tick too slow because you didn't move your body and leg together in one smooth motion LIKE HE'S BEEN SCREAMING AT YOU TO DO FOR THE PAST THREE DAYS — well, then you start to wonder. You wonder why in the name of Gruun the fate of the whole world seems to depend on why you need to lower your spear just a half-tick faster, and why you even signed on for this, and why you should even care about these stupid made-up little rules they make you follow just so you can go up and stand on a little piece of grass they put a little fence around and call the Glorious Field.

But then — that's when a letter comes. That's what pulls you back and, I guess, reminds you that you're not just a lonely "I" being torn apart by the Blue Wood. It's like Sgt. Sculler put it: Every worthwhile thing you'll ever do comes from your connections with others. An individual is just a spark; it's the bonds between us that build the flame. That's what letters do — they're like arteries connecting you to the web you're a part of, and like arteries, they pump blood back into you and give you strength.

To my surprise, my first mail call contained two letters. The first was from my mom. I've still got that letter, and I'm going to copy it down right here, because I think it was the first time I ever felt like I hadn't let my mom down:

"Dear Lash

"I received your first letter from training three days ago, and I wanted to write to you the very second I read it because I knew that the only part from you was your signature."

I had a hazy memory of the first night we were there. I remembered that one of the endless documents they had us sign that first night was a letter home, telling our families we'd arrived. I have no idea what it actually said; it was prewritten in a delicate scribe's hand that looked nothing like my normal jagged scrawl.

"When I saw that, it immediately reminded me of that awful day back in the gaol, when they browbeat you into signing that confession."

That wasn't how I remembered it, of course, but they say every boy is a saint in the eyes of his mother.

"Aunt Twos actually found me crying over it — my tears smudged the ink so much it blotted out the part with the return address, which of course sent me off crying again. But Aunt Twos said there was no reason to worry, because Footman Loze would know where to send it.

"Of course, I rushed over to the chapel immediately, because I was determined to get in touch with you and get in touch with those horrid Raiders too. I thought they were supposed to be building my boy into a man, and here they were forcing him to sign a letter already written, as if he's some kind of prisoner!

"But Footman Loze, praise his sandals, sat with me and talked to me and calmed me down. He said he had a friend of his, a fellow Footman, had served in the Raiders, and he sent me to talk to him. You might remember his friend from your time at the Temple School — he was one of your teachers, Footman Tan."

Oh, you'd better believe I remembered. My ass actually started feeling sore at the mention of his name.

The next part, the first time I read it, I thought it might have been my mom's idea of a joke.

"Well, Footman Tan was so gracious and so polite to me — he wasn't anything like those mean teachers you used to tell me about who used to yell at you and beat you every day at Temple School. He was so kind and understanding when I came to him with my worries about you. I'm sure it probably has to do with that awful scar that runs across his head and face — I'm willing to bet people treat him terribly for that, and that's probably why he's such a gentle person."

If it hadn't been for her mention of his scar, I would have thought my mom was talking about a different Footman Tan.

"Of course, knowing he taught at the Temple School, I immediately asked if he'd ever had you as a student, and I was surprised and overjoyed when he said he had, and that he remembered you. He told me you'd always been one of his favorite students, and that you were really a good boy with a good heart and that Auld Father had suffered Gruun to lay just a few more obstacles on the Path for you than for other boys.

"He said he even shared your taste in literature, and said he'd always found you reading those books about Vast the Brutal — remember those nasty little books I used to scold you for reading? Well, he showed me an entire bookshelf filled with them! He told me they actually weren't bad books, and that they were actually quite clever, because they were filled with important moral lessons, but told in a way that would appeal to young boys. He said that of course he had to take such books away from you when he caught you reading them in class, because they weren't appropriate for Auld Father's house, but that there was nothing wrong with boys reading them when they were out of school.

"His face lit up with a great smile when I told him where you were. Of course I told him of all my worries about you, and I told him about that awful letter, and he said it was nothing to worry about, that it was pre-written simply to save time, because they keep you very busy there during your first few days.

"He told me that a boy like you would have no trouble in the Raiders, and that I'd be overjoyed when I finally saw you.

"Thinking about you, and how this is your first adventure away from home, made me remember how excited I was when I first came to the capital — it must be something like what you're going through! How wonderful you must feel right now!

"Footman Tan asked me to pray with him, and he offered the most beautiful prayer I've ever heard to give you strength and encouragement during your training. I wish I could remember it well enough to write it down."

I chuckled at that, wondering what my mom would think of the prayers they made us recite here in the Blue Wood.

"Before I left, he told me to hold off a few days before writing to you, because for the first couple of weeks you wouldn't even have time to read any letters. But after that, he said, I should write to you as often as I was able, because he said my words would be a blessing to you. I can't imagine your poor old mother's words being a blessing to anybody, but I did as he asked and waited until two Sevendays had passed to write this.

"Lash, I am so proud of you. I was so scared for you at first, and all I could think of was those awful men doing terrible things to my beautiful boy. But if a man like Footman Tan thinks this is what's best for you — well, that is calming to my soul.

"May Auld Father guide your feet,

"Love, Mom"

The second letter I got was an odd one. The address was written in an extravagant but neat hand, and claimed to be from Rupens, my old pal from the Stonegate Clubs. I knew for a fact that Rupens couldn't read, much less write — and definitely not with such a practiced script. I opened it up and read it, puzzled.

The letter inside continued in the same neat, flowery text:

"Hey you Molan bastard this is Rupens. I'm a scribe now, ha ha! Just kidding, I hired that Professor Omi guy from The Dead Scorpion to write this. He didn't want to help me at first but I threatened to knock out those shiny teeth of his and string them around my neck and then he was okay with it and we settled on a price and now he's writing this, which it's all fancy and shit."

In parentheses, Professor Omi had written:

"Your friend has a fascinating style of negotiation, involving drunkenly wrapping his fingers around my neck and squeezing while screaming at me. I am not sure the fellow understands his own strength. He's still quite drunk, so what you read here is a more or less exact transcription of his words."

The letter continued:

"Sorry about the whole shit with Pip, but they were threatening your old boys with three months in the City Gaol, and we figured since you've done served time in that school at the top of the hill it wouldn't be nothing for you to serve three months. Taygor said to me you've been sent off to join the army or some shit and I didn't believe him, so the other day when after I finished giving a bit of the old push pull and pump to this little twat that lives in the rooming house with your mom, I asked her about it and she said yeah it was true and that your mom was all torn up over it. She said she could get me a place to send you a letter at and since I know you like to read I thought I'd give you something on what we've been up to since you've been away.

"Nabbing Pip really raised the stock of the Stonegate Clubs. The night they hustled you off to the City Gaol, Lusseau took the whole gang to Mallee's and rented out the Grand Chamber, where we had a big bash and Pip himself was there sitting on the throne for the guest of honor. Somebody had made up a little Black Star sloucher for him to wear, and at one point Lusseau was standing on the table giving a speech and he stopped and said 'oh, fuck, I've got to piss. Open wide, Pip!' And he whipped out his cock and just started whizzing all over the little bastard. He even tried to strike that little pose Pip has, with both his arms up, except when he did that he had to let go of his cock and his piss went off to the side and landed in Lyco's mug. And you know how Lyco is like, and he was all 'get this shit away from me' and he pushed over the mug as he jumped out of the way to dodge Lusseau's piss. It was the funniest fucking thing I've ever seen. Later after Lyco passed out, we poured a pint of warm ale through that hole in the back of Pip's head so the statue would piss all over Lyco's face, and of course he immediately ran to the washroom to rinse off his face, only to find we'd all pissed in the washbowl. He came stumbling out of the washroom and threw up all over Madam Mallee's new dress. I thought she was going to throw us out until Lusseau flipped her two gold pieces and told her to have a couple of girls give Lyco a bath.

"Of course, it didn't take the Black Stars long to figure out who'd taken Pip, though we probably helped them out a bit with the way we were all walking around acting like the new swinging dicks of the Warrens. After they jumped a couple of our guys on Weaver's Row, Lusseau had us knock over a gin merchant who was paying them for protection. And that's when things got real bad and the Tritons stepped in and made us hand back Pip. Then they set up a warehouse fight between us and the Black Stars to give everybody a chance to burn off any grudge we still had. By Gruun's reamed-out asshole if that wasn't a corker. I lost two teeth and Lyco got his nose broken, but he said it was worth it because he took a chunk out of one Black Star's face with his teeth. He said I should tell you to hurry up and bribe someone at that army camp you're at so you can get out of there already and get back here where you belong.

"Well I gotta hit the bar for another pint and go talk to some of the other guys so I'm gonna say bye now. Stonegate Clubs forever motherfucker!"

Underneath this, there was another note from Professor Omi:

"I know this is no business of mine, but my priestly instincts have not been entirely extinguished, and I feel compelled to offer you a bit of advice: Don't throw your life away by falling back in with these degenerates. I recognized the address your friend gave me — if you're with the Raiders, I think it's fair to say you're looking for something more out of life than anything you'll find here in this dung-heap. As I believe they put it in your religion, stay on that 'Path' and you won't go wrong."

There was no need for him to add that. After what my mom wrote, the letter from Rupens just filled me with shame.

But it wasn't the shame that caused me to keep that letter. It was the fear — the fear that, if I failed in the Raiders, if I failed at the Blue Wood, then that life was all I had to look forward to (after a stint in prison, of course). Drinking and fighting and whoring until I either died early or ended up as another one of those old men stumbling out of the public halls, sleeping in the streets and pissing himself. Oh, if I proved myself as a capable thug, there was the chance I might get called up to join the Tritons — but I knew there was slim chance of that. I was a mean bastard and could hold my own in a fight, but the beating I'd given that old man which had led to me ending up with the Raiders, and the way that made me feel — I think I knew then that I didn't have what it took to make it as a full-fledged gangster. And even if I did, I figured that the price was too high. The Raiders asked a lot, but they didn't ask me to murder my own soul to join them. Toughen it, strengthen it, cleanse it and forge it into something new, yes, but not destroy it.

I put the letter from Rupens down, and realized I felt dirty. Everything around me seemed dirty. I spent the rest of my personal time that night polishing my gear.

34

It was our first time in full pads, and it was the worst day for it — hot and muggy as a demon's bowels. I would have actually preferred to be out drilling, but we were locked up in the arena.

Only Toad — Recruit Evin, who got his nickname because Sgt. Taba took note of his widely-spaced eyes — was outside. He'd tripped and knocked over a bunch of spears, so Sgt. Taba had given him a broom and assigned him to "sweep away the sunlight" so our spears could relax in the shade. This involved running back and forth waving a broom in the air yelling "Go away, sun! Leave our spears alone!" over and over. We could still hear him even with the heavy door of the arena shut tight.

Up until now, we'd been practicing moves, or sparring with dummies. A few of us, including myself, had been picked to serve as human punching bags so DCs could demonstrate particular techniques, but that was the closest we got to an actual live opponent. Now we'd donned unwieldy sparring armor covered with thick cushions. Wearing it actually made me long for my regular armor — I'd been getting accustomed to its weight, and it allowed much more freedom of movement. Though they were lighter, the pads were much more restrictive; every movement had to be firm and deliberate, with little ability to adjust or fine-tune things. I don't know if that was on purpose, or just a lucky accident of the design, but I understood immediately that this would force me to think about each movement and commit — no second-guesses, no take-backs.

It was also — I can't stress this enough — incredibly hot. For the four millionth time since we'd arrived, Sgt. Taba was lecturing us on hydration.

"I've hauled away dead bodies from a battlefield that didn't have a scratch on them — the guys just dropped dead of heat sickness," he said. "It's the dumbest thing in the world. Nobody has ever won a fight because he passed up a drink of water, ladies, so if you feel thirsty, drink. Now you should each have a full canteen;

I want you to grab it and pop the cork and down the entire thing, starting three... two...now!"

Everybody raised their canteen to their lips. After we finished, we turned them upside down above our heads to prove they were empty. Satisfied, Taba paired us up with sparring partners. And wouldn't you know it — I got paired with Parsa.

"I'm gonna enjoy this, you Molan piece of shit," he growled at me as we squared off. I sighed and gripped my wooden practice sword and shield, trying to keep the lessons straight: Ignore his head, keep your eyes focused on your opponent's weapon and his waist — "his torso will tell you where the rest of him is going," as Sgt. Taba had put it.

The whistle blew, and the sparring started.

Ignoring what they'd been trying to teach us, Parsa charged forward like a bull, not even trying to protect himself. Now, that might have worked if he'd been a big, fast, beefy guy like Rupens from back in the Warrens, but Parsa was compact and slow. If it hadn't been for the pads, I could have jumped quickly aside and clotheslined him, but I settled for a short, sharp parry, which allowed me to move in and body check him with my shoulder, knocking him to the ground.

I offered a hand to help him up, but he batted it away and pulled himself back to his feet.

"Look, man," I told him, "I'm sorry for bopping you on the head with my spear at first, but I've got the hang of it now — it's been, what, a week since last time I accidentally hit you? Come on and let's drop it and be pals, alright? Whaddya say?"

He fixed me with a chilly stare.

"We're not friends," he said, and dropped into a defensive stance. I shook my head and prepared to face him.

Five minutes later, I'd knocked him down twice, spun him around and got a kill stroke on his back, and slipped past his defense and gotten a kill stroke on his liver. He was 0 for 5 against me, panting heavily, about to lose his temper. It's not that I was a great swordsman or anything — it's just that Parsa was so overcome with emotion that he tended to signal his moves in advance. He'd be a pushover in a card game like Cooper's Crown.

"Can I show you something?" I asked, thinking I'd give him a little bit of Warrens wisdom to help him out. He looked up at me with quiet rage.

Camlin stepped up and put a hand on his squad leader's shoulder.

"Hey, boss. Mind if I step in? You can switch with me and spar with Recruit Wym over there."

Parsa didn't take his eyes off me.

"Have at it," he said, then shoved Camlin's hand away as he turned to head over to where Recruit Wym was. Sgt. Taba didn't stop us from swapping opponents, so I guess it must have been okay.

I turned to Camlin.

"What's with that guy? Why does he have it out for me?"

Camlin's face was blank as he dropped back into a sparring stance.

"You really think you know what's going on, don't you?" he asked.

I fell back into my own stance.

"Count of three. One, two, three!"

I barely had time to think before I found myself on my back, Camlin's wooden blade at my throat.

"Good one. You caught me off guard," I said, getting up. We lined up again, I counted off, and in no time Camlin's wooden blade was against my throat — though at least now I was still standing.

After showing up Parsa, now it was my turn to lose. Three more bouts, three more quick kill strokes for Camlin. He had barely broken a sweat.

I tried again to be friendly.

"Damn, you're pretty good. You've done this before, haven't you?"

He didn't respond — he simply adopted a sparring stance, ready to go again. Before I could get ready, the screech of Sgt. Taba's whistle pulled my attention away.

"Okay. We're going to change it up a little. Those of you on my left — stay where you are. Those of you on my right — that's those of you over here closest to the west wall, for you turd-tappers who can't tell the difference — put your sparring swords back on the weapons racks and grab a dagger. Yes, I said a dagger. Any day now, come on — they're right there on the bottom of the rack. And everyone will be on the sparring line in three…two…now. Okay, that was…" — Taba waited a beat — "…adequate."

Staring straight at me, with no emotion, Camlin cut loose a huge fart. The room burst into laughter, and even Sgt. Taba smiled.

Camlin's face was a stone mask. I thought I maybe caught the beginning of a smile, but it could have been my imagination.

Sgt. Taba marched up to Camlin and looked up at him.

"Holy GOBLIN NUTS, Camlin, what in the name of Gruun's asshole did you eat?"

I couldn't see Taba's face, but I could tell by his voice he was on the verge of laughter, despite his shouting.

"You just bought the whole platoon a three-mile run after we finish up here. And since it will probably take a week to air out the arena after that, you bought yourself a new name. From now on, Recruit Camlin Of The Five Houses will be known as Recruit Skunk! Auld Father knows there's no way a smell like that could come from the perfumed asshole of a noble. Holy shit, Recruit, and I mean that literally."

Sgt. Taba walked away shaking his head, trying to suppress a smile.

Even armed with nothing but a dagger, my newly-named opponent was a formidable foe, winning the next six matches. Every time I thought I had him, by the time my blade reached the spot where I was aiming, he'd moved somewhere else.

Watching his body for hints of his next movement was useless. I was in the process of losing a seventh match when Sgt. Taba blew a whistle and told us to put our sparring gear away.

I tried to congratulate Skunk, but he just turned his back on me.

Later that night during personal time, I was in front of the washroom mirror shaving. I'd adopted the habit of shaving the night before in order to save time the next morning. That's another thing about training: You're always looking for shortcuts and tricks. If you don't, there's no way you'll make it. I remember Recruit Teryn figured out that the blade of the fighting knives they'd issued us were exactly 6 inches long, which was the precise distance that your bunk was supposed to be from your footlocker, while our canteens were exactly 15 inches long, which is precisely the distance that your bunk was supposed to be from the wall. Up until then, most guys hadn't been paying much attention to Teryn, but after that he picked up the nickname "Professor" — or just "Prof" — and became the go-to guy for anything technical.

Anyway, I was there shaving, and Camlin, or "Skunk," came in and began preparing a washbasin to do the same thing. Thinking maybe he'd cooled off a bit from that afternoon, I tried again to congratulate him.

"Hey man that was some intense shit back in the arena. You were fucking impressive! I think maybe you could teach Sgt. Taba a thing…"

His hands dropped to the washbasin and he stared straight into the mirror and let out a loud, annoyed huff, then turned to me.

"Are you fucking done?"

"Hey man, I'm just trying to…"

"Are you harassing my swordsman, rat?" came a voice from behind me. I wheeled around; it was Parsa coming in from the latrine, still adjusting his belt. He came over and stood on the other side of me, mirroring Skunk's hostile glare. I looked back and forth between the two of them, the highborn noble and the rustic farm boy, united in hatred of the street trash.

"What the fuck are you even doing here?" Parsa asked.

"Fuck you."

"You know you don't belong here, rat. Why keep pretending?"

I got up in Parsa's face, popped my eyes out to flash some crazy. We just looked at each other for several seconds, breathing slowly. My instincts kicked in and I tensed up, ready for any surprise moves. But nothing came.

After a moment, I just whispered: "I'm from the Warrens, motherfucker. I'm the realest motherfucker you've ever seen."

Parsa just smiled, then Skunk gathered up his shaving gear and put his hand on his squad leader's shoulder. Parsa shrugged it off and looked at me for a few breaths more, then he and Skunk turned and left the room. I thought about yelling something as they walked away, but I just went back to shaving.

35

It was either the day after that, or the next, that something bizarre happened, which only made sense much later. After noon chow, Sculler marched us over to one of the stone buildings clustered around the center of base.

The building was long and flat, and had no windows. Unlike most of the other buildings, this one had no signs that might have told you its purpose. It just had a small, plain white sign with black lettering that read: "27-8." If I'd thought about it at all, I probably would have assumed it was a storage building.

Herding us inside, it proved to contain a long hallway with small rooms off to either side, each with a large wooden door, and each one containing a table, chair, a sheet of papers, an inkpot and a pen. At the very end of the hall was a big brass bell. Every recruit was sent to a separate room, closing the door behind him. The walls between rooms were thick enough to prevent any whispered conversations.

"When you hear the bell ring — and not a moment before — you will pick up and look at the sheet of papers in front of you and follow the instructions," Sculler had told us. "When the bell rings a second time — no matter what you are doing — you will stop, put everything down on the desk, and leave the room, and assemble in formation right here, facing north. Finally — and this is very important — once the bell rings and you leave your room, you will not speak to any other recruits about what happened here, including fellow recruits in your platoon. You will not breathe a word of it to anybody at Fort Harrel unless asked about it by a superior. The penalty for this is immediate expulsion from training, and from the Raiders. Is that understood?"

It was. Both Sculler and Taba seemed to be in an unusually grave mood, so it was clear that whatever this was, it was serious.

It sounded like this would be a written test — we'd already had some of those, all covering material in the Hand Book. I had done...well, average, I suppose.

But those tests had been given back at barracks. What was up with this? Were they trying to keep us from cheating? They needn't have bothered. Once Sgt. Scull-er explained the flogging that awaited anybody caught cheating on tests — al-though we'd all seen floggings before, he said, we'd never seen one performed by a trained Raider disciplinary officer — that was all the deterrent we needed.

I was thinking about all of this as I closed the door to my little room and looked down at the sheet of paper on the desk. There were a series of questions written on it. I looked at the first one: "Explain the correct storage procedure for incendiary paste in the following conditions: A. Hot and dry weather. B. Hot and wet weather. C. Cold and dry weather."

So it was another test, I decided. I sat down at the desk and waited. The bell rang, I readied my quill, and picked up the paper...

...and the text changed.

I put down the paper. The text changed back. I picked up the paper again. Once again, the letters on the page melted before my eyes and reformed into something new. The new text read:

"Do not be alarmed. Hold the palm of your hand against this stack of papers for 5 seconds to allow the new letters to set, then continue the examination as you normally would."

I put the paper down, and the message vanished again, replaced by the original questions.

Okay. I thought back to Professor Omi and his card. So this was some kind of magic, I thought.

I placed my palm on the stack of papers. Again, the text changed back. I silently counted to 5, very slowly, then removed my hand. This time, the letters remained. Shaking my head, I picked up my quill again and began the test. It was entirely unlike any test I'd ever seen before.

Many of the questions didn't make any sense. One I remember was, "you are walking through a meadow, and a gnome appears and offers you a flower. A troll emerges from the forest and eats the gnome. What color was the flower?" Anoth-er was, "you have a box filled with stones. You count them, revealing 62 marble stones and 81 onyx stones. If there were any granite stones, which there are not, would there be 5, 22, or some other number?"

Then there were some that weren't even questions, just statements: "There are four bowls, each filled with water. The water is at a different level in each bowl." And...? I think I wrote down that the water was cold. What else was I supposed to do?

Some weren't even text — they were just collections of symbols or numbers. A few of them seemed like they were supposed to be puzzles, but not quite — al-most as if there was a piece missing, which I could almost visualize in my head. I sketched out the image I saw in my head, hoping that might be the right answer.

Then there were pages that were almost completely blank, which I thought at first might be a mistake, but each page was numbered. Some feeling in the back of my skull drove me to write or draw on those pages, too, though I couldn't explain why. I remember I drew a picture of a nesting bird on one of them. That turned out to be a good idea, because a question a few pages later referred back to that page and asked me what color the bird's egg was. Huh? How did it know that's what I'd draw? If I'd drawn something else, would the question have been different?

I still had several pages left when I heard the bell ring. I got up and headed out to form up with the rest of One One Five. On the way, I searched the faces of my fellow recruits, wondering if any of them had an experience anything like mine. If any had, they weren't showing it. Sculler marched us back to the arena and, after an especially brutal workout with meels, gave us the rest of the afternoon in the arena to spar.

36

Parsa and Skunk continued to give me shit over the next several days.
They hid one of my boots one night, making me late for morning inspection on the drill deck. I finally found my boot at the bottom of my footlocker, underneath my spare clothes. I hadn't placed it there — nobody would ever place their boots there; they were supposed to be placed on top of your footlocker, exactly in the middle, toes facing the center of the room. That was exactly how I'd placed them the night before, after I'd spent my "personal time" cleaning them, along with my armor.

I knew it was Parsa and Skunk, and they knew that I knew — Skunk had been on fire watch that night. I made it a point to hide my footlocker key under my mattress after that, so they couldn't pull something like that again.

A fat lot of good it did — bastards somehow managed to unlock my foot locker without using a key.

"Holy fuck, Lips," Sgt. Taba said when I came back from midday chow to find my footlocker sitting outside on the front stoop of the barracks. "You left your footlocker unlocked. Imagine if that footlocker had maps of troop movements. Imagine those maps were stolen because you forgot to lock your footlocker. Lips, your entire unit has now been killed by an enemy ambush!"

I tried, in vain, to stick up for myself.

"Sir, Recruit Pearl clearly remembers locking his footlocker this morning. Recruit Pearl suspects he is the victim of a prank."

Even though I had to look down to see him, the way Sgt. Taba's veins popped up from his skin when he got angry made it feel like I was staring up at a giant.

"Recruit, if you queef another excuse out of your face-cunt I'm going to fuck it with my fist. I don't give a fuck if an army of gnomes crawled in here and unlocked your footlocker. You are responsible for the security of your fuckin' gear, and because YOU failed to UNFUCK YOURSELF, your brother Raiders are paying the price."

He turned to face the rest of the platoon.

"Do you men like being dead because recruit Lips left his footlocker unlocked? I can only speak for myself here, but I think it fucking SUCKS. I think the only cure is a good workout with meels in the arena. Come on ladies, inside, be ready in two minutes — starting now. Oh, Lips — not you. Maybe you should check inside your footlocker. You do have the key, don't you?"

I did, of course, and when I opened it up, it was empty — except for a utility sack, and a note. I recognized the sharp but elegant script as belonging to Sgt. Sculler. It read:

Congratulations, Recruit Pearl. Thanks to your carelessness, you've been selected for an important commando mission: You'll need to retrieve the important Crown property that the enemy has pilfered from your footlocker.

Because this mission will be conducted deep inside enemy territory, you will need to practice stealth and evasion tactics. Using the combat crawl, proceed to the following location...

...which was, I don't remember — I think it might have been the maintenance office. When I got to my assigned location, I had to recite the chain of command backwards, starting from Father General, starting the whole thing over every time I made a mistake. Then, they'd give me one piece of my gear — the utility sack was for me to carry everything — and send me off to another location to fetch the next piece. There were other dumb things too, like how any time an officer came near me I had to stand on one leg and hold my arms out crooked and shout "nothing here but us trees!" in order to demonstrate my "expert camouflage skills."

A couple of junior officers — they couldn't have been much older than me — thought it would be funny to fuck around with me once when I was doing this, holding a long "argument" about "credible reports" of "enemy spies" in the area — all while I was standing on one aching leg, about to fall over.

One got right up in my face: "I'm pretty sure I see an enemy spy over here!"

And the other one was all, "no, look, that's a tree! Look how still it is! If it moves or breathes — then you'll know it's a spy!"

And they stood there waiting for me to make a movement or breathe.

They tried to keep a straight face — until they finally burst out laughing and just walked off.

It was sergeants who were the worst. They'd always pull me aside and smoke me for molehilling — that's what they call having your ass too high in the air when doing a combat crawl.

"Who the fuck are your DCs?" they'd always want to know.

"Sir! This recruit's DCs are Sgt. Taba and Sgt. Sculler!"

"Bullshit, recruit! I ought to see the outline of Sgt. Taba's boot permanently imprinted in your ass by now! Which wet-fart platoon are you with?"

"Sir this recruit is with Platoon One One Five under Sgt. Taba and Sgt. Sculler!"

"By His Foot, recruit, I can't wait to rib them about what dribble-dicks they've got under their command. They're gonna smoke you so fucking hard you'll have to turn yourself inside out."

I didn't finish my "mission" until well after evening chow. Prof managed to smuggle out a few rolls from the chow hall so I wouldn't go hungry.

During personal time that evening, I confronted Parsa.

"Look, man, I don't know what your fucking problem is, but cut it out. For fuck's sake, you guys are getting the shit kicked out of you every time you cause me to fuck up. What do you get out of it, man? What's your fucking angle?"

Parsa, who was lying on his bunk reading The Walk, slowly stood up and got in my face.

"That's all life is to you, isn't it, rat? Angles. That's what you're always looking for, isn't it?"

While I could feel my hands curling into fists, I kept them locked at my sides. "I don't know who you think I am, but I'm pretty sure you've got it figured wrong. I can keep playing these games as long as you can."

"Oh I think I've got you figured out pretty good."

I noticed everybody in the room had gone silent. They were sitting or standing there looking at us, obviously waiting for something to start.

That's when Gorgeous stood up.

"Guys," he said gravely, "before anything happens, I just want to remind you of something."

He paused. When we didn't react, he continued: "I'm serious. Guys, look at me."

We turned to look at him. The whole floor was as silent as a tomb.

"I know how strongly you two feel about this, but I think you need to remember something," he said, then paused again.

"I've just been reading the Raider Hand Book, and Regulation Number 142 says that sexual and romantic relationships between Raiders are expressly forbidden, and even minor expressions of romantic affection like kissing can, in some cases, be grounds for dismissal."

Now, I actually just copied the text of Regulation Number 142 straight from the Raider Hand Book right there, but in real life, I think Gorgeous might have gotten less than halfway through reciting it before the whole room erupted into laughter. I actually don't think he managed to finish before laughing himself. I smiled, and I think Parsa smiled, though I didn't bother to look, because I turned around and went back over to my bunk.

I thought the whole dispute was over.

37

The next morning, when we were rushing out to assemble for drill practice, I went to retrieve my spear. As always, they were lined up leaning against the side of the building in a neat row, all in order.

I grabbed my spear from the spot where I'd placed it the night before, swinging it around while preparing to run to my place on the flagstones of the drill deck to get into formation.

But when I finished swinging it around, I felt a strange springy feeling run along the wooden shaft.

"Look out!" someone yelled. Another — Prof, as it turned out — had the presence of mind to shout the proper words: "Down! Down! Down!"

While it hadn't yet quite become a reflex, our response to that phrase had gotten down to a speed you could measure in eye blinks: Everybody immediately hit the dirt, helmets firmly held against their skulls. As I felt my face slam into the ground, I simultaneously heard a metallic clanging coming from the flagstones of the drill deck.

Sgt. Sculler's boots came thumping down the front steps of the building.

"What in St. Rom's name is going on here?" he bellowed.

We started to look up from our spots along the ground.

"Sir, the tip of Lips' spear just flew off," someone offered. I looked over where I'd tossed my spear on the ground. Sure enough, the long metal tip was gone.

"Okay, you idiots stay put. Where did it land? Is anybody hurt?"

The thin voice of Recruit Wym — his voice matched his stature, as he was the smallest non-dwarf in One One Five — called out, "it landed over next to this recruit, sir. This recruit is unharmed."

"Okay. Anybody else?"

No response.

"Okay. Get up, you mouth-breathers. Get up and come over here to the sand pits, line up, we're going to learn a little…hold up, damn it, hold up, what's gotten into you, Lips?"

In a blind rage, I had gotten up and rushed over to Parsa, ready to give him a good punch in the jaw, when Prof and Gorgeous grabbed me and held me back. Parsa had seen me coming and was ready to deliver a few blows of his own, but Skunk stepped in front of his squad leader, pushing him back. I heard him growl to Parsa, "Not yet. Remember?"

Sgt. Sculler stepped in between us and drew his impressive frame up to its full height, then bellowed in a voice loud enough to start an avalanche, "THAT'S ENOUGH!"

He looked at me, looked at Parsa.

"You two," he said. "I want to see both of you standing at attention outside The Cage in two minutes, starting now."

He hadn't even finished his sentence before we were both sprinting to the building. Behind me, I could hear Sgt. Sculler starting to say something to the rest of One One Five, no doubt giving them some miserable orders to follow while he was gone.

Parsa didn't look at me, or even acknowledge me. He just stood there beside the door to The Cage, staring straight ahead. I did the same, though inside my skull I was nervous and fidgety.

Then I heard Sculler's boots clomping across the room and over to where we stood. He acted like he didn't see us; merely unlocked the door to The Cage and went inside.

From where I was standing, I couldn't see inside, but I could hear him rustling around. I heard furniture scraping against the floor. Then:

"Recruit Pearl, come in."

I went in and stood at attention. Inside, Sarge was sitting at a desk at the far end of the room.

"Sir! Recruit Pearl reporting as ordered!"

"At ease, recruit. Close the door."

I did, then turned around to face Sarge.

The Cage was slightly larger than I expected. To the left was a bed, made up to perfect Raider standards. Above it was a small bookshelf; I didn't dare look long enough to figure out a title.

Further down the right wall were five or six maps. I recognized one as a map of Garlund; it was littered with tiny colored flags, which I guess marked troop positions. The other maps were unfamiliar to me, although one bore the title "FORT HARREL" in large block letters — so I assumed it must have been a map of my then-current home.

Taking up much of the back wall were two large vertical cabinets, much larger than our footlockers. They were both closed and locked, but their function was clear enough from the names affixed to each one: "SCULLER" and "TABA."

To the side, there was a small door, which I later learned concealed a private shower and latrine. At the time, I hadn't even noticed that I never saw the DCs showering, shaving or shitting. They just seemed so damn impressive and intimidating that an exemption from normal grooming and bodily functions seemed natural.

Sgt. Sculler hadn't budged from his desk, hadn't even looked up. He was scratching something into a notebook. Finally, he finished whatever he'd been writing, and closed the book. As he was putting away the pen, without looking at me, he said, "Recruit Pearl, can you explain to me what the fuck is going on between you and Recruit Parsa?"

He then looked directly at me, his expression blank.

"Sir," I said, "Parsa doesn't like m...pardon, sir. Parsa doesn't like this recruit."

Sculler's face spread into his usual wide, pussy-melting grin.

"Well from what I saw out there I'd reckon he doesn't have much reason to. You were about to jump him, weren't you? Isn't that what I saw out there?"

"Yes, sir. But Recruit Parsa...sir, this recruit believes Recruit Parsa sabotaged his spear."

"So Parsa was the one responsible for that disgrace out there just now, is that what you're saying?"

"Sir, this recruit doesn't know exactly — what this recruit means is that he isn't certain Parsa himself performed the sabotage, but he believes Parsa...was responsible."

"You think he ordered one of his squad members to do it?"

"Sir, this recruit does not know."

"I see."

He spread his hands out on his desk, and studied them for a moment. Then he continued.

"Recruit Pearl, do you consider yourself blameless in this matter?"

"Sir, this recruit is not blameless for trying to attack Parsa. That was a clear mistake on the part of this recruit."

"Well I'm glad that I at least don't have to explain that much to you. But what about leading up to that?"

I blinked. Was he trying to suggest I'd brought the harassment on myself?

"Sir, this recruit, um, may have gotten off on the wrong foot with Parsa?"

"Are you asking me or telling me, Pearl?"

I tried again.

"Um, sir. Sir, this recruit believes Recruit Parsa's actions stem from this recruit unintentionally irritating Recruit Parsa."

Sarge raised a finger. "Aha. A spark glimmers in the pupil's eye. I gather from your background that you're a practical fellow, so I'll spare you an academic discussion, and instead I'll just point to that bed over there. You see it? Go ahead, look at it."

I looked at it.

"Good. Now, how many legs does it have?"

"Four, sir."

"Good. It might surprise you to know that we occasionally get recruits who can't even answer that correctly. Now. Would it still be a bed if I cut one of those legs off it?"

"Um," I said. I was about to follow that up with something, but I didn't.

"It's not a trick question, recruit."

I thought about my words, then answered.

"Sir, it would be a bed. But it would be a really shitty bed."

"Yes it would. What if I didn't cut one of the legs off, but Sgt. Taba did. Would that change the outcome?"

"No, sir. It would still be a shitty bed."

Sculler eyed me for a moment; I think he was wondering if I'd understood his point. I thought I did.

"Good. Now, Recruit Pearl, I am going to punish you. There is no way around that; you tried to attack another recruit, which is against our rules. But I am hopeful that this punishment will be educational for you. Because I think you show promise, Recruit Pearl. If we can manage to straighten you out, you might make a halfway decent Raider."

"Yes, sir."

"Okay. Now go get your spear and see to it that the point is securely fastened. We'll discuss your punishment later. Dismissed."

I turned around and reached for the door handle, when I heard: "Oh, and Recruit Pearl? Not that this excuses anything, but if it had been me in your position, I would have given Recruit Parsa a knuckle sandwich."

I waited for a moment to see if he'd add anything, but he didn't, so I left, leaving the door open. I heard him summoning Recruit Parsa as I headed out of the barracks.

I FOUND THE REST of One One Five practicing wounded carry drills in the sand pit: One guy would carry a "wounded" comrade across the sand pit, then the "wounded" guy, having made a miraculous recovery, would carry his now-wounded rescuer back to the other side. It had only been a few minutes, but most of the guys were already caked with sand and looking miserable. After getting my spear together, I went over and joined them. Since the whole thing had been my fault to begin with, I volunteered to pair with Gorgeous, because he was the beefiest guy in the platoon. The others probably would have forced me to pair with him anyway, but I figured I might as well save them the trouble.

My fellow platoonmates not only agreed to my proposal, they graciously allowed me to go to the front of the line. They were kind enough to offer plenty of jeers and curses, to let me know just how much they believed in me.

I couldn't blame them. I would have done the same if I'd been in their boots.

Gorgeous let himself go limp, and I struggled to lift his huge frame onto my shoulders. It turned out to be easier than it looked — maybe all that time lifting those stone spheres and practicing with meels had paid off.

I took a few wobbly steps forward — then collapsed flat on my face as soon as I stepped into the soft, unstable sand. That brought a round of laughs; even Gorgeous, who was supposed to be limp and unconscious, couldn't stifle his laughter.

I pulled myself to my feet. With some effort, I managed to get a stable footing in the sand, and — after several false starts — I managed to pull Gorgeous onto my shoulders.

After a bit of trial and error, I was able to walk through the sand with Gorgeous on my back by crouching. This kept me from falling, but it was incredibly slow, and after a few steps I felt my thighs start to burn.

By the time I reached the halfway point, the laughter had stopped. I was about to give up when I heard someone whisper "good job." That gave me another tiny burst of energy, and I took a couple of more steps. Then I heard: "Come on, Lips. Come on!"

By this point I could feel nothing but hot pain all through my legs. I felt certain I was damaging something; I was going to tear a muscle and be unable to walk and get kicked out of training. But fuck it. I didn't care. If I was going to get sent packing, I was going to let those fuckers know just what a Warrens rat was made of. I owed it to myself. I owed it to the Warrens. I owed it to my mom. I owed it to my King.

I owed it to Auld Father.

A few more steps, and I started to hear whoops and shouts of encouragement. I don't want to make it sound like the whole platoon was cheering me on, but with each step I took, more folks joined in. By the time I reached the end of the sandpit, my vision was going blurry, and it required a surge of willpower just to lift each foot and swing it forward, but I had maybe half of One One Five cheering me on.

I noticed Skunk wasn't among them. He just stood there, arms folded across his chest, watching me. He looked deep in thought.

That was the last thing I remembered seeing, just as my foot finally touched solid ground.

The next thing I knew, my face was being splashed with water. I sputtered, reached up and pushed away the canteen that had been shoved in my face. I blinked. Gorgeous's dopey grin filled up my view.

"Damn, brother. That was tight. You got sea balance, brother. You ever ride a board?"

"What? What the fuck are you talking about?"

"A board, man. Surfboard. You're Molan, aren't you?"

He offered me a hand. I took it, and he pulled me to my feet.

"Yeah. I mean I'm half-Molan," I said, feeling the soreness up and down my legs. "My dad was Molan."

"He ever teach you to ride a board, man? Some people say the Molans invented surfing — even if we perfected it in Lyndan."

I shook my head.

"Never knew my dad," I said. "And we don't have surfing in Solta. The coast is too rocky."

"Shit, dude. That was impressive. I felt sure you weren't going to be able to make the last dozen feet there. But you kept on going. You a motherfuckin' hoss, Lips."

"Thanks, Gorgeous."

"Okay, my turn. You just relax and I'll carry you back across the pit..."

The air was split by a sudden "HUHteeeeeeeen-CHUN!" We all went ramrod straight, as if somebody had yanked us all up by the top of our heads.

It was Sgt. Sculler, who'd returned with Parsa.

"Recruit Skunk! Front and center!"

Skunk loped on over and planted himself in front of the DC.

"Recruit Camlin reporting as ordered, sir!"

"Skunk, Recruit Parsa has been relieved of squadron command. You have been promoted to squad commander. Try not to fuck it up."

"Yes, sir!"

Sculler looked around at the rest of us, caked in sand and sweat.

"You animals look like a pile of puke and a pile of shit had a baby. I want to see you in formation on the drill pad in exactly 30 seconds starting now. Get going!"

I FOUND OUT ABOUT my punishment after evening chow. Sgt. Taba pulled me aside and brought me over to the edge of the forest behind the barracks building. There he showed me a large tree.

"This tree has probably been here for more than 100 years, recruit. It's seen thousands of recruits come through here. But your fuckups caused it to die of a broken heart."

I could see Sgt. Taba trying to hold back a chuckle while he gave this little speech. He clearly found the situation hilarious.

"So thanks to you, recruit, we're going to have to cut down this tree and use it for firewood. And you're going to be the one to do it."

I knew by now that there was a catch. And Sgt. Taba didn't disappoint. He presented me with a rusty fighting knife — identical to the one I wore as part of my gear, but blunt and badly worn with age.

"Here's what you'll use," he said, with the most punchable smile you've ever seen.

"Is this recruit permitted to sharpen it?" I asked.

"You can, if you think that will help. But you'll have to do it on your own time. Right now, you need to start cutting — chopping, whatever. And keep at it until I come back and get you."

"What if the recruit finishes cutting it down before then?"

Taba looked at me, then looked at the tree. The trunk was so wide that if it had been hollow, it could have held two men. He looked back at me. "You'll need that sense of humor, recruit."

I chopped away for at least an hour before that damn klanger came back. I'd managed to hack out a small dent.

Taba looked it over carefully.

"Well, hopefully you can do better than that tomorrow," he finally said.

"Tomorrow?"

"Oh, yes, you'll be at this until you manage to cut all the way through, recruit. And just felling the tree won't be enough, either. I want a full cut. I don't want to see anything here but a flat stump."

"Sir, that will take months."

He looked at the small dent I'd made.

"It will if that's the best you can do each day."

38

"Sir, what is it?"

Sgt. Taba sat with his eyes gleaming in front of the crazy looking set of structures in front of us.

"Recruit, I am glad you asked."

EARLIER THAT DAY, AFTER morning chow, Sgt. Taba had brought us back to barracks and had us stow our battle gear.

"We're going on a quest, boys," he announced brightly. "You booger-lickers know what a quest is, don't you? It will be like in those books for toddlers, the ones about the wandering knight with the blue helmet — what's his name?"

"Sir Chaucy," Prof answered.

"Yes! Sir Chaucy! I'm surprised you didn't answer, Lips. Aren't those about your reading level?"

"Sir, they are if you say so."

"Holy shit, Lips — spoken like a true recruit. We might actually make a Raider out of you yet."

Sgt. Taba started us out on a run, belting out chants as we went along. We tried to keep up as best we could; luckily, he stopped before the strain caused us to slack off, which would have given him another reason to smoke us.

Sgt. Taba might have been a dwarf, but he sure didn't run like one. He could keep pace with all but the fastest humans, and he never seemed to tire — he barely even broke a sweat. By contrast, the other dwarves in One One Five always visibly struggled to keep up during runs, and inevitably one or two of them would end up lagging behind.

This time was no different. Prof and another dwarf, Limul — "Ostral, son of Octin, of the House of Limul" — started to struggle, and then began to fall away from the rest of us.

Limul's squad leader, Blockhead — otherwise known as Recruit Rahlee, a long and lanky human who'd grown up with Limul in southern Selva — shouted over his shoulder, "Hey, Limul, wait until your sister gets a look at me when we get home after this. I'm gonna find out if it's true what they say about klanger titties!"

That did the trick. Limul was the most dwarf-like of our dwarven recruits — he had bright red hair and the classic dwarven berserker temper, which Blockhead loved to toy with. I looked over my shoulder to see an angry, crimson-faced dwarf furiously pumping his arms and legs to get closer to us.

Blockhead saw it too.

"Woo! Look at that little klanger run! Come on klanger, come and kick my ass if you can reach that high! Come on!"

Blockhead easily kept out of Limul's reach, alternately sprinting ahead and then running rings around his angry pursuer.

They'd be friends again in an hour. This was something that had been going on between them for years.

That left Prof still back there, puffing away. Me and Gorgeous fell back to keep pace with him and offer him encouragement — and try to gradually pull him back to the pace of the rest of the group.

"I'm...not...cut out..." he wheezed.

"Neither am I, Prof," I said. "I'm trying to figure out why Taba's so good at this, since he's a dwarf — maybe you can help me out."

"I...wouldn't...know..."

"I think I know," Gorgeous said. "I just can't figure out which farm animal his dad stuffed the ol' wizard's wand into to cause THAT" — he gestured toward the front, where Taba was still effortlessly pounding along — "...to pop out."

Prof coughed out a laugh.

"It...couldn't...be...a...whew..." Professor took a few chestfuls of air and continued: "It...couldn't...be...a...draft...horse...because...he's...still...too...short..."

"That's the spirit, Prof. I'm thinking it must have been a sow. Look at those thighs of his: they're like basted hams."

At that, Gorgeous picked up the pace a bit more, and I matched him. Prof clenched his jaw and pulled even with us.

"No...not...a...sow..." he finally said.

"Really? Maybe a cow, then. Those big old muscle titties of his might as well be udders."

Prof pulled in more chestfuls of air and pulled forward some more. Me and Gorgeous kept alongside him. After a minute, he finally said, "no...Taba's...mom... definitely...an...ass. Nothing...else...that...fucking...stubborn."

Gorgeous let loose a belly laugh, me and Prof joined in, and Gorgeous started moving a little faster. You could see that Prof was proud of getting a laugh out of

Gorgeous, and I think that gave him the spark he needed to match our pace. We caught up with the rest of the group.

I think Prof rode that feeling of pride the rest of the way. Every time his little body started to flag, Gorgeous would get his mind back on track.

"You know," he said at one point, "I never noticed, but Taba's ears do seem a little long." Another time he simply mimicked the braying sounds of a stubborn pack animal.

I don't think any of the rest of us would have made it through training if it hadn't been for Gorgeous.

It was a good thing he kept Prof going that day, because I was noticing that this wasn't some ordinary run. We'd already run past Fort Harrel's main cluster of buildings, past the great statue of Major Braborn, and past the locked gates that led to the Glorious Field.

When we reached the stables, it was the farthest south I'd ever been on the base — and we kept going. We ran past rows and rows of crops, which I later found out were one of the main sources of our food at the chow hall. We then turned west along a well-groomed trail leading into the woods. It looked like we were about to start heading into the Striped Mountain foothills when we abruptly turned north again, crossed a bridge across a small creek, and then came into a clearing, where a jumble of weird wooden constructions stood.

THAT WAS WHERE SOMEONE had asked Sgt. Taba what it was.

"This," he said, pivoting on a heel to look at it all, "is the Blue Wood's obstacle course. These signs..." — he pointed to a wooden arrow painted Raider blue, indicating a gravel path — "...help you to figure out where to go. The objective is quite simple: Follow the path from right here where I'm standing until you cross the finish line, surmounting any and all obstacles that impede your progress."

The obstacles were all built of wood and ropes. From where I was standing, the first few looked fairly easy, but after that things started to look iffy. There was one very tall tower with a small platform at the top; looking at it, I could see no obvious way to get to that platform. Maybe it was just the angle from which I was looking at it.

Taba had us form up by squads, then explained we'd have a staggered start — one squad would go, then five minutes later the next squad would go, then five minutes later the next squad, and so on.

"The squad record for completing the course is 41 minutes, 5 seconds," he said. "With you guys, I'm planning on taking a three-hour nap at the finish."

Since we were Squad Three, we went third. Sgt. Taba blew his whistle and we were off.

The first obstacle was just a simple wall; we had to hoist ourselves over it and keep going. After that was a wooden beam over a mud pit. As our squad commander, Recruit Gorgeous decided to go first. Gorgeous proved to be as nimble as he was handsome — he lost his footing several times while trying to cross. He never actually fell off into the pit, but one time right near the end he came close enough to pull a gasp out of us.

The rest of us made it over with no trouble, and it was on to the next obstacle: We had to climb up rope netting to a high platform, then shimmy down a rope on the other side.

It proved to be harder than it looked, because the rope netting was springy and hung very loose. There was a lot of swaying, and I'll admit that when I got about halfway up, I froze. With encouragement from my squadmates, though, I finally managed to climb the rest of the way. I had to force myself not to look down.

Next came a mess of barbed wire that we had to crawl under. That might have been easy, except part of the crawl also went through a tunnel underneath an earthen berm, so not only were we crawling just inches from sharp barbs, we were in the dark. If that wasn't enough, the tunnel wasn't straight; it took a few turns. Taking point, Recruit Gorgeous had to find the way by feel, then we'd pass the word back through the line until each man had successfully navigated around each bend. It was about as much of a clusterfuck as you'd expect.

When we finally emerged from the tunnel, we found ourselves in front of a tower. It wasn't the really tall one I'd seen earlier, but looking up at this one, the same dilemma presented itself.

Before I could say anything, Gorgeous spoke the exact words that were going through my head.

"How the fuck are we supposed to climb that thing?" he said, scratching his head.

After an awkward moment's pause, Prof spoke: "You guys are pulling my leg now, right?"

We turned to look at him.

Gorgeous: "Pulling your leg? How?"

"You guys really can't get up there?"

Another awkward pause. Then Gorgeous quietly said, "you can?"

Prof looked back and forth, then sighed and ran up to the base of the tower...

...and scampered right up a sheer vertical wall, with no foot- or handholds that I could see.

Even if we'd been able to climb that wall — which we couldn't — that still didn't bring us to the top. There were a set of widely-spaced horizontal bars of some sort sticking out in the air; you'd have to somehow navigate those, then somehow jump across a gap and then maneuver to reach another sheer wall which led to the top.

I watched in amazement as Prof leaped through the air and grabbed the first bar, then flung himself through the air from one bar to the next, like he was a monkey at the Royal Zoo.

When he came to the gap, he swung himself back and forth to build up momentum, then hurled his body across the gap, where his hand caught a teeny-tiny ledge.

"Fuck me," Gorgeous said. "Did you guys know he could do that?"

With perfect calm, Prof hung there from the tiny ledge with one hand, studying his surroundings. He looked down at us.

"Can you guys see a ledge or something?"

I squinted. There was something...yeah, it was another tiny ledge. It was around a sharp corner from where Prof was hanging.

"Yeah, it's around that corner there to your right — you can't see it?"

"No, I'm gonna have to do this blind. I'll need you guys to spot for me. Is it higher or lower than the ledge I'm hanging on now?"

Gorgeous piped up.

"Prof, as your, uh, squad commander, I'm going to have to ask you what the fuck? Are you crazy? There's got to be a, uh, safer way, right?"

Prof looked around some more.

"Not that I can see. Come on, we're wasting time. Is the next ledge higher or lower?"

"Definitely higher," I said.

"How much higher?"

"Um..."

"Is it above my head?"

"Uh...yes."

"By how much?"

"It's hard to judge from here, but...I'd say about a foot?"

Still hanging from just a single hand, Prof took a good look at the corner.

"Okay. About a foot. Would you say it's more than three feet?"

"No, definitely not."

"Okay. Here goes..."

And before we could say anything, that motherfucking klanger just threw himself around the corner and caught hold of the tiny ledge — again with just one hand.

There was another blind handhold where we had to spot for him, then he reached the second sheer wall and once again just zipped right up it like he was some kind of insect.

We cheered as he vaulted onto the platform. He reached down and tossed something over the side — it turned out to be a rope ladder for the rest of us.

WHAT I DIDN'T KNOW, but Prof explained later, was that climbing skill is native to dwarves.

"Our homeland, where our savage cousins still live, is in the mountains and ice of the far south," he said. "It's said that our climbing ability comes from our Tikei blood. They needed it to navigate the caves where they lived deep within the earth."

"Tikei?" I asked.

"Our ancestors, who were the children of Lorm, the god of the dwarves."

"You don't worship Auld Father?"

"Well, I do. My family does. Most of us dwarves who live among the humans are descendants of outcasts from the dwarven homeland, and most of us follow the Path. But we still tell the stories of the old faith, mainly to entertain children."

I was still confused. "But…how can you do that and still follow the Path? Keeping the stories of Gruun's demons alive…isn't that…I don't know. Immoral?"

"Where in The Walk does it say all stories have to be moral? We don't do it because it's moral. We do it because it's *us*. I can still remember my grandfather — who was a regular zealot for Auld Father! — telling me the stories of Lorm when I was barely old enough to walk."

"Barely able to walk — but how was your climbing?" I asked with a smile.

"Oh, I could climb to the ceiling and get around by swinging from one hand-hold to the next while I was still crawling. Like I said, it's in our blood. I mean, you should see the dwarven cities in the far south. They're built around sheer cliff faces or sharp hillsides — in the farthest parts south, near the pole, they're even carved into the ice."

"So why were you so surprised that we couldn't climb that obstacle?"

He shrugged.

"I knew that you guys didn't have our climbing ability, but I guess I never really appreciated just how, well — handicapped you guys really are, when it comes to that. I mean, even with our short legs, we can usually keep up with you guys on foot — we just have to try a little harder. I guess I thought it was the same way with you ogres and climbing."

"Nah, brother." I looked at his arms. "Shit, those meels must be a breeze for you — or pushups! Fuck that must be like, nothing for you guys."

"Correct. I'd been wondering about that, why they keep making us do them. Now I think I see why. That must kill those pussy-ass arms of yours."

"Fuck off. Now I see why they make you klangers do so many damn squats."

WHEN EVERYBODY HAD REACHED the top platform, we found a rope which we could lower down the other side; the rope was connected to a set of pulleys so that when it was lowered, the rope ladder was pulled back up behind us.

As we were about to shimmy down the rope to head to the next obstacle, Squad Four crawled out of the tunnel.

I could see Blockhead, their squad leader, looking up at us with confusion as Limul and the others emerged behind him.

"Hey Lips," he said. "How the fuck do we get up there?"

I smiled and shook my head, and started to turn away, then thought of something. I turned back and shouted, "Hey Blockhead, don't listen to anything Limul says! He's full of shit!"

The rest of the obstacle course was like that — most of the obstacles were set up to test both our muscles and our teamwork.

The only other thing I should mention is what happened when we got to that really tall tower. That one was stacked with puzzles — there was one part where the only way to advance was for Prof to carry each of us on his back.

The last bit, though, was the kicker. After studying it for a moment, we decided we would have to throw Prof across a large gap so he could grab a handhold. If we managed that, Prof would then climb up a sheer wall and lower a set of stairs — we could see them folded up, hanging above our heads — down to allow the rest of us to reach the top.

We were nervous, but Prof insisted he could handle it.

"Just throw me, damn it. With all of you working together, it should be more than enough to get me across there. Shit, a pair of dwarves could hurl me that far easily. Seven of you stick-armed clowns ought to be enough to get it done."

With that kind of encouragement, we lifted the little klanger bastard up.

"On the count of three!" Gorgeous said. "One! Two! Three!"

And with that, Prof went sailing over the side — except with less than full force. Three of us hadn't thrown him. They'd been waiting to toss at the command of "throw," after the count of three, but the others — including me — had thrown on the three.

We only sorted that out later, of course. At that exact moment, Prof was flying through the air with half the momentum he needed, and we rushed to the edge to watch him flailing as he arced downward, down, down, down towards the ground.

"I can't look," Gorgeous said, and turned away, but I watched in cold, frightened silence, certain that I was about to see someone die — a death for which I would be responsible. It felt like the whole world had stopped.

Then, as Prof's body began to near the ground, it slowed. It got slower and slower until he was able to extend his legs and land gently on the ground, as if his fall had been a simple hop.

A man I'd never seen before, wearing an officer's cap, stepped out of the forest and walked over to Prof, and they talked for a moment. We couldn't hear what they were saying, but the man seemed to be making sure Prof was okay.

"Dude," someone said. "That's a fucking battle mage."

"How can you tell?"

"That staff he's carrying — that's a mage's staff."

Gorgeous piped up. He was no longer shielding his eyes in fear. "No, he's right. I can see the markings on his uniform. Not just any battle mage — that's a master wizard."

"No shit? What's he doing here?"

"Probably for something like, well — that. To keep us from killing ourselves."

I looked around at the woods.

"Wow, do you think there are more of them? Are they just hiding out there, watching us?"

Before anybody could answer, Prof came running over to the tower and quickly clambered back up to where we were. Without us weighing him down, he made the whole climb in less than a minute.

When he reached us, he sighed, shook his head in disgust, and said, "you assholes are the worst dwarf tossers I've ever seen."

WHEN WE GOT TO the end of the course, Taba was standing there with Sgt. Sculler. Taba was looking at his watch. Sculler was holding a pen in one hand and had a large open book cradled in his other arm.

"One hour, thirty-seven minutes and 3 seconds," Taba said, without even bothering to look up. Sculler made a notation in the book.

"Congratulations, you animals," Sculler said, not looking up. "That was the second slowest time this week. Maybe next time we can round up a group of crippled street urchins and have you race them, though I wouldn't put my money on you guys."

39

Later that day, we finally got our platoon standard. There was a little ceremony with Lt. Col. Ilos, the guy in charge at Fort Harrel, and then they sent us on our way back to the barracks.

Even though it was a small flag and not particularly fancy, I knew enough about fabrics to know it couldn't have been cheap — I was pretty sure it was made of Lyndan silk. Everybody else seemed properly awed by it, too. Prof himself confided to me later that he got a little misty-eyed while carrying it, and even Gorgeous was unusually reverential when we finally arrived back at barracks.

"Be careful!" he hissed, consulting the Raider Hand Book for proper flag etiquette. "Don't let it touch the ground!"

Auld Father help us, we tried to be solemn, but we couldn't resist whooping and hollering and making a ruckus. Sculler and Taba stood back and didn't intervene.

On the far wall of the bunk room, next to the big clock, there were a set of hooks jutting out of the wall. Most of us had wondered over the previous few weeks what they were for, but without even being told, we now understood. Gorgeous and Parsa hoisted Prof onto their shoulders and carried him to the far end of the bunk room, where he carefully hung our new standard, accompanied by loud cheers.

Suddenly, Toad's voice cut through the noise.

"Sgt. Sculler!" he said, "this recruit would like to make a request!"

"Go ahead, recruit."

"Sir — assuming this recruit's platoonmates are okay with it — this recruit thinks we should do something to mark this occasion."

"What did you have in mind, recruit?"

Everyone grew silent. Toad looked around at the rest of us, took a deep breath, then said:

"Sir...this recruit notices that Death Row is looking a little dry..."

That drew whoops and cheers. Toad continued:

"Sir, this recruit thinks a sweatbox session is in order."

The cheers got louder.

"Sir, this recruit thinks Platoon One One Five could put enough drops on Death Row to earn 20 extra minutes of free time tonight."

The cheers rose to a pitch, and then formed into a chant of "One! One! Five! One! One! Five!" At that moment, we felt like we could have kicked the ever-loving shit out of any platoon in Fort Harrel.

Sculler's face broke out in a wide grin. He turned to Taba.

"Sgt. Taba, let's see what these swingin' dicks are made of."

The whole platoon roared in approval.

They smoked the blood and piss right out of us, but when they finished, Sculler counted off 32 drops of moisture on Death Row.

OF COURSE, 32 EXTRA minutes of personal time for me just meant more time working on the tree I was supposed to be chopping down. That evening, I pulled out my rusty old chopping knife — I'd sharpened it as much as I could, but there was only so much you could do with it — and on my way out, I cruised on over to Parsa's bunk.

Parsa was reading a letter he'd received that afternoon at mail call. He looked up at me as I approached. He tried to look bored, but he was hiding something.

I hadn't had time to speak with him since our tussle from the day before that had led to him losing command of his squad. Thinking maybe a bit of humility would have mellowed him, I decided to try again to smooth things over.

"Hey man," I said. "No hard feelings, brother."

Skunk suddenly stepped in between us. I was forced to step back to give him enough room.

He looked down at me with a firm, serious face.

"You need to speak to one of my squad members, you come to me," he said coldly.

I just turned around and left.

40

After 433 years, the Raiders have learned a thing or two about training, and it was only much later that I realized just how much they've managed to get it down to what I believe Footman Sesh would call "metrical doctrine." I told him that's just a fancy way of saying they know their shit. Anyway, looking back, it makes sense that just as soon as we were starting to feel a little bit like our own gang, they'd put our newfound spirit to the test.

Even though there's actually a pretty strict schedule with Raider training, nobody ever tells the recruits about it, so they never see any of the milestones coming. So when we came up on our next big test, not more than three days after the obstacle course, we had no warning that anything was up. Now when I think back on it, I do seem to recall something different about our DCs — they did seem a little bit edgier, to the extent either of them could be edgy about anything. Maybe Sculler's smile wasn't quite as shiny, and Taba seemed a little bit more pissed off than usual.

The day started out pretty normally. Wake up, shave, shit and shower. Sculler led us on a run, then it was off to morning chow.

Then we headed back to the arena. But instead of a workout or weapons sparring, Sgt. Taba surprised us by inviting anybody who dared to come and fight him.

"No weapons, no pads, and no pulling punches, ladies, I want you to bring everything you've got," he barked.

After nobody else volunteered — we all remembered "A-1 Avor" — Gorgeous gamely looked around and stepped forward.

"Man, you fellas disappoint me," he said, and breaking into a grin, announced, "I'm gonna show you how a REAL man gets his ass kicked."

We whooped and roared in approval, and Gorgeous did indeed show us how he got his ass kicked — though it didn't escape anyone's notice that Taba didn't brutally crush him the way he had the late, unlamented Avor. This was a friendly contest, not a street fight.

After Gorgeous's bravely futile performance, Recruit Blockhead finally sighed and volunteered to face Taba next.

I think everybody was expecting Blockhead to get his ass kicked. But when the fight began, it was surprising to see how fast he was. Blockhead was already one of the better fighters in the platoon, but without pads slowing him down, his movements and reflexes were much sharper, and it was clear Sgt. Taba was having to work a bit to avoid his blows. Maybe all our training really was starting to pay off.

After maybe a minute of sparring, with Blockhead trying to land a hit on Taba and Taba just flicking his little dwarf frame this way and that, dodging his hands and feet, there finally came a time when the DC was just a half-tick too slow.

The sound of meat smacking meat felt like a thunderclap as Blockhead's fist connected with Taba's shoulder, sending the dwarf staggering. Gasps and sounds of "oooooooo" came forth from our platoon.

Blockhead halted for a second, apparently wondering if he'd done something wrong, but that was all the time Sgt. Taba needed to bounce back and take him apart as methodically as he'd done with Gorgeous. But the shock of seeing one of our own manage to lay a hand on Sgt. Taba — who we'd come to think of as invincible — was powerful.

At that point, all eyes turned to Skunk. Whatever else you might say about our resident highborn, it had become clear during our weeks of training that he was downright deadly in the arena. He was good enough that Taba and Sculler often took it upon themselves to spar with him rather than have him waste his time beating the rest of us. How would he fare against Taba in a straight contest, with nothing holding him back? Skunk just smiled and shook his head, and then the spell was broken when another recruit stepped up to volunteer to be the next to get his ass heroically beaten. Again, he made a good showing, but there was no way he was going to beat Taba. Still, the fact that some of us were getting good enough to at least make the little bastard work for it was exhilarating. I reckon that by the time we all headed off to midday chow, we felt like One One Five was the baddest band of motherfuckers that ever strapped on boots.

When we got to midday chow, we saw another group of fresh recruits who'd just come from intake, hauling their buckets and gear. By His Foot, they were so dirty! Did we really look that dirty on our first day? And they were so disorganized, shuffling along with no order or rhythm — nothing like the finely tuned instrument that was Platoon One One Five. A DC was screaming at them that they were the lousiest sacks of shit he'd ever seen in all his time in the Raiders. And at that moment, I thought he was right. I mean, there's no way we ever looked that bad, right?

Boy, were we about to get a lesson in humility.

After midday chow, we went back to the barracks and got geared up in full battle rattle. Nothing unusual about that — we assumed we were looking at another afternoon of endless spear drills.

Sgt. Sculler then appeared, and joined Taba in leading us on a march — taking us *away* from the drill deck and back toward the main buildings at the center of the base. When we got there, we marched west, towards another part of the base I'd never been to before. We marched through a copse of trees and emerged in a clearing with a very large marble-covered drill area, several times the size of our little drill pad back at barracks.

Sculler marched us to the northern end of the drill area and had us turn and halt — though he didn't give the "at ease" command. Instead, he kept us there standing at attention.

We were facing west, and at the other side of the drill area, we could see a small raised platform. There were three officers standing there, along with what I assumed were their assistants. Of the officers, I recognized Lt. Col. Ilos; the other two — a colonel and a no-shit general, with a shiny gold dragon on his hat and everything — I didn't recognize.

"Dude," I heard Gorgeous whisper. "That's a fuckin' general."

"Yeah, I can see."

"What the crap is all this about? It must be important."

Not more than a minute after Sculler had brought us to a halt, another platoon of recruits came marching into the clearing. Once they got close, I recognized them. We all did. We saw them every day at chow, and every Sevenday at chapel.

"It's Platoon Two One Five," Prof muttered.

After they had arrived and been brought to a halt, another minute passed, and Platoon Three One Five came marching in. Once they'd been brought to a halt, Lt. Col Ilos stepped forward on the platform and addressed us.

"Gentlemen! Welcome to Fort Harrel's parade ground. For the past several weeks, your Drill Commanders have been instructing you in the finer points of spear drilling. Now I know many of you probably believe that this is a waste of time in an era of war wizards, steam-powered factories and chemical explosives, but I assure you that it is still quite relevant to the Raiders.

"Every few years, some clever young adjutant presents the Raider Command Staff with a carefully-reasoned proposal for eliminating spear drills from our training curriculum. Every time they bring up the same arguments: The changing nature of war, the pressing need for greater specialized training, the newer and more sophisticated tools of combat.

"And every time that happens, the general in charge of training and doctrine slaps it down. I've personally witnessed Father General Temushi himself dress down a staff officer for submitting such a suggestion. That's because spear drills are not about learning a form of combat — they're about learning a form of thinking, a mindset.

"Today, you gentlemen have the opportunity to demonstrate to us what you have learned so far. We will study you closely, and we will rank you. Those of you ranked first can walk a little taller, and those of you ranked last will have the motivation to work that much harder."

Prof snorted. "Those clowns don't have a fuckin' chance," he said, loud enough that Sculler and Taba had to have heard him. There were lot of "fuck yeahs" and "fuckin' A's" muttered in response. We were clean, mean One-Fifteen. We were tighter than a maiden's cunt.

Our platoon went first, and for the first time since I'd picked up a spear, I thought I finally understood how it all went together. Sculler gave commands, and it was like our bodies were yoked together with steel rods — everybody snapped in at the same time. Every time I made a move, it seemed like I was surrounded by 34 mirrors that exactly matched me. I only noticed two errors: Once I could hear somebody behind me fall slightly out of step for just a moment, but he quickly caught up. Another time I noticed from the corner of my eye that Limul was a hair too slow on the "charge spear" command. But other than that, we seemed better than I could ever remember us being. Once Sculler had steered us back to our starting point, I felt like we had the whole thing sewn up. We'd been about as close to perfect as I could ever imagine. I couldn't stop thinking to myself, "Look at us. Just look at us. We look like Raiders — we look like real Raiders."

We watched our two rival platoons go through their own drill routines. Platoon Two One Five was better than I was expecting, but they still didn't look as put together as we did. One of their guys in particular was always just a little bit too slow, just the tiniest bit out of sync with the others. I squinted to get a good look at him. He had a freckled face and a sad looking excuse for a chin.

I wasn't the only one who noticed.

"That freckled fucker's gonna cost them," I heard Blockhead mutter.

Next up was Three One Five, and they were just awful. Sgt. Taba was standing a few feet off to my side, and even though he was silent, I got the sensation that he was seething. Any second I expected him to go charging out onto the parade field and smack down Three One Five's own sergeant and light into his troops. If our platoon had done such a shitty job, I believe Taba would have made us build him a tower so he could personally throw each of us off it.

"You wanna fuck around and wear a pretty uniform, so go join the hawk cavalry," he'd probably tell us as we went sailing through the air.

Once Three One Five finished, Lt. Col. Ilos and the two other officers briefly went off to one side and conferred among themselves. Then the two senior brass returned to attention, and Ilos stepped forward to announce the result.

After carefully watching all three of our platoons, he said, they'd determined that first place went to...

...Two One Five.

"Bullshit!" Parsa hissed under his breath, and for once I wanted to hug the guy.

Well, I had to admit Two One Five had been pretty good; maybe they looked better than us from a different angle. Then Ilos announced the second place, and it was THREE MOTHERFUCKING ONE MOTHERFUCKING FIVE.

Off to the side, I heard Sgt. Taba's boots scrape as he stiffened. Gorgeous said, loud enough for both Taba and Sculler to hear, "Fuck off!"

"Recruit," Sculler growled. But there was an edge in his voice that wasn't directed at us.

I could believe, just barely, that Two One Five might have seemed better than us. I don't think they *were* better, but I could believe they seemed that way. But there was no way I could believe that about Three One Five. There was no way that was on the level; I don't know if it was a bribe or a favor or what, but I can't believe anybody with functioning eyes thought we were THIRD.

Lt. Col. Ilos puked out some bullshit about how all three platoons had done a great job and he had no doubt we'd continue to make him proud, but I barely listened. We marched back to the barracks feeling glum and defeated.

When we arrived, Platoon One One Three — who occupied the barracks directly across the drill pad from our own — was out admiring themselves in their newly-arrived dress uniforms. They looked like they'd stepped right out of a recruiting mural, and were taking turns posing for each other.

One One Five had weeks to go before we were even measured for our dress blues. And for a brief moment, I wasn't sure I wanted to go on with this. This was bullshit. Everything we'd done, everything we'd worked for seemed like bullshit.

I thought about the tree I was cutting down with my rusty knife. I tried to calculate how much more time I had. There was no way I'd make it in time. I'd probably be held back, recirculated back to a new platoon.

It was all bullshit.

Sgt. Sculler marched us into the barracks and had us line up, as if for inspection. Taba, stone-faced, stood at the back. Sculler paced back and forth for a minute — I guess he was gathering his thoughts. For once, he was not smiling.

Then he pulled up a stool and sat down on it. His grin returned.

"Boys," he said, "at ease. Gather around me here. Let me tell you something about the Raiders — not just the Raiders, the military in general."

We crowded in around him, some sitting on the floor, some plopped down on bunks. I noticed that Skunk continued to stand.

Sculler said, "there's a certain purity to what we do here at the Blue Wood. For many of you, this might be the first time in your lives that you've been judged on the basis of your merit alone — not by how much money you have, who your ancestors were, what you look like, or who your parents know."

I looked over at Skunk. As usual, he betrayed nothing of what he might have been thinking. Sculler went on: "But the thing is, the rest of the world, it's still out there. None of us can escape it. We have to operate in the world. It's part of our mission. And those who leave here wearing Raider Blue are going to find the world after this disappointing in many ways. And sometimes, well — sometimes, despite our best efforts, the disappointing things of the outside world come to us here — right here, on our own sacred soil. It's frustrating, but it's something we have to live with. Look at it as a learning opportunity. It's a taste of what you will have to deal with once you leave this place and are trying to do your job on the battlefield. One of the paradoxes of life is that war is not and never has been a thing of virtue, but a true warrior is the last and best refuge of virtue in the maelstrom of treachery, evil, horror and dishonor we call war — and hopefully, prayerfully in the equally treacherous arena we mistakenly call peace.

"Because ultimately, that's our task in the world — we bring the purity of this place, the purity of our devotion to Auld Father, out into the world, that we might serve as a cleansing force. It is our bodies, our skills and our weapons that win battles, but it is our purity, honor and discipline that win the only battle that matters — the battle to bring Auld Father's peace to all of creation. You will lose battles, but you must never lose that — because that is the force which ultimately redeems the world and makes battle unnecessary. That's what separates the Raiders from all other warriors: We strive ever for victory, but even our defeats are victories, as long as we stay true to ourselves."

He paused, looking at us, seeming to gauge our response. Then he continued.

"But there are defeats suffered on the battlefield, and there are defeats whose cause lies elsewhere. And those are the hardest to deal with. The only way to deal with them is to become even better — to perform so well and achieve such greatness that, with Auld Father's help, the petty things of the outside world are forced to step back and let Auld Father alone determine the victor.

"And in case there's any doubt about it, I just want to say that in the mind of myself and Sgt. Taba, there was only one clear victor out on that parade ground today, and it wasn't Platoon Two One Five."

As we whooped in approval, Sculler stood up, and pointed to the wall where our standard hung proudly.

"That victory medallion belongs on OUR WALL," he bellowed, "and I know that next time, that's where it will be. Can I get an A-MEN?"

"A-MEN!" we roared, and started chanting: "One-Fifteen! One-Fifteen!"

Sculler waved his hands to quiet us.

"I like that spirit. And since I believe you boys won fair and square — and nothing will convince me otherwise — you all get 20 extra minutes personal time tonight."

Even though I knew that just meant more time out back with my tree, I cheered along with everyone else.

Recruit Limul got on the floor and started doing push-ups. Prof turned to me.

"Let's really show them something. Stand on my back!"

I was about to ask him what he meant when he fell to the ground and started doing pushups as well. I immediately stepped onto the dwarf's shoulders. He didn't even break stride, and I actually found myself having to sway to keep my balance. The little bastard was right about that arm strength.

Blockhead went and stood on Limul's shoulders, and then Gorgeous joined me standing on Prof's back. Pretty soon every dwarf in the room was doing pushups with as many guys on his back as he could fit, with us hooting encouragement. We were trying to figure out how to add more weight — the little klangers kept shouting challenges — when a laughing Sgt. Sculler finally stepped in and told us to cut it out.

41

That night after lights out, I got up to visit the latrine. I noticed Prof's bunk was empty.

Toad was on fire watch. On the way back from the latrine I asked him about Prof.

"He's outside. Watching the light show," was the answer.

Of course, we weren't supposed to leave the bunkroom after lights out except to visit the latrine, and while Sgt. Taba (who'd originally laid down that rule) never specified a punishment, I was pretty sure that death would be a preferable fate. That said, none of the doors in the building were locked, and everybody ventured outside at night at least once. Sometimes you just needed a walk in the cool night air to gather your bearings. Sometimes you'd even run into guys from the other platoons in our little quadrant who were doing the same thing; that was always a good way to catch up on gossip and get a sense of what might lay ahead.

I went out that night wondering about this "light show" business. As I made my way outside as quietly as possible, I spied Prof over near the drill deck. Actually, I could smell him before I saw him; he was smoking his pipe. The embers from the burning blackleaf as he took another puff showed me exactly where he was.

"What's a goat-raping klanger like you doing out here at this hour of the night?" I called — mostly to avoid sneaking up and startling him.

"Romancing livestock is more of a human thing, from what I've heard," he retorted.

"Yeah, if you've ever seen a bull, you know where we get it from. Seriously, what's up? Toad said something about a light show."

Prof took another puff, lighting up his face, then gestured south.

"You see it? Look at the part where the treeline meets the sky."

I squinted. "Oh, yeah. Oh! Wow, is that — holy shit, is that a dragon?"

"It's not real. If it were, the whole base would be on high alert now."

I watched for a few more seconds. As my eyes adjusted to the light, I could make it out more clearly.

"How do they fake it?" I finally asked.

Prof took a long drag, and then blew a few smoke rings.

"They use a lot of different things. High sorcerers are quite skilled at illusion spells, of course, but for something like a dragon, well...ever heard of djinn?"

"Of course, but...aren't djinn..."

"Servants of Gruun. Yes, if you believe the legends."

I stiffened. "You don't? I thought you said you kneeled for Auld Father."

Even though I'd never had any strong feelings about religion before, I was starting to feel what Footman Sesh calls "a sense of propriety" about religious stuff. It was seeping into my bones and muscles — Auld Father and the Path just seemed like they were always on the side of right, and whatever was against them was the side of wrong. That didn't mean I was going to clean up my act, but — well, it kept me pointed in the right direction, I suppose.

I guess Prof noticed my reaction; he let out a chuckle.

"Yes, of course I do. But haven't you read The Walk? I see you reading it every Sevenday. There's nothing at all in there about djinn."

I was sure that had to be wrong, and made a note to myself to look it up later.

"So?" I said, trying to sound like I knew what I was talking about. "They trick people, don't they? Doesn't that make them servants of Gruun?"

The glow of the embers in his pipe revealed Prof's smile.

"Maybe so. But 'where the word of Auld Father is silent, the mind will build its own empires.'"

I don't actually know if that was a quote from somewhere, but the way he said it made it sound like it was. I pretended to think it over for moment before I responded:

"Okay. So the Raiders are fine with djinn."

"Oh, I wouldn't say they're fine with them. Just realistic. No sane warrior would deny himself a tool used by his enemy."

"True — but I've never heard of a djinn east of the Striped Mountains. All the stories I've ever heard about them are from Garlund."

"Correct. That is where they are originally from — whatever they are. But numerous specimens have been smuggled east."

"Really? How many? And why doesn't the King use them in this war over in Garlund?"

I looked back over at the not-real dragon in the distance.

"You've been reading too many two-coppers," Prof said. "A djinn has no power to affect the real world. All they have control of is perception — their only way of affecting the world is by manipulating mortals to do their bidding, and they do that by tempting mortal beings through illusion. That's why they can only be handled by a very experienced mage protected by powerful ward spells."

"Okay, so what do they have to do with that dragon? It's just a djinn illusion?"

"Yup. What you're seeing is called 'Terminal Phase.' It's the last stage before graduation. A platoon has to undergo a mock combat operation. The Raider sorcerers use their own illusion spells, but they also use an illusion-working djinn to enhance the realism."

Several bright explosions bloomed up on the horizon, followed a moment later by loud "pops." Then the dragon swooped in, and a massive explosion bulged up from the distant trees — a moment after that, we felt a rumbling boom.

"That was an illusion too?" I asked.

"Most likely."

"So are we going to have to fight a dragon? I mean, an illusion of one?"

"Maybe. Maybe not. I suspect it's different for each group."

"How do you know all this stuff?"

He shrugged.

"Some of it I've read about. Others — well, you hear things, as a dwarf."

"You guys have your own little thing, huh?"

He smiled, and for a second I thought I might have seen his eyes twinkling in the dark. "Humans tend to be more careless about what they say around us. Maybe it's because they don't realize we're there — being so short and all."

"Since you hear stuff: What's the deal with Skunk and Parsa? Why do they hate my guts so much?"

Prof took another puff, and sat thoughtfully for a second. There were more explosions in the distance — smaller this time, followed a moment later by popping noises. The "battle," if that was what you could call it, seemed to be dying down.

"Well, in the first place, you didn't hear this from me. In fact, it would probably be better for everyone if you didn't hear this at all."

"I want to know."

"Understood, and understandable. Speaking just from what I've seen and heard, I don't think it's you, specifically, that they have a problem with. I think it's more what you represent."

"Okay. I can see that with Skunk — he's a spoiled rich kid who doesn't want to be around gutter trash. I'm still confused about Parsa."

"You shouldn't be so hard on Recruit Camlin," Prof said, pointedly using Skunk's real name. "His life hasn't been as great as you probably think."

"Pardon me if I can't quite warm up to a guy who grew up with five houses and an army of servants at his beck and call."

Another smile. "Ah, my overgrown friend, you clearly know nothing of the perfumed world of the nobility."

"You're damn right I don't. If I had that much money…"

"...You'd probably be much like Recruit Camlin's ancestor, Kvan, the Lord of Goldmarch."

"Where have I heard that name...?"

"From the founding of Selva, of course. You did say you attended the Temple School? I assume they made you study that. Kvan was the barbarian chief who rescued King Laelmor, then helped him unite the kingdom. Come now, you're from Solta. If nothing else, you know it from the parade they have every King's Day."

"THAT was Skunk's ancestor? Now you're just fucking with me."

"Not at all. And his family has the documents to prove it."

I suddenly had a lot more questions about Skunk, but before I could get to them, I asked about Parsa.

"Ah. Now that's an interesting one. How much do you know about Parsa?"

"I mean, he's from that place, what did he call it...Caford. They grow oats. His people are farmers."

Prof patted my arm.

"'Were' farmers," he corrected. "There aren't actually that many farmers left, in the conventional sense."

I vaguely knew what he was talking about. "Yeah. It's mostly done with magic these days, right?"

"That's a simplistic way of putting it, but yes. Like everything else, the need for manual labor has been massively reduced. It's...well, you grew up in Solta. Didn't you ever wonder why the King pays for the public halls? Or the public games?"

"Because that's his job, I thought. He's the father of the nation, as Auld Father is the father of all people."

"Yes, but..." Prof stopped, and shook his head. "I can see you don't follow politics."

I shrugged. "Why should I? It's just nobles fighting nobles. It doesn't affect anything where I come from."

"That's not true, but I can see why you would say that. But I'm getting sidetracked. My point is, Parsa is — his family, you see..."

Prof trailed off.

"Yes?" I said, nudging him back to the topic at hand.

"Parsa has lost much."

"Too bad for him. I never had much."

"He lost his father."

"I never knew mine."

"No, I don't think you understand. He LOST his father. Or perhaps you could say his father lost himself."

He looked at me seriously, seeing if I took his meaning. I thought I understood, but I wasn't quite sure.

"An accident...?"

There was a long pause. Then: "That's probably what Parsa would say. If you were to ask him." Pause. "Which you shouldn't."

I thought about that. Then Prof continued: "Anyway, the point is, for both Parsa and Skunk, this — the Raiders — is the end of the line. This is the last chance they'll have to build a life of honor. They resent you because you're a reminder of how far they have fallen. And they also fear that any failure on your part will attach itself to them — or that any failure on their part will associate them with you. They don't intend to blow this chance, and they don't intend to let you blow this chance for them."

I turned that over in my mind.

"I understand. But this is my last chance, too. And if I blow it here, I won't be headed back to a pretty farm village or a gilded mansion. I'm just headed back to the Warrens — or worse." I thought about the suspended sentence hanging over my head. "They might think this is the bottom, but trust me, there's much, much further they could fall. I know."

Prof nodded. "Oh, I'm well aware of that. But you asked about Parsa and Skunk. You need to convince them."

"How? The fuckers won't even talk to me."

"That, my good man, is what we're all here for. I don't know the answer any more than you do. I just know we have to find it if we're ever going to get out of this place."

I looked once more at the horizon. The light show seemed to be dying down.

"I'll see you tomorrow, Prof."

He nodded and took another puff. I headed back to the fourth floor and crawled in my bunk. I fell asleep and tried to summon up a dream of the Molan warrior, but that dream wouldn't come. Instead I just dreamed I was back in the shit-stained streets of the Warrens.

42

The next few days, I was like a block of ice. I focused myself completely on carrying out every order, performing every task as flawlessly as possible.

I did it partly because of what Prof had told me, but partly because I felt Platoon One One Five deserved nothing less.

Now that the drill competition was over, Taba and Sculler began to lay off on the drilling a little; we usually only drilled once a day. Even so, we still carried the platoon standard with us everywhere we went, and it was like a constant reminder that fucking up was not an individual act. You didn't disgrace yourself — you disgraced our standard. And the shame of doing that was much scarier than anything the DCs could scare me with.

As for Parsa and Skunk — I gave them a wide berth. I guess I felt sorry for Parsa, in a way. I wasn't sure how I felt about Skunk, who I'd noticed was beginning to excel at...well, nearly everything. He'd come a long way from the guy who had broken down crying his second day at the Wood.

"Shit, Recruit Skunk," Sgt. Taba said to him at one point after pausing to give Skunk a sudden quiz on trumpet and drum battlefield signals. "You keep that up, maybe you can buck for an officer's shield. Then you won't have to work for a living."

Taba smiled when he said that, obviously proud of his own joke. I would have smiled in response, if it had been me. But Skunk remained a silent enigma.

Parsa, on the other hand, was gradually becoming a royal fuckup.

THE WHOLE THING STARTED with Parsa's shoes. See, way back on our first day, when they were piling all of our gear in our buckets, one of the pieces of gear they issued us was a set of dress shoes to wear during services at the chapel, because obviously they don't want you clomping into the sacred precinct of Auld Father in a pair of filthy sandals or boots.

The thing is, though, one of the first things you learn in the Raiders — I was smoked probably a dozen times my first week for violations — is how to pack your shit.

Your footlocker is supposed to be packed in a very specific way. At the time I thought it was just another damn rule they invented so they'd have an excuse to bust our asses for breaking it, but I eventually learned that the point, like everything else in training, was to get us in the habit of thinking like a Raider. Say if your squad is carrying all their gear on their backs, and you suddenly come under attack, it turns out that it can help to have your gear packed in a certain way.

It's not even just about having all your weapons stashed where they're easy to get to. Depending on what kind of pack you're carrying, what you're facing, and what gear you've got with you, a squad can use their packs to form a barrier, or steps to climb over an obstacle. In the right circumstances you can even use a loaded pack as a weapon. But like I said, at the time it just seemed like another of the endless rules they hit you with every time you turn around.

And on this particular day, for whatever reason, Sgt. Taba decided to do a spot inspection of Parsa's footlocker. They could do that at any time, even when you weren't around — there weren't any secrets in the Raiders. Why Parsa, and why just then, I don't know, though I don't think it was an accident.

Parsa dutifully opened his footlocker, then immediately snapped to attention beside it, not touching anything. As if he knew exactly what to look for, Sculler lifted the gray formal tunic and trousers for Sevenday services out of their normal place, to find that the dress shoes were not there.

Taba slammed the footlocker shut, stepped up on top of it and got as close to Parsa's face as his small stature would allow.

"Recruit, would you mind informing me why your dress shoes are not packed in their proper place in your footlocker?"

"Sir? Um, sir. Sir..."

"Sir. Sir. Sir. You got a stutter, recruit?" Taba's voice was low, but boiling. "Answer the question."

"Sir, this recruit does not know."

"Well, think, recruit. They didn't just walk themselves right the fuck out the fuckin' door. So I assume you put them somewhere."

"Um..."

"'Um?' Is that a place, recruit? Is that where you put your shoes?"

"No, sir."

"Then where are they? Remember your first day here, recruit? What was one of the first things you learned to do with your equipment?"

"Immediately produce any item when it is requested, sir."

"Okay. If I tell you, 'Recruit Parsa, produce your shoes,' can you do that right this second?"

"No, sir."

"What if I give you 10 seconds?"

"Possibly, sir."

"What about five minutes?"

"Yes, sir."

"Five minutes."

Taba turned and stepped off the footlocker and began walking away. "Five minutes. If I give you *five minutes*, you can put your hands on your shoes, which are only so damn important that they're the only thing allowed on your feet when you're in Auld Father's house. Five minutes to put your hands on what just might be the most important piece of equipment you've been issued."

Taba wheeled around, his face twisted in rage. He stormed back to where Parsa stood, jumping up on the footlocker.

"Tell you what, recruit, why don't I give you five *hours*? Why not all fuckin' day? It's not like we've got anything important to do. Recruit Parsa, I do not believe you want to be a Raider. I believe you were just walking down the street one day and you looked over and you saw a Raider coming down the other side of the street with two of the finest pieces of pussy you've ever seen in your life. And I believe you asked yourself, holy fuck, that's two times as much pussy as I've ever had in my life, how do I get that much pussy? And I believe you saw that Raider's uniform and thought if you had those shiny buttons on your chest, you'd have a piece of fine-ass stink glued to each arm just like that Raider. I believe you broke up with your right hand on that day, Recruit Parsa, and I believe you went down to the recruiting office and signed your induction papers with your left hand, because your right hand was too heartbroken to cooperate. I think you're here just to get that uniform, Recruit Parsa, and I think you want that uniform because you think it means you'll be ass-deep in pussy all day long, even though you'll never be ass-deep in pussy, you'll never even be toe-deep in pussy, because you'll never wear that uniform. Do you know why I think that, Recruit Parsa?"

Sgt. Taba was inches from Parsa's face. I expected him to take a deep breath after he finished rapidly spitting out all those words, but he was silent. But that made sense — DCs didn't have hearts; why would they need lungs?

"Sir," Parsa stammered, "c-could you repeat the question?"

"Am I not SPEAKING CLEARLY enough for you, Recruit Parsa?"

"No, sir. I just..."

"RECRUIT PARSA DID YOU JUST SAY 'I?'" Taba wailed. He wheeled around and looked up and down the bunkroom where we were all, nervously, at attention.

"I WANT EVERY SINGLE ONE OF YOU SHITHEELS OUTSIDE IN FORMATION IN TWO MINUTES."

Outside, it was storming, and the rain was coming down in buckets, and at that moment most of us weren't even dressed properly. There was some slight shuffling, as if none of us could really believe…

"THAT MEANS NOW," Taba bellowed, adding "you too, Parsa." The shuffling turned into a scramble.

Back home on the coast, we used to get huge squalls in late summer. But this storm was worse than that. The sky was covered in soot-black clouds, and they were angrily dumping out water that smacked into us in fat, stinging drops. It was like the sky itself was pissed at us on Sgt. Taba's behalf. The thunder and lightning rattled our teeth.

Training in the rain was nothing new, of course, but we'd never been out before in weather like this. In the few seconds it took us to charge out of the building and assume formation, our clothes were thoroughly soaked. Surely Taba wasn't going to have us out in this for very long, I thought. He'll smoke us for a few minutes to make a point, and then call us back inside.

Taba came stomping out, looked us over with disgust, and then marched us over to the Toothpick — the long wooden log we sometimes used for training.

Taba ordered us to lift it up. With a heave-ho, we lifted it onto our shoulders. The bark was both slippery and sharp, making it nearly impossible to grip in the middle of the downpour. I was far from the only one with blood streaming down my wrist as I settled the load onto my shoulder, where it instantly caused a dull pain. The rough bark scratched annoyingly against my ear.

Taba had us start marching. Hauling the toothpick was shitty even in good weather, but in the middle of a howling storm, it was awful. Every sense I had was being simultaneously hammered — my body was cold, wet, and wracked with pain; my eyes struggled to see through the damp gray air, and my ears were filled with screams of Sgt. Taba punctuated every minute or so by a roar of thunder.

"Got yourselves a standard now, and you think it's all easy sailing from now on," Taba snapped. "I see how you clowns just float back and forth to chow, looking proud as a flock of peacocks. I see the way you look at the new platoon, One One Six, when they're out there fucking up their drilling. Like they're not even fit to touch your damn shadows. Well guess what, ladies? You're still recruits, you're still shit, you're still not fit to look down on anyone."

At first, I had no idea where Taba was taking us. All I could focus on was the cold and wet and the throbbing pain in my shoulder. I barely paid attention to where we were headed, taking care only to avoid slipping on the muddy ground.

But our destination was soon unmistakable. Taba was driving us straight towards the statue of Major Braborn that loomed at the center of camp.

If you ever find yourself at the Wood, the statue will probably be the first thing you notice — it was probably the biggest statue I'd ever seen up to that point in my life, and it's supposed to show the Major giving thanks to Auld Father after defeating the last dragon east of the Striped Mountains. He's dressed in old-fashioned looking armor, with his helmet off so you can see his face, and he's in a position of prayer — down on one knee, face turned to the sky, with both arms outstretched as if ready to receive a blessing. His right hand is still clutching his sword, as if he were ready to start swinging it again at a moment's notice. One thing that stands out is his very un-Raider-like full beard and long mane of hair, but apparently that wasn't against regulations 202 years ago.

Anyway, the statue is perched at the top of a steep, steep manmade hill that overlooks the heart of Fort Harrel. Beyond it lie the foothills of the Striped Mountains, forming a dramatic backdrop to Major Braborn's heroic pose.

Sgt. Taba marched us up to the bottom of the long slope that angled sharply up to the summit where the statue was perched, and commanded us to drop the Toothpick.

"Since you're all so eager to stand on the Glorious Field, I'll tell you what," he began. "I'll let you stand there today. No need to go through with any of this training bullshit, since all of you are obviously too good for it. No, you ladies can join the Eternal Band right now!"

He looked at us, apparently understanding our skepticism, and suddenly smiled. Reaching into the pocket on his breast — which I'd imagined was just for show — he pulled out a shiny golden key.

"This," he announced, "is the key that unlocks the Turquoise Gate to the Glorious Field. A copy of this key is presented to every Drill Commander at the Blue Wood.

"Now I'm sure a bunch of big-brained scholars such as yourselves will understand that this key is primarily intended as a symbol. It shows that we, and we alone, are the gatekeepers of the Glorious Field. We, and we alone, determine who walks onto that sacred turf.

"But here's a little fact for you long-beard scholars — I'm speaking figuratively there, that's a concept you beardless long-beard scholars should understand — here's a fact for you: A symbol is only effective inasmuch as it corresponds with the truth."

Footman Sesh tells me that's a "bastardization" — that's the word he used — of a quote from some long-beard named "Elantus," for those of you long-beards who care about that sort of thing. Anyway, Sgt. Taba went on:

"And doubt not that this key I hold in my hand has the power to unlock the gates of the Glorious Field. It is not only fitted to the tumblers of that lock; it also disables the magical spells used to hold the lock fast. It is within my power today — it is within my power at any time of my choosing — to unlock those gates and allow you to pass the grand archway, and administer the Raider's Oath.

"And since you sacks of shit are so eager to stand there, I'm going to make it easy for you. All you have to do is roll the Toothpick up that hill. You can see from here, there's a space right below the statue where this piece of wood should rest comfortably."

Following Sgt. Sculler's gestures, I could clearly see a little flat outcropping next to the toe of Major Braborn's boot. The slope of the hill turned almost vertical near the crest to form the outcropping; getting the Toothpick up there would mean pushing it over that sharp ridge — assuming we could get it that far.

I guess we must have looked kind of dumb just standing there looking up at the Major, so Taba finally butted in with: "Go on. What are you ladies waiting for? Push it up there!"

After an uncomfortable pause, Skunk stepped forward.

"We'll have the best chance if we do it crosswise to the slope — that way, we use every man's full strength. Come on, let's get it in place."

A roar of thunder shuddered earth and sky as we lifted the toothpick and positioned it at the bottom of the slope — as if Auld Father were mocking us. The wind picked up, and the rain, which had been falling in thick raindrops, came at us from the side in a stinging spray.

"Everybody together now, on three," Skunk announced. "One. Two. THREE!"

We shoved our shoulders hard into the side of the wooden beam, and began grinding our feet into the earth. The Toothpick rolled a few feet up the side of the hill.

When we'd first arrived at the Blue Wood, the hillside we were now trying to scale had been awash in wildflowers, as if Auld Father himself had emptied a paint pot all over the side. But the bloom was off the flowers now, and the soles of our boots found only the slick green stalks that had once held them. And by His Foot, were they slick. They would have made poor footing even if they were dry, but soaked with rain, it was like trying to climb through oil. Men kept slipping and falling, but every time they did, they would pick themselves up and press their shoulders anew against the huge slab of wood. The dwarves among us found that their upper limb strength counted for little; though their arms were far more powerful, their legs were only about as strong as a human's, and though they had better balance, their feet slipped on the slick greenery just as much as ours did.

We had managed to push the toothpick about 10 feet up the side of the hill when we finally lost control. I don't know how it happened, but I remember several men to my left suddenly falling, one after the other, and then pumping my legs furiously against the ground as the full weight of the log kept pushing me down, down, down the hill, until I lost my footing and the damn thing knocked me back and rolled right over me. The weight of it chipped a tooth and gashed my face. Blood filled up my mouth and was pouring out of a cut in my cheek. I stood up, spit out the tooth chip, and swallowed a mouthful of blood.

Sgt. Taba glowered at us from underneath his DC hat, the yellow feather hanging limply in the soaking rain.

"And here you ladyboys thought you were something special. You thought you'd accomplished something. Why I bet you bastards felt like the Reckoner himself."

Skunk stood up. He had a massive cut over his eye which was bleeding down the side of his face, and a swelling bruise on his jaw.

"Sgt. Taba, with your permission, One One Five would like to try again."

Taba looked Skunk up and down.

"Recruit Skunk, I don't see a corporal's cross on your collar. Since when are you the leader of this outfit?"

Skunk ignored Taba's mocking tone.

"Sir, this recruit makes no claim to be a leader," Skunk began. "This recruit believes he speaks for all the men" — he emphasized "men" — "in One One Five when he says we are clean and mean and we belong on the Glorious Field. And we can damn well prove it right now."

"Fuck yeah," somebody shouted in response.

Taba looked around, one eyelid cocked.

"That didn't sound…"

Like a sudden crack of lightning, the shouted reply came back in unison: "FUCK YEAH, SIR!"

Taba shook his head and extended his arm.

"By all means, Recruit *Camlin*." He emphasized Skunk's real name with a sneer.

We immediately lifted up the Toothpick — which had rolled some distance away — and carried it over to the base of the hill, where we lined up against it, shoulders pressed hard into the side.

"Okay, men, this time, we need to dig those boots deep into the ground. Don't take a step forward until you've got your other foot lodged as deep and hard in the earth as you can. Get ready. On three!" Skunk's voice sang out, overflowing with confidence. And the confidence was infectious. I felt a surge of determination flow through my body and into my limbs as he shouted, "One! Two! THREE!"

We pressed hard into the craggy bark, and mashed our boots deep into the rain-soaked ground with each step. I didn't even bother to mark our progress; I just focused all my might on finding one deep, firm foothold after another and using it to press forward.

We passed the point where we'd failed the first time — I could tell because the tracks of our previous effort suddenly ended. We kept pressing further, further. I had no idea where we were, but it felt like we were making good progress. I felt sure that within a few minutes, we'd be standing at the crest of the hill, waiting for Sgt. Taba to bow in humility and retrieve the little key from his pocket…

Suddenly, the ground beneath us gave way. It was no use trying to find a foothold; the earth itself was sliding downward. The gashes where we'd plunged our boots into the mud had loosened the earth and caused a mudslide. We were helpless to stop the weight of the Toothpick as it fell back and rolled right over us again. The only saving grace was that the mud was now soft enough that the massive log's weight didn't injure us — it just pushed us down into the wet soil.

When I got up again, I looked up at the hillside. We'd managed to push the toothpick maybe a quarter of the way to the top.

"Pathetic," Taba spat.

We huddled together, covered with mud, bruises and shame. A clap of thunder put a sharp point on our disgrace.

"I shouldn't do this," Taba began, his voice softening somewhat, though the anger and disappointment were still there, "but I'm going to give you boys a heads up." We were back to being "boys," so I guess it wasn't all bad.

"I've got a soft spot for this platoon, if only because you boys have heart. You can't find your own asses with a map and a compass, but you've got heart. Unfortunately, the soldier who's all heart is the one who ends up bleeding to death. The soldiers who win battles are built of iron and ice. Heart is something you leave at home, because you'll need it when you come back. But it has no place on the battlefield.

"Let me tell you why you failed just now. You failed because all of you, you're still an 'I.' Like Recruit Parsa, you still think this whole thing is all about you. Well, look at where that got you. You're here now because Recruit Parsa still thinks he's an 'I,' and you failed to reach the Glorious Field because every one of you still thinks he's an 'I.' Look at Recruit Skunk there, already measuring himself for a lieutenant's uniform."

Skunk was angry, and seemed to shrink in reaction to Taba's comment.

"Sgt. Sculler told you once before that no individual ever accomplished anything — what you accomplish together determines who you are. And what you are now is jack shit.

"If you want to be something more than jack shit — if you want to be a Raider — you'd better stop thinking of yourselves and start thinking of One One Five. That standard hanging on the wall in the bunkroom is who you are, and just having it there isn't what makes you a fucking swinging dick. It's what YOU — you as a group — do that that makes it mean something. Now pick up the Toothpick and start marching it back to barracks. I mean double time, damn it!"

When we got back to the barracks, everybody's footlocker had been opened, and everybody's gear had been tossed about everywhere. Even the beds, mattresses and sheets had been tossed everywhere. Sgt. Sculler stood at the far end of the bunkroom smiling.

We spent the rest of the day getting everything back in order. We didn't even get a break to go to chow — Sculler had bread, soup and water brought from the mess hall, and we had 15 minutes to eat; anything left was dumped in a barrel and carted away to feed the hogs at the fort's farm.

When we finally got everything squared away, we had a few minutes left of personal time before lights out. I grabbed my dull knife and headed out back to keep working on my tree.

43

Before lights out, Sgt. Taba told us to rest up, because the next day would be a "Raider Scramble."

None of us had any idea what a "Raider Scramble" might be, but it sounded exciting. We'd reached a point in training when anything novel was "exciting." I went to bed thinking it might be something like the obstacle course.

You could almost hear the excitement fizzle the next morning when we were standing for inspection when Sgt. Taba came out of The Cage wheeling a large cart stuffed with mops, towels, brushes, soap, solvent, wax — everything you could possibly imagine you'd ever need for cleaning a barracks.

"Welcome to your first battle," Taba announced. "I know you boys are fired up to get your cherries popped. After this you'll probably want to run to the nearest skin sketcher and get a commemorative tattoo."

That damn little klanger thoroughly enjoyed his little speech, full of stupid damn jokes that I'm sure he thought were hilarious, but dropped like a lead anchor among us. Oh, how he smiled while going on about how the dirt and grime had us surrounded, and only a mass frontal assault would be enough to win the day. He made cleaning floors sound like the time the Raiders had stormed the fortress at Zinman's Crossing.

"By the time of evening chow, I fully expect we'll be in a position to dictate the terms of our enemy's surrender," Taba concluded. "We'll have smashed their vanguard and rolled up resistance from one corner of this floor to the other. Because what are Raiders above all else?"

"Clean, sir!" came the reflexive reply. We put some punch in it, even though none of us was feeling particularly fired up.

Taba retreated into The Cage, assuring us that he and Sgt. Sculler would be popping in from time to time to make "strategic adjustments" as the "battle" unfolded.

As soon as the door shut and locked, Recruit Limul stepped forward.

"OK guys, look, I spent eight summers helping my aunt clean houses in the merchants' quarters back in Komat, so here's how we're going to do this..."

I GOT PAIRED UP with Gorgeous to move all the bunks to one side of the room so that the floor could be scrubbed.

"I wonder what kind of wood this is," Gorgeous asked aloud as we hauled one of the bunks to the far end of the room.

"Why? You a carpenter?"

"Of sorts."

"What do you mean?"

And that's where I learned all about Gorgeous's passion for surfing.

He was originally from Lyndan, over on Selva's northeastern coast. His dad was some kind of famous painter — a few guys, including Sgt. Sculler, had actually heard of the man.

But Gorgeous himself had no talent for art, at least of the serious kind. He was good at silly cartoons of the sort you might find scrawled inside a toilet stall — I've still got one he did, titled "One One Five's Cutest Couple," showing a rat and an ogre kissing. The rat, of course, was supposed to be me — because I'm from the Warrens, get it? The ogre was supposed to be Parsa. His stocky, hairy body drew more than one comparison to those monsters.

Gorgeous explained how, growing up as a somewhat rich and very aimless kid along Lyndan's famous coastline, he'd quickly fallen in with the surfer crowd. Despite his father's connections, he'd failed out of one school after another, and then failed at one job after another, all because of his devotion to surfing. Unlike Parsa and Skunk, he didn't seem too weighed down about his past — he just treated the ups and downs of his life as a great adventure.

Though I've read books that say otherwise, Gorgeous insisted that surfing had been invented in Lyndan, because the Song Cedars that grew thick along the coast there furnished the perfect material for creating surfboards — true surfers, he said confidently, knew that no other wood was suitable for riding the waves.

That was what sparked his interest in the wood. It reminded him of the wood they used to make surfboards back in Lyndan.

"The grain isn't quite right, though," he explained. "It's not from a Song Cedar, but I think it might be a related breed."

Gorgeous told me that boot camp was the longest he'd been without a surfboard since he'd first started carrying one around everywhere about the time of his ninth summer.

"Why the Raiders, though?" I asked. "Why not the navy? Wouldn't that be a more natural fit for a surfer?"

"That's what I thought at first, too," he said. "But the more I thought about it, the more I realized if I was ever going to amount to anything, I'd need a clean break from the waves. Surfing, man, it's a life. It's kind of a family. And, well, I knew if I was going to amount to anything my dad could be proud of, I'd need to find another family."

"So you're done with surfing?"

"Shit no! If this whole war business heats up, we might get sent to Garlund! GARLUND, brother! We might even be heading to the northern coast. You know about the beaches there? Best surfing in the world, from what I hear."

We were in the middle of moving one of the bunks. I stopped, which forced him to stop. I looked at him.

"Do you really think they're gonna let you take a surfboard to Garlund?"

"Dude, I'll find a way. And if not — shit, I've heard the trees in Garlund aren't bad for surfboards. And if that's not an option, well..."

He looked down at the bunk.

"I don't reckon the Raiders are going to miss a few of these bunks if they disappear."

He smiled. I smiled back and started moving the bunk again. Something fell out of it.

"Hold up," I said. Gorgeous saw it too — it was a piece of folded-up paper. It was sitting on the ground right next to my foot. I looked at Gorgeous, he nodded, and we set the bunk down. I picked up the paper, unfolded it, and read it.

"So what's it say?" Gorgeous asked.

I re-folded it and stuffed it in my pocket.

"Let's finish this first."

SGT. TABA EMERGED FROM The Cage right before midday chow to inspect our progress. He stalked back and forth between the bunkroom and the washroom several times. I sneaked a few glances at him, but his face was empty of any sign of feeling. Finally he ordered everyone to stop, and marched us over to the arena for chow — again, trucked out to our barracks from the mess hall. It was sandwiches and water — but Taba shocked us by giving us a FULL HOUR for lunch. And we didn't have to sit stiff and silent like we were in the mess hall. He explicitly told us we were "at liberty" for the entire hour — "because you're gonna need it," he added, with a hint of a grin.

I found a spot at the back of the arena that had some privacy and pulled out the note I'd stashed in my pocket. The reason I'd put it there was because of the first two words I saw when I unfolded it: "Dear Gralen."

"Gralen" was Parsa's first name.

I'd been butting heads with Parsa from the moment I'd arrived. Here was a chance to get inside his head. "To understand your enemy's thoughts is to see the path to victory," Vast the Brutal once said.

I unfolded the letter and read. Later I made my own copy, so instead of trying to explain it in my own words, I'll just put it down here exactly as it was written:

Dear Gralen,

I have just finished reading your last letter, and after some brief reflection, here is my response: No. If you return to Caford without bearing the blue of the Raiders, what choice do I have?

Oh, Gralen. Dear one! Honesty forces me to confess that your honeyed words are singularly moving. That gentle soul of yours, wrapped in such a plain and honest figure, is what originally stirred my affections and won you my hand.

But however pleasing your words may be to my soul, they are but dry and empty air to my body. Should Auld Father grant me children, are my breasts to nurse them with the milk of your poetry? When winter comes, is my naked flesh to be warmed with the praise of a well-turned verse?

I know from our tumblings in the grove last winter that you are fully a male, and as a male, I am sure you know far more than I that these treasures of mine are not to be surrendered lightly. As delightful as it was to sport with that eager wand, a woman must stake her future on something more than a firm hilt and soft sighs. You above all should know that, from the stories that are still told about your family.

You need not beseech me with your lamentations about the cruel winds that have blown through our corner of the kingdom. Well I know them, for half or more of my male relations are now permanently ensconced at the local public hall, spending their days in a wine goblet only to stumble home with cakes and meats for their families to enjoy while they sleep it off before going forth again. Your finely-spun expressions of grief could scarcely make more of an impression on me than the pools of vomit I have had to clean up or the crying children I have had to help soothe.

My friendship and goodwill I give to you freely, but for the bonds of matrimony and the pleasures of intimacy I must regrettably assign a price. If, as you say, you still retain the honor of your blood in spite of the present diminution of your family name, then I expect you shall be able to pay it. I am not wise in the ways of men; as a woman, I can only advise you to call upon whatever inner resources have carried you this far to see you through to the conclusion of this "crucible," as you call it.

With warmest regards,

Dessa

I closed the letter and thought hard about that. Even though the problems Parsa was having weren't something I had any experience with, I realized I could put together something from the jumble of feelings in my own skull that made me feel something like what he was feeling.

I thought back to Kanin, the rich girl I'd known back in Solta. She'd managed to stir something in me that had made me wish for something more — something that, in my case, seemed well out of my reach. But thinking of her, and the beautiful warm illusion I'd felt just being close to her, was enough to make me understand why my mom still wore her wedding band.

But Parsa, it appeared, was on the verge of winning his dream girl, of achieving what to me was only a distant mirage. And now he was watching it slip away — unless he could make it out of the Wood.

I was still thinking about it when Sgt. Taba re-emerged from wherever he went to relax by torturing orphans and told us to form up. I carefully folded up the note and put it back in my pocket, not sure if I should give it back to Parsa or not. That's when I noticed that Taba was dressed in full battle armor.

I jogged over and took my place in formation.

Sgt. Taba had discouraging news. It seemed that while we'd been resting and recuperating, there had been a terrible setback. The tide of the battle had turned, and our only hope was in a last, desperate assault. He told us to gear up for battle, and then meet him back out front in 15 minutes "starting NOW, two, three…"

Before he got to four we were on our way. We didn't have to go very far: We found all our footlockers and gear neatly stacked up just outside the arena. No wonder he'd given us a long lunch.

Once we were strapped up, Sgt. Taba had us gather in a circle around the sand pit. He had used his sword to draw a crude map in the sand of the barracks layout. He used rocks as markers to lay out the "plan of attack," with each squad being instructed to "clear and secure" its zone. Squad Three of Platoon One One Five of the Recruit Training Battalion was assigned the crucial task of clearing the washroom.

And yes, we had to do it all in full battle rattle.

I have to give Taba credit: Not once did he tip his hand or display the slightest indication that he was anything but completely serious about all this. He even gave a little speech about how he didn't expect to meet us all on the other side, and he wasn't sure he'd be there himself, but he knew we would all fight valiantly to the last man. I almost expected to see a tear in his fucking eye. The little klanger could have had a second career as a stage-monger in some traveling theater troupe.

It probably goes without saying that we arrived at the barracks to discover that Sgt. Taba had undone all our work, and then some. Mud — where did he get mud, and where did he get so much of it? — had been splattered everywhere. This was no ordinary mud, either; it was some gooey, sticky shit that was impossible to clean up. I later overheard Taba bragging to some other DCs about his "special recipe."

Damn klangers.

A little while later I was standing there in full armor, polishing the inside of a copper wash basin when I looked over to see Gorgeous standing motionless, looking into the bowl at the end of the row.

"Hey chief, you see something in there?" I asked.

"Just my dignity."

"What?"

He suddenly looked up at me, as if waking up from a trance, and waved me over. Sitting in the bowl was a truly enormous log of shit.

"Fuck! You think Taba did that?"

"I don't see how. It's nearly as long as he is tall."

He looked at me with dead seriousness. "You think we should maybe go check on him? I mean he might be hurt...you know, after that..."

He nodded down at the turd.

We both tried to remain stone-faced for as long as possible, but Gorgeous finally burst out laughing, and I joined in.

"By His Foot, the smell!" I said. "What the hell does that muscle-headed bastard eat?"

"Something vile, no doubt." He looked down again at the turd. "You know, I thought I was going to come here and learn to kill people. And now...this."

"Chief," I said, clapping him on the back, "I've already learned to kill. I'll kill as many fuckers as they want if it means I'll never have to come back here."

ABOUT THE TIME WE would have gone to evening chow, Sgt. Sculler appeared, along with a team of mess workers hauling a cauldron of stew and a sack of bread. Taba had pulled a vanishing act.

Sculler had us all gather around him while we gulped down our meals. He didn't eat anything himself; he just sat there sipping what I guess was tea from a little cup that he had perched on a saucer he was carrying around.

"How are you boys enjoying your first Raider Scramble?" he began.

A chorus of groans greeted him. He just flashed his pearly teeth, then took another sip.

"Yeah, Sgt. Taba can get a bit into it, can't he? But there's a serious point to all this, and it's not just to keep you looking sharp and snappy. Recruit Rahlee, how many Raiders died in the sacking of Ophur?"

Raider History wasn't Blockhead's strong point, but Prof had been tutoring him for the past week during personal time. After a pause he said, "Sir, about 300."

"Three hundred twenty-seven, to be precise," Sculler said. "And do you know how many died in the occupation afterward?"

"Sir?"

"The 11th Raider Regiment occupied the fortress for four months after the sacking. Do you know how many died during the occupation?"

Blockhead stood there for several moments, looking uncomfortable. Beads of sweat began to appear on his forehead.

"That's okay, Recruit. You're not supposed to know; it's not in the Raider Hand Book. But the correct answer is 1,101. They died because a plague broke out during the occupation and could not be controlled, all because of lax sanitation procedures. With over half the regiment dead, the fortress had to be abandoned. Which led to many other bad things."

Blockhead scratched his head and asked the question that was going through my head.

"Sir, what does sanitation have to do with plague?"

Sculler looked thoughtful.

"We're not really sure. I've heard doctors of medicine say that it's because of vapors or fumes emitted by the dirt, but I prefer the explanation of the Footmen: It's Auld Father's way of expressing his displeasure with us for defiling our dwellings. To lie down in dirt and filth is to be no better than a wild beast, and Auld Father clearly placed his children above the beasts. When we lower ourselves to the level of animals, Auld Father uses his powers to chastise us."

That, I have to admit, made sense. It would explain why the Warrens was such a miserable place — looking back, it actually makes me kind of sick to think of how nasty the place was, what with everybody pissing and shitting in the street and never even catching whiff of a bar of soap. Some of the people who lived there were not much different than animals, actually — by His Foot, hadn't I been little more than an animal when I was running with a gang?

"But whatever the cause," Sculler continued, "we know from long experience that clean soldiers are healthy soldiers. A Raider who isn't snapping the bones and slitting the throats of the enemy is not doing his job, and he can't do his job when he's laid up in a sick bed. The point, for any of you who haven't figured it out, is that if you think the only enemies you face are clothed in flesh and carrying a sword and shield, you better wise the fuck up or get the fuck out of my Raiders.

"And that, boys, is why you stay clean. You live clean. This was your first Raider Scramble, but it will not be your last. Get used to them, because they are every bit as important as a battle. In our eyes, a Scramble IS a battle. Because to be a Raider is to be what?"

"CLEAN, SIR!" came the shouted reply.

"If you've got dirt under your fingernails, are you clean?"

"NO, SIR!"

"If you've got mud all over your armor, are you clean?"

"NO, SIR!"

"If you don't wipe your ass after you take a shit, are you clean?"

"NO, SIR!"

"Good. Any questions?"

Limul spoke up.

"Are we done, sir? With the...the Scramble?" His eyes flicked over to the massive clock on the wall.

Sculler, catching the movement, smiled and took another sip of his tea.

"You know, I could tell you boys what I think, tell you exactly when, or if, I think you're done. Or I could tell you to tell me when you think you're done, and smoke you if I think you fall short.

"But you know what? I'm not going to let you know either way."

He held out his cup and saucer, and one of the mess workers, who I'd forgotten were even there, suddenly appeared to take it from his hand.

"See, the thing is, you won't always have a DC to hold your hand and tell you if you're doing it right. A lot of times you will be the only man on the scene, and the only one who can judge if the job has been done." He began walking over to The Cage.

"I'm going to turn in for the night," he said. "You boys decide if you're done, or when you're done. You decide if you'd do better than those men at Ophul. When you think Auld Father would approve, you can go ahead and hit the sack."

He went inside and closed the door, and the mess workers collected up our bowls and spoons and left. We looked at the clock on the wall. We had an hour and a half until what would have been lights out.

It was impossible to look at that clock without seeing our standard hanging on the wall next to it. Finally, Skunk stepped forward.

"Let's get back to work," he said.

A little more than four hours later, we climbed into bed.

44

I should probably mention that our training wasn't all about fighting and getting smoked until we could barely move. There were also etiquette lessons.

I know, okay? For all the jokes about us recruits being "girls" who would be
better off in a "finishing school," the Raiders run their own honest-to-Auld Father
finishing school. The official explanation is about something called the "ethos" of
the Raiders, but I think Sgt. Sculler's explanation was better: "If any of you sad
pukes ever get to meet the King, you need to at least be able to fake being someone
the Raiders can be proud of. You carry the weight of 433 years of Raider swinging
dicks, and if you embarrass us, the spirits of all dead Raiders will be so fucking
pissed off they'll spend the rest of your life butt-fucking your soul."

THAT, OF COURSE, WASN'T how Mrs. Gern explained things.

Mrs. Gern was the wife of General Gern, who was the commander of the Blue
Wood, and she was the one who taught etiquette classes. Classes were held in the
main hall at HQ every Sixday, following midday chow.

Mrs. Gern was a tall, thin woman who wore her long gray hair pulled tightly back and piled extravagantly atop her head. She looked far too hard-edged to
have come from noble blood — it was clear from her face and hands that she'd
done plenty of real work in her time — but despite that, she carried herself with
the kind of grace and firmness you'd see in a royal. Her clothes were modest but
looked as crisply put together as any DC's uniform. She spoke with a highborn
accent, but again, you could tell it wasn't natural for her — you could hear her
putting a bit of effort to get the pronunciation just right, like a stage actor.

For some reason, Sgt. Sculler and Taba never accompanied us to etiquette lessons
— though if you thought you could get away with farting around, you learned
quick that anything you did found its way back to the ears of the DCs. And let's just

say, one punishing session with meels was all it took to keep that from happening again.

Not that the threat of punishment was necessary — I actually think there were some guys who were more frightened of Mrs. Gern than they were of the DCs. She was that intimidating.

"A Raider is not called to be skilled in arms alone," she told us. "In ages past, the great knights were both masters of the arts of war and masters of the arts of peace."

It was interesting, I thought, that she said "in ages past." As far as I knew, we still had "knights" — though truth be told, the only "knights" I'd ever seen were mostly ancient, white-haired men who marched in the King's Day parade. But the way Mrs. Gern said it, I took it to mean that we Raiders were the ones who were supposed to be filling the boots of these "knights" of the past. I guess that was kind of flattering, but I also thought that if anybody came at me with some bullshit about taking a vow of chastity, they could take that and stuff it right up their ass.

Mrs. Gern never said anything to us about chastity, though she might well have, given her elaborate instructions on how we were to treat "ladies." There was a correct way to greet a lady, a correct way to address a lady, a correct way to take her hand, a correct way to walk with her, even — Auld Father's mercy — a correct way to dance with one.

Yes, our "etiquette" classes included dancing lessons. I could only imagine what Lyco would say, watching me play-act as if I were at some royal fuck-knows-what, pretending Recruit Toad was Lady Ice-Cunt of so-and-so. I had to go through the whole routine of bowing, taking "her" hand (if offered), proposing a dance, leading "her" out to the dance floor, and leading "her" through a dance. Then we switched roles, and I would get to play the "lady."

During the dancing lessons, a small group of musicians in crisp Raider formal dress provided the music. Even though it was the kind of dainty music you'd think would only be played by poofters, all of the musicians were built like ogres. The guy playing the cello looked like he could crush my skull with his fist. They didn't speak a word, and responded only to commands from Mrs. Gern; they acted like the rest of us didn't exist.

I don't know how you long-beards feel about all this, but I can tell you that normal people are probably pissing their pants laughing when imagining how this all looked. I'd laugh, too, if I hadn't had to go through with it. It would have felt good to laugh about it at the time, but as I said, it was made clear to us that anyone who didn't take the whole thing stone-serious was signing his own death warrant.

As for Mrs. Gern, she was no more impressed with anything we did than Sgt. Sculler or Sgt. Taba were.

"An officer would be drummed out of the Raiders for such disgraceful footwork," she told one recruit after a minuet. "But for an enlisted man, it is..." She paused, then rolled her eyes. "...sufficient. I *suppose*."

The only person who seemed to mildly impress her was Skunk, who had of course been taking etiquette classes his whole life in one or another of his family's houses. But even he didn't quite rise to her standards.

"Recruit...Camlin, did you say?" she said, studying the form of his bow. "You are of the House of Camlin, I believe?"

"Indeed, my lady," he said, speaking with a stiff formal tone as if it were second nature. He drew himself up proudly. "This recruit's father is the Duke of Cercel."

The old woman looked him up and down, clearly unimpressed.

"You have sisters, I believe?"

"Yes, my lady. Three of them."

"Good. There's hope for the nobility yet," she said, as she shook her head and walked away.

If Mrs. Gern had ever been told that there are people who think the point of dancing is to have an excuse to feel a girl up, or who think that dancing is supposed to be a prelude to fucking, she gave no hint of it. She made formal events sound like dreary chores, about as exciting as a Winter Solstice service. If this was what life for a highborn was like, I wanted no part of it.

The dull sense of duty seemed to extend to anything that a normal person might enjoy — such as eating, for example. Not that we got to eat in Mrs. Gern's class — we just sat there with empty plates while we heard all about the mouth-watering dishes we *might* be served if we ever got to attend a formal event, which I reckoned would be "never," for me. There was a bit of excitement on the day Mrs. Gern informed us we'd be learning about wine and spirits — followed by the crushing news that we wouldn't actually be permitted to *drink* any.

I knew about table manners, of course — my mother had sent me off to bed more than a few times when I'd been acting up at the common room dinner table back at the rooming house. I was good enough with the basics that I didn't raise eyebrows among my classmates at the Temple School.

I had some inkling that there was more to it than that, though, if you went to something like a fancy dinner at the Palace, but I had no idea there were so many rules — or so many utensils. I couldn't get over the fact that there were four different types of forks, or that they had different types of cups and glasses for different drinks. It all seemed so pointless to me. And one day I made the mistake of saying so out loud.

"You have a problem, Recruit Pearl?" Mrs. Gern said when she overheard my grumbling. She was at the far end of the table, but her hearing was better than a DC's. The woman could have heard a cat tip-toeing on silk from a mile away.

There was no point in denying it. I held up the knife I was holding.

"Mrs. Gern, this recruit doesn't understand. This knife here seems like it's just fine on its own. It's sharp and it cuts well. Why does this recruit need a separate knife for fish?"

She replied, "why, in the course of a military engagement, does one choose a sword rather than a longbow, or a billhook rather than a mace?"

That was a good point, I thought — different tools for different jobs. Still, we weren't talking about the intricacies of killing a man who was actively trying to kill you. We were talking about dinner. I mustered up my courage.

"This recruit understands the lady's point, but..."

Mrs. Gern looked at me calmly, as if she knew what I was trying to say, which I didn't. Damn it. How would Footman Tan have put it?

"...this recruit...doesn't quite see the analogy."

Analogy! That was a good Footman Tan word if I'd ever heard one!

"Elaborate, if you will," she said.

I sighed. "Well, the weapons a man uses are usually matched to his skills, and the type of fighting he does. This..." — I indicated the table setting — "...just seems complicated for the sake of being complicated. Why this way and not another way? Why not just use one knife, one fork, one spoon? Whatever good comes from having a slightly different design for a dessert spoon seems...small."

I looked at my plate and imagined a dessert sitting there. If one had suddenly appeared just then, I wouldn't have bothered with a spoon. I would have stuffed it into my mouth with just my hands.

"That," she said, "is your error, Recruit Pearl. You are attempting to use reason for a realm where reason has no purchase."

Huh? Did she just say what she thought she said?

Figuring there was no way I could possibly dig myself any deeper, I pressed on.

"Is...is the lady saying that table etiquette is not reasonable? That it...doesn't make any sense?"

I heard a few murmurs from my fellow recruits. Someone kicked me under the table. But Mrs. Gern simply smiled.

"No, Recruit Pearl, I said nothing of the sort. I simply said reason does not apply here. Etiquette is a matter of tradition, not reason. It may have its origins in reason — it is said that the tradition of placing knives on the right side of the plate harkens back to more primitive times, when a warrior might need his knife at the ready in case of an attack — that assumes, of course, that all warriors are right-handed.

"Tradition may or may not be reasonable — but that is not why we follow it. No worthwhile tradition remains static; every good custom should remain amenable to reform. But the habits of the past are not handed down to us to make our lives easier. Recruit Camlin," — she turned suddenly to Skunk — "you should be able to answer this, assuming noble upbringing has taught you anything. What benefit do men derive from manners?"

Skunk responded instantly, as if the words had been burned into him by habit: "Manners serve to elevate us, my lady."

"But your are of noble blood, Recruit Camlin. You are already elevated. What use are manners to one such as you?"

Again, Skunk rattled off a perfect answer, barely stopping to think: "Manners are not the property of the nobility, my lady. They are the rightful estate of every good servant of our blessed King."

Mrs. Gern nodded, then turned to me.

"The purpose of etiquette, Recruit Pearl, is not to burden you with useless rules about which knife to use. The purpose is to civilize you; nay, to fashion you into an exemplar of Auld Father's people.

"A civilization is built on rules — it is built on 'no,'" she continued. "'No' is the beginning of civilization, because only a civilized man — a controlled man, a thinking man, a man in full possession of his powers — has the ability to say it. Creatures such as goblins, or some lesser humans, which cannot say 'no,' cannot build a civilization. Do you know what we call a man who lacks the ability to say 'no,' Recruit Pearl?"

"A savage?" I offered.

"Close, but not exactly. We call such a man a 'slave.'"

She let that word hang there in the air for a moment. Slavery had been outlawed in our kingdom for more than a hundred years.

"Yes, I said 'slave,'" she continued. "Do not think we do not still have them. Whether a man is a slave to another man or a slave to some passion inside of him, the result is the same: He becomes little more than a brutish beast. And any civilization which loses the power to say 'no' will descend into barbarism."

Mrs. Gern stood up. Because she hadn't excused herself, we all stood up with her. It was automatic at this point.

She looked over us sternly. "In war, 'yes' is the cry of defeat. It is the white flag: 'yes, I will accept your terms, I will do as you say.' The crown of victory goes to the last man to say 'no.' And a Raider should be able to say 'no' much harder than any other man."

45

One day I was talking with a few of the guys outside the chapel after Sevenday services — they were asking me about the Palace, which they'd only seen in pictures. I was about to tell them about the time I met the King when a recruit from another platoon approached me.

"You're from Solta?"

"Yeah," I said, looking him up and down. I'd seen him around; he was in one of the platoons in our section of the camp — one of the ones that was several weeks ahead of us in training. "You too?"

"Yep. Which part?"

I paused. "The Warrens," I said.

"No shit? Me too. I think I recognize you. You're from the eastside, aren't you?"

"Yeah."

"I'm westside. Which gang did you roll with?"

I stiffened. Did I come all the way to the Blue Wood just to get in a damn Warrens scrap?

"Stonegate Clubs," I finally said.

"Burnhouse Butchers," he said, flashing their gang sign. "I don't think we ever had much friction with you guys, but I heard about you. They said you were pretty hardcore."

I instinctively slipped on my fuck-you Clubs face, the look that says to folks, "come on and try it, motherfucker."

"Maybe," I said. I noticed the guys I'd been talking with suddenly looked tense. They'd never seen this side of me.

The newcomer put on a face to match mine, and stepped up to me. I tensed up, waiting for him to take a swing.

Then he suddenly broke out in a broad smile.

"Motherfucker," he said, slapping me on the shoulder. "Can you believe we used to fight over shit like that? Come here, man..."

He gave me a bear hug, which I very tentatively returned.

"I'm Fent," he said.

"Lash," I said, shaking his hand. "One One Four?"

"One One Three."

"Oh, shit. You guys only have — what, three more weeks?"

"Yep. In a few days we head out for field exercises."

"Man, we've got a ways to go to get where you are. You got any advice?"

"Oh, yeah. In about three weeks, I think, they'll march you out to the lake for sparring day. Remember the drill trials against the other platoons?"

I looked at the One One Five guys I'd just been talking to. They frowned. I looked back at Fent.

"Yeah."

"Same thing, except it'll be one-on-one, hand-to-hand, like in the arena."

"Dummy weapons?"

"Yeah. Except it won't be with normal sparring pads. The padding you'll wear is lighter, supposed to move and feel more like normal battle armor."

I nodded. "We'll be fighting guys from another platoon?" I wanted to fight someone from Two One Five; I had a score to settle with those shitbirds.

"They'll mix things up; some of you will fight guys from one platoon, some will fight guys from the other platoon. They'll have judges watching every fight."

Little Recruit Wym piped up: "Do they separate you into weight classes?"

Fent laughed. "By Gruun! No, they don't use weight classes! There's no weight classes in battle! Everything's pure luck of the draw!"

Wym shuddered.

"So how do they determine the winner?"

"At the end of the day the judges will put their heads together and, based on total performance of the whole platoon, they'll pick one for third place. The two remaining platoons face off in a three-round tag-team match."

I'd seen tag-team matches in the pits over in the Improvement District back in Solta, but that was usually teams of three, maybe four guys at most.

"You can tag anybody?" I asked.

"Anybody in your platoon, yeah."

"Good to know."

The next day, we were sparring in the arena. Usually Taba had the reins when we were in the arena — it had finally dawned on us that this was something like Taba's specialty. But today, Taba was nowhere to be seen; instead, Sgt. Sculler was strutting silently in and out between the different matchups, his hands folded behind his back, and his usual smile looking strangely subdued. Unlike Taba, he stayed mostly silent, not stopping to make adjustments or offer critiques.

He's sizing us up, I realized. *He wants to see if we're ready for sparring day.*

I couldn't read his expression, tell if he was disappointed or pleased. He just seemed to be thinking.

Well there's not much we can do at this point, I thought to myself. *We've either got this or we don't. All we can do is try to make sure we're sharp for the...*

I looked over at Parsa. He'd just gotten his ass kicked by Blockhead, and Skunk was trying again to teach him how to block and pivot to a new stance. He'd been going at it all morning.

I could see the problem, even if Skunk couldn't. Parsa moved like a wrestler — watching him, I suspected he had a fair bit of experience with it. Skunk was an incredible swordsman, but the style of swordfighting he was trying to teach Parsa was something closer to dancing. Parsa didn't have the finesse or agility for it.

I strode over and patted Skunk on the shoulder. He wheeled around and fixed me with an evil glare.

"Look," I said. "Can we just put the whole grudge aside for a moment? You've heard sparring day is coming up?"

"So?"

"So we want to win, right? Let me teach Parsa."

The glare got worse.

"You can't be serious."

"Hey, look, everybody knows you're the best fighter in the platoon." He seemed to soften a bit at that, so I went on. "You're great, nobody wants to take that away from you. But Parsa is never gonna learn this..." — I almost said *shit*, but caught myself — "...*complicated style* you're trying to teach him. Maybe if you had a year or so, he could figure it out, but we've got maybe a week or two. So let me teach him."

"What makes you think you'd be better?"

"Let's just say you pick up a few things down in the toilet district of Solta. I can teach him...let's call them 'shortcuts.' He won't be anybody's idea of a master swordsman, but he'll be able to hold his own."

Skunk seemed to turn the idea over in his mind for a moment. He looked over at Parsa.

"You okay with that?" he asked.

Parsa didn't look okay with it, but he, too, seemed to give it some thought. He tried to look hardened, but he couldn't hide the look of defeat in his eyes. Finally, he shrugged.

"Sure."

Skunk took me aside. Leaning in and speaking in a low voice to keep from being overheard, he growled, "I don't fucking like you, but that doesn't mean I don't recognize there's a use for guys like you. You're a tough motherfucker, and in some ways you've grown on me...don't give me that look. We are not fucking pals."

I didn't know I had a "look," but I did my best to put it away.

"Like I said, I recognize what you've got. So I'm letting you handle him. But you'd better fucking deliver. Or else."

I had no idea what the "or else" was, and I doubted Skunk was in any position to be handing out "elses" — but then again, he *did* come from nobility. They had levers and strings to pull that the rest of us could barely conceive of. But then again, I was about as low as they come in Selva. How much worse off could I be than I was before I came here?

I got up in Skunk's face, gave him the dead-eyed look I'd give a rival gang member.

"I can handle it," I said.

I walked over to Parsa. "So you gonna teach me to paint my face and do one of your tribal war dances?" he asked. Fucker had some balls, trying to grief me about my Molan blood.

"Good," I said. "Different time and place, you'd be swallowing your own teeth for talking like that to me, but that shows me you've got an attitude and you're fearless. We can do something with that."

"Yeah? What are you gonna..."

I sucker punched him in the ribs between his pads before he could finish. To his credit, he didn't go down. Instead, he dropped into a wrestler's crouch and tried to bring me to the ground, but I pushed him away with the tip of my dummy sword.

"You can take pain, too. Good, good."

He straightened up, rubbing his side and eyeing me warily. I could read his eyes. He was looking for an opportunity to strike when I was distracted.

I made a scolding motion with my sword.

"You could try, and you might even manage to lay a hand on me. But I'll make sure you pay for it."

He hesitated. "Look, if this is some kind of...if you're just..." He trailed off, and didn't finish the sentence. Instead, he fixed me with an angry, defeated look, then turned and started to stalk away.

"Hey," I said. I walked after him, and laid a hand on his shoulder.

I knew what was coming next, but it still caught me by surprise. He pivoted off one foot and threw his whole body into me, and I was instantly on the floor, face down, fighting to get up. But he had me pinned solid.

Flecks of spit flew out of his mouth as he screamed in my ear. I couldn't see his face, but I'm sure if I could it would have been redder than a sporting girl's cunt at the end of the night on payday.

"What the fuck is it? What the fuck is it?" he yelled, and the pain in his voice was clear as a bell. "You're just playing fucking games with me? Who the fuck do you think I am? Who are you to fuck with me, you rat-shit scaleback?"

A chorus of "ooooooohs" swelled up around the room. "Rat-shit" was bad enough, but the last time anybody had called me "scaleback," he'd been left with a limp and his eye had been swollen shut for a week. If there hadn't been witnesses...

Out of the corner of my eye, I could see everyone gathering in a circle around me and Parsa. From somewhere in the back of the room, I heard Sgt. Sculler: "You ladyboys need me to pull you apart before you start kissing?"

Parsa let me go, jumped up and stared at me. He had about 12 different emotions running across his face, none of them good. I couldn't tell if he was going to cry or rip my throat out.

I wondered for a second if I should tip my hand, let him know I had some idea of what he was going through.

But I quickly decided against it. I pulled myself up, and I could feel every eye in the arena on me. They all knew what "scaleback" meant, and they were clearly expecting me to take some payback out of Parsa's ass.

I took a deep breath. *This isn't The Warrens, Lash. It's not about you,* I told myself. And where had living by the code of The Warrens ever gotten me?

I smiled, and tried to make it look genuine.

"It's alright," I said. I looked over at Sgt. Sculler. "It's okay, sir. This recruit was... testing Recruit Parsa. And Recruit Parsa passed."

Sculler just nodded. I got the feeling he knew what I was doing better than I did.

I walked up to Parsa, who was still eyeing me like a cornered fighting dog. I held up my palms — easy there, fella.

"I'm not going to trick you, man. I swear. I'm just trying to get those Raider Blues, same as you, so I can get out of this place. I think I can help you. Remember, if one of us fails, we all fail. Right?"

"Right."

"And I don't want to fail. Do you?"

He looked like he was thinking — probably going over in his head again the consequences of failure.

"No."

"Good, now come over here," I said, leading him off to a relatively quiet corner.

"Oh, and one more thing," I said over my shoulder. "You ever call me 'scaleback' again I'm gonna put my foot so far up your ass I'll be able to use your guts as galoshes."

MOST OF WHAT I showed Parsa involved adapting his wrestling instincts to fighting with a sword. He might not be able to pull off lots of fancy blade work like Skunk could, but as I knew from long experience from brawling back in the Warrens, a weapon was only as useful as the hand holding it.

Knowing that, I counseled him to take the fight close in, make sure the other guy didn't have much opportunity to swing his weapon. In a real fight with real blades, that would be dangerous — but then again, in a real fight, we'd be wearing armor.

And we wouldn't be using real blades on sparring day. Sure, you lost points every time your opponent landed a blow, so theoretically, Parsa could lose a fight on points. But I'd also been in enough brawls to know that fights aren't really won based on theory, or "points," and I suspected the judges would know that, too. Not that this made things any easier — even a dummy wooden blade can be plenty scary when someone's swinging one at you in anger, and even with pads, it's no fun to get hit with one. But Parsa was tough, and I knew from how he'd pinned me that once he got inside the other guy's blade — once he got up close — he'd be formidable.

"Just focus everything on taking the other guy's weapons out of the fight," I told him. "Once you've got control, that's when you use your blade to finish him. Sure, you'll take some blows from his sword. It will hurt, and they'll hit you pretty hard on points. But if you end it, that won't matter."

It took him a few days, but by the end of that week, he was able to match me. A few more days and he could beat me every single time.

I knew, of course, that most of what I showed him would be useless against a sword master like Skunk — but there weren't many of those among Raider recruits, and I was gambling on the likelihood Parsa wouldn't have to face one. Just get through training — that was the goal. For now, if he was good enough to beat me, I figured he was good enough to hold his own against whoever they threw against him. If he wanted to go toe-to-toe with someone like Skunk, he could work on that in his own time.

46

We noticed, of course, that the DCs had been giving us extra time in the arena; we took that as proof that fight day was nearly upon us.

And we were ready. The next Sevenday in chapel, we walked a little taller, moved a little sharper. We couldn't help but size up our competition in Two One Five and Three One Five. We wondered if they knew what was coming up — if they knew what kind of grinder they were about to be fed into when they faced us.

All through the invocation and the reading of The Walk, I was mentally running through my combat exercises. I was debating who I should spar with later when I noticed Footman Glaine ascending the pulpit.

Wait a minute — Footman Glaine? That was my first clue something was up. He was the Footman Magnus for the Blue Wood. He'd been the one who'd given the sermon to us our first day here, though I'd barely seen him since. I didn't even know his name until our third week of training, when for some reason he'd shown up at the chow hall to lead prayers.

On this day, he began by telling us about time — about how we thought it belonged to us, but all the time we had was really a grant from Auld Father.

"Just like the quartermaster issues you your gear, Auld Father issues each one of us an allotment of time in this life. And just like you are expected to use your gear to mold yourself into a Raider, Auld Father expects you to use your time to better serve him by continuing to ascend the Path, and to help others in their own ascent," Glaine said.

"Now, as recruits, I know you gentlemen are probably more aware than most that your time is not your own," he said, smiling. That brought chuckles from the assembly.

He continued: "But just as you have submitted yourself to the discipline of higher masters, so must your masters submit to a higher discipline. And so must their own masters, even up to and including our King. For time does not belong to any mortal man; it is solely the servant and instrument of Auld Father. The man who claims dominion over it rejects the loving hand of our Patriarch."

This was beginning to sound familiar. I noticed some of the other recruits around me paying closer attention than normal, as if they knew where this was going. I thought back to my years in Temple School, trying to remember where I'd heard this before.

"This evening at sundown marks the beginning of Vernet — that dark time when our blessed Father slept, and could not hear his children's cries," Glaine said.

Ah, I thought. *That was it.* I remembered it from Temple School — I knew it was somewhere around this time of year, but my thoughts had been focused so much on whatever torment the DCs had placed in front of me that I hadn't had time to think it might be coming up.

Not that I knew much about it — Footman Tan would probably have killed me twice for this, but all I knew about Vernet was that it was three days when the Temple School — the whole Temple complex, actually — was completely closed, and the streets in some parts of the city were quieter for some reason. All it meant to me was three days where I didn't have to worry about the Footmen lecturers coming after me with their leather straps.

"The holy labors which you gentlemen are engaged in do not exempt you from putting those labors aside during this period — indeed, as Auld Father's sword in this world, it could be said you have a special obligation to submit yourselves to this most solemn ordinance."

"Accordingly, after your evening meal tonight, you will return to your barracks and find your Vernet robes. Beginning at midnight tonight, you will mark the Three Days of Darkness. I advise you to take this seriously, because the Raiders certainly take it seriously, even during wartime."

"Why? Because war is a passing thing, like a snowstorm. The Path is eternal. Do we cease our journey on the Path simply because we are caught in a blizzard? Are we excused from our duty merely because it is inconvenient? Does a Raider run from a battle merely because to march forward exposes him to danger? Even a cowardly man can summon up the courage to face death if you give him a shield and a sword. How much more courageous, then, is the man who faces it on his knees, his arms open in prayer."

"We do this, not just in memory of the Three Days of Darkness, but to reaffirm that a Raider serves a cause higher than the petty feuds of men; a Raider is consecrated to the service of Auld Father. And when His service requires it, we will put the affairs of men aside."

The rest of that day was normal, if more quiet than usual. Taba and Sculler mostly laid off us. A lot of guys read mail, or wrote letters. I spent a healthy part of the afternoon working on my tree.

When we came back to barracks after evening chow, we each found a dark gray cloak folded up on our bunks. Sgt. Sculler commanded us to strip off everything — even underclothes — and don our cloaks.

The cloaks were made of rough fabric, and though clean, they looked worn. We looked like a band of beggars at the city gates. Sculler had us gather around him and sit on the floor.

His customary grin gone, he looked back and forth at our ragged group, like some cold-hearted judge.

"Recruit Parsa," he finally said, "can you stand and refresh our memories about the Three Days of Darkness?"

Parsa, of course, was by far the most religious among us; that was almost surely why Sgt. Sculler had called on him. He stood up, closed his eyes for a moment and drew in a deep breath, then exhaled. He opened his eyes and looked at us.

"As Footman Rom tells us in Chapter Two of The Walk, 'during man's infancy, Auld Father still dwelt among his children, giving them gentle guidance and instruction from his own blessed mouth. And it was in those days that at each sunset, he would return to the summit of Mount Cord to rest, coming down from his summit each morning to spend his waking hours with his beloved progeny.

"'But it came to pass that one night, Auld Father's eternal foe, Gruun, slew the bluebird whose song awoke Auld Father from his rest at the dawn of each day. And as the new day dawned, Auld Father did not awaken, and did not descend from the mountain to dwell among his children.

"'And cut free from Auld Father's discipline, his children fell prey to Gruun, and the manifold snares he had unleashed into the world to torment and destroy Auld Father's beloved creations: Hatred, fear, anger, greed, lust, murder, and all the other cancers which consume the hearts of men.

"'And so it was that for three days and three nights Auld Father slumbered, cut off from his creation, unable either to comfort or chastise his beloved young. And on the fourth day, he awakened, and descended the mountain to find a horror of desecration.

"'For behold, under the cruel sway of Gruun's whispered seductions, the people had fallen upon each other in a debauchery of violence, shedding the blood of their brothers until the streams and brooks of the forests were cloaked in scarlet. And out of every 100 people who had been alive on earth, 99 lay slain at the foot of Mount Cord.

"'But those who were not slain, and who yet drew breath, had fled from Gruun's evil bewitchment to a dark cave at the foot of the Holy Mountain. And it was there that Auld Father found them, huddled together in darkness — naked, cold and afraid. In their anguish, they had prayed for three days and three nights for their loving Father to rescue them; and for three days and three nights, only silence and darkness answered.

"'And it was with these, his most faithful children, that Auld Father resolved to raise his people up from childhood, so that they could learn to walk straight, with hearts locked fast against the enchanting horrors of Gruun. And thus he established the Path, that all who seek him could one day join him in maturity atop His Holy Mountain.'"

Sgt. Sculler nodded in approval, and Parsa resumed his seat on the ground.

"And that," Sculler began, "is what we will commemorate with Vernet. Now I know that some of you probably mark this occasion back home, but the way Raiders do it is a bit different…"

AFTER SGT. SCULLER HAD explained everything, he gave us the rest of the evening off. A few guys talked or read, but most of us just checked and rechecked our equipment and bunk areas to make sure everything was flawless. Even though the DCs would supposedly be taking part in Vernet, we'd all developed a healthy Raider paranoia about being caught unprepared. What if Sgt. Taba had to come back to the barracks for some reason, and found the folds on somebody's bunk weren't perfectly crisp? Three whole days would give that klanger way too much time to dream up some diabolically clever punishment; nobody wanted to give him an excuse.

Then, at midnight came the silence. For the next three days, speech was forbidden.

We collected up the only items we were permitted to take with us. Along with the robes we wore, we could take our canteens (both main and backup), our swords (because a Raider should always be armed, even when he's at peace) and our copies of The Walk.

Oh, and soap, of course. As many bars as we wanted to carry. Auld Father forbid any Raiders ever be caught without soap.

But no food. That was the other thing about how Raiders marked Vernet — we'd be fasting the whole time. Back home in the Warrens, my mother had occasionally made us fast during holy days, but I'd never taken it seriously and had always found a way to sneak some food without her knowing — or perhaps she did know it, now that I think about it. But that wouldn't cut it here. This time, I'd have to endure the real thing for three whole days — the better to remind us of the privation Auld Father's children had suffered.

As soon as we'd collected our things and were standing at attention, as if on cue, Sculler and Taba emerged from The Cage dressed in their own robes. I had an urge to snicker when I first saw them, but I managed to hold it back. Still, seeing them looking as wretched as the rest of us was amusing.

Maintaining silence, they led us out to the front of the building, where a group of ox-trolleys had been drawn up. Along with the other two platoons in our building, we queued up and took seats aboard the trolleys. Once everybody was in place, the DCs exchanged hand signals with the drovers, and the ox-trolleys heaved off.

Our own little group soon joined a procession of trolleys winding their way through the camp toward the mountains. We made our way past the statue of Major Braborn — the steep, slick slopes leading up to it seemed to mock us as we passed by. All around the camp proper, men were setting up small shelters — the traditional way Raiders marked Vernet. But since we were recruits marking our first Vernet, Sgt. Sculler told us they had something unique planned for us.

We went around the rim of Fort Harrel's main pasture lands, through a thick copse of trees toward a sheer face of rock that loomed up over us. For several minutes, it was confusing — the caravan seemed to be plodding slowly towards that huge stand of rock. But as we drew within a bowshot of the base, the path took a sharp turn to the left, then down a small slope and around a gentle bend that followed a large, tumbling stream. We came up another hill and emerged into a canyon almost perfectly hidden among the folds of the rocks of the Striped Mountains.

The floor of the canyon was wide enough for many small meadows and stands of trees, and it seemed to slope on and upward for several miles; if I strained my neck, I could see a slope far in the distance where the floor seemed to narrow and then jut sharply up, becoming lost in a forest that swaddled the lower reaches of a massive, snow-capped peak.

Yet despite its generous size, the canyon was still small and well-hidden enough that it would have been nearly impossible to locate until you literally stumbled into it. I found out later that it was in fact the beginning of the High Anvil Pass — one of the five "great" passes across the Striped Mountains. I know that's probably nothing new to you long-beards, but up until then, I was only dimly aware that it had once been possible to cross the Striped Mountains on foot.

The canyon itself was awe-inspiring. The rocky sides rose up sharply, like the walls of an enormous fortress. Here and there I saw what looked like dark spots in the walls. Were those…holes? In some parts they were bunched together in a way that sort of resembled a honeycomb.

I realized then that these must be the "cells" Sgt. Sculler had told us about earlier. He hadn't given us a detailed explanation — he'd just said we'd be reporting to our "cells," where we were to remain for the duration of Vernet. (Footman Sesh says I should mention how that canyon and those cells were where Footman Ivak and his followers hid during the persecutions of King Bolt II. I don't know what any of that means, but Footman Sesh says you long-beards will know what I'm talking about and will be impressed.)

The whole caravan trundled along through the dark hours of the early day. The sun rose, and I got a better view of the incredible sights of the hidden canyon. Finally, around mid-morning, the drovers and DCs started flashing hand signals back and forth, and the whole thing came to a stop.

We were in the middle of a broad meadow broken up by small clumps of trees; the stream that ran through the canyon had formed a large pool there, and stepping down off the ox-cart, I marveled at how clear the water was. Even though I'd spent my whole life next to the sea, this was unlike anything I'd ever seen. The whole pool was maybe 50 feet across, and deep enough in the middle that the tallest man could have stood at the bottom and raised his arms without his fingertips breaking the surface. And yet the water was so perfectly clear that I could see the tiny rocks strewn along the bottom just as if I were looking at them through a shop window.

I felt a firm hand on my shoulder, and turned to see Gorgeous. He gestured with his head, to where most of One One Five was already walking back to the cliffside. As we made our way across to the rock face, the ox-trolleys turned around and headed back towards the Blue Wood.

"Find a cell and settle in," Sculler had told us back at barracks. It took me about an hour to actually find one; unlike the close-set, honeycomb-looking groups of cells nearer the canyon entrance, the cells in this part were set well apart from each other, and many were actually well-hidden — clearly, the intention here was to encourage solitude.

The one I finally found was partially hidden by a tall tree with a mass of spreading roots that made it a challenge to climb in and out; more than once during our "sojourn," as Prof called it, I hit my shins on those damn roots. I could have chosen a cell higher up along the rocky sides of the canyon, but I figured if I wasn't going to be able to eat for three days, it would be smart to pick a place where I wouldn't have to do much climbing.

Crawling in for the first time, I found the cell set up much as Sgt. Sculler had described it. There was a flat spot at the entrance which was clearly where I'd be spending my time in meditation and study; the rocks and soil there had obviously been well-worn by the butts of generations of Raider recruits. Further back was a long, flat depression in the dirt floor where I guessed I'd be sleeping. And even further back was a big pile of dirt covered over with cave mushrooms and who knew what other nasty stuff. That would be my latrine.

I know I'm not supposed to say this, but I was actually sort of looking forward to this part — for the first time since arriving at training, I'd be able to take a shit in peace. There was an old but sturdy shovel leaning against a rock, which I could use to hide the shameful evidence that I was not yet able to sustain my body purely on air, pain and the blood of my enemies.

The first thing, Sculler had emphasized, was to thoroughly search through your cell for indications it was already occupied.

"It's no fun to be awakened at night to find a bear in the process of chewing your leg off," he'd told us, with a gray and bland tone as if this was something that happened all the time.

No droppings, no animal tracks, no bones or half-devoured corpses were anywhere to be found in my little hole. That didn't necessarily mean it was unoccupied, Sculler had told us, but it lowered the odds. I thought I had caught a bit of a grin when he said that, but he turned away before I could get a good look.

Prayer, study, meditation. That was our assignment for the next three days. No food, but we could go down to the stream and refill our canteens.

I wasn't sure about the prayer part. I knew a lot of people prayed to Auld Father to ask for things, but that felt strange to me. It might be because of my Temple School days, when the Footmen used to lecture us about how miserable children like us had no business asking Auld Father for anything, and any prayers we had should be dedicated to thanking Him for not having come into the world crippled or diseased, because we were so wicked that even that would be a mercy for us.

I didn't tell them, of course, that I *had* actually come into the world that way when I'd been born blind, and that by giving me my sight, the Patriarch had given me at least one thing I could genuinely thank him for. But even if that hadn't been true, there was a part of me that felt too proud to go before even Auld Father with the kind of prayers that make you sound like a beggar. So I just recited the prayers I'd been taught all my life, even if I didn't know what half the words meant. Settling into my little spot at the entrance, I quietly mumbled out an old prayer from Temple School — the one about asking Auld Father to strengthen our limbs and hearts for the journey ahead. That sounded like something a Raider would pray; somehow the usual blood and guts Raider prayer didn't seem right for this situation. I resolved to repeat the process every morning and evening; I figured that ought to be enough for the Blessed Father; if he wanted me to put on a show for him, he would have led me to become a Footman.

That left study and meditation. I had to ask Prof what "meditation" meant, and at first I didn't quite understand his explanation. He said you sat and thought about things, and I told him the Footmen back at Temple School used to call that "daydreaming" and would thrash my backside raw when they caught me doing it.

"No, it's not that!" he exclaimed. "It's...it's kind of like daydreaming with a purpose, I guess. Like daydreaming at prayer."

I just looked at him. I guess he could tell I had no idea what that bullshit meant, so he quickly added, "look — just read a few pages from The Walk. Just open it at random and read something. Then sit and think about that for a long time."

That still sounded a lot like daydreaming, but I sort of got where he was going with it.

So after my prayer, I figured I'd have lunch and then get to the "study and meditation" part. Then I remembered that, shit, I wouldn't be having lunch. Or dinner, or breakfast the next day.

My stomach grumbled just then. I realized that this was the first time since we'd left for our sojourn that I'd thought about food.

It wouldn't be the last time.

47

I pushed aside my thoughts of hunger. *Suck it up, pussy,* I thought. *It's not like you'll be going on a ten-mile hump in full battle rattle later.*

Following Prof's suggestion, I pulled out my copy of The Walk and found a page at random. As it happened, it was Journeys of Rom, Book III — the part where Footman Ellu is talking about his arrival with Footman Rom at the town of Swar, in the land of Kassor. It just now occurred to me that I have no idea where "Swar" is, so I asked Footman Sesh about it, and he showed me where it is on a map — only he said it's called "Saromo" today, which means "blessing of Rom" in the Auld Tongue.

Anyway, instead of trying to tell you in my own words, I'll copy out what I read just as it's written here in Scripture:

And after leaving the city of Agellos, which continued to shut its ears to our joyful message, we made our way to the town of Swar, where we were told that our messengers had won many lost souls back to Auld Father's Path, and there was a great hunger to learn more of the signs and wisdom that mark well the way to the summit.

When we arrived, the magistrate himself greeted us on the road with three white steeds, strong and swift, from the finest bloodlines of the Kanassi breeders.

The magistrate fell to his knees before us and welcomed us to his fair town, and related that he had some months before dedicated himself to the Path when one of our emissaries had invoked the name of Auld Father to heal his daughter, after the shamans and priests of the river gods had been powerless to do so.

Rom raised the man to his feet, explaining that he was neither a king nor Auld Father, but just a normal man, and thus not deserving of such high honors.

The magistrate then insisted that we all three mount his great steeds, that we might ride into Swar in glory, to mark Auld Father's triumphant entry to the city. But Rom gently chid-ed the magistrate, explaining that it was not Auld Father, but merely two of his humble ser-

vants, and they were not there to bring Auld Father, but to bid His children to return to Him.

"And as for these mighty stallions," Rom said, "they are indeed fine creatures, and worthy mounts for a wise and just officer such as yourself. But these two shoes upon my feet have been the faithful beasts of burden that have carried me here from far Garlund, across the high mountains and through the dark lands of the forest-brutes, and across the breadth of this fertile and well-tended country. Having come so far with only my legs, I require not the legs of your fine herd to carry me but a little further. For in following the Path, man has no animal to carry him, nor any cart or wagon or chariot; though Auld Father has cleared the way, man alone must walk it."

The magistrate was a hearty man, and given to good humor, so he took no offense at Rom's words. Instead, he invited us, once we had reached the city, to join him at his great hall for the evening meal, where we could share the gift of Auld Father's wisdom with the many children who had found their way back to the true and ancient faith.

And it came to pass that night during the meal, that a young man appeared among the guests, and with him was an old man, gray of hair and with a tired spirit, and looking upon the multitude with bitterness.

The young man's clothing marked him as one of wealth. And during the evening, the young man listened eagerly to Rom's teachings, and asked of him many hard questions, which revealed to all that he was also sharp of mind, and much given to thought.

And Footman Rom found himself affected by the young man, who reminded him much of his own youth. But he was more stirred by the strange sight of the tired old man, who maintained a haughty cast despite his wretched appearance.

So Footman Rom asked the youth about the man, who had the appearance of being his servant. The proud young man announced to the assembly that the man was indeed his bond-servant, and furthermore that the man was also his own father.

And Footman Rom was amazed at this, and asked the young man how this had come to pass. The proud youth said that after he had been guided back to the true Path, he had clashed with his father, who continued to worship the river gods, and had mocked the ways of Auld Father, dismissing them as lies.

And their discord became so great that the young man left his father's house, and came to the town of Swar, where he became a laborer for a wealthy merchant, one who had also been returned to the Path. And the wealthy merchant was much taken with the youth, who worked hard and was distinguished by his cleverness and talents. And after five years, the youth had been raised to authority over all the merchant's many affairs, and was regarded with awe for his great skill as an administrator, for he had fattened the gold sacks of his employer many times over.

Now it happened that this merchant had but one child, a daughter renowned for her grace and comeliness, who had received the attentions of many men of noble birth, from storied houses all across the kingdom. And it was believed by all that once the daughter came of age, the father would have her married to one of these many nobles.

But to the astonishment of many, he consented that his young laborer should marry his daughter, and after his death should inherit all of his wealth and many holdings. And this was judged a happy and propitious decision, because it was known that the daughter and the young man had great affection for one another, and as even Auld Father has declared, the graft of mutual love engenders the most fruitful and harmonious marriages.

And so it came to pass that the two were wed, and not long after this, the merchant died, and his possessions passed to the young man, who showed his gratitude by dedicating a temple to Auld Father, the first in that part of Kassor; a temple which was even then being built, and of which the magistrate had boasted earlier.

"You have indeed been fortunate," Footman Rom said, "but again I ask of you: How came your father to be your own bondsman?"

And the young man explained that on a certain day about a year before, he had chanced to be traveling through the market of Swar, and it had been the day upon which the magistrate offered up the bond-service of those men who had been imprisoned for their great debts. While traveling through the marketplace, the young man was astonished to see that one of the imprisoned men was his own father.

Querying the bailiff, he discovered that his father, who had once owned many fields and flocks and was reckoned a great man among his neighbors, had lost nearly all of his holdings in a great river flood, the mightiest that had been seen in those parts within the memory of all who were then living; yea, even those of 90 and nine years.

And though the father had been renowned for his wise stewardship of his lands and his flocks and all his many possessions, yet there remained nothing of value left for him to pay his lenders, and no hope of re-establishing himself, for he had lost many of his best workers in the flood, and those he had not lost had abandoned him for want of payment. And so the father had been imprisoned, and had expected to live out his days in the city dungeons — for his debts were great, and it was thought that none would be willing to pay so great a price for so meager a servant.

The young man asked his father, standing there in heavy chains, if he still followed the river gods, who had taken from him all of his great wealth and even his good name. The father told the son that he still did follow them, and even now prayed to them, asking them to restore him to his former state.

The young man then waited for his father to come to the auction block, and quickly offered up a bid beyond what any had expected, paying off all of his father's debts and all interest on them. The father's bond-service was thus given over to the son, who instead of freeing his aged father, insisted on taking the old man into his house as a servant. The young man said with great haughtiness that he intended his actions to be an example to others, most especially his father, about the judgements of Auld Father.

"For is it not true that Auld Father rewards those who follow the Path, while Gruun repays those who honor his many puppets with woe and despair?" the young man asserted, clearly expecting that Footman Rom would be greatly impressed with this.

But Footman Rom was grieved, for he reminded the young man that he had neglected Auld Father's Third Law: "The guiding hand of Auld Father flows through the loving hands of the parents. Children who reject their loving parents have lost the Path."

But the young man protested: How could his father be a loving parent if he counseled others to seek after the servants of the eternal foe, who leads men not on the Path to the summit of the Holy Mountain, but to the black road into the deep hollows of darkness?

And Rom rebuked him, asking him sharply if he knew why Auld Father had decreed the Third Law. And the young man admitted that he did not know.

"You say that it was your great skill and cleverness that raised you from humble beginnings in the service of your late patron to master of his household," Rom said. "From where did you learn these things? From whose mouth did you receive this instruction? From whose hands did you receive these gifts, which you have put to such great use?"

The young man answered, "All I have been blessed with, I have received from the hands of Auld Father."

Footman Rom shook his head, and pointed to the old man, whose face had lost its disdainful aspect, and now looked at Rom in great confusion.

"It is that man there who bequeathed to you your blessings; unknown even to him, he was the instrument of Auld Father's will, and it is to him you should direct your gratitude."

"For it is not Auld Father, but Gruun who seeks to separate father from son, mother from daughter, brother from brother. Auld Father seeks not to cut us away from our past, but to reconnect us with it. How could it be otherwise? For His is the true Path that was laid out at the beginning of time, and all of Gruun's false religions are but novelties, which can only grow and prosper among those who have been tricked into forgetting the old and true way."

"As Auld Father is our original loving Father, all parents who love their children and raise them in righteous ways serve him, even if they know it not. And all parents who hate and destroy their children are servants of Gruun, even if their mouths are filled with Auld Father's name. For Auld Father's way is called the The Path, and like a path made by men, a traveler on it will have a path behind him as well as a path in front of him. But while the true Path has only one ending, it has many beginnings, one for each of Auld Father's lost children. And any path that has brought us to Auld Father's way is part of the true Path, and should be honored for where it has brought us, even as we may scorn the darkness it led us through."

And when he finished, the assembled people were amazed, for none had ever heard such a strange teaching from the many other priests and holy men who swarmed about the land. And they were further amazed to see the young man unlock the bondsman's collar from around his father's neck, and toss it into the fire; and he then fell to the ground and kissed the feet of his own father, and begged that he might be forgiven.

The old man, with tears flowing from his eyes, bid the young man rise, and announced to the assembled multitude that over the years, he had watched his son from afar. And he had felt gladness in his heart to see his son rise in the esteem of men, for he recognized in all the youth's actions the things he had taught him from childhood. And even as he had made offerings to them, he had feared to confess to the river gods the pride he felt in his own son, fearing their wrath should they know he loved his son who had rejected them. He said that he had looked upon his misfortunes as a judgment from the river gods, those wicked servants of Gruun.

And he there renounced those devils, for he perceived now the hand of Auld Father in all of these things, and he desired to follow the true Path of the one who is the Father of all. It is said that he lived on for many more years as an honored guest in his son's house, and that his wisdom helped his son bring yet greater and richer increase to his estate.

I put down the Scripture then. Even though I'd heard that story a thousand times or more, I think that was the first time I'd ever read it just as it was written in The Walk. I guess what surprised me most at first was all the stuff it didn't say. Like the story didn't actually say what the "young man" or his patron did; it just said he was a rich merchant. Every time they told the story to us as children, they always said he was a dealer in fine fabrics, and the paintings I'd seen always showed the "young man" dressed in colorful clothes that looked like something you see nobles and kings wearing in their old portraits. I asked Footman Sesh about that, and he said it's an old tradition, but I got him to admit that nobody actually knows if it's all true or not.

But what really stuck in my head was the part about the young man's father. Footman Rom was really, really worked up about how important it was that the rich little jackass needed to drop his attitude and be tight with his dad.

I guess I couldn't avoid thinking about my own dad. What was he like? What would I say to him if I met him? What would he say to me? Would he approve of who I'd become — or would he be ashamed?

Footman Rom had been all about how the Path behind you is as important as the Path in front of you, and the way I took it, he didn't mean just you, but your parents and their parents and all your people going back for as far back as they were a people.

But I didn't have a people — not one I'd ever met. My mother said little about her own people. And I didn't know the first thing about my dad's people, the Molans — I mean, I knew the tales about the Strongbloods, of course. I had seen them down around the docks working with the ships, and now and then you saw a rich-looking one around the Palace District. But beyond that, I didn't really know anything about them.

It was fine for Footman Rom to get sore at the young man in the story — at least that guy knew his dad. But what would Footman Rom say to me? The only path behind me was the Warrens.

For the rest of that day, I thought — meditated, I guess you'd say — about how I'd like to ask Rom about that. I remember being pretty pissed off about it, pissed off enough that if Footman Rom himself had suddenly shown up in person I'd probably have punched him — forgive me, Auld Father.

As the sun went down and the shadows grew long, I suddenly realized that this was the first time in my life I'd ever spent the night out of doors, out in the wild, completely alone.

48

Being alone might have bothered me more if I wasn't so cursed hungry. I have to admit, compared to some of the things I've been through since, one crummy day without food — especially a day where I didn't even have to do any real work — seems like a day in a palace feather-bed. But even growing up as poor as I did, the King had always seen that there was bread enough for every soul under his scepter, so an empty stomach was a new experience.

By this point in training, I'd gotten to the point where I pretty much fell asleep as soon as I hit my bunk and slept soundly until wake-up call, but for some reason that first night of Vernet was rough. I don't know if it was having to sleep on the ground, or if it was the nervous worry about waking up to find some animal in my cave with me, or something else. The weird nighttime sounds didn't help. At one point that night I woke up and heard a howling or wailing in the far-off distance — at least I hoped it was in the far-off distance.

I awoke the next morning shivering. Pulling my cloak tight around myself, I made my way to the front of my cell.

It had been raining heavily — the ground outside was soaked — and the view outside was nothing but thick fog. I mumbled a prayer and read some more from The Walk, without paying much attention. I don't remember what I read this time — my mind was knocked off track by the cold against my skin and the growling in my stomach, and I couldn't stop staring out into the fog. It reminded me of the fog that sometimes came up from the ocean back in Solta.

Except it never got this cold back home, I thought. Still, something seemed familiar about this — looking out into the fog, it felt like if I got up and walked out there through it, I would find myself at the edge of a great ocean. I could almost smell the briny salt air and hear the crash of waves — but if I tried to focus on either, the feeling went away. It seemed to hover there just on the edge of my mind, like a buzzing insect bobbing around behind your head.

Then the fog lifted, and the illusion was gone. And I wanted a bowl of Twoday Tripe from the mess hall — I was that hungry. It looked and tasted nasty — well, back then I thought it did — but all I could think of was how it made you feel full afterward. Nothing else they served at mess did quite as good a job at putting a plug in your appetite. Sgt. Sculler had told us you knew you were a true Raider when you ate Twoday Tripe and actually enjoyed it. I wasn't there yet, but I think that was the moment I started to turn that corner.

The rain started up again, in real heavy sheets. After a few minutes, a spout of water started pouring down from above the entrance to my cell, turning the path that led up to my little den into a stream that led down into the valley. I glanced at my watch — it was still midmorning! Would it be cheating if I crawled back to my dirt bed and went back to sleep?

I decided it would. I flipped open my copy of The Walk and tried to read some more, but I couldn't concentrate. Some feeling wouldn't let go of me — it was kind of a sad feeling, except I wasn't sure what I had to feel sad about. And then I realized what it was: I was feeling lonely.

I've never been one of the types who has to go around slapping every person on the back and flapping my lips through every conversation. I guess if I was forced at knifepoint to put a word on it, I'd say I'm "shy," but I hate that word because it makes me sound like a pussy.

But being "shy" — ugh, it feels nasty just to write that — doesn't mean you hate people. I asked Footman Sesh about it just to be sure, and he said the word you long-beards use for someone who hates people is "misanthrope." Anyway, being shy isn't the same as that — it just means you're a lot more careful of the people you call "friends," instead of gang members or gang molls or folks around the block you say hi to.

Shy folks still need people, though. By His Foot, everybody needs people. I remember a phrase I heard somewhere back in Temple School — "a mountain peak stands alone, yet still it stands upon the rocks below."

Every time I think of that line, I try to picture a mountain peak just hanging there in midair, not connected to anything below it. I remember back in Temple School that Footman Tan once said the summit of the Holy Mountain is a little bit like that — hanging out in midair, I mean. Not exactly like that, because that would be stupid — but it's the same idea. It's because Auld Father, being the creator of the world, is the only thing not connected to it. Footman Tan also said that's why only the faithful can ever complete the Path — because once you walk as far along it as a mortal being can using nothing but his own powers, you still need a ladder to reach the summit, and that ladder is what they call "faith."

But I'm getting off course here. What I was saying is that it's all connected, and so shy people need people too, even if it's only a few people. And when you don't have people, you don't feel any connection to anything else. And that's when you start feeling lonely, which is what I was feeling then.

It occurred to me that this might be something like the point of this whole Vernet business. I opened up the part of The Walk that Parsa had recited to us, about the Three Days of Darkness. I started reading, and I came to this part:

And cut free from Auld Father's discipline, his children fell prey to Gruun...

The word "discipline" jumped off the page at me. That was what I'd spent these past weeks at the Wood learning to observe...and learning to hate. And yet now, for three days, I was completely free of it. I was free of everything — even the need to worry about food. And instead of feeling like I'd been freed from chains, I was eaten up with a need to just talk to someone, even just see another face.

But all I had was myself and my little cell.

It finally stopped raining, and the sun came out. I shook off all my fucked-up feelings and said another prayer, then spent more time "meditating," still not entirely sure if I was doing it right. If I'm being honest, I actually spent the time just looking at the forest outside. There was a patch of flowers not far from the opening of my cell, and I noticed bees buzzing around them. Back in Temple School, Footman Ulas once told us that bees got their food from flowers, and I told him I didn't believe it, because how stupid is that? Food from flowers? But he insisted it was true and I decided not to argue with him because I didn't want another beating.

Now here were a bunch of the little bastards, and fuck me if they didn't look like a bunch of pickers going through a fresh trash heap in Craller Square. A regular feast they were having. It made me feel hungry just looking at it.

I spent the rest of the day looking out at the woods and trying to think good religious thoughts, but as the day wore on it was harder for me to ignore my rumbling stomach. When night fell on that second day, all I could think of was a big, hot cut of meat sitting on a plate in front of me. I said one final prayer, not even thinking about the words, and shuffled back to my sleeping area. I hadn't realized how tired I felt until I actually stood up and tried to walk. When I finally put my head down, I fell asleep pretty quickly — still dreaming of food.

49

I remember waking up at dawn the morning of the third day feeling frightened about the dreams I'd had the night before — but I couldn't remember anything about them. I just knew that when I opened my eyes and felt the dirt beneath me, I felt gripped by fear. It felt like I'd been running away from something.

It was still very dark, and I tried to go back to sleep, but after a few minutes it became clear that my body wasn't going to cooperate. I had to piss and take a shit, and my grumbling hunger was starting to wake up from whatever slumber had kept it occupied during the night.

My morning labors done, I dragged my bones back to the front of the cave, said some prayers, and opened up The Walk to read a passage that I could spend time "meditating" about.

Since all I could think about was food, I decided I might as well read about it. I thumbed through my copy until I found the story about the time Footman Rom was captured by the great steppe chieftain while traveling to Lynd. You longbeards all know the story, but I was mainly interested in the part where the chieftain boasts about his favorite wife, who runs his household and instructs all his many children, and is the finest kitchenmaster in all the world — and to prove it he commands her to prepare a great feast for Footman Rom.

There's this part where it goes on for like five pages talking about all the different courses of the meal, and describing all the exotic dishes and the rare ingredients that were used. That was the part I wanted to read about. I know you longbeards know all about that part, so I won't bore you with it, and I'll skip ahead to the crap that you'll probably think was really important for my spiritual journey.

So after they've finished the meal, the chieftain has Footman Rom put back in chains and brought before him, right? And he's there with his big pipe, smoking moonfeather, and bragging to Footman Rom about all his power and wealth, saying, "hey, look at all this stuff Vipraal the serpent god gave me, how is your Auld

Father supposed to compete with this?" So Rom asks him why he worships Vipraal, and he said it's because his father did, and his grandfather, and his great-grandfather and so on. And Rom asks, well why did they all worship him? And of course the chieftain is all like, "because Vipraal lets us live free and doesn't have all the stupid laws your civilized gods have, because we're the great warriors of the high plains and we don't like being tied down."

Anyway, I was reading through that stuff and not really paying much attention when I came to this part. Again, I'll just copy it out directly:

But Footman Rom had heard stories of the chieftain, and affecting ignorance, he asked the steppe lord if his father had lived in a great tent of fine and intricate fabrics, such as the one where they now reposed. And the chieftain said, with swelling pride, that he had not: "My father's tent was but a small canopy of goatskin, and it was but one room; and even though he was first among his kinsman, his was not different in kind from that of the lowliest of his clan."

"Was it the same with your grandfather, and his father before him?" Rom asked. And the chieftain said it was the same, and had been for generations, yea unto the beginning of the world.

"What then of your father's flocks? For I saw as you brought me here that your own flocks wax great, and it is said that even the poorest among your kinsman can boast of ten and one she-goats, and an unblemished ram, and an ass, and a house for his hens, and a white stallion to bear him into battle beside your eminence." And the chieftain said proudly that the flocks of his poorest kinsmen were richer than any known in his father's time, though his father had been first among his tribe, and it had been thus for generations, unto the time of the first men.

Rom then asked the chieftain about his sparkling jewels and rich robes — the heavy rings that shone on his fingers, and the cords of pearls and gold draped about his neck, and the fine and colorful fabrics which flowed about his body.

"Was it your father's custom to clothe himself with such regalia? Surely it must have been, for I have seen that even the servant who carries your footstool; nay, even the men who bridle the horses of your warriors are clad in silk, and adorn their ears with precious stones, and have buckles on their boots of the finest silver." But once again, the chieftain said that no man of his father's time had felt such cloth upon his skin, or possessed any bauble of such luster; his father had shroud himself in clothes of yak skin and jute, and knew gold and silver only from the coins stolen from unwary travelers. And it had been thus even in the time of his most distant ancestors, from when, as he claimed, Vipraal had first placed the egg Quay'opay in the high heavens to light the day.

"Your lordship," Rom asked, "how is it that Vipraal did not bestow such riches on your forefathers, if they were indeed as faithful as you say?"

The great chieftain laughed, and said none before himself had understood the power of the steppe tribes.

"It was I who taught them to put aside their quarrels, for as a scattered host we were but fingers poking at our neighbors, but when closed together we were a mighty fist!" the chieftain declared. "It was I who taught them to ceaselessly hone their skills, for as indolent hunters we were but mangy dogs living off our neighbors' scraps, but with cultivation we were as the mighty lions of the mountains! It was I, foolish holy man, who tempered them with strenuous discipline, for it is only hot fire that can forge hard steel!"

"I am sorry," Rom said, "but I am confused. Your lordship praises the indulgent license of your god Vipraal, but you say it was the heavy yoke of your rule which lifted up your people and made them into a race of princes. Your god burdens you with no laws and forbids you no enjoyments, yet he was pleased to let your many forefathers quarrel against each other in poverty. By your own telling, it was only your strict hand which made your men respected and feared."

When Footman Rom finished, the chieftain's prideful tongue had departed him, and he sent Footman Rom back to his tent with instructions that he be treated with hospitality.

"You speak true words, holy man, and I must have time to think on these things," he said.

I stopped reading about there. Anyway, you know the rest of the story, about how Footman Rom converted the chieftain and his whole tribe, which is supposedly why the tribes eventually took over Lyndan and turned it into the first city whose whole people swore allegiance to Auld Father.

I sat there for some time thinking about what I'd read. The image of that proud chieftain stuck with me, which I figured was a sign I was supposed to meditate on it.

Around midmorning, I took a swig from my backup canteen — I had emptied my main canteen on the first day. All that came out was a little trickle.

Well, there's an excuse to do something different, I thought, so I decided to make my way down to the pool I'd seen on that first day of Vernet. They had said we could refill our canteens, after all. I paused before stepping out of my cell, wondering if I should take my sword with me. Wasn't a Raider always supposed to be armed? For no reason I can explain, I decided to leave my sword in my cell.

Making my way through the trees, I encountered Limul coming back bearing his own canteens. We exchanged glances. No speaking was allowed. He shrugged, and I shrugged, and we went our separate ways. As he walked away, I noticed he wasn't carrying his sword, either. That made me feel a little better, like I'd made the right decision after all.

As I got closer to the pool, I noticed a robed figure sitting along the bank. When I was within a stone's throw of the water, I saw that it was Skunk.

He didn't even look up, didn't even seem to notice I was there. He had a small twig in his hand, sprouting small leaves and a few little flowers. He was just turning it back and forth in his hand, looking at it.

I waited for what felt like several minutes, expecting him to notice me. I mean, I was standing only a few paces away. But he just continued to stare at the twig. He turned his head at one point and seemed to stare at something in the distance, on the far side of the canyon. I looked and didn't see anything there. Then he went back to staring at the twig.

That shit was creeping me out, so I went ahead and filled both my canteens. I looked once more at him as I started to leave; he still seemed to be lost in a trance. I did note, though, that Skunk had been sure to bring his sword, which was sheathed in its scabbard and propped on a rock within easy reach — almost as if he were expecting to have to draw it.

The sky rumbled, and I looked up — though it had been sunny all morning, the clouds were starting to roll in. I looked east; the clouds back towards Fort Harrel were beginning to get dark and ugly.

Fuck that, I thought. At least I don't have to drill in the rain during this nonsense. I picked up the pace and made my way back to the treeline. Before I disappeared into the woods, I took one last look back at Skunk. He was still sitting beside the pool, still holding his twig — but he was now looking off to the east at the gathering storm clouds.

I was in such a hurry to get back to shelter that I got a little off course trying to find my way back to my cell. Give me a break — it was well-hidden, and it was only my second time having to find it. I emerged into a small glade on the slope of the canyon and could immediately tell I was too high up. Using the features of the canyon walls as a rough guide, I estimated that my own little cave was downslope and about a hundred yards further to the west — I saw what I was certain was the tree whose roots partly hid the opening to my cell.

The sky rumbled again, and I felt a single raindrop strike the back of my neck. I was about to start hustling off towards my cave when I saw something moving through the underbrush.

At first, I was certain it was Skunk — or one of the other recruits. I'd seen some squirrels and even something that I later learned was a badger, but this was much larger than that. I thought back to what Sgt. Sculler had said about bears. Oh, shit, was this a bear? I felt a chill run across me, and I could actually feel my heart jumping in my chest.

After a moment, I started to calm down. It couldn't be a bear, I realized. I'd seen bears, and whatever this was, it wasn't making enough noise coming through the brush to be a bear. I was starting to think it think it might be another recruit fucking with me when it finally stepped out from behind a bush.

It was a wolf.

It was a big fucking wolf. Its fur was almost all black, which is why I'd had trouble seeing it in the brush. Did I mention that it was big? I'd seen paintings of wolves and I knew they looked something like dogs, but by Gruun, none of the pictures I'd seen showed how big they were. It didn't look like something I could chase off by yelling and throwing a rock.

The wolf gave me a strange look, kind of like it wasn't expecting to see me. My heart was thumping wildly again, and my thoughts raced as I tried to think of what to do. My instinct was to reach for a sword or knife, except…I didn't have one.

Fuck.

I finally decided that all I could do was fight the cursed thing like I'd fight a man; I dropped into a defensive posture and stretched my fingers, staring the beast directly in the face. I don't know how to read what a wolf is thinking, but if it had been a human, I think you'd call its look "quizzical." I mean, the thing looked at me like I was bright purple and had two heads.

We sat there and looked at each other for a few moments; neither of us moving. I was beginning to wonder if I should start yelling — either to scare it (which didn't seem likely) or just to summon help.

Then suddenly the wolf's ears spiked straight up. It took a step to the side and craned its neck, like I was in its way. Then it dropped down into a low crouch, seeming to melt into the brush. I could still see its snout and its piercing gold eyes, though — once you'd seen and recognized them, they seemed to glow even in bright daylight.

The animal's eyes stared at me, then flicked over to something else. Then back to me. Then back to the other thing. Then back to me.

My street-fighting instincts told me not to stop looking, not to turn around and try to see what the wolf was looking at — if it was anything like a human, it would see that as an opening to strike.

I slowly started to back away, keeping my eyes fixed on the animal's eyes. Right about then, it occurred to me I'd read somewhere that wolves hunt in packs. I tried to sneak a few glances around the edges of the clearing, hoping my adversary wouldn't notice.

There. Another form was moving through the brush to my left. I saw a patch of fur just as it disappeared behind a tree. So he wasn't alone.

I was getting closer to the edge of the clearing now, trying to think of my next move. Even I knew there was no way I was about to outrun a wolf. I was figuring once I reached the trees I could look for a sturdy stick or rock to use as a weapon, then start yelling for help. Maybe I could snap off a branch. I was close enough to the edge of the clearing that the tree canopy was above me now; my eyes still locked in a stare with the wolf, I reached up and felt around, trying to grab one. My hand wrapped around a nice, thick branch and I began pulling, and…

Everything happened really fast. The idea came to me and, in the excitement of the moment I turned around and looked up at the tree. Then I heard crunching leaves and snapped back to my surroundings; I whirled around and saw a flash of something to my right and instinctively ducked. There was a rush of air and a snarl as something whisked over my head just as I ducked. I whipped around and saw a third wolf stumbling to a landing and wheeling around to face me. I looked and saw the first wolf — the big black one — bounding across the clearing. I immediately began scrambling up the tree — which had been the bright idea I'd had that had distracted me in the first place. The black wolf snapped its jaws into the edge of one of my sandals, barely missing my skin. The wolf yanked its head back and the sandal slipped off, and I kept climbing.

That little bit of luck gave me just enough time to pull myself high enough into the tree that the wolves couldn't reach me. And then I kept climbing. When I stopped to look back down, I saw the pack jumping up and scratching at the trunk, snapping their jaws and snarling. The black one let out a couple of low, throaty barks that shook me like a bell.

I'd never crawled up a tree before, but I'd spent enough time clambering up and down the buildings of the Warrens that I found it came second nature to me. Unfortunately, I also immediately learned an important lesson about climbing trees — the higher up you go, the iffier things get.

In my initial burst of terror, I'd climbed about halfway to the top. But the wind from the gathering storm was beginning to cause the trees to sway wildly. This high up, the swaying was making me uncomfortable; I could actually hear the creaking of the wood as it bent back and forth. Also, the branches I was standing on were pretty flimsy; I wasn't sure if they'd hold. But I didn't dare climb back down. I wasn't sure how high those wolves could jump if they had a mind to.

Then the rain started. Thin drops for a few seconds, then suddenly the clouds opened up. I looked up; the dark, angry clouds were starting to unroll across the sky. As the rain got worse, the sky suddenly grew very dark. There was more thunder; it made me think of the rumbling stomach of a troll about to carve me up and eat me for dinner.

The rain made it even harder to stand on the small, thin branches this high in the tree. I looked down, hopeful the storm might be enough to chase away the pack of wolves. No such luck. They were circling around the base of the tree like a pack of sharks around a fishing trawler, looking up at me and snarling. I counted five of them. The big black one — which I guessed must have been the leader — stood back a bit from the others. Its huge golden eyes did not seem the least bit bothered. Its gaze seemed to say, *take all the time you want. I can wait as long as you like.*

Finally, the branches were getting so wet that my bare foot kept slipping off. I looked down at the black wolf, and saw my lost sandal sitting right at its feet, chewed almost in half. Sighing, I started to climb down to try to get a better stance on some of the lower limbs. That got the wolves worked up again, and they started snarling and jumping up again, their claws scraping the lowest branches.

I settled in on some thicker branches about six feet below where I'd been before. These branches were thick enough to allow my feet a better grip, but they still bent uncomfortably under my weight. Most importantly, though, they were still well out of range of those hungry, snapping jaws at the base of the trunk.

That was when I finally realized that since I was no longer in imminent danger, I could safely call for help. Wait — would that be breaking the oath I'd taken to remain silent? Shit. I turned it over in my mind, then looked down at the wolves. One of them barked.

Fuck it, I thought. I started screaming as loud as my lungs could manage. I screamed and screamed until I was out of breath.

The only answer I got was more thunder, followed by a pounding wave of rain that soaked through my cloak to my skin — almost as if the storm itself was screaming back a challenge at me. Would anybody be able to hear me through the storm, I wondered?

The dogs back in the Warrens had always been frightened of storms, but the wolves at the bottom of my tree just seemed to be whipped into an even greater fury. Their sopping fur seemed to reveal why: They were actually quite thin, as if they hadn't had a good meal in weeks. Eventually the rain seemed to be getting to them, and they took shelter under some nearby shrubs. They still kept looking at me, though — the gaze of the big black leader was always fixed on me whenever I looked.

I tried screaming some more, but my shouts seemed to get lost in the rain and thunder. I'll just have to wait it out, I thought, looking over at the wolves. They'd obviously made the same decision.

The weather didn't bother me at first — it wouldn't be the first time I'd been caught out in a rainstorm. But as the minutes piled up into an hour and kept on going, the rain kept on at a steady, soaking pace. The thunder seemed to relax, but the skies continued to pour out like a broken aqueduct. My soggy cloak grew more uncomfortable, and I was starting to get cold. It wasn't my imagination — I could feel it in my toes and fingers: The temperature was starting to drop.

Then something else loomed up in my mind: I was getting very, very tired. This was — what day was it again? Day three. I'd now gone two days without food. Which wouldn't be so bad if I'd been back in my Vernet cell, where I could relax and "meditate," or even just sleep. But I was up a tree, holding on for dear life.

I started to feel unsteady from exhaustion. Then my hand slipped off the trunk and I wobbled crazily for a second until I grabbed another branch to steady myself. I sighed — I could be stuck here for hours, I realized, and there was no way I could focus on maintaining my balance that whole time.

The branches below were thicker. A few at the very bottom, which still bore scratch marks from the wolves' paws, were thick enough that I could probably stretch out and lie down on one — which might have been downright peaceful if I hadn't had a band of predators just below, hungering for my flesh.

Still, I couldn't stay where I was. I started climbing down. The wolves immediately noticed, sitting up and running over to the trunk. They planted themselves on their haunches and glared up at me, licking their chops in anticipation. The black one made a mighty leap and managed to wrap its front paws around one of the lowest branches, its back feet crazily scratching at the trunk. It growled and snapped its jaws again before losing its grip and dropping back down.

Okay, I thought, so the lowest branches are off limits. I found a branch that was maybe four feet above the lowest branches; it was thick enough that I could sit down, dropping one leg over either side and resting my back against the trunk. After a moment, the rain dropped off to a gentle sprinkle, the thunder to a sleepy murmur. My body felt incredibly drowsy; I didn't want to fall asleep, but I thought maybe if I just closed my eyes, just for a second…

I don't know how long I was out. It might have been awhile, because I think the sky was a little darker when I woke up. I say "I think" because I wasn't really paying attention to that; what woke me up was the sensation of falling. All I know was that I snapped instantly awake just as I felt my leg slide away from the branch.

From some place that my sleep-dulled mind could not touch, my training-sharpened reflexes took control, twisting my falling body and forcing my arms and legs to reach for where they knew a limb should be. The limb was there, and my body wrapped around it in a tight bear hug just as my brain became fully aware of what was happening. And the first clear thought I had was that a wolf's teeth were about to close around my hand or wrist.

If I was one of those poets with ten thousand flowery-sounding words in my head, I could probably describe the next part better. All I know is that the next few seconds were strange. I was awake and knew what was going on, but it felt like it was happening in a dream. Somehow, my body scrambled up into a standing position on the branch. I saw the snout of the black wolf, lips curled back, teeth shining, rising up from the ground as if it had grown a pair of wings. I kicked it in the face with my one remaining sandal, sending it flailing to the ground, only to see another snarling mouth rising up in its place. I pulled myself up onto the branch where I had fallen asleep, but as soon as I threw a leg over and started to pull myself into a standing position, it just…snapped.

There was a branch a few feet away from me at about chest height; I hurled myself across to it and grabbed it firmly with both hands. Then I immediately cursed myself for not wrapping myself around the trunk instead; this branch wasn't big enough for my weight. It started to bend at a frightening angle. I looked around, but I couldn't see any other branch I could get to that looked safe. There was a branch below that I thought about taking a chance with, but I scratched that idea as soon as I saw several of the wolves managed to clear it with their heads. I might just as well have been served up to those wolves on a spit.

At that moment, the wind suddenly picked up. The tree itself began to sway, and the branch I was on began to make loud cracking sounds. I knew I didn't have much longer.

I made my mind up to go out fighting. I clenched my jaw and stared down at the wolves, which had assembled in a neat circle on the ground — as if they expected their next meal to be promptly delivered at any moment. But before it went to blood, I looked straight up at the sky. The rain falling down toward me formed a shape like a crown. I bit off a few short words, which I remember as if I just spoke them: "Auld Father, if you are there..."

I hung there for a second, trying to think of what to say next. Then I heard something. Actually, I don't think I heard it so much as sensed it.

I looked down — the wolves must have sensed it, too, because not a single one was looking up at me. Instead, their heads were all turned to something on the other side of the clearing. A few of them started to crouch down in anticipation. I looked in the direction they were looking. At first I didn't see anything. Then, I saw a quick rustle of branches and a deer suddenly stepped full into the clearing. It was a silver deer — I recognized the breed by the sheen of its coat, which was longer and shaggier than a normal deer. It looked around for a moment, then — I would swear this before Auld Father — it looked directly at me.

After locking eyes with me, the animal seemed to turn coolly to regard the pack of wolves, whose fur I could see bristling in excitement.

With something that looked an awful lot like contempt, it bounded away into the forest, and the wolves shot off after it as if propelled from a huntsman's bow. As their barks and snarls disappeared off into the trees, I heard a snap from the branch I was hanging from, and it slowly drooped down until I felt my feet on the dirt. At the exact moment I safely touched the ground, the whole branch snapped off and fell. I backed away and looked around, expecting the wolves to come back. But all I could hear was a few barks moving away in the distance.

For some reason, I grabbed what was left of my chewed-up sandal — maybe I could show it to Sgt. Sculler to explain what happened — and I began running in the direction of my cell. I don't know how I suddenly knew where it was, but my running feet quickly took me right to the entrance.

I was free now, but didn't feel better. I grabbed my sword and yanked it out of its scabbard, and backed slowly into my cell. I kept my sword gripped tightly in my hand, pointed back toward the entrance — my eyes hunted for every movement, my ears focused on every snatch of sound.

The storm started up again, more ferociously than before. The sound of the rain coming in was like a muted roar. Thunder rumbled, and lightning came crashing down. I just huddled there in the darkness, my only comfort coming from the blade in my trembling hand. It would not be the last time in my life I'd found myself in such a bind, but it was the last and only time I faced it alone.

AT SOME POINT I fell asleep. I don't remember when it happened, but I remember the dream I had.

I was in a boat again, one of Molan design, paddling through a gray, cold ocean. I remember the boat had an interesting design painted on its surface — a long silvery sea serpent, with four horns and a mouth full of long, thin teeth.

Looking ahead, I could see another craft like mine, holding the same man I'd seen before in my dreams. He was paddling away — his thick, muscular arms seemed to propel his boat away at an unnatural speed.

I paddled after him. I worked the oars until my muscles burned. For some reason I couldn't explain, I felt like I had to catch this man. I felt like I had to tell him something, or maybe ask him about something — though I wasn't sure what it was.

He was paddling toward some land in the distance. In the misty spray of the cold sea, it was difficult to tell if it was an island or part of a larger land mass. All I could see was a rocky beach; everything beyond was shrouded by fog.

As I got closer to the shore, the ocean swells began to overwhelm me. I lost sight of the other man in his boat, and almost lost sight of the land itself. I carefully guided my craft down the side of one wave only to feel myself dropping — a huge hill of water suddenly thrust up before me, and before I could react, I was thrown out of my boat and sent tumbling deep under the waves.

I swam desperately for the surface, pulling my head into the air and looking around. My boat was gone — pulled down into the depths, I supposed. Then I spied the land I'd been trying to reach a couple of hundred feet off to my left. I began swimming towards it, fighting the waves the entire time. More than once I was pulled under, but I always managed to fight my way back to the air. Each time, the land was a little bit closer.

Finally, I was close enough that I felt the sharp, rocky seafloor beneath my feet. I fought the enormous tow of the receding ocean trying to pull me back, willing my painful arms and legs to pull me forward.

I fought my way onto the shore, past the reach of the water, and fell to my hands and knees. I spent a long time just catching my breath. When I looked up, I saw something further up on the shore ahead, just at the point where the curtain of mist blotted out everything beyond. I pulled myself up and walked towards it.

Getting closer, I recognized it as the form of a man. He was laying face down on the ground, not moving. I realized it was the man I'd seen before in the boat — the one I'd been trying to catch up with. I started running towards him — I had to see if he was okay.

Reaching the collapsed form, I leaned over and felt the flesh — it was cold to the touch. The man was dead, and it seemed he had been dead for quite some time. I put both my hands on him to try to turn him over, to get a look at his face.

"Leave him," a voice said. "You have done all you can."

The voice sounded familiar. I looked up. There was another man standing there beside me, who had seemingly appeared out of nowhere. I looked around to see where he had come from. All I saw was a muddy trail leading away from the shore into the mist, but there were no footprints on it.

I looked up at the man who had spoken to me and was startled to see the face of the King! He looked just as he had back in Solta, the time I had given him the sealed letter — except now he had a crown on his head, the way he always did in paintings. I immediately got on my knees before him and bowed my head.

"Your Majesty," I blurted out.

I felt his hand touch my shoulder, and then I looked up at him. The way he smiled at me seemed to wash away my pain and fear.

"My Lord," I said, my breath catching in my throat.

He placed a hand on my head. "Rise, my child," he said, with an air of perfect love.

I stood, looking at him. His smile was broad and generous, and gave me such peace. I turned back to the man lying on the ground. I pointed: "Is he...?"

"He was a good and faithful servant," the King said.

I looked my King directly in the eye. I wanted to say something — I think it might have been what I wanted to say to the man in the boat, who now lay dead at my feet. But before I could say anything, the King just shook his head, still smiling.

"I am merely a servant myself," he said, "as we all are." Then he looked over at the path leading away from the shore. He pointed at it, and looked back at me.

"That is the way. Come, let us go together."

From a scabbard at his side, he drew a great, flaming sword, the light of which caused the crown atop his head to sparkle. Nodding to me, he turned and began to run down the path.

50

"Lips. Lips. Hey — Lips!"

I felt someone shaking me and opened my eyes to see Limul. I sat up with a start.

"Come on!" he said. "Get your sword there and let's get going! The wagons are waiting! They brought us bread and when we got back they're taking us straight to the mess hall! Everybody else is almost loaded up!"

I shook off my slumber and looked at him.

"Sorry. I was just having a strange dream," I said.

"Yeah, I think everybody had weird dreams last night. I always have weird dreams on an empty stomach. Anyway, that's not going to be a problem much longer. By His Foot, I'm starving. Come on!"

When we got to the wagons, Sgt. Sculler was standing there looking at some sort of checklist.

"Recruit Pearl was where this recruit thought he was, sir!" Limul announced. "He was still asleep — he must not have heard the horn."

Sculler glared at me, looking me up and down.

"Recruit, what happened to your other sandal?" he asked, and I was about to explain, but he quickly turned back to his list.

"That leaves Recruits Camlin and Parsa. Has anybody seen those two?"

"Sir, this recruit saw Skunk...Recruit Camlin...here yesterday at the stream."

Sculler glared at me again. "Sir," I continued, "this recruit volunteers to go find him. This recruit believes that wherever Skunk is, Parsa can't be far away."

There was laughter from the guys in the cart, which was quickly cut short by a stern look from Sarge. Then he looked at me and simply nodded. Even though I had no idea where either one of them might be, something drew me back to the clearing where I'd encountered the wolves. This time I walked into the clearing slowly, with my sword drawn.

Nothing was in the clearing. I searched around and found several trails leading away from the clearing, each bearing sandal prints. There was no way to know which one might be right, or if any of them might be right.

I was examining one of the trails when I noticed a fresh, sharp hoof print in the center of it, just a stone's throw away. I'll be the first to tell you that I have no idea what a silver deer's hoof print is supposed to look like, but studying it, I decided it could have been from one. I glanced up at the sky and let out a sigh, and Auld Father curse me, I couldn't keep from rolling my eyes. Then I followed that path deeper into the forest.

It led on past a set of huge boulders that for some reason were just sitting there in the forest. I imagined they might have been the remains of some ancient avalanche from the sharp cliffs above, but it must have been a long time ago — they were now shielded by the canopies of tall trees, and bore thick coats of moss. I was making my way around one huge rock the size of a small building when I heard voices. I followed them to a small ridge that led up through the trees to the base of one of the cliffs. As I grew closer, I could distinctly hear Parsa's voice — along with a softer voice that I assumed must have been Skunk's.

The voices were coming from near a huge tree which had fallen over, exposing a massive spread of roots. As I made my way past the roots, the voices stopped. I guess they heard my feet crunching the underbrush.

The top of Parsa's head poked up above some brush, and making my way through it I found myself at the mouth of a hole that had apparently been carved right into the solid rock face of the cliff.

Parsa looked at me. "You're missing a sandal," he said.

"We're leaving. Everybody else is already on the cart. What's the holdup?"

Parsa gestured to the cave.

"Skunk, what's the holdup?" he asked.

"Is that Lips?" came a voice from inside.

"Naw, it's Footman fuckin' Rom," I said. "I'm here to show you the Path. It leads out of this fuckin' cave and down to the ox-cart that's taking us back to the Blue Wood."

There was no answer for a moment, then: "Eat my dick and balls, Lips. Eat them until you fucking gag."

"I had your mom gagging last night."

I heard a weary chuckle from inside.

"Guess I asked for that. Hey, come on back here, Lips. Hey Parsa? Head back to the cart."

"I'm not going anywhere," Parsa said.

"Go on, I'll be there in a minute. I just want to talk to this fuckin' scaleback for a moment."

Parsa looked at me, and then silently walked off. I crawled back into the cave.

It was not too different from mine, but more narrow. There was a space at the front to sit and read and "meditate," and a pile of dirt at the back to bury your shit.

Skunk was sitting in what I took to be the sleeping area. He was sitting cross legged, but his sword was out of its scabbard. He held it up and pointed it at me as I approached. I stopped.

"Did you have a dream last night?" he asked. He had a weary smile on his face.

"Yeah, man. I think we all did. It was all this meditating and not eating and shit. Come on..."

I stepped toward him, but he raised his sword again.

"You think I'm a piece of shit," he said. It wasn't a question; it was a statement.

"Well sort of," I admitted. "Less than I did when we first got here. What's your point?"

Skunk ignored the question. "I had a dream last night too."

"Yeah, I know. Like I said, everybody did. I think that was part of the whole process..."

"I don't have to leave this cave, you know," he said, interrupting me.

"Uh, yeah. Yeah you kind of do, unless you want Sculler to come up here and drag you out. And you and I both know there won't be enough left of your ass after that to stuff in a thimble and mail back home to your parents."

"To my mom," he said. "I don't think my dad would care."

"Are you coming or not?"

"I hated you too, Pearl, when I first got here. I still don't know if I really like you. But I don't hate you."

"Okay."

He pointed his sword back towards the entrance.

"I spent a lot of time looking out at that world out there. Maybe I don't want to go back. Maybe I want to live as a hermit out here, praying and meditating. Just have them bring me food every few days."

"Oh, you don't want that," I quickly said, thinking of the wolves. The force of my answer seemed to surprise him.

"What makes you so certain?"

I thought about telling him what had happened. Instead I just shrugged. "Something I read in The Walk," I added.

He nodded.

"Where did you go to school, Pearl? Where did you learn to read and write?"

"The Temple School. In Solta."

"Really."

"Yes."

"Did you know Footman Tan?"

"Yeah...yeah, he was one of the teachers there. I had several classes with him. Why do you ask?"

He shook his head, smiling.

"I know his family. He comes from nobility, like me."

"I had no idea he was rich."

"He's not. Not anymore, at least. He had to give that all up when he joined the brotherhood."

He stared past me towards the mouth of the cave in disgust.

"Look, man," I finally said. "I don't know about what you've got going on out...there. Outside the Blue Wood, I mean. But right now, we're *here*. I...we..."

As I tried to think of the right words to say, Skunk looked up at me, seeming to get a kick out of my struggle.

"We're all in this together, man," I finally said. "We're all we've got. Now can you pick your ass up and come with me and make me look good in front of Sculler?"

He sighed and began picking up his things.

When we got back to the wagons, Skunk and Gorgeous were summarily demoted from squad commanders — Gorgeous because of my "lack of discipline," and Skunk because of his own. Skunk got replaced with Recruit Berchin, and in place of Gorgeous, Sculler gave command of Squad Three to Prof.

Skunk looked relieved. Gorgeous didn't seem to care. And Prof looked thoughtful.

Everybody was talking and joking more than normal on the ride back. I guess three days of silence helps to loosen the tongue. We couldn't wait to get back to the relative comfort of our old bunkroom.

A few more people mentioned my missing sandal. But for some reason, I just didn't want to talk about it. Maybe I was afraid that telling the story would make me look like an idiot. Or maybe I was afraid it would make me look like a badass. I'm not sure which would have been worse.

It wasn't until we got back and we were heading into the mess hall that I asked to speak to Sgt. Sculler alone. He pulled me around the corner.

"Recruit Pearl, you have something to say?"

I pulled out the mangled remains of my sandal. For the first and only time since I'd been at training, I saw something like surprise cross Sculler's face.

"This recruit had an encounter with a pack of wolves, sir. This recruit climbed a tree to escape from them, but one of them managed to get m...the Crown's sandal. Sir."

"Thank you for reporting this, recruit," Sculler said, taking the sandal from my hand to examine it. "How exactly did you manage to escape?"

"Sir, the fortunate appearance of a silver deer distracted the wolves and allowed this recruit to escape."

Sculler was turning the sandal over in his hand, but when I mentioned a "silver deer," he paused.

"You're sure it was a silver deer?" he said, eyeing me carefully. "It couldn't have been a normal deer? Or possibly a mountain goat? They're easily confused with silver deer, because of the coat."

"Sir, the recruit doesn't think so. It looked like the image on the Prince of the Forest playing card. And there's a pair of them at Royal Zoo in Solta, so I've seen a live one. Also, there's a big painting of a silver deer in the Royal Museum of Solta; the recruit remembers seeing it as a boy. This animal looked just like the one in that painting."

"I am familiar with that painting..." Sculler muttered, not looking at me. Then his head suddenly snapped up.

"Thank you for bringing this to my attention, recruit. Now go join your platoon in the mess hall. Dismissed."

I snapped to attention, did an about face and went in to join One One Five for what was, by Raider standards, a sumptuous feast.

After marching back to our barracks, showering and switching into proper Raider recruit attire, a beaming Sgt. Taba had us strap on full battle gear, grab our spears and spend the rest of the day drilling.

51

Of course, all anybody could talk about was sparring day. Even though we weren't really supposed to know what was coming next, it had become an open secret, and when we asked Sgt. Taba for extra time in the arena to train, he only half-managed to hide his satisfaction.

But instead of dumping everybody right into the melee, they gave us a couple of days to get back in the rhythm of training. I noticed that both Sculler and Taba were on hand to give us some final pointers and help make any last-minute adjustments to everybody's technique.

What I saw made *me* feel good about our chances, at least. Wym, the little guy who'd been so worried about fighting guys bigger than him, had been practicing like a madman, and it had paid off. That initial fear had been all the fuel he needed to become quite a tough little scrapper, and his newfound talent had transformed his personality. Now he was constantly challenging our biggest guys every time he got the chance; Taba actually had to force him to spar with smaller guys.

Among our other guys, Limul and Prof were busy reminding anyone who might have forgotten just why dwarves have such a fearsome reputation as brawlers. To get our heads in the right place, we had Gorgeous — when he wasn't fighting anyone, he lightened the mood with his nonstop commentary, taking time out to give people pointers on the fine art of trash-talking opponents.

And then there was Skunk. Our highborn recruit with the five houses was so good that Sculler and Taba were now sparring with him personally nearly all the time, since none of us could present him with a challenge. I kind of felt sorry for whoever had to face him.

But only kind of.

We also did a couple more things in the days leading up to sparring day. One, we got measured for our dress uniforms. Any sense of celebration was washed away by Sgt. Taba's subsequent "uniform inspection" of our regular gear. Three days without food — and weeks of hard training — meant our gear now had less-than-perfect fit. Cloth now hung loosely where flab had been, and in other places, our newly-pumped-up muscles made things too tight. After smoking us good — including leading us on a long march while carrying the Toothpick — we spent a long night making adjustments to our clothes. Prof's tailoring experience made it easier for our squad. I noticed he took to command quite naturally, and was actually much better than Gorgeous had been. Prof didn't say much, but he paid attention to everything, and he now put that knowledge to good use.

"Lips, rip out that seam — it's not straight enough. Use the blade of your sword as a guide. Toad, you're getting there — just keep doing what you're doing. Gorgeous..." — Prof paused, looking up into the eyes of his immediate predecessor — "...by Gruun, what is that on your face?"

"Acne," Gorgeous said, and then let out a belch. "If you think this is bad, you should see the pimples on my ass."

"By His Foot, Gorgeous, you are an ugly son of a bitch. Why don't you go slam your face against that wall until I can stand to look at you?"

"Sure thing, boss. How ugly am I going for — your sister after she gets kicked milking the cow, or your mom after she won't blow your old man?"

Everybody froze. The two stared at each other, faces unreadable. Then they both broke up laughing.

Prof looked at the work Gorgeous had done to adjust his clothes. "You're actually doing a great job there — hey, if this Raider thing doesn't work out for you, you might have a future as a tailor. But you could do a little better making up your bunk."

"Sir, consider it done."

IT STARTED JUST LIKE any other day — Taba came in banging on his drum, and ran us through exercises with meels. The exercises were noticeably less strenuous than usual — the idea, I suppose, was to loosen us up.

After breakfast, Sculler appeared, and he and Taba led us on a march — so far, no different from any other day. Except this time, on the route where we would normally have turned right to head back to our barracks, we turned left. Taba — who was in the lead, with Sculler back off to the side, trying to be inconspicuous — gave no indication that anything was up: Just another day of training, no different from any other. In fact, I don't think any of us realized there was anything different until we headed down an unfamiliar road through a thick forest in the northern part of the base. Wym sneaked a look over his shoulder at me and nodded: This was it.

The forest we made our way through was very thick, with some of the largest trees we'd seen on base. The shade was actually cool and refreshing, and the trees were filled with the songs of birds. Had we been anywhere else, I would have called it a pleasant stroll.

We marched for a long time through the forest — well over an hour. Finally, though, we could see an open space through the trees off to the side. Then I heard water gently lapping at a shoreline. We emerged into a big, open area beside a large lake whose smooth surface reflected the tall, snow-capped peak which rose sharply in the distance.

We were in a broad, flat area cleared of trees. Several roads led out of the woods from different directions into this common area.

Up ahead, along the shore of the lake was a wide strip of sand. In the sand were three large, circular areas marked out by wooden fences. Each ring had a small raised portion where three or four men could stand and get a clear view of the fights — for the judges, I learned. There were also a number of carts pulled up nearby, loaded up with mock weapons and armor.

As before, One One Five was the first to arrive. We had barely gotten settled when the next group arrived. As they got close, I couldn't turn my head to get a good look at them, but from the corner of my eye, I knew from the colors of their standard — green and gold — that it was Three One Five.

After they'd arranged themselves in formation, we had to wait a couple of minutes before Two One Five arrived. And when they did, I wasn't sure if I should be worried or elated.

Two One Five was cocky, that was obvious. You could see it in those shit-eating grins they had, which almost begged you to punch them. If nothing else, fighting them would be satisfying.

Did all that confidence mean they knew something we didn't, or were they still riding the high from coming in first the last time? One thing was certain, though — their discipline had taken a hit. Their guidon held their standard — red and gold — at a sloppy angle. Several of their guys were noticeably out of step while marching. I couldn't get a look at Taba from where I was standing, but I'm sure his butt cheeks were clenched in rage.

Once everybody was in place at attention, Lt. Col Ilos appeared and gave a little speech laying out the rules: No hits to the groin. Only two fighters in the ring at a time. No interference from anyone outside the ring. And so on, blah blah blah. We knew all of it. We were itching to kick some ass.

"This isn't the Royal Games," Ilos explained. "There's no tournament brackets in battle." Matches would be set up by random draw, continuing until everybody in all three platoons had a chance to fight at least once. There was no time limit; matches continued until one fighter submitted, or was off his feet for at least 15 consecutive seconds, whether through pinning, knockout, exhaustion, whatever. No fighting a man off his feet if he was not fighting back. Since the numbers weren't even, a few "lucky" guys would have to fight more than once.

After all that, the judges would huddle together and then eliminate one platoon. The decision was made purely based on the judges' estimate of each platoon's fighting skill, not how many fights they won.

For the last fight, it was a tag-team match. Each platoon got to choose which fighter they wanted to start, and each platoon got three "tags" — opportunities to switch out fighters in the course of the fight. The fighter in the ring could choose anybody he wanted. The winner of the last fight was the champion platoon, and brought home the victory medallion to hang on its bunkroom wall beneath its standard.

That medallion belonged on *our* wall.

Matchups were drawn at random out of buckets. The first guy up from our platoon was Wym.

After all the time Wym had spent preparing to fight someone much larger, his big fight seemed somewhat anticlimactic...at first. He was matched with a guy from Two One Five who was not much bigger than he was. When we saw his opponent, our guys started whooping in triumph before the judge could even blow his whistle to start the match. I'd seen Wym take down Gorgeous more than once — how hard could this dude be?

Plenty hard, as it turned out. Wym's opponent might have been slight, but he was fast. At one point in the fight, he came close to the side of the ring where I was watching. In between his pads, I could see that despite his small frame, the guy was wrapped in tight, sinewy muscles. He started by landing a whole series of good, solid hits. I wasn't sure little Wym was going to recover.

But I needn't have worried. Fighting bigger guys had taught Wym how to take a hit — and he wasn't exactly slow himself. After a couple of minutes, it became clear that though his opponent was fast, speed was basically his only advantage. He was lousy with his balance, and Wym eventually picked up on that. After getting repeatedly dumped on his ass, the guy must have realized he was getting nowhere, and he quickly submitted.

My name came up in the next draw. I wish I could sit here and tell you it was some kind of an epic brawl for the ages, but Auld Father's truth, it was about as bad as a gentle breeze on a warm day in the Warrens.

My opponent was some guy from Three One Five. I gathered from the cheering from his comrades that he was supposed to be some kind of hotshot. And indeed, when the whistle blew he came out doing some kind of whirling, weaving, jumping crap that told me he'd probably watched too many Sulan-style boxing matches like the kind I'd seen at the Royal Games. I guess I was supposed to be intimidated, but all I could think of was that he looked like a dancing girl on stage at Mallee's.

I closed in on him quickly and easily brushed aside his fancy moves with my shield. Then I gave a him a few good whacks on the head with my wooden sword and used the hilt to give him a good, hard pop in the kidney. From the way he reacted, I could tell he'd never taken hits like that before. A few more hits and a good kick and he submitted. I'd barely broken a sweat.

Fent was right about the padding — it was much lighter and looser than what we normally sparred with. Our training gear felt like molasses next to this stuff. I don't want to say I could move twice as fast as I could in training gear, but it sure felt that way. It reminded me a bit of the homemade padding we'd sometimes use in street brawls back home.

Unfortunately, being lighter, it wasn't as good at soaking up blows. My opponent did get a couple of clean hits on my forearm, and they stung. I still felt a dull pain an hour later.

I missed Skunk's fight, since his was at the same time as mine, but everyone told me it had been downright jaw-dropping. His opponent had apparently been pretty good and fearsome, but Skunk had made a mockery of the guy.

"He didn't even look like he was trying," Limul said, shaking his head.

There was one fight, though, that I was determined to see: Parsa.

Over the preceding weeks, I'd watched Parsa progress. He was no longer the wavering, easily-overwhelmed fighter I'd had to start with. I'd managed to shape him into a very respectable brawler who could have easily held his own in a no-holds-barred street fight. I was 90 percent sure he could handle anybody he might have to face. If he could close the gap with his opponent and get inside his swing, his wrestling instincts would deliver the rest.

I say "90 percent," though, because I knew there was one kind of opponent he couldn't handle: A very sharp, well-trained technical fighter like Skunk — or Sculler and Taba, for that matter. He wasn't very good at hiding his moves — even I could see them coming from a mile away. He was fast and strong enough that it usually didn't matter, but against someone with training...

"Training," as Skunk explained it to me, "gives you options. I've trained under an experienced fightmaster since I was six summers in age. So I have a lot of options."

And a fighter who signals moves well in advance, the way Parsa did, gives you more time to consider your options.

"Every extra second I have — every extra half-second — gives me more of an edge," Skunk said.

So Parsa ought to be fine, I thought...if he doesn't have to fight someone like Skunk.

I was watching Prof fight when I heard Parsa's name announced. As much as I wanted to stay — Prof's bout was actually pretty exciting — I rushed off to the ring at the far end. I imagine I felt something like a dad about to watch his son take his first steps.

Parsa was pulling on his helmet as I reached the side of the ring. I grabbed his head and whispered a few words of advice — "close fast, get inside" — then turned to see who he'd be up against.

At first glance, I felt a sense of relief. The guy from Two One Five looked like a real meathead. Big but kind of soft — the kind of clumsy ox who mostly fights with his weight. But as he came closer, I started to feel a nervous tremble in my gut.

Peeking out from beneath his pads, he sported numerous scars. I recognized the pattern — it was the kind of wounds I'd seen a thousand times on pit fighters back in the Improvement District. I wasn't sure how a pit fighter managed to get into the Raiders — they're not exactly known for being very bright, and this one didn't look any different — but I knew Parsa's chances were not good.

The judge blew the whistle, and Parsa and his foe came on hard. Parsa did just as I'd trained, and tried to close the gap, but his opponent swung his wooden sword quick and hard, sending Parsa sprawling.

Parsa leaped back up only to be bashed back down with his opponent's shield. I recognized the moves — the guy was a baton fighter, and a damn good one. The way he held his sword and shield was odd — it wouldn't have worked against an opponent with a real sword, because he made almost no attempt to protect his legs. But armed with nothing but lumber, he was ferocious.

Again and again, I watched Parsa stand up and bravely charge the guy, and again he sent Parsa sprawling into the sand. At one point, Parsa got up and I could see the sand caked around a nasty open cut on his cheek. I'd spent hours training Parsa to ignore his instincts to duck and dodge blows, telling him he could take it, that nobody could hit him hard enough to do any real damage. And he'd taken the lesson to heart.

But by teaching him that, I'd left him with a giant hole in his fighting skills, and this motherfucker was charging right through it again and again, bashing Parsa around the ring like a toy.

Parsa never gave up. Each time he went down, he tried to get up again. But after a few minutes, the pain and exhaustion started to get the better of him. I watched as tried for the umpteenth time to pull himself to his feet, but his opponent just slammed a foot down on his back and pressed him down into the sand. He struggled with every ounce of strength he had, but it wasn't enough. Ten seconds went by, 15. And it was over.

I rushed over to help him out of the ring, throwing my arm around him to try to give some encouragement, but as soon as he saw my face, he shoved me away.

"Fuck off, scaleback," he hissed as he stalked off to the aid station to get his cuts bandaged.

The looks I received from the other guys in my platoon were hard to read. Some seemed sorry for me; others looked at me in disgust. I looked around for Skunk — not because I was eager to see him, but just because, well — I guess I was looking for forgiveness. I finally saw him walking around the edge of the ring, his face a mask of stone. I came up to him and greeted him, and he looked at me with something like pity — but it was the kind of pity that comes from great disappointment. He sighed and brushed past me, heading over to the aid station to join Parsa.

The fights went on for another couple of hours. I watched a few more, though I was in too much of a daze to pay much attention. From what I could see, not many of the guys from Three One Five could quite put it together — a few of them were pretty good, but they hadn't spent nearly as much time in their arena as we had, and it showed. The guys from Two One Five were very good — easily a match for us. I don't think anybody was much surprised when the judges announced Three One Five was out of the running.

SO THE BIG MATCH would be between us and Two One Five. They gave us an hour to talk things over and agree on a strategy.

To me, the strategy was obvious, and I said so: We should send Skunk out there as our first fighter. He could probably win the whole thing by himself without tagging any of us.

"Yeah, we all saw what a fucking mastermind you are, Lips," somebody snarled. I bristled, but didn't argue.

I felt a hand on my arm and turned to see Prof. He gave me a nod, then turned to the group.

"I wouldn't be so quick to dismiss Lips; he's right that Skunk is the one who's going to win this for us," he said.

Skunk was leaning against the ring fence, his arms crossed. He didn't say a word. If he was flattered by Prof's comment, he didn't show it.

Prof continued. "But I agree we shouldn't put him out there first. We don't know what could happen once that whistle blows; the way I see it, our job here is to minimize the ways things could go wrong. I think we should wear Two One Five down, then send Skunk in to wrap it up."

There were nods and murmurs of approval. It was interesting to see how everyone so easily deferred to Prof, and how naturally the role of command seemed to come to him. Maybe that klanger's big brain was useful for something other than books.

"So who leads off, then?" Wym asked, obviously hoping it would be himself. For a guy who was so scared a few weeks before, he'd really developed a passion for scrapping; he was born-again hard. He'd be great to have at your shoulder in a street fight.

"Wym, you are a bona-fide bone-crunching badass, and I admire the hell out of you, but this isn't the best job for you. What we need is three guys who can take a lot of damage and give a lot back. We want to plow the road free of obstacles for Skunk," Prof said. "I'd suggest we start off with Gorgeous."

Gorgeous let loose a big grin and did a little dance, then flexed his muscles and posed like a statue. We whooped in approval.

"Not only am I gonna put my padded boot up some red-and-gold Two One Five ass, I'm gonna look sexy when I do it," Gorgeous boasted.

Prof smiled, and continued. "That's exactly what we want, Gorgeous. If there's anybody who knows how to take a hit with style, it's you."

"Shit. Ain't nobody gonna lay a finger on me."

"Well if you can pull that off, that's great, but the idea is to wear them down. Ideally, we want the first guy to pack it in and get them to use their first tag. Rope-a-dope, you might say."

Prof was clever. He knew how Gorgeous's ego would react to "rope-a-dope."

"Hey hey hey, I ain't no string puppet," he said.

"We don't want you to be. Not exactly. We want you to get them riled up. So they won't think straight. So they slip up."

Gorgeous stroked his chin. "Gotcha. So I retire the first guy. Then what?"

"Just last as long as you can, then tag out."

"What makes you think I'm gonna need to tag out?"

"Call it a hunch."

"Okay. Hunch, then. Who do I tag?"

"I'd say we go with Blockhead."

Blockhead looked up.

"Huh? Why me?"

"Well — call it another hunch. I saw you fight that big son of a bitch from Three One Five earlier."

"But...I lost."

"Right. But you lasted a good 10 minutes with him, at least."

"Yeah..."

"How many else of you saw that fight?" Maybe half the hands went up. "Okay, how many of you could have lasted 10 minutes with that guy?"

Every hand went back down.

"Five minutes?" Prof pressed.

No hands were raised. Prof folded his arms in satisfaction.

"Blockhead — no offense, but your name fits."

Blockhead shrugged. Prof went on: "Block here might not be the best fighter we've got, but he takes hard hits and gives them right back. We want him to soak up damage and hopefully get the next guy to tag out, and hopefully the guy after that. Then he'll tag Skunk, who'll come in and clean up."

Everybody looked at Skunk. He still looked unimpressed.

"Sounds like a good idea, but I think you're forgetting something," Skunk said.

Prof smiled — almost like he was expecting this. He gestured to Skunk to continue.

Skunk sighed. "Two," he said, holding up two fingers. "That's two tags. We get three. If I get my ass kicked, you got someone in mind to send in after me?"

"Oh, no, you're definitely our cleanup, Skunk. Whatever happens, you'll be the last one standing."

"I'm still not hearing an answer to my question."

"Ah. Yes. Block, if you're getting absolutely killed out there and they haven't used their second tag, you'll tag in Lips."

Nobody said anything, but from the nervous shuffling, you could tell they wanted to.

"No, hear me out. Lips, how old were you when you first got punched in the mouth?"

I thought back. "Eight summers. Or maybe nine. No, wait — I remember now. It was eight. Definitely eight."

Then with no warning at all, Prof whirled around and took a swing at me. I jumped back to avoid it.

"Hey, what in Gruun's name..."

Prof folded his arms again. "Except for Skunk, Lips has been fighting for longer than any of us have, and more importantly is the way he learned to fight."

"How do you mean?" Gorgeous asked.

Prof looked at me. "Correct me if I'm wrong here, Lips, but where you come from, you had to be ready for somebody to jump you at any time, right?"

"Yeah..."

"There's probably not a lot of cheap shots anyone could pull on you, right? Look at how you were able to dodge that punch I threw."

"You weren't exactly moving like a scorpion's stinger."

"Granted. But still, you had no reason to expect I would do that. And you still reacted just right."

"I can't do that all the time," I said, then nodded at Skunk: "He's the one who can dodge raindrops."

"Right, but the point is, you're tough and you're no stranger to this. In a fight, you're not an expert in anything, but you're pretty good at everything. Am I wrong?"

I thought for a moment.

"No," I answered honestly.

"Right. You can take a hit almost as good as Blockhead, and you should be able to at least hold your own no matter what crazy stuff they throw at you. That's all we need. You know the ballista play in skram?"

"Shit, dwarf. Remember who you're talking to."

"It's like that: You're the secondary. You just set everything up, and Skunk comes in and delivers the win."

"But I probably won't have to, though."

"I doubt it. I think Gorgeous and Blockhead can handle this, but I think we should have you as backup — just in case."

"Just in case."

"Yeah."

I looked at Skunk. "What do you think?" I asked.

Skunk straightened up, looked around — all eyes were on him.

"What I think," he said, "is that I'm ready to go out there and show Two One Five, and that son of a bitch Sgt. Sculler, and that asshole Sgt. Taba, and all those ball-licking officers with their damn medals just who the meanest, leanest, and cleanest outfit in all of the Blue Fucking Wood really is."

I'm pretty sure you could have heard the cheers all the way to Solta.

PROF HAD EVERYBODY DON sparring pads and have shields and swords ready. I wasn't sure there would be enough to outfit our entire platoon, but surprisingly, there were.

The quartermaster didn't seem the least bit surprised when we all lined up to get gear.

"He knows," Prof explained. "He's seen this before."

I didn't quite understand what Prof was getting at until we arrived at the ring where the fight would take place. It was the one in the center, the largest of the three.

It was getting dark, so they set up torches along the rails that marked out the ring. As we drew up alongside it, I saw that Two One Five had only six fighters outfitted in sparring pads. They looked at us in confusion.

Ohhhhhh, I thought to myself. *They've got no idea who our fighters are, since we're all in gear. They don't know what to expect.*

That was Prof: Always thinking ahead.

After they explained the rules one last time, Lt. Col. Ilos asked, "One One Five, have your first fighter come forward."

Gorgeous leaped over the railing in one fluid motion. Once in the ring, he immediately began strutting and posing, accompanied by loud hoots and whistles from our side. Prof had told him to prance around like a Kanassi stallion — not that Gorgeous needed any encouragement, but he did seem to give it an extra bit of flair.

After a minute or so of this, one of the judges motioned for us to calm down, which we did reluctantly. When we were quiet, he turned to Two One Five and asked them to send their guy out.

"Their guy" was by far the largest in their platoon, standing a full head taller than the next-tallest recruit. He certainly wasn't an athlete — instead of leaping over the railing like Gorgeous, he sort of rolled over it like a side of beef coming through a slaughterhouse. After 14 weeks of training, you couldn't call the guy "fat," but he was still pretty beefy. His frame was powerful, but these weren't training muscles — from his rough skin, it was obvious he was used to some kind of backbreaking work. Looking at him, I was reminded of the stevedores down at the docks back home.

He moved slowly but purposefully through the ring. When he turned to salute his fellows, they let loose with a low, challenging roar. Their mockery for us was unmistakable. I felt my face grow hot. Boy, if I got in that ring...

The judge called for their side to pipe down, and after everything was calm, he ordered the fighters to their places. He blew the whistle, and it began.

As soon as I saw Two One Five's ox take his first few swings, I knew Gorgeous had the fight in the bag. Gorgeous knew it, too, and he mercilessly toyed with his foe, dodging blows with exaggerated flourishes like he was some dancer at a Royal Ball, and jabbing and striking with deliberately showy, over-the-top attacks. He made sure to mug for the crowd at every opportunity — a dumb move in normal circumstances, since it left him wide open to attack. But his opponent was slow enough that he was never in any real trouble, and anyway, the clown show was part of our strategy.

I was beginning to wonder why they'd sent the big oaf out there to begin with when Gorgeous made a bad step at one point. The extra step he needed to regain his balance was all the time his opponent needed.

He landed a good, solid hit on Gorgeous's side. Gorgeous — who wasn't small himself — was lifted up off his feet. The meaty "thunk" of the hit was bad enough that even I felt it. Gorgeous flew up in the air at least two feet. There were gasps on our side; Two One Five let out another arrogant roar.

It was a terrific blow, and when Gorgeous landed, he was moving noticeably slower. The wincing look on his face showed he was in a good bit of pain.

Gorgeous quickly regained his good spirits — though maybe they weren't quite as good as before. He reined in the clown act a little bit to concentrate on fighting — though he made sure to throw in a few faces and mocking gestures every now and then.

It turned out that bell-ringing blows was the only tool in the big guy's kit. He managed to land a couple more glancing blows, and while Gorgeous told me later that they stung like fire, he was able to keep going. A few more minutes of Gorgeous's act and the ox was out of wind. Those hard swings began to take their toll, and every time he slowed down to catch his breath, Gorgeous was right there pressing him. His opponent was finally reduced to having to just hold up his shield and back away to avoid attacks.

The big man finally made his way to the side of the ring and tagged a comrade, who whipped over the side and began a furious assault on Gorgeous.

The new opponent looked like he might have stepped right off a Raiders recruiting poster. He'd chosen a full-face sparring helmet — better for protection, but it obstructs your vision — so I couldn't make out his face. Maybe he looked like a troll underneath — but you could see even with his padding that the rest of him was built like a statue.

Gorgeous fought back, but this guy was really, really good. From the looks of it, he'd had a lot of practice — he was very precise and technical, and after a minute or so it was clear that Gorgeous was no match for him.

In fact, the way he was fighting reminded me of Skunk. He couldn't be that good, could he? I looked over at Skunk. He was carefully studying Gorgeous's opponent, but if he was worried, you couldn't read it.

Gorgeous's antics were gone now, and he fought valiantly for awhile, somehow never losing his smile. But after a few more minutes, it was clear he was done. He did a merry little dance over to the side of the ring and, almost like it was an afterthought, tagged in Blockhead.

Gorgeous leaped out of the ring like a conquering champion, with plenty of cheers and backslaps from our guys. Even though he'd just been convincingly outmatched, from the way he carried himself — and from the reaction we gave him — you'd think he'd just won the whole thing for us.

At first, it didn't seem like things were going well for Blockhead. He wasn't as slow as the big guy Two One Five had led with, but he sure wasn't quick, either. Two One Five's golden boy mostly ducked and dodged his swings with ease.

But as Blockhead shrugged off one blow after another and kept on coming, it became clear that Prof's plan was still sound. Golden boy's weakness soon became clear — he was so reliant on his technique that he had no soul, no heart. Even though he was obviously not low-born, I recognized the type from back in the Warrens: His fight is all about a terrific opening, but there's no follow-through. Once it's clear that his opponent isn't intimidated by his skill, he doesn't have any other cards to play.

And whether it was from golden boy starting to get tired or Blockhead finally picking up on his opponent's rhythm enough to catch him when he slipped, our man started to get in a few good blows of his own.

Blockhead couldn't deliver massive earth-shakers like Two One Five's first fighter, but he hit hard enough. And he seemed as much a stranger to pain as a deaf man is to sound. At one point, he made a bad misstep that left him wide open, and golden boy went right for it, delivering a powerful head blow with his wooden sword that probably would have knocked a guy like Prof unconscious. But Blockhead just shook his head like he'd gotten dust in his eye and then kept on coming.

They fought for what felt like a long time — it was by far the longest match I'd seen all day. Blockhead was like a stonemason working a block of granite — at first, it doesn't look like he's getting much done, just a chip here and a flake there, but he keeps at it and keeps at it and before you know it you see the work taking

shape. Chip by chip, Blockhead wore down golden boy, until at last the fellow started looking groggy. Blockhead was shaking off another of his blows when golden
boy shook his head and jogged over to the railing and tagged in a new fighter.

Our side cheered, of course, but my own voice was cut short when I saw Two
One Five's next man jump into the ring. It was the guy who'd fought Parsa — that
blasted pit fighter with all the scars.

He came in fast and immediately started doing damage. Blockhead managed
to get in a few good hits, but this was a guy who had made his living sponging up
pain, and it showed. Two One Five recognized what was going on, too and they
began to whoop and jeer at us as Blockhead started to get his ass kicked.

The guy was so, so fast. Blockhead just couldn't keep up, and he was getting
pounded.

At first, Blockhead held up the same before, and it looked like we might be in
for another long, dragged-out fight as each man slowly wore down his opponent.

But then Two One Five's man suddenly delivered a quick volley of attacks that left
Blockhead staggering. He fell down...and this time, he didn't spring right back up.

The judge started the count: "One! Two! Three!" For the first few seconds,
Blockhead didn't even move. Then we saw his arm twitch, and he slowly pulled
himself to his feet, lifting himself to a standing right at 10.

From the moment Blockhead was back on his feet, his opponent came roaring in
and began another relentless assault. Blockhead was visibly struggling to keep up
with him, and when he got knocked down a second time, I wasn't sure he'd get up.

The count started again. I watched as Blockhead slowly pulled himself to all
fours, shaking his head again from dizziness. He took a few deep breaths, and started to crawl over to the railing. I raced over and he tagged me in as soon as he was
within arm's length. I leaped over the railing and into the ring, prepared to die.

52

There was, of course, no way I was going to beat this guy, I thought, but I kept reminding myself of the strategy: Just plow the road for Skunk. Get in there and do as much damage as you can for as long as you can, then hand it over to our ace to finish. It looked like Skunk was going to have a harder job than we expected, but my job was to make it less of a chore than it needed to be.

I was in no mood to start getting pounded right away, so I started out rope-a-doping him, dancing and dodging in and out of range. Unfortunately, unlike Gorgeous, I am not any kind of natural entertainer, so I didn't have any taunts or goofy hamming to keep the crowd entertained. I heard a chorus of boos coming from Two One Five. Then a chant started: "Fight! Fight! Fight! Fight!"

I had hoped that I might be able to use this act to get into my foe's head, but after a few minutes it became clear it wasn't working. He remained unmoved; he had seen it all before. He wasn't about to waste any of his strength or energy on one of my bullshit fake-outs.

So that's how it was gonna be: I would have to play the punching bag. I'd have to put myself in there and get clobbered until I couldn't take it anymore and then hope he didn't have enough firewood left in the shed to burn though Skunk.

I took a long, deep sigh. This was gonna *hurt*.

But by Auld Father, I was gonna make him work for it.

I faked to my left, and at the last moment I switched and tried to get a jab in past his shield. He saw it coming a mile away, and I felt my sword arm brutally slapped away. Then he gave me a good kick in the knee and then knocked me to the ground with his shield.

That was pretty much what I expected, but by Gruun, I didn't expect his blows to sting so bad. The sparring pads were next to useless.

But I'd fallen in such a way that my opponent mostly blocked the view of the judges. So I made like I was grabbing at my knee — believe me, it wasn't a stretch to sell that one — and I grabbed a handful of sand and threw it right in his face.

Oh, yeah. I see I forgot to mention earlier that throwing sand in the eyes was against the rules. I didn't care. Look, the Raiders could hand me all the rules they wanted to about how to eat, how to sleep, how to take a shit and how to wipe my ass, and I was fine with all of it. But if the spirit of Major Braborn was looking down on me, I find it hard to believe he was gonna have much of a problem if I had to break a few rules to get one over on the enemy. What had Taba told us that time when he'd taken apart "A-1" Avor? "War's got nothing to do with how smooth you are, how cool you look, or how many points you can score," he'd said. "Whether you do it as a gentleman or whether you do it as a snake doesn't really matter."

Well, I'd decided I was going to be a snake.

Of course, I used my opponent's sudden confusion to give him a solid thwack on the skull and a few more in the torso.

I don't know if the judges saw what I did — like I said, the guy's back was to them — but most everybody else saw it. There was a brief moment of weird silence right after it happened, as if nobody knew quite how to react. Then I heard a loud round of boos from Two One Five, along with some nervous sounding cheers from my side.

Then the dumbass did something I didn't expect. He turned to the judge's stand and held his hands out, as if to say, "What the fuck, man?"

And doing so, he turned his back to me. He just stood there and gave me a perfect clean shot. So of course I did what any Warrens brawler would have done: I took a running leap and crashed into the center of his back, boots first.

I don't want to sound like I'm bragging here, but I am pretty sure that got the biggest, loudest reaction of the night from the crowd.

Mr. Human Cockfighter went down, and I launched into an attack on him while he was still flat on his face. This was another no-no — the rules said no fighting a man on the ground unless he was fighting back.

This time, there's no way the judges could have missed it. I thought I'd just get a few licks in until I heard the whistle sound, but no whistle came. So I continued kicking and striking him until he, too, belatedly realized the judges weren't going to save him, and finally flipped himself over and started fighting back. Once he actually did start fighting back, he was quickly back on his feet and getting the best of me, but in the meantime I'd managed to rough him up pretty good, I thought.

Maybe so, but I'd also managed to whip him into a boiling rage. His face flushed red and he bellowed in anger.

"I'm going to kick your scaleback ass all the way back to the ocean then cut you into chum and feed you to your cousins," he barked, which sent the guys from Two One Five into a spasm of taunts and curses. "You'll wish you could sprout fins like your bitch-hag of a mother to swim away."

I flashed the biggest grin I could muster. "At least my mom isn't roasting on a spit with an apple in her mouth like yours!" I said with a wink, and it was shortly after those words left my lips that everything went black. I never even saw the hit coming.

Sitting here right now, I can still call up the throb-throb-throb hammering inside my skull that I felt when I opened my eyes and realized I was on the ground. I can't have been out of it more than a second or two, because I heard the judge's count start at the same time I became aware of the throbbing, coming in perfect sync with it: "One (throb)! Two (throb)! Three (throb!)" And so on. Even though I couldn't actually remember getting hit, or being knocked to the ground, when I asked Prof about it later, he said Pit Fighter had caught me real good with the edge of his shield.

But at just that moment, I was laid out on the sand with a head that felt like a troll was using it for a drum.

I started to move my hand, but felt a big foot come down hard on my sword arm.

"Oh, no, you're not going to pull that one on me twice, you scaleback shit," Pit Fighter growled.

Which was fine, because it put his leg in the perfect position for me to lean over and bite it.

The way the guy yelled, you'd think he'd never been bit before — I mean, it's not unheard of in a pit fight. Maybe he still thought this was a fair fight.

Oh, that's right. I forgot to say, biting was "against the rules," too. Prof told me later that when I chomped Pit Fighter's ankle, he saw the head DC for Two One Five start shoving people aside to charge over to the judge's stand and start protesting. The judges, Prof said, just waved him away.

Anyway, while my foe was howling and grabbing at his foot, and all the clowns in Two One Five were booing me, I leaped back up and grabbed my sword — but not my shield. Instead, with my head still throbbing, I gave my opponent a hard kick and then took my wooden-bladed sparring sword in two hands — blade first. I gripped it hard; had it been a real sword, I would have sliced my hands to ribbons.

Then with both hands, I gave it a good swing, using the heavy steel handle to deliver a good thwack right to my opponent's head.

Hey, I aimed for the thickest part of his helmet. It couldn't have been any worse than what he'd already done to me.

He fumbled around for his shield and sword, grabbing both before I could get in another hit. But even with his guard up and blade ready, I could see he was still a bit dizzy. The way my own head felt, I didn't think I was going to last much longer, so I thought I'd take one more big, crowd-pleasing blow. I swung hard. He saw it coming, and raised his shield to block it, but I don't think he was prepared for the force of the blow, because it sent him staggering and he tipped over. With my last bit of strength I surged forward and kicked him in the ribs. I felt a satisfying beefy slap as my foot connected, but I was done.

I started edging my way slowly to the side of the ring, so I could quickly tag in Skunk. I watched Pit Fighter pull himself back to his feet and shake his head; I was certain he was going to come charging right at me. I gave a quick glance over my shoulder, seeing Skunk move himself into position. As soon as my opponent started his attack, I planned to whip around and tag Skunk, then pull myself over the railing and collapse in pain and exhaustion.

But Pit Fighter didn't charge me. He stood there, looking at me with his head cocked. He paced back and forth, apparently trying to size up the situation. Then he shook his head, turned his back on me and walked over to the side of the ring in disgust. I straightened up. Was he going to tag out? Did I just...beat a professional fighter?

He turned back and gave me one last look. It was a mixture of anger and something else — frustration, maybe? He turned and tagged in a new guy, who climbed into the ring with slow, steely resolve.

I could have taken two quick steps and tagged in Skunk. My body was already half-turned to do just that. But seeing this new opponent, something made me turn back to face him. The throbbing pain in my head was still there, but it was crowded out by curiosity.

So this was the recruit Two One Five was counting on to carry them to victory. I assumed that, like us, they would have been smart enough to save their best guy for last.

The fellow walking purposefully across the ring towards me didn't look intimidating. He was a dwarf, and not a terribly tough-looking one, either. He wasn't wrapped in bulging muscle like Sgt. Taba; in fact, he was actually shorter and thinner than Prof.

I'd fought Prof enough times not to be fooled by the size — that dwarven upper-body strength is no joke. One good hit could send you flying. But what dwarves have in strength, they lack in speed. Fighting them is mostly about learning to read their physical cues, then moving safely out of the way before they actually hit you. With a little practice, it's not too difficult for many humans.

So yeah, I admit my curiosity outweighed my better judgment. I began walking over to meet this odd new opponent. I put my sword and shield up and got into a fighting stance, not really sure what to expect.

As I got within a few steps of him, he suddenly speeded up his pace and closed the distance very quickly. That was the last thing I clearly remember.

Okay, you know how I just said dwarves were slow? This one wasn't slow.

The next thing I knew I was on my back, with everything feeling fuzzy. I could hear a count-off, but it seemed to be in the distance. Everything seemed to be in the distance. I pulled myself up and looked around; I realized I was nowhere near where I'd been standing, which was approximately where my dwarven opponent now had his feet planted.

He had...thrown me. He'd somehow used his shield and sword to pick me up and throw me to the other side of the ring. That by itself wasn't surprising — like I said, dwarves are strong. But I couldn't even remember him making a move; he'd been so fast that the whole thing was over before I realized it.

Seeing him stalk towards me like a beast about to devour its prey, I got up, dropped my shield, and flipped my sword around to use as a club again, like I'd done with the last guy. The dwarf was between me and the side of the ring where Skunk stood at the ready. I didn't know what this new enemy's deal was, but I knew I wasn't cut out to handle it. All I could think of was my throbbing head.

My goal was just to get across the ring and tag Skunk and get out of there; I figured that the prospect of getting hit with that thick metal handle would convince this guy to give me enough space to make my exit. I gave the backwards sword a good swing as if to emphasize I was serious.

The dwarf stopped, and cocked his head. I could see him smiling.

The smile seemed to say, "I've got you right where I want you," and I believed it. I began edging my way across the ring, back towards the spot where I'd seen Skunk moving. I didn't dare glance back to make sure I had it right; I was certain that was all the opening this klanger bastard would need to get the drop on me.

Then the dwarf held up his arms and, in a fuck-you flourish worthy of Gorgeous, he dropped his sword and shield. The roar of excitement this raised among Two One Five's recruits told me all I needed to know about what this meant. He started pacing calmly toward me, and when I saw him start to drop into a fighting stance I swung as fast and hard as I could. All my weapon found was empty air — not that I cared; I was just trying to buy time. I let the sword fly out of my hands and turned to lunge for the side of the ring, ready to tag Skunk...when I found myself being whirled around and slammed backwards into the sand.

I tried to move, but I was held fast. A massively powerful force pressed my legs and torso into the soft sand; try as I might, they would not move. I lifted my sword arm, only to feel it slammed violently down; it, too, was now held fast. I tried my shield arm; I could move my fingers, but the forearm was caught in a steel-like grip that dug into my flesh.

I felt hot flesh and scratchy stubble against my face, and loud, moist breathing. A muffled voice said, "Give up. Give up, there's no fighting this. There's no way out. Just give up like the pussy you are."

I don't know who you are reading this. When I get done with this, I imagine Footman Sesh is going to have it filed away in one of those endless cave-like libraries you scholars have, the ones where long-beard doctors and professors spend their days shuffling around in the darkness, finding their way by lamplight, sweeping away the dust and spiderwebs from numberless sheaves of bound paper read by nobody until they crumble into moldy ruins. Sitting here scratching out these words with my pen, I cannot imagine why any soul blessed or cursed by Auld Father might ever want to read them. And that's the only reason I'm saying this, I'm admitting right now that, reader, I was about to give up. I was about to stop fighting and let the count roll out until it was all over.

And then the fucker *had* to call me a scaleback. He said, "Just imagine you're back on whatever shit-smeared beach you call home, scaleback. Just relax and think of the ocean." And though I couldn't move my limbs, I could move my eyes. I saw, just a few feet away, an upside-down face leaning over the ringside railing looking down at me. I saw another face beside it, saying something and reaching out a hand to me, but it was the face directly above me that I was focused on. And at that moment, I knew. I don't know how I knew, but I did. I knew what to do.

I felt the dwarf's sweaty, panting face pressed against mine. So I stuck out my tongue and began licking it, jabbing the tip of my tongue into his nostril.

"Ew! Ewwwwww!" he yelped, and without thinking, he reflexively lifted his hand to push my tongue away, freeing my shield arm for a moment.

It was all I needed. My hand shot out and I tagged not Skunk, who was straining to reach me...

...But Parsa, who was standing right there like a figure in some half-forgotten dream.

53

Everybody around us suddenly got quiet, and there was a moment where everything seemed to stand still, as if nobody was sure what to do. Then I saw Parsa leap over the railing and I felt the powerful force that held me motionless suddenly release. Then I felt many pairs of hands clasp my body and pull me up and over the railing, and then drop me rudely back to the ground. All was blurry for a few moments, while I struggled to get to my feet. My ears were filled with the sounds of my fellow recruits...cheering.

Once I was standing again, things started to come back into focus. I had my back to the ring. I turned around and tried to shove my way to the railing to get a better view. When I finally managed to get into a position where I could see, I looked around and saw Parsa and his opponent on the ground, locked in a ferocious grappling contest.

The dwarf seemed to have Parsa pinned tight, but when I looked at his face, Parsa seemed utterly calm. He slowly maneuvered his limbs into position, then suddenly flipped his opponent over. A few seconds later he had the dwarf pinned on his back. Parsa had his foe in a tight bear hug, preventing him from taking advantage of his powerful arms.

The judges started the count. When they reached "nine" the dwarf's face turned red and angry, and he let out a huge roar and began struggling. Just before the count hit 15, he managed to free himself and get to his feet. He backed up swiftly, putting distance between himself and Parsa, but never letting Parsa out of his sight.

The two circled each other warily. When the dwarf came close to his discarded shield and sword, he quickly picked them up. Parsa responded by picking up his shield — but not his sword.

Crouching low behind his shield, Parsa advanced quickly at the dwarf, who used his own shield to try to push Parsa away. Then in a lightning-fast movement, he thrust his sword past the edge of Parsa's shield and jabbed him hard in the ribs.

Parsa visibly staggered, and dropped back. His shield dipped slightly, and the dwarf gave him a hard thwack in the head, causing him to drop several more wobbly steps back.

The dwarf moved in quickly and tried another fast jab with his sword. Again, I watched Parsa stagger from a blow to the ribs. Then the dwarf let fly with a volley of blows — Parsa tried blocking them with his shield, but he just wasn't fast enough. The dwarf used his shield to give Parsa a huge shove, and One One Five's champion was thrown onto his back in the sand. Instead of immediately jumping on Parsa to pin him, the dwarf turned to the crowd and raised his sword and shield in a triumphant gesture. Two One Five shouted their approval.

I heard insulting murmurs from my side — guys questioning my intelligence, my ancestry, my species. "Scaleback" was uttered a few times. I ignored all of it. If I was wrong, I deserved it.

Was I wrong? The sense of serene assurance I'd felt in my gut when I'd tagged in Parsa was fading fast.

As Parsa lay on his back, I watched the rising and falling of his chest; he was breathing hard, but there was still a spark of defiance in his eyes. While his opponent soaked in the cheers of the crowd, he pulled himself up, and slowly planted his feet in a firmly balanced fighting stance — it was a low, wide crouch which would make it hard for him to move, but also hard to knock down. The dwarf turned to face him, sized him up, and gave a contemptuous smile.

Parsa's lips moved, but I was too far away to hear what he said, or even get a good read on his expression — it might have been a smile, or it might have been a grimace of pain. But what he did next left no room for doubt: He thrust his empty hand out and made a bold "come here" gesture.

The dwarf grinned, and quickly stepped over to face him, dropping into a fighting stance as he got within striking distance. Again, he lashed out with his sword and struck Parsa in the ribs before Parsa could move his shield to block him. Parsa winced, but didn't budge from his stance. He moved his shield to prevent another blow from that direction, but the dwarf responded by twisting his body and thrusting his sword into Parsa's other side — normally a risky move, but Parsa was in no condition to take advantage of it. He simply shrunk behind his shield, waiting for the next blow.

The dwarf was now bobbing around, offering quick feints, apparently at ease with his enemy, as if he'd finally got the measure of him. He made another quick strike with his sword, and a loud "oof" from Parsa made it clear the blow had connected.

But when the dwarf tried to cock his sword arm for another blow, he found he couldn't move it.

When the dwarf had struck with his sword, Parsa used his free hand to grab his opponent's wrist, and he was twisting it. The look of surprise on the dwarf's face when he realized what had happened told me everything I needed to know. It dawned on me then why Parsa was fighting with only his shield: he'd been waiting for this opening. This time, the dwarf's strike had been just a hair too slow.

What happened next happened so fast that I'm not sure if I actually remember seeing it, or if my memory is just filling in the blanks. Parsa pulled the dwarf's arm and twisted it further, spinning his enemy around. He then used a leg sweep to trip his opponent and send him face-first into the ground. Then he used his own shield to lock down the dwarf's shield arm while still twisting his sword arm. He then drove his knee into the dwarf's back, pinning him hard against the sand.

In an eye blink, Parsa had gone from being a punching bag to rendering his opponent helpless; the dwarf kicked and squirmed, but couldn't manage to budge. One of his powerful dwarf arms was twisted back in pain, and the other was locked between his own shield and his opponent's.

The judge counted to 15, and it was all over.

I was knocked to the ground as the guys around me surged over the railing to get to Parsa and lift him onto their shoulders. As I got up, I looked over and saw the head DC for Two One Five next to the judge's stand, his face purple with rage. Lt. Col. Ilos jumped down from the stand and whispered something in the DC's ear, and the man's face went blank. He turned and walked away stiffly.

Everybody from One One Five was crowding around Parsa to congratulate him, but I had something else in mind. I went to go find the pit fighter. I got several "accidental" shoves and jabs from guys in Two One Five as I made my way through the crowd, but I finally found him over near the quartermaster's wagon, pulling off the last of his sparring pads.

"Hey," I said. He turned to look at me.

"Hey, good fight, man," he said. "You're a nasty fighter, but I can't say I blame you. I'd have done the same if I could have gotten away with it."

"Yeah, about that. I have a question."

"Okay."

"What's the First Raider Command?"

"The what?"

"The First Raider Command. Come on. 'I am the sword of Auld Father...'"

He looked at me blankly. I stared at him, nodded, and walked away.

I figured the next person I needed to see was Skunk. I found him standing on the side of the ring, in an animated discussion with Prof. As they saw me getting closer, they both stopped talking and looked directly at me.

I put my hand on Skunk's shoulder.

"Look man, I know I was supposed to..."

I didn't finish my sentence, as Skunk caught me square in the jaw with his clenched fist. I was thrown back, but I caught myself before falling on my ass, dropping into a crouch. I sprung at Skunk, grabbing him in the midsection and trying to throw him to the ground. I knew I didn't stand a chance against Skunk, but I was past the point of caring about pain and figured I'd get in a few good hits before he completely knocked me out.

But after a few seconds I felt hands around my arms and waist dragging me away. I looked and saw Skunk in the same predicament. By this time we were both seeing red, and we both struggled for a moment, but once it was clear neither one of us was going anywhere, we both relaxed — though our platoonmates still held us fast.

"WHAT THE FUCK IS GOING ON HERE?" roared Sgt. Sculler as he shoved his way through the crowd and stood between us. With that, I finally felt the hands gripping me loosen.

"Sir, Recruits Camlin and Pearl are just roughhousing," Prof announced, as if he had the whole situation under control.

"Everything okay with your recruits, Sergeant?" I turned to see Lt. Col. Ilos, who had suddenly appeared beside Sculler. For once, Sgt. Sculler looked as surprised as I was.

"What? No, sir, my boys were just being Raiders; you know how they get."

Sculler tied a bow on his excuse by flashing his huge smile, which caused Ilos to chuckle.

"Understood, but try to have them save it for the battlefield, Sergeant."

"Yes, sir; sometimes, they just can't contain themselves. You two," — he gestured at me and Skunk — "come with me."

SGT. SCULLER FOUND A spot behind an ox cart to give us a little privacy. As soon as we were alone, the grin disappeared.

"Recruit Camlin, would you like to explain to me what just happened back there?"

"Sir, Recruit Pearl did not follow the plan we had agreed upon beforehand. It is this recruit's view that Pearl's decision endangered One One Five's chance at victory."

"Recruit Camlin," Sculler asked slowly, "were you the man in the ring?"

Skunk stiffened. "No, sir."

Sculler relaxed his frown. "Camlin, you're smart. I had hoped that by now you would have picked up on the fact that plans don't win battles — men do. Recruit Pearl was the man on the scene, and he made the call based on the information he had."

"But sir..."

Sculler cut him off with a look, then turned to me.

"Pearl, Recruit Camlin claims you deviated from the plan. Explain yourself. And it had better be good."

"Sir, it was this recruit's judgment that Recruit Parsa was better equipped to handle the opponent than Sku...Recruit Camlin."

"So Recruit Camlin was originally set to be your cleanup, but you tagged in Recruit Parsa."

"Yes, sir."

"And you made this decision why, Recruit Pearl?"

I looked at Skunk, then back at Sgt. Sculler. I realized for the first time that I couldn't explain why I'd chosen Parsa. It was just a feeling that had come upon me in a rush; at the exact moment I'd made my decision, my mind was in a fog, but tagging Parsa had for some reason seemed like the only natural choice in the world. But here afterward, thinking clearly, it seemed like insanity.

I mumbled something about Parsa being a wrestler.

"And?"

I took in a deep breath, to try and organize my jumbled thoughts.

"Recruit Camlin is a very, very skilled fighter, sir," I began. "But the opponent in this case was a dwarf with an obvious wrestling background. Had he been able to get close enough, this recruit believes the opponent could have used his upper body strength to overwhelm Recruit Camlin."

Skunk snorted. "He wouldn't have gotten anywhere near..." A flick of the eyes from Sculler cut him off in mid-sentence.

"And you thought Parsa would be better able to handle the opponent?"

"Sir, the recruit made a snap judgment that Parsa would be a better choice."

"You're sure you weren't letting personal feelings sway your judgment?"

I blinked in confusion. "Sir?"

"You've been assisting Recruit Parsa in training the past few weeks. Are you sure you just weren't trying to give your star pupil a chance to shine and make you look good?"

Was that it? Now that Sculler had pointed it out, it did occur to me that I might have had that thought somewhere in the back of my mind. But Auld Father's Truth, I still don't have a clear idea of why I tagged Parsa. I just know it came to me as a sudden inspiration.

I answered as truthfully as I could: "Sir, this recruit just did what he thought was best at the time."

Sculler eyed me carefully for a moment. "That's all you can do, recruit. Did One One Five achieve victory?" he looked back and forth between me and Skunk.

Finally, Skunk spoke: "We were triumphant, sir."

"Then Recruit Pearl made the right call. In the last analysis, victory or defeat is the only evidence available to us."

Sculler began to turn, as if preparing to dismiss us, but then stopped. He looked at me.

"Recruit Pearl, you look like you have something else on your mind."

I gathered up my courage and spoke: "Sir, this recruit believes Two One Five is guilty of cheating."

Sculler eyed me closely. "Some might say the same thing about you, Pearl."

"No, sir, what the recruit means is that...that..."

I struggled to come up with a way to say it that wouldn't sound too outrageous.

"Sir, the recruit believes Two One Five's cheating...does not originate with its recruits."

"Are you accusing a Raider Drill Commander of misconduct, Recruit Pearl?"

"Sir...I...sir, this recruit doesn't know. Sir, the recruit spoke to one of Two One Five's fighters after the match. The recruit does not believe the fighter is a member of the Raiders or even a recruit. Sir."

Sculler's eyes narrowed. He turned to Skunk.

"Recruit Camlin, you're dismissed."

Skunk looked at me, then back at the Sergeant.

"Yes, sir," he said, and left.

With Skunk gone, Sculler got right up into my face.

"Now just what grounds do you have to make such an outrageous accusation, recruit?"

"Sir, the guy I...the guy this recruit fought with all the scars — he's a professional pit fighter from Solta."

"Maybe he decided to change careers."

"He didn't know the First Raider Command, sir. Also — when this recruit bit his leg..." — I waited for a second to see if Sculler would say anything about that — "...this recruit noticed the tattoo on his ankle. He's one of Bynn Kizer's fighters. Kizer doesn't let his fighters leave his service without either burning off their Kizer tattoo — if he likes them — or cutting off a finger if he doesn't. This guy had all his fingers and still had his Kizer tattoo, which means he's still in Kizer's stable. If this recruit had to guess, he'd say that he was hired out to fight as a ringer for Two One Five."

I paused for a second, then added: "He's probably not the only one."

Sculler was silent for a long time, just staring at me. I could hear his measured breathing.

Finally, he spoke: "Recruit, our King is dead."

54

I looked at Sgt. Sculler, trying to figure out what he meant. It sounded like he'd just said that the King was dead. Was that some kind of code?

"S-s-sir?" I stammered. I was sure I was misunderstanding things.

"Our Royal Sovereign, the leader of our nation, is dead. He was killed a week ago in a battle with the Arcanter. Most of the forces he was leading were wiped out or captured. The Arcanter now controls nearly everything west of the Striped Mountains." He said the last part with a nod at the majestic peaks rising up just west of us.

He paused for a moment, as if he was going to leave it at that. But then he added, "Officers and training staff were told about it this morning. The rest of you will get the official word at a chapel service first thing tomorrow."

"What...what does this mean?"

"It means, recruit, that a second Great War has now begun. It means that, most likely, you and everyone in One One Five, Two One Five, Three One Five, and many of the men you see around you here at Fort Harrel will be sent to fight in Garlund. And many of you will die there."

"Does that include you?"

Sculler sighed, and for the first time since I'd met him, he seemed to talk to me like a fellow human, and not just a piece of meat.

"I don't know yet, recruit. It will depend on what the Father General and his staff determine about the needs of the service. It's possible that they will decide I would do a better job here preparing more young men to be shipped off to get slaughtered."

Sculler spit out the last part with contempt. He wants to go, I realized. He wants to go, but he probably won't.

But I would be going. And it didn't sound like there was much hope that I would be coming home.

"Why are you telling me this?"

"I'm not exactly sure, recruit. I guess I'm trying to say that this is how things work in the real world, once you leave training. If you leave here wearing Raider Blue, I mean."

"How things work? You mean…cheating?"

Sculler sighed. "Sgt. Wulock's character is not a secret. It is also not your concern, recruit."

"Sgt. Wulock?"

"The head DC for Two One Five. The man you just accused of cheating."

I stiffened. "Seeing as this recruit was just on the receiving end of that cheating, he thinks it IS his concern. Sir."

"And you HANDLED the situation, didn't you, recruit? You were presented with a problem, and you found a solution. You didn't just send it up the chain of command. You dealt with it on the spot. Like a Raider would."

"Yes, sir."

"The point is, recruit…the point is that in war, you'll face this sort of thing all the time. The enemy certainly isn't going to respect any rulebook — that goes without saying. But there will even be times when it feels like the enemy is wearing the same uniform that you are. You deal with it. You get the job done. Like you just did."

"By cheating?"

"Sgt. Wulock might say so."

I studied Sculler's face. It was inscrutable.

"But you don't agree," I ventured.

He looked at me a long time before answering.

"Recruit," he finally said, "by this time next year, you will probably be dead on some battlefield in Garlund, and I will be training another bunch of boys to go die right after you. The world is much bigger than Sgt. Wulock's career. It's much bigger than a medallion hanging on a wall back at One One Five's barracks. If a piece of metal on your chest or a letter of reprimand in your file are the limits of your horizon, then none of it really matters anyway."

He waited a moment, and added: "Recruit, for any problem, there's a right way, a wrong way, and a Raider way. If you want someone to sort it out for you, I suggest you pray to Auld Father."

Sculler didn't need to tell me not to share what he'd said with the rest of the platoon. I tried to put on a good face for the rest of the night.

Sgt. Taba took command shortly after my conversation with Sculler. He made us run the whole way back to the barracks, but the spiritual surge from our victory made the whole thing seem effortless. When we got back, Skunk apologized for punching me.

"Don't worry about it," I told him. "If I'd been in your shoes, I would have done the same thing."

My interaction with Parsa was more limited.

We found ourselves standing next to each other as Gorgeous showed off his previously-unrevealed skill at juggling.

"Thanks," Parsa said.

"No, thank you," I said, "for not making me look like the biggest fuckup on two legs."

EVEN THOUGH I KNEW in advance what they would tell us, the chapel service the next day was sobering. It was the first and only time I saw the entire chapel filled — there were so many people that there weren't enough seats. Hundreds of people had to stand. I was told later that nearly every person on base was in attendance.

Everybody who had one arrived in their full dress uniform. Since we didn't yet have ours, we were obviously exempt, though Sgt. Taba's uniform inspection that morning of our Sevenday garments had been especially brutal.

The recruits were all seated in the very front, closest to the pulpit. I think they wanted to emphasize that whatever came next, we recruits were probably going to bear the brunt of it.

The first speaker was General Gern, the commander of Fort Harrel — I'd never seen him before, but I knew about him from his wife's etiquette class. He soberly informed the assembly what I already knew: The King had fallen in battle not more than a few days before. Even as we sat there, his body was on its way back across the Glass Ocean, to be buried with honors in the capital.

When he pronounced the words that the King was dead, they barely had time to escape his lips before gasps erupted from all over the spacious hall. As he continued with the grim news, I heard quiet sobbing. A few people, including a couple of recruits, were so overcome they got up and left the building in obvious distress. Nobody tried to stop them.

I even felt my own eyes getting a little damp around the edges. But a question was gnawing at me. Gen. Gern said the battle had been only a few days ago. The body was practically still warm; how had the word had arrived so quickly? I knew courier gulls were fast, but they still took more than a week to cross the Glass Ocean. When I asked Prof about it later, he chalked it up to magic — high-level enchanters, he said, could broadcast their thoughts and have them picked up by others of their kind anywhere in the world.

"Wouldn't something like that put the Crown Post out of business?" I asked.

He shook his head. "It's not secure. If they send out their thoughts, anyone else of sufficient magical skill can pick them up. Even if you try to disguise the message, say by using a code, they can still read the thoughts behind it directly."

"So there's no privacy."

"Nope. You can use it for things like this. But not for anything you're trying to keep secret."

Well, there was no way something like this could be kept secret.

Gen. Gern went on to explain how it had happened. As he told it, our King had been in charge of a combined force made up of Selvan troops along with the bulk of the Suzer's forces. The King and the troops under his command were supposed to draw the Arcanter into a trap; once they had the Arcanter where they wanted him, the Suzer and his elite guard would then sweep in from the north to catch the enemy by surprise.

I'm not really smart enough to understand all the details of what happened, but through some combination of military genius and dark magic, the Arcanter had completely crushed both armies. Our King had been killed; the Suzer had barely escaped with his life.

What came next was uncertain, but one thing WAS certain — there was no making peace with the Arcanter.

"The darkest evil which has ever threatened this world," was how the next speaker — Footman Glaine, the Footman Magnus — described him.

There had long been rumors and whispers about the Arcanter's bloody rule, but now Footman Glaine talked about it openly, accusing the tyrant of brutality on a mass scale — and confirming that he did indeed wield the terrifying power of necromancy, fueled by the oceans of blood from his innocent victims. The thought of his cruel yoke upon the free men of the east sent a chill through the whole temple.

The message was clear: We could go and fight the Arcanter in Garlund, or we could wait for him to grow in strength and power until one day — a day not very far off, to judge from how things were going — we would have to fight him here, on our own lands. There was no other choice.

After spending a good hour painting a picture of terror and despair, though, the Footman Magnus suddenly switched gears.

"I have heard it said," he shouted, "or to be more accurate, I have heard it shamefully whispered that the woes of the west are no concern of ours. Why should the fate of the Suzer and his blasphemous faith be of any consequence to the faithful followers of Auld Father?

"But lest we forget — Footman Rom himself was born in the west, and came to us bearing the gift of the true faith whose ways had been forgotten in the land of his birth. And it was Footman Rom himself who prophesied that the true faith would one day return to roll back the fog that has descended on his homeland, to make way for the clear light which shows us the Path to Auld Father.

"And that, my dear brothers of the Path, that is why I am privileged to stand before you today, and offer you not tidings of despair, but tidings of hope, which in the fulness of time shall blossom into tidings of victory. Recruits, Raiders, Footmen, and all who serve Auld Father: The Reckoner HAS ARISEN."

Footman Glaine barked the last two words, slamming his fist on the lectern for each one. The echoing of his words was swallowed up by the sounds coming from the crowd. I remember feeling numb at first, but then the numbness drowning in a surge of excitement. Then everybody started talking — I remember Toad loudly asking what it meant: "Does this mean we're not going to Garlund? Does this mean we don't have to fight? Does the Reckoner even need us to beat the Arcanter?"

Footman Glaine motioned for everybody to calm down, but it took awhile — while all it took was a look from Sculler to shut us up, there were other people in the temple who required more direct encouragement.

"I know that all of you have many questions," Glaine said, "and in time they will all be answered. But for the moment we are able to say little, lest the Arcanter or his spies attempt to thwart us. Gruun's demons may try to prevent our eventual victory, and they may even achieve enough to believe that they have succeeded. But those of the true faith can be confident that no matter how dark the days ahead, our triumph is assured. Because on the day the light went out in the west, it was, after so many countless eons, rekindled in the east. As a single candle pushes away the most powerful darkness, and can in time sire an unquenchable flame, so today know that Auld Father's mighty scythe has been found, and shall return to clear the fields so his faith can be planted there again.

"My brothers, our King has fallen! But the first shoots of our victory have now emerged!"

The whole temple shook with the shouts of joy and rapturous oaths to Auld Father.

That was the moment when I finally allowed myself to savor One One Five's victory at the sparring ring. I had held off feeling proud before, even beneath my smiles, because I was still brooding over the talk I'd had with Sgt. Sculler. The DC's talk with me was the first hint anyone had given to me since arriving at training that the answer to all questions could not be found in either The Walk or the Raider Hand Book.

But now — now those thoughts had been washed away like dust clouds in a downpour. I was a blade forged and sharpened, and I knew now the throat I was made to cut, the blood I was meant to spill, and the heart I was meant to skewer. And I lived now to be unsheathed.

55

The big fight was over; the sparring medallion now hung on our wall. We knew in our hearts the drill medallion belonged there, too — but that was out of our hands.

By this time, everybody knew what was ahead. We knew that we'd be conducting mock field exercises with the other two platoons, where we'd march out into the wilds and experience life as an army on campaign. After several weeks of that, we'd come back and spend a few weeks finishing up — we'd finally get our dress uniforms, for one. And at the very end, we'd face the big "light show": Terminal Phase. All three platoons would participate in a full mock combat drill, complete with an illusory enemy supplied by whatever the Raider wizards and their djinn could conjure up. It was more symbolic than anything; nobody expected a company of recruits to actually mount a credible military operation. It was a "test of our mettle" — that's the phrase you kept hearing. After passing this "test," we'd collect our buckets and march out to the pit to welcome the next batch of recruits, the way we'd been greeted so many weeks before. Then we'd get our duty assignments, and it was off to our regular service in the Raiders.

But it was no longer a mystery what those duty assignments would probably be.

ONE SEVENDAY A FEW weeks after sparring day, Sgt. Sculler came striding out of The Cage and immediately fixed his eyes on me.

"Lips, you don't look like you're doing anything useful. Get over here," he ordered.

I quickly folded up the letter I'd gotten from my mom, in which she'd been explaining that, no, she wouldn't be able to make it to my graduation — not that I had actually expected her to make the trip all the way from Solta. I hustled to the front of the room to see what the DC wanted this time.

He handed me a small leather satchel; the knot that held it shut bore a wax seal.

"Get this over to HQ on the double. Be back before we leave for chow."

I glanced at the clock on the wall. I figured I had plenty of time.

"Any particular place at HQ, sir?"

"Just show it to them and tell them who it's from; they'll send you to the right place."

"Yes, sir."

That made it sound easy, but the first person I spoke to at HQ — a scared-looking private manning a desk — had no idea where I should go and seemed in a hurry to have me leave. Whatever my business was, he was eager not to have any involvement with it.

A disgusted-looking lieutenant finally directed me to "sorting," which turned out to be at the far back of one of the largest stone buildings. I had gotten it into my head that whatever I was carrying was of vital importance, since Sculler evidently didn't want to wait for the afternoon delivery rounds. It was as if I was once again back in Solta wearing my old Post Man's Cap, dropping off a letter to some high government minister.

That illusion evaporated once I actually reached the sorting room, though. It was a large, barn-like space filled with numbered bins, with three very tired-looking privates dashing back and forth between them ferrying documents and packages.

I stopped one of them and showed him my cargo. He seemed shocked to see me there, and quickly examined the satchel.

"Oh," he said, his momentary excitement gone. "Yeah. Just put that in this bin here."

He motioned to a bin a few steps away, which already had six or seven identical-looking looking satchels.

"There's no...hurry on these?" I asked.

He shrugged. "I mean...sort of. But not really."

So much for an important errand. I found the exit and was making my way back to the barracks when I rounded a corner and was greeted by a curious sight.

About a bowshot away, I saw Skunk standing rigidly at attention, and a DC I didn't recognize was in his face screaming at him. Two more sergeants stood nearby watching, occasionally joining in.

I remembered then that Sculler had sent Skunk on an errand earlier, about an hour before he'd sent me out. I had no idea what he'd been sent to do, but whatever it was, it looked like it had been hard work — Skunk's uniform was dirty and wrinkled and he was covered in sweat.

I stopped to watch. It reminded me of the swarming attacks we'd been subjected to from DCs the first day of training.

Trying to piece things together from the spittle-flecked roars of the sergeant who seemed to be in charge, it sounded like Skunk's disastrous appearance had gotten him in trouble.

"I cannot believe they're gonna let a fuckin' disgrace like you in the fuckin' Raiders!" the sergeant screamed. "Look at this fuckin' disgrace of a uniform!"

He gave Skunk a shove, and that's when I noticed the sergeant was a bit unsteady on his feet. Shit, I realized — the son of a bitch is drunk. So were the other two with him.

That took a second to digest, because I realized up until that moment I couldn't even imagine a DC being drunk. I was pretty sure that alcohol turned to water the second it touched Sgt. Sculler's lips; as for Taba, I suspected that his blood was pure acid and he pissed snake venom, so I couldn't imagine alcohol could have done much to him.

"What unit are you with, you waste of a fucking orgasm?" the sergeant asked, and Skunk dutifully rattled off: "Recruit Camlin belongs to Training Platoon One One Five of the Recruit Training Regiment at Fort Harrel, sir."

"One One Five, huh? I heard about you cocksuckers. Heard you were the ones that ruined Wulock's streak. You guys must be made of steel. You guys must really able to take a punch..."

At that he gave Skunk a hard jab right in the stomach that caused him to double over in pain. The other two sergeants roared at that, but Skunk quickly pulled himself up and back to attention, prepared to take more abuse.

Skunk's main tormentor paced back and forth a few times, eyeing him, taking mock swings at him to try to get him to flinch. Skunk was a statue.

Finally, the sergeant's face brightened.

"Squats, recruit. On my count. One! Two! Three!"

Skunk immediately began doing deep knee bends, following along with the sergeant's rhythm. I hesitated for just a second, but I knew what I had to do. Even if I didn't want to. I boldly walked up and took my place to Skunk's left, and began doing squats in sync with him.

The sergeant immediately called things to a halt.

"What the fuck is this?" he asked, stepping up to me. He was close enough to me now that I could smell the whiskey on his breath. "Are you his fuckin' twin or something?"

I didn't flinch.

"Recruit Pearl belongs to Training Platoon One One Five of the..."

"Wait, wait, hold on a second here. Recruit 'Pearl?' What kind of faggot name is that? Fuck me, guys, I think this is his girlfriend! I bet they tickle each other's turds with their dickholes after lights out!"

The sergeant whooped like he thought he'd just made the funniest joke in the history of the Raiders.

I snuck a glance at Skunk. He gave me a quick what-in-the-name-of-Auld-Father-do-you-think-you-are-doing look. I snapped my eyes back to where they were pointed straight ahead. Still laughing, the sergeant then sucker-punched me in the gut. Just as Skunk had, I pulled myself back to attention, grinding my teeth and forcing myself to ignore the pain.

"Give me your fucking swords," the sergeant growled.

I felt a twitch in my muscles and was about to unhook my sword when some instinct stopped me. I noticed Skunk wasn't moving, either.

Then I remembered: According to the Raider Hand Book, there were only two instances when a Raider was required to hand over his weapon: When told by a superior, "present your weapon for inspection," or when told by a superior, "surrender your weapon." (If an enemy demanded surrender, the decision to comply or resist fell to "the senior ranking man on the scene.")

The drunk sergeant — I saw the name "Lyon" on his lapel — had not given us a lawful order. At least I didn't think so. At the moment, I wasn't entirely sure — I was just following Skunk's lead.

It took a second for Sergeant Lyon to realize we were not going to comply.

"Are you two fucking DEAF?!" he roared. "I said GIVE ME YOUR FUCKING SWORDS."

Neither one of us moved.

The sergeant stepped up to Skunk and tried to grab the sword and scabbard hanging from his waist. Skunk resisted. I actually turned my head in surprise to watch as the two men struggled with the blade for several seconds. Finally the sergeant struck Skunk several times and wrenched the weapon away, then shoved him to the ground. One of the other two sergeants suddenly grabbed me and held my arms behind my back as the other pulled my own sword away. He handed it to Sergeant Lyon, who was looking at Skunk's sword while the recruit picked himself up and returned to attention. When the other sergeant released me, I did the same.

Sergeant Lyon paced back and forth slowly in front of us, pulling each sword from its scabbard and examining it closely. He pulled a hair from his head and used it to test the sharpness of each blade.

"Very nice work, boys. Look at that polish — I can see my reflection."

He then turned to look at us, and tossed our swords and scabbards into a cart path. I didn't have to look; the wet "thwock" told me that one or both blades had landed in a fresh pile of ox dung.

"Recruits: Present your weapons for inspection," he said.

Me and Skunk looked at each other, then walked over to fetch our swords. Our tormentors followed close behind. We picked up our swords — I tried to wipe some of the dung off mine — carefully sheathed them, and presented them in the official manner.

Sgt. Lyon once made a big show of it, as if he were Lt. Col. Ilos doing a formal review. At one point, he lifted my blade to his nose and sniffed a spot of dung, then frowned. After a minute or two, he handed the blades back and put his hands on his hips.

"No, sir, this will not do at all," he said. "Not at all." He glanced over his shoulder at one of the other sergeants. "What are we going to do about this, Sgt. Hist?"

"Seems to me these recruits need some extra conditioning," came the reply.

"Just to focus their minds," the other one added.

Lyon scratched his chin thoughtfully.

"Conditioning...Conditioning..." he murmured, and looked up at the sky as if deep in thought. It was all a stupid game, of course; me and Skunk both knew exactly what was coming next.

He turned to us and smiled.

"I've got it!" he said. "Push-ups!"

"Strengthens the arms," said Sgt. Hist.

"Might help them polish those blades properly," said the third one.

"Outstanding!" Lyon added. "Men: On the ground, on my count..."

Reflexively, me and Skunk immediately dropped to the ground and assumed push-up position — where we found ourselves face to face with the pile of ox dung where our swords had just been. Most of my right hand had sunk deep into a steaming pile of shit, but at least I was better off than Skunk — the way he was positioned, he would have to repeatedly shove his face into a small mound of the stuff on every downstroke. Lyon began counting off — "One! Two! Raider! Blue!" — and we followed along.

By this point I could do 50 pushups before I even started to get tired, and could probably pass 150 before my arms gave out. I imagined Skunk wasn't much different. So the actual physical work was no big deal. It was just having your face shoved in shit that was the problem. And dealing with that was just a matter of sheer iron will — not a problem of those of us who'd made it this far.

I don't know how long I'd been going before I suddenly heard Sgt. Taba's voice, somewhere off to the side. I can't remember exactly what he said — I just remember his surprised tone. I remember it because it was so genuine — while Taba often put on a good show of acting surprised, mostly when we fucked up, you always sort of knew it was an act. So hearing real surprise coming from him was something new.

But it's what came next that really caught me off guard. With no warning, somebody dropped down on my left and began doing push-ups in time with me. I glanced over and saw it was Gorgeous. And then I saw other One One Five recruits joining him. For a moment there I actually slipped and missed a push-up, because I was so confused at what was going on. If anybody noticed, they didn't say anything.

I looked to my right, past Skunk, and saw other guys from One One Five joining in. I noticed that Parsa had a particularly fresh mound of ox shit that he had to keep pressing against his forehead.

For a minute or so, there was no sound except the strained breathing of recruits from One One Five and the "squish" of skin hitting shit. I don't remember the count; I don't even remember feeling tired. Instead, I felt something new and strange. It was as if a new well of strength had been opened up somewhere inside me.

Finally, I heard Taba's normal, gruff voice. The surprise was gone: "All right. That's enough, guys. Get up and fall in."

We quickly assembled ourselves into marching formation. Taba walked back and forth, studying us, before he announced, "there's a water tap over by the main stables — the wooden building on the far side of the main HQ. Go over there and clean yourselves up as best you can — don't worry about the sign — then report to the mess hall. I'll meet you over there in 20."

The "sign" next to the large water tap and attached hose said "LIVESTOCK ONLY," but we followed Taba's instructions. While we were waiting our turn, Gorgeous explained that Taba had been leading One One Five to the mess hall when they'd rounded a corner and came upon the scene with me and Skunk and the drunk sergeants.

"You could tell they were drunk?" I asked.

"You could smell the whiskey on them from 50 feet away," Gorgeous said.

He explained that Wym was the one who started it — after they'd watched us for a few moments and grasped what was going on, Wym was the one who'd broken out of formation to run over and join us in push-ups. When everyone else saw what he was doing, they immediately joined in.

"Taba didn't tell you to do it?"

"Nobody told us to do it. It just seemed like the natural thing to do. I mean, we're fuckin' One One Five, right?"

LATER THAT EVENING, I grabbed my rusty knife and headed outside to work on my tree out back. I was just starting to hack away when I heard a commotion from over near the barracks. Then I heard Prof's voice: "Hey Lips! Hold up!"

I turned to ask what the problem was and saw every single man in One One Five headed towards me. Every single one of them was carrying his utility knife.

"Okay, guys, line up in two files, marching order," Prof chirped, with something that sounded almost like authority. "We work in pairs, one man on either side, alternating swings. When you get tired, stop and head to the back of the line; the next man steps up and takes your place. Don't forget to sharpen your blades while you're waiting for your next turn. Lips, you've already done enough — you hang back."

Using my rusty knife, I'd managed to cut maybe a quarter of the way through the trunk. But with sharpened knives and a continuous churn of new arms ready to swing hard until they wore themselves out, the rest of One One Five managed to double my work in less than 15 minutes.

It took about an hour; there was a loud cracking sound, and everybody stepped back, waiting to see which way the tree would fall. It leaned over and started coming down where everybody was lined up. There were curses and laughter as everybody ran to get out of the way; the soft ground shook as the big tree slammed into it to the cheers of tired recruits. The trunk didn't snap off cleanly; there was still a thin, bent strip of wood and bark attached to the stump. Without missing a beat, the next pair of recruits hustled over and hacked off the last part.

Stepping close to look at the result, I felt a hand on my shoulder. I turned to see Skunk eyeing me. He didn't seem happy or angry or anything — just serious. He just nodded; I slowly nodded back, adding a smile as if to say, hey, lighten up. He looked down at the tree, shook his head and laughed.

"Taba's in The Cage right now," Gorgeous said, his booming voice instantly grabbing everyone's attention. "Should we go get him and let him know?"

Most seemed to think that was a great idea, and we were about to head off when Skunk finally spoke up.

"Actually," he said. "I've got a better idea."

WHEN TABA CAME IN the next morning banging his drum to wake us up, his face seemed to be an entirely new shade of red. That usually wasn't a good sign.

At first there was nothing out of the ordinary — shave, shit, shower, straighten our bunks; by the time we were in uniform, we thought maybe we were in the clear. Taba walked up and down the center of the bunkroom, only calling out a few infractions.

He finally returned to the front of the room and I was about to breathe a sigh of relief when he suddenly stopped.

"Oh, one last thing," he said casually. Then it came: "WOULD ANYBODY LIKE TO EXPLAIN TO ME WHY THERE IS A CUT-DOWN TREE AT THE FEET OF MAJOR BRABORN'S STATUE?"

It was what you long-beards call a "rhetorical question," of course, and I don't think Gorgeous did us any favors when he burst out laughing as soon as Taba asked it. Needless to say, Taba dropped us and smoked us within an inch of our lives that morning, closing the windows and giving us the full sweatbox treatment.

And you want to know something? I was grinning the whole time.

56

We spent several weeks doing mock field campaigns, and this one started off like any of the others. We left early, not even going in for chow — we had to eat on the march. After loading up with all of our gear, including supplies, Sculler and Taba marched us north into the forest. When we got to the site of the sparring rings, we were joined by Two One Five and Three One Five, being led by their own DCs.

By the time we broke for midday chow, my legs were burning, and I was about ready to collapse. We were supposed to get an hour to rest and gulp down some water along with dried meat or crackers, but of course Taba tapped me for picket duty. Me, Limul and Wym were tasked with patrolling the path ahead, to "prevent a surprise attack" by the enemy. I looked enviously at the rest of guys stretching out on their backs in the shade.

"Just think of how much better you'll sleep tonight," Limul said, punching me in the arm.

"Yeah," I sighed. Well, at least I didn't have to carry my supply pack for picket duty — after hauling it on my back all morning, suddenly my armor didn't feel so heavy anymore. I pulled some seeds out of a pouch to munch on while we went ahead to find a suitable lookout perch.

I was trying to enjoy the outdoors, which were still a novelty to a city boy like me, but Wym wouldn't shut up. All he wanted to talk about was the war.

"How long do you think it will take before we see some action? I mean, after we graduate." Ever since he'd found he could hold his own in a fight, Wym's confidence about himself had actually become a bit irritating. He was downright eager to test himself against new challenges.

"Not for a while, if you're lucky," Limul said.

"'If I'm lucky?'"

"Well, the way things are going, you might be sent in with the first wave. By His

Foot, that will be a meat-grinder." He looked at Wym gravely. "If that happens, you won't have much time to prepare. You'll just have to listen to the more experienced guys in your unit and try not to get in the way." I think he was hoping to shake up Wym, but the little guy wasn't intimidated.

"What makes you such an expert?" I asked.

Limul snorted. "My older brothers are both Raiders. They're in Agellos right now. That's where they're assembling the fleet they'll use to cross the ocean for the main invasion."

"When does it launch?"

"Not sure. Nobody knows. It could be launching right this second, for all anybody knows. Last I heard, they're still preparing."

"But still. They wouldn't waste fresh-out-of-training troops in the first wave."

"Not normally," Limul agreed, "but they're running short on seasoned troops right now. A lot of veteran troops got wiped out along with the King in the last expedition. This expedition will be at least ten times the size of that one, so at least some of the guys in the first wave will be as green as a spring meadow."

He smiled at me and Wym and winked. "I'm sure *you* two will be fine, though."

I rolled my eyes. "Why don't you kiss the spring meadow growing on my ass, klanger?" I said.

"I don't do that for scalebacks," Limul said. "Can't stand the fucking fish smell."

"Can't help the smell, man. It's 'cause we're always ass-deep in klanger pussy."

Limul laughed and shook his head.

WE CONTINUED TO MARCH the rest of the day and on into the evening. Even though it looks tiny on most of the maps I've seen, the Blue Wood is actually about a five-day march on foot from north to south — and that's with a light load, with most of the heavy supplies being hauled by ox-cart. The way we were outfitted, with every last piece of equipment being hauled on someone's back, you'd be lucky to do it in a week.

I was hoping we'd get to whatever our destination was by nightfall, but no such luck: That night we did an "on march" encampment, meaning as much equipment as possible had to remain stowed, so the detachment could be ready to go as quickly as possible when we got up to continue our march the next morning. That meant no tents, no fires, no cooking — find the best shelter you could, drop your pack and go to sleep. It was a cold and rainy night, so we were gonna be miserable.

I found a tree with a nice, wide spread to keep out as much rain as possible, stripped off the heaviest bits of my armor, and collapsed into the dirt. The last thing I remembered that night was Sgt. Wulock, the DC of Two One Five, bellowing orders to some poor saps who were up for first watch that night. Throughout the day, I had dimly become aware that Sgt. Wulock was the "commander" of this field exercise, with the DCs from the other platoons following his lead. The previous field exercises we'd done had been led by either Sgt. Sculler or the head DC for Three One Five, whose name I can't even remember. This was the first one where that shitheel Wulock was in charge.

I already knew Wulock didn't like me, because I'd fucked up his perfect record. And now he was calling the shots. All I could do was try to keep my head down and I'd have to try and stay out of his way. I remembered what Sgt. Sculler had said: There's a right way, a wrong way, and a Raider way. If you want to know which one to follow, pray to Auld Father.

I did just that right before falling into a deep sleep.

IT WAS STILL DRIZZLING when whistles sounded to wake us up. Without thinking much, I pulled on my armor and gear and made my way to the assembly point for One One Five. We'd been in front for the first day's march; today we brought up the rear. I was still wiping gunk from my eyes when we started marching.

The light rain also brought a cool air that would have been nice for marching, if it had stuck around. But we hadn't gone a mile before the sun burst through the clouds, then burned them away until we were walking under a completely open sky, and it seemed like the sun had orders to give us a few extra doses of heat. I was soaked in sweat by mid-morning. The extra canteens of water we were saddled with suddenly seemed like a blessing.

Unlike the first day, we didn't stop for lunch, because, as the DCs assured us, it was "only a little bit farther." But it was very late in the day before we finally reached our ultimate destination. After marching across a broad plain covered mostly with tall grass that reached up to my chin, we scaled a tall but gently sloped ridgeline which was topped with a thicket of trees. Upon reaching the top of the ridge, we finally came to a halt.

I noticed Parsa gazing in amazement at the land on the other side of the ridge. It was mostly green, gently rolling grasslands, with small hills and rises crowned with peaceful-looking groves of trees.

"You look like you recognize this place," I told him.

"Never seen it before in my life."

"Then what's up with that face?"

For a moment I didn't think he'd heard me, but then he looked down and shook his head.

"Just...this is..." He shook his head again. "It reminds me of home. Where I come from, the man who owned this land would be..."

I waited for a moment, unsure if I should say anything. But I went ahead: "Would be what?"

Parsa shook his head again. "He'd be lucky," he said, and walked away.

The ridge we were standing on ran down from the Striped Mountains; standing in the right spot, you could see where it continued on up into the high, rocky peaks, many miles distant. Our orders were to establish a base camp and fortify the ridge-line in anticipation of an attack from the north. There were reports that enemy forces were on the move and were expected to make an advance across this ridge in order to blah blah blah, I don't fucking remember, and it doesn't matter. There was no enemy, but we were supposed to play along. We'd already been through this kind of thing several times in the preceding weeks. The enemy wasn't the point; it was to get us accustomed to life on campaign. If there was time, they might split us into teams and do some "capture the flag" exercises to introduce us to basic field tactics.

"Fortifying" is one of those words that sounds like it might almost be fun, as in "hey, we're gonna build a fort!" What it means in practice is lots and lots and lots of digging. Then when you're done with digging, you dig some more. After that, there's more digging. Trenches, foxholes, tunnels, berms and barriers — and most importantly, latrines. When setting up camp, that's always the very first thing that gets built — and it's not just because everybody's in a hurry to take a dump.

"The latrine needs to be located in one of the most secure areas of your camp," Sgt. Sculler had explained. "Let me tell you, the last thing you want is to be pinned down in a position where the enemy can deny you access to your own latrine. You can dig your own hole in a pinch, but there's only so much room in a trench or foxhole for people to be digging holes. Things get really nasty really quick."

But of course, a latrine is only one part of it, for Raiders. Because as they never tired of reminding us: Raiders are CLEAN.

"If you maggots think for a second we're gonna let up on hygiene just because we're out in the dirt, you've got another thing coming," Taba had snarled at us during our first field exercise. "Just because you're living down in the dirt doesn't mean you're a filthy animal. Take some damn pride in yourselves."

Now, at this point, you might be thinking to yourself: They've got soap, because Raiders are never without soap. Some Raiders even have bars of soap placed in their coffins, just in case. But where do they get water?

And there you have one of the great conundrums of life in the field. You need water — not just to stay clean, but to cook food and keep people from dying of thirst. On low-lying ground, it's easier to find sources of water, like lakes and streams and rivers. But low ground makes you more vulnerable to attack. High ground, like the ridge we were on, is more defensible, but it's often farther away from water. A high, defensible position with ready access to fresh water, like a spring, is a dream come true, but you are rarely that lucky.

So picking a location to camp is usually a compromise. You want a place that's easily defensible, but with reasonably good access to water. I found out later that clever commanders can often anticipate an enemy's movements simply by having a thorough knowledge of all water sources in the region.

That's probably more than you ever wanted to know about this stuff, but what it boils down to is that setting up on high ground, like we were doing, meant doing water supply runs. There was a stream about a mile in back of our position, on the far side of the plain of tall grass we'd had to march through. After latrines had been dug, I got put on "camel duty."

Among the gear we brought with on field exercises were five very large waterskins. After filling one, you sling it underneath a long pole. One man lifts from the front and the other from the back, and you haul it back to camp — along with two or three smaller waterskins slung across your body, larger than the normal canteen. Which is why it's called camel duty. It had to be done at least three times a day. Luckily, nobody had to do it more than once a day. (Usually...)

I got tapped along with Blockhead and a bunch of guys from the other platoons to do the first run that evening. While the walk to the stream was easy, the walk back was a killer. Even though it was still light when we headed out, it took longer than we'd expected to fill the big waterskins and get them hitched up. The last bit of sunlight winked out just as we were starting to head back.

Only the smallest moon, Tarissa, was out that night, so we might as well have been walking blindfolded; the only reason we were able to make our way back was because we'd cleared a trail through the high grass leading up to the foot of the ridge.

Even though the weight soon had my muscles burning, I was actually in a chipper mood, because I was thinking to myself that I'd made it. Well, not yet — not officially. There were still two more weeks left, with Terminal Phase looming at the end. But I couldn't imagine there were any more challenges they could throw at me that I wouldn't be able to handle. I could already see myself standing on the Glorious Field, extending my sword as I recited the Raider Oath: Today I stand before all men in the eyes of Auld Father, to declare...

I stepped in a soft piece of ground and suddenly lurched to the side. I managed to catch my balance and bounce back before falling over and dropping my end of the pole, but I felt a shock of pain run through my shoulder as the weight shifted. I sucked in a deep breath to keep from yelping in pain.

"You okay up there, Lips?" Blockhead asked.

"Yeah, fine...just..." I gritted my teeth as I felt another sharp jolt of pain.

Maybe talking would take my mind off it, I thought.

"Hey, Block," I said. "What's the first thing you're gonna do when you get out of here?"

"Dude, I'll tell you something. Somewhere out there, there's a barrel of ale the size of this sack of water. I'm gonna find it and drink it all and then sleep for a week. What about you?"

Up until that moment, my goal had been a lot like Blockhead's, but for some reason, hearing him describe it — picturing in my mind the sight of Blockhead's big, fleshy body sprawled out in some inn, snoring after downing a whole barrel of ale — made me shiver. *What if Taba caught me like that, I thought. Shit, that klanger bastard is going to be living in my head for the rest of my life, isn't he?*

I must have been silent for awhile, because I heard Blockhead ask, "Lips? You sure that stumble back there…"

"Naw man, sorry. Just thinking. I think the first thing I want to do when I get out of here is go see…"

I almost said "my mom," because that was what I was thinking. But I caught myself.

"…my old friends," I said. "Back in the Warrens. I want to show off my new uniform. I'll look finer than any gangster in Craller Square in a new sloucher."

"Craller Square? Sloucher? What the fuck are you talking about?"

I was about to launch into an explanation of gang life back in the Warrens when I suddenly heard something.

It was…singing?

"Hey, do you hear that?" I asked.

"Yeah. It's coming from the top of the ridge."

We had just left the tall grass and were about to start making our way up to the camp. I could make out the orange glow of campfires on the trees at the top; that's where the singing was coming from. As we drew closer, I could hear something else — a lute. A lute!

"Who the fuck has a lute?" I exclaimed. "How did they even manage to bring it all this way?"

I realized that in the whole time I'd been at the Blue Wood, I hadn't once heard music other than beating drums, signal horns, the formal dancing music in Mrs. Gern's etiquette class, and a few hymns sung at the chapel. Hearing the sort of music I would have heard in the real world, like you'd hear over mugs of ale at a tavern, was eerily spellbinding. Even though I'd been dreading the haul up to the top of the ridge, I was so curious and captivated by this odd new thing that I barely noticed the burning in my legs and shoulder as we muscled the waterskin up the slope to our encampment. After securing the sack to a designated tree, the recruit in charge of supplies — a greasy little klanger from Three One Five — gave us the good news that we were off duty until 5 the next morning — when we'd immediately head out on another camel run. Blockhead went to get some sleep, while I made my way over to the campfire where the music was coming from.

As I drew closer, the singer started up a new song, and this one brought ripples of laughter from the small group assembled around the fire. I could make out the lyrics as I grew closer — it was an obscene little ditty about a Raider in the role of a dashing knight, rescuing a lady locked in a tower by an evil sorceress — and what he did with the lady *and* the sorceress afterward.

As I finally joined the little crowd, I saw the singer was a recruit from Two One

Five. I didn't know his name, but I recognized his smarmy grin and sleepy-looking eyes from the mess hall, where he was usually getting screamed at and smoked by one of the DCs. From the little I'd seen of him, I'd gathered that he was Two One Five's resident smartass — but I was surprised to find that he was a halfway decent singer, too.

The lute player turned out to be none other than Gorgeous. I knew he'd mentioned being able to play music, but I was still confused about where he'd acquired a lute.

I looked around for somebody I recognized and found Toad a few steps away. I sauntered over and posed the question to him.

"Bro," he said. "You're not gonna believe this, but it's Sculler's!" The way his eyes widened told me he was telling the truth, even if he didn't fully believe it himself.

"Sarge? No shit?"

"Yeah! He came by while he was making the rounds and checking the guys on night duty — we're off duty now, so we were just sitting around the fire shooting the shit — and he asked if anybody knew how to play, and Gorgeous said he knew how. So Sculler disappears for a bit and then comes back and hands him this lute and tells him not to break it, because it was his second-favorite lute, and just make sure it was sitting outside his tent tomorrow morning. Then he just walked off."

I stood silent for a second, trying to absorb this new information into my image of Sculler.

The guy singing brought his bawdy tune to a close, accompanied by snorts and guffaws and slaps on the back. When things died down, Gorgeous stood and held up the lute.

"Hey, I don't want anyone to feel like I'm hogging this thing. Can any of you other degenerates play?"

From somewhere far on the edge, where the fire's light started to fall off into shadow, a voice came: "Parsa can play. He can sing, too."

I recognized the voice as Skunk's, but I couldn't see him — he was tucked away too far in the darkness.

Eyes swiveled around to focus on Parsa, who was wrapped in a thick cloak, staring intently at the flames. There were some moments of silence, but he didn't respond.

Gorgeous held out the lute to him.

"Parsa? Wanna give it a try?"

The voice seemed to rouse him from his reverie, and he looked at the lute, then looked around at everyone staring at him. He sighed.

"Sure," he said, taking the lute, and strumming it quickly, making adjustments to the tuning.

"What do you guys want to hear?" he asked, without looking up. I noticed that he was amazingly focused on making small adjustments to the lute, stopping to hold it up to his ear and pluck the strings, listening for — whatever lute players listen for, I guess.

A voice I didn't recognize — it must have been someone from one of the other platoons — said, "Home!"

Parsa looked up at that. "Home?"

There were murmurs of approval around the circle; I spoke up: "Sing something from where you grew up."

I thought maybe it might buck up his spirits. What do I know?

Parsa looked at me, and then looked around at the expectant faces. He nodded, and bit his lip, as if he was thinking.

"Okay. I've got one," he said, holding the lute up to his ear one last time to check the sound. Then he drew in his breath and started strumming a haunting tune with incredible skill. There was an audible "whoa" from several people around the campfire as his fingers danced over the strings with the style of a seasoned performer.

I watched a shape emerge from the shadows into the firelight: It was Skunk. He wore an expression of surprise — not even he had expected this, apparently.

Parsa began singing. He was...well, he was quite good. His singing wasn't in the same league as his playing, but it was certainly nothing to be ashamed of.

I don't remember the exact words, but the song was about a man traveling in a faraway land. He was on a quest of some kind, although the song wasn't very specific about that. It was more about his dreams of his homeland, and how he feared he would never see it again. There was a refrain that was something about asking the stars in the sky to tell him of the changing seasons back home; I asked Footman Sesh about it, and he said it sounded like a version of a traditional folk song he knew from his own childhood.

Everybody was very quiet throughout the entire song, and they remained quiet for several seconds after the last notes of the song drifted away. Looking around, I could see the telltale glint of moisture in the eyes of some of the guys standing around the fire. I hadn't been hit that hard by it — at least I don't think I was. But I knew what some of those guys were feeling.

Thinking I should lighten the mood, I spoke up: "Shit, Parsa. You got any other hidden talents we should know about?"

There was some muffled laughter. A few people made some jokes. But it was clear the night was over. Gradually, one by one, we drifted away from the blaze. Parsa was one of the last to leave, taking the lute with him — presumably to make sure it got returned to Sculler.

I poured some water over the fire and headed off to find a place to sack out. I saw Skunk was still standing there. I couldn't make out the expression on his face in the darkness.

57

In a lot of ways, camp life was almost like a vacation from normal training. I wouldn't go so far as to call it easy, but after our strictly-regimented days back at the barracks, it felt leisurely by comparison.

Not that we didn't work hard. There's always work to be done around a military camp — in addition to camel duty, there's firewood that needs to be collected, trenches that need digging, fortifications to be built or strengthened. There's guard duty around the camp and patrols around the local area.

Everything is a chore. I was excited at first when me, Prof and Gorgeous got picked for patrol duty the next day, because I was thinking about the fun we'd have away from the eyes of the DCs — but then Sgt. Sculler informed us that one of our duties during this patrol would be to forage for food. After sketching out a route on our map, Sculler showed us a type of wild tuber that he said grew in the area and handed us some sacks.

"Your patrol isn't finished until those sacks are full," he said, and dismissed us.

The patrol ended up taking most of the afternoon. But the thing was, there was nobody screaming at us, nobody to smoke us if we did anything wrong or got our gear smudged or scratched. Not that we would have done anything out of line — we'd long since reached the point where keeping everything tight, clean and sharp was as natural and automatic as breathing. But there was an incredible relief at not having somebody breathing down our necks every waking moment.

And we could shoot the shit all we wanted! That's what I mean about it feeling a little like a vacation. Everything still ran with discipline — this was the Raiders, after all — but at the same time, everything was more laid back. As long as you did your job, nobody really hassled you.

Our patrol route had a series of checkpoints. At each checkpoint we were supposed to leave a small white stone; the next patrol would collect those stones, and leave black ones; the one after that would collect those and leave red ones, and so on — that was how camp HQ kept tabs on the patrol rotation. At one checkpoint, Gorgeous was writing out a description of where he'd cached his marker stone, and I noticed Prof off by himself lost in thought.

That wasn't like him, I thought. Well, the "lost in thought" part was like him, but not while we were on duty. I picked up a stick and sneaked up behind him, signaling to Gorgeous to keep quiet and not spoil the surprise. When I got close enough, I gave him a sharp poke. He jumped.

"Congratulations, recruit. You've just been killed by one of the Arcanter's scout troops," I said, patting him on the shoulder to try to calm him down.

He sighed. "I guess I deserved that."

"Hey, man. Don't take it so hard. I'm sure you'll get me next time. Seriously though, what were you thinking about? You looked like your mind had flown off to the Holy Mountain."

"I'm just thinking about Wulock. I'm trying to understand."

"What's to understand? Guy's an asshole. Sometimes assholes finish first. You might know that if you hadn't spent your whole life in a book."

"Says the guy who's read every single Vast the Brutal two-copper."

"You know what I mean."

I waited for him to reply, but he seemed like he was starting to drift again.

"Hey," I said, interrupting him again. "What about Sgt. Wulock?"

Prof scratched his cheek. "It's just the guy seems like a walking mockery of everything they've been trying to teach us here. I mean, Sculler and Taba are assholes, but they're not hypocrites. They live and breathe the Raider code, and they make you want to live up to their example. But Wulock's not like that at all. I mean he's a hardass just like every other DC, but he just...he just..."

"He's all about himself," Gorgeous said. He'd finished his business with the marker stone and was brushing past us headed to a nearby tree, where he began to take a leak.

"He's a glory hound," Gorgeous said over his shoulder. "But he comes by it honestly. You guys notice that white thing he's got pinned on his collar?"

I thought back to the last time I'd seen Wulock up close. It had been just that morning when I'd been coming back from the latrine.

Wulock was on the short side. The little bit of graying hair on his balding head was kept neatly cropped, and his leathery skin looked like it had been pulled too tight over his skull. His thin lips seemed locked in a permanent scowl, like every other DC, but unlike the others, there were no signs he might have ever cracked a smile. Instead of laugh lines, the only creases were on his forehead, which always seemed to be knotted with worry above his dark, angry eyes.

Seeing him coming up the path, I'd stopped and stepped to the side to let him pass, snapping to attention and greeting him with a "Good morning, sergeant!", but he'd just shot by without even acknowledging me. Now that I was thinking about it, I did remember a small round white pin of some sort on his collar.

"Yeah," I said, the picture coming back to me. "What is that, a star?"

"Flower," Gorgeous said, turning back to focus on taking a piss.

Heading off for the next checkpoint, Gorgeous shed some more light on the subject as we strolled along.

"It's supposed to be a Ferian's Bonnet flower. You know about those, right Prof?"

"I've heard of them," Prof said. "I think they're rare..."

"I'll say. They only bloom naturally in the spring after a wildfire."

Prof nodded. "So what's the significance?"

"It's shows Wulock's a member of the Order of the Inferno."

"What in the name of Gruun's cock is that?" I asked. "It's not in the Raider Hand Book." I'd memorized every piece of uniform insignia in the book once I'd realized just how damn important all those distinctions were among Raiders.

"It's not an official thing — he wouldn't wear it on his full dress uniform. But they tolerate him wearing it on his regular duty uniform. They wouldn't dare tell him to take it off, on account of what it symbolizes."

"And that is?"

"It's worn by the survivors of the Fifth Legion."

Prof let out a low whistle. "The Ghost Legion," he said.

That was something that *was* covered in the Hand Book. Something close to 80 percent of them died in the Battle of Hermit's Creek, during the last great goblin eruption. That had been, what, 25 years ago? But I remembered that it was the Fifth Legion's sacrifice that guaranteed the battle's ultimate success.

"Wulock was one of them?" I asked.

"One of the few still in active service, from what I hear," Gorgeous said. "Took out a goblin sorcerer by himself, supposedly."

"Bullshit," Prof said.

"Hey, I didn't say I knew for sure. Just what I heard."

I could see Prof was still thinking about this, so I spoke up. "He's a fucking war hero, that's what you're saying?"

"Not just a war hero. That guy has been through the deepest, darkest bowels of Gruundeep and came out the other side. He's seen things most of us can't even imagine."

"So that makes him exempt from the Raider Code, then? All the shit they've been preaching to us about honor and discipline — we can toss it into the rubbish tip just because he walked away from a battle when nobody else did? And how do we know how he survived, anyway? Maybe the men who lived up to the code were the ones who didn't make it home."

Gorgeous just shrugged. I turned to Prof, thinking he might say something to back me up, but he'd become very quiet. After a moment he spoke.

"Can't have a Raider Code if there are no Raiders," he said gloomily.

We got back to camp as the sun was beginning to dip behind the Striped Mountains. The last mile or so was exhausting; we'd managed to find a large patch of the tubers Sculler had shown us, and we'd filled our sacks, but hauling them back wore us out.

The only good part was that it got us out of camel duty. Instead, we got the "easy" job of helping man the forward post during night watch. When Taba gave us our orders, I was about to ask "when are we supposed to sleep?" when Gorgeous went ahead and asked the question before I could.

Taba's eyes looked like they would pop out of his head.

"Sleep? SLEEP?" he bellowed. "Do you think the Arcanter's men out there are going to be sporting enough to schedule an assault when we've all had time to get fucking rested and ready? Does this look like a fucking roadside inn to you, recruit? Do you want me to get you a fucking pillow and tuck you in for the night?"

Taba had been so mellow the past few days that I'd forgotten what a terror he could be when he got wound up. His little dwarven face turned several shades of red as he laid into Gorgeous, whose beefy frame seemed to shrink right before my eyes.

Just then, Sgt. Wulock appeared out of nowhere, in the creepy way the DCs always do.

"Something wrong, Sgt. Taba?" he asked.

Taba cut short his tirade and stepped back. Nodding to indicate Gorgeous, he explained: "The recruit here expressed concern that being assigned night watch will interfere with his ability to be adequately rested and relaxed in the event of an attack by the enemy."

Wulock was silent for a moment, and I stole a look at the pin on his collar. I was close enough to see that it was, indeed, in the shape of a flower. As I studied it, I also noticed something else that I'd never noticed before: A massive scar running across his neck.

Suddenly, Wulock turned his head, and for the briefest moment our eyes met. I still remember those eyes: They were the color of burnished steel. I immediately snapped back to attention, eyes facing forward. I practically burned a hole in a nearby tree with my locked-in stare.

My ears still took everything in, though. Wulock finally spoke. He was firm but weirdly sympathetic: "Recruit, there will be three of you in each foxhole out there. You can sleep in shifts — one man sleeps, the other two keep watch. Work the schedule out among yourselves. Just don't snore."

There was some nervous laughter at that. Then he continued.

"Sgt. Taba is just doing his job, recruit, but honestly, I wouldn't worry too much about it. If the enemy launches a real assault, you'll be dead even if you're wide awake. Your only job is to alert the rest of us before you die."

And with that, he took the signal whistle which Taba was holding, looked it over, and handed it to Gorgeous.

"Good luck," he said, and then turned on his heels and walked away.

58

"Man, FUCK Taba," Gorgeous said as we made our way out to the post — though he carefully waited until we were out of earshot of the main camp. "That little fucking klanger..."

Prof loudly cleared his throat.

"Sorry, Prof," Gorgeous said. "I didn't mean you. I mean, there's dwarves, and then there's...there's fuckin' *klangers*, man. You know?"

"Yeah, I know," Prof replied. "Fuckin' klangers. Assholes so tight you can't even get a needle up there, right?"

"Yeah. Yeah, you know what I'm saying!"

"Fuckin' klangers. They'll take the skin off a working man's ass just to make an extra copper," Prof continued. "And no fuckin' sense of humor, either. And sensitive as shit, right?"

"Yeah! See, you know what I'm talking about?"

As we reached the forward watch posts, Prof walked up to Gorgeous and stared straight up into his face. "You use the word 'klanger' one more time and I'll cut you off at the kneecaps."

They stared at each other for a long time. Then Gorgeous broke out in a grin and slapped Prof on the back.

"Man, Prof, I do believe you would," he said.

The forward post consisted of four foxholes; I got put in the far left one. My companions were Gorgeous and Wym, who was still undergoing his metamorphosis into the perfect recruiting-mural Raider. I'd caught him that morning practicing pull-ups on a tree branch.

"What in Gruun's name are you doing?" I asked when I saw what he was up to.

He ignored me until he finished, then dropped to the ground and looked at me with an intense smile.

"'More sweat in camp, less blood in battle,'" he said proudly. It was a quote from the Raider Hand Book.

At the foxhole, Wym immediately volunteered for first watch. So me and Gorgeous had to decide between us who got to sleep the first shift. I looked over at Gorgeous — I could barely keep my eyes open, but I wasn't going to fight him. He rolled his eyes.

"I'll be your second," he told Wym. "Lips, go ahead and sack out."

When Gorgeous finally woke me up, I was confused at first about where I was. It was a very dark night — none of the moons were out. And it was quiet in that way that freaked out city dwellers like me. All I could hear was the sound of insects. Gorgeous yawned, curled up in the dirt, and after awhile the symphony of insects were joined by the soft sound of his whistle-like snoring.

"I wish I could sleep like that," Wym muttered.

I settled in beside him, squinting and waiting for my eyes to adjust to the dark. But even when I could start to make things out, they were still little more than dark shapes. I knew there was a small tree standing by itself about 100 yards in front of us and off to the left, but I couldn't see it. By His Foot, I couldn't even see Wym, and he was right beside me.

After awhile I started to get bored. I thought about cracking a joke, but then I remembered that the whole point of this was to be silent, so the last thing anybody needed to do was start laughing. Instead, I just whispered the obvious: "I can barely see anything out here."

"Yeah," Wym said. "How are we even supposed to know if something's up?"

"Well, I think if this was the real thing, we'd probably have a mage in our outfit. That would help. He could use nightsight or something. Or maybe a warding spell. I guess you could also rig up something out there to make noise if people were moving over it — dried foliage or something like that."

Wym didn't immediately respond, so I don't know if he bought that. Since I couldn't even see him to gauge a reaction, I assumed the conversation was over. I was starting to settle in to stare back out into the darkness when he spoke up again.

"You think it'll be like this?"

"Like what?"

"I don't know — waiting, I guess. Just...waiting."

"And working your ass off."

"Yeah, that too. But I mean...is this what it feels like? I mean, before a battle?"

"I'm not sure I follow."

"Just...you know when you're standing someplace way up high, and you look over the edge, and it gives you the shivers? Like some part of you wants to jump?"

"Sure."

"I'm just wondering if that's what it's like right before. Right before it all goes down."

"You're asking the wrong guy, man. And anyway, you shouldn't be feeling something like that anyhow. It's not like we're on the verge of battle out here. What are we gonna fight — a bunch of rocks and trees?"

"I know, I know. I just want to be ready. When it happens."

"Dude, that's the whole reason we're here."

Wym didn't have anything to say to that, so we sat in silence for awhile. I tried to focus on staying alert, but it was hard — even if you could fight off the urge to sleep, the cool, peaceful night air tended to cause your thoughts to drift. I was dreaming of getting back to Solta and sitting down for a fat, juicy leg of mutton and a big mug of ale when I was brought back into the moment by the rustling of some grass.

I can't really explain what made it catch my attention. I guess I'd been listening to the natural rustle caused by the breeze for more than an hour, so I suppose the slightly different sound caused by a moving creature stood out.

My muscles tensed. I leaned over to Wym and when I put my hand on him I could feel the tightness of his body, too.

"I've got my knife out," I whispered as quietly as I could. "You've got the whistle. Have it ready if anything crazy happens." I think I felt him nod, but it was too dark to be certain.

We waited. The soft sound of Gorgeous's snoring was suddenly nerve-wracking. I was worried waking him up might make more noise, but I decided to risk it. I kicked him lightly.

The snoring stopped. I dropped beside him and slapped my hand over his mouth.

"It's okay, it's just me. Something is out there. We just heard it. Nod if you understand."

I felt his head move, and I removed my hand. I pulled myself up, poking my head up over the edge of the foxhole to try to get a good look. It was useless — all I saw was darkness.

I sensed Gorgeous pull himself up and move beside me. I leaned over and felt his ear, and cupped my hands over it. I whispered, "Wym's got the whistle. If anything happens, he'll let loose." I waited a second, then added: "I can't see shit out here." Again I felt his head nod.

We waited, and waited some more. All we heard was the normal rustling of the grass. I was beginning to think it might be a false alarm, but then I heard it again — this time, it was unmistakable. There was something moving out there. Whatever it was, it was close.

Gorgeous put a hand on my shoulder, as if to steady me, then he spoke: "Ocean," he said. His voice was calm and clear, but not loud.

"Seashore," came the reply — low but distinct.

"Ocean" was the challenge phrase of the day, and "seashore" was the counter-sign. So that meant we were talking to one of our own...theoretically.

Raider doctrine, though, was that our mystery visitor could have simply tortured one of our comrades to get the correct countersign — not to mention, a clever fellow could have probably guessed it. So there was a second challenge phrase, and Gorgeous reeled it off as naturally as any performer at the theater: "Damn, brother. Had me rattled there."

But our mystery visitor rasped out the right response: "Snakes rattle, brother; men don't." If the reply had been anything else, me and Gorgeous were supposed to immediately jump out of the foxhole to attack, while Wym sounded the alarm. But...this was an exercise. So if the stranger hadn't known the right phrase...

I shook my head; no time to think about that now. Gorgeous grabbed my shoulder and motioned for me to climb out of the foxhole; I did so. As soon as I cleared the rim, I could hear our visitor rustling through the grass toward me. I made my way towards the sound and eventually found him, and helped him back into the foxhole. I could tell from when I brushed against him that he was a dwarf, but his armor was oddly ill-fitting.

Once he'd joined us in our foxhole, Gorgeous asked him what in the name of Auld Father's Foot was going on.

"I'm from..." he began, in a strangely nasal voice, and Gorgeous immediately shushed him.

"Quiet!" Gorgeous rasped. "This is a forward post."

"Gotcha," the visitor said in a whisper. "Sorry about this. Name's Frenlen. I'm from Three One Five. I got separated from my unit on a scouting patrol and got lost."

"How the fuck did you get separated?" I asked. "You're supposed to maintain sightlines on patrol."

Then Wym suddenly spoke up: "And how come your unit didn't report you missing when they checked in?"

"They probably DID — when they checked in, which I imagine was probably not more than a few minutes ago. Our patrol was running way late. They wanted us to gather these damn tubers..."

Me and Gorgeous groaned almost simultaneously.

"You guys too?" Gorgeous asked. Then he added, "We lucked out, I guess. We stumbled on a big patch of them about halfway through our patrol."

Frenlen seemed to take that in for a moment, then said, "Shit, I don't even know..." There was a rustling sound, as if he was adjusting his clothes. Then he said, "I've got a few here in my pack, but Auld Father knows if my squadmates found enough to bring back." He paused, and then asked, "Have you guys ever tried these things?"

"Nope," I said.

"Never," said Gorgeous.

"No idea," said Wym.

Frenlen said he was hungry and was thinking about trying one, but I said it probably wouldn't be smart to eat one raw.

"Oh — yeah. Yeah I wouldn't have thought of that. You guys in One One Five are pretty smart. You know your shit. It must be because of your DCs, huh?"

Gorgeous audibly snorted. I chuckled. Wym just sighed.

"What — you guys don't like your DCs? I mean, I guess nobody does, but there's no way your guys could be as bad as ours. Man, Sgt. Baryl, our second, is a fuckin' monster. Sometimes I think he gets off on giving us shit."

"Trust me, he's a daydream compared to Sgt. Taba," Gorgeous moaned.

"Oh yeah? He's the dwarf, right? Like me? Word among us dwarves is that he goes easy on the humans."

I was close enough to feel Gorgeous' hot breath. I could tell he was about to pop.

Frenlen continued. "I mean, some of the stories I've heard, they say you guys got it lucky — that Taba, he's supposed to be a creampuff. They say if you're in his platoon, you've got it made. They say..."

"I don't know who or where you've been hearing that," Gorgeous interrupted, "but let me tell you about that fucker Taba. That little bastard is the most annoying little cunt I've ever met. I've shot loads bigger than him. He's a shitstain covered in muscles, who walks around like he's invincible because he has that feather in his hat."

"Let me tell you something," he continued. "If I ever meet that runt in a tavern without his uniform on — let me tell you what I'll do. I'm gonna come up behind him and cold-cock his arrogant little ass and then beat him like I was his daddy. Not that the punk has a fuckin' daddy. Not a person, anyway. He's the product of unnatural barnyard relations."

"Wow, this Taba really gets on your nerves, doesn't he?"

"He gets on everybody's nerves. There's not a man in One One Five who doesn't want to take a swing right at his teeth while he's screaming at us. I bet the only reason he can open his mouth that wide is because he likes stuffing it with horse cock. Shit, I bet he gives you a run for your money, right Lips?"

Gorgeous was on a roll, so I played along. "Yup. Learned everything I know from him."

That got a laugh — as much of a laugh as you could get while trying to be quiet, anyway.

"Fuck me, man. Sounds like your Taba's a demon." Frenlen said. "Well I gotta get back. Keep going this way, I take it?"

Gorgeous got him going in the right direction, then stretched out across the back of the foxhole once again.

"Good job, you guys. Remind me to tell Taba tomorrow. Now unless someone's coming at you with a war hammer, don't fucking wake me up until the next shift."

THE NEXT MORNING AFTER we reported in, Gorgeous grabbed me and Wym and dragged us off to find Sgt. Taba.

When we found him, he was shaving — he was shirtless, displaying his intimidating muscles, and he had a huge knife that had the flat edge polished to a brilliant shine, which he was using as a mirror.

He listened patiently as Gorgeous laid out the entire story about how we'd intercepted Frenlen, and about how he'd gotten the challenge phrases right, so we'd sent him on his way. Taba showed no emotion throughout the whole thing, continuing to carefully shave while studying his reflection in the knife blade.

"Sgt. Taba, sir, this recruit thinks his fellow recruits are to be commended for their quick, alert work out there last night," Gorgeous concluded.

Apparently finished shaving, Taba toweled off his face and took another look at his reflection in the blade, admiring the job he'd done. He was still admiring himself when he spoke.

"So this 'Frenlen' — you said you just let him go?"

"Sir, the recruits did so. This recruit directed him back to the camp."

"I see. Without searching him?"

"Sir?"

"You said you directed him back to the camp. Did you search him?"

"Sir...he knew the passphrases. We — the recruits believed he was a friendly."

"I see. But you didn't search him."

Gorgeous looked at us blankly, then turned back to Taba, who was still admiring himself.

"Sir — the recruits did not."

"It did not occur to you that you might be talking to an enemy who might have managed to learn the passphrases?"

"Sir, it did not."

"I see. What did he look like?"

Gorgeous blinked. Now he was nervous.

"Um. Sir, the recruit does not know. It was too dark."

There was a good long pause before Taba said, in a distinct nasally tone, "Snakes rattle, brother. Men don't."

Uh-oh.

I looked at Gorgeous, who still didn't seem to grasp what was happening.

Taba dabbed at his face with a towel, then put away his knife and threw the towel over his shoulder. He turned to face Gorgeous with a huge smile.

"'That Taba, he's supposed to be a creampuff,'" Taba said, again in the nasally voice.

"Frenlen's" voice.

Then Gorgeous' face fell, and he visibly slumped.

Taba gave him a friendly punch.

"Cheer up, recruit. Today is gonna be fun! I don't know about you, but it's gonna be the most fun I've had in weeks!"

Remember how I said camp life was kind of like a vacation? Well the vacation ended there. First, Taba patiently explained to us what we *should* have done in the situation we'd found ourselves in. Since "Frenlen" was not known to any of us, we should have either bound his hands and immediately sent him back to camp with an escort, or we should have detained him for the duration of our watch and brought him back with us in the morning; in either case, we should have kept him under our control until his identity could be confirmed.

The Raider Hand Book hadn't explained it in exactly those words, of course — it just said to "verify the identity" of anyone approaching our post, which we thought we'd done. As we discovered, though, there are many, many situations where the instructions in the Hand Book are just a starting point, and the model Raider is supposed to use his intelligence, initiative and creativity (as well as hints and advice from other Raiders) to fill in the rest.

We paid for our mistake, of course. After Taba had dropped the dogshit out of us, we got a full day of the worst duty assignments he could dream up — not all of them strictly "necessary" for camp operations. All I'll say is if anybody ever tells you you're about to "wheel the break piles," run as fast as you can in the opposite direction.

59

The next day, the three of us — me, Wym and Gorgeous — were still on Sgt. Taba's shit list. We had to be up before dawn for camel duty. I was taking a piss and trying not to fall back asleep when I heard the first noise. It sounded a bit like thunder. In fact, I thought it was thunder, at first. But it sounded close — and I hadn't seen any lightning.

"Hey Gorgeous, what was that?" I asked after I finished my business.

"Thunder, sounded like."

Wym chipped in. "I don't think so. There was no lightning."

Then another boom came. And another. They sounded too short and sharp to be thunder. Then came a series of loud "cracks."

Then all was silent.

"Maybe it is thunder," I said. It was still dark out, but the sky was full of menacing clouds. "It looks like we're gonna get rain, anyway."

We met up with some guys from Three One Five who we'd be working camel duty with. Just as we headed off, there was another loud crack.

"What the fuck is that?" one of our new companions asked.

"It's gotta be thunder," Gorgeous said. "Look at the clouds."

"That doesn't sound like thunder," the guy said.

We were still arguing about it an hour later while hauling the waterskins back to camp when we heard another sound.

Gorgeous heard it first. He stopped our caravan and told everybody to shut up.

At first I didn't hear anything. But after a moment, I heard a faint sound that I immediately recognized: Hoofbeats from a horse running at full gallop.

"Single rider," Wym said. "He's moving fast."

By this time the sky was beginning to show light, even though it was filled with thick, low-hanging clouds. I turned and looked back down the trail. The mist still hung thick near the ground, but as the hoofbeats grew louder, a shape emerged.

It was a horse with a rider, of course, but there was something strange about it. The thick fog meant I didn't get a clear look until it was almost upon us.

The rider was...well, he was slumped over the back of the horse. He looked very weak. At first I thought he might be dead, but as he drew close, he pulled himself up and tried to rein in his steed, but the effort caused him to lose his balance, and he fell off. The horse continued to gallop on and quickly disappeared back into the mist.

We ran over to check on him. He was clad in armor and his shoulders bore a corporal's crest. It was quickly apparent why he'd been slumping — laying face down, you could see an arrow shaft sticking out from his back.

Gorgeous snapped off the shaft, and gently turned the man over. His face was very pale, and his lips looked sickly, but he was still breathing.

"Sergeant...Wulock...where..." the man gasped, looking around at our faces.

"He's not far. We'll bring you to him," Gorgeous assured him. "Come on, guys, everybody pitch in."

We dropped the waterskins and hoisted the wounded man onto our shoulders and carried him back to camp. When we arrived at HQ — a large hole dug into the ground, with a makeshift roof of branches and moss to keep out the rain — the recruit on guard duty at first refused to let us in.

"He's fucking dying!" Wym shouted, looking like he was about to start throwing punches. He started to move toward the guard, but quickly pulled back. He kept shouting at the guard, though, until Sgt. Wulock himself suddenly emerged from the dugout and everybody shut up and snapped to attention.

"What in St. Rom's name is going on here?" he bellowed.

He listened carefully as we explained what had happened, then turned to the recruit on guard duty.

"Fetch Sgt. Taba. He has training as a medic. The rest of you, bring this man inside."

The dugout was lit with several lanterns. There was a large, flat rock inside that served as a makeshift table; we placed the wounded man atop it, with a rolled-up blanket supporting his head.

He looked around groggily, until his eyes focused on Sgt. Wulock.

"Sergeant...are the recruits...okay?"

Wulock looked around.

"We haven't done the morning review yet, but...what's going on?"

The man struggled to pull himself up, and grasped for a canteen laying off to the side. I grabbed it and handed it to him, and he took several large gulps. Handing it back to me, he continued.

"Arcanter's men. They came...they came out of the High Anvil Pass. The whole camp has been overrun."

"Was that what we heard earlier?" I blurted out. Wulock gave me a look.

"When we were heading out on camel duty earlier — we heard something that sounded like thunder," I explained.

"Explosions," the corporal said. "They have high sorcerers with them. There are...I saw hundreds destroyed..."

Wulock's eyes narrowed. "Why are you here, corporal?"

"Sent...by Lt. Col. Ilos...I have..."

He patted around his uniform, searching for something, then pulled a folded piece of paper from somewhere under his shirt.

Wulock opened the paper and turned away from us to read it. Just then, Taba ducked into the dugout.

"Sgt. Wulock, one of the recruits informed me that...oh." He ran over to the man and did some medic-type things I didn't understand.

He looked at Wulock, who still had his back turned.

"Sergeant?" he asked. But Wulock kept his back turned, kept reading the piece of paper.

The wounded man finally spoke up.

"With your permission, sir," he said, "I would like to close my eyes for a moment."

NOT MORE THAN AN hour later, all three platoons were on the move. The last I saw of the wounded man was when I was ushered out of the dugout and sent to retrieve Sgt. Sculler. Nobody told us what happened to the man, but I assumed the obvious.

Our orders, which the rider had given to Sgt. Wulock, were to head to a village nearby to find horses so we could send out riders to raise an alert. Sgt. Sculler wasn't smiling, which was our first sign that this was serious. Wulock said we had to move quickly — enemy scouts might stumble upon our position at any minute.

We carried only our swords, spears, shields, canteens and whatever food we could stuff in our pouches. Instead of shouldering our spears, we trailed them — holding them by the neck of the pointed steel head while dragging the long shaft along behind. And instead of marching in formation, they had us humping it single-file through heavy forest — to better hide our movement, Sculler said.

In some places, there wasn't even a trail. It was a new experience — unlike drill, walking single-file with trailed spears meant we had to keep our distance.

"Give the man in front some space," Taba said — although for once, he wasn't shouting. "Keep a good distance. You guys can cram up and buttfuck each other all you want when this is all over."

Back at our camp, everything else was left in place. We even left fires burning — carefully shielded to avoid burning down the forest, of course. Anybody approaching our fortified ridge would have expected to catch us by surprise.

Sgt. Wulock put One One Five at the front — and Skunk was at the very front, walking point for all of us.

We stuck to the trees and avoided open spaces as much as possible. We only stopped twice — to allow the DCs to study their maps and discuss potential routes. They seemed to put a lot of trust in Skunk to know what he was doing.

Even as it grew dark, we kept moving. The DCs had a few lanterns, but they seemed wary about handing them out. Skunk got one because he was walking point, but the rest of us just had to use the light from one moon to see where we were going. Only Tarissa, the smallest, was out that night, so it wasn't much help. We were on a trail, if you could call it that. I mean, there was an obvious path where the rocks and brush were less thick, but from all the overgrowth, it didn't look like it had been used in some time.

It was nearing midnight when we heard it: A series of booms, then pops and cracks. It sounded like distant fireworks. Word went up and down the line and we halted and hit the dirt.

We couldn't actually see much of anything — we were deep in the forest, and the tall trees blocked out our view. We could see flashes in the sky, though, and it was pretty obvious that they weren't from lightning.

Since Taba was the only dwarf DC, he got the job of finding the highest tree nearby and climbing it to see what was going on. In the moonlight, I could see him scurry his way to the top like a monkey. He sat there for what seemed like several minutes, clasped effortlessly to the tall crown as it swayed in the night breeze. I thought back to my encounter with the wolves. Would have been a lot easier with klanger arms...

The pops and cracks and flashes of light continued while he was up there. Finally, he slid back down and headed off, I guess to talk to Sgt. Wulock. A bit later, word came down the line to dig in and "prepare to engage." That was all they said, "prepare to engage." It was the first time I ever heard that phrase, and I have never liked hearing it since.

We were on relatively high ground, which I knew was supposed to give us an advantage — at least that's what everyone said. The pops and cracks and lights stopped, and were gradually replaced by the maddening, whispery chirps and clicks of the nighttime forest.

A bit later, Sgt. Sculler came by. He was cheerful and supernaturally calm. He brought everybody in close together, and showed us where to dig in and where to point our spears.

Prof asked him what was going on.

"What was that with the lights and explosions?" he asked.

"High sorcerer," Sculler said casually. "That was him destroying our camp back on the ridge."

He said it as normally as if he was telling you the time of day, or who'd won last week's skram game.

I spoke up, asking the obvious: "How are we supposed to fight a high sorcerer?"

I couldn't make out his face in the moonlight, but the tone of his voice seemed to carry a fatherly grin: "I don't expect you'll have to. They don't know where we are — if they did, they would have sent him here."

"Then why are we dug in? Who are we supposed to fight?"

"They have teams of scouts searching the area. There's one a little bit to the west of us. Hopefully they'll miss us, but we're in a good defensive spot now, and it's best to be prepared," he said.

Gorgeous asked it before I could.

"What if they don't miss us?" he said.

I couldn't see the grin, but I could hear it in Sculler's voice: "Like I said: It's best to be prepared."

He moved on down the line to talk to the next squad. On his way back, he stopped once more to talk to us.

"Don't worry — Taba thinks there are less than ten of them. We've got them badly outnumbered. We should easily be able to take them, if it comes to that."

He hesitated for a second, then added: "Just one thing — don't run. Hold your position, face the enemy and keep fighting. If we need to retreat, we'll do it in an orderly fashion. But don't turn tail and run. In every battle I've ever fought in, most of the bodies we buried died from wounds in their backs."

And with that, he was gone.

THE WAITING IS THE WORST.

The actual fighting is hard to remember. You can only call up brief images — you use those to tell the story, but you don't actually remember the story happening the way you tell it. All you remember are brief flashes.

But the waiting — oh, the waiting. You remember every second of that, because it seems like it lasts forever.

So I remember the waiting, and I remember it very clearly. We'd quickly dug out a shallow trench with our shields, and I remember spending an eternity just looking out there into the moonlit forest, trying to see the enemy.

But it was the sounds that told the real story. The shadows cast by the moonlight revealed nothing, but the sounds — was it because I was a city boy that I picked up on unusual sounds? Or did country boys hear things that I couldn't? I don't know.

The sound came first. After an hour or so of listening to the nighttime forest, the sudden snapping and crunching of feet along the forest floor was unmistakable.

They were somewhere in front of us, on lower ground. I couldn't tell exactly how far away they were, but if I could hear them, they couldn't be that far. The sounds grew closer, and I noticed something off about them. At first I was wondering if Taba's estimate of "less than ten" scouts might have been too low, except...except as the sound grew close, it wasn't the number of footfalls crunching through the brush — it was the weight of those footfalls that seemed off.

Prof was to my right. I felt for his shoulder, then leaned over and whispered in his ear, as softly as possible, "are they on horseback?" In the darkness he made some motion that I took to be a shrug.

Something must have tipped off our opponents, because the sounds suddenly stopped. Everything was silent for a bit, then I heard something that sounded like speech, but it was low and I couldn't make out any words.

Then everything went quiet again. It lasted for a minute or more, the silence as taut as a drawn bowstring. Suddenly, I heard a few short, sharp words in a tongue I didn't recognize, followed by a quick series of whistles. And then big, heavy footfalls, in quick rhythm, coming quickly towards us. I remember a few heartbeats of confusion, as I tried to identify the sound. It was a throng of creatures too big to be human, but without the orderly, staccato thrum of horses' hooves.

They would be upon us in moments, but I could not call up in my mind any kind of image of what I was about to face.

And then someone — one of the DCs, I guess — threw a flare-dust charge in the air. There was a soft "pop," and the darkness was suddenly cut through with thousands of impossibly bright little pinpoints of light that drifted lazily on the night air. Each one was like a tiny sun throwing light and shadows everywhere, and I suddenly saw what we were facing.

They were wolves. Only...not like the ones I'd seen before. Not like ANY I'd seen before.

The shaggy beasts shooting towards us were each the size of a large horse. And I noticed there was something strange about their faces.

The sudden light from the flare dust must have startled them, because they all quickly stopped and howled. I could clearly see three of them, but could tell from the sounds that there had to be more than that.

There was more shouting from somewhere behind the wolves, again in a strange tongue, followed by more whistles. The animals quickly lowered their heads and bounded forward again.

Instinctively, I gripped my spear tighter. So did everyone else — as the creatures drew closer, they were suddenly confronted with a nest of steel points.

The wolf closest to me was approaching the line to my right. As it saw the bristling row of spears, it stopped short, growled, and let out a tremendous roar. That's when I got a good look at its face.

It had an extra pair of eyes set into its head, and the four eyeballs were moving independently, sweeping the area around it. Not only that, there was a fifth eye set right in the middle of its forehead, which seemed to glow an angry red.

It was a five-eyed wolf.

All my life, I'd heard that they were nothing but a ghost story to scare children. And yet here was one crouched in front of me, all fur and fangs. Something told me there would be no climbing a tree to escape this time, and no silver deer to be a distraction. This creature looked like it could snap a deer in half with its jaws.

The animal snarled at the row of spears, then made a huge leap, completely clearing our line — I was close enough to feel its fur brush me as it moved by. I looked back over my shoulder and saw the wolf wheeling itself around to charge us from the back. I barely had time to gasp before it had leapt off its haunches and was sailing through the air directly towards me.

By some sudden instinct, I lifted the shaft of my spear and rammed the butt end of the weapon at the wolf's body, as hard as I could. In that panic-filled moment I had somehow grasped that I had no time to swing my spear around. The sharp bounce of the shaft told me that I'd struck something firm but pliable, and a short yelp told me the beast didn't like it. I saw its furry shape tumble to the side, and it hit the ground with a "whump" heavy enough that I felt it in the ground.

I dropped the spear and unsheathed my sword. I crouched and groped around for my shield, never taking my eyes off the animal, which rolled itself to its feet, gave its fur a quick shake, and fixed me with its unholy gaze. It leaned back on its haunches as if to spring upon me.

I still hadn't found my shield, and was still on my knees, and I didn't dare let down my guard even for the second or so it would take me to stand up, knowing that was all the time it would take for my foe to be upon me. I thrust my sword out, prepared to stab the animal when it struck. I was murmuring the first words of a prayer and expecting the next sensation I felt to be the animal's jaws clenching the life from my throat when it suddenly made a leap to the side.

I quickly saw why. Prof and Gorgeous were charging at it with their spears — with the sharp spearheads pointed the RIGHT way, thank the Father. In the terror of the moment, I had briefly forgotten that I was not alone out here this time.

The wolf was in a powerful crouch, the hair around its neck flaring out. It let out a snarl, as if challenging my squadmates. Then Limul appeared, moving steadily toward the animal from the other side, slowly waving the tip of his own spear in a taunting motion. I snatched up my own spear and joined him.

"Careful," Limul said. "He sees everything with those eyes. The only way to catch him is to…"

A shape suddenly dropped out of the trees onto the wolf's back, and it let out a howl.

"Now!" Limul shouted. "Get him now while he's…"

He didn't finish the sentence — he didn't have to. As soon as the wolf's eyes turned away, Gorgeous charged in with his spear and pushed it deep into the creature's side. The rest of us were close behind; I pushed the shaft of the spear with every bit of strength I had. The flesh was surprisingly tough, but after a moment I felt the point slide through into something soft.

The animal let out a roar and began struggling; I fought to hold onto the shaft of my spear as it bucked around, getting slammed in my own ribs a few times for my efforts. Its massive head swung back and forth while its jaws snapped furiously, and I was close enough to feel its hot breath, but as long as I held fast to my spear it couldn't contort its body enough to reach me.

At one point it seemed to fix me with two of its demonic eyes as it struggled. The gaze was pure bloodlust. I responded by giving my spear an extra twist and jerk while I bellowed curses at it.

I was feeling my strength begin to give way when the wolf suddenly gave a strained gurgle. The shaft of my spear quivered a few times, then stopped.

A figure slid off the wolf's back — Sgt. Taba. He was sweating, breathing heavily and covered with blood. For a moment he seemed to be in a daze, but then he shook his head and looked around at us. He looked over at the dead monster, then stepped back over to it and pulled himself up the side of the carcass. He felt around in the thick fur, then pulled out a bloody sword. A weak spray of blood shot out of the wound after he pulled his weapon out.

Taba looked around at us.

"What are you fuckers waiting for?" he said, and he charged off towards the sound of another animal snarling and roaring somewhere close by, amid the shouts and curses of other recruits.

Just as he set off, the last bits of flare dust blinked out, and we were headed into darkness — it took a few moments for my eyes to adjust to the moonlight, but the way forward was easy enough — Taba's steady footsteps crunched across the ground just ahead, and the barking and bellowing of another furious struggle grew louder.

I don't know how I was able to keep moving forward. I should have been terrified; if you'd snatched me up off the streets of the Warrens and dropped me directly into this mess, I would have probably curled up into a ball and cried. But my mind was in a different place right there, in that moment — it was like I was in some kind of trance.

All I was aware of was my heart beating, my breathing, and a need to go, go, go forward and find something to fight. My limbs tingled with anticipation. I was somewhere beyond fear. I was an arrow fired sharp and straight from a bow, singing toward a target, and for some reason I was calm even though it all felt completely out of my hands.

As we drew closer to one of the creatures, it let out a yelp of pain, then a loud, plaintive whimper. It continued to wail and whimper as we got closer — a terrible and icy sound. I saw the huge, fur-covered form just ahead and ran toward it, gripping my spear to strike. But then the creature's terrified cries suddenly stopped, and I saw a human figure fall back from the hulk of fur, landing in the dirt.

Once again, a dark shape soared out from somewhere in the trees and landed atop the animal: Taba again. In the dark and confusion, he had somehow managed to clamber up into the treetops again for another attack from above. But this time the animal he landed on had been felled before he could strike. He stood up slowly, balancing himself on the creature's back. He prodded it with his sword. The body made a few sad, reflexive kicks, but there was no life behind the movement.

"Dead," Taba said, and jumped down.

Everyone turned to the figure who'd fallen into the dirt. He was pulling himself to his feet, and he made his way over to the remains of his foe. Taba struck a match, and we could see the figure's face: It was Skunk. He was badly bruised, dirty, and breathing heavily, but otherwise unhurt. The look in his eyes was one I recognized — he was shocked that he was still alive. It had been the same feeling I'd felt right after my squadmates had driven back the beast just before it pounced on me.

"You took this thing down by yourself?" Taba asked.

"I...yeah. I...the recruit was trying to lure it away from the rest of his squad."

"And you thought you could handle it alone?"

Skunk was visibly shaking. From fear? From excitement? Maybe both. "The recruit wasn't sure — this recruit has..."

"You can say 'I,' Recruit Camlin," Taba suddenly said, with a softness I didn't think he was capable of.

"Sorry, sir. This rec...I've hunted Dire Boars before, on my father's estate. They're about the same size as these...these..."

He stopped and looked at the dead carcass.

"I didn't think these were real, sir."

"Real, and deadly. They use them to hunt in Garlund. The twin pairs of eyes give them an almost-circular field of view, and the single eye in the forehead..." — Taba swung the match over to show us — "...can see in total darkness. It stays closed during the day."

"And now they're using them to hunt us," Skunk said.

"Are there any left?" I heard myself asking. I was still riding the rush of battle.

Taba motioned with his hand for us to be quiet, and listened for a moment.

"This way," he finally said, and we followed him off into the brush.

IT TURNED OUT THERE were six creatures in all. Two had been killed by our fellow recruits by the time we got to them, and in battling the remaining two I was little more than a spectator — though I like to think that our simply being there and standing by with spears gave the other squads the spirit they needed to finally overcome those horrible beasts. Wym dispatched the last one by worming under it and using his knife to slice open an artery near its groin — a move he surmised would work from time he'd spent working in a slaughterhouse. It had left him drenched in blood, looking like a nightmarish ghoul, but when someone pointed out his terrifying appearance he took it as a compliment and began preening for us.

"I only wish I had a mirror," he said.

The vile demons dispensed with, we rounded everyone up and took a headcount. Everyone had survived, although some folks had been beaten up badly. Talk immediately turned to going after the beasts' handlers — presumably, those had been the voices we'd heard before the attack.

Sgt. Wulock quashed that idea.

"They're long gone now — probably to alert their commander about our location. We need to get moving as quickly as possible."

It was obvious from the murmurs around me that Wulock's decision didn't sit well with everybody, but he was in charge. He had that collar pin. He belonged to the Order of the Inferno. Who could question his judgment?

I gathered up everything I'd dropped — my shield, my canteens and a few pouches stuffed with food, and my spear. At least I hoped it was my spear. It was hard to tell after all the confusion. We were forming up to begin marching again when I heard a crackling noise. It sounded a bit like a chunk of meat frying.

I looked around. Parsa was right in front of me, and in the dim light I could see he looked as confused as I was.

"Did you hear that?" I asked.

"Yeah. That was..."

It started up again, much louder this time.

"What in Gruun's name..." Parsa said.

There were loud popping sounds, each one accompanied by sparks flying out of thin air. I was about to say something when a bolt of lightning shot out of the empty sky — there were no clouds — and struck the ground far to the left of us. It was accompanied by an ear-splitting "boom" that shook the very ground we were standing on; for a brief moment, the entire forest around us was lit up so brightly it seemed like the sun itself had temporarily appeared and fallen to the ground.

For a moment I couldn't move — I thought for sure this must be some freak of nature, and there was nothing to do but stand and gawk. But then there was more crackling, more popping, growing louder, and another bolt of lightning shot out of the sky — but this one didn't disappear. It stood like a column, reaching up into the sky, its crooked shape constantly changing. The light filled the forest, causing the trees all around to cast long, sharp black shadows.

My ears hurt — a long, continuous cracking sound ripped through everything. Even my bones seemed to be humming. I slapped my palms over my ears and looked up.

At the top of the lightning column was a glowing blue orb. It was quickly descending — as it drew closer to the ground, I could see a figure inside of it. It was a man of maybe 30 summers. He had bright red hair, and wore a dark-colored outfit. In one of his hands he held a long staff, with one end glowing brightly.

I saw Parsa shouting something, so I leaned in to hear him better. Just above the roar I could make out his words: "HIGH SORCERER." I'd never actually *seen* a high sorcerer before — only read about them. But the figure floating to the ground looked about the way I imagined one would look.

As he dropped further down, the figure extended his feet as if preparing to land. I saw Parsa draw his sword and pull up his shield, as if he were preparing for combat. I grabbed him and screamed into his ear: "WHAT ARE YOU DOING?"

He looked at me with a smile of wonder, as if gazing upon a beautiful sunset. "I'M NOT GOING TO DIE DOING NOTHING," he yelled back, and he began charging toward the spot where the sorcerer was landing. For a second I just stood there looking at him, but then I found myself gripping my own sword and shield and charging after him, my mind still searching for a reason while my limbs went ahead and carried me forward.

Parsa was maybe a dozen strides away from the sorcerer, his sword raised to strike, when the mage's foot touched the ground. Then there was a flash and the next thing I knew I was lying on my back, seeing the stars through the branches of the trees above.

The next minute or so is hard to describe. There was a hum. At first I thought it might have just been from the rush of blood in my head, but it grew louder, and I felt it all over my skin and through my body. My vision suddenly got blurry, and everything seemed bathed in a bright purple mist.

I sat up and noticed that something felt different, but I couldn't immediately place what it was. The humming stopped, my vision went back to normal, and I heard a powerful but friendly voice.

"Congratulations, gentlemen," it said. "You have just passed your final test."

60

I turned to the sound of the voice, which proved to belong to the sorcerer. A soft glow emanated from the tip of his staff, and he looked relaxed and unthreatening — unlike the vision of mighty power that had ridden down out of the heavens on a lighting bolt. But I could see from his clothing and shock of red hair that it was the same man.

Parsa, who like me was pulling himself back to his feet, was the first one to speak. I think he spoke for everybody when he sputtered, "What the fuck?"

The sorcerer just smiled.

I picked up my sword and approached the man nervously. Parsa seemed to be standing there a little dazed. I moved in and stood next to him, and we exchanged a look, then turned back to the sorcerer. He seemed amused by the whole thing.

"Aren't you men going to salute Maj. Tyvin?" another voice suddenly said, and we turned and saw Lt. Col Ilos emerging from the brush in a crisp dress uniform, accompanied by a band of junior flunkies.

I turned back to the sorcerer, and for the first time I noticed that his clothing was actually some kind of uniform. And on his collar were the stylized escutcheons of a major. Shit.

Both me and Parsa almost instantly snapped to attention and saluted, though I was just a tick slower because I started to sheathe my sword before thinking better of it and simply dropping it in the dirt.

Both Lt. Col. Ilos and Maj. Tyvin let out a hearty laugh, and Ilos told us both to relax. Then he called out to all the other recruits to come gather around him.

"Come in here, guys, you'll want to see this."

As the others emerged out of the forest, I saw that all their bruises and scrapes had disappeared. Wym was no longer drenched in blood — in fact, everybody's armor and weapons looked clean.

It was then that I noticed that all the aches and strains all over my body from our recent battle were gone. I felt as new and refreshed as if I'd just rolled out of an overstuffed feather bed in a palace after sleeping for two days straight.

Our DCs appeared wearing knowing smiles. Wulock had us do a count off to make sure everybody was present, then Ilos told everybody to take a load off.

"Sit your asses down, you bastards," he said. "You've earned it."

It turned out that everything — the whole "invasion" — the strange sounds, the attacks, even our wounds — were our "light show," like the one I'd watched with Prof that night out in front of the barracks, where we'd watched. We'd just completed Terminal Phase.

"That wasn't real?" I said. "That was — an illusion?"

"Yes, and lucky for you it was," Wulock said. "Auld Father help us if there'd been a real invasion and we'd had to rely on you clowns. If Maj. Tyvin had been an enemy sorcerer, every single one of you would have been dead."

"Sgt. Wulock is right, of course," Lt. Ilos said. "But the point of this exercise wasn't to defeat a high sorcerer, something none of you would have been equipped to deal with anyway. That is a lesson for another day.

"The important thing is, you stared into the face of battle, worked as a team and held your ground. You did not fall apart, and did not abandon each other. You have shown you are worthy of becoming Raiders."

There were murmurs from the group. A lot of us were still trying to decide if this was just another mindfuck. I kept waiting for the part where they started screaming at us and smoked the shit out of us for a good half-hour.

Not everyone was so nervous, though. "There's no invasion?" Toad asked.

Ilos answered him calmly. "No invasion across the mountains. No attack. No wolves. No sorcerer — well, except for Maj. Tyvin here, who thank goodness is on our side. Oh, and just over that hill back there we have a train of ox carts to take you back to the main base. So no more marching, at least tonight."

That was the first good news I'd had in days. I'm a bit ashamed to say this, but I cried a little — not straight up bawling; just little tears around the corners of my eyes. It was all I could do to relieve the tension. But within seconds, the crying turned to laughter. I looked at Parsa, looked at Skunk, looked at Prof. They were all smiling too.

It was Wym who finally asked the question that was on everyone's mind. "Sir? I...this recruit thought Terminal Phase wasn't for another two weeks."

Ilos nodded solemnly. "As you gentlemen know, we're at war now." He said the last four words slowly, and let them hang there for a moment, to let them sink in. Then he continued. "And that has created certain...pressures upon us. We now have a backlog of new recruits, and to speed things along, it was decided to shorten your schedule. I assure you, the decision to send you into Terminal Phase without warning was not one that was made lightly. But it was the opinion of your Drill Commanders that you would be equal to the task." He shot a look at our DCs, who stood to the side now, grouped together, eyeing us with a look that might have been pride, if I thought they were capable of such a thing.

"The good news is, though, that your graduation has been moved up. In two days, all of you will be standing on the hallowed ground of the Glorious Field."

It took a second for that to sink in, but when it did, guys began clapping and whooping, which slowly built to a loud, sustained cheer. At that point I really did start crying. I looked over at the DCs. And for the first time since I'd set foot into the Wood, they were smiling — genuinely smiling. Even Sgt. Wulock wore a tight little grin.

Finally, after things settled down, someone asked how they'd created the illusion. Was it Maj. Tyvin?

"Oh, Maj. Tyvin helped, I can assure you of that," Ilos said, patting the major on the shoulder. "But ultimately, no mortal sorcerer can create an illusion like the one you fellows just lived through. Let me show you guys the coolest thing you've ever seen."

He motioned to somebody behind him. Two corporals emerged, carrying a large, cast iron vessel of elaborate design. One of the corporals, I noted, was the "wounded" rider whose appearance had set this whole thing off.

The vessel had a squat body that tapered up into a thin but short neck, and the neck had some kind of valve built into it.

The vessel had two large rings on either side for carrying, and I could see each corporal straining with both arms to hold either ring. They set it down in front of Ilos.

"You guys might want to stand back for this," Ilos said, and gave a nod.

One of the corporals worked a latch and removed a stopper from the vessel's neck, then backed quickly away. His companion released the valve and quickly backed away in the other direction.

A darkly glowing purple smoke poured out of the neck of the vessel, producing a thick, but sweet-smelling cloud, exactly like the purple mist I'd seen earlier. The cloud slowly took shape, until it gradually took the form of a huge...man?

Not a man, though it had the general shape of a man from the waist up. Below the waist, the thing's body curled away into a ribbon of smoke that trailed back into the iron vessel.

Above the waist, the proportions were off — it had a thick, barrel-shaped torso and massive, beast-like arms. It must have been at least 20 feet tall.

Weirdest of all was the head — if you could call it that. The head was attached directly to the shoulders, with no neck — it protruded like a small dome. If you'd seen it from behind, you might have thought you were looking at a hunchback.

The head had no face, really. There was the suggestion of a face, like somebody had started to form one, but nothing you could call a mouth or nose. What it did have were eyes — great red slashes on either side of the face. Against the dark purple of the rest of its body, the bright red glow of the eyes looked downright evil.

There were gasps, and some guys began to back away and mutter prayers to Auld Father. Ilos just chuckled.

"Relax, relax! It's just our djinn. We call him Smoky. Allow me to demonstrate. Smoky?"

The giant form turned slowly and looked at Ilos, who said something to it in a strange language I'd never heard before. It nodded, and clapped its hands.

There was a pitter-pattering sound from out in the dark, and suddenly a huge golden scorpion, the size of a large dog, came scampering up. It began snapping its claws at different recruits, whipping out its tail to try and sting them as they jumped out of the way.

Gorgeous in particular was shaken up. He quickly drew his sword and began waving it in the creature's direction.

"Keep that thing away from me!" he wailed, and the tone of his voice expressed sheer terror.

"Calm down, recruit, let me get you some help!" Ilos laughed. As soon as he did so, a huge dark shape came soaring out of the darkness and landed right atop the snapping scorpion with a growl.

It was a five-eyed wolf — just like the ones we'd fought earlier. The hairy beast grabbed the scorpion's tail in its massive jaws and began flinging it about. The scorpion's shell cracked several times with a gooey-sounding "crunch." When it was nothing more than a twitching mass, its foe ripped its tail from its body in a final gesture of victory.

The fur-covered beast then turned to look at us, the writhing tail still held firmly in its jaws.

I stepped forward, approaching the great beast. Somebody tried to hold me back, but I shrugged them off. I drew in closer; the great animal's eyes all turned to focus on me.

I reached out and rubbed its fur. To my surprise, it felt solid.

Incredible. No wonder, I thought, that djinn are considered so dangerous. I later found out that there have been people who imprisoned djinn and forced them to spin fantasies, only to end up dying of starvation because they couldn't pull themselves away from the captivating illusions long enough to eat or drink.

An illusion, I learned, can be the most powerful magic of all.

61

I guess that at this point, I'm supposed to tell you all about the Raider graduation, and about how I finally took my place in the long blue line on the Glorious Field. But to be honest, the whole thing didn't leave much of an impression on me. For one, because they'd moved up the date, nobody had friends or family there to congratulate them; the visitor's seats sat completely empty. And anyway, we already *felt* like full Raiders. The ceremony just seemed like — what would Footman Sesh call it? — a "formality."

It went about like you'd expect. It was a sunny day, and everyone in all three platoons was dressed sharp and shiny for the occasion.

Lt. Ilos made a little speech. He apologized about having to move the graduation. Footman Glaine preached a sermon about duty, another variation of the one we'd already heard him preach countless times before, then offered prayers to Auld Father. Then General Gern said a few words and pronounced us Raiders in good standing. From then on, we were no longer "recruits"; we all had the title "private." A handful of guys, including Skunk and Prof, were named "private, first class" because of their exceptional performance in training — the rest of us would have to wait to get promoted to that rank. And Prof was awarded the purple sash for being judged the top recruit from our platoon. The look of shock on his face when he went up to accept it drew laughs from the rest of us. He was the only guy there who didn't seem to realize how much he deserved it.

I wrote my mother a letter describing everything. I think she was probably more excited, though, by the signed letter she received from Father General Temushi himself, which she had framed to hang on her wall. It congratulated her on being "one of the most honored mothers of our blessed Kingdom," for having given birth to "a brave and mighty warrior, who will carry the great name of our people and enlarge their honor by rendering justice, establishing peace and proclaiming the name of Auld Father with his blade."

Anyway, like I said, the ceremony was almost an afterthought, at least for me. What I remember more — what really stuck with me — was something from the night before.

We knew we were supposed to go out to greet the newest recruits at the rubbish pit, the same way we'd been greeted when we first arrived. Of course, we needed to get into the proper spirit for the occasion, so Gorgeous — speaking for all of us — told Sgt. Taba, "sir, these recruits respectfully ask you to smoke the trollshit out of us." He happily obliged, screwing on his meanest DC face and screaming his little dwarven lungs out, but even he was having trouble hiding his smile.

When we were done, we walked out, bodies sweating and muscles aching, to "welcome" the newest recruits. Some guys in our platoon went through the trouble of shitting in their buckets, though I only went as far as scrounging some nasty scraps from the mess hall.

As we rounded the side of the receiving building, I saw the row of massive ox trolleys sitting there beside the pit, and remembered the lean, tough-looking guys who had welcomed us that first night. The thought that I was now one of those tough bastards didn't seem real — it felt like just yesterday that I'd been down in that pit. It felt like just yesterday, but at the same time, it felt like centuries. I'm not sure I would even know what to say to the nervous little jackass who'd first come through the gates of this place all those months ago.

The guys in the ox trolleys were just like we had been. I heard some of them quietly sobbing, while others were shouting challenges at us, trying to hide their fear behind bravado. When they finally pulled the pins and dumped them all into the pit, those were the guys I was laughing at. I was laughing because they didn't even know yet that this was the easiest part.

As I was dumping the contents of my bucket over their heads, I spied one face that I recognized.

It was the ringer — the pit fighter that Sgt. Wulock had brought in on sparring day to try to mess us up. He was standing there looking as confused as anybody else.

I called out to him. "Hey buddy? Remember me?"

He didn't respond at first, so I added, "You with the muscles, dumbass!"

That seemed to reach through his thick skull, and he looked around and then fixed his eyes on me.

"Uh. Yeah. Yeah, I remember you."

"What are you doing back here? Didn't get enough of an ass-whipping last time?"

He looked at me and blinked.

"The war," he finally said. "I...I wanted to do my part. And I remembered how you guys were such badasses. I figured if I was going to fight, it could only be with you guys. I mean, look at me!" He struck a pose. "You telling me the Raiders don't want a weapon like this?"

I grinned, tossed him my bucket in a friendly gesture, and told him to tell that to the first sergeant he saw.

"Really?" he asked.

"Yeah. I can guarantee they will agree with you. They might even let you skip some of the harder stuff."

He smiled. "Thanks man! Good to know!"

I fought like crazy to hold in my laughter until we got back to the barracks. But when I finished laughing, that's when it hit me — the thing I couldn't stop thinking about.

The rubbish pit this time was a lot longer than it had been when I'd started training — at some point over the past six months, it had been extended. It had to be, because the line of trolleys bringing in new recruits was now twice as long.

PART THREE

RAIDER

62

When Lt. Col. Ilos had given us the good news about our early graduation, he'd carefully neglected to tell us the bad news: We wouldn't get to go home immediately. With the whole realm now on war footing, and many more recruits coming in, our first assignment as newly-minted Raiders would be working to upgrade Fort Harrel to accommodate a literal army.

While a few guys like Prof managed to get assigned as clerks, and Skunk even got tasked with helping train new recruits in sparring — they were still short on DCs to handle everything, apparently — most of us got herded into "labor companies." Most days we were out from sunup to sunset clearing forests, hauling supplies, helping with construction, and generally just performing whatever grunt work was needed to get the place ready to churn out new Raiders on a scale unseen since the Great War.

Since they didn't have any barracks for us — they needed every available space to house the recruits — they lodged us in tents, four men per tent. (Sergeants got individual tents that they didn't have to share; officers got wooden cabins.) I suppose the best I can say is that it was comfier than a field encampment, though chilly nights made me think back longingly to our old stone quarters.

Most of the work I did was pretty forgettable, but I did get to spend a couple of memorable weeks helping build a new "auxiliary chapel." The brass decided that the old chapel, despite being the largest building on base, was no longer big enough for Sevenday services without packing everyone in butts to nuts, so they decided to throw up a second chapel to help with the overflow. The new building was little more than four stone walls enclosing a huge space with a roof thrown over it. It reminded me of a vast livestock stable more than a house of Auld Father, but Footman Glaine assured us with the proper consecration it would be sufficient "for the duration of the war."

That was another thing. They were now talking about the war lasting two, maybe even three years, instead of the "few weeks" everyone was throwing around when I first fell off the ox trolley.

On days we didn't work, we still went on marches and did weapons training, just to "keep us sharp," they told us. It was rougher than work detail, but since we were now officially Raiders, we no longer had to worry about DCs constantly riding us into the ground. The guy bossing me around now, Sgt. Kutko, looked old enough to be Sgt. Sculler's dad. He had actually been a retired Raider (there are no "former" Raiders), but volunteered for re-enlistment after the death of the King.

Sgt. Kutko had a barrel chest and a jowly face that made me think of a deflated balloon. He wasn't all gleaming and sharp like our Sculler and Taba, but he still looked more put together than any of us newly-minted Raiders could manage. Though I never saw him smile, even when cracking a joke, he had those kind old man's eyes that you could imagine putting a child at ease. He looked like the sort of man you might have confided in if you met him in a bar out in the civilian world, though he always kept his distance from us.

He could be as strict about the rules as any DC, but as long as you kept your head down and did your job, you wouldn't have trouble with him. "This isn't a nursery," he told us, "and you aren't babies. I expect you to know enough at this point that I don't have to tell you to shake it after you take a piss."

When people did do something to get on his bad side, I never saw him raise his voice, and I only once saw him smoke somebody. But since he was in charge of the duty roster each day, he had other ways to punish you. One time, a private who was caught breaking the rules about having alcohol in camp got a whole week of latrine duty. This was, I should point out, latrine duty *for all* of *Fort Harrel*. I can assure you that this private — I seem to recall his name as "Pvt. Pearl" — was extra careful about the rules for the rest of his time there.

But the biggest difference was that we now got "off duty" time. Your options for what to do were pretty limited — there was a tavern for enlisted men, and as you can imagine, it was always packed. But it wasn't the kind of vomit-soaked piss-bucket brawl hall where you'd normally expect to find a bunch of bleeding, broken-toothed Raiders blowing off steam — the Blue Wood had strict rules about excessive drunkenness, and there were no women to chat up, dance with or fight over. The wine and ale on tap was watered down, anyway.

There was a library, and while I did check out a couple of books, the selection of volumes wasn't put together with entertainment in mind. It was mostly stuff for officers — history, geography, strategy and tactics, engineering, and magical arcana, along with lots of religion and philosophy. Real long-beard scholar crap.

Although there were always cards or dice games going on, there were no stakes, because gambling was strictly forbidden. What most people ended up doing with their free time was playing skram — we even got a small league going, and the team I was on (The Blue Boogers) even made it to the finals. When people weren't doing that, they'd read and write letters, or stand around campfires gossiping and arguing.

An always-popular topic was this mysterious "Reckoner" who was supposed to guarantee us victory. The consensus was that he must be some kind of powerful mage — after all, the Arcanter was said to be a fearsome spellcaster wielding the powers of necromancy, so it would only make sense if our side had a mighty sorcerer of our own. From my encounter with Maj. Tyvin — who was said to be merely run-of-the-mill, as High Sorcerers go; supposedly there were other sorcerers who were vastly more powerful — that sounded like a pretty fair guess. But other people were sure the Reckoner was merely a superb warrior with no special magic — perhaps a charismatic general who wouldn't so much defeat the Arcanter in single combat as use his superior wisdom to lead us to victory. "The army of the faithful will be Auld Father's sword; the Reckoner will merely wield it" was how one extremely pompous private, a former member of Two One Five, put it at the end of a long-winded lecture. Still others held that the Reckoner would be some kind of holy man, possibly an ordained Footman, who would defeat the Arcanter simply by calling forth a miracle from Auld Father himself.

"How would that be different from just a really powerful sorcerer?" I onced asked Parsa, who, being a bit of a Walk-thumper, tended to take this view of things. He gave me an earful about how vulgar magic was merely the clever manipulation of natural laws, and thus subject to limits — which was completely different from a manifestation of divine power, which was without any limits. I thought about that and responded with one of those questions we'd pester the Footmen with back in Temple School: Is Auld Father powerful enough to create a rock that He cannot lift?

Parsa gave me a look. "Fuck you," he said, while I burst out laughing.

One particularly cold night, we got on the subject again while gathered around a campfire, and somebody asked Skunk his thoughts on the whole thing, being a highborn and all.

I can remember the look on his face, as he sat there sipping a mug of warm mead. He gave a soft chuckle, and then grew serious, staring straight into the fire.

He said: "What I think is that I really, really hope this whole war isn't riding on just one man."

63

And then, finally, we were allowed to leave. And I don't know which had changed more — us, or the world beyond the gates of the Blue Wood.

As the ox-trolley lumbered over the crest of a hill, I finally got a look at my old home city. The first thing I noticed was all the smoke and haze around the place. Did the air always look like that? Or did it just seem different because of where I'd been?

Then as we got closer, I saw the people. Thousands of them, clustered out around the walls. On what used to be a field of rolling pasture, something like a small town had sprung up. Actually it was more like a camp, with tents and caravan wagons and hastily slapped-together wooden buildings, but it was the size of it that made me think of a town.

The drover must have seen me staring, because he started explaining: "It's the war. The Regency Council has opened up the royal treasuries like a spigot; everybody's burning to get revenge for the death of the King, and they're sparing no expense to get the job done. It's meant plenty of work for all the tradesmen and factories in the city — that's why you see all the smoke."

Skunk, who'd been watching the scene with his usual reserve, said "So these are...workers?"

The drover laughed. "Oh, goodness no!" He gestured back to the overloaded trolley, which was packed with bodies — most of whom were clearly not Raiders. "These are the workers. Been pouring in for weeks now."

We'd left the Blue Wood the same way we'd come in: Aboard a train of ox-trolleys — normal ones, not the ones with the trick hinges they'd brought us in on.

Our instructions were to report to camp in three weeks at Agellos — the great port city of the south, and the heart of the preparations for the invasion. In the entire history of the world, nothing like the invasion had ever been attempted — the mightiest armada ever assembled would launch forth from the eastern coast and sail across the Glass Ocean to storm the coast of Garlund. It sounded crazy, but compared to trying to march an army across the Striped Mountains, it was downright sensible.

While some guys were eager to head straight for Agellos and get their first taste of life as full-fledged Raiders, our superiors all sounded the same note: It would be better for all of us to put in at least a few days at home first.

"Go back, see your family," Sgt. Kutko said. "Get things in order. Say your good-byes — a lot of you won't get another chance." You could tell by the look in his eyes he meant that last part.

After leaving the camp, we gradually split up as different guys went different ways to get back home. We promised to have a One One Five reunion when we got to Agellos — though our "official" standard had been retired at the end of training, Blockhead said he could whip up some copies to give us the next time he saw us.

By the time we reached Solta, Skunk was the only other One One Fiver left. I asked him if that's where his family's "summer home" was. He flipped me off.

"No, that's where my dad's main house is. He's stationed in the capital and he wanted to see me first thing; I haven't seen him in..." He thought for a moment, then shook his head. "It's been almost two years," he finally said.

Our train of ox-trolleys was now passing right through the middle of the "camp" outside the main gates, and I was still trying to figure out who all these squatters were.

"So if these people aren't workers," I asked the drover, "who are they? Why are they here?"

The drover looked around with weary disgust.

"Well, I think of them as fleas on the capital's ass." Seeing I didn't quite get his meaning, he went on. "Like I said, ever since the war flames started burning hot, there's been lots of money to go around. From the crown, it goes to the tradesmen and builders and merchants and privateers. And from there it makes its way down to the soldiers and workers. And once they get it, well..."

He looked at me with a gleam in his eye.

"They want to spend it," I said. He nodded.

"Seems like there'd be enough for them to spend it on in the city," I said, thinking out loud.

"Oh, for most things. But the Lord Mayor does prefer to maintain a certain amount of respectability within the city walls. And some of the men prefer entertainments that are...less than respectable."

"So this is, what would you call it, a red light district?" Skunk asked.

"I thought we already had something like that down in the Warrens," I said.

"Oh, the Warrens! Wait until you see what's happening there!"

I thought about that for a few minutes, then said out loud, to nobody in partic-ular, "Where does the Crown get the money for all this?"

I knew the Crown was rich, of course, but all I could think of was all the "improvements" that were supposed to be made down in the Warrens that never got done because, it was said, the Crown didn't have the money.

Skunk chuckled and patted me on the back.

"Friend, you do not want to know," he said. "You really don't."

Actually getting through the gates took some time — nobody got in without a pass, and the guards were making sure to check every single one. It took a good hour, at least, for them to finally wave through our ox-trolley — and there was a train of nine more behind ours. I understood then why, when we'd set out that morning, the drover had encouraged me and Skunk to ride in the lead cart.

Once inside, though, it was quickly obvious just how much had changed. Every street seemed to be a hive of activity. Everybody seemed to be moving with a purpose — it was like the morning of market day, except it was late afternoon in the middle of the week. Most of the people seemed to be hauling things or running errands, but there were many who were in fresh work clothes who seemed to be on their way to a job.

"Is this a shift change?" I asked the drover.

The drover laughed. "Shift change? Oh, no, I made sure we got in before that. We've still got over two hours until most of the afternoon shift gets off."

Skunk just looked over the whole scene with an enormous grin. When he shook his head and chuckled, I asked him what he found so amusing.

"It's just like my great-uncle used to say, when I'd ask him to tell me stories about the Great War," he said. "I always wanted to hear about the legendary battles he'd fought in, but he'd always just look grim and say, 'Would that something less terrible could move men so.'"

He looked at me, and continued. "What he meant..."

"I know. I got it."

"Well, it's just I never really understood until just now. Not really."

The ox-trolley carried us as far as the grand arcade, which seemed to have been turned into a makeshift depot, with baggage trains and ox-trolleys loading and unloading on every square inch of ground. I gave Skunk a handshake before I headed off.

"Come see me before you go," Skunk said. He must have seen the look on my face, because he added, "Don't look at me that way. I just meant to get a drink. It's not like I'm going to invite you to sleep in my house and fuck my sister, you Warrens scum."

I pretended to be serious. "Do you think she would fuck me?"

He returned the serious gaze. "Probably. But there's no way I could let my Raider buddy put Crown Property at risk that way."

We both busted out laughing. Skunk gave me his address, and I promised to swing by the first time I had the chance.

64

I was still mulling over my options for where to stay while I was back home. But before anything else, I wanted to see my mom.

Getting back to the Warrens took longer than I'd expected. In addition to all the usual street traffic, there were also different bands of soldiers marching on many of the larger avenues. "Marching" might be a bit of a stretch — they weren't doing anything a Raider would recognize as marching after a few days in the Blue Wood, but they were moving in something that might have been Sgt. Taba's bad dream of a formation and following commands from "sergeants" who would have caused Sculler to die of shame if he could have seen them.

These were, I later learned, "auxiliary" units. Real military units were stationed elsewhere, in key positions. But as I came to understand, during war, there's always a shortage of qualified men, but never a shortage of volunteers.

And so, for the greater glory of the realm, wealthy and powerful men would organize their own units, which they'd humbly offer up to "assist" the Crown. (I've heard that such efforts can help to greatly relieve a wealthy man's taxes — but as I know nothing of that, I won't speculate.) Not all of these units are trash — some actually turn out to hold their own quite well in battle if they manage to get some decent training. But decent training was another thing that was in short supply.

At any rate, I encountered several platoons, companies and even what could have been battalions out marching on the streets, trying and largely failing to conduct the sort of basic maneuvers that we'd learned on our first day in the Blue Wood. I uttered a silent prayer to Auld Father, asking that he never allow me to go into battle alongside any of them.

When I arrived in the Warrens, I saw what the drover meant about all the changes. Half of the buildings had been torn down and were being rebuilt. I was shocked to find that the big granite block in Craller Square had been completely cleared away, and there was some large brick building being put up in its place. I hailed one of the workmen and asked what it was for, and he said he'd been told it was for a "refinery." Of what sort, he couldn't tell me.

I finally made my way over to the rooming house. When I was walking up to it, it seemed so much smaller than I remembered, next to all the construction I saw everywhere. It was a strange feeling — when I was a child, and my mother used to take me up to the roof to look out at the harbor, it seemed like the rooming house was one of the tallest buildings in the whole world. But here in the middle of this whirlwind of activity, it seemed almost tiny.

I opened the front door; the entry parlor was empty. I called out, and after some commotion behind the pantry doors, Aunt Twos appeared.

"Lash!" she said, as if my appearance had been a surprise. I'd sent a letter to my mom about my coming visit, but who knows if that made it through.

I merely bowed to Aunt Twos — exactly the way it had been instilled in me during Mrs. Gern's class. It was instinctive: when I looked at her afterward, she seemed surprised.

"I...I almost didn't recognize you for a second there! My, how you've... changed!" she said. "Let me go get your mother..."

She began to make her way to the stairs, but I could already hear footsteps tapping hurriedly above my head, and just as Aunt Twos reached the bottom of the stairs, my mother rounded the first landing and appeared. I forgot to bow to her because the look on her face caught me off guard. She looked shocked — like she'd seen a ghost.

"Lash?" she said, her voice trembling.

"Mom!" I held out my arms wide to give her a hug. She made her way down the stairs slowly at first, the look of shock still frozen on her face. About half-way down, though, her face softened and she hurried down the last few steps and threw her arms around me and began crying.

When she finally composed herself, she kept looking at me, as if she still couldn't quite believe what she was seeing.

"Oh, Lash, my boy, you look...you like your ..."

She stopped, and simply stared at me, then hugged me again.

Aunt Twos said I was welcome to stay for the evening meal, but it wouldn't be for another two hours. I told her that was fine — me and mom had a lot to catch up on. We sat in the parlor and I told her all about the training, and about the guys I'd met, and about where I'd be heading next. She filled me in on all the changes that had been going on while I'd been gone.

The death of the King had apparently shaken the people quite deeply — the grand hall of the palace was still draped in black, and even all these months later there were still people leaving flowers and candles and letters on the steps outside.

The whole kingdom had quickly been seized with a desire to avenge the King's honor, and as I'd seen already, the city had been transformed into a great work-shop of war. Everyone was hiring, and people were streaming in from across the realm to work in the factories — the blacksmith across the street, Mr. Dour, who'd had a single apprentice when I'd left, now had a staff of 20; he'd bought the old bakery and torn it down and was building a new workshop there. The owners of the bakery had bought the old warehouse down the street and torn it down, and were now building a huge new bakery to supply the army.

They'd nearly tripled their weekly output at the factory where my mother worked and hired at least 100 more women — many of them lived at the rooming house. The woman who had my old bed in mom's room worked the day shift there — I'd meet her if I stayed for the evening meal. Which brought up another question: Where, my mom asked, would I be staying?

Before I could answer, I had a sudden flash of realization.

"I...mom, where are all the..." — I tried to think of how to phrase it — "...all the, um, guys from around the neighborhood?"

She gave me a forced smile.

"Well, a lot of young men volunteered for the military, or started working jobs. A lot of the new work pays very well," she said.

I couldn't see any of the guys from my old gang volunteering for any kind of hitch in the military, and I couldn't see any of them working a regular job, either.

"What about the ones who...don't do any of that?"

The smile grew tighter. "Well, I suppose many of them are around. You probably didn't see them because they try to stay off the streets as much as possible these days. The press gangs come through pretty regularly, and any men of the right age who are found out on the street are bound to get swept up."

Press gangs? They had those sometimes when I was a little kid — groups of "royal deputies" who would sweep through the Warrens and grab a few strong-looking young men to "volunteer" for the Royal Navy or Army. But I hadn't heard of one coming through in years.

"Why do they need press gangs? I thought you said they had lots of volunteers."

"Oh, for fighting outfits, they have all they need and more. They have to turn people away! That's why you have all those crazy-quilt groups out on the streets marching. But there's still a lot of work to be done, work that a lot of people don't want to do — they need miners, they need loggers..."

"Labor companies," I mumbled.

"What?"

"Oh, nothing. That's what I've been doing since graduation. They called us labor companies."

"Well, I guess that's what it is, then."

"Not many volunteers for that," I said.

"Well, it would not appear so. All I know is that when the press gangs come through, any man they find without a valid worker's ID gets put on the cart and hauled away."

I thought about that.

"Any man?" I asked. I wasn't worried about myself — it was pretty obvious from my uniform that I was already spoken for — but there were others I wondered about.

She nodded. "Any man. Even the drunks. I've even seen them take old men."

So that's what was different, I realized — I'd noticed a change around the Warrens that I couldn't really describe, but I knew then what it was — all the layabouts and drunks had been swept away; now, all the men I saw looked like they had a sense of purpose.

I was musing about that when my mom asked again where I'd be staying. I snapped back to proper military bearing. "No worries," I told her. "I've got arrangements for tonight. The Crown has taken care of that."

We talked a little bit longer, but I eventually made my apologies and had to leave. I wasn't particularly happy to do so. I'd already noticed the looks I'd gotten from some younger women while I was wearing my Raider dress uniform, and I knew I'd probably get a lot more of those looks if I stayed for supper. I'd be lying if I said I didn't find it kind of exciting.

But aside from the fact that I wasn't sure how to handle that kind of attention in front of my mom, I had a deadline: The Crown had a special barracks set aside for military men "in transit," traveling between assignments, but you had to show up at a certain address at a certain time, and you couldn't be late. I'd decided that rather than pay for lodging — seeing all the crowds of new people, I wasn't quite sure what would be available, or how much it might cost — it would probably be best to take the Crown up on its offer.

The address turned out to be a tidy little square in the Bronze Terraces, one I used to go through every day on my way to the Temple School. When I got there, I counted five other Raiders, and about a dozen men from other branches. I stood off by myself; all of the other men looked a lot older and more experienced.

The man who drove up in the cart right at 6:30 looked quite young, though — my age, maybe even younger. When the other men piled into the back, I volunteered to sit in front with him. We spent the journey talking about all the changes in the city.

He told me he'd been a drover's assistant when the Black Day had arrived — that was what they called the day when the King's death had been announced. After hearing the news, he'd immediately quit his job and volunteered for the army. After standing in line for 10 hours, he'd finally spoken to an army officer who spent about 10 seconds listening to his background before immediately assigning him to a transport battalion.

"I'm actually lucky," he explained, puffing out his chest, "because I'm still an official member of the Royal Army. A lot of the guys who waited to sign up ended up in the auxiliaries." At that, he nodded at a handful of "auxiliaries" in brightly-colored uniforms who were stumbling around drunk along the sidewalk.

I looked at the drunks, then looked back at him.

"Did they give you any training, though?" I asked. "I mean, it's about a lot more than a uniform, you know."

"Oh, Gruun's asshole, you'd better believe it! They trained us good and hard! Worst two weeks of my life! Why do you think I don't look like those degenerates?" He sounded like he wanted to spit while he looked back at them.

I said nothing, and just smiled.

When we finally got to our "barracks," though, I suddenly started laughing out loud.

"What's so funny?" the drover asked.

"Oh, nothing. It's just that it looks…familiar."

Our barracks, it turned out, were the old City Gaol, where I'd been held before being shipped off to the Raiders.

I could see that the drover was giving me a skeptical eye.

"It's a long story," I said. "But trust me, if I told you the whole thing, you'd think it was funny, too."

I REMEMBERED THE EXACT number of my old cell, and asked the desk clerk if it would be possible to bunk there. He raised an eyebrow that looked like it hadn't moved in years.

"Why," he asked, "do you want to bunk there?"

I lied and said that it was my family's lucky number. He rolled his eyes and then looked down at the ledger in front of him.

"I was going to give you a room by yourself," he said, looking me up and down, "but if you want that one, there's one bunk left. I'll warn you, there are three other men bunked there."

I told him that was okay, and made my way up the stairs to my old cell. It was a bit strange seeing the place with no guards — and no locked doors. When I swung open the door to my old cave, I half-expected to see Jop sit up from his bunk and greet me.

But nobody sat up. The only greeting I got was the snores of my three fellow bunkmates; I could tell instantly from the way they had their stuff arranged that none of them were in the Raiders.

I sighed. I removed my uniform and neatly folded it, stowed it in my pack, and climbed into bed and went to sleep.

65

I awoke early the next morning and instinctively began making up my bed; I was almost halfway done before I remembered I was no longer in the Blue Wood. I looked around the cell and saw that all three of my fellow bunkmates were still fast asleep.

I wondered what I was doing for a moment, but when I looked down at my bunk, I saw it was halfway done — I figured I might as well finish the job. After that I went looking for a shower or bath. There were no guards along the halls, like there'd been when I was locked up; I finally found my way down to the desk clerk and asked him where the washroom was.

He looked at me with sad, sleepy eyes. "You must be a Raider," he said.

"Why do you say that?"

He gave me a lazy roll of the eyes.

"Only RAIDERS," he said with a whine, "ever ask where the washroom is."

And with that he directed me down to the stairs to the basement. As I made my way down to the washroom, it occurred to me that the desk clerk had smelled pretty rank. In fact, nearly every person I'd met since coming back into Solta — every man, at least — had smelled pretty awful. Had they always smelled that bad, I wondered?

My morning routine finished, I carefully checked my new dress uniform — I still half-expected a DC to jump out from behind a pillar somewhere and start screaming at me about how my buttons were crooked — and once I was satisfied I didn't look like a complete disgrace, I was out to look around the city.

First thing, I thought I'd go find the old gang. It was Sixeve, so I thought I'd look them up at Rainbow's Court — or wherever else St. Pola's was playing that day. But when I got to the arena, I discovered all skram games had been canceled — the entire season's worth!

"The war," was the only explanation I got.

If there were no skram games, then Gruun only knew where the guys were at that hour of the morning. Still, I found myself being drawn back to the Warrens. I decided to go look up my old pal the Post Master. I figured at the very least, he'd have some good gossip.

When I walked up the desk in his office, he was feeding a large courier gull — a retired bird he kept as a pet. He gave me one glance and straightened up.

"Good day, sir," he said with an air of deep respect. "How can I be of service to you today?"

It was obvious he didn't recognize me.

"Calm down, boss, it's me, your old errand boy."

"Lash?"

His eyes went wide, and he looked me up and down. "By His Foot, what's happened to you? Come over, here, boy, and have a drink! I've just whipped up a pot of tea!"

He spent the rest of the morning giving me a sense of what had been going on in the wider world since I'd been gone. I'd never been much for politics, but apparently there was a lot of intrigue with the Regency Council. There was a faction in the palace that was skeptical about the war, and some even suggested approaching the Arcanter about a treaty and calling off the invasion.

What business of it was ours, they said, if the cat worshippers were under siege? That was the price they paid for turning their backs on the true faith. Didn't the Arcanter's success demonstrate that he had the support of the people? Who knew — maybe the Arcanter would be friendlier to our religion than the Suzer and his lackeys.

And had anybody spoken to the Arcanter? How did we even know he was an enemy? Did we accept that just on the say-so of the faithless cat worshippers?

This was all very different from the picture they'd painted for us back at the Blue Wood, where it was just accepted without question that the Arcanter was purest evil and it was the duty of the faithful to march against him and destroy him. I asked the Post Master what he thought of all that talk.

He shook his head gravely. "My father was killed in the Great War," he said. "I still remember every Sevenday when they published the lists of war dead, and all the wailing and tears. Mothers would see all of their children wiped out in a single day. It's not something I'm eager to live through again."

"So you agree with these guys — what did you say they call themselves?"

"The 'owls.' That's what everybody's been calling them."

"The owls, then. You agree with them?"

He leaned back and petted the blue feathers of his pet gull, which looked at him and squawked with what I thought was affection. He smiled at the bird, then took a sip of tea. "I'm not saying I can't see their point of view — because I can. Like I said, I remember the Great War, even if I was just a little boy at the time. It's strange to look out and think that so many of the people I see out there on the streets have no memory of it. So many of them don't know..."

He was quiet for several seconds, and I thought for a moment that he was finished, but then he continued: "But I fear we may be at a crossroads here. I feel this may be one of those moments where our descendants will look back on and judge us on what we chose at this desperate hour."

"So you support the war. You agree with the invasion?"

"I believe the Arcanter must be destroyed. If it takes a great invasion to do that, then yes, I support it."

I turned that over in my mind. "You're holding something back. You have some doubts," I observed.

"Not doubts — not like what you're thinking. See — well, let me put it this way: On Sixeve, I like to have a drink at this place over on the far side of the harbor — The Maiden's Comb. You know of it?"

I reached back in my mind. "I think so. In the Palace District, right?"

"No, but just on the edge. It was one of my regular haunts back when I worked in the Palace Complex, and I still have friends who work there; that's where we meet up. But it's also in the heart of the Crab Quarter, where many of the refugees from Garlund live."

"I see. And?"

"Well, many of them are regulars there, too. I've spoken with quite a few of them over the past few years. I've heard the stories they tell about the Arcanter."

I'd heard a lot of stories about the Arcanter, too. "I've heard he roasts infants alive and eats them for his supper," I said — one of the grislier details I'd heard repeated in whispers as if they were Auld Father's own words.

The Post Master rolled his eyes and shook his head.

"The newspapers are full of stories like that these days. I heard the same stories about the dwarves back during the Great War."

"But you don't believe them?"

He shook his head again. "No. But speaking to the exiles — they leave little doubt that the Arcanter is a great threat. But it is the kind of threat he represents that worries me."

"You mean...his use of necromancy?"

He wrinkled his brow. "Well, that's certainly worrisome. But that's not what I'm thinking of."

"So what, then?"

He took another sip and leaned back. His eyes grew distant.

"It would take a man with a much finer tongue than mine to put it into words," he finally said. "It's a kind of — Auld Father made man, he made him a certain way, you know? And Gruun, he's always trying to draw us away from that."

"I know. I went to Temple School. They made us read..."

"Yes, I know all about what it says in The Walk. But this is something else. Gru-un is forever trying to lead us away. The Walk says he does that because he is at war with Auld Father, which I don't doubt. But what if — what if there's more to it than that?"

"I don't follow."

He sat thoughtfully for a moment, then said: "I mean, what if — what if Gru-un isn't just trying to lead us away to spite Auld Father? What if Gruun wants to make an entirely new type of man?"

That sounded familiar. "Like — you mean like how people say the goblins were once men? Or was it men used to be goblins..."

"Something like that. I was thinking more of the dwarves and the elves. You know, elves say the dwarves were once their elven brothers, eons ago. But they broke away and followed a different path..."

"Don't ever let a dwarf hear you say that," I said.

"Oh, believe me, I know! I used to work with them over in the Palace Complex. Fussiest bastards you ever saw..."

And with that, he was off on another of his stories. The whole business about the Arcanter was forgotten as quickly as it had come along.

When I finally left him around lunchtime, I still wasn't quite ready to go hunting for the old gang. I figured I had a few hours to kill before they'd be in regular form, so I decided to make one more stop. I turned and aimed my feet toward the tall spires which stood atop the highest point of the city — might as well pay a visit to the place that, more than anything else, had paved my way out of the Warrens and into the Blue Wood.

I followed the old route I used to take to the Temple School, looking for the book cart I used to steal two-coppers from, thinking I might purchase something from the owner to kind of quietly make amends. His cart was no longer there — not that there would have been room for it with all the crowds moving busily through the streets. I was about to keep going on my way until I turned around and noticed that the building across the street looked different. It had never stood out before, but it looked like it had been freshly cleaned and painted — well, partially painted. There was a section where the new coat of paint abruptly ended, making it clear it was a work in progress.

Inside the newly-cleaned windows, I could see bookshelves — and there above the door there was a crudely drawn sign that said "Bookshop." There was a newly-installed wrought-iron hanger extending out from the side of the building that was clearly intended to hold a much larger sign, but I guessed that, like the unfinished paint job, it too was a work in progress.

The sense of an interrupted project continued inside, where there were rows and rows of newly-built shelves, though only about half of them were full. The empty rows of shelves were crammed with books piled haphazardly on the floor, or big wooden crates of books that were in various states of being unloaded. There was a harried-looking young boy clambering around the maze unloading boxes and placing books on shelves, stopping every few seconds to consult a piece of paper.

I was trying to decide whether or not to interrupt the youngster when he finally noticed me standing in the doorway.

"Oh, I'm just the stock clerk," he said in a high, scratchy voice that made him sound almost like a girl. "Mr. Yoll is in the back!"

He pointed off to the far left side of the store. "The aisle marked 'Royal History.' Go all the way to the back; he's at his desk."

I'd never known the name of the man who operated the cart, but when I followed the boy's directions and made my way back, the "Mr. Yoll" turned out to be the very same one I'd known from my thieving days. Apparently the war money was lifting up even people who had nothing to do with war.

"Mr. Yoll" had, of course, managed to catch me thieving a few times back then, and had taken to chasing me away from his cart whenever he'd noticed me creeping up on his cart — not that I ever let that stop me; I had Warrens blood too deep in my veins. When I presented myself at his desk, I was worried he was going to chase me away just like the old times.

He was making notations in a big ledger of some kind when I approached. Without looking up, he raised one finger, signaling me to wait. I instinctively fell into parade rest.

He made a few more jots in the ledger, then smiled broadly. I noticed his clothes, while not exactly fashionable, no longer looked tattered and worn. He looked up at me, still smiling.

That had been the moment I'd been half-dreading, but whether it was because I was older, or because of the uniform — probably both — his face betrayed no sign of recognition.

"Can I help you, sir?" he said brightly.

I decided to test my luck. "Aren't you the fellow who used to have the book cart just across the street?"

His eyes narrowed slightly, as if he was sizing me up, trying to remember me. But it was just for a brief moment; a heartbeat later, his eyes popped back open and it was obvious that any recognition he might have had was long gone.

"Yes, yes, I had a cart for many years. But..." — he paused, obviously trying to decide how much of his business he wanted to reveal — "...well, with all the people who've come into the city recently, I've been quite fortunate, Auld Father be praised!"

He made the sign of the arrow.

I gave him an empty smile. "Well it's good to see you're doing so well. I'm looking for, um...pardon me, this isn't my usual interest...are you familiar with books about a character named 'Vast the Brutal?'"

Mr. Yoll clapped his hands together. "Ah, now THAT brings back some memories! Back when I had a simple cart, those were among the strongest sellers!"

He gave me a huge, genuine-looking smile. "If you'll go back towards the door of the shop, look for the row of shelves marked 'Adventure,'" he said. "I think they're organized by series. If I'm not mistaken, 'Vast the Brutal' books should be close to the back of the aisle — right before it switches over to 'romance' stories."

I gave him a polite nod and then followed his directions. I wasn't expecting to find anything, since I believed I'd read every single Vast the Brutal tale ever written. But to my surprise, I found a couple of Vast books I'd never heard of before — and they both looked pretty old. I excitedly snapped up both volumes and headed back to the owner's desk. I wasn't interested in haggling — I was ready to pay the asking price and be on my way. But I came up short when I rounded the corner of the aisle that led back to where he sat.

There was somebody there, talking to him. The conversation was quite animated. It was hard to make things out from the front of the shop, but as I quietly moved closer, I could see the new person by the light of his desk lamp: It was a girl. As I got closer, I saw there was a large sack on the floor next to her; it was clear from the outlines of the contents that it was full of books.

I edged closer, turning my head to the side so I could hear the conversation.

I heard the girl say: "...a perfectly good collection. You won't find a finer series of volumes in all of Solta!"

The shopkeeper replied: "Perhaps so, but I've already got three other sets, and I've only got limited shelf space here. We've got books coming in every day! I'll tell you what, I'll make a deal with you. Three gold pieces for the entire set. That's a huge sacrifice for me, but maybe it will help you out."

The girl let out a sigh of disgust, and with much effort, picked up the bag and started down the aisle toward me. As she moved closer, I stepped out of the way to give her room, and she looked up at me — and I recognized her.

"Kanin," I blurted out involuntarily.

Her eyes widened a bit. "You...you're...you're..." She trailed off.

"I used to deliver packages..." I stammered.

Her eyes grew wider still.

"Lash?" she said, smiling. "Lash Pearl?"

It caught me by surprise when she said that. I couldn't remember the last time anybody had remembered my full name.

Looking back, I probably should have corrected her: "Private Pearl, of the Raiders." But I was too intoxicated in the feeling of the moment.

"The very same," I said. "Surprised you remember me." My gaze flicked back to Mr. Yoll, to see if his memory might have been jogged, but after a brief smile, he went back to his ledger.

I looked down at the sack she was struggling to carry. "What seems to be the problem?" I asked.

She looked down at the sack.

"Oh...it's nothing."

"Nothing?" I said with a grin.

She smiled back, and seemed to soften a bit. "Oh, you know...I mean I'm certain you know, with the war and all...it's just that father's business has been soft lately..."

I looked around. "Seems like business has been booming everywhere," I said.

She blushed. "Oh, well, yes, the war has been good for...business. But..."

She trailed off and blushed again.

"Hasn't your father secured any contracts?" I asked knowingly. It was complete bullshit. I still had no idea what her father did for a living.

I could immediately tell I'd said the wrong thing, though. She gave me a nervous smile, then started to make an excuse to leave.

"Hold on," I said, looking down at the sack she held. "That looks awful heavy. At least let me take it...and escort you home."

She gave me a confused smile, and then nodded. I put down the books I'd planned to buy — "I'll be back for these later!" I shouted to Mr. Yoll, who responded with a wave without looking up — and took the sack from her hands and headed for the door.

Kanin's house was a good 30 blocks away. As we made our way through the streets, I got the basics of the story in dribs and drabs.

Her father's business, she said, was in antiquities. That was what was in all the packages I was always bringing to her house — historical items secured from all across Selva, and beyond. He'd done a brisk business...at least back then.

Ever since the news of the King's death and the upsurge in war preparations, the demand for "luxuries" such as the items her father sold had dropped off dramatically. There had even been stories in the papers, she explained, of wealthy families donating valuable antiques to be melted down to supply metal for the war effort.

"I don't know if they're true," she said. "I have my doubts, personally. But all the same, nobody wants to be very conspicuous with these things. So father's business is...not what it was. We had to let most of our servants go last month — not that they were interested in staying; they immediately got higher-paying jobs elsewhere because of the war.

"I keep telling my father that with only a few servants around, we really ought to sell our house and find something more sensible, but of course he won't hear of it. He's too attached to the old place."

"It is a very nice place."

"It's just a house," she scoffed. "Just a pile of bricks and stone. A house is any place with a roof. What makes a home is the people inside it. Wasn't that true with your house growing up?"

I told her it was, deliberately gliding over the fact that my "house" had been rooming house with a family of some 70-odd women. I didn't want to scare her off by letting her know just how far down in the gutter I came from.

And anyway, I hadn't lied to her — I could see from the looks she kept sneaking at my uniform that my clothes had made my introduction for me, and seeing as I'd earned the right to wear that uniform, I saw no reason to correct any misconceptions. If she asked me about my background, I'd be straight with her — but there was nothing wrong with enjoying the moment while it lasted, was there?

"Why the Raiders, then?" she suddenly asked.

"I beg your pardon?"

"Why the Raiders? Most men who want to fight just join the army, or become sailors — if they're accepted, at least. The ones who aren't join the auxiliaries..." She said "auxiliaries" with a dismissive scoff. "So why the Raiders? I hear they're quite strict."

"Extremely strict," I said, "and we like it that way."

That seemed to catch her a little off guard. "I see. But if you just want to serve the Crown, why go through all the trouble?"

It took me a second to realize that she had no idea what it took to join the Raiders. "Well...there wasn't a war going on when I joined up. I mean, not like there is now."

"How do you mean?"

"The King was still alive when I...reported for training. Nobody had any reason to suspect...I mean nobody thought..."

"So you didn't just get swept up and join in the heat of the moment, then?"

I hesitated. "No," I said. "Actually, I just got back from training yesterday. I'm only here at home for a few days, then I head off to Agellos to join preparations for the invasion."

"Oh," she said.

Oh.

Oh? What in the name of His Foot does "oh" mean?

Now I was lost. I decided to change the subject.

"So, you wanted to sell your books, then?"

"Not MY books, really. My late mother's books. It's the collected works of Fenson. He's a Footman-philosopher my mother liked."

I recognized the name "Fenson." I reached back in my memory for something...

"Fenson," I said. "'The Arguments?'"

She looked a little flustered at that. "Well yes, that's one volume. But these are his complete works."

She tapped the heavy sack I held in my hand.

"You've...read Fenson?" she asked warily. I could tell she didn't quite believe me.

"Oh, not...not actually. We just...discussed him at the Wood."

"'The Wood?'"

"I'm sorry, Fort Harrel. They call it 'The Blue Wood.'" I paused. "That's where I was in training."

"Raiders talk about philosophy?"

"Not...well...nobody ever used the word 'philosophy,'" I said, trying to explain it without digging myself in deeper. "But we did talk about...what it meant, you know, to be a Raider. What it meant to serve the Crown. And Fenson's name came up. You know, about how we...we need...we need to be cultivated? Like Kassflowers." I hoped that sounded convincing enough, because I'd pretty much reached the end of everything I knew about this Fenson guy.

She seemed to think about that for a moment. "That makes sense, now that I think of it. Anyway, most people have only heard of 'The Arguments.' But he wrote much more than that. Many of his more obscure works are difficult to find. I had thought they might fetch a nice price at the bookseller, but it appears not." She looked at me coyly. "So what does a Raider read, then? If not Fenson's 'Arguments?'"

I thought about making something up — the old Lash probably would have tried to spin her a line of bullshit. But my Raider training kicked in: Honesty was always the safest, if scariest, course of action.

"Well, probably nothing a girl like you would read. I've always liked adventure tales — my favorite was Vast the Brutal..."

"'A girl like me?'" she said with a scowl. "Do you still see me as the silly girl who doesn't understand skram?"

I just blinked. "I didn't..."

She pressed on, ignoring me. "Do you think I read only proper romances about virtuous, chaste young ladies being rescued by handsome princes?"

"Well...I don't know," I said. I didn't add that most girls where I came from never read anything.

She rolled her eyes. "Ugh. That's what my *father* thinks I should read."

I felt a little stung. "Well, what *do* you read?"

"Nothing like that 'Vast the Brutal.' Honestly, you men are so predictable. Big men with muscles, carrying on with women with bosoms out to here." She thrust out her arms like she was holding a giant pair of tits.

What could I say? I shrugged.

To my surprise, she laughed at my reaction.

"Oh, don't get me wrong, I understand it," she said. "Who wants to read something dull? But I prefer something more...intellectually stimulating. Have you ever heard of Clanton Clave?"

I said I hadn't.

"He writes books about a circle of sorcerers — well, first of all, the stories take place on a different planet..."

"Like one of the moons?"

"'One of the moons?' Well...I guess you could say that. I mean everybody knows that the moons are all just barren rock..."

"They are?"

She gave me a look, then something seemed to dawn on her.

"Oh, I guess they wouldn't teach that in the Raiders, would they? I'm sorry, it's just..."

She started to blush. That blush. As much as I liked how she looked when she did that, I tried to smooth things over. "I think I know what you mean by a different planet. Like we're all living on a big ball that goes around the sun..."

"Right! Our planet is called 'Cianu.'"

"Huh?"

"'CIANU,' she said slowly, seeming quite impressed with herself. "At least that's what the scholars call it. It's an ancient word in the Auld Tongue — I think it's usually translated as 'warm home,' but I'm not sure that captures the full meaning..."

"Cianu..." I said. I'd never known our ball actually had a name. "Right. But, as I was saying — there are others that go around the sun, but you can't see them, except as stars..."

"Oh but you can see them!" she interrupted. "With a telescope!"

"You've gotta be shi...you're pulling my leg. You can barely see Mule Island from here with a spyglass, and it's right offshore from us."

"No, not a *spyglass*, silly! A *telescope*! Like the one my father has! It's much larger than a spyglass. And anyway, the reason it's hard to see Mule Island is because it's over the curve of the horizon." Then she launched into an explanation of the moons and the stars that I couldn't really follow, but I just nodded and pretended she was making sense, because honestly, it was just nice to look at her face when she was excited. She had more freckles than you'd expect from someone her age, and her top lip was a little too large to match the bottom, but the way it curled up when she laughed couldn't help but make me grin right back.

She was pretty, okay? I don't have a poet's talent for these things, but I'll try to make you see her: She had reddish-blonde hair, and was a bit taller than I would have gone for if I'd been prowling for girls in a tavern. Also skinnier, but don't call up some image of one of those bony, graceful ladies floating around the Palace District. There was a big swingy clop to the way she moved, like she was stepping over puddles that weren't there. The DCs back at training would have melted from fury at her "improper gait" and would have spent a week screaming it out of her — and for that I thank Auld Father that there are no female Raiders, because the way she looked when she did it could not have made me feel any giddier.

As we'd been walking, I'd noticed that as the houses became nicer, there had

been a change in the way people looked at us. Everywhere else I'd been so far, people saw my uniform and seemed to give a subtle nod of respect. But now people
were giving me the same kind of suspicious looks I'd gotten when I wandered out
of the Warrens as a young kid.

Then I realized: It was my appearance. They didn't see many scalebacks around
these parts of the city, and when they did, they weren't getting friendly with a
proper-looking maiden. I saw a severe-looking woman about my mother's age
giving me a foul look as I walked by. I responded by standing a little straighter
and puffing out my chest a little more — because fuck you, that's why. Anyway, it
didn't seem to matter to Kanin. At least I didn't think it did.

"Here's my house up here," she finally said. "I don't think father's home yet. I
think I can talk Mr. Jess — he's the chief steward — into letting us into the obser-
vatory so I can show you father's telescope."

"Oh, you probably shouldn't do that. If your father has forbidden it..."

"Oh, it's just a silly rule. Rules are made to be broken, right?"

"Actually," I said. "I don't think that they are."

She gave me a strange sort of smile at that.

We didn't go in the front; instead, she led me around to the servant's entrance
I remembered so well, and into the kitchen where we'd had tea so many times.
To my surprise, the kitchen wasn't empty. Instead, there was a plump middle-age
woman scurrying about, checking different dishes in various states of preparation.

"Mrs. Lodi!" Kanin said brightly. "Is father home?"

"Oh, yes m'lady," she said with a quick bow. "Got home just a few minutes ago."

Kanin gave an obviously forced smile.

"Oh, delightful! I thought for sure he'd be late because of his meeting with Mr.
Peris. Is father feeling well?"

The cook gave us a look that wasn't a smile, but didn't quite fall over into a
frown. Kanin just nodded.

"Oh, Mrs. Lodi, I almost forgot! This is my friend Mr. Pearl!"

I took Mrs. Lodi's hand and gave her a bow, feeling like Mrs. Gern's eyes were
burning a hole in me from across the miles. Mrs. Lodi gave me a smile and a slight
curtsy.

"A Raider! My son hopes to join your ranks some day, Mr. Pearl," she said.

Putting on my best Palace District voice, I said, "Well I haven't been one for very
long, but if I ever have the good fortune to meet your son, I'll be happy to tell him
everything I know."

She blushed, and gave Kanin a look and a wink.

Kanin led me through the door into the main part of her house. I felt a tingle
of something like fear, because it was the first time I'd had a chance to see any of
her house past the kitchen. We went down a long hallway, then up a tight staircase.
At the top, we emerged into a large room that I took to be the main entrance hall.

The door we came out of was set beneath a wide, carved wooden staircase beneath an elegant chandelier the size of an ox-trolley wheel. Kanin quickly ushered me towards another large room that opened up on one side of the entrance parlor.

Before we went in, she paused for a moment, looked at me, and then looked at the sack of books I was carrying. Moving quietly, she took it from out of my hands and stashed it beneath a thickly-padded bench beside the small door we'd just come through. She held a finger up to her lips, then wheeled around and strode purposefully into the room.

"Father!" she chirped brightly. "What a pleasant surprise to see you home early!"

The room she led me into was elegantly furnished, yet cozy. I don't know much about fancy houses, but I think it's what they call a "study." Except it was hard to see how one could ever get much real studying done there, seeing as it was obviously set up for comfort. There was a large desk at one end, flanked by some locked cabinets — the locks looked pretty flimsy to my Warrens-trained eyes, but I suppose they were there more for the peace of mind of the owner. The desk was polished and empty except for a few unopened letters and a copy of a newspaper — the Capital Ledger, I noted. Aside from the few things atop it, the desk looked like it had hardly been touched.

The walls of the room were rich, dark wood, and were lined on two sides with bookcases. One of the bookcases had a set of carved doors built into it; the doors were open, revealing several bottles of spirits and some drinkware.

At one end of the room, a large window looked out on the street; a table and chairs were set in front of it. The rest of the furniture in the room consisted of sumptuous-looking overstuffed chairs and couches, with a handful of small tables which looked like they were meant to hold drinks or cigars — I noticed several ashtrays, all empty.

All the way at the other end of the room was a large fireplace, and hanging above it was a large oil painting of a young man who looked to be about my age, clad in a Raider uniform not much different from the one I was wearing; from the markings, he was a lieutenant.

I was so transfixed by the painting that I almost didn't notice the wiry man sitting in an overstuffed chair near the fireplace. His clear, ringing voice quickly caught my attention.

"Kanin, my dear! Come let me see you!"

He set down a drink he'd been holding on a side table and sprang up to cross the room and meet his daughter. He was slightly shorter than Kanin, but with her same too-long limbs; he had a clean-shaven face and an elegantly styled shock of graying hair. His clothes, while not the finest I've ever seen, were obviously costly, if a bit old. They'd been impeccably maintained, though.

After greeting his daughter, he turned to look at me. Although his wrinkled face was probably at least a decade older than my mother's, he still had the sparkling eyes and open smile of a young man.

"Who is this fine fellow you've brought home?" he asked. He looked at my collar. "Private, correct? Not Private First Class?"

"No, sir. Not yet."

"Ah, yes," he said, leaning in slightly to study my collar. "I can see the triangle is silver, not gold. It's hard to tell in this light. Mr. Jess should be around any second now to set the lights for the evening — I'm sorry, Private, I didn't catch your name?"

"This is Lash Pearl, father," Kanin interjected. "He used to make deliveries for the Crown Post."

"Rush deliveries only, actually," I said, bowing slightly. "I wasn't an official deliveryman. I was an...adjunct."

I hoped I used that word correctly.

"Well, Private Pearl, I'm Hewlan Mils. A pleasure to make your acquaintance!" He shook my hand vigorously. I got the sense that his manner wasn't entirely genuine. I'd noticed the glass he'd put on the table was quite full of whiskey; it didn't feel like he was celebrating.

"I noticed you looking at the portrait there," he said, nodding to indicate the oil painting. The man in the picture bore a clear resemblance to Mr. Mils — he had the same sparkling eyes, the same build, and his reddish-blond hair — the same shade as Kanin's — was done in a similar style.

"Yes, sir. I was wondering about it," I said. "Is that you?"

Mr. Mils' smile crinkled a little at the corners, and he shook his head.

"No, no, not me, I'm afraid. I was never cut out for life in the military." He turned and admired the portrait for a moment. "No, that's my younger brother..."

His voice seemed to trail off as he stared at the portrait. I was about to ask if his brother was still in the Raiders, and what rank he held today, when he turned abruptly to face me and said brightly, "To what do we owe the pleasure, Private Pearl?"

I opened my mouth to answer, but Kanin quickly cut in, "I was at the Palace District exchange, looking at the new dresses — I simply must have a new dress for the Harvest Ball, father! — and I ran into Private Pearl. He's on a brief assignment here before he heads off to Agellos." She didn't explain why I was going to Agellos; I had picked up that most people in the city understood "going to Agellos" meant you were going to be part of the great invasion.

"He was kind enough to escort me back, since it was getting late and some of the auxiliaries...well, you know how they get around this hour..."

She gave me a look which seemed to acknowledge she wasn't being entirely truthful, then turned back to her father. He was beaming. He stepped up and put his hands on my shoulders, looked me up and down, then took my hands in his.

"Thank you, Private, for doing that." He looked warmly at his daughter, then back at me. "I assure you, any man wearing the uniform of the Raiders is welcome in this house."

He looked at me almost tenderly, then looked at Kanin, then back at me.

"Oh, father?" Kanin said, once again seeming to interrupt some unspoken train of thought he was having. "I was wondering if it would be too much trouble if I could show Private Pearl your telescope?"

Mr. Mils looked at her blankly, still smiling. She continued: "Private Pearl was telling me about the spyglasses they use in the Raiders, and I told him about your telescope. I thought it might be interesting for him to see it, just to compare the two."

I went along with it. "Yes, I understand it works on the same principle," I bull-shitted. "I'm curious to see the difference."

Mr. Mils' smile crinkled again. "Of course," he said. "Will Private Pearl...be staying for dinner?"

I looked quickly at Kanin, and before I could even form a thought, she answered, "No, Private Pearl has another engagement, unfortunately, but...it's possible he may be able to dine with us later this week." She flicked her eyes to me, then back to Mr. Mils. "Assuming that you approve, father?"

Mr. Mils looked back at me and gave me a soft punch in the shoulder. "Not a problem with me. We shall miss your company this evening, Private!"

As Kanin led me up the stairs, I tried to come up with a question to express my utter confusion.

"I don't have a prior engagement," I said. "Did I say something..."

"Oh, no, I'm sorry, you didn't do anything wrong. I just saw how hard Mrs. Lodi was working and I didn't want to burden her with an extra guest."

"I see..."

Seeming to sense the bewilderment in my voice, Kanin explained, "She's not usually that overwhelmed. She's taking extra care with the meal tonight because of the day father has had."

"I see," I said again, not seeing.

Kanin sighed. "My father was hoping to close a sale with Mr. Peris for a collection of the early Fesian era...for some antiques. It didn't go well..."

I didn't answer, because I didn't know what to say. Kanin suddenly stopped. We were on a landing between the second and third floors. She looked at me, and in the dying light of the afternoon, I could see that her eyes were moist. She wasn't crying yet — she looked at me with great strength. But I could see she was on the verge.

Feeling like I should do something, I stepped forward and embraced her. It was something I'd dreamed of doing countless times before, but the circumstances drained much of the excitement from the moment.

She responded stiffly at first, but after a moment her body seemed to relax in my arms, and I felt her embrace me.

She sighed deeply, then stepped back, gave me a smile, and said, "It's right up here!" Her bright, chirpy tone made it sound like nothing had passed between us. Bewildered, I followed her up the last set of stairs.

At the top, a set of doors opened into a wide room that was a perfect circle. The ceiling was a great dome, and in the center of the room was something that had the shape and proportions of a spyglass, but much larger. It must have been at least 30 feet from one end to the other, and it was mounted on some kind of stand with a mess of gears like the kind you'd see in a tower clock.

I looked around the room.

"How do you use it to see anything, though?" I asked.

"Oh, that's the best part! Father hired an engineer from the Royal Academy to design this!" Kanin said excitedly.

She scurried over to one of the walls where there was a large circular handwheel which she began turning with much difficulty. I went over to try to help her, but she elbowed me away. After the first half-turn, it began to spin quite easily.

From above us, I heard a creaking sound, and a large slit opened up in the dome, exposing the large end of the "telescope" to the sky, which was quickly growing dark. I knew that Siran, the second-largest moon, would be high in the sky and quite bright this evening — but it would be in the eastern sky, and the "telescope" was pointed towards the west.

I told Kanin, "Siran..." but she cut me off with "On it!" and scurried over to another handwheel, which she began spinning with ease.

To my amazement, the telescope and the dome above began turning together. I was stunned that such a small girl could move such a vast apparatus by herself. I looked up in wonder as the whole thing slowly rotated into position. "How does..."

"It's a system of counterweights!" she said excitedly. "Even a child can do it!"

Looking over at her, I saw she was focused on a big round dial set into the wall, the size of a large dinner plate. It looked a bit like a clock, but there was only one hand, and it moved rather slowly. When it finally reached a point she seemed satisfied with, she scurried over to the stand that held the telescope, spinning more handwheels and looking at another pair of dials. Then she rushed over to the small end of the telescope, looked in the eyepiece, and beckoned me over.

"Come quick!" she said.

I came over and followed her instructions, looking into the eyepiece. I found myself looking at something like the barren rocky surface you'd see on the side of a cliff. It was covered with tiny little circular pockmarks. But the image was... moving.

"Hey," I said after a moment. "Hey, I think something slipped, all I can see is black. I think."

"Hold on," she said, elbowing me out of the way. She peered into the eyepiece, then rushed over to the handwheels attached to the telescope stand and made some adjustments. She came back over, peeked in the eyepiece again, and then hastened me to look again.

This time I saw more of the pockmarks, along with something — it looked a little bit like drawings I'd seen on maps.

"Is that a mountain range?" I asked.

"Yes!" she said, clapping her hands in excitement. I pulled away from the eyepiece.

"There are mountains on Siran...?" I asked, but she quickly motioned for me to look back at the eyepiece, so I did so.

"Wow, I think I see...I think I see...are those rocks?"

"Those are boulders from the eruptions!" she squealed. "Siran is volcanically active! It's rare, but every so often you can catch an eruption in progress!"

I looked up again from the eyepiece. She made a scoffing sound, and pushed me out of the way, bending down to look into the eyepiece herself. Auld Father forgive me, but as she bent over, I took the opportunity to admire her figure. She was unlike any girl I'd ever seen in the Warrens. Despite her gawkiness, her lines were clean, strong and smooth.

"It's moved away again," she said, standing up to look at me. I hoped she didn't notice how my eyes flicked upward from her chest to meet her face. "Anyway, you see how marvelous it is! On dark nights you can even see the other planets!"

"I thought the moons were planets."

"No, silly, it's...oh, it's a long story. Probably nothing you Raiders would be interested in." She playfully slapped my shoulder and gave me a wily glance.

There was a moment there when I hesitated, trying to decide what to do, but my thoughts were interrupted by the sudden sound of boots coming up the stairs. I turned to see Mr. Mils coming into the room.

"Ah, so Kanin has been showing you...let's see, it's Siran tonight, isn't it?" he said, looking past us at the telescope and all its equipment.

"Kanin said there are...volcanoes there?" I looked at her, not sure I had understood her correctly.

"Yes!" Mr. Mils said, ignoring the telescope and looking up through the slit in the dome above us. "Yes, quite fascinating to watch! This isn't the time of year for them, though. You should see it in the early spring! If you're lucky, it's quite the show!"

66

After leaving Kanin's home, I made my way back to the Warrens to visit my mom before she left for her night shift at the factory. The next day was Sevenday, and I promised her I'd take her to service.

"Not the local chapel — I'll hire a carriage for us and we'll go to service at the Temple," I said.

After seeing her off for the night, I decided it was finally time to go see if I could find the old gang of louts. It was Sixeve, so I knew if there was any night I'd find them out on the streets, this would be it. Not even press gangs worked on Sixeve.

The first place I went was our old haunt, the Anders Arms, but it had been closed down and converted into a worker's bunkhouse. The One-Legged Rooster down the street was closed, too, but there was a crudely-scrawled sign on the door that said they'd reopened over in the Improvement District.

The old Improvement District was something else. All the public halls were packed — from the accents and even different languages, I gathered that they were mostly new arrivals. When I came to the old flatlands, a big open space that used to be a rubbish tip, everything was taken up by hastily-erected tents and merchant's wagons. It was like a mirror image of the camp I'd seen outside the city gates.

Several of the largest tents were clearly taverns, so I hunted about for a name I recognized. It didn't take long for me find one with a crude sign that read, "The On-Legid Roostur." Ducking in, I immediately recognized the man stationed behind the hastily-constructed "bar" as Cobbee, the proprietor of the old Rooster. The place was busy, but I managed to find an open space at the bar and signaled for a mug of ale.

Cobbee handed me a mug and gave me a nod of recognition, but quickly moved on to other customers — I had planned to ask him if he knew where I could find any of my old gang, but it was obvious I'd have to wait for things to slow down a bit before I got a chance to talk to him.

I sipped my ale and turned to look around at the rest of the new Rooster. There was a bard in one corner strumming some kind of stringed instrument and belting out lewd songs, which some of the drunker patrons were singing along with. There were a couple of dirty billiards tables that looked like they'd been pulled out of the old rubbish tip — actually, a lot of the furniture looked like it had come out of there, and knowing Cobbee, it probably had.

There were some makeshift dartboards hanging on one side of the tent. At one table, a group of men were jabbering at each other in a language I didn't understand while they played some kind of game I'd never seen, with a board decorated with triangles and circles and little figurines carved in the shape of horses.

What caught my eye finally, though, was a table of fellows in bright green and blue military garb — members of one of those "auxiliary" units who were always out in the streets playing pretend-soldier.

There were four of them huddled around a table, and they were all staring at me over large pints of ale. They didn't look happy.

I realized I'd seen some of them earlier that day, out clogging up the streets while "marching." I was trying to remember where I'd seen them when the largest one got up, followed a second later by the other three. They walked over to where I was standing. I looked around to see if anybody could give me a clue what was going on, but nobody else seemed to be paying attention.

The big fellow came and stood right next to me, staring at me and breathing hard. His breath smelled heavily of ale, and I noticed he was a little unsteady, even as he tried to stand still and intimidate me. I continued to lean casually against the bar.

The big guy eyed me for several uncomfortable seconds. I was about to say something when he finally spoke up.

"Raider," he said, looking me up and down.

"Yup. I can see you're a military man yourself," I said, saluting him with my mug before I took another sip.

"Probably think that uniform makes you pretty special," the guy said. I noted his eyes were unfocused, but the way they were darting about, and the way the muscles in his hand were lazily twitching, he might as well have been shouting to the whole bar that he was thinking about hitting me.

Wondering what in Auld Father's name his problem was, I decided he and his pals were sloshed enough that I could afford to toy with them. Besides, it was already obvious from their lack of scars that none of them were Warrens regulars.

"It's not the uniform," I said. "But now that you mention it, yeah, wearing this does make me feel pretty special." I topped that off with a wink.

"I don't care what you're fucking wearing," he said, leaning in closer. "I don't fucking like scalebacks."

Had he been from the Warrens, he'd already have been on the floor with a broken nose for that, but I gave him a little more rope to hang himself with.

"And we especially don't like scalebacks in our part of the city," said one of his buddies.

"And we really, really don't like scalebacks coming near our women," the big one said.

Oh.

Oh.

So that's what this was about. I remembered now where I'd seen them: They'd gone marching by when I was escorting Kanin home. I hadn't paid any attention to them, but I'd gotten enough dirty looks from the other people in the neighborhood to get the idea that I wasn't wanted there. I didn't know why Kanin and her father weren't bothered by it, but her neighbors surely were.

I lifted my mug to take a sip, trying to look as casual as possible, then said with a cheerful grin: "You know what they say. Once a girl's had a *fish-bone*, nothing else is ever good enough."

I don't know if you could fairly call what came next a "punch." He swung his arm hard, and I easily ducked under it. I had enough time after that to carefully set my mug down on the bar before he could try anything else.

He next tried to ram into me with his body, but I easily stepped aside and gave him a quick strike to the knee which caused him to fall forward. There was a "crack" as his jaw slammed into the bar, and he fell to the dirt floor like a limp sack.

I turned to face the other three, who were momentarily stunned at what had just happened to their comrade. The bar suddenly got quiet as everyone turned to look at the sudden commotion.

Two of the drunk crew launched themselves at me, but I used my foot to slide a chair into their path, which they both stumbled over. I kneed the closest one in the face and tossed him into the side of a large keg of ale, which cracked and began leaking. The next one I grabbed in a firm headlock. He was squirming helplessly when I looked up to see where the fourth one had gone.

I quickly found him. He had stepped back from the fight, and had somehow managed to produce a huge knife — whether he'd been carrying it on him or had lifted it off another patron, I couldn't tell.

That was when I got worried. Not for myself — it was obvious from the way the fellow moved that he had no idea how to properly use a knife — but for my uniform. The Raider dress uniform I was wearing was the only one I owned. I had been hopeful I could get through this mess without damaging it, but if some asshole was going to pull a knife on me, I might have to change things up. My uniform might end up getting ripped, or even stained. I was already totaling up the costs in my head — I'd have to pay for the keg of ale I'd just broken, and I might have to buy a new uniform. I'd only been back in Solta one day, and it seemed I was already going to burn through what little cash I'd managed to put away since graduation.

If these sons of a she-troll fuck up my uniform, I told myself, I'm going to make this worth it. I was about to give these guys a Warrens welcome when somebody smashed a bottle of ale over the head of the guy holding the knife, sending him sprawling on the floor. And from out of the crowd, holding the broken bottle, stepped my old gang buddy Taygor.

67

I'd been on the lookout for guys wearing gang slouchers, but Taygor wasn't wearing one. Instead, he was dressed in a subdued-looking black outfit with silver accents. Even though it didn't call attention to itself, the fabrics were finer than what you normally saw in this part of the city.

With the help of Taygor, Cobbee and a few other patrons, we sent the four troublemakers packing.

"Don't let me catch your ass in the Warrens again," Taygor told the big one. "This ain't your part of town."

The lunk nodded in terror, then looked over at me.

"And don't mess with our friends," Taygor added. I noted the "our," and the four of them booked it down the street as if a pack of hounds were nipping at their heels.

I offered to pay Cobbee for the broken keg, but he looked at Taygor respectfully and smiled at me and said, "Don't worry about it."

"Come on, you filthy beast," Taygor told me. "Let me take you somewhere special."

I followed Taygor through a maze of back alleys just off the main street of the Improvement District. I noted that the rats that scurried out of the way looked particularly well-fed.

We came out next to a sleepy-looking public hall. There weren't very many patrons, and the ones who were there looked like the kind of run-down old men you saw in such places back before I left. The whole place smelled like piss and shit. Nobody glanced at us as we walked past their tables.

There was one serving wench, an older woman in a dingy dress that tried to pass off her lumpy figure as curvy; it didn't fool anybody. To my surprise, Taygor greeted her warmly, and they exchanged pecks on the cheek. She stepped aside and allowed us to pass through a small doorway where a stained gray curtain hung.

We passed through something that looked like a kitchen, though it was obvious nobody had done any cooking there in years. Most of the space was taken up with crate after crate and barrel after barrel of free, crown-supplied wine and ale— the same piss served up in every other public hall.

At the back of the room, hidden behind a stack of barrels, we came to a thick door. Taygor rapped on it — two knocks, a pause, and then three knocks. A tiny slit opened, and I could see a pair of eyes looking out at us. The slit closed, and I heard a heavy bar being moved on the other side of the door. A very large man who had the scars and tattoos of a veteran pit fighter opened the door and waved us inside. He didn't give Taygor a second look, but he looked at my uniform warily.

"We have to keep a low profile these days," Taygor explained. "I'm sure you've probably heard about the press gangs, but the crown has been cracking down on everything pretty hard — they say they want things to be pleasant for all the new workers. Of course we can still operate — we just have to be quieter about it." He nodded at his new clothes. "Nobody wears slouchers on the streets anymore."

I'd already managed to piece that much together, but there was still something different about Taygor. Part of it was his manner, but part of it was the way everybody treated him — like the way Cobbee had just waved off the thing with the keg.

We came through another set of doors, and suddenly it was like I was back in the old Warrens. EVERY man in the place aside from us was wearing a sloucher, and reading the buttons, I realized that several were from rival gangs. I looked over at Taygor, and he understood my confusion immediately.

"This is neutral ground," he said. "At least for gangs on the eastside." He pointed out banners hanging on one of the walls; every eastside gang was represented, including the Clubs.

As we approached the bar, I noticed several guys respectfully step away to give us room. The bar itself was very nice, covered with fine carvings. As soon as we sat down on our stools, the bartender placed a pair of ice-cold mugs of ale in front of us. As he did so, he gave a quick smile and nod to Taygor.

As I sipped my ale, I noticed that a long mirror ran behind the bar, with different bottles of spirits lined up in front of it. When I looked at the mirror, I had a sudden moment of confusion. I noticed a lean but strong-looking man in a Raider uniform, and for the briefest second, I didn't realize I was looking at my own reflection.

I slowly put down my mug of ale and studied myself. It was the first time I'd gotten a good look at myself dressed up as an honest-to-Auld-Father Raider. The person staring back at me no longer looked like a boy. He looked like a serious man, the kind of man you look at and just automatically assume is in charge. My face seemed stronger and more chiseled than I remembered it, and my chest and shoulders seemed to have swelled — nobody was about to confuse me with Sgt. Taba, but there were definitely muscles there that hadn't been there before. I looked at the other faces in the room — many of which I recognized. Suddenly, they all looked so young and so...silly. Not children, but...not men.

I looked at the reflection of Taygor, who was smiling back at me. He was the only one who looked changed — though it wasn't the same. Then I caught a glint of light coming from something on his chest. I turned away from the reflection and looked at the real article. Pinned to his chest was a stylized image of a small silver trident.

"You're a Triton," I said.

"Well, a candidate, actually. If things go well, next year I'll be able to wear the black pin."

"How long?"

"I've actually been an associate for a few years now, but of course you're not allowed to advertise that."

"That's how you got us into the Dead Scorpion," I said.

He just raised his glass and winked. "Once I'm a full member — if I'm a full member — I'll be able to bring a few others into the Tritons," he said. "I was thinking of a few guys from the Clubs. Not just anybody, of course. I was thinking Rupens would be good for muscle. And I was thinking you'd make a good lieutenant. To me, of course."

"What would I have to do?"

He looked me up and down. "Lose that uniform, for starters."

That raised my hackles a bit.

"I made a commitment," I said.

"Yes, I know, and that's one of the reasons I respect you! That, and if you survive this war, you'll have seen enough blood that you won't flinch at doing what's necessary. Honor your commitment! Just know that when you get back, there will be a place for you here in Solta."

"If I get back. And if you get to wear the black pin."

"You worry about the first one. You let me worry about the second."

I sipped my ale and thought about that for a moment when we were suddenly interrupted by a drunk, filthy looking guy in a Stonegate Clubs sloucher.

"Hey, Taygor," he slurred. "Who's your — fuck my mother, is that Lasssss?" He was so drunk he couldn't form the last part of my name, so he drew out the "ssssss."

At first, I couldn't place him — his face was unshaven and his gaze was bloodshot and unfocused. But when he moved closer, I was hit with a heavy whiff of fragrant oils, ladled on thick enough to cover up the stench of a man who'd gone days without washing. There was only one guy I knew in the Warrens who used oils like that.

"Lyco," I said, punching him in the shoulder. I was instinctively worried about touching him and getting any of his filth on my uniform. I realized that I'd never noticed the stench before — the scents he wore always covered it up, and my sense of smell hadn't ever detected it. But after five months in the Raiders, it was impossible to miss.

Lyco threw his arm around me, not noticing my discomfort. "So has this son of a whore been bragging to you about making the Tritons?"

"Oh, he might have mentioned it."

That's when it finally clicked for me — the way everybody had been so deferential to Taygor, the thing about "our friends" that had shaken up the guys back at the Rooster. Growing up, I'd always known the Tritons were a big deal, but never having dealt face to face with a real one, I didn't know just how big.

"Get your ass over here, Lassss," Lyco said. "Come and say hi to everybody! Hey guys, it's Lassss!"

Taygor gave me a smile as I allowed Lyco to hustle me over to a corner of the saloon, where a bunch of the old gang were gathered. I looked at the faces; there were some younger ones that were new to me, but the older ones — including Lusseau — were nowhere to be found. I knew a few were probably in prison — they'd finally reached the point where they couldn't use the rowdy youngster excuse. Others might be dead.

I realized that the guys my age were starting to become the old guard, which meant the end of the line. Which meant...what? Taygor had managed to make it to the next level, and maybe a few others would. But what happened to the rest?

And then, of course, I remembered the hopeless, broken old men that had always filled the public halls, drowning in cheap, crown-supplied wine.

There was a ratty-looking old sofa in the corner, and they offered me a place on it. As soon as I sat down, I suddenly had company. On one side of me was a young girl I didn't recognize. On the other was Salah — Salah, the first girl I'd ever been with.

She looked older and more worn than the last time I'd seen her. She was smoking one of the big cigarettes that I remembered Aunt Twos used to like. I suspected that Salah's skin wouldn't look great, if I could see it — she had covered it up with what looked like a pound of makeup. She more than made up for it, though, with the revealing dress she was wearing — her body was still good enough that I felt an immediate stiffening in my crotch.

At that sensation, a stern voice in my head reminded me that my dick was still Crown property.

"Look at you!" Salah squealed, mashing one of her tits into my arm. "That uniform makes you look so hot."

She held her face close to mine, and all I could smell was the disgusting aroma of cigarettes. "Isn't he hot, Luscia?" she said.

The younger girl on my other side leaned closer, her breath thick with the smell of ale. She placed a hand on my chest — her nails were badly chipped and the skin looked dry. "I've never been with a Raider before," she said. She sounded like she was trying to mimic Salah's tone, but she was too over the top.

Even so, I couldn't keep my eyes off her huge, and quite inviting cleavage. That voice in my head reminding me about who owned my dick got louder. I was on the verge of telling that voice to shut up for an hour or three when I felt something cold and wet on my neck. I sat up, sending Salah and Luscia back into the sofa in a fit of giggles as I turned around to see what happened. Lyco was sitting there, somehow looking horrified while also cracking up.

"Oh, shit, Lassss, I'm sorry," said. "That was my fault dude. I was leaning over to try to get a look at Luscia's tits and I spilled some ale. Dude. Is your uniform okay?"

"It's fine," I lied, thinking about all the work I'd have to put into getting it clean again. "What the fuck, dude?"

"Hey, come on, man, let me get you another ale..."

I sat there with everyone for about an hour, sipping my ale and trying to enjoy things with the old gang. There was talk about maybe going to see a dog fight, but I lied and said I had to be back early. In truth, I just couldn't stand the dirt, the grime, the smells — being filthy just made me feel weird. I'm sure if I drank enough the feeling would have gone away — but I didn't *want* to drink enough.

I looked at Salah — she'd once been so beautiful. She still was beautiful, in a way, but she didn't look like she'd be that way for much longer. And there was Lyco — I tried to imagine Lyco as a Raider. With his fussiness about appearance, he would have at least mastered the basics, and I bet if someone like Sgt. Sculler could get him to widen his focus a bit, he would have been a solid, sharp edge on Auld Father's blade.

Such a waste.

Before I made an excuse to head out, I looked across the room at Taygor. He was still holding the same mug of ale, and I bet if I'd checked, it would still be mostly full. He stood in that tavern as a pillar of perfect calm in the eye of a storm. There, I thought to myself, is a man who has his life together. But why?

I tried to imagine him in the middle of a storm, stuck up a tree, with a pack of hungry wolves looking to devour him. How would he handle it? For some reason, I was sure he'd handle it well.

I waved goodbye, and he raised his mug and nodded. There was something about his eyes...

It was only much, much later that I realized what I saw there. Taygor would never find himself stuck in that tree. Because he would be one of the wolves.

68

I spent much of the rest of the night cleaning and prepping my dress uniform, since there was no way I was taking my mom to the Temple looking like just another clown in military garb. The actual cleaning wasn't too bad, but drying and then getting it properly pressed was a pain in the ass. I had to dry it by the barracks fireplace, which took forever, then carefully smooth the fabric and brush out the lint.

I managed to grab a few hours of sleep before once again waking up automatically at dawn. My bunkmates were all still snoring; I realized I hadn't yet seen one of them awake. Checking my watch, I realized I could have slept another hour and a half. I tried, but after a few minutes I gave up — I was too restless. I headed down to the basement to wash up.

On my way back upstairs I noticed a slight man in frilly clothes speaking with the desk clerk. The clerk looked bewildered.

"Are you absolutely sure you have the right address?" he said.

The strangely dressed man sighed.

"I am QUITE sure," he said with a polished accent. "My instructions are to deliver this message to the hand of a Mr. Pearl..."

My ears perked up.

"I'm Mr. Pearl," I said. I was standing there dressed in nothing but a towel; from the way he looked at me, I could tell he would have rather been faced with a goblin.

"Mr. LASHAN Pearl?" he asked, as if he was praying I'd say no.

"Only one I know of," I said.

He sighed and rolled his eyes. "I have been instructed to present you with... this." He held out a small envelope. The way he clasped it by the tips of his fingers told me he didn't want to get any closer to me than he had to.

I stepped closer, hoping to make him more uncomfortable, and took the envelope from him.

"To whom do I owe the pleasure?" I asked.

He sighed again.

"Everything should be there," he said. "Now if you'll excuse me, I must be on my way." He left in a hurry, his ridiculous frilly clothes flapping along with him.

I had an idea what was in the envelope — I'd seen this whole scene play out among rich people enough times to have some notion of it. I took it upstairs where I could open it in private.

I was either hoping or dreading it was from Kanin, or perhaps her father — I say "both" because I wasn't sure what either one might want to say to me. But when I opened it up, I read:

The presence of PVT. LASHAN PEARL
is requested tomorrow evening (Firstday 3 of the Eighth Month, Year 1627)
at a reception in honor of

PVT. BERRIT CAMLIN

the son of LORD NETHAN CAMLIN IX, 9th Duke of Cercel, Margrave of Komat,
Land Secretary of the Regency Council and Arch-Colonel (Emeritus) of the Royal Cavalry.

One guest permitted. Formal dress.

Below the last line, Skunk had scribbled: "Lash — Raider dress uniform is fine! Come at 7!"

WHEN THE CARRIAGE I'D hired arrived at the temple, I was surprised by the number of people who were there.

"It's not one of the holy days," I told my mom. "Why is there such a crowd?"

She gave me a look of surprise and I think a little bit of pride. Before the Raiders, I hadn't paid any attention to the holy calendar, but since Raiders marked ALL feast days and holy days, I'd since practically memorized it.

"Oh, it's been like this every week since the Black Day," she explained, fingering the arrow she wore around her neck. "People come for so many reasons — some are grieving loved ones lost in the fighting, some are praying for Auld Father's wisdom to guide the Regency Council. For many of the new workers, it's a reminder of home. And of course, many are worried about their men who will be going off to join the fight."

She gave me a pat on the shoulder at that. I smiled, and helped her out of the carriage.

The service itself was shorter than what I was used to — mom explained it was because no work was officially permitted on Sevenday, so the Footman Magnus of Solta wanted to make sure all the workers in the city had an opportunity that day to rest. The Temple was more packed with worshippers than I'd ever seen it — extra benches and chairs had been brought in to accommodate the huge crowds.

There were only two hymns and then a short sermon, then we touched our feet to the sacred soil and the congregation was dismissed.

After the service, I asked one of the Footmen if he knew where I could find Footman Tan; I wanted to show off my uniform to the old bastard and thank him for calming down my mother. The man frowned and pulled me aside.

"Are you a friend of Footman Tan?"

"A former student."

"I see," he said. "I'm afraid I have some bad news."

I'D NEVER BEEN TO the Royal Mausoleum before. If you've ever been to Solta, it's built right above the Palace District, perched on a cliff that gives it a commanding view of the harbor and the city. They say that it's built on the location of the original palace, which was sited there because it's on the most defensible piece of land in the entire city, and that later kings moved the palace closer to the harbor to make it more easily accessible. Because so many royals were still buried there, though, they changed it into a mausoleum. The only reason I'd even heard of it was because you could see its dome jutting up from almost every part of the city, and it was often used as a landmark when giving directions.

They told me Footman Tan had died of a fever he'd caught very suddenly. A group of newcomers to the city had arrived afflicted with some illness, and they'd been put in quarantine.

The group had all come from the same village, and by the time they reached the gates of Solta, they knew they were dying. Many of the survivors wanted to make sure their feet were firmly on the Path before they passed from this world. Footman Tan volunteered to take charge of their care during their last days. He had begun showing signs of the illness only a few hours before the last two died. Within a week, he was dead himself.

For some reason, I'd always thought that only royalty were buried in the Royal Mausoleum — I mean, it's right in the name, right? But it turns out the royal tombs are only a small part of the building — they're all placed in the Grand Crypt, the part that towers over the rest with its big white dome. But the building itself is actually much larger, and the rest of it holds the remains of other honored citizens.

After following the directions the Footman at the Temple had given us, I found out why Footman Tan had been buried there. The little inscription on the marble plaque that marked his tomb noted his rank when he'd retired from the Raiders

— First Sergeant, which made perfect sense — and also noted he'd earned the Order of St. Mersa.

The Crimson Star. Every man who'd earned it, no matter what branch of service, was entitled to interment in the Royal Mausoleum at Crown expense.

The Footman at the Temple had allowed me to go through Footman Tan's effects. Most of the stuff had no meaning to me, but I did find a few things I took with me — his leather strap, which I'd been beaten with countless times, and his copy of The Walk, which I have carried with me ever since. I also looked through his collection of Vast the Brutal books. I'd read all the ones he had, but one in particular looked familiar. It was the story about Vast rescuing a princess from a giant spider with wings — the one he'd beaten me for reading in class all those years ago.

There was a note sticking out of it. I pulled it out and read it.

"Confiscated from L. Pearl," it said. I asked the Footman about it, and he said Footman Tan would sometimes confiscate things from students and return them at a later time.

"When was 'a later time?'"

"I believe it was when he felt like they'd earned it back," he said with a shrug.

There was a little carved-out niche above the plaque on Footman Tan's tomb where people could leave things. I saw flowers placed in many of them. But in the niche above his, I placed his old leather strap, along with the Vast the Brutal book he'd taken from me.

"I don't know if I've earned this back," I whispered quietly, running my fingers across the inscription of his name. "Maybe someday you can tell me." I want it known for the record that I didn't cry at that moment, but I did feel my eyes getting a little moist.

"What did you say, dear?" my mother asked.

"Nothing, mom. It's nothing." I gave her a hug, and took her back to the waiting carriage.

I was about to ask the driver to take us back to the Warrens, when I realized where we were. If I was this close, there was no reason not to chance it.

"Take us back to the Warrens," I said, "but on the way back, can I ask you to take a slight detour?"

69

A few minutes before 7 the next evening, I walked up to the gate of the biggest house I'd ever seen, with Kanin on my arm. I hadn't been planning on taking anyone with me to the reception that evening, but something about the experience at the mausoleum made me feel like I should take a chance with her, no matter how remote.

To my immense relief, she'd accepted. And now, here we were, about to enter the wealthiest, most lavish affair I'd ever been to in my entire life. If that didn't make an impression on her, nothing would.

The servant — he was wearing the same frilly clothes as the man who'd delivered my invitation, although he looked much younger — looked me up and down and smiled. To my surprise, he acted like my presence was perfectly natural.

He asked for my name.

"Private Lashan Pearl," I said, "and Miss Kanin Mils." I tried to deepen my voice a bit to make it sound more mature. He looked down at a piece of paper, then looked up quickly.

"Right this way, sir!" he said, opening the gate. "Follow the pathway through the garden, then up the steps; one of the attendants will assist you from there."

The "garden" was more like a miniature forest — even though the walk was less than a couple hundred feet, the whole way was shaded by trees that were obviously quite old.

"How does a boy from the Warrens get invited to a party thrown by a member of the Regency Council?" Kanin asked, giving me a playful jab.

I was caught off guard by her question, though. "How did you...I never said..."

"That you were from the Warrens?" giving her voice an exaggerated edge of snobbiness.

"Yes. That."

"I'm not as stupid as I look, you know."

"I never said you were..."

"Hush, I'm just teasing. Here, there's the attendant up ahead. Let's see how well a Warrens rat handles this one!" she said with a giggle. It was, thank goodness, a friendly giggle.

Skunk's house — or rather, his father's house — was familiar to me, it turned out. I'd never been inside it, but it was hard for anybody who passed through the Palace District to avoid noticing it. The home was easily the largest and most ornate of the homes of the nobility. Though it might as well have been a shack in comparison to the palace, it was still one of the most striking buildings in the whole city, and had actually become something of a landmark. Newcomers who passed by inevitably stopped to admire the intricate stonework, particularly the two massive bear sculptures that flanked the main entrance gate — as Skunk later explained, the bear had long been the family's symbol, going all the way back to his barbarian ancestors.

Much later, I learned from Footman Sesh that the word "Kvan," the name of Skunk's barbarian ancestor, was actually the word for "bear" in the Auld Tongue, and "Camlin" is related to a word in the Auld Tongue meaning "fierce and strong."

When we were brought into the main hall (I made sure to walk with Kanin on my arm exactly as Mrs. Gern had taught us), I scanned the crowd for a familiar face. I noticed Skunk at the same moment he noticed me — he excused himself and came over to greet me and Kanin.

Skunk cleaned up VERY well. He was, of course, dressed in a Raider formal uniform that matched my own, but his face and hair looked like something you'd see in a painting. Kanin was obviously quite impressed with him, but she must have seen the jealousy on my face, because she leaned over and whispered to me, "He's wearing makeup!" I tried to get a good look, but I never did decide if she was right, or if she was just telling me so I wouldn't feel so bad next to him.

As it turned out, the stated purpose of the whole event was supposedly to mark Skunk's becoming a Raider. There was a second, more important purpose, though — raising money for the war effort. Many people, I found out, had actually paid money to get on the guest list, and once inside, there were numerous opportunities to spend money — there was an auction; a room on the second floor was set aside for gambling; guests could pay to join a wine tasting being held in the Duke's private cellar; another fee got one a guided tour of the Duke's art collection — you get the idea.

When I asked Skunk about it, he just shook his head and rolled his eyes.

"I told you before, you don't want to know about what it takes to finance a war," he said. He did give me a small admittance card so I could take Kanin on the art collection tour, though.

When they were taking us through the sculpture hall, I told Kanin that if I ever had that much money, there was no way I'd go around spending it on such nonsense.

"Oh, but you would," she said. "You don't understand — it costs money to be this rich."

I gave her a look. She continued, "It takes a lot more than money to be rich — to be a noble. The more money you have, the more you have to spend."

"That's ridiculous."

"No, I'm quite serious. If you have a fortune and don't spend it, the Crown will take much of it in taxes — especially now, with the war. But of course, if you *do* spend it before the Crown can tax it, the Crown will expect you to pay your dues in other ways. Have you ever heard the saying, 'the man born with wings carries the heaviest burden?'"

"Of course."

"Then be glad you were born without wings."

I thought about that.

"What if I refused to fly?"

"What?"

"What if I was born with wings, burdened with the weight of all these duties, and I refused to fly?"

She looked at me, then looked me up and down.

"From what I've been told," she said, "that's a thought that would never occur to a Raider."

I met a lot of people that I suppose I should have known of, but I didn't. Kanin, Auld Father bless her, guided me through all of it. At dinner, I noted that many of my supposed superiors had table manners that would have gotten them a verbal thrashing from Mrs. Gern. Kanin gave me a look of surprise — a good surprise, I hoped — when she saw I knew which fork, spoon and knife to use with which dish.

Afterwards, we were ushered into a hall for an after-dinner concert, during which we were served dessert. It was during this that Skunk suddenly appeared and asked Kanin if he could borrow me for a second.

He ushered me out onto a large balcony with a magnificent view of the bay.

"Man, Lips, where did a hobo like you find such a gorgeous piece of..."

"She's a friend — one I happen to like," I said, cutting him off. "Don't get any ideas."

"Hey, hey, I got it, man. I understand."

I studied his face. He seemed genuinely apologetic. I walked over to the railing of the balcony.

"What's up?" I asked.

He joined me at the railing.

"I mean...I just needed a break. From this," he said, gesturing over his shoulder.

"If this is what it's like every day, no wonder."

"No, I don't mean...ah, forget it."

We looked out at the bay for a few seconds. I got the feeling I'd kind of pissed him off.

"No, man, look. Look, dude. I'm sorry. I'm just not used to this," I said. "You gotta remember, this is pretty far from what I come from."

"It's not exactly what I'm used to, either. I've spent most of my life as an embarrassment to my dad. I kind of still am, but...hey, I never asked, where are you headed?"

"Agellos. Same as you."

"No, I mean..."

"I know what you meant. Where are *you* headed?"

"I asked first."

"You asked first because you don't want to say."

Skunk was silent for a few seconds after that. I broke the tension by answering his question: "They want me to be a mage."

Skunk stood up in surprise. "No shit? How did that happen?"

I turned my back to the bay and leaned against the railing. I thought for a moment if I should tell Skunk, but I decided it wouldn't hurt.

"It was the day before graduation. I'd gotten my assignment card — they wanted me for infantry, big surprise — but then Sgt. Sculler called me into The Cage.

"He closed the door and had me sit down. 'Recruit Pearl,' he said, 'have you ever thought about becoming a mage?'

"I told him I doubted I had any ability for it. I mean, I've read about how people with chantic powers usually know from a very young age — being able to move very small objects with their mind, being able to read the thoughts of others, that sort of thing. I told him I'd never had anything like that.

"So he told me about that weird test they gave us — the written one, where we were each put in our own little room."

"Yeah. I wondered about that, why all the secrecy."

"Yours wasn't...weird?"

"No. What was yours like?"

I quickly gave Skunk a rundown of the strange experience I'd had, with the changing ink. According to Sgt. Sculler, the changing ink was an indication I possessed a latent magic ability. The rest of the questions — the strange stuff that didn't make any sense — was intended to test the strength of that ability.

"So, what are you saying — that I aced it?" I'd asked Sculler. "Are you saying I get to be a high sorcerer, like Maj. Tyvin?"

In fact, Sculler informed me, I'd failed — but only by one point. Normally that would be enough to kill any chance I had of becoming a mage — but there were two problems.

The first problem was that there was a war going on, and they needed mages. Not every mage, he pointed out, was a powerful sorcerer. Even among those born with magic ability, that kind of skill was out of the ordinary. But there were plenty of magical tasks that needed doing, and having those of "more modest magical endowments," as he put it, handle those duties helped free up the sorcerers, wizards, warlocks and thaumaturges to do what they did best — drowning the enemy in giant oceans of ass-kicking.

Okay. So they needed people to do the magical equivalent of emptying latrines, and hey, a filthy Warrens kid with a bit of fairy blood in his veins looked like a good fit, is what I didn't say in response. Got it.

The second problem was, I'd told him about being cornered by a pack of wolves, then being saved when they were led away by a silver deer.

Sculler told me that immediately after we got back from our Vernet seclusion, a hunting party had been sent out and had killed the wolves, which were indeed underfed. They'd probably migrated down out of the mountains to try their luck preying on the Fort Harrel's livestock, or anything else they might have managed to scrounge up. The Raiders were in my debt for bringing it to their attention, Sculler said. He didn't add that the "anything else" had come close to including me, or possibly some other unlucky recruit.

He was interested in the silver deer, though. Sculler said that silver deer were believed to be entirely gone from that part of the Kingdom; it was *believed* that the closest wild population was at least 200 miles to the south.

"One might say it was as if you conjured one up, recruit," he said evenly.

"I don't know about that, sir. Don't animals sometimes wander pretty far from their normal range?" I thought I'd remembered reading that somewhere.

"It's not impossible that a single specimen might have wandered this far north," he allowed.

"I think that's probably it, sir. I think I was just lucky. I mean, there's no way I'm going to conjure up a silver deer right here in this room."

Sculler responded by pulling something out of his desk and held it out to me.

"Recruit, pick a card."

I pulled one at random out of the deck and looked at it.

"Which card did you draw, recruit?"

"The Prince of the Forest, sir."

"A silver deer, in other words."

"Yes sir. But I hardly think that luck of the draw..."

Sculler then spread the cards out on the table, face up.

They were all blank. I dropped the card I was holding, and as soon as it left my fingers it went blank, too. I picked up another card. Another silver deer card. I picked up another, and another, until I'd picked up eight silver deer cards in a row. There were only seven silver deer cards to a deck.

"Try thinking of another card, recruit."

I thought of the Green Man — there was only one per deck. I picked up a card I'd previously picked up, and the Green Man appeared. I picked up another, holding both at the same time — *two* Green Man cards. I concentrated, and changed one to a Red Fowl and the other to a Blue Fowl. I showed them to Sgt. Sculler.

"What do you know? The Duchess Pair." I smiled and studied the cards carefully, trying to see if there was anything about the ink. I noticed the paper had a metallic sheen. "Is this a trick deck?"

Sculler picked up several of the cards and fanned them out for me to see. They remained blank. "Not for me."

Sculler gave me a choice — infantry, or mage. He said he'd go with whichever choice I made.

"If your score had been higher, you wouldn't have a choice," he said. "I would have just assigned you to mage duty, and that would have been it. But because you missed it by just one point — and because you clearly have some hidden talent for it — I'm letting you decide something that very few recruits ever get a chance to decide."

I tried to read his face, but it was impenetrable.

"How many mages do the Raiders require?" I asked. "If they need me, I'm at their service. But if it's all the same, sir, I'd prefer to be infantry."

That was an honest answer. Chantic abilities held no interest for me; all I wanted to do was fight. I would have been happy hefting a sword and being cut down in single combat.

But it wasn't about me — that was what had been burned into me by the Raiders. What was best for Lash Pearl wasn't necessarily best for my team, my platoon, my company, my regiment. And so on.

I told Sculler as much, and he nodded, and told me what he thought was best for the Raiders.

"And so," I told Skunk, "I'm going to be a battlemage."

"I see."

"So what about you? Where are you headed?"

Skunk smiled, and looked out at the gorgeous view.

"Sculler called me into The Cage, too," he said. "He wanted to submit my name as a candidate to the ORC."

He paused and looked at me, and I think he quickly saw that I was confused.

"ORC — Officer Review Council," he said. "To fast-track me for an officer's post. He said that many, many had been lost...with the King." Then he turned back to look at the harbor.

"But that's not the only reason," I said. He didn't answer. "It's also because...because you're a noble." He looked for a moment like he was about to turn around, but he kept his back turned.

I don't know how I knew, but I knew: "You said no."

"I said no."

A moment passed. Finally I asked, "Why?"

He took in a deep breath, turned around, and nodded in the direction of the house. "You see all those paintings in there?"

"You mean in the gallery? Yeah I took Kanin..."

"No, not in the gallery. I mean all the paintings in the halls, the dining room, the reception area — all those."

I thought back. "Yeah. A bunch of rich guys."

"The ones in uniform."

I shrugged. "Cavalry officers," I said. "Relatives of yours, right?"

Skunk looked down. "My ancestors," he said. "My family, going back at least eight generations."

I was puzzled. "So? That's certainly nothing to be ashamed of."

"I'm not ashamed of it. I'm proud of it. But..."

I waited for him to continue. "But what?" I prodded.

He sighed and shrugged.

"I'm different," he finally said. "I've always known it. My dad has always known it. I'm not like those guys in there hanging on those walls."

"But you joined the Raiders. And...and you did well."

"I did. But none of those men in those pictures are wearing Raider blue."

He stared out at the harbor for a moment, then stood up straight. "I talked all of this over with Sculler, and believe it or not, the old bastard understood. That motherfucker was a lot smarter than any of us ever realized. Anyway, he gave me another option."

I was getting a weird feeling. It almost felt like Skunk was ready to throw himself off the balcony. I instinctively stepped closer, ready to grab him if he did anything stupid.

"Dude. Why are you telling me all this?"

For a moment he looked like he might be in a trance, but then he gave me a friendly smile.

"It's just...well, when you get to Agellos, to get ready for the invasion, you probably won't see me. I mean, I'll be there — but I won't be somewhere that you'll probably run into me."

"We were all supposed to meet when we get there. Remember? The One One Five reunion."

"I know. I'll try to make it if I can. But if I'm not there...don't worry about me. I'm not abandoning you. Auld Father willing, I'll see you guys in Garlund."

I didn't know what to say, so I just said, "You okay, man?"

He smiled, waited a few seconds, then patted me on the back.

"I'm fine, you Molan bastard. Get in there and be with your woman."

AFTER THE RECEPTION, I noted that Arban and Siran were in the sky that night, and I told Kanin it seemed like a waste not to take in the view in the company of one as knowledgeable as herself.

"Oh really," she said, giving me a smiling side-eye. "And just where would you propose we go? To get the best view, I mean."

"Well, that contraption of your father's, that telescope, wouldn't that be best?"

"Perhaps…not there. Not tonight." I noticed she was distractedly looking away when she said that. In truth I didn't care about the moons; I was just looking for an excuse to spend more time with her.

"Well…well the Palace District Promenade then," I said quickly. It was on a high point with a view not blocked by any buildings, so it would be a good place for moon watching, I thought.

"You don't fool me, sir," she teased. "I know I'm not the first lady friend you've taken there."

I laughed and told her truthfully I'd never taken a single girl there before in my life.

"Oh? What is so special about me that I have earned such an honor?"

I stiffened. "Well for one thing, they would have run off anybody like me, especially at this time of night."

The moonlight was bright enough for me to see her blush.

"I'm sorry," she quickly said.

"No, no. Don't apologize. But will you go with me?"

Not 10 minutes and one quick carriage ride later, we were on the Promenade, with the city and the harbor spread out below us.

"I'm surprised there aren't more people here," I said. There had been three couples along the Promenade when we arrived, and one left shortly after we got there. From their dress and what little I could pick up of their whispered conversations, they all seemed like Palace District types, which made me a bit wary. But when we passed one of them, the man gave a respectful nod, and I quickly remembered the effect my uniform had on people. It put me at ease.

Well, as much as it was possible to feel at ease with Kanin there. When we stepped out of the carriage, the way she gripped my arm and smiled at me gave me shivers in a way I'd never felt before.

What was it about her? Since I'd been back, I'd noticed plenty of admiring looks from cute girls who wouldn't have given me a second glance if they'd known I was a Warrens rat. But beyond the novelty factor, they didn't catch my fancy the way Kanin did. I was looking at her and thinking about this when she noticed I wasn't focused on the moons.

"Shouldn't you be looking skyward?" she said, and gave me a wide smile. I remember her mismatched lips were parted slightly, and there was just a tiny glint of moonlight on her teeth. And I think that was it, that was the moment I knew what it was. She was looking at me and seeing, well…me. Just me. Not what I was wearing, or where I had grown up, or who my father had been. Just as it had been back when we used to have tea in her kitchen while I tried to explain skram to her, she had brushed aside all the things about me that other people couldn't see past — that even I couldn't see past — with a brisk sweep of one of her gawky, too-long arms.

Except her arms didn't look too long now; the cut of her pale pink gown combined with the long gloves she wore made her look graceful, even regal. ("My old bridesmaid's dress from my cousin's wedding!" she'd whispered to me at one point.) And this regal beauty was now looking at me — just me, just plain old Lash — and was delighted by what she saw.

She seemed to see something there that I couldn't. Maybe she always had. But now I felt that very thing welling up within me: A great spirit asserting its claim. But it wasn't something new or strange; it was more like when the feeling of numbness fades from a sleeping limb, a thing that had been there all along. I saw the way she looked me, and I knew then I could be the man who deserved that; I *wanted* to be that.

But I didn't know how to say it. Even now I don't know how to say it; I'm reading these words on parchment and they fall short. She was looking as if she expected me to say something, and I was fumbling for the words.

"You look beautiful," was all I could come up with.

She blushed again. "I'm sure any girl would look fetching with a handsome gent like you as her squire," she said, giving my arm a playful squeeze. I caught a quick flash of surprise in her face as she felt the firmness of the muscle beneath the fabric, and I turned quickly away lest she notice my grin of pride.

"So the moons," I said, changing the subject, and looking up at the twin sentinels. "I think I can sort of make out those mountain ranges, now that I know what to look for. But I'm wondering about the circular features I see — there are a lot more of them on Siran, but you can see them on Arban as well."

"Craters," she said, following my gaze. "Father says they are caused by the impact of huge rocks on the surface. See how they almost seem like ripples on the surface of a pond, if you throw stones into it? Except there's no water, there's just dirt, so instead of fading away, the ripples just stay frozen there; what's left is called a crater."

I squinted.

"I see what you mean. But…where do these rocks come from?"

"Oh, they're flying through the aether up there, all about us! They're too tiny to see from this distance. But sometimes they crash into the moons — sometimes they even crash here into Cianu! That's what causes shooting stars! Father says most of them burn up completely while they are high up in the aether, but some of the larger ones make it to the ground. People have even recovered them!"

"I've heard of rocks like those." I studied the surface of the moons for a few more moments. "Those...craters? Is that what you called them? They look like what you see when a heavy missile from a trebuchet strikes a soft patch of earth. But if you can see them from here...the rocks that made them must have been enormous!"

"Father says they could have been hundreds of feet wide. Some of the craters you see are dozens of miles across!"

I shook my head and chuckled. "If only we could enlist Auld Father to toss a few of those rocks down at the Arcanter..."

Kanin grew quiet, and I saw she was no longer looking at the sky. She noticed me looking, gave me a quick smile, and released her hand from my arm as she took in the lights of the city, her face once again serious.

"Does it scare you," she finally said.

"What? Facing the Arcanter? Well I'm sure it won't be pleasant, but..."

"No, I mean...knowing that you could die. Over there."

"I could die right here in Solta tomorrow. A runaway cart could roll right over me..."

"Fatalism doesn't suit you," she said softly, cutting me off.

I was quiet for a long time. I could have given another flippant response, but I knew she'd see right through it, and I could see how serious she suddenly was. I wanted to give the most honest response I could.

"I guess...I don't know if I've ever really thought about it."

I put my hand on her shoulder, but she remained still. I sighed, and sat down on a nearby bench.

"To tell you the truth, until...well, before..." I tried to figure out how to explain it all to her. "Before...I joined the Raiders. Before then. Before then, I don't think I ever thought about dying, because to worry about dying...you have to worry about the future. And I didn't see any future for myself worth caring about."

I sighed. "It was all just a game, like a round of cards. You know the game will be over, eventually. But you don't think about it. You just enjoy it while you can, until the last card is drawn. And...and that's it."

"What changed," she said, her back to me.

I thought about my mother, and the Post Master, and Footman Tan, and Auld Father. I thought about my life in the Warrens. I thought about being born blind, then being cured.

But more than anything, I thought about our fallen King, when he placed that golden coin in my hand. And I brightened. "Someone else saw it differently, and told me so. And I guess, little by little, I've come to see it, too."

She sat down beside me. She touched my hand with her own, then pulled it away.

"And now…this. This war," she said. She shrugged, and gave me a forced smile. "At the reception…I overheard two elderly ladies talking. They were admiring you and your friend, and the other young men there in uniform. One of them said, 'It's so tragic when we lose them at that age.' And the other said, 'So many of them won't be with us this time next year. This will be their last golden moment. You just want to shake them, and tell them to enjoy every second of it.'"

I didn't speak. I didn't know what to say. In all the time since I'd first known I would be headed off to war, the idea of death — I mean the reality of it, the idea that I would be gone, or with Auld Father on His Holy Mountain or whatever, while the rest of the world would just carry on — until that moment, I'd never thought about it, even for the briefest moment. It's not that I'd never thought of *dying* — it's just that when I did, it was as another Raider milestone: A glorious death in battle, like the kind you see in old paintings or read about in the Raider Hand Book. And that would be it — the last card is revealed; the game is over.

But here, for the first time in my life, I could feel myself beginning to form some murky notions about my own future — notions that seemed to center on this woman sitting beside me. And now she was reminding me that I might not *have* a future — at least, not for much longer.

I felt a chill. "What are you trying to tell me?"

Please don't say you won't see me, I thought. Please don't send me away. Please don't say I'm not worth the risk. Please don't say you've had fun, but…

"I don't know," she said. She looked at me, then turned away and repeated, "I don't know."

Ah, it was like that. She just couldn't say it. So it would be up to me.

I sighed, preparing myself to bring things to an honorable close. I was already forming plans to drop her off at home, gracefully bid her farewell, and go drown my cares in a tavern down in the Improvement District when she suddenly stood up, and said "This will not do." She began tugging at my uniform to get me to stand up.

"What?"

"This will not do!" she repeated, with a sudden firmness. "Get up! Dance with me here, the way you did back at the reception! Where did you learn to dance that way?"

I shrugged, got up, and put her through the fanciest dance moves I could remember from Mrs. Gern's class. I wasn't thinking straight, and I could just picture Mrs. Gern scowling at my shoddy footwork. But after a few minutes I had Kanin squealing with laughter again. For a moment it felt like the rest of the world had faded away — it was just us two, dancing to silent music in the light of the moon, with the city and the war and everything else a distant memory.

"By His Foot, you are marvelous!" she exclaimed. When I finished wheeling her through a particularly tricky number, I was surprised to hear clapping. I turned and looked, and one of the other couples on the Promenade was applauding us.

My heart was racing now. I wiped the perspiration from my brow and turned to Kanin, who had one arm about me and was glowing with the widest, most achingly lovely smile, and at that moment I didn't have a care in the world. She was flushed, I could see her neck pulsing as she caught her breath; her eyes widened and...

I immediately took her in my arms and kissed her, and the hungry way she returned it made my whole body shudder.

Shortly afterward, we were back sitting on the bench and looking up at the moons. Now she was leaning against me, her hand softly stroking my chest and playing with the buttons of my uniform.

We talked, in a way we'd never been able to talk before. She told me about her life with her quirky and somewhat absentminded father, and all the famous and strange people they had hosted in their home. She told of the headaches she'd given her dad with her schooling, and while it was far different from what I'd put my mom through, I could see the parallels: Both our parents had wanted something greater for us, and we'd both been too headstrong to exactly follow the path they'd laid out.

For my part, I told her about my time at the Temple School, which surprised her a little bit — in a good way, apparently. "My, Mr. Pearl," she said, with a new look in her eye. "You really are quite the anomaly, aren't you?" (I didn't know what "anomaly" meant, but Footman Sesh says it's a good thing in this context.)

I told her about growing up in the Warrens, though I tried to skip over some of the uglier stuff. I admitted I'd been in a gang, but told her it wasn't like all the stuff she might have read in the papers. And anyway, I said truthfully, that life was now far behind me.

She was particularly fascinated by all the brawling I'd done. "I don't think I've ever met a man who has so much as thrown a punch in anger," she said. "The boys I knew could trade fine-sounding insults, but it always struck me as hollow."

"I wouldn't be so quick to judge them," I told her, thinking of Skunk. "You can find a hard man under those soft manners, sometimes."

"Mmmmm," she said, running her hand over my chest.

"No, I meant..."

"I know what you meant."

I kissed her again. After several more passionate minutes, we had to come up for air.

I looked at her, at her flushed face and funny smile, and I laughed.

"I hope this isn't my golden moment," I said, "because I want a lot more moments like this."

She pulled my face closer. "If it is, we'd better make sure it's worth it." And she hungrily pressed her lips to mine.

70

Three days later, I caught an ox-trolley caravan headed from Solta to Agellos. For some reason, watching the walls of the city disappear over the horizon wasn't quite as unnerving this time. After the Blue Wood, I was pretty sure I could handle anything.

On the morning I was set to leave, I went to visit my mother. I told her I wouldn't have much time, but she insisted. She said it was important.

The dawn sky was still gray when we sat down in the front parlor of the rooming house. I remember it was cold — the first cold day of the year.

My mother came down the stairs looking tired — it was obvious she'd just returned from her job at the factory. It was the first time I noticed the wisps of white just barely beginning to show in her red hair. When she saw me, she brightened.

We sat down on the couches in the parlor — she sat directly across from me and stared at me for a minute, still smiling.

"For much of your life, I feared this moment would never come," she finally said.

"You make it sound like going off to war is a good thing, mom."

"No...no, I don't mean that." She sighed. "One thing my mother told me: 'There will always be wars. Men will always find an excuse to fight.' No, I always knew that. I've known ever since your father..."

She trailed off, and looked into the distance for just a brief second. Then her gaze snapped back to me.

"Actually, that is what I wanted to talk to you about."

There was a small tea table between us; mom reached out and placed something on to it. When she pulled her hand away, I saw that it was a small pearl. But it wasn't like any pearl I'd ever seen. It was a dark red, but the way the light seemed to bounce off it was extraordinary. It almost glowed — as if it was wrapped in a tiny flame.

"Your father gave this to me when I was pregnant with you," she said. "He said if he never came back, that I was to give it to you when you became a man."

"How did he know you wouldn't have a daughter?"

She smiled, and looked down at the pearl.

"I remember I asked him that, and he laughed — the same laugh that you have." She looked back at me. "He said that he knew. And...I think I knew, too."

I picked it up and studied it.

"So...it's a pearl?"

"Not just any pearl. A fire pearl — the rarest kind. There were many times over the years I thought about selling it, but...when I prayed to Auld Father about it, he seemed to guide my heart away from that."

"I've never heard of them," I said.

"They're only found in a specific type of oyster that lives off the coast of your father's homeland. He told me that when a Molan boy feels he has reached manhood, he goes searching for one. These oysters — apparently they live very deep in the water, and even if you know where to find one, it requires a skilled swimmer to dive and fetch it. And even then, it might take dozens of dives before you find one that contains a pearl. He said it was very exhausting. He said it was the closest he'd ever felt to death throughout his whole life."

"And when you find one — you're a man?"

"Yes. You present it to the tribal elders, and there's a ceremony. If you're never able to find one, they'll still have a ceremony for you when you reach a certain age, but...well, he said it's not quite the same. People don't look at you quite the same way. The men who do it the way he did — they are something special. He said they're called 'pearls.'"

I had a sudden realization.

"That's...that's where our name comes from. You said..."

"I know what I said."

I looked again at the pearl, then back at her, a bit confused.

"So...I'm a man now? That's what this means?"

"Your father said I would know."

I looked down at my uniform.

"Not because of that," she said, as if reading my thoughts. "Or rather, not only because of that. It's...there's been something different about you these past few days. I don't know how to put it into words; it's something I think only a woman can understand."

"A woman?"

"Yes. I wasn't sure I saw it at first. But I'm sure I do now."

She pushed the pearl into my palm, and closed my fist around it. Then we closed our eyes, lifted our heads, and she offered up a prayer.

My last meeting with Kanin had been the evening before. We promised to write each other. But before that, I asked her if it bothered her that I was a half-Molan.

She put her hand on my cheek and smiled. "There was a time it might have been a problem — I mean, I don't mind it at all, but I know others do, and there was a time that would have caused me to be more cautious.

"But this war...the death of the King...I guess it's made a lot of things clear to me. There were people I once respected whose opinions seem worth far less to me now. But now, none of that matters."

She paused, looked at me, then turned away. There was a long, awkward moment before she said, her back still turned to me: "We let the last of our servants go today. We'll be selling the house."

I moved to comfort her, but she turned and intercepted me, pushing me away.

"It's okay. It really is. Father has a new place — not in such a nice neighborhood, but..."

"But not in the Warrens," I said.

"You know I wasn't thinking that."

"Maybe not exactly that. But you're grateful you won't be living in a slum."

"And why shouldn't I? Wouldn't you feel the same?"

"I'm sorry, it's just force of habit. I'm used to people looking down on me."

"You of all people should know I don't look down on you," she said, stepping quickly toward me, and before I knew what had happened, she had embraced me and was passionately kissing me. I didn't think she'd ever stop; her thin fingers dug into my flesh and gripped me fiercely.

Thinking about it still made me light-headed; I was still a bit dizzy several days later. I think riding the high from that moment was what kept me from realizing until we rolled into Agellos that I might have seen my home for the last time in my life.

I don't know how many of you long-beards have been to Solta, but I'm betting that nearly all of you have been to Agellos. Still, I think I ought to tell you what it felt like through my eyes, both for any of you who haven't been there and for any who might be curious about how I felt when I first saw it.

Coming into the city for the first time isn't anything dramatic, because there's no hills or anything to give you a view — all the land for miles around is just flat. I remember it was shortly before midday when we first rolled up to the city wall.

It was a bit confusing at first, because the caravan rolled up to this gatehouse that was in the middle of an endless pine-scrub forest in what seemed like the middle of nowhere. Because everything was flat, all you could see in any direction was endless stands of pine scrub, interrupted by the occasional marsh or lake. So when the caravan drew up to this gatehouse, my first thought was that it might be some isolated frontier fort, maybe a sentinel outpost for the main city. It was only as we got closer that I saw that it was part of a wall that extended far out to either side.

Because our caravan was a special express that came direct from Solta, getting approval from the guards didn't take very long. Soldiers went up and down the row of ox trolleys doing spot checks, carefully studied the caravan boss's papers, then waved us through. The whole process took maybe a half-hour.

And that was my introduction to the famed walls of Agellos, supposedly the longest city wall east of the Striped Mountains. Truthfully, it didn't seem very impressive, at least what I saw of it, because the gatehouse was far outside the city and what I saw of the walls disappeared into the endless scrub pines.

"Is that really it?" I asked a traveling companion. Betca was a dwarf who was coming to Agellos to help his cousin, whose foundry was overwhelmed with work in preparation for the invasion. "I always thought it would be — you know, a lot more impressive."

"It does the job," he told me. "All the land around is flat, so there's no need to make it that high — just make it really, really long. Now the walls of Murak, that's something you should see..."

I took another look at the wall as we passed through the gatehouse and trundled on into more endless pine scrub. "Why does it look so funny?" I asked Betca.

"It's the way it's made," he said. "You're from Solta — there's plenty of stone quarries around there, so they can build walls out of stone. But here, there's not much stone to be found. If you want to build a wall, you have to build it out of concrete. You know what concrete is, don't you?"

I told him I did — some of the newer parts of the palace back in Solta were built from it.

"But that doesn't look like any concrete I've ever seen," I said.

"That's because it's mixed with shells and pebbles from the seashore. It's not as strong, but it's strong enough, and it's much cheaper — the kind you know from back in Solta is made with ash."

After we'd passed the wall, we traveled through miles of empty scrub forest before we started seeing some buildings. At first, they were all spread out — it looked like we might be coming into a small village. I noticed that the trees rapidly thinned out, and most of the first buildings we saw seemed to be wood mills of various kinds, gradually eating their way into the vast forests that surrounded the city.

The more we traveled, the more buildings there were — lumber mills gave way to turpentine mills and paper mills, which gave way to normal businesses and houses that slowly grew denser until they were all packed close together, like a proper city. Still, it was hard to get a sense of the sheer size of the place, because of the flat terrain. I noticed that all the buildings were at least two stories, with most having three stories and many rising to four and five, or even more.

"Flooding can be real bad here during storm season," Betca explained. "In the case of flooding, people will haul everything important up to the second or third floors until the waters recede."

It wasn't until I reached the actual coastline that I was able to appreciate the size of Agellos. All my life, I'd heard that it was the largest city in the east — six or seven or even ten times the size of Solta, depending on who you asked. When our caravan finally came to halt in a large cargo transfer station, we were within sight of the water, but it was still some distance away.

I still had several hours until I had to report for duty, so as soon as I grabbed my gear I headed out towards the ocean. I walked out onto a long dock and looked back at the land — on either side, stretching to the north and south, there were nothing but buildings as far as the eye could see.

To the south, I saw a spire that rose high above everything else, which I immediately recognized: The famous Sailors' Chapel of Agellos. The pictures and paintings I'd seen scarcely did it justice. It was much, much larger than the Sailor's Chapel I'd known back in Solta. In sheer size, it rivaled the main Temple back in Solta — which wasn't surprising, as it had been built to honor the men who, more than any others, were responsible for the city's great wealth.

The scale of those men's contribution became obvious once my attention turned to the ships in the vast harbor. By Auld Father, the ships! There were more ships there than I'd ever seen in one place in my entire life, even when they filled the harbor of Solta during the week of King's Day. Most of the ones I saw nearby were fishing or cargo vessels, but farther north, there were hundreds of warships of every type I'd ever heard of — many of strange design.

I was still staring dumbfounded at all this when I heard a piercing screech, and turned to see a flight of hawk cavalry soaring in low from out over the ocean. They were close enough that I could see their riders as they came near. I waved to the lead rider, not sure if he'd even notice me, but to my surprise he made a Raider hand signal — we usually tell non-Raiders it means "OK," but every true Raider knows it means "fuck yeah." I saw as he flew directly overhead that he was dressed in Raider colors.

I scanned the rest of the sky and saw dozens more flights of hawk cavalry, some just dots in the far distance — only their tight formations set them apart from flocks of seabirds.

I remembered that back in the Blue Wood, Parsa had drawn a hawk cavalry posting. Of the 12 guys in our old platoon who'd requested it, including me, he'd been one of only two to get tapped for it. Prof said it was probably because he already had a background working with animals on a farm.

I wondered for a second if he might be out there in one of those formations, but then realized that as a greenie like me, they were probably still teaching him which end of a hawk was which. I chuckled at the thought. I could just see his temper building as some smart-ass lectured him on making sure the beak was in front.

Looking around at everything, it seemed like we were invincible. It was, as everyone kept saying, the most massive armada in the history of the world. What sorcery of the Arcanter could possibly stand up to all of this?

71

The only instructions I had were to report to "the military district." The people I stopped to ask for directions all just told me to head north.

After walking for a couple of miles, I came to an entire section of the city surrounded by an imposing fence. The fence sported a number of warning signs promising untold tortures to anyone trying to break through. I followed the fence until I came to a gate manned by some surly-looking guards.

"Private Lashan Pearl, reporting for duty!" I told the guard, showing him my assignment ticket.

He barely glanced at it, then looked at me with disgust.

"New arrivals have to go through Gate 1. It's two miles down that way," he droned, as if he'd said it a thousand times already. He pointed further west down the fence line.

I looked at the gate I was standing at. There was no indication of a number.

"How will I know I'm at the right gate?" I asked.

"Just keep going. You'll know." He turned away from me and shuffled back to his post.

I followed the fence west. I came to another gate that looked exactly like the first one. I checked my watch — I was cutting it close. Not wanting to risk this one, I picked up my pace and kept heading down the fence until I came to a much larger gate with two lanes of traffic — one going in, and the other going out. It had a rough-hewn archway passing over both lanes painted with the words "Camp Driftwood." Below that was scrawled the words "next stop Garlund — no pussy for 5,577 miles!"

I figured this was the right place.

There was a line of carts and people waiting to be admitted through the gate. I tried heading to the front to let the guards know that I was a new arrival and was in a hurry, but they just told me to get in line with the others. I shuffled my way to the back; it took over an hour until the guards got to me. By the time I reached the gate, I was already incredibly late.

"Name," a guard holding a sheaf of papers said, without looking at me.

"Private Lashan Pearl, reporting for duty," I said. I held out my assignment ticket.

The guard looked up and studied it for a brief moment, then went back to the sheaf of papers.

"You're clear. Raiders report to sector 8-L."

"Where is sector..."

"Move," he snapped. "You're holding up the line!"

I hurried inside and decided to follow along with where most of the rest of the people seemed to be headed. We were on what obviously used to be a normal commercial street that had been taken over by the military. You could see where signs for various military units had been nailed over the signs of the original buildings.

Although a few buildings were made from the funny concrete I'd seen, most were made of wood. The wood was weather-beaten and sagging — I later learned that "Camp Driftwood" had originally just been "Driftwood" — or "the Drift," to locals. It had been the old slums of Agellos — their version of the Warrens. With the coming of the invasion, the decision had been made to eject all the residents and turn the whole area into a military district. Auld Father knows none of the respectable parts of the city were going to surrender their homes and businesses for the war effort, and the slumlords who owned much of the property saw an opportunity to sell off their holdings for a big profit.

After a few blocks, the crowd emptied out into something like a main square. At the far end, I saw an enormous wooden board which was covered with hundreds of signs. I made my way over to it and found what I guess you'd call the camp bulletin board. The whole thing was covered with a bewildering mess of orders, proclamations, advertisements, notices, newsletters, and even jokes and lewd pictures. I found one large wooden sheet on which was painted a map of Camp Driftwood.

It wasn't a very good map, as I'd eventually find out, but it was good enough that anybody new to the camp could use it to find where they were going. I located "sector 8-L," which was in the northeastern part of the camp, memorized the directions as best I could, and hurried off to report for duty. At that point, I was over an hour late, so I was preparing myself for the ass-chewing to end all ass-chewings.

To get to Sector 8-L, you had to keep going north until the buildings started to thin out, giving way to endless rows of tents. As the buildings started to disappear, I noticed that the ground beneath me changed from sandy soil to just plain sand.

I finally came to a small gate labeled "8-L," with two bored-looking guards. I showed them my assignment ticket, and they told me to go to the mess tent in section C.

"Where is section..."

"Just keep moving," the guard told me. "You'll find it."

I shrugged and went in. I was in no hurry to face the inevitable wrath of who-ever I was reporting to.

I found another bulletin board, this one much smaller than the first one. Among the many postings, I found a new one that said "One One Five Reunion! Here tonight at 7:30! (RAIDER DRESS UNIFORM — INCLUDING SWORDS! — PLEASE!)"

The last bit threw me off, but as late as I was, I figured there was no way I'd make it, so I picked up a pencil tied to the board and scrawled — "can't make it, but I'm here — Lash." I found directions on the board to section C and headed off to meet my doom.

The mess tent in section C wasn't hard to find — it was by far the largest tent in that area. I straightened up and marched inside, expecting to meet a sergeant with veins and eyeballs about to pop with rage.

Instead, I found a lot of guys lounging around. Some were snoring. There was a sergeant there — even if you couldn't read his insignia, it was obvious from his bulging muscles. But he wasn't screaming.

He was leaning back in his chair, reading a book — the writing was in some language I didn't recognize, and he was silently whispering phrases over and over. His thinning hair was streaked with gray, and he wore a pair of reading spectacles.

He looked up at me.

"Nine Nine Three?" he said.

"Um...what?"

"Your assignment ticket," he said, casually getting up and approaching me. "Does it say Nine Nine Three?"

I showed it to him. He studied it.

"Oh, good, you're the mage we're missing. I was wondering when you'd get here. Go take a load off with the other guys. Lieutenant will be here eventually."

He picked his book up, paused, then checked his watch and looked up at me again. "Oh, yeah, don't worry about being late today. This isn't the Wood. We got-ta deal with a bunch of paper-pushing dickwads here, so we're a little looser."

I blinked, then he flexed his muscles and cracked his neck. "Just don't be late to muster. Ever. We might be a little looser here, but we're still fucking Raiders. Don't forget it."

That was my introduction to Sgt. Ergin.

I went and introduced myself to the other guys. Nearly all of them were recent grads, though one guy, a huge bastard, had already been in the Raiders for more than a year.

One of the guys who was snoozing turned out to be Fent — the guy from the Warrens who'd been just ahead of me at the Wood. About an hour after I reported in, Wym showed up. There were a couple of other guys I recognized from Three One Five, and one I recognized from Two One Five — he looked at me and Wym in disgust. Wym immediately confronted him.

"You got a fucking problem?" Wym asked. The guy was a dwarf; even though Wym was short by human standards, this guy's head barely reached the bottom of Wym's neck. "You still sore about us thumping your cheating asses back at the Wood?"

I stepped in to try to defuse things.

"Hey, man, don't worry about Wym." I looked down at his name tag; it read "Vaanzur." It sounded like a name from among the ice dwarves of the far south, the "savages" we'd fought in the Great War, but I didn't want to make assumptions. "He's just eager to kick some ass. Hey, Wym, save it for the Arcanter, buddy!"

Wym seemed to calm down, but still eyed his antagonist warily. I decided then that whenever we finally went into battle, I wanted Wym by my side.

"Vaanzur" still looked coiled to strike. "Hey, hey, we're on the same side here," I told him. "What's the problem?"

He was still eyeing Wym, but turned his gaze to meet mine.

"I'm Lash. Lash Pearl," I said, extending my hand. "This is Wym. Wym Clovar."

He looked down at my hand, but didn't shake it.

"Dral," he said. "Son of Duul."

"Of the…House of…" I looked quickly down at his name tag again. "…Vaanzur?"

His eyes narrowed. "That's what the name tag says. But you don't get to call me that."

"Dral it is. Where are you from, pal?"

His eyes flicked back and forth between me and Wym.

"Who the fuck cares," he said, and stalked off to the corner of the tent to brood.

I looked at Wym. "Don't even think about it," I told him.

A few more guys straggled in — enough, I noted, to form a proper platoon. It was another hour and a half before Sgt. Ergin suddenly stood ramrod straight and barked "Officer on the floor! Huhteeeeen-CHUN!" Every single man, including the guys who were apparently asleep, popped right up and stood at attention.

The man who entered the tent looked a few years older than me, but his tired eyes looked a decade older. He was about medium height, but he looked much smaller because of his thin face and gangly frame. His hair was brownish and mussed, and he looked like he hadn't slept in days.

"At ease," he said. "Thank you, Sgt. Ergin. Is everyone here?"

"Platoon Nine Nine Three is now at full strength, all accounted for," Sgt. Ergin said.

The new man, who sported a lieutenant's insignia, looked at Sgt. Ergin with surprise.

"The stump humpers actually delivered everyone, did they? I was expecting a few stragglers," he said. Then he turned to us. "I'm Lt. Kretek, and this is Sector 8-L of Camp Driftwood. This isn't the Wood, so you guys don't have to walk around on pins and needles. Just stay clean and do what you're told and do it quick, like a bunch of A-1 fucking Raiders, and you'll be okay. We don't smoke anybody here — we haven't got time for that shit — but if you are a consistent fuck up you'll end up in the brig. And trust me, you don't want that.

"Here's the schedule: Starting tomorrow, you'll report to utility training — Sgt. Ergin will tell you where to go. I don't want any bitching about what you're assigned — we need tailors and clerks as much as we need livestock wranglers and armorers. You're all doing your part. Of course, you mages will be off learning your hocus-pocus shit."

He said the last part with a smile, which gave everyone room to laugh.

"The day after that," he said, "you'll report to me, and we'll start invasion prep. That's when you'll learn how to actually put your skills to use on a battlefield. From now until we sail out, you'll alternate days — utility one day, invasion prep the next, and so on. You'll have Sevenday off — though I expect every one of you to show up for chapel like proper Raiders."

There was a long pause as he looked back and forth at us.

"You will also be at liberty every Sixeve — *at my discretion.*" He gave that last part heavy emphasis. "Don't think it's automatic. We will train right through the night if I think it's necessary. So take this shit seriously."

He turned to Sgt. Ergin.

"The sergeant will show you to your quarters. Once you've gotten your gear stowed to his satisfaction, you're at liberty for the evening. Just remember: Muster is at 7 tomorrow, and you'd better be clean and fucking mean. You're Raiders — act like it. That's all."

He turned and left. From the look on his face, it seemed like it would be several more days before he got to sleep.

Sgt. Ergin marched us over to the quartermaster's tent, where they outfitted us with the gear we'd need for the invasion — swords, armor, and everything else. To my great relief, it was all brand new — nothing like the worn out, sweaty-smelling gear we'd had back at the Wood.

Then we got our assignments. As if Auld Father wanted to torture me, Wym and Dral were my squadmates. When Sarge brought us to our tent, I made sure to take the bunk between them.

Luckily, our squad leader was much easier to get along with. Corporal Hust Q'amim — "call me Wheels," he said; "don't give me that corporal shit" — was easily seven feet tall — I'm pretty sure he was the tallest Raider I ever saw. Despite his height, he was lean — though in uniform, his looks were deceiving. When he stripped off his shirt, his thin frame was covered in wiry muscles. The thing that caught my attention, though, was his skin — it was similar to my own. I asked him if he had Molan blood, and he laughed.

"Not a drop," he said, "though if you believe the stories, our people are related."

It turned out he was a Toman. My father was a Molan — from the islands off the eastern coast of Selva. Hust's people, the Tomans, were from the islands off the western coast of Garlund.

I'd read about it before — supposedly, many eons ago, the Glass Ocean was much lower than it is today, and there was a chain of islands that allowed easy contact between the peoples of the eastern and western coasts. There were some who claimed the Molans and the Tomans were once a common people, though I knew that Molans of the present denied it. I didn't know what Tomans thought about that.

"What are you doing on this side of the Striped Mountains?" I asked.

He laughed. "You easterners don't know anything, do you?" he said.

He explained that over a century before, Footmen had arrived on the Toman islands preaching the truth of Auld Father. While many Tomans rejected the missionaries, preferring the sea gods of their ancestors, many had enthusiastically embraced the true faith.

"They called us 'conversos,'" he said. "If they'd only left us alone, everything would have been very different."

I dimly remembered having heard the story before, but hearing it from Wheels's lips made it vividly real to me.

"Those who clung to the worship of Gruun's fish demons were jealous of those who accepted the truth," Wheels said, "and they banded together with the worshipers of the Suzer's cat worshipers to crush us. The faithful fought bravely, but thousands were slaughtered. By the grace of Auld Father, acting through his blessed servant, the King of Selva, we were delivered."

"Yeah, the King agreed to bring you here and gave you guys...they gave you that land in Kon. It's just north of here," I said. I tried to choose my words carefully. "Beautiful country, I've heard."

Wheels gave a deep, hearty laugh. He slapped me on the shoulder. "My Molan friend, the King dumped us into a shithole swamp! Oh, do not be ashamed — our people have learned to be quite happy there! That swamp is all I've ever known — all I know of our homeland is what I hear in songs and stories!"

He saw the look on my face, and burst into another round of laughter. He took another look at me, and then doubled over again in guffaws.

"Ah, you Molan dog, don't give me that look. When we arrive with the Reckoner, you shall witness the greatest event in history, as the Tomans finally bring Auld Father's light to the blind men who once drove us out!"

72

At one minute before 7:30 that evening, me and Wym arrived in front of the 8-L bulletin board. I was sick and damn tired of wearing my dress blues and was eager to start wearing something less constricting, but I had Wym scope out my uniform before we left. He found a few stray threads on mine, which I made sure to clip off, but his looked immaculate.

I hadn't taken out my ceremonial sword since graduation; I felt a sense of reverence when I took it out of its wooden case and polished it for presentation. I had no idea why they wanted me to bring it, but I wasn't about to bring it out of its sheath in public unless it looked perfect.

When we arrived at the appointed spot, every graduate of One One Five was there — except for Skunk.

Nobody seemed to notice his absence, though. Everybody was crowded around Parsa, who had brought the dashing-looking helmet he wore as a hawk cavalryman to show off to everyone.

"Just issued it to me today!" he boasted.

"What's going on?" I asked. "Why are we all dressed up?"

Gorgeous pounded me on the back; I stiffened and pretended it didn't hurt.

"Didn't you hear, Lips?" he said. "Parsa is getting hitched tonight!"

There were several chapels sprinkled throughout Camp Driftwood, but we made our way to the largest one — it wasn't hard to find, as its spire made it the tallest building in the camp.

The ceremony itself was fairly modest. Nobody from Parsa's family was there — except for the rest of us in One One Five — and there were only about a half-dozen from the family of his bride, Dessa. When she first came into the chapel, the gasp of the crowd was sharp and powerful — the girl was absolutely stunning.

The dress she wore was nothing fancy — in fact, now that I think back on it, you might even have called it cheap. But on her, it might as well have cost a fortune

— I'm quite sure there are many wealthy girls who wouldn't have looked half as gorgeous in a dress ten times the price.

Dessa was short and slim, with a long mane of curly blonde hair. Her smile was wide and actually gave me an ache of longing — there was a promise of joy there that made me think of Kanin.

The only part that was off was her eyes. They were small and sharp — even angry, even when she smiled. I sensed that she would be a stern wife, but knowing Parsa, I'm pretty sure that's the kind of wife he wanted. I had little doubt they would be happy together.

The Footman, who wore a chaplain's uniform, gave a brief homily and conducted the wedding. As the couple left the chapel, us Raiders stood in two opposing rows at the exit and did a sword arch.

I don't know if any of you long-beards have ever seen the sword arch, at least as it's done by the Raiders, so I'll describe it. We followed tradition, putting the dwarves at the end of each row, so the couple would have to duck low to pass under their blades.

Prof was at the very end of the row on the bride's side, with Limul opposite. As the couple ducked to pass under the last few blades, Prof and Limul dropped their swords to block the couple.

Following tradition, Prof raised the tip of his blade to the bride's chin, prodding her face back and forward to get a good look at it.

"Why would a fine and fair lass such as yourself take a brute like Private Parsa?" he said, following the script.

"But I beg your pardon, kind sir; once a maid has kissed a Raider, her good sense is but petals taken away by the wind!" Dessa replied, also on script.

Then Limul spoke his words: "The maid has been warned; the Crown grants its approval."

Limul then raised his sword to Parsa's throat, and pressed the sharp end against it — the sharpened edge lightly nicked the skin, causing a tiny trickle of blood.

"Let that be a reminder of the fate that awaits any Raider who dishonors his bride!" Limul said.

It was impossible for anybody to say the next line without a smile: "Now go forth and make more Raiders, Private!" Limul said, and he dropped his sword again and pointed the tip at Parsa's crotch. "Remember that *this* is still the Property of the Crown!"

That brought a laugh from the small group — even from the chaplain. Then Prof and Limul raised their swords to allow the couple to pass under them and into their waiting carriage.

I described the whole thing in my first letter to Kanin. She wrote back that it was "a sight I should like to see in person someday."

"There is, I'll grant, something about a kiss from a Raider," she added. "With such a keen power afoot, one is surprised that the good sense of half the poor maidens of Agellos has not yet been put to full flight!"

Well, she didn't have anything to worry about on my account. But I couldn't answer for whatever my brothers in arms might be getting up to. In Agellos, opportunities abounded.

After the wedding couple had left that evening, the rest of us went out drinking. There were a dozen bars inside Camp Driftwood and probably a hundred more outside within a few blocks of the gate, but Limul swore he'd found the best one — a ramshackle old saloon called The Pirate's Prayer, which looked like something out of a Vast the Brutal story.

From the second we walked in, it was obvious we weren't in a "military" bar — the patrons all looked like locals, and they looked like a very rough crowd. Entering in full Raider dress uniforms — complete with swords — we looked as out of place as a pile of turds on the buffet at a fancy royal ball.

When we came in, every eye in the place turned to look at us suspiciously.

"Limul, are you sure about..." Prof said, but then Limul elbowed his way to the front and bellowed, "We're celebrating, boys! Next round of drinks is on me!"

The patrons roared in approval, and it quickly became apparent that Limul was already friends with everyone in the place. I just want to take this moment to say that the stories they tell about those klanger bastards are true — there's not a tavern anywhere in the world, no matter how frightening, where they aren't welcome.

As I took a place at the bar, a huge, beefy giant of a man threw his arm around me and pulled me against his bare chest, which was covered with thick, black hair.

"Any friend of Limul's," he bellowed, "is a friend of mine!"

He scuffed up my hair, and his powerful grip made it feel like my skull was about to be crushed. When he finally let me go, I had to pick strands of his chest hair out of my teeth.

I looked up at him. For some reason he had a string tied around his head with dozens and dozens of keys. You read that right — keys, like the kind you use to open a lock. He wore them around his completely bare head like a crown. Whenever I asked why that was, I was told "long story, I'll tell you later." But he never did tell me later.

At the moment, though, I saw there was a fresh, cold mug of ale already sitting in front of me, the foam pouring off the head. I picked it up and made a toast to my new friend.

Several hours later, I was sitting at the bar with Prof and Gorgeous. It was last call, and we were sipping our last mugs of ale. To my right, the Key King was passed out on the bar.

Other patrons, including a couple of Raiders, sat passed out at various tables. Over in one corner, Limul and the other patrons who were still conscious were drunkenly competing to see who could balance a Raider sword on his nose for the longest time. One of the regulars was arguing with Limul, saying his fat dwarven beak gave him an unfair advantage; Limul kept responding by making some point about the art of metalsmithing that seemed to have nothing to do with anything.

I was staring at the mirror behind the bar. I don't want to brag, but even smashed, the three of us looked pretty impressive in our dress blues.

"So how's this going to work with Parsa being married?" I asked. "Does he, I don't know — does he go live with Dessa? Do they find a room somewhere and set up house?"

"Dessa and her family are leaving day after tomorrow," Prof said. "He spends tonight and tomorrow with her, then he's back in 8-L — just another Raider like the rest of us."

I shook my head and took a long drink of ale.

"That doesn't seem right," I said. "I mean, this invasion — she could be a widow within months."

Prof shrugged. "They're in love. They've been in love since they were kids. It's what they wanted. Me, I don't know if I could do it. I don't know if I could go off to Garlund, go off to war, with something like that hanging over my head. I mean — shit, how can you focus? You go into this shit, you gotta be ready to die. How can you be ready to die if you've got a family?"

I couldn't avoid thinking about Kanin. I wondered what it would be like to be a husband — a good husband, the kind I'd never seen before. I knew those kind of men were out there.

Gorgeous let out a loud, long belch.

"Lips, you ain't got to worry about nothing," he said. "Ain't no pussy going to hitch itself to your ugly scaleback ass."

Prof spit out his ale laughing, and after a moment, Gorgeous joined in. I set my mug down and tried to look serious, but fuck if I didn't start laughing too.

There are very few people I will say this about, so don't get any ideas. But I'll say this about Gorgeous and Prof and the other shitstains in One One Five: Those fuckers had earned the right to call me a scaleback.

73

Don't. Ever. Fucking. Do. That. Again.

That's all I could think of the next morning. Waking up with a massive hangover, I'd shit/shaved/showered, gotten my bunk squared away, then followed the directions through Camp Driftwood to arrive at a tent labeled, "MR-C." I'd expected a classroom of some sort, but the inside of the tent was completely bare except for a chalkboard at one end and a large wooden box that was closed with a heavy padlock. This was Combat Mage Training, Day 1.

I was the last one to arrive; there were 20 other men in the tent when I got there, and every single one of them looked alert and alive — not a single one looked like they'd spent the night before in an alcoholic haze. When I came in the tent flap, the first guy I saw recoiled from my no-doubt-bloodshot eyes. I didn't say anything; all I could think of was the massive, throbbing pain in my head.

Everyone was gathered around the mysterious box, though they kept a respectful distance. I shuffled my way to the very back of the group. There was no point in attracting attention in my state.

I checked my watch nervously every couple of minutes. The time for the class to start came and went. I started to tense in anticipation of getting smoked for being late, until my bleary mind reminded me that I was actually on time — I'd been early, even. It was the instructor who was late.

As I was beginning to understand, the real world doesn't operate like the Blue Wood.

More than 15 minutes after the class was supposed to start, the tent flap opened. Everybody in the room quickly turned to face the new arrival. I don't know what everyone else was expecting, but I was expecting some kind of tall, distinguished-looking gray-haired man in a Raider uniform. They don't allow beards in the Raiders, of course, but I was expecting to see, well, you know — a long-bearded old wizard. But maybe without the beard.

What walked into the tent was an elf. His hair was not gray — it was green, and much, much longer than regulation. Like all elves, he was short — dwarven height — and at first glance, he looked like a human child. The pointed ears and large, oddly-shaped eyes were the only immediate giveaway. Once he drew closer, his weathered skin made it clear he was much older than anyone else present — if he'd been a human, I would have guessed him to be about 60, which meant he was probably about 120.

The other thing that stuck out was that he wasn't dressed in a Raider uniform. Elves aren't allowed in the Raiders, of course, but this elf had no military clothing whatsoever. He was clad only in a rough-fabric tunic and short breeches and a worn leather belt — he looked like most other elves I'd encountered in my life, both male and female. He was almost — I'm using a word Footman Sesh taught me, so I hope I'm using it right — a "caricature" of an elf, looking like he'd just climbed down from the trees of the Lyndan Marsh and strolled right into our camp. An elaborate elven tattoo covered his right forearm. The only thing that seemed out of place was the long wooden staff he carried, with a smooth, carved crystal set into the head, held in place by delicate-looking steel prongs.

He strode forcefully into the center of the group, perching himself on top of the locked wooden box.

"My name is Gostor," he said. "And yes, I'm an elf. And no, I'm not a Raider. Any questions?"

One guy in the front row — Private Wernar, another mage in my platoon — raised his hand. Gostor pointed at him with his staff.

"Yes?"

Wernar mumbled out a question: "Why aren't you a Raider?"

"Elves can't be Raiders," Gostor said, then bopped the private on the head with his staff. Hard. The guy doubled over and came up rubbing the top of his head.

"But I don't think that's quite what you meant," the elf continued, "and that, my friends, is the first and most important lesson of magic: Precision. You MUST..."

He bonked Wernar on the head for emphasis.

"ALWAYS..."

— bonk —

"BE..."

— bonk —

"ABSOLUTELY..."

— bonk —

"CLEAR..."

— bonk —

"WITH..."

— bonk —

"YOUR..."

— bonk —

"SPELLS!"

— bonk.

He stood, looked around us, then held out the staff again, touching it lightly on Wernar's skull, which the private was rubbing while moaning in pain.

The crystal glowed a soft green, and Wernar suddenly stopped rubbing his head and stood up.

"The pain...it just..."

"It was lifted, and it won't return — unless you injure your head again," Gostor said. "If you'd been badly wounded, the pain would eventually return — but you would have been able to fight for another hour or so before it came back. But that's another discussion!"

He quickly turned his back on the private and began pacing back and forth atop the box.

"What our subject really meant to ask...what was your name? Ah, I see your tag. What Private Wernar meant to ask was why an elf, who isn't even in the military, is instructing a bunch of buck private mages in spellcraft. This is a question above your pay grade, but because it's our first day, and I'm in a generous mood, I'll explain.

"There's a war going on, and the best combat mages are needed elsewhere. Some are preparing for the invasion, others are needed to teach skills to more advanced students.

"But somebody needs to teach those of you who will be fed first into the meat grinder, in the no-doubt-vain hope that you might learn a thing or two that will help you or your companions survive. So they've brought in outside help to introduce you to the basics."

He stopped, looked around at us, as if daring anyone to say anything. Then he continued.

"I am not a combat mage," he said. "I am what your people refer to as an elven cleric. We have a different word for it in our own tongue.

"Now you may be wondering what an elven cleric can teach any of you about being a combat mage. Well, in the first place, much of what you grunts will be doing will be warding, healing and protection spells. So this is my bailiwick.

"In the second place, I've been practicing spellcraft for more than 100 of your 'years,' as you call them. Apparently this is an impressive figure among your kind, and even among those degenerate dwarves you insist on consorting with."

I looked around to see if we had any dwarves with us — we didn't.

"The point is," Gostor continued, "that in all the time I've been working with the magical arts, I've learned more than most of you humans will ever know. I'm sure there are a few of you standing here who will one day exceed my powers. You humans are quick learners — which is good, since you never seem to stick around long. But looking at you now, I wouldn't lay odds on any of you in this room."

He let that sink in, then jumped down off the box.

"Now, let me introduce you to the tool of your trade."

He touched the tip of his staff to the lock on the wooden box, and it snapped open. Then the top swung open on its hinges, as if moved by invisible hands.

Inside were racks full of wooden staves exactly like the one in Gostor's hand — except instead of crystals, each one was mounted with an intricately carved metal ingot.

Gostor stuck his staff in the sand and produced a little notebook, and began passing out staves to each man present. He recorded the serial number on each staff, along with the name of the Raider it was assigned to. He encouraged us to swing them about and point with them and try to cast spells.

"I'm quite sure none of you will manage to hurt yourselves," he said.

When he got to me, he said, "Had some fun last night, did we private?" He didn't look up at me when he said it.

"A little, sir. A fellow private was getting married."

He shook his head.

"You humans. Always in a hurry," he sighed.

When everybody had been assigned a staff, the elf retrieved his own and pointed it at the box, which still held several unassigned staves. The doors swung shut and the lock reset itself.

We didn't learn any spells the first day. Instead, the whole day was dedicated to learning about our new weapons, along with the theory of magic.

There are some who claim anyone can learn magic with enough study — "but we have neither the time nor the resources to put that theory to the test," Gostor explained. "What is known is that certain people are naturally born with a greater facility for it."

As Gostor explained it, it has something to do with a different cast of mind — an intuitive ability to grasp ideas in multiple mystical dimensions and then manipulate them to create effects in the "real world." This ability could be tested — that was the point of the weird exam we'd all been given back in the Wood. It wasn't a test you could cheat on or pass through dumb luck — you really had to have a latent magic ability in order to pass it.

And just passing it wasn't enough — the Raiders had their own ideas about who was best cut out to be a mage, and they didn't necessarily think everybody who showed latent powers was ready to wield a staff. For those of us present, though, the Raiders had determined that we were the sort of men they trusted with magic.

"In the hands of the greatest mages," Gostor said gravely, "the mystic ways are the greatest, most terrible power the world has ever known." After a pregnant pause, he added, "I have no worries about any of you, though."

Truly understanding the mystical dimensions enough to work magical wonders took years of careful study, he explained.

"I've already seen all your files, and I don't see the makings of any future thaumaturges or even warlocks among you," he said.

As he put it, all we needed to know was that:

1. There are parts of reality you can't see;

2. You can change unseen things in a way that causes the things you can see to change;

3. We all had the power to do that.

Not completely on our own, of course — "If you could do that," he said, "you wouldn't be men — you would be gods."

And that, he said, was where the staves came in. To directly access and fully control the mystic dimensions required additional components — almost like keys, he said.

The first part was the vognon — "The common term, in your language, is 'spell.' That is the mental component which connects your mind to the mystical dimension."

But a spell alone was not sufficient. One needed an additional element — "a bridge, you might say, between the mind and the mystical dimension. That bridge is what you are holding in your hand right now — your mage's staff."

And with that, he pointed his staff back at the wooden box, which unlocked itself, then locked itself back.

"Each of your staves was crafted by an expert dwarven smith, specifically to allow you to access the mystical dimensions. The ingot — the 'telluric' component of spellcasting — is replaceable, as using magic will cause it to degrade."

"What about yours?" Private Wernar asked brightly, making sure to add in a thick dollop of sass. "Was yours made by degenerate dwarves?"

That brought a loud "ooooooooo!" from everyone else, but Gostor ignored it.

"No," he said firmly. "I made my staff and shaped its crystal with my own hands, like my forefathers before me. No dwarf has ever put his filthy fingers on it."

"But..."

"I don't have time to explain it," he snapped. "Let's just say your staves will be more than enough for what's in store."

Gostor also informed us that from there on out, we had to carry our staves with us wherever we went on base. Our staves, he explained, would replace the spears that other Raiders carried. I could only pray that whatever Gostor taught us would hold off a five-eyed wolf as well as a spear.

74

Wheels told us not to worry about the first day of invasion prep.
"It's just going to be about covering the basics," he said. I already
knew enough to know that meant trouble.

FIVE HOURS AFTER I'D rolled out of bed, I was soaking wet and it felt like I'd
inhaled enough saltwater to sprout gills.

"What in the fuck was that?" Sgt. Ergin shouted, as I pulled myself out of the
water for the umpteenth time. My muscles were already on fire from having to
move through the water in full armor.

I climbed back into the boat and asked Wheels, "Does saltwater damage our
gear?"

"Oh fuck yeah," he said with a grin. "You'll be cleaning it for a couple of hours
when we get back."

Just the basics, he'd told us.

The invasion, at least our part of it, was going to be an amphibious assault.
That meant getting everybody good and comfortable with operating in boats, in
the water. Lesson No. 1: How to get in and out of a landing boat in full armor. For
those of you long-beards who've never even worn armor, let me assure you that
however hard you might think this sounds, it's still a fuckload harder than you
can believe.

Still, having grown up along the coast, I was better off than Wym — at least I
was used to being in the water.

"Remember that day we did water training back in the Wood, man," I told him.
"They taught us that stuff for a reason."

He spat out a mouthful of seawater as I helped him climb back on board the
boat.

"I never thought I'd actually have to use that, dude," he said.

"Hey, at least you don't have to carry this," I said, waving my staff at him. I turned to Wheels. "Hey, corporal — won't saltwater destroy my staff? It's some kind of delicate handcrafted bullshit."

"You bet your ass it will," he said. "But I wouldn't worry. You'll probably be killed before that ever becomes a problem."

When we finally finished around sunset, I think we were just maybe starting to get the hang of operating in the water. Sgt. Ergin told us not to get comfortable, because they'd be feeding us a completely different bag of dicks next time.

"But Sarge, Lips loves dicks," Wym said. "That's how he got his name."

"Give him a break, he's a mage," Sarge said. "Haven't you heard that's where they get their magic powers? They get it from drinking powerful magic 'potions' from the dicks of real Raiders."

"Pity we don't have female mages," Wheels said.

SGT. ERGIN WAS NOTHING like our DCs back at the Wood. Not that he wasn't a fucking hard ass — it was just that he didn't seem to delight in torturing us every chance he got. When we fucked something up, he mainly just looked disgusted, and if we kept fucking up, he'd step in to "pull that damn head of yours out of your ass," as he put it.

At first I thought that was strange, but when I thought about it later, it actually made sense. Sgt. Sculler and Sgt. Taba were taking a bunch of nasty civilians and turning them into clean and mean Raiders. They had to torture us because they were taking everything in us that wasn't a Raider and crushing it until it stopped breathing.

By the time we got to Agellos, that process was supposed to be done. The Wood had built us into the best men it knew how. Sgt. Ergin didn't need to scream or smoke us. He just had to let us know we were letting down the Wood, letting down that big statue of Major Braborn, letting down the Raiders. That was worse than any sweatbox session he could have put us through.

What really interested me, though, was Lt. Kretek. He'd been with us the whole day, doing everything we did. It was pretty clear he had already been through this drill countless times; he effortlessly went through all the same exercises. But he barely spoke to us, except a short talk in the morning, explaining what we were doing and how it fit into the larger picture.

"The most dangerous and vulnerable part of an amphibious assault," he explained, "is the time between when you board the landing craft and when you pull onto the shore. That's when the enemy will have the easiest time hitting you, and you'll have almost no ability to hit back. Auld Father, in His infinite wisdom, neglected to supply us with fins."

Throughout the rest of the day, he spoke mainly to Sgt. Ergin, only occasionally stepping in to offer a few words of advice. As a fairly small guy himself, he'd given Wym some pointers on the best way to pull himself on board a boat.

On our way back to our tent, I'd spied a mage sporting a useful-looking back sling for his sword scabbard and stopped to ask him where I could scrounge up one.

"Fuck off, greenie," was his only reply.

Later that evening, while we were all working on cleaning our gear, Lt. Kretek came by to check up on us. He gave us a little talk about how important it was to guard against saltwater damage, and he was about to leave when I finally decided to risk asking him a question.

"Sir, I was wondering where I could get one of those back scabbards for my sword. I have to wield this staff, and having my sword hanging from my belt makes things harder." Private Wernar chimed in, seconding my complaint.

Lt. Kretek looked at us somberly.

"The back scabbards you're talking about are not official issue, and are actually discouraged by the general staff, being against regulation," he began. After he saw the discouraged look on our faces, he continued.

"It's an unfortunate fact that, because of the urgency of our mission, we have had to overlook some lapses in proper equipment procedure. Very, very unfortunate. If our situation were not so dire, I can assure you these infractions would be sternly and quickly corrected.

"Yes, it's very unfortunate that so many of our mages have found that this deviation from protocol is so useful, and — they claim — makes them more effective. So I want to make myself perfectly clear.

"I would NOT advise any of the mages under my command to adopt this unauthorized equipment, ESPECIALLY if they believe it would make them more effective. I would furthermore NOT advise them to seek out Sgt. Macsin, who can usually be found after normal hours drinking at the Rusted Anchor pub, usually on the second stool from the end, working on a bottle of Ytter's.

"I would strongly urge the mages under my command NOT to consult with Sgt. Macsin about the best way to modify a regulation scabbard, or about procuring one that's already been modified. I can assure them that if they follow this course of action, there will be severe consequences. Assuming, of course, that I ever hear about it.

"Now, if any of my mages were to show up for exercises wearing such equipment, I'm afraid there's little I could do about it at this time. But," he said, lowering his voice and adopting a threatening tone, "once the invasion has succeeded, and we've all come back from Garlund alive, it will be a very, very different story."

He stared daggers at us when he said that. Then he gave the tiniest bit of a smile, winked, and then left.

75

When we filed into the tent the next day, Gostor immediately noted the way me and Wernar had our swords slung on our backs.

"Nice back scabbards," he said. He pointed them out to the rest of the assembled group.

"The rest of you might want to look into getting those," he said. "It's not like you'll be using your swords much anyway."

Though nobody said anything, you could feel that they were about to, and Gostor headed them off.

"Yeah, I know what your damn regulations say. Follow them if you want. I'm just telling you what I think. But I'm sure my experience is nothing compared to the wisdom of the Raider general staff," he sneered.

While he was saying that, I noticed Gostor's forearm. Since he'd already singled me out, I figured what the hell and spoke up: "Hey...sir."

"You don't have don't have to sir me. Gostor is fine. I'm not in your blasted Raiders."

"Sir...I mean Mister, um, Gostor...the tattoo on your forearm — it's changed. The other day it showed a fish, didn't it?"

He held up his arm for everyone to see. The tattoo there clearly showed a bird. Before our eyes, we watched the lines move and join and split and reform themselves into the stylized picture of the fish I remembered from the day before.

"You mean like this?" he said. There were several audible gasps, but others cheered and whooped.

Gostor rolled his eyes. "Look," he said, "I'm only going to go over this once, because I know there are some of you who don't know much about elves. We elves can change our skin. It's an inborn ability. And like any other ability, it's something that gets better with practice. And I've had a lot of practice," he said. With that, his skin suddenly changed to blend in with the chalkboard he was standing in front of. When there were several gasps, something that looked like a smile of satisfaction seemed to pass over his face — what I could make out of it — but I might have been imagining that.

His skin switched back to normal — the bird image returning to his forearm, I noticed.

"We don't follow your…strange religion, either, and there are many other ways in which our races diverge. But we have enough in common that there are truths we can communicate to each other. There are valuable things I have learned from humans and even — though may the gods forgive me for saying it — *dwarves*."

The way he said "dwarves" sounded like he was spitting out a mouthful of rancid food.

There was a long pause as he eyed us all gravely.

"But I'm quite confident there's nothing I can learn from any of you," he finally said. "So shut your mouths and open your ears, and maybe you won't all end up being slaughtered."

After exhaustively reviewing the previous lesson — Gostor was big on repetition; he'd have made a fine DC back at the Wood — our instructor suddenly announced that we'd be casting our first spell.

Some moron pointed his staff at a buddy and whispered "FOOOOM!" Gostor, who had his back turned, whipped around and glared at the assembled pupils.

"Oh, don't be mistaken. If any of you think I'm about to show any of you how to do a fireball or a lightning bolt spell, you might as well go back to those ridiculous 'stories' you humans like to 'read' — as if a story could ever be captured in ink!

"Let me lay this out for all of you as simply as possible: You're here mainly to learn how to keep your comrades from being massacred. That will be your chief task as a novice battlemage. If you can learn to do that without screwing up, then, and only then, will I give you some insight into…more antagonistic uses of the mystical dimensions."

That didn't particularly bother me, but I noticed that several of the guys around me looked kind of disappointed.

The first spell we were to learn, Gostor said, was "deflection."

"Battles are won with swords, axes, maces, warhammers," Gostor explained. "Success is always — always — rooted in one thing: Boots on the ground. So the very first thing an enemy will try to do is stop your boots from ever getting close to his ground."

Gostor was at the back of the tent when he said that, and he punctuated it by suddenly producing a dagger and sending it flying into the blackboard. It happened so fast that the first thing I noticed was the quivering blade which suddenly appeared stuck in the blackboard; it took me an awkward moment to make the connection between that sudden sight and the instructor standing in the back of the room.

When I finally put it together, I realized with a chill that the blade had passed just inches above my head. If Gostor had been off only a few finger-widths, I could have been dead without ever having realized what was going on.

"That," Gostor said, pointing across the tent at the still-quivering blade, "is what you need to learn to prevent."

In all the two-copper books I'd read, wizards always worked their spells by saying a bunch of magic words. While that method would indeed work, our instructor explained, it was rarely used in the real world.

"The problem with verbal spellcasting should be obvious. An alert and clever enemy can steal your vognon — the mental component of your spell — if he doesn't already know it. He can then use it against you. Now many times that doesn't really matter, because the vognon of many spells are widely known — some of the simplest ones are known even among laymen. But as any veteran of magical combat can tell you, there are times when it profits you to be able to cast a spell that your opponent cannot duplicate or respond to.

"There are magic users out there who will prattle on about the need for correct intonation and meter when speaking a vognon aloud, but that is mostly sloth droppings — excuse me, I believe the term among your race is 'bullshit.' It is indeed true that incredible precision is crucial in casting the highest, most powerful spells, which can only be handled by prime enchanters. But none of the spells you're learning will be anything like that. And because you never want to give an enemy the slightest advantage in any fight, we'll be dispensing with the abracadabra nonsense."

Instead of words, we'd be casting with symbols — to cast a spell, you had to visualize a series of weird symbols in your mind, in a particular sequence. It sounds strange, but once you've learned the process, it becomes as natural as speaking.

Gostor singled me out of the group to demonstrate. First, he handed me a sack of pebbles. Then he walked to the other side of the tent.

"Pull a pebble out of the bag and throw it at me," he said.

Not sure if I fully understood his instruction, I limply tossed a pebble at him. It fell well short of where he was standing.

"I said throw it *at* me," he said. I pulled another stone from the pouch and tossed it somewhat closer, but it still fell short.

"I SAID AT ME, YOU SON OF A SOLTAN WHORE," Gostor bellowed, his voice dropping much lower than seemed possible for such a small body.

I paused for a second, feeling chills of rage pulse through my body — which is no doubt exactly what he intended. I pulled out a pebble and flung it right at his smirking face, thinking I'd surely break at least one of his frail little elven bones.

But Gostor just pointed his staff at the rock as it sailed through the air, and it curved harmlessly off to the side, smacking into the side of the tent.

"Good. Again, you piece of Warrens vomit."

I hurled another rock. This time I really was trying to hurt him, but again he pointed his staff and effortlessly directed the rock off to the side.

"Again!" he barked, and I threw another stone, then another, and another. After less than a minute, I was pulling handfuls of rocks out of the bag and hurling them at Gostor as hard as I could, and the damn elf simply flicked them all aside in midair with his staff, as if he might have been waving away specks of dust.

After that demonstration, he walked over to a display board at the side of the tent that was covered with a sheet. He pulled the sheet away, revealing the rebus — the series of symbols — necessary to work a simple deflection spell.

"Memorize it well," he said.

As I said, it took a bit of getting used to at first. The symbols were very simple (the more complex the design, the harder to memorize, and thus the more powerful, Gostor explained), but the task of mentally invoking them, one after the other, in the correct order, was a strange feeling. I know nothing of music myself, but other mages who are musically inclined tell me that when they were first learning to cast spells with symbols, it felt like a skilled musician trying to learn a new and unfamiliar instrument. You know, in theory, how it's supposed to work, but actually making yourself do it is a different matter.

I'll never forget the first time I actually got it to work. I was paired with Wernar; he had a sack of pebbles, and he was tossing them to me to deflect. He'd already thrown more than a dozen, and every time I tried to move one in midair, it just kept sailing straight at me, and I kept having to step out of the way.

I was beginning to get tired, but my frustration was at a boiling point. I told Wernar to throw another one, and — how do I explain it? I mentally ran through the rebus, and for some reason the mental pictures were razor sharp this time. And then to my astonishment, I saw the pebble curving off to the side — I could even control the arc of its flight by moving my staff. It was incredible. I immediately told Wernar to toss another pebble at me, and I managed to do it again — not quite as precisely this time, but good enough.

I'd done it. I'd finally gotten it — I had worked an actual, by-Auld-Father's-Fucking-Foot spell.

I watched as the pebble I'd deflected plopped into the sand, close to where I'd pointed with my staff.

"Excellent," I heard Gostor say. "I was wondering when you'd finally catch up, Private Pearl." I looked around the practice yard and saw that every other mage was already well on their way to honing their newfound skill — I was literally the last one to figure it out.

A single point. I'd failed the exam back at the Wood by just one point. But Sgt. Sculler thought there was enough there to work with to put me in with these guys. It was gratifying to learn he wasn't completely wrong — whatever magic ability is, I had enough to keep up. I'd just have to work twice as hard at it as everyone else.

I smiled at that thought. For Lashan Pearl, that would be a piece of cake.

76

Honestly, the next three months were a giant blur. The two things I remember most clearly are being drenched in seawater and endless, endless repetitions of a handful of spells until they were forever burned into the lining of my skull.

Oh, and the potions. By His Foot, the potions. But I'll get to that later. The thing that I remember most clearly is the spells.

Take that deflection spell, for instance. After a few hours, I thought I'd managed to get pretty good at it.

Nope. For one, I learned that there are multiple types of deflection spells. Some work on projectiles; others work against other spells. Then there are counter-deflection spells, and counter-counter-deflection spells, and so on, apparently — though mercifully we didn't have to go too far down that rabbit hole.

But the most important thing about learning spells is really *learning* them.

"It's not enough to know a spell," Gostor barked at us. "Anybody with magic talent and a telluric charm can work a spell. In a battle, your spellcasting has to be sharpened down to the point where it's a reflex — before you even know you're casting a spell, you should be almost done casting it."

I understood what he was saying, of course — every Raider did; it was why, first thing after waking up each morning, every last one of us automatically made up our bunks to Blue Wood standard, even before we took a shit or wiped the crust out of our eyes. I understood it, yes, but that blasted elf made us live it.

"The difference between a master and a dabbler," Gostor explained, "is that a dabbler practices his art until he knows how to do it perfectly, then stops. A master practices until he no longer even remembers how to do it wrong."

So once we'd "perfected" the basics of spellcasting, Gostor's teaching was all about drill, drill, drill and more drill. And when you were done with that, there was more drill. Break time only meant drilling with something different. I'm not joking — even during the half-hour we had for lunch, we still had to practice casting while we were eating our meals.

On days when Gostor had us, the only time we weren't casting spells was when we went to use the latrine. And even then, you found yourself reflexively trying to use deflection spells to help aim the stream of your piss, until you realized you weren't holding your staff — you were holding your dick.

I don't think I was the first or the last mage private who secretly wondered about using his mage staff in the latrine. I'm quite sure more than a few have probably tried it.

By the end, I was starting to see spell rebuses in my sleep. It got to the point where I knew to wake up because my sleep-soaked mind was sending me an endless reel of spell rebuses, one after the other — some which I recognized, and some which I'd never seen but seemed to follow some strange logic. I'm told that's sometimes how prime enchanters actually stumble upon new spells — by seeing them flash across their dreams that way, after countless hours of study.

Auld Father be praised that my staff wasn't in reach when that happened to me. I mean, you know how fucked-up dreams are. Who knows what I might have accidentally done to myself or my comrades.

I mentioned the potions — that was the other thing we learned with Gostor. One of the duties of a combat mage is to serve as a medic. Normally, that involves nothing more than a few healing spells — the idea is to either give your man the ability to keep on fighting, or keep him alive until a real doctor could see him.

But spells aren't always the best battlefield treatment — for one thing, you might lose your mage staff and not be able to work any spells. So we had to learn the basics of binding wounds and setting bones, along with mixing potions, elixirs and unguents. We'd be able to carry a few pre-prepared vials with us, but those could quickly run out. So a lot of times, we'd have to be mixing our own from what materials we could find.

It doesn't sound like that would be very hard — I mean, how does it always go in the stories? Wing of kobold, eye of fairyworm? You just put them in a cauldron and stir, right?

Well, I'm here to tell you, it's a lot harder than that. For a lot of potions, you have to get the amounts exactly right, and preparing them isn't just a matter of throwing them into a pot and stirring them together. Gostor compared it to a chef preparing a meal — and that's immediately a mark against me, because I couldn't cook for shit. Aunt Rossie had tried to teach me a few times back at the rooming house, but I always ended up ruining whatever recipe she set me to make.

Luckily, Gostor was apparently accustomed to teaching lunk-headed Raiders, who wouldn't know their way around a cooking area even if it was part of the Raider Hand Book. He patiently took us through the basics of potion preparation. Distillation, steeping, fermenting, stewing, milling, assaying, dissolving, diluting, concentrating, thickening, thinning, drying, soaking, flaking, congealing — it was dull, dull work, but Gostor made you do it over and over again until you got it right.

It was frustrating, because you usually couldn't tell by sight or smell if you were doing it right. You only knew if you'd pulled it off when you were finished and Gostor came by and dropped some grains of powder or poured some liquid into your concoction and it changed the right color.

I grew to hate potion work, though I'm told there are some among you long-bearded scholars who can't get enough of it. I've heard there are men and even women who will spend days or weeks trying to perfect some concoction. But I dreaded every day that blasted elf had us in the lab. At least with spellcraft, you can see the results immediately. I'll take a hundred days on a battlefield to avoid just a single day having to whip up some damned draught of soothing.

WHEN I WASN'T MESSING around with spells or potions, though, I was out on the ocean with my unit, getting soaking, coughing, sputtering, choking wet…and cold. Those three months happened to be during the winter. Granted, Agellos has pretty mild winters, but if you're spending eight to 10 hours battling the waves in a small, leaky landing boat, constantly soaked in cold seawater, "mild" doesn't mean much. I could only thank Auld Father that we had warm campfires and hot showers to look forward to back at camp.

We practiced with landing boats in every conceivable condition — rain and shine, night and day. Calm water or crashing, tumbling waves.

You had to get in them, get out of them, launch them and land them in full armor. There were endless hours of rowing. We had to learn to board the landing boats from land, board them from troop-carrying ships, or board them while you were flailing about in the water. We had to learn to move from one landing boat to another while on the water. We had to learn to operate landing boats that were heavily overloaded with men and supplies.

And you were always wet. Even though I'd grown up by the ocean, I was quickly getting good and damn sick of it. I was at the point where I was ready to storm onto the shore of Garlund and go kill the Arcanter himself with my bare hands just so I'd never have to climb into another landing boat for the rest of my life.

Kanin was fascinated by the tools we were using to coordinate the assault. When you're trying to wrangle thousands of men across a large area, you have to fall back on the basics — sound, color and light. On a regular battlefield, that meant bugles, flags and lanterns. No fancy courier gulls or magic mind-messaging for the grunts.

But for this operation, everything had been scaled up, with massive, ship-borne horns and huge signal barges which could send up columns of dyed smoke during the day and used powerful mounted lighthouse beacons at night. Kanin thought it sounded like an immensely exciting spectacle. "Great, rolling clouds of smoke in red, green or who knows what other colors! Horns as loud as thunderclaps! The pageantry sounds more exciting than any King's Day here in the capital!"

I told her it *was* exciting, but it brought wails of protest from locals. Lord General Cullven, the architect of the invasion, was said to spend much of his mornings hearing a stream of complaints from the civilian leaders of the city. When soldiers and sailors weren't corrupting the morals of the fair maidens of Agellos, we were frightening children and livestock. But General Cullven only needed to remind the locals of their ever-swelling coffers and coin-purses, for which they had us grunts to thank.

I'll say this, though: Grunts talk a lot of shit about their officers, and a lot of it is true. But through all of those wet and endless days, Lt. Kretek was right there with us the whole time.

"I know this seems like a cruel joke," he once said, right before we were about to launch out onto a foaming, wind-whipped sea for what felt like the 7,000th time in a row, "but you gotta remember — when we hit the shore in Garlund, we've got just one chance to get this right. If there's anything we're likely to fuck up, it's best to find it out now — not then. Let's get it so that when we set foot in Garlund, we're wearing boots with five full fathoms of fuck you."

And when we cheered him for that, he didn't smile or nod or take a moment to enjoy it. He just climbed right back in that boat with us to do it all again.

THERE WAS ONE THING that bothered me, though. Although we spent endless hours and days practicing landings, we didn't spend a lot of time on what we'd do once we reached dry land.

"We're the greenies," Wheels said. "They expect us to go and die so our corpses can pave the road that the vets will ride over on their way to victory."

I must have made a face, because when he looked at me, he let out another of his loud guffaws. "Hey, cheer up, man. Think of *all the pussy* those guys are gonna get when this is over!" He slapped me hard on the back like a big brother. "Just think: WE are the ones who'll make that possible! They'll be so grateful, they might even show up for the memorial parade for a couple of years before they forget we ever existed."

"That better be some really good pussy," I said.

"Trust me, hoss — it will be the best you'll never have!"

I left that part out of the letters I wrote to Kanin.

77

On nights we had off, I mostly hung with the guys from my platoon. At first it was just because I wanted to keep an eye on Wym — I didn't want him to getting into it with Dral. I figured one way to redirect their hostility was to teach them to play cards.

Helpfully, Lt. Kretek had a standing rule that there was to be no gambling — between members of the platoon, at any rate.

"If you want to lose your money to somebody from some other outfit, I'm not going to stop you," he said. "The only rule I have is: DON'T CHEAT. You don't get to soil the name of my platoon."

"What if somebody cheats us?" I asked.

"If it's another Raider, you tell me. I'll deal with it."

Since there was no money on the line, we used seashells — there was no shortage of those in Agellos. Luckily, Wym and Dral quickly became enthusiastic players, and most evenings found them hunched over the table in our squad tent playing Cooper's Crown. Bonding over cards seemed to take the steam out of their rivalry, but there were occasional hiccups. I remember one night Dral wanted to switch things up and play a dwarven version of Cooper's Crown called Farrier's Fork.

I knew about Farrier's Fork, and told Dral I didn't think it was such a great idea.

"Humans — always looking out for your own," he snorted. "Afraid your boy here can't handle a more aggressive game?"

Farrier's Fork did indeed have a faster pace, and didn't reward hesitation. I could see why dwarves would prefer it. Dral probably thought he'd have an edge. But Wym wasn't about to shrink from a challenge.

My fellow One One Fiver did indeed lose the first dozen or so games. But once he managed to absorb some of the subtleties of the rules, his play rapidly improved. If there was one thing Wym had in abundance, it was boldness — some might have even called it foolhardiness. And that's exactly what it took to prevail at Farrier's Fork.

One evening a few days after Dral had introduced the game, I was sitting on my bunk reading a letter from Kanin when I suddenly noticed things had grown very quiet. I looked over at the table and saw a huge pile of shells on Wym's side, and only a handful on the table in front of Dral.

Dral was turning a deep shade of red — a giveaway that he was about to burst with rage. I quickly got up and moved closer, ready to jump in.

"Everything cool over here, guys?" I asked.

Dral didn't look at me — he just stared at the cards on the table. He looked at the cards Wym had revealed, then back at his own.

"Might I suggest," he said calmly, "that we go back to playing Cooper's Crown?"

THE GANG FROM ONE One Five still managed to get together, though — Prof would cook up some crazy scheme for our rare days off and post a notice about it on the 8-L bulletin board, and everybody who hadn't drawn extra duty would show up.

One time Prof got word of a particular beach nearby where the waves were supposed to be really impressive, so he came up with the idea of everyone from One One Five going out there so Gorgeous could teach us how to surf. As far as I knew, nobody in Agellos had ever even heard of surfing, so I was surprised when I showed up at the gate after chapel on a bright and sunny Sevenday and Prof produced five of what he swore were authentic Lyndan Coast surfboards.

Then Gorgeous showed up toting his own board.

"How in the name of Gruun's asshole did you convince them to let you bring that in here?" I asked.

Gorgeous broke out in a wide grin. "When I showed up here with my board, Sarge was tearing my fucking head off about it, but then, Major Lowey, the battalion commander, just happened to be stopping by to check on things. And it turns out Maj. Lowey's a surfhead from Lyndan just like me, and he told Sarge that it was cool. Dude even brought me into his command tent one day to show me his board. He's as pumped to ride those waves over in Garlund as I am."

He turned to look at the boards Prof had brought, examining them skeptically.

"Well, the wood is right. They're not really that great — too heavy, and the shape is weird. They look like they'll be pretty stable, though — good for beginners."

He showed off his own board. It sported a stylized picture of a Raider helmet and crossed swords, painted in the colors of our standard from back in the Blue Wood. The words "One One Five" were written above the design in menacing-looking letters; underneath was written "Kings of the Ring."

"Painted it myself just the other week," he said proudly.

The beach itself was on the far north of Agellos, just beyond the shipbuilding district. On our way there, in between our teasing him about life as a married man, Parsa entertained us with stories of hawk cavalry training. He was flying regular missions now, but he still had a ways to go before he'd be fully ready for combat.

"Two days from now, I'll be doing my first ship mission," he explained. "I'll have to fly out and land aboard a ship that's underway, then stow Dessie — she's my mount; I named her after my wife — below decks, spend the night, then rig her up and fly back the next morning."

"Cavalry hawks on a boat? What's the point?" I asked.

"That's how we're getting them across the ocean. They don't have enough range to fly there. They've got special aviary ships rigged up that can hold two entire flights below deck."

"Will the hawks even stand for that? I mean, being cooped up like that?"

"The females will. That's why only females can be used as mounts — they're the only ones who can be successfully tamed. The males are a lot bigger and stronger, but they're impossible to control — shame, because they'd be awesome in combat. Anyway, the ladies will still get regular flights for training and exercise once we're underway at sea. They'll be in a lot better shape than the horses we're bringing, that's for sure."

When we finally got to the beach, I wasn't sure how Gorgeous would react — I'd seen much bigger waves back home, but I don't know what surfers are looking for.

But Gorgeous was happy with it. "Shit, Prof, you done good," he said as he stood on a rise, looking out at white foam of the crashing waves that interrupted the dark blue of the ocean's surface. "I didn't think it was possible to find waves like this around here."

Prof pointed out the newly-constructed seawall that had been built for the shipbuilding district.

"I think it's somehow funneling waves toward this stretch of coast, and strengthening them. It's an accident."

"A happy one," Gorgeous said.

Most of the guys gave the surfing thing a few tries and then found something else to do. A bunch of local kids — including several girls — showed up around mid-afternoon, and that ended up drawing most of the attention. As the sun was dropping towards the horizon, the only ones who were still out there on the water were me, Gorgeous, and Limul.

You wouldn't think a dwarf would be much for surfing, since a lot of them are scared to even ride in boats. But for whatever reason, Limul took to surfing like a fish to water — I don't think I'd ever seen the little bastard have so much fun.

"By His Foot, that's a rush!" he exclaimed after wiping out from a huge wave. "Did you see that? Did you see how long I held on in that barrel?"

"Very sweet, my man," Gorgeous said. "You looked like a natural out there." Gorgeous had found a convert.

As for myself — I have no idea if my surfing did any credit to my Molan ancestors, but Gorgeous seemed pleased with it, and I enjoyed it a lot more than I thought I would. The best moment for me was right at the end, when it was starting to get dark and we were all about to head in to shore. I was looking back, and I saw what looked like a perfect wave starting to build. On a whim, I turned around and paddled out to try and catch it.

I'd had problems all day with dropping in — Gorgeous made it look so easy when he did it, and after some practice, Limul seemed to look pretty smooth, too. But every time I tried, I always felt wobbly; it always took me a few awkward moments to find my balance.

But for some reason, this time I found the wave, stood up and immediately got the balance right. I think Gorgeous called it "finding the groove." I let out a loud whoop as the wave began to curl over and I rode along it. The board felt like it was actually gliding on air — I remember thinking to myself, "this must be what birds feel like. This must be what it's like to fly." Even now, I can still look back in my memory and summon up the feeling of that moment.

When I wrote to Kanin about it later, I told her it was the most carefree moment I'd had since leaving home. I wanted to write, "It was almost like being in your arms again," but my quill wavered for a moment over the paper, and I snatched the thought back, and then switched to something else — I can't remember what.

WHEN WE WERE HEADING back through the shipyards at the end of the day, I asked Prof why all the ships they were building looked so strange. All of them had a bunch of metal equipment mounted on their decks, and they had funny-looking circular bits of metal sticking out of their sterns.

"They're steamships," he explained. "Certainly you've seen them in Solta?"

"Only a few. They didn't look like these, though. The ones I've seen didn't look like they could carry more than a few men at a time. And shouldn't they have those things on top to let out all the smoke? Don't they need coal? I haven't seen any smoke from coal burning since I got here."

"Right. These are much bigger than the steamships you've seen, but there's no way we'd ever have enough coal to power them all."

"So…doesn't a steam engine need heat?"

I couldn't pretend to understand how a steam engine worked, but I knew for sure that they needed *steam*. And I knew you needed a lot of heat to generate enough steam to power a steam engine, and I imagined you needed a lot more to power a steam engine that would push a massive ship like the ones we were walking past.

Prof looked at me in surprise. "Don't you know? I thought you were a mage."

"I don't know."

Prof shook his head and patted my arm.

"Magic, my Molan friend. They're using magic. The same magic you manipulate with your staff."

"They can...they can do that?"

"Apparently so. It has to be carefully supervised by a Master Wizard — or so I'm told — but they perfected the process a couple of years ago. After the death of the King, they started building these things as fast as they could make them. They're supposed to give us a big edge — at least that's the plan."

"How so?"

"Supposedly, they can cross the Moon Sea in about two months, give or take — about half the time it takes for most sailing ships. And that means they don't have to carry as many provisions for the crew and passengers. Which means they can carry more cargo. And more cargo opens up new possibilities."

"Such as?"

"Well, beyond carrying a lot more troops and equipment, they can mount trebuchets and catapults on them. And of course, that's how Parsa and his buddies in the hawk cavalry are getting to Garlund."

I looked around for Parsa, but didn't see him — someone said he'd had to leave early. It was right about then that Wym pointed out a place ahead with a large, colorful sign that said "The Salty Strumpet." There was a picture of a bosomy girl on the sign with a dress that seemed to just barely cover her chest.

"Hey, I've heard about that place!" he shouted. "We have to check it out!"

I eyed the place warily. Nearly all of the men going in and out were sailors — even if they weren't in uniform, those heavily-muscled arms were a dead giveaway. I wasn't sure a bunch of Raiders carrying surfboards were going to be welcomed in a navy joint.

I tried to put up a protest, but Wym was insistent, and everybody else was too distracted by the painting of the girl to listen to me. So we went on in.

After passing through a couple of curtains, we emerged into a place with a bar and a large, well-lighted stage.

Now I doubt this place is still there after all this time, so I don't think I'm putting anybody in any danger by saying this. But there were girls dancing up on that stage who didn't have a single stitch of clothes on. They were as naked as the day they were born.

I looked over at Prof. "How...how is this legal? Doesn't the Lord Mayor..."

"Oh, the Lord Mayor of Agellos just passed his 91st summer. I doubt he's much concerned with this," Prof said.

"You know what I mean. How is this allowed?"

I was pretty sure there was something in The Walk that forbade this sort of thing, even if I didn't know the exact chapter and verse. If there wasn't, well, there should be.

All the time I was thinking this, I was staring at the big, perfectly-shaped bouncing bosoms of the raven-haired dancer on the far left side of the stage. Auld Father forgive me, but I'm inclined to say it's at least partly His fault for creating a woman of such perfect proportions. Footman Sesh will say it's blasphemy, but speaking in truth, our Great Father deserves some sort of prayer of thanks for making a woman like that — I don't think I could have done as fine a job even with my own imagination. Looking at her, I felt a powerful swelling in my crotch.

Prof almost doubled over in laughter.

"Your face! If you could only see your face!" he said. "'How is this allowed?' Fuck, Lips, you are the funniest thing I've seen in weeks!"

I tried to shoot him a nasty glare, but that just made him laugh even more.

"A Warrens boy gets religion!" he said. "Oh, this is one for the history books!"

In truth, there was a time when none of this would have particularly bothered me, but I'd actually been spending a lot of time with Kanin on my mind. I had been slowly coming around to the idea of asking for her hand in marriage. I still didn't know how much longer we had until the invasion, but if we were still in Agellos in a few more months, it might be possible for me to take a week of leave. Perhaps, if I could come home to Solta, or if she could travel here...assuming she would even agree to my proposal...

My head had been filled with those thoughts lately, so being in there, in that place — it felt like I was somehow betraying her. I thought again about Parsa — the only married man from our old platoon. Would that Walk-thumping bastard have allowed himself to be talked into coming into a place like this?

And speaking of Scripture, I'd been doing a lot of thinking about that — what Prof called "getting religion." I'd even taken to reading a few pages from The Walk at the beginning of each day and right before I dropped off to sleep at night. If I was going to be a husband, didn't I need to be thinking about that? I'd spent my whole life thinking of myself, and I was starting to realize that the thing that really separates adults from children is that adults worry about the people around them, while children worry only about themselves. I could feel that fire pearl I had tucked in my pocket, and I remembered what my mom said about me being a man.

Not that thinking of others makes you a better person, of course. I was pretty sure Taygor worried a lot about other people — that's why I think he seemed so mature when I met him after coming home. I was sure he probably worried quite a bit about the people around him — but not because he was looking out for their best interests.

I looked over at Prof, who was still laughing at me. His laughter quickly faded when he saw how serious I was.

"What is it, man? You haven't been like this since Skunk and Parsa were riding your ass back at the Wood."

"I just don't want to fuck up," I finally said.

I don't know how much that told Prof, but he seemed to soften a bit after I said it.

"Lips, man — you are the last guy I would ever expect to fuck up." He looked around at the other guys in our group. "And if you need to justify this to yourself, look at it this way — we're the fuckers who helped drag that part of yourself into the open, kicking and screaming. Before us, your whole life was a fuck-up. All our lives were. And look at us now." He took another look at our surroundings, and added, "in the larger sense, I mean."

"Yeah," I said. "Look at us. In a few months we could all be laying hacked to pieces on some battlefield on the other side of the ocean."

"Can you think of a better way to go?"

"Yeah, laying in a soft bed in my mansion at the age of 99."

"Well okay. Granted. But what's your second choice?"

I wanted to chuckle at that, but I held it in.

"You'd be a good Footman, Prof," I said.

"Maybe someday. But for now let's go over to that bar and get some ale. You can stare at my sexy face instead of those girls' jugs."

I was able to relax a bit after that. I didn't watch the girls — not much, at least — and instead tried to pick Prof's brain about what else he knew about the invasion.

"How do you know all this stuff?" I asked at one point.

"Told you before, bro — dwarves have their own grapevine."

After a couple of hours, Wym suddenly got into an argument with a few sailors, and me and Prof rushed over to handle it. There were some punches thrown — I don't remember who threw the first one — but the last thing I remember was Gorgeous bellowing, "I told you to keep your hands off my board, asshole!"

WHEN I WOKE UP a few hours later, I was in a cell with the other guys from One One Five. I had a massive headache, and when I touched my face, it was tender in spots from the bruising.

"What in the name of Gruun's bloody asshole happened?" I asked, though it was more or less obvious.

"Guy was cheating at cards," Wym said. "I called him out and he got mad."

"And that's when the fun started!" Limul exclaimed with a grin. Even with his face banged up, he looked like he was having a blast.

"Oh, man, CO's gonna kill us," I said. "I've gotta be at mage training tomorrow morning."

"You'll be back in plenty of time," Prof said. "They're gonna be letting us out in another hour or so. Somebody paid our fines."

"Who?"

Prof shrugged. "They wouldn't say."

It wasn't even midnight when we got out. On the way back, Limul said, "I've got an idea."

After a bit of searching, we found a tattoo guy who agreed to stay open for a little longer — for a price.

"Can you do this design?" Limul asked him.

He looked at it, looked back at Limul. "Piece of cake."

And that's how we all ended up getting matching shoulder tattoos of the insignia on Gorgeous's surfboard.

"Kings of the Ring," Wym said, admiring his new ink. "I don't care if I get killed on the first day. I already know who I am."

78

We knew the invasion had to be getting close when they moved us from our tents and had us start sleeping on the ships. They tried to make it sound routine, like it was a question of freeing up space on shore for storage, but that was obviously a cover story. We started getting lectures about keeping quiet about things, not revealing too much information — there were reports that the Arcanter had spies in Agellos.

I don't know why you would have even needed spies — even if you weren't in the military, it was pretty obvious what was going on. There were thousands of troops being put aboard vessels, and every day, newly-built ships were coming into the harbor and being loaded down with stores. They were even starting to practice loading livestock onto the ships and keeping them there for longer periods of time, to get them accustomed to shipboard life.

Bunking on a ship was in some ways not so different from bunking in tents on land. The biggest difference, of course, was that things were a lot tighter. Troops were stuffed into the front of the ship — we had our own section which was sort of separate from the rest of the ship, where regular sailors weren't allowed except during emergencies. Ship officers, of course, could come into our area whenever they wanted, though they rarely did.

Onboard, our area was treated essentially as a separate camp. We kept to the same schedule and same routines we had on land, though getting off and on the ship was a problem for ships that weren't docked. Even in a city the size of Agellos, there's only so much dock space, and most of the ships were moored in the harbor. They ran a regular ferry service with smaller landing boats to get us back and forth to land. If you'd been out partying and missed the last ferry back to your ship, you were in for a world of trouble.

Most ships carried a company of troops, though that varied — there were some larger vessels that carried a lot more, and some — like aviary ships or trebuchet and ballista platforms — that carried a lot fewer. I still hadn't seen the aviary ships, but the missile boats were obvious.

"Have they ever done this before? Mounted artillery on boats?" I asked Sgt. Ergin.

"Nope. Like everything else we're doing here, it's all one grand experiment. You mages do experiments, don't you?"

I wasn't THAT kind of mage — not yet — but I knew what he was talking about.

"Yeah, but most of our experiments end up destroying the lab," I said.

IT WAS SHORTLY AFTER we started bunking on the boats that I finally got to try my first attack spell.

There was no warning about it. Gostor just gave us a different location to report to that day, and when we got there, it turned out to be a spellcasting range. It was a wide packed-dirt field surrounded by a thick stone wall. At the far end of the field were a series of targets which ranged from small leather spheres up to a large stone structure that I guess was supposed to represent part of a castle. Most of the targets were wooden dummies which were obviously supposed to be "enemy soldiers."

Nearly all of the targets showed heavy burn markings, which got me excited when I first saw them. I was hoping we were finally going to learn to throw fireballs.

But we weren't going to learn fireball casting — at least not that day. Gostor rolled his eyes when someone — that someone might have been me — asked about it.

"We're here to teach you how to be effective on a battlefield, not to stage tricks to impress a harlot in some tavern," he said. "Fire spells have their uses, but they're more spectacle than anything else. You need to master something more useful."

That "something" turned out to be a freeze blast. It didn't sound very exciting — and didn't look very exciting, either. You pointed your staff and did the spell, then a column of what looked like white smoke shot out from the end of the staff at whatever you were aiming at.

Gostor could see we were skeptical, so he had one of us — that unnamed dummy who asked about the fireball — go and stand near the other target dummies. He let forth a quick blast, and the dummy — the human one — felt a sudden, intense chill. When he tried to react, he discovered it was difficult to move. He wasn't frozen in place, but the sensation (or, so I'm told) is like having a huge bucket of the coldest water you've ever felt get dumped all over you. It takes a moment for your limbs to adjust. When the dummy tried to walk back to join the group, Gostor gave him another blast, and suddenly his feet were encased in a block of ice. The big dummy tipped over and fell on his dumb face.

Okay, so freeze blast turned out to be a useful spell. Gostor claimed experienced enchanters could cast freeze blasts powerful enough to kill a target instantly, "...

but I'm not worried about any of you managing to do that."

Another handy thing about a freeze blast, Gostor pointed out, was that it had a wide area of effect, and with practice, it had much greater range than most other spells. "It can also be used to extinguish fires," he added as an afterthought.

Like any spell, you got better at it with practice. At first I could only sustain a blast for about a second, and only send it a few feet, but by the end of the day I was launching several-second shots from one end of the range and hitting the targets on the other side. We also practiced casting the spells on each other, trying to duplicate the trick of catching the other guy's feet in a block of ice. A few guys managed to pull it off that same day, but it was a week before I could manage it. As usual, I was the last one to master it.

There's no doubt it was a useful spell, and in hindsight, it makes sense that they'd want us to master it before anything else. But for whatever reason, I wasn't going to feel like a true combat mage until I could point that damn staff and shoot big, bright balls of orange flame out the fucking end.

79

"Private Vaanzur, would you mind explaining what the fuck this is?" Sgt. Ergin bellowed.

It was evening, and we were in our shipboard quarters. I remember because I was practicing swordfighting with Wym. Even though I was a mage, I still had to lug a sword around, so I figured I'd probably get some practice in with it. Wym had been sparring with me for a few weeks, and for the first time since arriving in Agellos, I felt like I was really holding my own in a fight with him.

"Impressive, young one," he teased. "Perhaps one day you'll be able to fight at my level."

I was about to remind him of what a scared little runt he'd been when I first saw him back at the Wood when Sgt. Ergin came bursting in holding a sack in one hand and an open box in the other.

Dral — Private Vaanzur — was sitting at a table trying to teach himself knife tricks — he tended to develop obsessions, and that was his latest one — when Sarge came roaring in.

"Sarge!" he said, leaping up. "What's wrong?"

"What's wrong?" Ergin said. "What's WRONG?!?"

He stormed across the tight confines of the hold and shoved the box in front of Dral's face.

"What in the name of Gruun's asshole is THIS?"

Dral leaned over and looked into the box.

"C-c-cookies. From my...mom? I guess?"

He reached out to try to check the name written on the box, but Sarge snatched the box away.

"What's the rule about sweets, Private Vaanzur?"

"That...that...you're not allowed to have them? Sent to you?"

"Right. And what's the penalty?"

Dral slumped in his chair and mechanically said, "'The recipient shall go topside and stand at the prow of the ship and sing the Raider Hymn with force and enthusiasm, that the whole world may be reminded that a Raider disdains all luxuries and comforts, his only joy being found in hard discipline and the exhilaration of battle.'"

Sarge gave Dral a "what are you waiting for?" look, and the private put away his knife and headed topside. As he left, Sarge turned to face us and said, "Mail call, boys, and when you get the chance, come up here and have a cookie, courtesy of Private Vaanzur's mother. I can tell you from experience — they're delicious."

I went back to practicing with Wym, only to hear Sarge call out my name. I dropped my dummy sword and bounded across the small hold to grab the letter from Sarge's hands.

I looked eagerly at the name on the message:

Kanin Mils.

"You gonna stand there all day drooling, Private Pearl?" I heard Sarge say. "Grab a cookie and get out of the way so I can finish handing these out."

Not really thinking, I grabbed a cookie and headed up topside, where I could already hear Dral belting out the Raider Hymn. I asked one of the sailors on deck for permission to climb up to the crow's nest.

The young man, who looked up from polishing a length of metal railing, was clearly unsure of how to respond.

"Um. I don't know."

"Just tell them a crazy Raider threatened to hit you," I said, and started climbing up the mast.

I needed to be alone to read this letter, and since I was stuck on a ship, the crow's nest was the most private place I could think of.

In the darkness atop the mast, with only the illumination of a small lantern, I read these words:

Dear Lash,
Your last letter was quite a surprise.

It shouldn't have been, I suppose. Because I know that the words you wrote are what we have been building towards. I've known for some time those words would be coming, and here they are: Black ink on white paper, a fact confronting me, and demanding an answer.

Even before your letter arrived — even when we first began writing to each other — I spent countless hours composing a reply in my head. I thought I knew what my reply would be, and I delighted in selecting just the right words, just the right shades of meaning.

But now that it has come, I find my pen being held in check. There are other things that must be considered. So many other things.

That sounds terribly evasive. I shouldn't be evasive with you; you have been nothing but honest with me — perhaps the most honest man I have ever known. I was deeply touched that you felt comfortable enough with me to share all the details of your upbringing; I know there are many men who would have taken pains to conceal such a background. But you have been completely transparent with me.

In return, I owe you an equal share of honesty. So let me start by giving you a fuller account of my own circumstances right now.

We moved into our new house last week — our "new" new house. It is the second time we have had to move since we left what I still think of as "our" home, the home I was born in, though I don't think I shall ever be able to set foot in it again.

Even though our new house is quite a step down from our previous one, father has found that our expenses are still beyond what we are taking in. Father's new job seemed to pay well enough at first, but lately it seems the price of everything has been climbing upward at an alarming pace. The Lord Mayor and the Regency Council have tried to pass laws and edicts, forbidding certain price increases and implementing rationing of food and other essentials. But even with all that, there seems to be little they can do.

The scribes in the papers Father reads say it's an inevitable consequence of the war, and they warn that the kingdom cannot sustain a long and costly campaign. I cannot pretend that I understand such matters; I just know that life for people such as us has gotten much more difficult, even as life for some others has become much sweeter.

Although Father forbade me to work for the longest time, things are dire enough now that he finally relented, and I start a new job as a clerk in a factory tomorrow. I was only fortunate enough to secure the job because the owner knew Father and had recently bought "our" old house. When I happened to chance by the other day, they were in the process of removing father's telescope to be sold for scrap.

I suppose what I'm trying to say, Lash, is that while you are still the man I remember, I fear I am not the woman you remember. And before you protest, it's incumbent on me to address another factor.

As much as I would like to put it out of my mind, there is the inescapable fact that you may not be with us much longer.

Every Sevenday at chapel, I give my deepest thanks to Auld Father that he has seen fit to create so many very brave men such as yourself, who have dedicated their lives to protecting His children as they make their way on the Path. And should you be called home in the course of your service, I should count it as a blessing, for your rest with Auld Father upon His Holy Mountain shall be well deserved.

But there remains the problem of those of us who still labor on our journey. And I fear surrendering my heart to a man whose face I shall never see again. There was a time when I might have found that romantic — a time when I lived in a great house, the daughter of a wealthy man, confident that I would be forever insulated from the great trials of life. Perhaps I could afford to indulge such a passionate fantasy then. But now I simply wake up each day wondering if I shall be able to put together an evening meal for my poor, tired father. I look at him each day and wonder how I should make my way in this world if he were lost to me.

I am enmeshed in a web of practical concerns, and your letters, as much as I cherish them, seem like reminders of another time. I cannot live in another time, in either the past or the future. I am forced to live in the present.

Here is where we come to the part that is hardest for me to write, because the truth of the matter is that I do care for you, Lash. I care for you more than you shall ever know. But I fear this world is calling each of us to different destinies. I think the best thing — for both of us — is to embrace those destinies. And I think that requires us to now say goodbye.

Please know that I pray for you, Lash — for you and all the other men who are preparing to pay the highest price for our land and our faith. You go to your destiny with my deepest blessings. Go knowing that wherever the Path takes you, the end shall be eternal life with Auld Father.

But please know that I have my own destiny to pursue, and please respect that to bind myself further to you would be to chase after ghosts. I must ask that you allow me to sever those bindings.

Please, do not be sad — let all the sadness fall back onto me. Unburden yourself of it, and go boldly forth to claim the treasures that I could not give to you.

Auld Father's blessings,

Kanin

I carefully folded the letter and placed it in my front pocket — right next to my father's flame pearl. For some reason, I wanted to place it close to my heart, even though my heart had just been shattered. I looked out at the harbor. The moon Siran was high in the sky that night, and I could see her reflection quivering on the soft surface of the waves. There was something beautiful about the way the reflection was blurred by my tears.

80

Well, I finally learned how to cast a fireball. It happened the very next day, as a matter of fact — when Gostor announced the day's lesson, several of us thought he was joking.

Since I had other things I was worrying about, it didn't turn out to be the landmark event I'd built up in my mind. Gostor revealed the vognon to us and even issued us spellbooks. This should have been another landmark, but again, I was so focused on my own troubles that it barely registered. I remember Wernar eagerly paging through the little leather book trying to see if there were any transmutation spells. To his disappointment, there weren't.

"You may study these spells on your own time, and you may experiment with any of them here on the casting range. Starting today, you may even use the casting range when you're off duty, assuming it's not being used for classes. But do NOT, under any circumstances, fool around with these spells anywhere else," he said.

"What about in battle?" Wernar asked.

Gostor looked around theatrically.

"Do you see a battle going on, Private?"

"No, but..."

"Private, I assure you: If you're in a battle, looking up spells in a spellbook will be the least of your concerns."

Fireball worked exactly as it sounds: You cast the spell and a big ball of flame shoots from the end of your staff. It flies and hits the target in a burst of flame. If you make it hot enough — you have to concentrate to make it hot enough — it can even cause the target to catch on fire. Assuming the target can burn.

You can even guide them to their target with a little practice — which is good, because when I first started casting them I discovered I couldn't aim for shit. You can make them fly faster or slower, or fire them in rapid succession — though making them faster lowers the intensity of the flame. A "loafer" — a fat, slow-moving ball that's pretty easy for a man to dodge — is generally the most powerful.

As I lobbed one fireball after another at the target, Gostor picked up on my lack of enthusiasm.

"Your pet lizard die or something, Private?" he asked.

"Something," I said.

Instead of spending time studying my spellbook, though — "Basic Combat Spellcraft" it said on the title page — I found myself spending more time reading my copy of The Walk. I don't really know why — I was searching for answers, I suppose, but I didn't even know how to form the questions.

That's when I started attending services regularly — not just on Seveneve morning, but every chance I could get. I'd attend in the evening, during the week — any time I could get a chance. Don't get the wrong idea — it's not like I had some grand awakening, like the kind you always hear about. I always sat in the back, and never really participated. But something about being there seemed to give me a sense of peace.

AS YOU CAN IMAGINE, I was in a foul mood when St. Jaspen's Day arrived. I didn't want anything to do with a celebration of love and romance, but as luck would have it, St. Jaspen is also the patron saint of Agellos, so it's one of the city's biggest holidays. Instead of a day of hard training to take my mind off things, Lord General Cullven saw fit to give all the soldiers and sailors the day off.

Wheels wanted to take a bunch of us from Nine Nine Three to a sporting house. He said that the sporting houses in the city — always ready to seize an opportunity — were running St. Jaspen's Day specials.

"You clowns have been too stiff lately," he announced during breakfast. "And if I know Raiders, the best way to loosen them up is with some top-shelf pussy." That got a roar of approval all around — except for Sarge. He just rolled his eyes; I looked down at his hand and noticed a wedding band on his finger.

Lt. Kretek didn't have a wedding band. He couldn't go with us, of course — officers aren't supposed to hang out with enlisted men off duty — but there was no reason he couldn't have found another sporting house running a special for officers. Even with the day off, though, he was still hard at work in the little semi-private cubby he had aboard the ship. I wondered sometimes if the poor guy ever took a break.

I'd been planning to go with the rest of the guys — why not use one woman to forget about another one, at least for awhile — but something moved me to change my mind at the last minute. Instead, I grabbed my mage's staff and decided to head to the spellcasting range. If they wouldn't force me to train so I could take my mind off my troubles, I'd just have to do it myself. I rode with the rest of the platoon in the ferry to the docks, and we went our separate ways.

I wanted to go to the range because I'd been having trouble with the shield spell. Gostor had stressed that it would be one of the most important spells we would use in combat, so I wanted to make sure I had it down cold.

The shield spell is actually an advanced version of a simple deflection spell; it creates a large shield-like barrier that is supposed to protect anything behind it.

"Like having a castle wall in your pocket," was how Gostor described it. When you did it right, you could actually see the faint shimmering rainbows of the shield structure hanging in midair, radiating outward from the tip of the staff like a weird umbrella; they reminded me a little of the rainbows you'd see in the mist of a fountain.

I say it's *supposed* to work that way because like any other spell, it varies with the skill of the spellcaster. The better you were, the larger the size of the shield you could cast, and the longer you could hold it in place. I wasn't very good at either.

Since I didn't have anybody to practice with, I had to use the range's projectile launcher to practice. It was powered by springs, like a giant clock, so you had to spend an exhausting few minutes winding it up, but once it was wound and loaded, you just pulled a lever and it lobbed sawdust-packed leather balls at you for a good ten minutes or so; you could use a second lever to control the speed. It wasn't the best solution, but since I didn't have another mage to shoot spells at me, it would have to do.

I went through four cycles with the machine, having to go through the tedious process of reloading and rewinding it each time. It seemed hopeless at first — I would throw up a shield barely large enough to protect just myself, and I could only hold it for a second or so; then the colors would wink out of sight and I'd have to dive for the lever before I got smacked in the face by a ball. I could never hold the spell long enough to stop more than a couple of missiles.

I sat down in the dirt in frustration. I wanted to cry, but I fought off the urge. It was a time for sweat, not tears. I thought about Wym back at the Wood, using his fear to build himself into a fighter. You can't let your feelings seduce you, weaken you. Feelings are fuel.

I gathered up all my anger and sadness, pulled myself off the ground, and reset the machine. And I kept going until the spell's rebus seemed to burn itself into my eyelids, and then I kept going some more.

Eventually — not quickly, but eventually — I could block three projectiles in a row. Then four. Then five. As I learned to hold it longer, the range of the shield expanded, until by the end of the day I was able to load up the machine, flip it on and cast a shield big enough to protect a dozen men and hold long enough to block seven or eight shots in a row. It still wasn't close to what the best students in Gostor's class could do — but I knew none of them worked as hard as I had to get there. That's the thing about starting from rock bottom — every step up is another victory.

When I finished, the sun was beginning to dip below the horizon. Physically, I was feeling drained — something I shared with my gear. I noticed that the ingot attached to the tip of my staff — the "telluric component" for my spellcasting — was beginning to look badly corroded, a sign that I didn't have many spells left; I'd need to go see the quartermaster first thing tomorrow to get a new one.

My thoughts were still in a jumble. It felt good to have finally made some progress, but I still had a long way to go. Near the end, I was feeling confident enough that I even tried out a few of the more advanced spells in my spellbook, but the results were pretty humbling. I tried levitating myself, and while I could feel the pull of gravity starting to loosen, I never actually left the ground. When I tried casting a lightning bolt, all I got were a few puny sparks that flickered in the air and then disappeared.

But beneath it all, I couldn't shake Kanin from my mind. All this time I'd been building up a vision of some kind of golden future that had kept me pushing forward, but now it was ripped away. It wasn't new for me, living without a future — but I knew now that I couldn't let myself fall back into that hole. I was beginning to understand why my mother clung so fiercely to the Path — it was the only thing that kept her going after my father was gone and she was left alone to raise me.

I found my footsteps leading me to the Sailor's Chapel. Since it was a holy day, I knew they'd have services all day. If spending the day drilling my mind could sharpen my spellcasting, perhaps drilling my spirit could fix my mind on Auld Father; his Path was all I had left.

The city streets were decked out for the occasion, filled with colorful lights and streamers. I ignored it all as I made my way, keeping my eyes fixed on the chapel's great spire. When I reached it, I just wanted to sit in the back and lose myself in the calm lights and soft music while I fought my soft, silent little battle with Auld Father: *You tossed me into this angry ocean they call life, and I've been kicking my legs and churning my hands ever since. What miserable rock do you expect me to aim for? Or do you just expect me to strain and strive and finally drown?*

It was the same prayer, in one form or another, I'd been offering for weeks. As I walked, I felt in my breast pocket the fire pearl, the only connection I had with my worldly father.

The Sailor's Chapel was fronted by a wide pavilion that came right up to a seawall that looked out on the harbor. It was a popular meeting spot, because it gave one of the most spectacular views in the entire city, and on this night, of course, it was filled with happy couples strolling along in a haze of blind bliss. I fought to ignore them; I was walking across the pavilion, gazing up at the belltower spire when I was surprised to hear someone shout my name. I turned to look, and found Parsa coming up the steps behind me, clad in crisp Raider dress uniform.

"Lash! Lash, what are you doing here?"

I hesitated before answering. "Just need to find some peace," I said.

"Well brother, you've come to the right place! Here, let me join you."

I shrugged and we went inside. At the door, an acolyte was handing out cards. He explained that each one was imprinted with the name of a different soldier or sailor who'd be taking part in the grand invasion.

"We ask you to offer up a prayer this evening for the safety of this brave warrior," he said. I took a card and looked at it, wondering idly if I might be lucky enough to draw a card with my own name. But no: The name printed in simple block letters on my card was "Capt. Brulen, son of Banden, of the House of Klang."

I showed it to Parsa. "Is that...could he be one of *the* Klangs?" I don't suppose I have to explain to you long-beard scholars that the Klangs were the notorious ice dwarf tribe whose infamy was the source of the term "klanger."

Parsa studied the card. "It's possible," he said. "You know some from their tribe fought on our side during the Great War. Most of them later changed their names... or so I've heard. But not all." He shrugged. "You know dwarves. Stubborn."

At the time, this was new information to me. I looked down at the card. The acolyte picked up on my unease. "Perhaps you'd like another card, sir..."

"No, no this one is fine," I told him. I took at a sign of Auld Father's sense of humor — a scaleback being called to offer up prayers for a literal klanger.

The inside of the Sailor's Chapel was vast. In fact, calling it a "chapel" really didn't do it justice. It was more on the scale of a proper city Temple. The actual city Temple that served Agellos was much larger even than this — supposedly it's the largest Patriarch Temple in the world — but it was further inland and, to my mind, far less impressive. There's a reason the Sailor's Chapel, and not the Temple, is the one on all the souvenir paintings.

There was still quite a bit of time until the next service, but Parsa insisted on dragging me inside; maybe he sensed that I needed to be away from all the starry romance out on the pavilion. Even though we were early, the whole place was still very full.

I wanted to hang near the back, but Parsa insisted we sit as close to the front as possible. From the looks we got, I could tell services at this hour didn't get many soldiers. Or maybe people were just surprised by my mage staff; since I wasn't about to take the ferry back to our ship just to stow it, I still had it with me, and it wasn't like the Chapel had a place to store it — at least no place I felt comfortable leaving it.

While we waited for the service to begin, Parsa closed his eyes and silently prayed. I can still remember the look on his face — calm, purposeful, and maybe the tiniest bit of satisfaction. Not self-satisfaction, mind you — I'd seen the look of vain pride enough times on that face to know. It was more a sense of happy relief from a man who had finally found his place.

The organist was playing a soothing hymn I remembered from childhood —

I don't know the name. While I waited, I studied the huge carved wooden arrow that hung at the head of the Chapel, above the altar: The sign of Auld Father. *It is by the arrow that we will know the Path*, my mother had always said.

Well, here I am, I thought. Here I am, Auld Father. Show me the Path.

The acolytes finally began making their way around the Chapel to dim the candles, and the organist brought the hymn to close. A thin, almost feminine-looking Footman with bright eyes stepped up to the pulpit and called everyone to order. I remember being surprised at first at how high-pitched his voice was, but I was quickly lulled by its powerful, musical tone. A hush fell over the crowd.

"I see many new faces here tonight," he said. For a second, it seemed like he was looking directly at me, but his gaze quickly moved on, taking in the rest of the congregation. "For those of you who are just joining us, we begin our meetings with a prayer."

We got on our knees, closed our eyes, and turned our faces upward. "Imagine you are looking up at the summit of the Holy Mountain," is how my mom always taught me to think of it.

The Footman began. "Auld Father, we call on you to bless us tonight…"

He was cut off in mid-sentence by the sound of the horns.

There had actually been some noise already — as the organist was playing, I had heard a faint noise that suggested a tolling bell tower. I had dismissed it, thinking it might be a trick of the organist's playing.

It was only later that I found out those were the bells on the outskirts of the city, warning of the attack. But even if I'd known what I was hearing, I'm not sure it would have registered. The outskirts of the city were to the *west* of us. If there was an attack — which there wouldn't be, we'd been told again and again — it would come from the *east*, out over the ocean.

But there was no mistaking the sound of the horns — they were the loud, low ship-mounted horns they used for signaling maneuvers.

The horns sounded again, in a regular pattern. I recognized it.

"That's the sound for a general alarm," I told Parsa. "Is this…is it a surprise drill, maybe?"

Parsa was listening carefully, and he looked very serious. All of a sudden I felt like I was looking at a man ten years older. The murmurs inside the church were growing.

"We should go outside and check," he finally said, and stood up straight. I warily joined him. As I followed him down the aisle to the back of the sanctuary, he made soothing, reassuring gestures to the other worshipers: Nothing to worry about, you've got us here, he seemed to be saying, and it seemed to work — several people responded with hopeful nods and smiles. I could only hope my own appearance was half as reassuring, because inside I had no idea what was going on.

Very gently, Parsa opened one of the ornate doors that led out onto the pavilion, and we stepped outside. The very first thing I saw was a group of infantry running by. They weren't marching — they were running, and not in any kind of order. Several of them were still strapping on their armor and shouting at the others to wait up.

Outside, the sound of the bells was now everywhere — it sounded as if half the bell towers in the city were ringing frantically. Many of the couples that had been strolling around the pavilion earlier were now gone, and the few who were left seemed to be in a hurry to leave. One very panicked-looking man with a bored-looking lady on his arm tried to hail a carriage that came tearing through the pavilion; he waved around a fat-looking coin purse to try to attract the attention of the driver, but the coach sped by without the reinsman even seeming to notice him.

The couple were some distance away. Parsa waved to catch their attention. "What's going on?" he shouted.

"It's nothing," shouted the woman. She turned and said something to her companion, then strode quickly across the pavilion to us while he remained where he was, still holding his coin purse and looking confused.

"She could do better than him," Parsa said as she made her way to us. "You should hit her up, Lash." After a pause, he added, "if you were into girls, that is."

"Fuck you, man." He was still giggling when she finally walked up the steps to where we were standing.

"Thank the Father," she said. "Can you escort us to safety?"

"Escort you...what's going on here?" Parsa said.

She let out a frustrated sigh. "Don't you hear the bells? The HORNS?"

I'd noticed the chorus of bells seemed to be growing.

"Yes, it's a general alarm. What's going on? We were inside the Chapel..."

Just then there was an ear-piercing screech. It seemed to come from the direction of the ocean. I looked, squinted, and then saw it: A whole flight of hawk cavalry coming in low across the water, their wings glinting in the light of the moon Arban. They were headed straight toward the pavilion where we were standing.

Parsa gazed at them in confusion. "If they stay that low they're going to..."

Then a geyser of flame erupted from somewhere out of the sky, its evil orange light casting deep shadows across the pavilion. I watched, dumbstruck, as the flames poured out like water from a giant hose onto the formation of great birds.

When the torrent of flame suddenly stopped, I wasn't sure at first what I was looking at. It looked at first like the flickering flames of a candelabra, but I quickly realized these flickers were actually moving, with great speed.

I realized as these were the great flaming bodies of the cavalry birds, still hurtling through the air on sheer momentum. As I watched them grow larger, I saw they were hurtling towards us. I saw that the flaming carcass of the lead hawk would slam directly into us in mere seconds. I heard a weird, drawn-out guttural sound that seemed like the beginning of a word; I realized later that it had come from the girl standing with me and Parsa. She'd been trying to force her lips to say something.

Then Parsa said, "Lash, I..."

I don't remember actually thinking about what happened next; whatever my body did, it just seemed to do on its own, without bothering to consult me. But what happened was I thrust out my mage staff and cast a deflection spell. I just... saw the spell rebus pass through my mind in bright, sharp forms, and for a moment I felt like a bystander as I watched the huge flaming mass of flesh and feathers swerve off to the side, where it tumbled right into the man standing there with his coin purse, then kept tumbling until it slammed into a building off right off to the side of the pavilion, next to the Sailor's Chapel. At nearly the same instant, all the other burning carcasses slammed into other buildings along the waterfront with a series of quick thuds that made the ground shake. And then I snapped back, and no longer felt like a bystander, and my ears suddenly hurt from a piercing scream that seemed just inches away. It was the woman who'd come to ask us for help; she was suddenly shrieking hysterically. I reached out to her to try to calm her down, but she pushed me away and continued to scream.

"What the fuck just happened?" I shouted. I remember for a few crazy moments my whole body was numb, and everything felt like something out of a dream. My mind was racing to try and fit what I was seeing into some kind of reality that made sense. Was it a training exercise? Some djinn-conjured illusion, like back in the Wood? I turned to Parsa, expecting him to be as panicked as I was, but he was surveying the scene with a strange sense of calm.

"Can you do anything about those flames?" he said, gesturing at the burning hulk closest to us, the one I'd managed to prevent from slamming into us — and into the Sailor's Chapel, I suddenly realized.

I mumbled something and began sprinting over to the fiery carcass, barely recognizable as an animal. As I got closer, my nostrils were overcome with an aroma that reminded me of roasted pheasant. That at least brought a smile; I used my mage staff to cast frost blasts while I tried to see if I could find a survivor, either the hawk rider or...the fellow with the coin purse. As I gradually got the blaze under control, I saw something that...well, it was human at one point; that was all I could say.

When I finally got the flames extinguished, I turned to the other carcasses, but it was hopeless; the buildings along the waterfront were already a growing inferno. I jogged back to the steps of the Sailor's Chapel. The worshipers had now emerged onto the steps, and were alternately gawking or panicking at the flames that were slowly engulfing the entire quarter; they'd been joined by people who, judging from their appearance, had escaped from the nearby burning buildings. Making my way up the steps of the Chapel, I passed by the girl who'd come to us for help earlier. She had fainted.

Parsa was conferring with the Footman, who was surveying the growing chaos with a cool reserve that would have made Sgt. Taba proud.

"You're sure it's not safer to just keep everyone here on the pavilion," the Footman asked. "If we move them over there along the seawall, they'll be well clear of the burning buildings, and they could be rescued by boat."

Parsa shook his head. "I don't know what's going on; I still don't know what happened to that flight of hawk cavalry. You know this city better than we do; if you can lead everyone out of here, me and Lash can serve as escorts. You've seen what he can do with that staff of his."

The Footman looked me up and down. "You have been a blessing from Auld Father indeed, young man," he said in that same high-pitched, musical tone.

"I don't know about that," I said. I was still thinking of the burned-up husk of a body I'd seen earlier.

Just then, the loud ship-borne horns started to fall silent. I looked out at the harbor, and for the first time noticed the confused mass of ships, all moving about in every direction.

"Is that it? Is it over?" someone wailed. For a moment, I thought it was. The bells were still ringing all over the city, but without the loud, low sound from the ship-borne horns, a weird calm seemed to settle over everything.

Then I heard a slow, rhythmic beating, strong enough that I could feel it in the air itself. Then a great gust of fire-warmed air swept over the whole crowd. Something made me look up, and I saw a huge red shape pass swiftly but silently overhead. The crowd became very quiet, except for stray gasps and whimpers.

It was a great red dragon, like something out of a storybook. It sailed out across the harbor in frightening silence. Then it let out a loud squawk, opened its jaws, and vomited out a torrent of flame onto a group of assembled ships.

It banked slowly across the harbor, its flaming breath carving a long arc of fire across the flotilla. As the curve of its flight brought it back around towards us, it turned its head and changed course, heading into a shallow dive right towards the crowded pavilion. I could see the dragon inhaling, its chest bulging out as it prepared to unleash another blast, and all around me the air was filled with screams.

This time, my instincts didn't kick in, so I can't blame it on that. I don't know what it was — maybe it was just the mesmerizing sight of those slowly opening jaws, the glow of the flame rising up in the back of the beast's throat, and the feeling that I was about to die. But whatever it was, I held up my mage's staff, visualized the rebus, and there was a feeling like a puzzle piece snapping perfectly into place. I saw the shield bloom out from my staff like a flower, and the dragon's fiery blast pour into it, and the flames just...broke against my spell like water against solid rock. The blast of flame continued as the vile creature swooped over our heads, but I followed it with my staff, blocking its attack the whole way.

"Lash," Parsa said. "Lash what the fuck..."

"Shut up and let me concentrate." The creature swept into a wide banking move-ment, preparing for another approach. I gripped my staff tighter, praying that I could block another attack. I glanced at the metal ingot attached to my staff; it was now pitted and white with corrosion. Not much more left. Would it be enough?

But before I could begin to summon my spell, a shape dived straight down out of the heavens and slammed into the dragon, knocking it out of its smooth glide. Suddenly, the beast was tumbling through the sky, locked in a furious struggle with something I couldn't quite make out.

"What is that? What just happened?"

"It's…it's a cavalry hawk," Parsa said. "I think it's from my unit. I think that's… that's my commander."

The pair of aerial opponents looked like they might fall straight into the har-bor, but at the last second the dragon managed to stretch out its wings, flapping furiously to keep airborne. The cavalry hawk had its claws sunk deep into the dragon's back, and as the duo came in close I could see the hawk's rider leaping from his saddle onto the evil lizard's back.

The battling duo now looked like they were going to smash into the pavilion di-rectly in front of us; I readied to throw up another shield spell to block any debris. But at the last moment, the dragon spread its wings and began flapping them furi-ously. The rush of air was powerful enough to knock people down. With powerful effort, the animal was able to guide itself up over the pavilion; its massive claws sprang open, and it managed to grasp the tall spire of the Sailor's Chapel and wrap its body around it. The cavalry hawk bit and scratched furiously, and the beast let out a roar which seemed to shake the ground we were standing on. Swinging its neck around, it closed its giant jaws around the body of the hawk, ripping the animal off its back…and tearing away a big chunk of its own wing in the process.

"Watch out for the blood! Watch out for the blood!" Parsa shouted as chunks of the flying lizard's wing fell and crashed into the pavement.

I watched in horror as the dark black blood that splashed across steps of the building and pavilion immediately ate through the carved rock. Some of the splat-ter struck a few bystanders, who shrieked in agony.

"It's acid," Parsa said.

I backed away from the building, trying to get a better look at the battle going on above me. The dragon shook the body of the cavalry hawk back and forth like a dog with a dishrag, then at last flung the feathered corpse away, where it crashed into the stones of the pavilion.

"What about the rider?" someone asked.

The dragon then let out another roar of pain, and turned its body to the other side. And then I saw it — the hawk's rider was hacking away at the animal's other wing with a sword.

Once again the scaly monster swung its neck around and clamped its jaws around the tiny figure on its back. The rider never even looked up, never even flinched, and was still hacking away at the wing even as the jaws crushed around him. The monster yanked him up and flung him down hard onto the pavilion below. As his sword clanged loudly on the stone paving, he landed with a thick thud that made me feel sick — somehow, knowing a living human body had caused that sound made my stomach drop.

I ran over to see if there was anything I could do, expecting the worst. To my utter shock, the man was still alive, though for how much longer I couldn't say. I closed my eyes and cast a healing spell on him, trying to force myself to make it as strong as possible. The tip of my staff glowed a powerful green, and he suddenly looked up at me.

"Thanks," he said, "but you shouldn't have. I'm afraid there's no way I'll make it."

"Well that's not for you to decide, Captain," Parsa said. The man raised his head, looking in the direction of the voice. "Private Parsa. Fancy seeing you here. Trust me, you'll do a lot more good if you can get to your mount instead of wasting time with me."

Parsa shook his head. "First things first, Captain," he said, stripping off the coat of his dress uniform and folding it into a pillow to put under the Captain's head. He turned to the Footman, speaking loudly enough for everyone in the crowd to hear him. "Father, we need you to lead these people out of here. And we need to get this man to a doctor."

The Footman nodded, and without even needing to be told, a group of burly fellows who looked like dockworkers picked up a nearby wooden bench to serve as a makeshift stretcher, and began loading the wounded man onto it. But the Captain suddenly started struggling and shouted: "Wait! Wait! The dragon! Look! It can't fly! It's trapped!"

We looked up, and saw the red-scaled beast still clutching the spire of the Sailor's Chapel. It was examining its wings, trying to flex them. It tried to flap one, and then the other, but they were both so badly damaged that it could only move them with difficulty.

"Somebody has to kill it!" the Captain said. "If it can't get away, it will go down fighting! It will destroy everything it can see!"

The beast was scanning the area around its makeshift perch. Above us in the sky, two more red dragons swooped overhead, pursued by flights of hawk cavalry. The dragons in flight let out a series of squawks, and the one atop the spire followed them with its gaze, and let out a series of squawks in answer.

"Get these people out of here!" Parsa barked, and the Footman clapped his hands and began striding quickly out of the pavilion, followed by the crowd of civilians. The dragon looked down at them, and reared back its head while its chest expanded, preparing to unleash another river of flame right onto their heads.

I didn't know if I could throw up another shield spell as powerful as the one I'd used before, but there was one spell I absolutely knew I could pull off. I aimed my staff and used every ounce of my mental powers to summon up the strongest freeze blast I had ever unleashed, aiming right at the creature's maw. I held it as long as I could, the blast of cold forming a streak of ice crystals right through the air itself. There was something almost beautiful about the way the crystals caught the light as they fell tinkling to the ground.

When I finally relented, collapsing to my knees with exhaustion, I looked up and saw the animal's jaws were frozen shut, a crust of shiny ice wrapped all around its head. The monster swung its head around in confusion, and I heard muffled sounds coming from its frozen hood.

"I don't think that will hold for very long," I said, and I could already see the dragon's fiery breath glowing through the ice.

"It should last long enough for most of these people to get out of range," Parsa said, indicating the civilians who were now being led quickly away by the Footman, who began belting out a rousing hymn, I suppose to lift everyone's spirits. We both stood there watching the procession for what felt like a long time, ignoring the increasingly furious growls and muffled roars far above our heads. There was something strangely heartwarming about the whole crazy parade.

"Lash..." Parsa finally said, his voice trailing off as he looked up at the beast far above our heads. I noticed he was now gripping the hawk cavalry Captain's sword; drops of its acid blood still dripped onto the Chapel steps, burning a pattern of tiny holes into the stone.

"Yeah, Parsa?"

He seemed to drift for a moment, then blinked, and quickly regained his presence of mind.

"Lash, we need to kill that thing."

81

"I assume you have some kind of plan," I said.

"Not really. We just need to get up there. We'll figure something out. We're fuckin' Raiders, right?"

I sighed. "That we fucking are."

Just then there was another loud horn blast. I looked out at the harbor and saw that it had come from a ship just offshore — long oars stuck out from its sides, paddling it closer to the seawall that abutted the pavilion.

I recognized the shape of the craft immediately — it was an artillery ship. There was a sound of groaning wood, and a catapult sent a big stone ball over our heads and crashing into the roof of the chapel. It missed the dragon by maybe a dozen yards. The beast let out a muffled roar, and I saw the ice around its mouth was glowing very red.

There was a "thunk" as a second catapult launched another stone soaring over our heads. This one also missed, but it seemed to further enrage the beast.

"Well, we've got a diversion," Parsa said. "Come on."

We pulled open the doors and made our way into the chapel. The spire was now directly above us, and the dragon's frenzied movements were causing the entire ceiling to sway, sending chips of wood and paint falling down like frost.

"Do you know how to get up there?" I asked.

"No idea, but there's gotta be a way, right? I think there's a door over here..."

Parsa began heading towards a side altar when I heard a loud crack, and a chunk from a ceiling beam began to fall down towards where he was standing. Purely by reflex, I hurled out a deflection spell, causing the falling beam to arc off to the side just as I yelled, "Parsa! Watch out!"

He turned just in time to see the beam crash into a row of pews in the main sanctuary.

"I knew that stupid stick of yours would come in handy," he said.

"I've got your stick right here," I said, flipping him the bird.

I looked around at the building.

"This kind of looks like the Temple in Solta," I said. "The design is different but...it seems to have the same layout."

"And that helps us how?"

"Follow me," I said.

I led Parsa over to a carved wooden relief set into a wall near one corner. It was a familiar scene of Footman Rom traveling through the Stalk Valley, preaching the ways of Auld Father to the barbarians of the wilderness.

The scene was decorated around the edges with flowers. I began grasping at each one.

"I think one of these is...here it is." I grabbed one flower and felt it turn slightly: A hidden doorknob. The panel opened up, revealing a staircase.

"How did you know..."

"I've seen it before."

Parsa grabbed a lantern, and we started to make our way up the dark, winding spiral. I felt sure we were heading to our deaths.

I PROBABLY SHOULD HAVE been scared. At other times, I would have been. But at that moment, I wasn't really thinking; my mind was still racing from the excitement of facing an actual, live dragon. As we made our way to the top, the dragon's roars suddenly got much louder.

"I think the ice is melted now," I said, and Parsa just grunted. There were also occasional "thumps" that shook the building, from what I guessed were catapult shots. As we got higher up the stairway, the structure around us shook more violently.

We were both nearly out of breath when we finally reached a tiny landing beneath a wooden hatch, small enough that I wasn't sure at first we'd be able to squeeze through it.

"What, did they build this for a dwarf?" Parsa asked.

The dragon's roar shook the timbers of the small landing.

"That will be the belfry on the other side," I said. "The dragon is wrapped around the spire, which is directly above it. I don't know how we're going to be able to reach him."

"We'll figure something out," Parsa said, grasping the latch. Before he opened it, he looked at me.

"Ready to kill a dragon?" he said with a smile, and I did my best to push away any feelings of fear.

He swung the hatch open, and we climbed into an open space that was filled with several bells of different sizes. The space was ringed with open arches that allowed us to look out around the city in all directions.

The scene we were looking out at was a massacre. Whole sections of Agellos were consumed in flames.

Looking out at the harbor, though, I was surprised to see that most of the ships seemed to have escaped unharmed — flights of hawk cavalry, along with groups of High Sorcerers using their magic to zip about through the air, were patrolling and quickly swarming any dragons that came near.

There was a series of huge, thundering "cracks" from further down the shore, and when I turned to look, I could see another dragon. There was a glowing blue sphere buzzing around it, blasting it with massive bolts of lightning — a high sorcerer at work. For a brief moment, I felt a sense of relief — it felt good to see people fighting back.

Then the whole belfry shook, the heavy bells beating a dull chorus as the dragon lurched about on the spire above us and launched a blast of flame out at the harbor. Its flames licked at the catapult ship, leaving it dotted with little fires, but the vessel seemed to be far enough away to escape the worst of the beast's wrath.

There was a sound of creaking wood, and another of its catapults launched a stone sphere through the air. As I watched it arc upwards, I climbed out of one of the arches of the belfry, hanging out so that I could look up at the dragon.

"Lash? Lash what the fuck are you doing?" Parsa asked.

"Hold on. I'm gonna try something…" I thrust out my staff to cast a deflection spell on the stone missile. Instead of pushing it away, though, I used all my powers of concentration to bend its flight toward the dragon. I visualized sending it straight into the great beast's ugly head.

The heavy stone sphere missed the dragon's head, but smacked squarely into one of its feet, which it was using to hold onto the spire. It roared in pain, and its great body slid downward off the spire, crashing onto the chapel's roof.

With only three good legs, the beast was now scrambling to keep from sliding off and falling to the ground.

I ran over to another arch in the belfry where I could look down at the evil animal. It was the third time in a row I'd managed to get the better of the thing. Maybe fighting dragons wasn't so hard after all?

"Take that you acid-blooded piece of shit!" I yelled, and launched a freeze blast at the tiles of the roof, coating them with a slick film of ice just as the lizard was trying to find its grip. It began sliding toward the edge of the roof, where its useless wings would be unable to stop it from plummeting to the stone pavement below.

I was feeling pretty pleased with myself until the beast suddenly stopped sliding. One of its great hind claws suddenly rose up and found a powerful grip on the edge of the roof, and it lifted itself up, shook its body, and then looked around — and fixed its eyes directly at me. And suddenly, I felt numb.

I don't know exactly what happened; all this time I'd been operating on pure intuition and reflex, but now it suddenly drained away. No spells came into my mind; I was paralyzed with shock as I watched the great scaled horror claw its way across the roof, its long neck stretching out to where I stood in the arch of belfry. It opened its maw wide, and I saw the shining, dripping teeth leaping toward me — and then I felt myself being pulled away and thrown to the floor.

There was a great crashing sound as stone and wood split when the beast's head smashed into the belfry, accompanied by the loud clang of the bells. I lifted my head and found myself looking down at the rough wood planks of the belfry floor, now shaking violently. Then the bells were drowned out by an ear-splitting shriek; it sounded different from the roars and squawks the creature had spit out before.

I shook off my momentary confusion, and pulled myself up. Something was wrong. The structure of the spire was now gently swaying, but the chaotic sounds of struggle had stopped. The ringing of the huge bells grew slower, softer, then died away.

I could hear the dragon moving, its huge bulk still sending tremors through the floor, but it was moving sluggishly. I could feel hot waves of its breath, but they were coming slowly, and there was a soft, low gurgling sound. I shook off my confusion, turned around, and was greeted with a scene of horror.

There was the massive face of the monster, wedged into the archway where I'd been standing just moments before. Its huge, dark green eyes moved listlessly, not focusing on anything. And hanging there from its mouth, I saw Parsa. The beast's huge teeth were clamped hard around his body.

"Parsa?" I said. "Parsa what the fuck..."

I looked and saw the bloody tip of the sword Parsa had been holding protruding from the top of the dragon's head. The animal's eyes stopped moving. A last, guttural rumble traveled up through its neck and escaped from its mouth in a hot gust that left burns on my skin, but the flame in its belly had been snuffed out for good.

I was startled by another sound — a gurgling from Parsa's throat. He was looking at me — and he was smiling. The gurgling sounded a little bit like...laughter. I ran over to him and tried to pull apart the huge jaws, but it was hopeless. I brushed a drop of black acid blood away from his face; my fingertips seared with pain, but I ignored it.

"Hey, man, that was something," I said. "You killed a fucking dragon. When you get home to your wife and your village, you'll be the fucking greatest hero. All the stuff with your dad..."

I stopped, remembering that I wasn't supposed to know about any of that.

His eyes focused on me, and he smiled wider.

He still had one free hand, and he used it to slap me, hard. When I turned my head back he reached out again and patted my head.

"This is nothing dude," I said. "I got a healing spell I can use. It'll put you together good enough that we can get you to a doctor, a real healer, and they'll be able to…just…hold on a second…"

I fumbled around on the ground until I found my mage staff, but when I was finally able to find it and aim it at him, he was gone.

Just then, I felt a thudding rhythm in the air, with a heavy gust of wind which was strong enough to stir the heavy bells again. I recognized the signs from before, and moved to one of the belfry's open arches. I looked up into the sky and saw the stars blinking out above as a massive dark shape passed overhead, and then out over the waters of the harbor.

It took a few moments to make out what I was looking at. At first I wondered if it might be a cloud of smoke from the burning city, but gradually the outlines of the shape became clear. The size was immense; it almost matched the size of the largest ships I'd seen in the harbor.

It was a massive black dragon, much larger than the red ones I'd seen so far. It arced slowly over the harbor, beating its massive wings, then veered back and pulled up as it glided over the great pavilion. Even though its huge wings were beating lazily, it somehow managed to hover there in the air, level with me, not more than a few hundred feet from where I stood. The thick scales gleamed, almost as if the creature's hide was wet, and its mouth glowed from heat, showing the sharp outlines of its rows of teeth.

There was a figure perched on the beast's back, riding it. The figure was clad in flowing black robes that whipped slowly in the gusts from the enormous wings.

The figure seemed to be studying me.

Fuck you, I thought. And then I thought it again, my anger rising up inside me: FUCK. YOU.

I wheeled my staff toward the dragon and its rider, let out a furious yell, and began shooting fireballs at it. I was terrible with fireballs, but somehow, in all my rage, I was able to whip up a truly impressive volley, an inferno of white-hot orbs that would have blasted through the stone walls of the casting range. I remember thinking that Gostor might have smiled in approval, if only he could have seen it.

The black figure astride the dragon made a motion with his hand, and the fireballs all sputtered out in midair. I aimed my staff again, but nothing happened. I tried launching a freeze blast: Still nothing. Finally, I saw the ingot mounted at the staff's head: It was flaking away and shot through with cracks and holes. There were no more spells left. I looked again at the black figure. He flicked his hand again, and my entire field of sight was suddenly filled with a pure, painful flash of white light. Then everything was dark. I felt my face, held up my hands before my eyes: Nothing. I had been struck blind.

82

I managed to find my way out of the belfry, down the long flight of stairs, and back out to the front of the Chapel using just my sense of touch. I left my mage staff behind, because who cared anymore — I clearly wouldn't be needing it. What did the Raiders need with a blind mage?

It wasn't until I was out on the pavilion that it occurred to me that blind men often made their way around using sticks. That mage staff would have come in handy. Fuck.

I sank to the ground, exhausted and dejected. I listened to the sounds of the chaos; it was clear that the fighting was beginning to wind down, but I knew the struggle against the flames would go on a lot longer. After an hour or so, a detachment from the city guard found me and brought me to a hastily-established camp for survivors, and had me lay down on some sort of rough canvas mat. I could hear moans, sobs and occasional screams from other people nearby.

At some point some long-bearded physician came by to check me out — I'm not kidding, he had an actual long beard which brushed against me as he was examining me. I just told him I'd been struck blind by a bright light. I didn't much feel like getting into the details.

I remember feeling his bony, dry fingers grasp my skull as he peeled back my eyelids to examine the damage.

"You say a bright light did this?" he asked, with deep skepticism in his voice.

"I could see just fine yesterday," I said. I didn't feel like explaining. "Earlier tonight I was admiring the spire of the Sailor's Chapel."

He huffed derisively. "No damage at all to his eyes," he muttered to somebody standing nearby. "No reason they shouldn't work as well as ours; possibly brain damage." Then to me, "I am sorry...to be the one to tell you this. But it doesn't look like you've sustained any major injuries...except for those burns on your fingers; can't say I'm surprised to see those, what with all the fires and...your condition."

I felt him stand up. "He can stay here for tonight," he said, again talking to somebody else. "Last thing we need right now is a blind man wandering around in this environment. But first thing tomorrow, he needs to be gone. We'll need this space for other casualties."

And then I heard him move to the next person.

I laid down and tried to think about what my life would be like now. Would Kanin...? No. That door was closed. If I could get someone to bring me back to Solta...but what would I do there? The only blind men I saw back home were street beggars. I knew not all blind people were like that, but...but...

I didn't know. I was still chewing over it all when sleep finally claimed my exhausted mind and body.

THAT NIGHT I HAD another dream. I found myself standing on a cold, rocky seashore under an overcast sky. The gray water churned and battered the shore; every so often one would crash violently enough to send up a web of spray that would reach to where I was standing, peppering me with icy little drops. I looked down at myself — once again I was clad in the well-worn garments of a Molan Strongblood. I felt at my chest, and there was a woven pocket there that contained something small and round. I didn't need to look at it to know it was a fire pearl.

A thick layer of fog hung over the water; I could not see more than a hundred feet, at most. Beyond that, all was hidden in mist. But it seemed to me that there was something or someone — out there lurking in the fog, just beyond the point where everything was swallowed up in gray. I had a powerful urge to find this person, somehow get to them. I wanted to tell them something, though I didn't know what. I somehow knew I would know what to say, when I was finally face to face with them.

I charged out into the surf and began swimming, but I could make no progress. The lashing waves were too strong. I tried three, four, five times. Each time the waves dumped me back onto the blanket of smooth little pebbles that covered the shoreline. I tried again, then again; I lost count of the number of times I tried to force myself past the pounding waves. Finally, I collapsed onto the shore. It wasn't exhaustion that made me collapse, just the overwhelming sense of futility.

After several minutes just sitting there and staring angrily into the waves, I noticed a man walking down the shore. He was a surprisingly young man, with a dark but wispy beard, clad in a simple, sturdy peasant's robe. He was shorter than I was, and had wide, clear, deep-set eyes and a laughing smile. He was waving at me as if he were an old friend.

I stood up and approached him slowly. As he drew close, he opened his arms in a welcoming gesture, and embraced me warmly.

"My friend! It has been so many years! You must tell me of the great things you have seen!"

"Have we...do we know each other?"

"You don't recognize me? Oh, but I don't suppose you would, after all this time."

"Who are you?"

He let out a laugh, then took my hand and clasped it in both of his.

"My friends call me 'Bet.' And since you are my friend, that is what you shall call me."

The name sounded familiar, but I couldn't quite remember where I'd heard it.

"Bet, then. I don't know what to tell you of the things I've seen. I don't know that any of them have been very special. I can't even..."

I turned to look out at the fog that still hung over the angry waves. I didn't finish the sentence. I didn't know how.

Bet stood there for a few moments, studying me.

"Ah. I see. One of his imps has managed to tap you again with his rotten finger. Honestly. I don't know why they bother. They know how this ends."

"What are you talking about?"

"I told you once before, not even the greatest of his demons will stand against the Father. And there are still things you have left to see."

I looked at him like he was crazy. Demons? And I couldn't very well 'see' much of anything, because...because...

Bet shifted his smiling gaze from my face, to something behind me. I turned, and just down the shore from where we were standing, not more than a few dozen yards away, there was a boat washing up onto the shore, a slim craft of Molan design. It was a little beat up, but still looked seaworthy enough to head back out onto the waves. I could see it was fitted out with gear, including a paddle strapped to the side. The boat had a design painted on it — a long silvery sea serpent, with four horns and a mouth full of long, thin teeth.

I woke up then, and my vision had returned.

83

When I got back to our quarters aboard ship, I saw something I'd never seen on a sergeant's face before: Relief. Sgt. Ergin tried to hide it, but the way his forehead wrinkled up was a dead giveaway.

"You were the only one unaccounted for, Private," he said. "We were about to send Dral out to check...to see if anybody else had heard about you."

I knew when he meant; when coming back through the city I'd seen men checking the identification tags of dead soldiers — little metal disks that were each stamped with a unique number that was recorded somewhere next to your name.

"I guess the Arcanter will have to try harder next time if he wants to kill this Raider, sir."

"Amen," he said, before dismissing me, and I went to catch up with my platoonmates.

Over the next couple of days, a clearer picture of what had happened gradually emerged. A flight of at least 20 dragons had attacked the city, flying in from the west. Presumably, they'd flown from Garlund over the Striped Mountains to make their way to where the invasion fleet was being assembled. It was a daring attack, and losses had been heavy — but if the aim had been to knock us out of the war, it had been a failure. Most of those who died hadn't been soldiers at all — they'd been innocent civilians. Later on, I learned that one of them had been Gostor, my grumpy old instructor. Apparently, he'd died a hero's death, using his own powers to single-handedly hold off three dragons, killing two of them, while other civilians escaped to safety. I could just imagine him in whatever afterlife awaits elves, looking down with bored contempt at my own efforts.

The sheer scale of the carnage had banished any uncertainty or skepticism among the fighting men: People were calling for blood, and we were ready to make sure they got it. Looming behind that, though, was the sudden knowledge that the mountains no longer formed the impregnable barrier we had long assumed. There were a few tense days while we waited for news from the rest of the kingdom, fearing that other cities had been attacked. But no, it had only been Agellos and the fleet — this time. But if the Arcanter could send dragons across the mountains, what else could he send? An entire army, even? I thought back to that final trial we'd faced back at the Blue Wood. But there was no djinn this time to snatch the illusion away.

WITH ALL THIS IN mind, the date for the fleet to embark was now set: It would be in a little less than two weeks. We were told to wrap up any final business we might have, and prepare for the eight to nine weeks we'd be at sea.

I didn't tell anybody about what had happened at the Sailor's Chapel, and haven't ever told anyone until now. I don't know why. I guess when I read accounts of it in the papers, I figured they told the story as I wanted it to be remembered — a brave young Raider, later identified as Parsa, had taken charge of the situation and defeated the dragon — "assisted at one point," one story said, "by an unidentified young mage."

Parsa was posthumously awarded the Crimson Star. Perhaps, I thought, his wife Dessa would have him interred at the Royal Mausoleum. But something told me Parsa wouldn't want that. I thought the only place he'd want to be buried would be in his own hometown back in Caford, close to the woman he'd fought so hard for.

I did find Parsa's unit, and asked the officer in charge (now that the Captain was dead) if I could be the one to write to Dessa, to deliver the news. The man I spoke to was a pale, bleary-eyed young Lieutenant, who looked every bit as overwhelmed with work as Lt. Kretek. He was only too happy to oblige.

I don't remember exactly what I wrote; I remember Prof helped me find the right words for the occasion, so I'm sure the result sounded much finer than anything I've written here. I didn't tell Dessa anything about what I'd seen, of course. At the time I didn't want to — I still don't really want to. But part of me is glad that I've finally been able to tell the full story. I hope nobody who reads this will feel that I've diminished my friend; I only wanted the record to show just how great of a hero he was.

The dragon at the Sailor's Chapel was one of 15 that had been killed. All of them had been red; while many people had reported seeing a giant black dragon with a human rider, everyone agreed that the black one hadn't attacked anything. It had just glided back and forth over the city and the harbor, silently observing. People argued back and forth over whether it had really been the Arcanter, or simply one of his minions. I didn't offer an opinion. But I was pretty sure I knew.

I CAN SEE FOOTMAN Sesh glaring at me now, pointing at the clock on the wall. Even though there's a lot more to the story I have to tell, he wants me to wrap things up so he can get a copy of this to his superiors. The last mail cart for two weeks is leaving in a couple of hours.

"You can finish it later," he said. "They'll want to see the first part, at least. So wrap things up."

Sure thing, Father.

THE LAST EVENING BEFORE we were ready to leave, Sgt. Ergin passed out postcards.

"This will be the last thing you have the chance to send before we ship out," he said. "If there's anything you really need to say to anyone…"

When he got to me, I hesitated. I'd written my last letter to my mother just the day before, and said all I felt I needed to say. Maybe I should write something to Kanin…?

But no. Now wasn't the time to go back down that path. I looked at Sgt. Ergin and shook my head, and waved away the offered card. "I'm good, thank you."

Instead, I made my way up to the deck of the ship, and looked out at the city. The spire of the Sailor's Chapel, despite being heavily damaged, still stood strong. I marveled again at the massive size of the fleet. It seemed to give one hope — the Arcanter would regret the storm that he had now unleashed. But part of me couldn't help but wonder if this hadn't been his plan all along.

I pushed the thought away. Such things were out of my control; all I could do was go where they told me to go and kill who they needed me to kill. I could only hope that it did some good.

I turned my back on the city and went to the ship's prow, now pointed at the far horizon. Eventually, I knew I would have to head back to my bunk below deck, but I stayed there on the prow for as long as I could, looking out over the ocean. I knew if I could only stand there long enough, I would be able to see the sunrise.